The Adventures of Elizabeth Stanton

Series   Volume 1

The Evolution of the Path

Vic Broquard

The Adventures of Elizabeth Stanton Series
Volume 1 The Evolution of the Path

Vic Broquard

Published by:
Broquard eBooks
http://Broquard-eBooks.com
author@Broquard-eBooks.com
103 Timberlane
East Peoria, IL 61611

Artwork by Crooked Willow Studios

For Morgan and L. Ron Hubbard

Table of Contents

Chapter 1 The Beginning

My name is Elizabeth Stanton at the moment but my dearest friends call me Bethany. You see, I am a being, an immortal spirit. I've lived in many bodies and will have as many more as I desire, assuming the world is not destroyed. In my group, I am revered as the Wid Bethany — the title which I took nearly nine hundred years ago. I am Truth and Knowledge. Yes, you may call me a witch, a demon or a heretic, but, in doing so, you mark yourself as just another Blind One. I chose this road — this path I follow — knowingly and willingly. I do it for all mankind, even you.

For me, it all began in 550 AH (After Hodhekansis, the legendary twins and founders of Megalos) in a small village called Uru in the northern hills of the rolling green hills of the Greenway here on Tarra. Who I was and where I've been before coming to Tarra is blocked in my memories. Believe me, I've tried to crack that black veil which hides more of my past from me. The earliest memories I can see are running and playing tag with other children in Uru one spring morning.

Uru at that period in history was one of the first farming settlements on Tarra as far as anyone knows. No written records date from before 558 AH. We know writing was invented by the great artist and philosopher Niccolo Helios, but this is getting ahead of the story. So let me begin properly with a description of the planet we all call home, Tarra.

Tarra is a blue-green world about eight thousand miles in diameter consisting of vast oceans and one enormous continent shaped much like a dog bone — that is, the two huge continents we call Eastern Tarra and Western Tarra are physically joined by one long, narrow, nearly impassable desert region that is some two hundred miles wide and three hundred miles long. Where this narrows joins the roughly circular lobes of the two continents, two towering mountain ranges block any passage into the desert region that goes by the name of the Desert of Desolation. On our side, Western Tarra, the eighteen thousand foot range is called Kathas, while on the Eastern side the similar range is named Helios Grande after the great Sun God himself. None of us really knows what lies in Eastern Tarra because no one has been there and returned, though I have heard tales of some who have tried.

Straddling the southern side of the Desert of Desolation is a huge island, Megalos, which is four hundred miles long but only one hundred miles at its greatest width. Here on the Western Tarra side, Megalos nearly touches the continent. The Sallow Firth, as it is called, is two miles wide yet only three feet deep at low tide! Yes, horses and people often walk across the Firth, but there are ferries for those with money. The eastern side of Megalos is some twenty miles from the rocky coast of Eastern Tarra, but here treacherous tides thunder against many hidden rocks in that wide channel. From the dawn of time, Megalos and Western Tarra share the annals of history, both good and bad.

Now Western Tarra is roughly divided into halves by the great Med Sea, which opens onto the ocean at the western most part of the continent. This pale blue sea is nearly eight hundred miles long; its width varies between fifty and a hundred miles. Along the northern shores of Med Sea lies the principalities of the Seven Sea Princes. On the eastern shore of the Med Sea is the arid land called Juda Arad, which stretches all the way to the Kathas mountain range. All across the southern shore of Med Sea lies the giant Red Desert uninhabited and presumed unpassable. South of the Red Desert lies the Southlands with rich, rolling green savannahs and forests, rich in animal life but with few people. The Southlands and Megalos share a close relationship as far back as anyone can remember, though not necessarily a good one.

North of the principalities of the Seven Sea Princes is a mountain range known as the Appian Way. These spectacular eight thousand foot tall peaks stretch nearly across all of Western Tarra dividing the continent in half. The lands above the Appian Way are divided by nature into three roughly equal sized areas. At the far north lies the cold but timbered lands called Volksholm. To the east is the Northern Steppes, an arid land home to nomadic horsemen, while to the west lies the Greenway, a land of contrasts. Greenway consists of heavily forested, rugged hills interspersed with lush green valleys. My original village of Uru lies in the north central portion of the Greenway.

Many islands both large and small dot the lengthy coastline. However, of note is the large island called West Reach, which lies some ten miles off the coast of the Greenway. It is a large island kingdom unto itself, though as my story begins, it is largely unpopulated.

The world when I first arrived here on Tarra was roughly divisible into three political camps. Megalos, rumored to be the cradle of civilization, has great marble-stone cities, is very hot during summers, and has produced the first great thinkers including the great artist Niccolo Helios. The principalities of the Seven Sea Princes are the feudal city-states of wealthy men who sail the Med Sea trading there as well as up and down the coastline of Western Tarra. Finally, all of the lands above the Appian Way are inhabited warring hunter-gatherer groups or primitive farming communities. However, everywhere, rule is by the strongest sword and the mightiest forces, of which the Megalos Centurions are reputed to be the best as my story begins.

When I first arrived in Uru, a small farming community of some hundred men, women and children, life itself was rough and precarious. My village is totally dependent upon crops that we raise. In contrast to us, bands of hunter-gatherers that we call Galts, horsemen who live nomadic lives in the Northern Steppes, often leave their horses behind and, on foot, raid our villages usually for food and women. Uru is often raided by these sword wielding wild men who disrupt our precarious existence. For if we are unable to raise enough food for the long winter, starvation looms quite real. Worse still are the raiding bands of the Axemen, which is our name for the burly, hairy men from the northern ice lands of Volksholm. These barbarians pillage, rape and steal leaving whole villages desolated when they return to their lands. It is not a pretty sight and we fear the Axemen more than the Galts.

It all began for me that late spring day in Uru, the first of June. (Note I'm converting our month names into yours to spare you from having to learn our calendar.) Barefoot and dressed in grey, coarse cloth pants and shirt as were all the other kids, I was running from the seeker, playing an exciting game of hide and seek. I remember the feel of the warm, soft, dry, powdery dirt flowing up between my toes as my feet touched the ground. I remember the warm wind that brought wonderful fragrances to my nose: the smell of grasses, wild flowers, trees and our crops. At that moment, life felt grand and worth living just to experience the natural wonders of the world. Such is the view of a six year old girl with long brown hair and blue eyes.

The village consisted of some twenty-five wooden buildings with thatched roofs, crude but easy to build; timber was plentiful. Creative building design was not visible in Uru; each building was pretty much patterned after the other. Every day just after dawn, the men left to tend the fields surrounding our village or the herd of sheep. The women did everything else, from the cooking of food, to the making of clothes, to the repairs of the homes. Only when something required the strong hands of a man did the women set aside that task, for we all knew the loss of a field hand meant less food during the winter. You could say we were a hardy folk, determined and resolute, though ever practical. And you would be correct.

That day, around noon, Hamas halted his raiding party atop the last high hill before our green valley, hiding themselves behind the broad oak trees. Hamas was tall and lean, strong of bone, mighty with the sword, and belonged to a tribe of Galts. Through physical force, cunning, and guts, he had become their leader. His pants and shirt were made of tough leather, as were those of the rest of his men. It served to protect them from combat wounds. Hamas had long black hair that could have used a good washing months ago. Indeed, even his leather stank from stale perspiration from long wearing.

Hamas had led his hunting party a long way from their home because all of the neighboring tribes were stronger than his. To survive, they had been ranging farther and farther afield. Today, he smiled as he surveyed the smoke curling from the homes and spied tiny men far away tending crops. He spat on the ground, "Ground diggers!"

Fenas, his second in command, replied, "Yeh, but they gots what we needs. Probably gots lots of stuff we can use. And plenty'o women to have fun with when we get done — maybe even take some of the prettier ones home as pets!" The other men chuckled. This was going to be easy prey.

Surveying the village, Hamas said, "Probably, all the men are way off in the fields. They ain't no good fighting even if they was down there. Only women, so here's the plan. We sneaks down this hill to the open fields. Then, we run straight into the village, killing any ground diggers we pass. That way, we's got the town, and the ground diggers gotta come push us out, which they caint. What's a pitchfork gonna do to my fine blade here?" He snickered and laughed, as did the others. This was going to be the easiest raid they ever had and profitable too. Quietly, his band of twenty-five fighters crept down the hillside using the oak and maple trees for cover as much as possible.

Within a few minutes, the woods ended, and the relatively flat grasslands opened up, dotted here and there with well-tended fields. "Okay, let's charge to the town! Kill anyone that resists us!" And yelling loudly, they began running the mile toward the village. Off to the right, a startled farmer stopped hoeing and looked in terror at the wild men charging his way, sunlight reflecting off their blades, which they waved menacingly in the air. He had the sense of mind to get his antler horn and blow a warning call, though it quickly ended as a blade cut his throat. However, several other nearby horns took up the warning call which echoed in the valley.

I was running mostly to force the warm dirt to puff up between my toes when I heard the horns echoing far off in the distance. I stopped to listen wondering what it meant. So did my friends. Thomas, the oldest, about eight, said it meant trouble was coming, "Maybe Galts!" His eyes opened wide, for he had seen them once. I had never seen any.

My mother came out of our house and screaming for us kids, "Raiders! Run to the central well and stay there! Come on Elizabeth, run!" Mom grabbed my hand and fairly pulled me to the communal well located in the center of Uru. She had my younger brother in her arm and dragged my little sister with her other hand. As we ran, I could see other women running out of their houses too, some with dish towels in hand, some with sewing stuff. Fear was on their faces as they frantically looked about for their children. I'd never seen such fear. It was chaos for a couple minutes. Mom saw her neighbor and cried out, "Mary Sue, Billy's here. What is it, Galts?"

"Oh thank heavens! Billy, you stay right there now!" his mother called out. I noticed the women were looking frantically in all directions, wondering from where the attack was to come. "Heaven's protect us! It's Galts!" she yelled, as she saw the first of the raiders just coming into town.

We turned to stare at these raiders. They looked so mean, so dirty, so bad, so terrible to me, but then I was only six. Mommy called out, "Ellen, we need you now, please!" I wondered what she meant. Ellen was perhaps the oldest woman in our village. We all called her grandmom because she looked the part. She always gave us kids cookies and treats and was often babysitting us when our mothers were really busy, like during the fall harvest time. I wondered what grandmom could do. Where were daddy and the other men? I just knew they would never get here in time to stop these bad men from hurting us. For the first time, I felt the twinge of fear that slowly grew until my legs were shaking so badly I could barely stand.

Ellen slowly walked out in front of us, positioning herself between us and the oncoming raiders. I heard her singing or chanting something. It sounded beautiful! Strong and sure was her voice. I'd never heard that song, so

I tried very hard to hear her words, but her back was to me. Then, Ellen called out loudly so even I could hear. "I call upon the eternal fires; come now before me!" Suddenly a great sheet of flames came down like a curtain surrounding us all in a giant circle. "I call upon the ice of winter; come now before me!" Now, a great wall of blue ice formed a smaller circle around all of us. It was smaller in diameter than the flames. "I call upon the lightning of the storm; come now before me." And then I heard a humming sound, and something bluish hung in the air all around us just inside of the blue ice wall. I stared at these marvelous things I'd never seen before and wondered what they were.

Hamas, leading the charge, pulled up short of the wall of flames. "What devilry is this?" he called out in dismay. His men, breathing heavily, came up behind him. All halted before the sheet of flames, many rubbed their eyes in total disbelief. One called out, "Devil Magic?"

"Nay, men, tis foolery. Fire cannot burn like this. It is just a trick of light. Charge right on through it men," he ordered. He led the way, as all charged into the flames. I heard their screams. The flames were real, and burned their hair and exposed flesh. However, it took them only a second to get through the flames. They halted before the ice wall barrier. We could see their blackened, smoking bodies, distorted through the ice — like wild beasts they seemed to me. I was almost petrified. I heard Hamas yell, "Hack your way through; it's only ice!" We watched their blades hacking away, ice bits flying in all directions.

Only then did Ellen speak. I've never heard her voice sound so harsh and stern, "Leave now or die! Beyond the ice lies only your death!" By now, several had made a good-sized hole in the ice wall, and Hamas urged them to bust through and hack the old woman down. Three charged through the ice only to meet the crackling blue energy. Three giant bolts of lightning arced from way over our heads down onto the men. Their bodies flew up into the air, jerking violently, and then landed lifeless on the ground, smoking and stinking. I was petrified, yet I could not take my eyes off them.

Hamas hesitated, wondering what magic was this. He'd never seen such before. Seeing his hesitation, Ellen spoke directly to him, "Let this be a lesson to you. Go now and never return. If you do not, I shall pluck out your eyes. Go, you have been warned. There will be no second warning." She stared at him and gave him a minute to decide his fate. Meanwhile, the other men had finished cracking the wall of ice. It fell crashing onto the ground, raising piles of dry dust, pieces of ice rebounding a couple inches into the air.

Seeing the ice barrier gone brought hope to Hamas. "All of you charge that old woman! Kill her now!" he ordered.

Instantly, Ellen spoke a musical chant that was very short. Grandmom Ellen raised her hands and pointed them toward Hamas. Two great black rods flew from her hands straight at his eyes, as though they were arrows like those my dad sometimes shoots while hunting. Both smashed into his eyeballs, destroying them. I'll never forget his horrid shriek! He vainly used his hands to pull the rods out of his eyes, but it was too late, the damage was done. He screamed real terror and staggered backwards, a blind man. Fenas saw his opportunity to become their leader, "Retreat, I'm in command now. Let's get out of here as fast as we can. Run for it!" One of his men asked what about Hamas. "Leave him; he's as good as dead now anyway!" The raiders left even faster than they had come, all except Hamas who was screaming wildly, staggering about, lost in a world of darkness.

I saw Ellen wave her hand through the air in an arc, and the flames vanished as if they never were there in the first place. I saw daddy and several other men running into the village, pitchforks, staffs, and rocks in hand. I heard daddy say, "They killed Hank, but he was able to sound the alarm before he died. We owe Hank our lives; all praise to Hank and his family! The women chanted, "All praise to Hank!" I saw his wife and son, Billy, begin to cry.

Ellen said, "So be it. Slay this one in return, for he was their leader." I tried to see what happened next, but mommy pulled me into her skirt, hiding me from it. I only saw a tiny bit; the men began beating him with their big sticks. I did hear the blows landing on his head though, and it sounded ghastly, so I'm glad mommy didn't let me see. Afterwards, I did see his head, which looked all bloody and smashed up like a dead chicken. Mommy took me home then, but I could see all the other men arriving and heard Ellen say, "Bury them, please." The last thing I heard was the sound of the four bodies being dragged out of Uru.

When we were safely inside, mommy ordered me, "Beth, you are to stay inside the rest of the day."

"But mommy," I protested not wanting to be cooped up inside all afternoon. She looked stern so I tried a different approach. "But mommy, what about all my chores? Who'll feed the chickens if I don't go outside?"

Her stern countenance melted, and she smiled, so I hoped she would not keep me inside. "Elizabeth, you are really a great help around here. You always do such a good job with your chores and are so conscientious about doing them. Okay, today, I'll do your chores, and you watch after your brother and sister for me instead." I frowned; this was not at all what I had wanted! Unable to think of anything else to try, I sighed and agreed.

Near sunset, I did get to go outside. Daddy came by to get us all, "Elizabeth, you come with me. We must pay our last respects to Hank, who died today saving all of you. Hold onto my hand. Sarah, you bring the young ones." Daddy sounded very sad, and mommy had tears in her eyes, as we went outside in the rosy evening. It felt good to be holding daddy's strong hand, safe too. As we walked to the eastern edge of the village, he explained to me, "We're burying Hank in our cemetery facing the rising of the sun. Ellen is conducting the ceremony, Beth, so don't talk to her. This is a very important thing that she is doing for Hank."

Naively, I asked, "Will Hank be coming back to us tomorrow when the sun comes up?" I heard mommy cry a little more, and I thought maybe I shouldn't have asked him that.

"No, Beth. He has died. Hank will be with us no more. Ellen says he is a free spirit now and can choose what he will do next, though I'm not sure, Beth. Sometimes, I think Ellen has strange ideas. But she *is* the village guardian and a very good one, so no one dares say anything ill of her." As we approached the burial grounds, dozens of torches were crackling, casting flickering lights. Everyone in the village gathered close in a semicircle around a freshly dug hole in the ground. I spied four other new mounds nearby — the four bad men, I supposed. In the center of the half circle, Ellen stood holding a torch in one hand and her wooden staff in the other. She had on her finest cloak, I observed, the one with the beautifully embroidered oak leaf clusters on it.

Behind her on a wooden bower lay Hank. I looked to see where he had gotten cut, but couldn't see anything. I guess they cleaned him up and dressed him in his finest clothes. When everyone was present, Ellen began to speak. I didn't understand much of what she said and played with my toes in the soft dirt instead. When she was done, everyone walked by Hank's body and said farewell words. When daddy and I came up close, I could see his neck was cut, and it scared me a little. I managed to swallow hard and say, "Goodbye Hank. Thank you for saving us." I think that made daddy feel good, because he patted me kindly on my back, as we moved on by so mommy could get close. She was crying quite a lot now. Then, we all went home.

Mommy fixed dinner, and I soon forgot about my fears. Instead, I resolved to talk to grandmom about those magical things she did today. I really wanted to be able to bring down fire as she did. That night, I had dreams of me standing tall and calling forth the fires of heaven.

Just as soon as I did my chores the next morning, I went straight to grandmom's house. "Good morning, Elizabeth," she said as I came up to her. She was feeding her chickens. "And how are you this fine morning?"

"Oh just fine after yesterday's fright," I replied. "Grandmom, can you teach me how to call down the fires of the gods like you did? I really, really, really want to do that! Please?" I begged in my very best fashion; even my eyes pleaded with her. I figured she would say perhaps when you are much older. Adults always say that, you know. I wasn't really prepared for her response.

She stopped feeding the chickens and looked me straight in my eyes. There was that same stern look on her face again, and I was suddenly afraid I had just said something very wrong. Instead, she asked me the silliest question, "Beth, where are you?" I didn't quite know how to answer her. I was just right here. She seemed to think that was what I was thinking, picked up a stick, and drew a picture of me in the dirt. "Here is your body. Show me where you are?" She still had that stern look on her face and in her voice, too. I figured this was important.

"Right here, grandmom," I pointed to above and back of my head on the ground.

I don't think that fully satisfied her because she then said, "Okay, here take the stick; draw for me where you are and how big you are in proportion to the body."

Oh, now I understood. "Oh that's easy!" I drew a big circle about three times the size of the head that she had made in the dirt, placing it above and behind the head.

"Oh my! I thought so!" she exclaimed in surprise, though it would be many years before I understood why she was so surprised by my simple answer. Because she was not being so stern any more, I relaxed. "Yes, I believe I can teach you how to bring down fire from the sky, Elizabeth." My heart skipped a beat; enthusiasm swelled in me. "But you are going to have to study many lessons, and study them very, very hard. Making fire answer your call isn't an easy thing to do. It is no light matter to study these things." The thought of having to study hard only slightly tempered my happiness. "However, first we must have your mom and dad's permission. They might not want you to do this."

Now my heart sunk. What would I do if they would not let me? It had never occurred to me that they might not want me to learn to bring down fire from the sky. She saw the forlorn look on my face, "Don't worry. Say nothing about this to them, Beth. I'll come by tonight after supper and talk to them. Now let's go see if the cookie jar still has any more cookies in it!" The mention of cookies brought my cheerfulness back, almost as much as hearing that she would ask my parents for me. I figured if anyone could persuade them, it would be grandmom. I helped myself to two cookies before I went out to play.

I found it hard to play with the others that day. My thoughts kept drifting toward grandmom's visit, hoping mom and dad would let her teach me. I wanted to tell the other children I was going to learn how to bring down fire, but I knew I shouldn't because I'd look like a fool if my parents forbid it. I kept my mouth shut and tried not to mess up the games too badly.

Soon, it was time for the afternoon chores, which, as usual, went very quickly for me. I love to be helpful and take care of our animals. However, I grew more and more excited over dinner, knowing that at any minute Ellen would knock on our door. I tried very hard to act normal so they would not suspect something and then force me to have to try to explain. Each minute seemed like an hour to me. Finally, as I helped put the dishes away, we heard a knock on our door, and my heart leaped into my throat.

I heard Ellen's familiar voice sternly saying, "Good evening, Helmut. May I have a word with you and Sarah? It's important and concerns Elizabeth." Dad ushered her in to the now clean table, and mom, as she usually did when Ellen came to visit, made her a cup of herb tea. When all three were seated at the table, Ellen motioned for me to come and sit beside her. I was so nervous I almost bumped her teacup! I sat motionless, holding my breath.

"Helmut, Sarah, Elizabeth has asked me to teach her my ways. She wants to learn my priestess skills." Masterfully, she paused a moment to let the significance of that pronouncement register. So it was priestess skills. I hadn't known what to call them until now. Mom's mouth opened but no sound came out. "As you know, being a priestess demands great abilities, great skills, great knowledge, great wisdom, and great dedication to helping others — all of which requires long hours of study. Only those of great spiritual abilities can pass the test."

For a moment, I began to wonder if I was doing the right thing. All this sounded so difficult to achieve. I thought, *Well, I do like helping others, and there is so much I want to know.* I always liked to learn how to do new things, so maybe this would not be so bad after all.

Dad's voice brought me back to the present, "You know, Ellen, that we and the whole village owe our existence to you. If you were not protecting us, Uru would have been destroyed years ago. We cannot turn down your request. But how do you know Beth has these spiritual abilities? She looks like any other child in the village to me. Are you really sure she would be able to do this? I don't want to have her fail or get hurt. She's my eldest, and I love her way too much to have any harm, disgrace, or embarrassment befall her."

"I know, Helmut," she consoled him. "You know I wouldn't even broach this subject with you if I wasn't totally certain Elizabeth has the necessary spiritual capabilities. Actually, I've had my eye on her since she was three, though I've never said a word about it. I've studied all the children in the village, Helmut. There are two others that might have some small chance of success, but I'm not willing to risk it with them. With Elizabeth, I'm completely certain she has what it takes to become a priestess. But only with your total consent, mind you."

"But we desperately need her here," mom put in. "She's a great help to the family." This was certainly true, I thought; I cannot count the number of times they told me that in order to live, we all must do our part, our share. "Surely, you can wait until she grows up. She's only six," she pleaded. My heart sank; surely, this was true. I was only six, and they need my help.

"Sarah, her age has nothing to do with her spiritual abilities. She has so much to learn, years and years' worth. We prefer new priestesses begin their training at an early age." Enthusiasm swelled in me once more; I was not too young! I became even more excited, for surely they would say yes! Ellen continued, "Otherwise, the neophyte might only be ready to take on the full responsibilities when they are forty and be able to provide help for only a few years. Besides, Sarah, I'm getting old. I can feel it in my bones. My time here is growing short. My fondest desire is to have a replacement for me before I pass on, for I love you all too much to see you slain or worse. All my life's work would thus become meaningless." Pass on? Did she mean she was going to go away like Hank and soon? No! I wanted to protest; you have to live long! We need you; we love you!

"Sarah, look deep into your heart," Ellen commanded. "Haven't you guessed Elizabeth was different, somehow destined for something such as this? Haven't you known it all along, perhaps attempting to hide the truth from yourself?" What did she mean by that I wondered? Did mom know years ago that I wanted to be like Ellen? How could that be? I only decided that yesterday.

Mom looked downcast as if her words rang true. Ellen added, "If nothing else, think of the high honor and respect she'll bring to your family —

you who raised her. I can think of no higher honor for a family." Mom managed a faint smile.

"You're right as always," mom finally said. "But I feel like I'm suddenly losing my precious daughter!"

"No, she'll still be here and helping you as usual. I'll train her during the children's playtime. That way, she can help her family survive," Ellen explained. "You aren't losing her; rather she'll get educated in her spare time. Again, I stress, this can only be if I have your complete and total agreement."

My parents looked at each other and then at me. I fidgeted. "Beth, honey," mom said, "are you completely, totally sure this is what you really, really want to do? It's not just because of the raiders coming here yesterday? Not because you got scared?"

Somehow, I knew what I would say next mattered a great deal to them and that it somehow would make or break my dream. So I said carefully, "Yes, I was scared yesterday, mommy. But that isn't the reason. I like to help others. Yesterday, everyone in the whole village was afraid, except Ellen. I want to be like Ellen so when it really, really, really matters, I *can* help. When I saw her bring down the fire from the sky, it reminded me there is *so* much that I want to know. And I really want to learn everything!"

A hush fell over the room. Ellen spoke ever so softly, "Sarah, there's your answer. Only a great spirit wants to dedicate their life to being able to help others when it really matters."

Mom had tears flowing down her eyes, and I didn't know why or how I had upset her. She came over to me and hugged me tightly. "Beth, if this is what you truly want, you have my blessing and support, honey." Dad hugged us both and caressed my hair. I was so happy; all my fears that they would forbid it evaporated.

Ellen said humbly, "Thank you both. I swear to you to do my very best in training her so you may be proud of your daughter and her accomplishments." Grandmom Ellen took my hand, which, of course, got my full attention. "Beth, tomorrow when it is playtime, come to my house, and we'll begin. However, tonight I leave you with your first caution. Speak not a word about this to anyone other than your mom and dad. For reasons I'll explain tomorrow, your life may depend upon not letting others know about our training sessions, at least right away."

Though I was surprised and somewhat bothered about her statement, I managed to promise I wouldn't say anything, but I wondered why it had to be so secret. However, Ellen had that adult look on her face that said, "We're done talking." She bade me go play with my siblings so they could chat about the crops.

The next day, June 3, 550 AH, was a day I'll never forget. Not even the passage of lifetimes has dulled that day in my memory. It was my first lesson, one that changed me forever. At the crack of dawn, I hopped out of bed, quickly dressed, and cheerily did my chores. I loved being outdoors and used every excuse I could invent to spend more time outside the house. Today, with a crystal clear, blue sky still twinged in the east with the fading rosy red of dawn, promised to be a perfect late spring day. As soon as I stepped outside, the odors of nearby cooking fires curling bluish smoke up into the crisp sky mingled with the smell of the woods, which lay just north and east of the village, and the various animals we all kept. I trotted out onto our dirt street. Constant foot and horse traffic trampled the ground into a fine powdery dirt in which I loved to squiggle my toes.

Each house had some grassy areas around them and several fenced in sections that housed chickens, rabbits, ducks, and geese. Already the sheep had been led out to the far northern pastures; several men took turns watching over the combined village flock. Everyone's goats walked freely everywhere munching on whatever they could find to eat. The goats kept the grass at a short height, and they also gave us our milk for the morning porridge. This was my first task, to milk our two goats, but first, I had to round them up which was easy; I carried two handfuls of corn meal to entice them to come to me. Ten minutes later, I carried the pottery pitcher inside for mom. Next, I hurried out to collect the eggs and feed the chickens. I saw several other older children doing much the same thing for their families. We waved but said nothing. It was quiet and peaceful; none of us liked breaking in on that silent time we had to ourselves.

With these beginning chores done, I begrudgingly went inside. As usual, mom had breakfast waiting. I helped myself to a bread roll, and quickly ate my porridge from the wooden bowls with my favorite wooden spoon. Our utensils were carved from wood because wood here was plentiful; besides no one in the village knew how to work with metals. Trading for them in nearby villages was too expensive for us. After I ate my fill, I helped mom feed my little brother and sister and then changed their clothes. Mom still did the diapers, though, thankfully! Next, I helped with the house cleaning and dishwashing. Finally, I heard the magic words from mom, "Okay, Beth, we're all done. Playtime." Only today, mom knew that meant something vastly more important to me. She smiled and added, "Have fun, and learn all you can!"

Out the door I ran. Several of my friends were already outside starting up a game of kick the ball. They yelled for me to join them. I yelled back I couldn't right now. I headed straight for Ellen's house. She was waiting for me on her chair on her porch. "Beautiful morning, Elizabeth," she greeted me. "I see you're all ready to get started." That was obvious. I sat down on the steps in front of her and listened eagerly, wondering what I would learn first.

"Beth, I have much I can teach you. However, you'll have to listen carefully and memorize what I say and how I say it. You see, one day, you may desperately need this information or you may find yourself instructing another like I'm doing with you. Therefore, I'll be repeating many things and then asking you to repeat them back to me exactly as I said them so I know you know it. All of our knowledge is transmitted verbally from one to another. This way, no outsider can ever steal that knowledge. There are some who would do just that and then abuse or misuse that knowledge. We are the keepers of knowledge and wisdom. So repeat back to me, 'We are the keepers of knowledge and wisdom.'" I did several times until I could say it effortlessly.

"Now then, your first lesson is perhaps the most important lesson I can ever share with you. All knowledge rests upon this foundation. It is actually a skill, Beth, a skill you must perfect first before anything else." I held my breath, half-expecting to learn how to bring down fire or something equally spectacular. "You must learn to observe what is really there. The rule is 'One must always observe what is actually present.' Now this sounds utterly simple, but it's hardly ever done by other,s which is the main reason they fail so often."

I guess I looked pretty crestfallen, observe? That meant to look. I always looked.

"Okay, Beth, let's see how you do. I want you to observe little Annette over there playing ball. Tell me what you actually see and only what you actually can see," said Ellen using her stern voice so I knew she meant business.

"Well, I see Annette playing with the brown ball, and she's running trying to kick it into the other kids so they are 'it,'" I said, certain I had it right.

"You're doing what everyone does; you're unconsciously making numerous assumptions and conclusions about what you're seeing, and as a result, you're not answering the question. You are concluding that you see Annette 'playing' and 'running,' and you are assuming based on prior knowledge that she is trying to kick the ball into the other kids. You're supplying prior ideas of what the goal of the game is. All I want is to know what it is that you actually see. I'll give you an example. I see a circular brown colored object that just bent in slightly there as it just touched the ground. It rose above the ground about as high as it was before it touched the ground. I see a dark spot that moves across the hemisphere from left to right and then disappears. I see another dark spot appearing a little later back on the left side, and it moves toward the bottom right. You see, it is a conclusion of the mind that it is a ball and that it is bouncing and rolling. Can you see the difference?"

"Oh I get it," I exclaimed, "I see Annette — no, rather I see a young girl — er no, I see a small person, compared to that house over there. The person has brown hair that comes down to her shoulders. I see a right shoulder and right arm with a hand with no fingers. I see a light brown garment that goes from where the hair stops down to her right knee. I see a flesh colored knee and ankle and two toes. I can see one small one that is closer to me and one next to it. I see a piece of something that is yellow mixed in with the brown hair. The hair isn't straight, but is wavy. It doesn't hang straight down but twists and turns as it goes from the top of the person downward. How's that?" I asked confident I was getting the hang of this observing thing.

"Good. How do you know her knee is flesh colored?" asked Ellen.

"Oh, I see. Because it is the same color, or nearly so, as my arm here, which I can see at the same time, and it looks like my arm," I replied.

"Precisely. You can say it is flesh colored because you can compare it right now with your arm. Now, how do you know it is hair that is hanging down? You did well on describing it, mind you. But how do you know it is hair?" she inquired. I thought about that one. "Is it not because you 'know' people have hair of their heads, and thus you conclude you are seeing her hair? What if a person did not have hair? Some men shave their heads. Could it not just as easily be a form of hat made from long horsehair? In fact, could not this person be completely bald but wearing something to cover her head? I know, you know Annette, but you must train yourself to observe, just observe, and see what is actually present and not form instant conclusions based upon prior ideas." I looked befuddled.

"Let me give you an example. Suppose you had a pet rabbit that had brownish fur. It was a very loving pet, and you took it to bed with you at night where it snuggled with you. Got the idea?" I nodded. "Now suppose you are out walking in the woods collecting firewood for your mom, and you spy a brown rabbit that looks like yours except it is drooling white saliva around its mouth. Since you are friendly with your rabbit and it is friendly with you, would you not try to befriend this rabbit and try to pet it? Would that not be a reasonable thing to do?"

"Sure! Maybe it needs a nice home," I concluded, not seeing any point to this example at all.

"Ah, and if you did pet it, you would likely be bitten and would almost certainly get so very sick that your body would die a most painful death, wracked in massive pain. That rabbit had a very bad disease, a sickness. What was different about that rabbit? The clue is in how I described it to you."

I thought hard and suddenly exclaimed, "You said it was drooling saliva around its mouth. Is that it?"

"Precisely, that means it was a very, very sick rabbit. If you learn to see what you see and not mechanically form conclusions, you can learn much, even how to bring down fire. But if you cannot learn to see exactly what you see, to observe only, then there is no way I can ever teach you how to do that or much else that is truly useful. Nature and the universe opens up to those who can observe it and see just what is there, and it closes down to those who see only what they want to see, think they see, or imagine what they see. It is such a simple skill, to observe the obvious, but very, very few people can actually do so. It's altogether too easy to superimpose yesterday's memories of Annette over the images of what you are seeing today, to conclude it's her hair you see because you felt it or combed it for her yesterday, and to assume she is playing ball to win. Perhaps, she enjoys being 'it'. By watching her, by observing her, you can tell the difference. Now watch her actions."

I looked hard, trying not to assume anything. That was very hard, because I loved to play the game and had so many memories of playing rushing into my head. After a couple minutes, I exclaimed, "Wait a minute! You are right! Three times, she had a certain kicking motion but when that boy there was real close to her and a dead cinch to be hit by any kick, she used a different motion that caused the ball to just barely miss him. Conclusion: she enjoys being 'it' and isn't completely trying to hit the other players. I never saw that before!"

"Very good," Ellen congratulated me on my observation. "Now, let's observe her face as much as we can."

"She's smiling and laughing — er, no, I see a pair of lips curving upwards at both ends, and they are open a little way because I see some white things between the lips," I corrected myself. And so went the entire afternoon. Ellen had me observing nearly everything in the village. Somehow, I realized I had never really looked at everything; I saw things now in a different light. We kept this observing the obvious thing going all week long, day after day. I got better and better at it. I think Ellen was impressed with how well and how quickly I took to just observing.

As I was about to head home late that first afternoon, Ellen finally explained, "Now perhaps you can see why you don't want to go around telling everyone that you are learning from me. Annette might be upset if you told others she enjoyed being 'it.' Some would be so envious of you that they might hurt you. People fear what they do not understand. So keep this training to yourself for your own safety." I agreed I would, and I was slowly beginning to see just what she meant.

That strenuous week of just observing and not concluding made a tremendous change in me. I began to notice things, subtle things, things that were in fact obvious, if only one looked. For example, I saw just how tired dad was when he returned from the fields at the end of the day. I saw how much my little brother's messy pants bothered mom one afternoon when she was trying to cook supper and had to stop and clean up the mess. I saw the neighbor boy, Timmy, was the one who often started all the arguments between us kids. Most importantly, I spotted when one of our precious goats just started to get sick from having eaten something it should not have. I spotted it, and we took her to Ellen who cured her. Both mom and dad thanked me repeatedly for having saved our goat.

At the end of the week, Ellen asked me what I had learned about observing. I went on and on about how it had actually rather opened my eyes. I could see things I had never before "seen" even though I had seen them with my eyes. From the big smile on Ellen's face and the white brightness in her eyes, I knew she was pleased. "Beth, you have done very, very well this week. I must say you have even exceeded my expectations, and that is saying something." I beamed with happiness.

Indeed, this simple action, seeing what is present only, is a lesson that has never left me during all these years. I swear it is the basis for everything in life. Over the years, I have only gotten better and better doing it. Now, it is second nature to me to just observe and knowingly conclude only after observations are completed. Such a simple thing and yet it is so incredibly valuable and important.

My second week's lessons comprised an orientation or tour of what it was that I was learning to be. "We call ourselves the druwid or the Guardians. The word wid means to know, see, or observe, which leads to wisdom. Dru refers to our oak tree forests, which abound all around here. However, the common folk simply refer to us as their local priest or priestess. I think only a couple men in our village actually refer to me as their Guardian, and those, I don't think, know what the title means, really. This week, you will." I grew excited knowing I was about to hear things no one else in the village had. Druwids — Guardians — both had a nice feel about them, I thought. I sat listening intently to Ellen.

"Beth, when I use the word 'man' or 'men,' I mean men, women and children — not just your dad. Also, if you do not understand something I say, stop me at once so we can get it explained so you do understand, okay?" I nodded and she continued, "All of us are immortal spiritual beings." I guess I must have looked rather blankly, for she stopped and waited for me to say something.

"What's immortal and what's a spiritual being?" I asked not really knowing what she was saying at all. I was me, of that I was sure.

"Immortal means living forever through all time. It is something that cannot die. As for a spiritual being, it means something that is not of this world, not made of matter, like your body. Here, close your eyes and see if you can find a picture of feeding your chickens this morning." She waited until I said I could see my memories of it very clearly. "Now what you are looking at are mental images you have made of the universe around you. Okay, now turn the chickens purple. Go ahead, get the chickens all purple." I laughed saying they look awfully silly being purple. "I'll bet they do. Now those mental pictures are ones you have invented, your imagination, for you know none of your chickens are actually purple, right. See the difference between your mind's pictures of the universe and those you create yourself?" I said it was rather obvious, and she continued, "Now who is looking at those pictures in your mind?"

"I am," I said rather awkwardly.

"That's you, Beth, you the spiritual being. Where are you located in terms of your body?"

"Oh, I'm still just above and back of my head. Isn't everyone?" I asked wondering what the point of all this was.

"Oh my no, Beth! First, that's you — the looker at the pictures. And you are immortal and cannot die."

"But Hank died a couple weeks ago when the bad men came," I said rather confused about this.

"No, Hank did not die; his body died. Hank has gone in search of a new baby body to inhabit. Yes, that is the cycle of life that is going on here on Tarra. It is the magic of Nature. Women give birth to a baby; they create new a life form. So thus a baby gets born or created or comes into existence. Slowly, it grows into adulthood. From then, it slowly ages and deteriorates or decays and at last finally dies. But we are not our bodies. What we do usually is grab hold of a new baby body and live out a life using it. When it dies, we leave that one and go in search of a new body. This is the Cycle of Life on Tarra. That's what it's officially called."

"So Hank is not actually dead? He's gone looking for a new baby body? I wonder where he went?" I asked mostly to myself.

"Ah, one of our most sacred duties is to help others to do just that. I believe Hank has taken my suggestion and gone to Karka, which is ten miles west and just a little north of here. I told him there was a mother in Karka who was about to give birth and gave him directions."

"Will he remember us? I mean when he gets his new body and all?" I wondered.

"Before I answer that one, let me finish answering your previous one. We Guardians all are located much as you are, above and behind our body's head. I have known only a very few beings that did not need a body to do things. What I mean is this: can you open my front door without using your body to do it?"

"No! That's not possible!" I said rather aghast at the suggestion that I could open her door all by myself.

"If you could, you would be looked upon as a god or goddess anywhere in Tarra! For that is godlike power indeed. Don't fret. I can't do it either. Yet, there is a third possibility. Many are just plain stuck inside their body's head! Your mom and dad are unfortunately both stuck tightly inside their heads. Therefore, I invite you to practice your observational skills and see for yourself. In fact, your assignment this week is to locate where each person is in terms of their body. Thus, we have here on Tarra a very strange situation. Very few are godlike. I've only personally known one, and he was basically acting as a guardian of an entire forest area. The vast majority are somehow stuck inside their heads, and many of those are being their body so solidly that they have lost track of who and what they really are, spiritual beings. We sometimes call them *headers* but that is a very derogatory term, so don't let me hear you calling them that." I promised, but committed the label to memory. I thought the word *headers* was somehow appropriate.

"And then there are the rare ones like you and me who are always outside the head operating the body from there," smiled Ellen looking kindly at me.

"Gosh, I should think it would be so very hard to be packed into these tiny heads. I wonder how they shrink themselves so they fit?" I mused trying to see how I could be small enough even to fit inside my head.

"That's very observant of you. None do so well when packed inside a head. And this is one thing the most powerful Guardians are working on — trying to find out why they are stuck inside and how to get them free once more. The rest of us are trying to protect, help, and guide those that are unfortunate enough to be stuck there. You see, Beth, we have observed that over time, more and more beings are becoming lodged inside their heads with a drastic reduction in their natural abilities. So our task is a kind of holding action — keep it from getting worse, while the brightest of us try to work out why it is occurring and how to reverse it."

"Wow!" I meant a lot with my exclamation. She was saying I was special, different from the others in my village. I found it hard to suppress feelings of self-importance. But also, I could not help but feel compassion for what my mom and dad must be going though. How awful they must feel to be stuck inside their little heads! "Can't we get them out of their heads? I mean my mom and dad."

"Only when their bodies die will they leave," Ellen answered using her stern voice so I knew this was important. "Until that time, it's our task, Beth, to help them in any way we can so they don't get any worse." Suddenly, my chores took on an even bigger role in my mind. I resolved to do them better and to try to do more to help mom.

"Now, as for whether Hank will remember us here or not, that is a very good question. If it were you or me, the answer would most certainly be yes. But with these others, the answer is sometimes yes, but mostly they forget. Why they forget, we don't yet know. Tis very sad indeed." Ellen seemed lost in her own thoughts for a moment. I waited patiently, thinking over all she had said.

"Ah yes. Where was I? Oh, I know. Now, the next thing you need to learn is there are many areas in which we all strive to exist and do well, even the *headers*. First, we all want to do well for ourselves, to live a good life. Then, we want to exist and do well as a family unit. Actually, the family unit is really the most basic building block on Tarra, for without families, there would be no new children, no new bodies for us to occupy when ours dies. The miracle of Nature only allows women to create the new life. So all throughout Tarra, women should be held a position of honor and great respect. Next, we all want to do well in our group. Here it is the village. But you are now part of the druwid group as well, and we want to succeed as a group too. We want all mankind to flourish and prosper. We want all the plants and animals to thrive and live their lives to the fullest. We even want the physical world of Tarra to do well and to thrive, even the dust in our street. I see how much you like the dust." Her comment took me by surprise; my cheeks got a bit hot. "And lastly, we, and the Guardians especially, want all spiritual beings to thrive and do well. Those are the seven areas in which a single person is seeking to flourish and do well. And seven is the Guardian's magic number! We call these the Seven Aspects of Existence." We spent another hour going over them until I could repeat them all back to her properly.

"Now, here is this week's assignment for you, Beth. Look around at everything you are doing and look at everything you see anyone else doing. Figure out into which Aspect that action falls. See if you can find anything that anyone does which lies outside these Seven. Also, while you are observing the others, see where they are located: inside their heads or outside like yourself."

"I can do the first easily," I replied, sticking my lower lip up a bit in frustration. "But I don't know how to see spiritual beings. How am I to see where they are if I can't see them?"

"Observe, Beth." I was afraid she'd say something un-useful like that.

"I'll give you a hint. Most beings have some kind of energy glow about them, like the aurora we sometimes see in the night sky. Look for their color. Now go and play with the other kids and practice these things."

Though I felt I still had no idea how actually to see another being, I could tell she was not going to give me any further clues. I thanked her and headed off to join the seeker game that was in progress in the middle of the main street. My little sister, Anne, who was only four was standing at the edge of our yard watching the older kids play. I could see she wanted to play too. I took her hand, and together we joined in the afternoon fun.

Thus, it began for me, my initiation into the Guardians. Ellen taught me many, many skills. By the time I was ten years old, my knowledge of woodland lore was second only to hers, which gained me a great deal of respect in Uru. I knew the constellations and the motions of the planets. I learned to navigate by the stars, predict the seasons, and even foretell the weather, and how our crops would produce come the autumn harvest time. But from my point of view, perhaps the most valuable skill she taught me was the art of healing.

At that time, I was young girl with a burning desire to help others in need. I devoted all the time I could possibly muster to learning everything I possibly could. According to Ellen, I excelled in the diagnosis and treatment of commonplace injuries encountered in my village. As far as I was concerned, my time was well spent, for I was able to save my dad's life.

It happened one July afternoon when I was ten. Several men came home from the fields very early, bearing my dad on a makeshift stretcher. Thomas broke the news to mom and me, "He didn't join us for lunch, ma'am. We went to check on him and found him like this: unconscious, barely breathing. We brought him here as fast as we could." The men laid him on the dining room table. I sensed mom's growing panic as she felt almost no pulse. "Helmut! Helmut, what's wrong? What's happened to you?" she cried, becoming frantic. I could sense mom's totally helpless feelings.

So I took charge, "Mom, go boil some water fast." I had no idea why we should have the hot water, but I had seen Ellen request it several times, and it gave mom something concrete to do. Quickly, I concentrated totally on observation. I could see no visible signs of a wound. A quick pass of my hand verified no bumps on his head. I pulled his shirt off to inspect his arms. Carefully, I looked him over from his fingers up to his neck and saw nothing out of the ordinary. I had mom help me pull off his boots, socks and pants.

Then, I spied something. He had an ugly black bulge above his right knee. Long black streaks ran on down his leg ending with what appeared to be two tiny pin pricks. "Adder bite, mom!" I diagnosed. She nearly fainted; an adder bite is nearly always fatal. Adders were the most poisonous snakes we had in our area. I grabbed dad's hunting knife and a wooden bowl, and climbed onto the table. Carefully, I cut into that black bulge, releasing some of the rancid poison. As rapidly as I could, I sucked on the bleeding 'X' I had made, spitting out mouthfuls of blood and poison into the bowl. Just then, Ellen came rushing into our house, but as expected, she observed before speaking or acting.

I looked over at her and she nodded, "Carry on; you are doing fine." When I thought I had it all out of the bulge, Ellen inspected my work and suggested I do several more areas down toward the initial bite. "Excellent work, Beth, you have saved your father's life. Now go wash all of the poison out of your mouth very carefully and dispose of the bowl. It is contaminated with the poison, and it'll be very hard to ever get all traces of the poison out of the wood itself. I'll finish up here." I did as I was told, for I was near to gagging from all the poison, and my mouth was getting numb from it as well.

When I came back inside from washing my mouth out by the well, the pungent odor of boiling herbs greeted my nostrils. Ellen instructed me in how to mix the herb juice with the clay compress, which we applied to the cuts I had made. She told mom that as the mud dried, it would tend to suck any residual poison from his leg. After she had explained to her how to care for him during the next twelve hours, Ellen left.

Only when quiet returned to our home, did mom hug me tightly. Between tears, she whispered, "Oh thank you Elizabeth! You saved him! Honey, I'm so proud of you and so glad you have studied so hard so you can heal. I promise you that you'll always have our full support in your training. Anything you ever need, you just ask me, okay? Anything," she repeated, but she was so choked up further words were impossible for her to say, and none was really needed. I hugged her back. I cannot describe just how great it felt to have made a difference in a matter of life and death. This was my first time and certainly not the last.

Chapter 2 Expanding Horizons

The first four years of my training were fun filled learning experiences. I just could not get enough of it. I swear for every new thing I learned, I discovered ten more things that I wanted and needed to learn! However, this year brought several major political and cultural changes that would drastically alter my world in Uru.

The year was now 554 AH. In order for you to appreciate the significance of these changes, you must grasp how our lives were lived before these events occurred. Uru was an early attempt at a self-sufficient farming community. We had very few metal items for we had no metalworkers in Uru and little funds to purchase them elsewhere. Mostly, the men had a small metal bladed knife and an axe for felling trees. All else we fashioned from wood in which the world around us abounded.

For example, my house, which is nearly identical to all of the other houses in Uru, might be called a pole house or a long house. It is twenty-five feet wide and a hundred long. Going down the center and firmly embedded in the ground are twenty-foot tall poles that support the massive timbers that run its length. Five-foot tall poles embedded in the ground form the side walls. Logs that have been crudely split into rough-hewn boards cover the sides and the two ends. Our two doors are in the middle of the two long sides. The large V-shaped roof is very steeply slanted and made of interwoven small supple branches from the same trees that were used for the poles and timbers. Secured to the top of this tree-branch cloth as I sometimes call it, are reams and reams of thatching. It has to be strong to support the weight of the snow, which can sometimes reach two-feet in depth. Some of the houses use a combination of mud and straw instead of the rough planks, but those few houses are not as good as ours is.

Inside, we have two floors; in the upstairs, reachable by ladders, are our sleeping rooms. Each house has a large stone stove that provides cooking and heating facilities. Mom has a sewing and weaving section where she makes all our clothes. The pantry consists of a large number of sealable clay jars full of grains, nuts, and so forth. By late autumn, the pantry is brimming with foods of all kinds. Yet by early spring, most is gone, save for the seed stock for the new year's crops. In spite of the fact that early spring means new life comes soon, for me, that time of year is not so much fun as I am always hungry. However, I must say that our crops have been doing better each year and it is not as bad as it was four years ago.

We all raise various animals to supplement the crops. Sheep provide us with food and clothing. Several times a year, the men go on deer hunts. We make use of nearly the entire kill. Besides meat, we get our leather from their hides, and all sorts of small things are made from the bones and antlers, as are all mom's sewing needles and such. Nothing is wasted ever.

Yes, you could say we live a harsh life, but it has the benefit of making all of us dependent upon one another. For example, when the adder bit dad earlier this year, all the other men tended his crops while he was recovering. Later that summer, one mother of five got very sick, so mom and two other mothers pitched in and fixed all their meals for her family. Yes, we have a very strong sense of community here in Uru.

What about rulers or governing men? We have none and need none. Ellen, our Guardian priestess, handles all such matters. If some trouble or problem develops, she finds the truth of the matter and, after explaining it to us, corrects it honorably. If outside trouble comes, usually from the Galt raiding parties, Ellen takes care of them by calling down fire from the sky.

However, this year, Ellen is noticeably getting older and slower afoot. The Galt raids have become a bit more frequent, which has alarmed everyone. Often now, I hear the adults discussing the matter among themselves, whereas four years ago, I never did. Being a druwid priestess in training, it also bothered me for I still wasn't able to call down fires from the sky.

Ellen came to our house just after dinner on June 20 asking to speak to my parents. "As you know, tomorrow is the summer solstice, the longest day of the year. Among my fellow Guardians, it's considered a holy day, and we have an evening celebration at the standing stones. I came to ask your permission to take Elizabeth with me this year so she may meet other priests and priestesses and share in our festivities. If you agree, we should leave by noon in order to get there in time, and I'll have her back here by noon the next day. I know that not having her around is a hardship and that you will both have to do her chores. But it is really an important part of her education to attend."

When I heard this, my excitement rose to a fevered pitch. I could hardly sit still! Finally, I was going to meet others and participate in one of our holy celebrations! Yet, I knew my being gone for two days would make everyone else have to work all the harder and felt a twinge of guilt at running off and making them do my work for me. I expect Ellen sensed that in my face, for she added, "And when we return, I'm sure Elizabeth will work extra shifts to make it all up to you."

I began to think of various ways I could beg and plead with them to let me go, figuring they would object. To my surprise, mom answered with no hesitation, "Sure she can go, Ellen. I've already promised her that anything she needs, I'll support her all the way. Should I send along some food with her? Is there anything else she'll need?" Mom asked. Neither she nor I had any idea whatsoever of what this celebration required of its participants.

"You could pack a light trail lunch, but nothing more," Ellen replied. "And thank you both." She noticed that dad was awfully quiet, and she guessed what was troubling him. "Helmut, are you concerned about the safety of Uru while I'm gone for two days?" She hit the mark. How she always seemed to know precisely what was troubling a person, I still didn't know, but I knew I still had a lot to learn. I realized just then that it would still be many years before I could hope to fill Ellen's role as village guardian. That was a humbling thought to me.

Dad chuckled and relaxed. Now I could see that he had been tense. *How could I have not observed that?* I asked myself. Right away, I knew the answer; I had been so excited about getting to go to a druwid festival that I had failed to observe even my parents! Dad said, "Yes, these Galt raids are getting more frequent. I don't know what we would do if they came while you were not here to protect us."

Ellen looked dad squarely in his eyes, "I'll let you in on a little secret, Helmut." I watched dad's eyes perk up. "There are many guardians in the wide world around Uru. Some have been sent to spy on the Galts. Take it from me, there'll be *no* raids during the time I'm gone. Other Guardians will see to that detail. You can spread the word to any others that are worried about my absence." From dad's expression, I could tell that this was a major revelation to him, that he was hearing something he considered very important about the Guardians. I wondered just how many druwids there actually were. I imagined some sneaking about the woods spying on the Galt settlements protecting us, yet unseen by us villagers. Ellen added, "We're trying to do something about these raiders. As yet, I'm not certain of its ultimate outcome. I can say no more though." Dad respected her brief explanation and seemed to find comfort in her hints. He thanked her generously for her words and for taking me to the celebration.

It was bedtime. As usual, Mom brushed my long hair before I climbed up the ladder into my bed. "Beth, I've made a surprise for you. I was going to wait for your birthday to give it to you, but I know you can really make good use of it now!"

Instead of relaxing during the hair brushing ritual, I naturally got very animated. "What? Can I see it now?" I think mom was just as excited about it as I was. She smiled and told me to hide my eyes while she fetched it from its hiding place.

"Happy early birthday, Beth," she exclaimed.

"Wow!" I declared. Mom had made me a leather backpack and a matching leather collecting bag. "These are terrific, mom! Thanks a million!"

"Yes, I knew you would sooner or later be going off wandering in the woods and would need a backpack. Since Ellen has been showing you what herbs to gather, I spied on her and modeled this collection pack to be just like hers!" mom proudly explained. "But that's not all; look inside the pack. Go on; hurry up! I can't stand all the waiting either!"

Quickly, I opened the fastener and looked inside, saw more leather and pulled out clothes! My jaw dropped. I held up a set of soft leather pants and a matching leather long sleeved blouse! "Go on; try them on. I'm sure they fit. I made them a bit large because you are growing like a weed, and I wanted them to last you a couple years."

"Mom, these are fantastic! I'll look like a true woodsman now! Oh thank you! Thank you!" I exclaimed, as I hastily slipped on the pants and then the blouse. Mom fussed with the fittings. Yes, they were just a bit large, especially the middle of the blouse, but that meant I could wear this precious outfit even longer before I outgrew it and had to hand it down to Anne.

"I'm still working on the matching belt," she explained. "So we'll just have to see if we can make one of your father's fit until I get yours finished. Yes, it does fit just the way I had intended. You should get a couple of years use from it." She added, "I wanted to make sure my little priestess looks really good when she goes out on official priestess business. I guess it meets with your approval."

"You bet, mom! This is the best outfit ever! One day, I hope to be able to sew just as good as you can!"

"Well, Beth, you are almost eleven. I had decided that on your eleventh birthday, I'd begin teaching you all about weaving and sewing. So in two weeks' time, you'll get your wish," she teased me. "Now, take them off, and let's get your hair brushed. You are going to have to brush your own hair while you are off on your trip with Ellen. I don't imagine she'll have time to do it." Even after the brushing and I had crawled up and into bed, I was anything but relaxed. On the contrary, I was wide awake. So much had happened in the last few hours that my mind was racing, thinking, and imagining what the morrow would bring.

Next morning after the chores were done and my little sister and brother went out to play, mom and I packed a few things I would need in my new pack. Then, while I changed into my new leather outfit, mom fixed a lunch sack for me. She said, "I know you really do need a metal knife, Beth, but they are so expensive. However, I think your father is trying to save up enough grain this fall to afford to get you one come harvest time. But you know crops. He might not have enough, so don't get your hopes up too high on getting a knife." I promised her that I wouldn't, but that dad was trying to get me one made me feel really proud and worthy.

"Hey, my pants match my moccasins!" I exclaimed, as I finished tying the laces.

"Yes, they do. Same batch of leather," mom explained. "When the men bring in the deer, we women try to match the hides before we divide them up among us. Who wants pants and tops that just don't match?" We both chuckled.

Promptly at noon, Ellen knocked on our door. I opened it, "How do I look?" I exclaimed, twirling around showing off my new outfit.

"My, my, you look terrific. I see your mom has been really busy," Ellen smiled and nodded her approval to Sarah. "I'll take good care of her, I promise," she added. Mom appreciated her words; I could tell from her facial expression. She came to the door and proudly watched us walk off through the village heading south. I noticed all the other children stopped their games to watch as well. I held my head high and tried to walk as stately as Ellen did, for I was representing my village now or so I considered.

We headed south on the well-worn trail the men used to go to the scattered fields that lay about our valley. I waived at my dad as we passed him, and I could see his face smiling at my new outfit. I sensed his pride in me as well. In a half hour, the wide trail had dwindled to a narrow track. Now that we had left all traces of our village behind, Ellen began speaking. "Okay, geography review time, Beth. Tell me about the area in which we are walking."

I took a deep breath and began reciting, "We're in the Valley of Ur, which is about twenty-five miles wide. The Blankford Hills rise up on the eastern side, while Kapa Ridge blocks the southwestern side. The track we're following leads to the village of Undel, which is about ten miles due south of Uru. About halfway there, a side track leads east by north for another ten miles to the fortified town of Redun, where King Randolf, the Mighty, dwells. The village of Karka lies almost due west of Uru. So are we heading to Undel?" I ended by asking where we were going.

"Very good. Exactly correct. But no, not Undel. We're going to a place that is holy to druwids, the Standing Stones of Garth. It is located out in the middle of Garth Valley, which is just on the other side of Kapa Ridge. The Standing Stones are about five miles from the village of Garth, which is southwest of the stones. So that means we must cross Kapa Ridge or else we must walk the very long way around. Either we go some twenty-five miles on these tracks to get there or take the shortcut over the ridge line and only have to go about ten miles total. Which will it be?"

Twenty-five miles seemed like an eternity to me. I've never gone anywhere near that far before. So I said, "I hope we go over Kapa Ridge. But where? Is there a path for us to follow?"

"You remember that small little shelter I showed you when we were out here last summer?" I nodded remembering a small wooden cabin barely eight feet square located out in the middle of nowhere in the forested lands on our side of Kapa Ridge. We had stopped there for a brief rest and had eaten a snack.

"Actually, there is an easy route over Kapa Ridge that begins just behind that cabin, Beth. Other druwids built that cabin many years ago as an emergency shelter for us when we travel about. This is a very important thing to know, Beth. All throughout the entire Greenway, we have built little cabins like this one. Inside, you will find blankets, a little food, and some firewood, if you know where to look for them. They are there for emergencies. Just remember to replenish what you take as soon as you are able. So remember, there's an emergency cabin strategically placed about every five miles or so, unless a village is nearby. Here, there is this cabin on the eastern side of Kapa Ridge and an identical one on the other side. We'll see them both and sleep in the other one later tonight. Now, observe nature as we walk. See if you can lead us straight to that cabin. I won't say a word."

I gulped. She was leaving it up to me to find that cabin! I'd only been there once before and that was a whole year ago! I wondered if she'd let us wander aimlessly about if I couldn't find it. However, the sunny day soon evaporated my worries, and I began just to observe once again. Life was beautiful. Green grasses waved in the gentle afternoon breeze. The forests, which grew on both sides of the hills on either side of the slowly narrowing valley, looked particularly beautiful to my eyes.

We had walked perhaps a little over two hours meeting no one when I spied the tiniest hint of a side trail leading straight west. This had to be it, so I headed off west down this path, hoping it was right. Ellen, as she promised, said nothing but followed me like a puppy. Slowly, we began climbing up the side of Kapa Ridge. Soon, we entered the cool, dry forest proper. Orangish granite rock outcrops appeared here and there. Oaks, maples, and a host of other trees predominated, hiding, sometimes dwarfing the stony ridge.

Then, I noticed something else. Ellen was walking more slowly than normal and her breathing was more labored. "Are you okay?" I asked, as I paused and turned to look at her.

"Yes, dear," she replied stoically. "It's just I'm getting very old. My days in this body are growing far too short, I fear. This is the Cycle of Life on Tarra," she replied. "Let's just go a bit slower, please, and I'll do just fine." So I went slower, adjusting my speed to one in which she could breathe almost normally. Suddenly, I spied it — the cabin! It was just as we had left it last year. I felt a surge of pride at having been able to find it. I realized that had I not been observing, I would never have found it.

"Congratulations, Beth. Very well done!" Ellen exclaimed. "Now, let's go inside. I think you'll find something there waiting for you," she teased me, her eyes twinkling as I glanced back at her. I opened the door and went inside; she was right behind me. "Open that chest on the floor by the bed." I did as she was told.

"Allow me to present you with your first druwid cloak, staff, and knife," she pronounced, as I quickly brought out the three things. My eyes must have shown my wild excitement, as I examined the magnificent woolen cloak, dyed to match my leather outfit. On the lapel, Ellen had embroidered a beautiful oaken cluster, our Guardian symbol. Next, I displayed my walking staff. It was light, yet strong. Ellen explained that it was oak and hand-carved with symbols of our group. Finally, lying on the bottom of the chest was a six-inch metal knife with a white bone handle in a leather sheath. "I hereby present you with your first staff, cloak, and matching knife; they are symbols of our group." I think I must have said thank you about a hundred times. I was just *so* overcome with happiness.

Ellen helped me fasten the cloak about my neck. "Yes, perfect fit, if I do say so myself. Of course, your mom and I were in this together," she teased. "I had to make sure these all matched your new leather outfit. She showed me where to fasten the knife to my belt. "Always carry your knife on your left side so you can fast draw it when needed with your right. That is, unless you are left handed, in which case, do it just the opposite," she explained, and fetched her staff which she had left lying in the corner. She put on her cloak so we matched and then led the way back out of the cabin. We looked just alike, save for the size and age difference.

"So now you are a fully-equipped druwid. Let's see if you can live up to your calling. Lead us to the next emergency cabin on the other side of Kapa Ridge. We are in dire trouble and need to make that cabin quickly."

"But I've never been there!" I protested. How on Tarra could I ever find it, I thought.

"Ah, we guardians are called upon to travel sometimes long distances and to places we've never been. What happens to us if we have an emergency, say are bitten by an adder? If we stand around and do nothing, we would surely perish. None of us knows where all the emergency cabins are located, especially when we are in unfamiliar lands. Yet, we all know how to find one. So pretend we are in trouble and find us the next cabin. You can do it. I've already given you a big clue. Now do it."

She was using her stern voice once again so I knew that ended the matter. I would have to try. So I began observing the ground in the vicinity of the cabin on the western side. I knew we had to climb up and over the ridge. I spied a faint track but could not tell if deer had made it or people. It headed up toward the ridgeline. So I took it. Off we went, Ellen following me. An hour later, we crested the ridge. Here few trees grew, and we had a breathtaking panorama view of the entire Ur valley. It was so spectacular that we both paused in silence for several minutes. Ellen finally commented, "Views like this are what makes life so worth living! Okay, let's get going. Lead on, Beth."

Down the other side we went, still following the barely visible path. An hour later amid dense oak trees, I spied another cabin and walked up to it. I felt a great sense of relief, but also I felt proud of my accomplishment. I had found it without any help from Ellen, save that it was located on the other side of the ridge. "Very well done indeed, Guardian Elizabeth," Ellen proclaimed and added, "You probably feel like you are ten feet tall about now! Enjoy that feeling, for you have accomplished what most men cannot. Now, let's go inside and eat our lunch snack. We still have a couple hours of walking to go yet to get to the stones, but it is all downhill, and I should be able to go much faster."

"However, we are not going to go faster. Instead, it is time you learn critical details of our organization so when we join the others, you'll understand the importance of this meeting," she said in her stern voice so there was no misunderstanding on my part. I began to wonder just how large our organization actually was and where all of the others were. So far, my only contact with the druwid was Ellen.

"When a novice such as yourself accomplishes successfully the skills of the fourth year of training, it is then time you're brought forth as a new member in our group. That is one of the reasons for this gathering, to introduce you to the others. Actually, I'm not alone as you probably thought. I've never been alone. I'm part of my Circle of Seven. All druwids are formed into Circles of Seven, without exception. Each Circle acts independently of the others and is our most basic building block, organizationally." This sounded fascinating. I listened carefully, committing everything to memory as fast as I could.

"Each Circle has seven members, though each of the seven has a different title, purpose, and function within the Circle. We all have the same basic training, skills, and knowledge, but we all have a different interest in life and so choose one of the seven specialties in which to concentrate our knowledge and efforts. Does this make sense to you so far?"

"Sure, so you have six other really close friends. I didn't know that. Can I meet them or is that not allowed? How come they never visit you or do you sometimes visit them?" I seemed to be asking questions that popped into my head. If I had close friends, I'd want to be with them a lot of the time.

"Let me finish and then answer your direct questions. Otherwise, it'll be hard for you to grasp my reply." I nodded okay, and she continued. "Our Circle is called the Circle of Blankford. Each Circle usually adopts a name corresponding to the area in which the leader of the Circle dwells. Blankford is about twelve miles northeast of Uru. We've never been there. Now the leader of the Circle bears the title of Wid. Their specialty is truth, knowledge, and wisdom, which is why they are called upon to lead the others in the Circle. A Wid searches always for more knowledge. Next, there is the Healer whose specialty is the healing arts. A Healer knows far more than I do about curing man's illnesses and accidents. The Loremaster's specialty is a thorough knowledge of woodland lore, the lore of the lands, including plants and animals — all of Nature. That is my title. I'm the Loremaster of my Circle."

I interrupted her, "So this means you know more about the woods than anybody else around here, right?" I felt pleased to be walking with her.

"Yes, that I do," she replied with a smile. "Next is the Planner, whose skills lay in designing all things, especially buildings and structures. These people are very good at working with figures. I would say all major buildings in the Greenway have had a Planner somewhere behind the scenes planning and directing its construction. Next is a very special job, the Communicator, whose specialty is telepathy or communicating via thoughts directly from one person to another across any distance. You see, it is our Communicator who keeps each of us informed, even though we're all in different villages. So even though you do not see my other Circle members, we are communicating and relaying messages through our Communicator. That is how I know that no Galts are going to attack Uru while I'm away. Next comes the Protector, whose specialty lies in all types of combat and fighting. He is a master swordsman at the very least. His job is to protect the rest of the Circle and is a vital position indeed."

"That sounds like a dangerous job!" I exclaimed, imagining some strong man valiantly fending off scores of Galts who were intent on harming Ellen.

"Yes, it is. Sometimes, I wish we had more than one Protector. Last but not least is the Judger, who is both a conjurer and an arbitrator. These people are highly skilled in the rendering of community decisions. Villages, as well as many leaders, often call upon them to make a binding judgment on some matter of vital importance. These people are also masters at getting those we protect to accept and go along with their decisions. Fortunately, in Uru, everyone just accepts my judgment calls and doesn't challenge them. If they did protest my decisions, I'd call in our Judger, who would handle the matter. But the Judger is also a conjurer, sort of a magician who can make things appear from thin air, I sometimes believe. The closest I can come to conjuring is to bring down the fire from the sky."

"Golly, I never realized there were so many different tasks we have to perform. They all sound really interesting, except for the fighter, the Protector. I really don't like fighting at all," I pronounced.

"Ah, neither do I, Beth, neither do I," Ellen said with a sigh. "So to answer your original questions, because of the Communicator, we're in touch with each other at least once a day. Since we all have a village to help support, it's difficult for all of us to get away at the same time to meet. We do so on our special days, such as this one, the summer solstice. However, from time to time, we visit each other, though we never broadcast our visits to the local villagers. It is a private affair, if you follow me."

"I think so, but I would still like more contact with my friends, though," I declared. "Say, is one of these others your husband? Are you married?" I'm not sure why I blurted this question out. I guess it was the discovery that they were a close Circle that prompted it.

Ellen didn't answer for a minute. I looked at her eyes, and they seemed vacant, distant. I concluded she was looking at her memories. Perhaps, I should not have asked her that. She sighed and said, "I was married to Samuel Stocks a long time ago. He was killed by Galts nearly twenty years ago. He was one of the initial planners of Uru's long houses, in fact."

"Now Beth, we're getting close to the Standing Stones, so I must hurry this up. The leader of our Circle, our Wid, is Mary Ann Twindle, who lives in Blankford. Our Healer is Clyde Bingham, who dwells in Undel, which lies directly south of Uru. I'm the Loremaster. Our Planner is Jason Whiteoak, who is protecting Petersville, about ten miles northwest of Uru. Our Communicator is Willow Windsong, who lives in Karka. Our Protector is Herbert Jackson of Garth. He is in charge this time of bringing all the food and festival gear. We each take turns bringing the supplies for the others. Our Judger is Frank Williams, who lives in Redun on the other side of the Blankford Hills. Yes, you'll meet all of them in a few minutes."

"Finally, each of us has an apprentice druwid that we are teaching. So you will have six others here of nearly your own age, though I think you are the youngest. Golly, we're running out of time. So let me say one more thing, since this is your fifth year, you may choose one of these seven areas in which to specialize. There is no rush in making any decision, mind you, and you do not even have to choose until you are ready to do so. Here, pause a moment. Look down the hill through the oak trees."

"Wow! The stones really are standing up like people! And I can see other people there too. I hope we're not late or anything!" I replied suddenly worrying that we were the last to arrive.

"No child, we're not late until the sun sets, and we still have an hour to spare," she chuckled. "Let's go down and join them." Rapidly, we closed the distance to the festival.

We were in a very isolated glade or clearing, miles and miles from any civilization. In the center stood seven huge gray stones, their bases buried in the ground, pointing finger-like to the sky. They seemed to form a pattern, though I could not tell exactly what. There were far more people present than I reckoned, based on Ellen's discussion. It didn't take long for me to see that many had brought their wives and husbands and other children. Seeing many other children running around between the stones made me feel right at home and comfortable.

As soon as we got closer, the deep voice of their Protector, Herbert, spoke up, "Ah, there you are Ellen, last as always. The rest are already here. No problems getting here, I take it?" He was a tall, muscular man. His arms seemed awfully big, nearly twice those of my dad. I concluded he was very strong indeed. I also guessed he was the Circle's Protector. I was right. He carried two swords and several knives, and was dressed in heavy leather, rather like the nasty Galts that had attacked our village.

"Guardian Beth, let me introduce our Protector, Herbert Jackson. He is also our host this time, and the man to see for all the food and drink you can eat," Ellen explained. "Herbert, this is Beth."

"Pleased to meet you," I said rather bashfully. I was not used to meeting new people. In fact, I cannot recall having done so before. I knew everyone in our village.

"Ah, you do look mighty fine, Beth, even better than the Loremaster said! Say, here's someone I want you to meet. Roy, come over here a minute." A boy, about a year older than me, hastily rushed to his side. Roy was dressed similar to me, leather pants and top. He also had a cloak nearly identical to mine. He had long blonde hair and blue eyes and stood about six inches taller than me. "Beth, this is my apprentice, Guardian Roy Ron Randell. Roy, this is Ellen's apprentice, Beth. Make sure she feels right at home here. That's your charge tonight."

"Pleased to meet you, Beth," he said smiling, glad to have beaten out all the other apprentices to be the one to look after me, though I did not learn that fact until later. "I'll tag along beside you. I know lots, so just ask me," he said enthusiastically. I smiled thanks at him.

"Ah there you are, Ellen, just in time," the alto voice of an unassuming woman interrupted us. She was a tall woman whose face showed the same age lines as did Ellen, so I guessed they were about the same age. She spoke before Ellen could, "I'm the Wid, Mary Ann Twindle. And you must be Elizabeth. Is that a new outfit you are wearing? It looks really good on you."

I blushed. How did she know it was my new outfit? We'd never met, but then I remembered she was their Wid and expected to know many, many things. All at once, I realized she must be able to observe far better than anyone else did in the Circle. I had already learned that only by observation comes knowledge. "Yes, ma'am. I'm Elizabeth. Yes, my mom just made it for me; it was supposed to be my birthday present. She gave it to me early because

I was coming here. I'm very pleased to meet you too," I finally remembered my manners. Somehow, I just felt really comfortable around her, almost as if she were my mother.

She then said, "And this is my apprentice Raphael Penton." He was probably twelve years old, stood a foot taller than me, was just as thin as I am, and had short black hair and the bluest eyes I had ever seen. His voice was soft as rain.

"Pleased to meet you, Elizabeth," he said formally, and I replied in kind. I took an immediate fancy to him. Perhaps, he was like an older brother to me that I never had, since I was the oldest in our family. By now, the rest of Ellen's Circle had walked over and a whirlwind of introductions followed.

Clyde Bingham, the Healer, was introduced to me next. He was very old with grey hair and full grey beard. His mind always seemed elsewhere, but I heard him asking Ellen if she had brought the herbs he had been seeking. Thus, I figured he must be trying to heal someone. His apprentice was Sarah Jane Greenleaf, a pretty girl of thirteen. She wore her blonde hair longer than mine and looked stunning. She paid me little attention, preferring to enchant the other young lads. After she danced off after another boy trying to get his attention, Roy whispered to me, "She's just a tease, you know, but she is going to be a great healer one day."

Jason Whiteoak, the Planner, was perhaps the same age as my dad, youthful and full of ideas. He was continually making sketches of things on some parchment and seemed putout to have to stop to be introduced. He was tall and sported a great mustache that curved upwards at both ends. His apprentice was Simon Donegal, who was two years older than I was. I noticed his observant eyes first. Here was one who missed nothing. He was tall and well-dressed, as if he was trying to appear older than he actually was. Simon had short black hair and black eyes. After the introduction, he moved off attempting to strike up conversations with the others in Ellen's Circle.

Frank Williams, the Judger, was an impressive man, whose eyes missed nothing. When he addressed me, he looked me squarely in the eyes. At once, I felt that I could hold nothing back from him. He had that effect on me. Later, Roy explained that he always had that effect on everyone; after all, that was his specialty, the arbitrator. His apprentice was Thomas Wilkins, who was thirteen. He was the most unassuming of the apprentices, quiet and thoughtful. He had brown hair and brown eyes. Thomas, like me, carried several leather packs and pouches in which to put things he gathered. I thought at once that he was likely specializing in woodland lore, and as if in confirmation of my conclusion, he spent much time chatting with Ellen about the forest trees near Uru.

Finally, I was introduced to Willow Windsong, their Communicator. She was thin as a corn stalk with long brown hair that hung nearly to her knees. Her brown eyes sparkled with life, and she had a voice that I fell in love with almost at once, mellow and commanding it was. "I keep us all together," Willow explained, as I sat nearly enchanted listening to her every word. While

I felt like Mary Ann could almost be my mother, Willow felt more like a loving older sister! I knew I loved both of them just as soon as I met them. "And this is my apprentice Communicator, Sandy Gaston."

Sandy was only a year older than I was with long black hair and very attractive black eyes. She was not as pretty as Sarah Jane was, but when she spoke, I listened, for it was very similar to Willow's voice. I could see that she was also learning to be a Communicator.

Before I could say much else, Mary Ann's voice commanded all, "Okay, it is time for the celebration to begin. The sun is setting. Please take your places by your stone. Mark the position of the last ray of the sun, please."

Ellen took my hand, "Come, you can stand with me. Here is my stone — well it doesn't have my name on it. I just usually stand here. Now watch the sun's rays strike that front stone top. See where it goes from there. It should strike my stone squarely in this hollow spot. It only happens at sunset on the summer solstice. These Standing Stones are really marking out our yearly calendar. I will explain that in detail later on. Now watch." I watched the ruddy red sun slowly reach the distant horizon. Its last rays struck the top of the stone that Mary Ann was beside. I saw the ray also hit the center of the hollow on our stone. Ellen seemed pleased with our observations.

Then, everyone ignited lanterns and torches, and the small glen burst into light. Now, I could see all the preparations. A wagon was decorated in flowers and ribbons. It was the food wagon. Nearby wooden tables were setup, and I smelled roasting lamb. It was suppertime, and I found myself ravishingly hungry. The adults and their spouses ate at the larger tables, leaving us seven apprentices to our own table. The other children were at yet another table. I think we all were hungry, for we said nearly nothing but stuffed ourselves on the rich food. For me, it was like a harvest time feast. Only then could we afford so much good food at one time.

Once we were all so full that we could not eat another morsel, an herb tea laced with honey was served. We all sat back, and the chatting began. Quickly, I observed these other six already knew each other. So I was the newcomer. Sarah Jane wanted to know how old I was, and I said I'd be eleven in two months. I guessed I was the youngest apprentice.

Sarah Jane then said coyly, "Well, now we know each other. I should tell you that I, Simon, and Thomas are all *seventh* year apprentices." She emphasized the seventh. "Roy, Raphael, and Sandy are only in their *sixth* year. So that makes you only a *fifth* year apprentice, Elizabeth." I felt she was attempting to put me into my place in their group.

To my surprise, Thomas piped up in my defense, "Hey, Sarah Jane, don't be so condescending with her. I've heard tell she has been doing feats in her fourth year that the rest of us barely mastered in our fifth year, like finding the safe cabins on your own. I remember you had a really hard time passing that, and I just heard Beth did it easily on her first try." I smiled at him in appreciation. However, that others would find it hard to find the safe cabins had never crossed my mind.

Roy interrupted him, "She probably doesn't know about our choices yet, seeing how she is only starting her fifth year. We should explain it for her." Several of the others nodded, and he turned to me and said, "Usually in our fifth year we decide on what we really want to specialize. I'm training to be a Protector. Raphael there, he has the knack for figures; he's already helped construct two buildings! And Sarah Jane is becoming a Healer, but sometimes she is a bit rude." Sarah Jane blushed; she knew he spoke the truth. With her peers, there was no hiding the truth of an action. "Simon, he's working on being a Judger, and from what I can see so far, he's got just the temperament for it. He's always settling arguments, even among us. Thomas, he definitely has a thing for a Loremaster. Did you notice he has already chatted with Ellen?"

"Well, I don't get to see her as much as I want," Thomas protested in his defense.

Roy continued, ignoring Thomas's protest, "Sandy is most definitely a Communicator type. It's spooky how she can read your mind, your thoughts! Be careful around her; you can't hide anything from her," he teased.

"Well I wouldn't be much of a Communicator if you could hide things from me, now would I?" she replied with a touch of feigned sarcasm. Everyone laughed with her. "So, Beth, have you chosen a path yet? If not, what are you really interested in?" Now it was out. They really wanted to know much more about me! I wasn't prepared for this.

"I only found out about all this today, I'm sorry. I've no idea at all. I know I just want to learn all about everything. I haven't found anything yet that I don't want to know more about and to understand, except fighting. I loathe fighting. We've had many Galt attacks on our village. I've seen dead men, and I didn't like it at all!"

"Wow!" exclaimed Sarah Jane, "You've seen *real* dead Galts?" From her tone and concern, I assumed she hadn't actually seen them.

"Yes, the worst one was four years ago. A whole bunch of them attacked Uru. I stood near Ellen as she brought down the fires from the sky and even blinded their leader," I explained. Suddenly, I observed I had everyone's full and complete attention. Roy was practically staring at me, grasping the full meaning of my every word. I thought he looked a bit silly, but then fighting was what he was studying. So I had to recount the entire affair, repeating several times the things that Ellen had done to protect us all that day. From the looks on their faces, I knew they were impressed. Perhaps, they'd never seen Ellen in action, assuming she was only knowledgeable about the forestlands. I caught Sarah Jane and Thomas occasionally glancing over at Ellen as I described the affair.

When I finished, Sandy, clearly upset about the gruesome details, changed the topic. I was most grateful to her for doing so. "So, Beth, you really are interested in nearly everything? Even the best way to sew a new dress or why it snows or why we have seasons or what's just over the next ridge?"

I laughed at the strange concatenation of ideas, "You bet. Golly, each one of them is really interesting. I'd really like to know about all of them. I want to know why my mom and dad are so stuck inside their heads, and if possible, free them. Why, there is just *so* much to learn! Healing is so very important; I need to know far more than I do now, though I did save my dad's life when he got bit by an adder." Instantly, Sarah Jane looked at me in a very different way; I sensed she had just accepted me somehow. "And well, you are all studying stuff that interests me — well, all except Roy. I hate fighting."

All at once, Sandy stood up and pronounced, "Gang, I think we have found our Wid at long last!" The others cheered, but I looked dumbfounded. "Look, Beth, you have just said exactly what a Wid would say. You and Mary Ann are both peas in the same pod; you want to know everything. She's always learning something new and often surprising! Though you haven't yet officially made your choice, I can't see how it could be anything other than the Wid for you!"

"Well, I suppose so," I replied a bit daunted by their enthusiasm.

"And a Wid would make us complete," Sandy continued. "We'd then have all the positions filled so we could form our own Circle!" Again, everyone cheered. So I assumed that this was somehow very important to them.

Sarah Jane detected my confusion and explained, "You see, once we've finished our tenth year, we can at any time after that form our own Circle, and then we get all sorts of freedoms. We can even sometimes choose our own geographical base of operations. We'd be a real Circle! And until you came along, we were so very worried about not having a Wid. If we cannot find one, we have to try to get one from some other Circle's apprentices and that can sometimes take a very long time. Wids are very hard to find, the rarest of us all, I've heard tell. While we all have to study lots, a Wid apprentice has to study ten times as much! I *know* I can't do that! It's all I can do to learn all about the healing arts! By the way, I agree with you, I don't like all the fighting either. If Roy and all the other men would just stop fighting altogether, it would cut the amount of work a Healer has to do nearly in half!"

"Yeh, yeh, yeh," broke in Roy, "You say that now, but just you wait until the Galts come charging at you with their swords. Then, you'll be plenty glad you have a Protector around!" She snickered, but knew he spoke wisely.

"Well, maybe the answer lies in designing better fortifications around our villages," broke in Raphael. "King Randolf, the Mighty, in Redun, has now built super fortification walls around the entire town! The wooden walls are ten feet tall and tipped with spikes so you can't climb over them. Very impressive, I'd say. That'll stop the Galts!"

Looking downcast, Thomas answered, "Yes, he's completely wiped a huge section of his nearby forest out making that huge barricade. Whoever heard of enclosing an entire town that is about a mile in diameter with a solid, massive wooden wall? It's not going to last long before the termites go to work eating it up. The loss of all those trees makes me sick. Trees don't go around killing people. We could all learn lots more from nature!"

"Yes, but I sure would feel lots safer if my house were inside such a stockade wall," declared Sandy. "I wonder if all the villages will follow his lead and make barrier walls to protect themselves too?"

"King Randolf has got an army of fighters to man the walls — lots of archers too," Raphael added. "In Blankford, there is only one man who has any fighter training, and he is mostly retired. So even if every village made a huge stockade around their dwellings, they would still be pretty much defenseless."

I saw my chance to say something of importance, so I jumped in, "In Uru, the men were all far off in the fields when the Galts attacked us. It was all over by the time my dad got back to the village. So without someone to defend the walls, what use would they really be?" Everyone nodded approval at my observation.

"Say, do you think there is any truth in the rumor we've been hearing that King Randolf is going to annex all the nearby lands and put them under his protection?" Simon cleverly asked what he had been wondering about for weeks. "I've seen some of his new cavalry patrolling near Petersville. Is there any truth to this, Thomas? You live there."

"Yes that's precisely what I've heard. It has Frank really upset and bothered. I don't think he fully trusts King Randolf or maybe that he doesn't think the King can realistically provide all that much protection," Thomas confided. "Honestly, I've never seen him so worried about anything before. It is hard to rile a Judger, I've discovered. Even if I totally screw up, he doesn't mind at all. Yet, this annexation business has him really bothered. I suspect that is one of the things our elders are discussing over there. I kind of wish we could hear what they are saying. It might be really interesting." We all glanced over at the adult's table. Sure enough, they were all talking in hushed serious voices that we could not quite hear.

Sandy brought us back to the present, "Well, I'm sure our mentors will tell us everything when the time is right for us to know. Willow always does." I took some comfort in that for I hated to only half find out about something that was important. I just had to know all about it.

At this point, the elders finished their discussion, and Mary Ann loudly announced, "Okay, it's time for music and dancing. Musicians, let's have some fun!" This came as a surprise to me. Not only did I have no idea what dancing was all about, but music? In Uru, we sometimes sang songs. Could that be what she meant? A bit of panic struck me; I was sure I did not know any of their songs.

Frank Williams began strumming on his lute, and Jason joined in playing a flute like instrument. The music was lively, friendly, and made one start tapping one's feet in time. The others got up from the table, broke into pairs, and began dancing about. "Come on, Beth; dance with me," pleaded Roy.

I must have looked very embarrassed. He said, "So you don't know how to dance; come on. I'll show you how. It's so easy babies can learn it in no time. Come on." So I took his offered hand and away we went into the open area. Actually, it was easy. He only had to show me how for a couple minutes, and I caught on quickly. However, he was always doing different moves just as soon as I had mastered the one we were on. He was relentless and thoroughly enjoying the fun.

I noticed the other families and children had joined in. Everyone was twirling around in time to the music. I soon lost myself in the gaiety. Three hours passed in almost no time! Finally, the music stopped. Mary Ann proclaimed, "All good things must have an ending. And so here we are. This is the end of our Summer Solstice party. Don't fret. The Autumnal Equinox is just around the corner. Thank you all for coming." And just as fast as the party started, it ended. Everyone began packing up, and I helped as I could.

Sandy came over to me and spoke very softly, "Beth, now that you are one of us and going to be our Wid, can I try to communicate to you? You know, practice my telepathy with you. I've got to practice it lots and lots so I can get very good at it."

"Sure, but I don't know anything about it or how you do it," I consoled her. "I don't expect I'd be a very good person for you to practice on, really," I replied, not knowing at all what was expected of me.

"Thanks, you don't have to do anything at first. I do the work. But you'll see," she happily answered. There was no time for further discussion, Ellen found me and beckoned me to come. "Bye, Beth!"

"Bye, Sandy. I hope I don't mess it up too badly," I answered, as I grabbed hold of Ellen's hand. Mentally, I quickly made sure I now had everything I'd brought with me, packs, cloak, knife, walking stick. Yes, I was not forgetting anything. Ellen hastily led me out of the glen and into the dark woods that lined the ridge. She held a lantern before us so we could see the path. It was very late at night for me. I had never been up quite this late before.

"Think you can find the emergency cabin on your own?" she asked. "It's much harder at night with so little light."

"I'm awfully tired, but I can try." Only now was fatigue setting in. I just wanted to lie down and sleep. I began observing the ground in front of us, wishing I had paid more attention to our path when we came down the ridge. Luck was with me or Ellen had at least put us on the right path. I spied an uprooted rock here, bent grass there, even a moccasin footprint occasionally. Keeping my mind focused on the trail had the benefit of keeping it from thinking about all that I had learned and experienced this evening. I managed to say, "I had more fun tonight than any other party I've even attended. Thanks for bringing me."

Because I went very slowly, Ellen was not overly taxed climbing up the ridge. I wondered if that had any significance in her asking me to find the path. In an hour, I had walked us right up to the dark door. "I've never been so glad to find a cabin before!" I exclaimed yawning heavily.

"Very, very well done, Beth," Ellen complimented, "You know, very few fifth years students could actually find it in the daytime, let alone at night. You are an amazing young woman! I see I had better fix you a bed and fast. You look like you are falling asleep on your feet." I knew she was teasing, but I was thankful she made up our beds. One minute after I laid down, I was soundly asleep vaguely remembering mom had told me I would have to brush my hair before bed this night. I imagined myself doing it instead.

I awoke to the smells of breakfast cooking. How much earlier Ellen had arisen, I could only guess. Still tired, I managed to get properly dressed and lent a hand. After the warming porridge and a cup of tea, I felt more alert. Thankfully, Ellen did brush my hair so I didn't present that slept-in-look to mom when I got home. I cleaned up the cabin, while she put everything back in its proper place, ready for the next person in need. By about eight o'clock, we were on the trail once more.

Again, going downhill was much easier on her, and we began to chat about the festival. I had so many questions I wanted to ask her that I didn't know where to begin. So I started in with the biggest one. "They all expect I'll be their Wid in training. Each of them told me about their special interests. None, it seems, wants to know everything. I can't imagine why. Can I be a Wid, Ellen? They seemed to think that's what I should be. It seemed to me that some would rather play than study hard, especially Sarah Jane. What do you think?"

"I must apologize, Beth, I should have gone over the different specialties with you long ago. I just didn't get around to it. Not much of an excuse is it?" she said rather lamely. "Yes, it's your choice but seeing just how much you have learned in so short of a time, I totally back your decision to become a Wid. I think you have just what is required to hold that position — an incessant desire to know all about things, everything. I suppose they told you in a few years they'll be ready to form their own Circle?" I nodded. "And they probably also told you they were really anxious to find someone to hold the Wid position?" Again, I nodded. "Just make sure that's something you desire. If so, I completely support your decision."

"I think so," I replied, "because I'd feel like I had blinders on, like a buggy horse, if I was to concentrate only on Healing or woodland lore. True, I want to know about them, but there is so much else to know. Like what is the aurora that we sometimes see in the night sky? I've so many questions that want answers."

"And you should seek those answers, Beth. Be true to your own purposes, and you'll do just fine. And yes, the Wid knows much and is very wise, but that comes from constantly learning new things. That's why not everyone is cut out to become a Wid. It takes a special person who is willing always to learn new things to become a Wid. I think you'll do just fine." Then she changed the topic. "One of the things we must do during your fifth year is travel around the local area and get you familiar with the other towns and villages. You can also visit with your new friends." Hearing that made my heart jump! I would get to see the world and my new friends.

"Leave it to me to find a way to make it acceptable to your parents for you to accompany me. We both know just how much they are depending on you as you get older. Your mom is expecting another baby this late fall, am I not correct?" I grinned; it was supposed to be a secret for a little while yet. "Well, with a new baby to take care of, she is going to need more help, though Anne and Ben are now getting old enough to help out lots. I'll just have to see what I can do. We should get out and about at least once a month until the snows come." Now that sounded terrific to me. I'd get to see at least one of my new friends each month, as well as see these six other nearby towns that I had only heard about — it sounded fabulous to me.

Soon our tiny track joined the main trail connecting Undel to the south with Uru to the north, and the going was much easier. Then, we got a terrific break. We had not gone more than a mile when Mr. Dockwater overtook us with his wagon. He had been on a seed buying trip to Undel and was returning. "Hail Ellen! How about a ride?"

Ellen turned around, "Henry, that is the best idea I've heard all day. Have you got room for both of us?"

"Sure do, ma'am. Whoa," he called out to the two buggy horses pressed into wagon drawing service. When he stopped, we climbed aboard. Ellen sat up front on the seat with him, while I nestled down on the soft sacks of new seed and other supplies in the rear. This was also my first ride in a wagon, except the fall hayrack party rides around Uru.

Mr. Dockwater seemed glad for the chance to talk to Ellen. "I've managed to commandeer quite a lot of last year's seed from folks in Undel. I went around and bartered everyone for all their excess, leftover seed they didn't plant this past spring. Ellen, I ended up with far more seed than you had hoped we'd manage to find! Nearly twice. Imagine that. So even if some doesn't sprout, like you suggested, we have more than enough to greatly expand our crops next spring."

"Now that *is* the best news I've heard in quite a while, Henry. You did very well indeed. If my predictions hold true, then Uru should be able to significantly expand the amount of produce, come next harvest time. We ought to have an overabundance of production. And that means every family should have enough extra to barter for much needed supplies, maybe even some metal plow blades, clothes, and maybe even better cooking gear."

"I see it as being better able to ride out hard times, if you take my meaning," Henry added. Ellen obviously did, but I didn't. Was he worrying about the Galts or something else? I didn't dare ask, though. "Do you think we would be able to have enough extra to buy another dozen plow horses?"

Ellen replied, "Like I've always said, concentrate on constantly expanding your production. Yes, but I really think one of you should take up the breeding of plow horses. That way Uru could produce its own horses in abundance. Each of you could then raise far more crops and have much more excess with which to barter for all sorts of things. But so far, none of you has exhibited any horse sense." Both chucked at her play on words. That's true, I thought; no one in Uru really knew about how to breed, raise, and train horses. So naturally, I wondered if I could learn to do that. If so, I could be helpful to my village. I resolved to remember to ask Ellen about it when we were alone.

Just as Ellen had promised mom, we arrived back in Uru around noon. At the outskirts, we saw my dad working in his fields, and we waved. After thanking Mr. Dockwater for the ride, Ellen walked me to my door so mom would see that we arrived safely, and then she left heading to her house. Just as soon as I was inside, mom wanted to know all about it. Excitedly, I told her I had a wonderful time, that I had learned to dance, heard beautiful music, met many others my own age, and even met the six other local Guardians. I think she was truly happy for me. "But mom, Roy, he's like me only a year older, he had an outfit nearly like mine! I'm so glad you made this for me. If I had been wearing my normal clothes, I'd have been *so* embarrassed. Thank you, mom." She beamed, and I knew she had long ago thought something like this may happen and had prepared for it. My respect for her increased.

Over lunch, she had me tell her all about it. I did, of course, but I left out some things I knew she probably shouldn't hear because she wouldn't understand, her not being an apprentice. Then, over supper I had to tell it all again to dad. He was just as excited as mom was. However, he seemed very interested when I described the other Guardians.

"Yes, dad. All six of them said I could call on them at any time for any help we might need," I explained. I think that impressed him the most. I saw a bit more hope appearing in his face.

"Beth, that is really interesting about how Redun has built a stockade around the whole town. I sure wish we could do that here. You can't imagine how I feel way out there in the fields plowing when you, Sarah, and the kids are back here. I worry all the time that Galts might attack and harm you long before I could get back here. So if we had a stockade around Uru, I sure would rest easier!"

"But dad, unless we had men with swords and stuff behind the walls, the walls alone would not do much," I countered. He nodded; he saw my point. "Don't worry dad, soon I'll be strong enough to help call down the fires from the sky and help Ellen defend Uru. Then, there'll be two of us to contend with," I pronounced solidly, though I wondered just when I would finally be able to conjure the flames. Ellen had never said when I would learn that. I put that in the mental file to ask Ellen the next time I saw her. Then, it was chores and bedtime. I was really tired, and my own bed felt more than cozy that evening.

Chapter 3 The Seeds Are Sown

The next few days after the solstice festival, Ellen was busy catching up on her chores and assisting the villagers sort, catalog, and store their new seed. It was vital to preserve the seed from rotting, fungus attacks, and rodents until it could be planted next spring. Ellen paid careful attention to all aspects of these various tasks. As a result, my training was put on hold, which was just as well, since I wanted to work extra hard on my chores to make up for having missed two days and then get in some games. I missed just playing simple games with the others.

However, midmorning games ended abruptly with the arrival of two dozen cavalry men from Redun. They rode into the middle of the village, dismounting right in the middle of our playing field, so we had to quit. The women, of course, all came outside to see these fine young warriors who were gaily dressed in the blue tunics with a brown bear emblazoned on their fronts. Shortly, the men out in the fields came running into the village, gathering with their wives. All the moms had already gathered their children together. One man, who did not look like a fighter, since he had no swords on him, appeared to be the one in charge. He was perhaps thirty with a black beard neatly trimmed. However, his eyes darted about so, I instantly disliked him.

He waited until the out of breath men had gathered before he spoke, "Good Uru folk, I'm Simon Waters, steward to King Randolf, the Mighty. We know these attacks by the Galts and perhaps the Icemen have been on the increase. As you know, King Randolf has fortified Redun with an impregnable wall around the entire town. In his wisdom, King Randolf has formed up an army of mighty cavalry well equipped, as you can see. Their purpose is to defend the provinces that swear allegiance to his Majesty. Yes, all you must do is swear your allegiance to him, and King Randolf will send his cavalry to patrol Uru and the surrounding lands. King Randolf guarantees his cavalry will keep your village safe. However, the cavalry does require upkeep, what with all the horses and men. So in return for his protection, the village will donate one tenth of the autumnal harvest each year to the King. It's a small price to pay for the guarantee of the safety of Uru. What say you?"

His offer, I could see without much observation, struck a chord with the men. Of course, all were more than a little worried about these surprise Galt attacks, worried about the safety of their wives and children, to say nothing of themselves. I could hear much whispering among the villagers. Old Thomas spoke up first, "My Lord, we're under the protection of the Guardians. Ellen has been doing an excellent job of defending the village. It costs us next to nothing. One tenth of our total crops is a mighty high price to pay." Catcalls of Aye's and Yes's echoed his sentiments. We were barely making it now; by spring, the food pantries were nearly empty. One tenth would really cause food shortages, unless we tightened our belts all year long.

I listened eagerly to hear how Simon would respond. "King Randolf doesn't doubt the excellent services the Guardians perform. Indeed, he has the services of a Guardian in Redun as well, Frank Williams, who you may know is the arbitrator of all injustices for this whole area." More Aye's greeted his pronouncements. "But, and this is very important, but the Guardians are growing old. Look at Ellen; how old is she? How much longer can she perform her tasks? And she is only one. What happens if a large raiding party comes, more than she can handle? King Randolf knows nearly nothing can stop two dozen well-trained, charging cavalrymen. And he does guarantee this force will always be on patrol around the greater Uru area. Even a large host of Galts would flee in fright! Further, if a devastating assault should ever come, the King has told me to tell you that you're welcome to come to the safety of Redun."

He lowered his voice, which only caused everyone to listen even more intently, "I'll let you in on a little secret. King Randolf is going to offer this for a limited time only. He only has so many cavalrymen ready to go on patrol at the moment. All the surrounding villages are getting this same offer this week. We still have to get to Blankford, Petersville and Karka, once we're done here. Already Undel has signed on, and two dozen cavalry have begun their patrols just this morning!" Now he raised his voice once more, "You don't have to make a hasty decision. King Randolf wants you to discuss it amongst yourselves. I assure you the King doesn't take the safety of his neighbors lightly. I'll be back in two days' time from the northern villages. At that time, I must have your answer. If you so swear, I guarantee you two dozen cavalrymen will begin the daily patrols around Uru within one day's time. So think about it. This is a fantastic offer that costs you only grain. Think of the security of your families. Until late tomorrow, I bid you all good day." As if that was a prearranged signal, the men in unison mounted their large horses — large from my point of view anyway. It was an impressive sight, though, seeing so many fighters acting as one unit. I had no doubt they could defend us against the Galts. As if to accentuate their force, they galloped out of the town, hoof beats thundering upon the ground.

So what I had learned from my new friends at the festival was true; King Randolf was expanding the area under his rule. I wondered what the adults would decide. I wanted to talk to Ellen to get her opinion, but naturally, others were already talking with her. Slowly, the men headed back out to the fields, and the women went indoors back to their activities. In the confusion, I lost track of Ellen, and since our interrupted game of seeker had already begun once again, I joined in the fun, putting this important decision into the back of my mind.

We had just finished lunch when all the village children, myself included, dashed outside to play once again. I had already fended off numerous questions such as "Could I being down the fires from the sky" from some of the older ones. Finally, I could just relax and join in the fun. But that did not last long. No sooner had the game started, when I heard in my mind

Beth? Beth? Sandy here. Testing. Are you getting this? Startled, I looked around to see where my new friend was; I was not expecting her to come to visit me so soon. But I didn't see her. *Beth? Sandy here. Testing. Testing. Am I getting through? Come in Beth.*

All at once, I realized Sandy was using her telepathy abilities to reach me. I instantly regretted I hadn't had time to ask her what I was supposed to do. I had no idea. So I said aloud, "I'm here. I heard. Loud and clear, Sandy. What am I supposed to do?" Two nearby kids looked at me rather strangely, but I ignored them.

Great! Oh you don't need to talk. Just think your sentences in your mind and I'll hear them, Sandy sent back. Her words appeared in my mind almost as if she were standing beside me saying them aloud to my ears.

Okay, that's better. Some of the guys are looking at me funny, as if I'm talking to myself. This is really great, Sandy! I thought carefully in my mind.

Whoa. Please slow down. I'm not very good at this yet. I only got about half of what you thought, she sent frantically back to me.

I repeated my thoughts very slowly. *Okay. — This — is — so — great! — Some — of — the — guys — were — looking — at — me — funny — as if — I — was — talking — to — myself. — This — is — really — great — Sandy!*

That's much better. Willow is a good teacher. She says I need lots of practice. The others in our group have grown tired of me chatting with them. So I thought I'd practice with you. Is that okay? Is now a good time?

Give — me — a — minute — to — get — to — somewhere — quiet. I thought carefully. "Anne, you take my place. I have to go to the bathroom." My sister didn't hesitate a second; she was very happy to get into the older children's seeker game. She gave me a big smile and told me not to hurry. I knew what she meant. Quickly, I walked over to the latrines, which were just outside the village to the east. *Okay — Sandy — I'm — back. — We — can — talk — all — we — want — to — now.*

That's good. Willow says you should try to send just a bit faster so I can get better at this. She says I can always ask you to repeat it if I don't get it. She also says perhaps it would help if you used shorter sentences. Anyway, yes, this is really, really a great way to chat! Sandy placed into my mind.

*This is **so** intimate,* I sent back. After a short pause, I added, *How do you do this? Is it hard to learn how? Could Willow teach me how?*

I'll ask her. I've been working on it for a year now. It takes a lot of concentration, that's for sure! Sometimes I get so frustrated with myself for not being able to do it right that I stomp the ground. Say have you heard the news? Galts attacked Blankford yesterday! Willow got the news from Mary Ann.

No! Was anyone hurt? Did she bring down fire on them to drive them off? I asked her. This was fabulous. I was getting news that maybe even Ellen hadn't heard. I was quickly beginning to love telepathy as a way to communicate. I just *had* to learn how to do this!

Don't know what she did. Willow didn't tell me. I did hear that Frank, the Judger, has been keeping a log of their attacks. He thinks he sees some kind of overall plan in their attacks. I've been trying to find out, but no luck so far. Say, when is the best time of day for us to chat like this? Willow says we should make a permanent time for this practicing. I know it can be awkward if you are in the middle of your lessons with Ellen.

I thought fast. I usually had my lessons midday and then all afternoon. Lunchtime was hectic. *How about in the mornings before midday and after supper? I'm usually doing chores or having quiet time in my bed. Say, the King's men were here this morning offering Uru protection in return for our allegiance and one tenth our crops each year.*

We know already. Willow's been in contact with Ellen. Okay if I can, I'll contact you again tonight then. Say, one little thing. I think Roy now has a crush on you! He hasn't talked about hardly anything else but you for the last two days! Gotta go. Bye for now. My face suddenly felt red-hot. It had never occurred to me that a boy might be interested in me. I was only nearly eleven. I was sure glad she broke her connection with me just then; it was embarrassing. I tried to forget about it, for now anyway.

Since I was at the latrine, I decided to use it anyway. I had just finished and was walking back to join the game, when a huge commotion greeted my ears, coming from the southern end of Uru. Naturally, I headed there as fast as I could run. The alarm had not sounded, so it must not be the Galts. I saw several men carrying another man. They were yelling for Ellen; I saw her running their way. I ran up as fast as I could go, trying to remember to practice my observations first before drawing conclusions.

"Galts attacked us in the fields," my dad hastily explained, as they laid Rupert onto the ground so Ellen could examine him. They had really cut him up badly. His leg was bleeding profusely from a very nasty slice. Quickly, Ellen, using her knife, cut away the upper part of his trousers exposing his whole leg. It looked bad from where I stood.

Ellen said, "First, we stop the bleeding. Here, tie his belt around the upper part of his leg. Yes, like that. Now, twist it tight so the bleeding will stop. Good. That's doing it. Here, Rupert, chew on this; I've got to see how bad it is, and this may hurt a lot." She wadded up a piece of his pants and stuck it between his teeth. I saw him bite down hard on it, expecting the worst.

Ellen noticed me observing and nodded to me. I was getting a lesson in the healing arts. "Okay, it is not life threatening just yet. It is a nasty wound. You have lost a lot of blood, Rupert, which is why you are so weak." Speaking to the others, she said, "We need to get him to my house so I can sew up the wound. But I'm going to have to go into the forest to find some plants to use in making a sterile compress to help ward off infection. That's going to be the biggest worry — will it get infected during the slow healing process? Helmut, you go fetch two bottles of wine, one for Rupert and one for me to use to sterilize the wound. The rest of you, carry him to my house. Beth, you hold the belt on his leg tight; we don't want him losing any more blood." With that, my dad took off to get the wine. I held on tightly to the belt, while the men carefully picked him up.

A few minutes later, Rupert was guzzling the wine, which made him very lightheaded very quickly. Once Ellen was sure he'd drunk enough, she put the bit of cloth back in his mouth. She poured the wine into a bowl and dunked her sewing needles and scissors into it. Then, she poured some more over the wound. Rupert let out a mighty moan and passed out. Quickly, Ellen went to work. First, she cleaned the wound thoroughly eventually pouring some water over it to make sure nothing was buried in the deep cut. Next, she methodically began sewing his flesh back together. I noticed most of the men looked rather greenish and quietly left her house. I agreed; it was awfully gruesome, but a healer has got to do their work and cannot afford to be squeamish. I found by concentrating on just observing, my stomach stayed calm. Ten minutes later, she finished and wrapped a clean cloth bandage around the whole wound and had me release the belt very slowly. We both watched for more bleeding. Only a small amount came out. Ellen seemed very satisfied.

She and I cleaned up the mess, covered him with a blanket, and stole outside quietly. "Beth, I'm going to have to go get some fresh herbs from the nearby northern forest. I should be gone no more than an hour at most. Meantime, go find his wife, Betsy, and tell her we have fixed him up. Have her make some liver soup. I know it sounds awful, but when he wakes up, he is going to be dehydrated and will need lots of liquids and assistance building up his blood. So he needs liver soup. He's not to eat solids for at least a couple days." I repeated her exact words back to her so she knew I had it right. Then, we were both off.

I did not have far to go, Betsy was just coming up to the door anxiously hoping for news. I told her what Ellen instructed, while Ellen hastily ducked out her back door heading to the north woods. I let her come inside to see how her husband was doing, but he was still unconscious. She was shaking so badly that I went with her to help her make the soup. In an hour, we had a small pot done and carried it over to Ellen's, and I lit a small warming fire in Ellen's stove to keep it warm for when he woke up. Together, we sat quietly beside Rupert, waiting for Ellen to return.

Time passed, actually quite a lot of time. Suddenly, in my mind I heard Sandy's frantic attempt to make contact with me. *Beth! Beth! You there? Beth! I have to talk to you right now! You there?* It startled me, but fortunately, Betsy was watching her husband and didn't see my startled look.

Yes, I'm here. Galts attacked us. Rupert got badly hurt. Ellen and I sewed him up. I'm waiting for Ellen to get back, I thought fairly slowly, remembering the Sandy could not pick up my thoughts if I went too fast.

Oh great! Willow wants me to tell you that Ellen's in big trouble. Willow says she's not responding to her communication. Something very bad has happened to her. Willow says you are to go and find her right now. Did you get all this? Am I coming through all right? Sandy sounded positively frightened. Her words or thoughts rather were shaky, though I picked them up.

Oh no! Okay, I'll go find her at once. Let you know when I have found her. Thanks, Sandy! I sent. To Betsy, I said quickly, "I think something bad has happened to Ellen. She should have been back long ago! I have to go find her right away! You stay here with Rupert. I think he is coming around. Remember, lots of fluids and a bit of the liver soup." Betsy had a very startled and worried look on her face.

"Take a bunch of men with you. I'll be all right. I'll watch Rupert. Oh, I do hope nothing serious has happened to Ellen. Without her, we have no defense against the Galts!" She was right. I became even more worried. It was not like Ellen to be so late. I suppressed a wave of panic and rushed out the door to find my dad.

My dad listened to my hasty pronouncement. He did not ask how I knew she was in trouble and for that, I was very grateful. He accepted my simple statement that she was to be gone less than an hour and now three had passed. I could sense his extreme worry; without Ellen, Uru was in danger. She had to be found fast. Dad said, "The whole village is depending on you to find her. Go and change into your leathers and bring your knife. I'll gather a bunch of men. Wait for me outside." He kissed Sarah and told her not to worry. He was worried and so was mom. I changed as fast as I could.

On my way out the door, I told mom, "I'll find her. Don't worry. Be back in no time." She hugged me tightly, and then I scooted out the door. It wasn't long before twelve men joined dad. Each had some kind of a weapon, mostly clubs and staves. Four men actually carried the captured Galt swords that we got four years ago.

Dad said, "Okay Beth, lead the way." I led them to the woods north of the village. As we got to the woods' edge, I had them all stand back and let me do some scouting. Actually, I was frantically trying to spy any signs of her passing. I tried to think where she may have headed, remembering all our trips into these woods. *Think!* I told myself. *She was after herbs. Herbs grew best in the shady places on the downward slopes of the Blankford Hills.* So I headed slightly westward. After a half mile, I picked up her trail! Faint it was, but bent grass here and there were sure signs she had passed this way. I even spied a footprint; it was made by a moccasin of just her size. Now, I was sure I was on the right trail. I think dad was actually impressed I could find Ellen's trail, though I pointed out these telltale signs to him.

She was following the usual deer track into the depths of the forest. We made good time. Another half hour and she left the path, but her trail now was even easier for me to follow. Then, I spied large boot scuff marks made by those who cared not for the forest and what they trampled. Galts! It had to be. I pointed these out to dad. An ominous silence fell. I pushed onwards following her trail. The Galts were following her. Even dad could see that and, glancing over my shoulder, I saw he was growing more worried by the minute. So was I, for that matter.

We rounded a large rock outcrop, and there lay Ellen on the ground. I panicked when I saw her. Three arrows protruded from her; one in her leg, two in her chest. She had a nasty cut on her forehead that had covered her entire face in blood, which was now partially dry. No motion did she make. I froze in horror. This could not be happening! I was never so grateful for an adult ever. Dad quickly took charge. Kneeling beside her, he said to the stunned men, "She's still alive. Come on; we have to get her back to Uru as quickly as possible. Give me a hand." He skillfully broke the arrow shafts off, and three men lifted her up. I spied her pack on the ground, bulging with the precious herbs she'd gathered. I surmised she had been taken by surprise. Actually, I was amazed at just how fast the strong men got us safely back to Ellen's house. It took less than twenty minutes.

By the time they had Ellen laid out on her kitchen table, I had recovered my senses, gotten over my shock. "Okay, I'll take it from here. I do hope I know enough healing to do this. Now let's see. Betsy, can you make us lots of boiling water." Ah, that old trick came in useful. It allowed the others to have something to do and gave me time to think and look. Obviously, the arrowheads had to come out. I just hoped they weren't in so deep that I'd have to deal with massive bleeding. I really did not yet understand how to handle internal bleeding. Though I now knew what had to be done, I had not the physical strength to do it. Good old dad. He saw me through it. Under my guidance, he pulled the three arrows out. It took his strong arms to do it, though. Using the hot water and a cloth, I carefully washed each hole clean and let them bleed some more. Ellen had told me the blood would help wash out any contaminants that may have entered. Who knows what that arrowhead had last been in before it entered Ellen, so I let all three seep for a time. Meanwhile, Betsy and I washed off the bloody face so I could see the extent of her head wound.

I sighed in relief. It was a sword cut, but not a deep one. Thankfully, I would not need to attempt clumsily to sew it up. I regretted I still hadn't really learned to sew. I had Betsy hold a clean cloth on the wound to stem its bleeding, while I went to look closely at what herbs she had managed to find. Perfect. What she had gotten for Rupert was also just what she would need as well. This part of the healing arts I knew well. First, I boiled the herbs for twenty minutes and then added some clay. After the clay had boiled and cooled down, I made mud plasters. Three small ones covered each of three arrow holes. A big one covered the gash in her forehead. Then, I tied clean cloths around each to hold everything in place.

Rupert watched the whole operation from the other side of the table. When I finished Ellen, I did the same to his leg and bandaged it up. "There you go, Rupert. Soon you will be good as new." Both thanked me profusely; I felt just a little bit embarrassed by their adoration.

It was now quite dark out. I'd missed supper. Thankfully, mom came by just as I was done with my two patients. She'd brought my dinner, and said, "Dad's coming over to wait up with you when I get back. We don't want to leave your brother and sister alone."

"Thanks, mom. I think Ellen will be just fine, at least I hope so. Rupert's already doing much better," I said, and then ate quickly. I was famished!

"Aye, you have a life saver there, Sarah. Mighty good one," Rupert said softly, for he was still very weak.

Mom's face spoke a thousand words to me. She was so proud of me. Mom said, "You stay the night here, Beth. I'm sure Ellen would want you to be here and look after these two. Betsy, if you want, I'll get Ali to stay with your children tonight so you can stay here. I'm sure Ellen wouldn't want Rupert moved about much just yet."

"Oh would you? That would ease my mind. Robert is fifteen and nearly a man, but I would sleep much better if an adult were there for the younger ones," she replied. I could tell mom's offer gave her tremendous relief.

"Consider it done," mom exclaimed. She picked up the dirty dishes and left to get Ali. Dad came back a short while later; he didn't say much, but did look over my handiwork, nodding his approval. Then, fatigue set in, and I fell asleep in his lap.

It must have been about ten that night when I awoke with a start. People were entering Ellen's door, startling dad who unintentionally woke me. I heard a familiar voice, "Is Ellen all right?" It was Clyde Bingham, the Healer of Ellen's Circle!

I rubbed the sleep out of my eyes, and said, "Yes, I have fixed her up. I'm *so* glad you are here. Can you please see if I did it properly? Please?" I was near to begging. Then, I noticed behind him stood Herbert Jackson, the Protector, armed to the teeth with weapons; Willow Windsong was at his side, looking most worried. Standing behind them I saw their apprentices, my new friends, Roy, Sandy and Sarah Jane; all looked very worried indeed.

"More light," Clyde spoke; dad and Betsy turned up the lanterns. Clyde and Sarah Jane both examined Ellen in great detail, muttering comments as they looked and probed. I felt small and nervous, worrying if I had somehow got it all wrong. Here was a real Healer! Plus, Sarah Jane was almost one herself. After their close examination, he asked to see the arrowheads. Both looked them over carefully. Finally, Clyde spoke to me. "Beth, my compliments. You have done a nearly perfect job. The only detail is should or should not her head wound be sewn up. Sarah Jane and I still can't make up our minds whether it should be or not. So congratulations, Beth. You did an excellent job."

I can't tell you how much relief I felt from his words. First, Ellen was not going to die, and second, I'd actually done the healing properly! I relaxed, only then realizing just how tense my muscles had been during their inspection. Clyde continued, "Now, let's have a look at Rupert." Again, both healers closely examined him. "Sarah Jane, notice how the stitches are laid out. Ellen's style. Never could get her to use proper ones. She keeps thinking it's a piece of cloth." Sarah Jane smiled and nodded. "Rupert, you need to drink lots of liquids for the next few days," Clyde explained.

"Yes, that's what Beth said that Ellen prescribed. That and that awful liver soup! Do I really have to drink liver soup?" Rupert whined.

"Hum, clever, Ellen," Clyde commented. "Well, that's Ellen for you. No, if you would prefer, you can eat some boiled liver in its place. In two days, I want you eating normal food, but always have a small portion of liver with each meal for the next week. It'll help your body rebuild what you've lost." Rupert probably didn't like liver, I surmised from his snarling glance at Clyde. He grumbled, but said he would. Betsy swore she would force feed him if he didn't mind.

"All right then, healing action complete," pronounced Clyde. "Willow, let the others know Ellen will recover." Willow nodded and closed her eyes. Suddenly, I realized she was probably using her telepathy skills to communicate to the others in their Circle. I watched her intently, but saw no clues about how telepathy was actually done.

Herbert then took charge. "You are Helmut, right?" he said to dad, who nodded. "Okay, we'll stay here with Ellen tonight. You can go home. But first would you please let every other family in Uru know that the Guardian Protector is now here. For tonight, Uru is being protected by three Guardians."

Dad was very impressed. He'd never seen any other Guardians other than Ellen. Now, he realized there were three more here in Uru. If one was enough to protect the village, think of what three could do if need be. "I don't know how to thank you all enough. You're a godsend to us all. I'll let everyone know. Tonight we'll sleep well, thanks to you. What about Beth? Should she stay a while yet?" Suddenly, I had the fear I'd be sent home before I could even talk to my new friends!

Willow replied, "If you don't mind, let her stay the night. I promise I'll watch over her as if she were my own daughter." Dad smiled; that was way more than enough to satisfy him. He thanked her and headed off to let the other families know their great fortune. As soon as he left, Willow said, "Come children; let's go make a large pot of cocoa. Then, we can all talk. I expect Beth has a lot to tell us all!" We got our cocoa supplies in trade, and I was told cocoa came from some place called the Spice Islands. I led them into the kitchen area and showed her where Ellen kept things. I heard Herbert go outside to stable up their horses.

Soon, we were sitting around the kitchen table. "This couldn't have come at a worse time," I began. "Only this morning the King's men came here wanting the village to swear allegiance to him. If we do, he'll keep a cavalry patrol around Uru everyday, but it'll cost us one tenth of our crops! They're supposed to come back for our decision sometime tomorrow."

Herbert pronounced, "I find the coincidence of their offer and the attack on Ellen a most suspicious one. If Uru didn't have the protection of Ellen, I'll bet the entire village would have signed up on the spot. How convenient it is to have Ellen nearly slain."

"Are you saying there is a connection?" asked Willow. "A conspiracy?"

"No, I guess not," the fighter sighed. "It's just I find it highly suspicious, that's all. I'll wager Uru will bow down to King Randolf tomorrow. Mark my words, this may not be a good thing at all. Uru may regret the day they swore allegiance to Randolf."

Clyde spoke up, "Well, it could make sense. Beth has already told us the Galts have attacked the village many times. They know about Ellen and her powers. So put yourself in their shoes for a moment. Wouldn't you want to devise a scheme to get her out of the way? Attack and wound but not kill a farmer. Surely, they would know she would be very likely to go in search of healing herbs. There, they would spring a trap and get rid of her. After that, Uru is theirs for the taking." Clyde's words sounded so true that I became fearful an attack was coming at any moment. Sarah Jane and Sandy also thought along similar lines.

"Careful what you say in front of the children," Willow chastised him. "You have the girls here half scared to death."

"Sorry, mum," he looked downcast. "Didn't intend to scare them, but simple logic," he didn't finish his sentence. We knew what he meant, and I for one found his theory highly plausible.

"If we're in for an attack," I spoke up, "shouldn't we tell someone?"

"Time enough for that later, Beth," Willow spoke quietly and softly, instilling a bit of calmness in us. "We've never known the Galts to attack at night. They can't see what they are doing. If there's to be an attack, it'll not come before morning. Time enough then. So in the meantime," she continued but was interrupted by Herbert.

"I'm going out to do a bit of reconnoitering. If they intend to attack in the morning early, they'd have to be camped nearby. Back in a while; I'll stay in contact, Willow." She nodded her consent, and he quietly left. Ellen moaned so Clyde went to her side.

Willow then changed the topic, "Okay, Beth you were telling us what happened, and how you were able to find Ellen. Please, continue." I noticed all three of my new friends were listening intently to my every word; that rather unnerved me. So I took a deep breath and began once more, describing how Ellen had worked healing on Rupert and had left him in my charge, while she went in search of the necessary herbs. I think the other apprentices were impressed with just how I was able to find her in the woods.

When I finished, Sandy exclaimed, "Now that was really great Beth. I know I couldn't have done what you did!"

Sarah Jane added, "Nor I. I'm sure I couldn't have found someone in the woods without having lots and lots more clues. I'm really glad you are on our team!" Hearing her validate my efforts made me feel much closer to her than ever before. Roy just grinned. I could tell he felt proud of me. I was beginning to think he was supporting me with the others. I smiled back at him.

"Thanks," I said meekly. "Willow, can anyone learn how to do this telepathy? From what little I've seen of it today, it's the most incredibly valuable skill! Can Ellen teach me how to do it? Does the rest of the Circle already know how to do it?" I flushed as I realized I was asking way too many questions that really should have been asked of my teacher, Ellen. Willow was

Sandy's instructor.

Willow, as usual, spoke softly, "Beth, telepathy is a rare gift. Most do not have it. However, those that do have the skill, those I can help develop it in them more fully, help them learn to control and master it. We usually do not test our apprentices for the gift until their fifth year before they make their specialty decision. In your case, Ellen has just not had the time to go over it with you and to test you. I know she intends to do so, just not when she had in mind. So if you do have the gift, I would be honored to help you with it." Her words were so comforting; if I had the gift, I now felt certain I'd get any needed training so I could properly communicate with others. But the real question remained, did I have the gift. I had no idea how to tell if I did.

"The hour has grown very late. Let's all get some sleep. Tomorrow promises to be an eventful day around here. Beth, where does Ellen keep her spare blankets?" So yawning, I got plenty of blankets for us all. I was sound asleep almost before I laid down.

I awoke to conversation among the adults. I listened. Herbert had returned and was talking in hushed voices to the others. "My guess is the Galts will be here around ten in the morning, but the queer thing is that I tracked a man who rode between the encampment of the cavalrymen and the Galts. He went to the Galt camp, stayed only a few minutes and then returned to the cavalry encampment. It was dark, so I didn't get a good look at whom it was, but I do smell a rat."

The voice of Willow then spoke, "So you're suggesting the Galts will attack here around midmorning. How soon would the cavalrymen get here? Any guess?"

"From their trails and from what Beth relayed of their plans, I'd say they intend to visit Blankford in the morning and be here sometime in the afternoon," Herbert concluded. I wondered how he could tell all of this. It convinced me even more that I had so very much more to learn.

Clyde commented, "Then, it's up to us to repel the Galts. Do you think we can do it before they get to the town proper? You know, keep fighting away from the folks that live here. They are already sorely tempted to become vassals of Randolf. I don't want to add to their worry. In my opinion, joining Randolf will be a very bad mistake."

"Yes, on that we're all agreed," the soft voice of Willow concurred, "but we must always remember it is their choice. We must let them have freewill to choose their own paths, even if we might choose another."

"I know, I know," Clyde interrupted, "or else we then become their masters, their rulers. Sometimes, I think that would not be such a bad idea, personally." He grumbled. "Hush, now, I think the children are stirring." I heard Roy getting up, and I decided to get up myself. The other girls were right behind us, leaving me wondering if they had overheard the adults as I had. Unfortunately, there was no way just now to ask.

Ellen wakened as did Rupert, so it was time for breakfast. "I should go do my chores before I eat," I said, and added, "that is, if you think it's safe for me to go out and do them."

"Sure, I'll see what I can fix. Sarah Jane, Sandy, you two lend me a hand in the kitchen," Willow said.

"Mind if I tag along, Beth? I can lend you a hand. Besides, I don't have anything else to do really," Roy quickly inserted not a bit bashfully. Somehow, I got the impression he wanted to talk to me alone. Willow gave her permission, so out we went into the early morning light. All around us, other children were coming out to feed chickens, gather eggs, milk the goats, and so on. Roy and I walked quickly to my house, just a couple houses down the street from Ellen's.

"Beth, I think you did splendidly yesterday. You really kept your head about you," Roy complimented me. "I think that is terrific. Many girls in my village would have been completely helpless and useless if they had to deal with all that you did."

I blushed from his kind words, but was not sure why I did. "Oh, it was just the good training Ellen has given me," I tried to make it sound normal, if anything around here was now normal. "Here, you collect the eggs, and I'll feed them. Careful you don't break any," I added, as I saw him fumble around slightly. "You have collected eggs before, haven't you?" I asked.

"Er, no not really," he admitted. So I showed him how to do it and laughed a bit at his clumsy methods of moving the hens off of their nests. Soon, he had filled the wooden bowl with nearly a dozen. Next, I had to milk the goats. Somehow, I knew he had never done that, so I let him watch.

"Say, just before I woke," Roy said, "I heard them talking about an attack or something. Did you hear any of it?" Roy asked. I told him all I had heard. He was impressed with the news. Just then, my sister came out, so we quickly began talking about what a nice day this one promised to be.

"Say thanks, Beth," Anne said, "I figured I was going to have to do your chores. I'll take these in to mom. Are you coming in to eat?"

"No, tell mom I'm still helping Ellen," I replied eager to get back to the others and see what else I could learn. Quickly, Roy and I headed back to Ellen's house.

Inside, Ellen was up and eating slowly. She was still in some pain; I could easily tell, but the mood was considerably more cheerful. Sandy and Sarah Jane did much to liven up the breakfast table with their constant talk.

"Well, Beth, I guess I owe you my life," Ellen finally said. I flushed and looked at my bowl. "You did very well. You found me and healed me. Most excellent. Thank you, Beth."

I smiled and gave her a hug. "You're still my grandmom," I said, not able to think of anything more appropriate on the spur of the moment.

Once we had eaten, Herbert became serious, and suddenly, we all listened to his every word. "Okay everyone. Time to go to work. I suspect another Galt attack this morning. We've decided to intercept them and drive them away before they can scare the village. So Roy, you're coming with me. Observe and learn. Clyde and Willow will also come. You three must stay here and protect Ellen in case we fail. Willow will keep Sandy informed. If something goes very wrong, Beth, you are charged with getting Ellen, Sandy, and Sarah Jane to safety. Head for a nearby safe cabin. Sandy can contact Mary Ann for help. Any questions?" He sounded so formal, so determined, so strong, how could he possibly fail, I wondered. But we all agreed.

Quickly, the three adults and Roy made their preparations and checked their weapons, at least the fighter and his young apprentice did. I marveled that Roy could actually handle a sword. It was a side of him I had not yet seen. "You be careful," I whispered to him as he was leaving. He smiled back and winked. Then, they were gone.

"See, I told you he has a crush on you," teased Sandy. She ignored my protest that I was too young, still a young girl only about to be eleven. Then, we helped Ellen back into bed. Once she was comfortable, she directed us to pack several backpacks with some of her things and some trail food.

I could tell that Ellen was preparing for the worst; should it come, both she and I knew just how difficult it would be to get her to safety. She could barely walk, and she had a massive headache, but this did give us something to do. We tried to conceal much of our true intentions from Betsy and Rupert who were in the front room.

Once all was readied, we three sat by Ellen's bedside waiting. None of us dared to talk much. We knew Sandy would need to concentrate fully in order not to miss any message from Willow. I found the waiting very nerve-wracking and discovered just how much I hate waiting. Ellen also sensed our worry and calmed us, "Patience, you must learn patience. I'm sure all will be well, children. After all, I've been protecting Uru by myself for many years now, and I'm not a Protector. Herbert is more than enough to drive them all away. With three druwids, the Galts don't have any chance."

Her words were comforting and made sense to me. I'd seen her in action several times now, but then Herbert's words came back to mind haunting me. Why did he warn us? As if reading my thoughts, Ellen whispered, "Herbert is always making sure we're fully prepared for any eventuality. He's overly cautious in his role as our Protector." I sensed Sandy and Sarah Jane relax a bit, so I tried to do so as well. Sarah Jane busied herself with checking on her two patients. Sandy was mentally maintaining contact with Willow — at least that was what I assumed, for her eyes had a sort of vacant stare.

Hearing men talking outside, I opened the door to see what was going on. At this hour, they ought to have been out working the fields. Today, however, they were all milling around the center of town talking amongst themselves. No imagination was needed to know what they were discussing. In only a few hours, the King's representative was coming back to get their reply to King Randolf's offer. I saw dad obviously arguing with several men. He looked a bit upset with the way things were going. Hence, I went back inside and told the others what was happening. Ellen just sighed. Little did I know just how this seemingly simple decision was going to affect my life. I was shortly to find out.

About eleven, Sandy became quite animated. "Gather round, all of you. I've got news from Willow." Instantly, we all sat on the floor beside Ellen's bed. "Willow has sent both Ellen and me the same message. I'm supposed to relay the message, and Ellen's supposed to make sure I relay it correctly. So here goes," she excitedly explained. However, I noticed a slight hesitancy in her voice. I assumed she was thinking something like "I hope I get it right." I don't think any of us apprentices really felt utterly certain of our newly acquired skills just yet.

"The battle is over. No one is hurt. The Galts came down the predicted trail and were intercepted by Herbert with Roy standing behind him. Clyde and Willow were much farther back. They shot a pair of arrows at the fighters. Both caught the arrows mid-flight and dropped them on the ground. The Galts seemed very surprised by our presence and hastily retreated as fast as they could go. Not more than ten minutes after they left, the King Randolf's cavalry came charging through. It would seem that they expected to meet the Galts shortly after the Galts would have reached the northern edge of Uru. Herbert finds this is exceedingly curious. The cavalry noticed us but didn't stop, also curious. They'll be arriving in Uru within a few minutes. On foot, we should be there in about a half an hour. End of message. There, how did I do?" asked Sandy. I could see she had her fingers crossed behind her back.

"Very well done," Ellen said softly. "You relayed the essential basics of the message properly. I'll let Willow know. So you see nothing to worry about. If the cavalry are coming here, I had better try to put in an appearance." She tried to sit up, but the throbbing in her head was so severe that she didn't make it. Sarah Jane tried to help her to a sitting position, but even that effort failed because her head to hurt so badly. Ellen quickly laid back down. "I guess I'm not going to put in an appearance after all."

"You did take a nasty head wound, Loremaster Ellen," Sarah Jane pronounced in her stern voice. "So I wouldn't recommend you leaving your bed today. Rest and let the body heal more. Sandy and Beth can go outside, listen in, and let you know what happens."

Ellen muttered a curse in a very quiet voice, and then protested, "Sarah Jane, I simply must witness this meeting. I have to see firsthand what happens, the facial expressions, the tone of voices, and all the subtle nuances of expressions used. This is a very critical meeting. But you are right. I'll never get this body up and outdoors." I could see Ellen thinking hard, wresting with some decision.

At last she spoke up, "Sandy, I'm afraid I need to ask something of you that normally is not taught to a Communicator until the eight year. I know you don't know what you need to do, but we'll have to improvise."

Sandy's eyes opened wide; she suddenly was about to participate in something that was totally new to her. She was as excited as I get when Ellen teaches me something new. I think Sarah Jane also knew just how Sandy was feeling. Ellen explained, "I want you to get close to the leader who does the talking. Beth knows him and can maneuver you both in close without attracting any attention. Then, I'll attempt a Mind Joining with you. When we join minds, I'll be looking through your eyes, hearing what you are hearing, and even feeling what you are feeling. True, my body will still be here on the bed, but I'll be directly observing via your body." All three of us had never heard of this Mind Joining, but it sounded absolutely terrific.

Ellen continued, "I know you do not know what you must do, so I'll try to do most of the work, if I can. My hurting head may well interfere. If it does, I'll break the connection. Also, you may also experience what I'm feeling. So if my pain is too much for you to block out, let me know, and I'll also break the connection. Is that acceptable, Sandy?"

"You bet!" Sandy exclaimed, but really, she had no idea what was to happen.

"So once you are in position, make contact with me just as if you were going to relay me a message. I'll take it from there, once the connection is made — or rather, I'll try. I'm *not* very good at this sort of thing. To be honest, Sandy, I've only successfully done it one other time with Willow. So don't be disappointed if I cannot do it. It has nothing to do with your skills, only mine. Again, Sandy, if you cannot tolerate it, just let me know mentally. It's a very unusual and sometimes frightening experience to have another connected to you by a Mind Join. With my head hurting as bad as it is, I'm not sure I can even make the connection, but I have to try." Ellen sighed. We sensed just how important this was to her. This was her village, her people that she had guarded for so many years.

No sooner had Ellen finished explaining this to Sandy than the thunderous sounds of galloping cavalry filled the room. Quickly, I led Sandy outside. They halted in the large open section in the middle of Uru where we children normally play. Today, all of the adults in the village were gathered around the two dozen riders.

Simon Waters, steward to King Randolf, the Mighty, once again was the sole spokesperson. "Well, we have some news for you. It seems the Guardians just deflected another Galt attack, this time from the north, just a couple miles from Uru. You really do need King Randolf's protection. So what is your decision?"

By now, I had Sandy up close, just behind several villagers so she could clearly see Simon. I saw her close her eyes and assumed she made contact. Then, she opened them and stared at Simon. I saw her wince and grimace in pain. Her hand went up to her forehead, feeling the same spot where Ellen's wound was located. Sandy's head twisted to one side as she fought the pain. I watched her jaw tighten and sensed she was fighting as hard as she could.

One man, Thomas, I think, though I couldn't see him clearly, spoke first. "We can't all agree. Most of us feel King Randolf's offer is most fair, but some are worried the patrols will provide only a fleeting protection. What happens if your forces are five miles to the south when they attack from the north?"

"Ah, this is just tactics, kind sir. I know you aren't familiar with how cavalry patrols are executed or carried out, but rest assured our patrols will detect an advancing Galt or Axemen party well before they can reach your village. We then dispatch sufficient forces to deal with them, to drive them off before they can harm anyone in Uru. In fact, you might not even see us for days. We don't ride through Uru frequently at all. That would tend to disrupt your lives. No, we'll be scouring the hills and nearby forests routinely. The patrols will hardly even be noticed by you, if at all."

"But what happens if we do get attacked and hurt," broke in one woman. "Must we still pay the tithe if we get hurt? What guarantee does the King make if we are attacked? Some of us are concerned about giving up so much of our crops and then not getting real protection in return."

"Ah fair lady," he spoke coyly, hedging his words, if you ask me, "we all do make errors, do we not? Haven't you made an error at some time in your life? Yes, you see we humans are not perfect. Mistakes can be and are made, from time to time. King Randolf expects some errors may occur. If you do get attacked and we fail to protect you, you may petition for some recompense in your annual tithe. I'm sure the King will be fair." I immediately wondered fair to whom? Simon really didn't answer her question. "And remember, one and all, if it gets too rough here in Uru, too dangerous, all who pledge their allegiance to the King are more than welcome to move into the fortress at Redun. In fact, any that want to permanently move into the total safety of Redun may do so at any time. The King will help you resettle, give you land to farm, and a secure home in which to dwell."

My dad then spoke up, "And what happens to those of us that do not want to go along with this plan of yours? Suppose the village agrees, but some who live here do not?"

"Oh that is simple, those who do not want to abide by the decision of Uru are free to move on to a place that better suits them," Simon stated, with just a hint of antagonism or sarcasm in his voice. I could not be sure which it was. "You see, if Uru agrees and one man does not, does that not cast suspicion on that man's motives? Perhaps, he's actually a spy for the Galts! King Randolf treats spies harshly, and rightly so, after all, would you want someone here in the village passing along key information to the enemy? Treasonous!" Here many voiced their agreement with that statement. My dad was quite silent, however.

Thomas spoke above the cheers, "Then, I think you have our answer. I believe Uru is ready to accept King Randolf's most kind offer of protection. Everyone in favor, say 'Yes.'" The number of voices was large and loud. When he asked for 'No's', utter silence greeted our ears in sharp contrast. I suddenly realized why. Anyone saying openly 'No' would instantly be branded a traitor, a spy! I had a queasy feeling in my stomach, but didn't know why.

Simon sat as tall as he could in his saddle. "I hereby proclaim Uru is now totally under the protection of King Randolf! You've made a very wise decision. As I promised yesterday, you may expect the routine patrols to begin tomorrow."

Thomas spoke up once more, "But what about our guardian? Is she still permitted to live here? To help us?"

I saw Simon glancing about the entire crowd as if looking for Ellen. He did not see her. "I don't see her, but King Randolf totally acknowledges the great benefits offered to us by the Guardians. He is host to the Judger himself and has given Frank a most spacious home within the safety of the fortress at Redun. Your relationship with your village guardian remains as it is. Have we not all been blessed with their healing aid at one time or another?" Many cheers supported his statement. "Okay, then farewell for now. Tomorrow you may see the patrol in outlying areas around Uru." With that, they nudged their horses forward and walked them out of town before increasing their pace to a gallop.

I had forgotten all about Sandy. As I turned to her, her face was full of tears, so great was the unexpected pain that she had been fighting. She seemed totally disoriented and near collapse. I put my arms around her to steady her and slowly walked her back into Ellen's house. As we got to the door, she had me pause so she could wipe her face. "I don't want to go in looking like this," she whispered to me. She had no sooner gotten her face dried when the other druwids and Roy came trotting up out of breath. They had made all haste to get here, but missed the entire meeting. I heard Herbert curse under his breath. We all went inside.

Sarah Jane looked very worried. "Ellen's gone unconscious!" she blurted out. Clyde rushed to her side and began examining the Loremaster.

"What happened to her?" he asked.

"She had a horrible head pain and could not even sit up. So she did something called a Mind Join with Sandy so she could see what happened at the meeting. Just a bit ago, she just seemed to pass out. Is she all right?" Sarah Jane was near panic; a patient in her care had just gone critical in her view, and she did not know what to do about it, how to heal her.

"My gods!" exclaimed Willow. Looking at Sandy, she said, "My gods!" a second time. Thus far, I had never heard Willow sound so upset or agitated. "Sandy, are you okay? You look awful!"

"Pain, pain, I was — somehow felt Ellen's head and chest. Pain — almost could not stand it. Was important to her. Had to try. Had to endure. But it hurts so bad!" Sandy was near exhaustion.

Quickly, Willow had her assistant lie down on several blankets forming makeshift bed. "I'm going to enter your mind and help sooth it, Sandy. Just relax, yes, that's a good girl." I watched her like a hawk, but could see Willow doing nothing at all. She just gazed down at her apprentice, but something was happening with Sandy. The pain, the tension seemed to melt away. In five minutes, she had relaxed and drifted into a deep sleep. Only then did Willow arise. She whispered, "Sandy will be just fine after a little rest. A Mind Join is only taught to eighth year apprentices! What was Ellen thinking?"

"I can answer that," I spoke up. "Ellen had protected Uru for a very long time. She was keenly interested in observing firsthand the meeting with Simon. I think she thought it was extremely important." That soothed Willow's concerns somewhat.

Clyde spoke up, "Ellen's just over exerted herself. She'll be okay after some rest, I predict. No damage done. Her wound is starting to men, but it's going to take several weeks before she is going to be capable of much action. Beth, it's up to you to tell us what happened at the meeting with Simon, the steward."

I spent about a half hour retelling all that I could, paying particular attention to just straight observations as much as possible. They, of course, had me repeat several statements, asked for clarifications, and my interpretations of several points. I had just finished when mom and dad came knocking on Ellen's door. "We brought you some hot soup for lunch," mom said. Good old mom, still thinking of us even when bigger events surrounded us all.

Both wanted to know how Ellen was doing. Clyde, not wanting to alarm them, said, "She's sleeping now. She really needs lots of sleep. It'll be perhaps several weeks before she is back to a reasonable normal. She's getting rather old, you know." I could see mom and dad completely accept this, which really was the truth of the matter.

Clyde continued, "Helmut, Sarah, we really do need to return to our villages now. However, I would like to leave both Ellen and Rupert in your daughter's care, at least for the time being, if that is acceptable to you? Neither should be moved for several days, and with their wounds, both need attending to, if you follow me."

"We'd be totally honored to have Beth help them. We owe so much to Ellen; it's the very least we can to," dad replied. "I'm extremely proud of Beth. Sure, you have our permission, but can I ask you a question?" Clyde nodded. "Have you heard about the meeting we just had with Simon, King Randolf's steward?" He said Beth had just filled them in on the details. "Do you think Ellen will be safe here in Uru for the next few weeks while she is recovering? Do you think that these so called patrols will actually stop the Galts?"

Herbert answered for Clyde. "Helmut, I'm confident under Beth's expert hands, both patients will do well and that both are totally safe here in Uru, at least for the next few weeks. If there are attacks in the next week and people here get hurt, wouldn't that look very bad upon the King's promised protection?" Dad nodded agreement. "As for the second question, I'll be honest with you. Like you, I'm very suspicious of this whole arrangement. Stay alert, and if you spot something amiss or unusual, please let Beth know, and she can contact me in particular." Dad took great comfort in that, and I felt twelve feet tall!

The guardians ate lunch, gathered their gear, and said their farewells. Clyde repeated the healing instructions to me to be doubly certain I fully grasped every detail. Roy was intentionally the last one out the door. Excitedly, he whispered to me, "I actually caught my first arrow flying at me! A Galt shot one at me, and I caught it! Isn't that something?" I gave him a congratulatory hug! While my idea would have been to try to get out of the arrow's path, a fighter's grand idea was to catch the darn thing. What a difference in viewpoints, I thought. After they left, a great silence fell in Ellen's home. Both patients were asleep, and Betsy had gone home to attend to her family. I felt just a little bit lonesome there all by myself. I really missed my new friends.

There was not much actually for me to do that day. Both of my patients slept mostly. Mom brought us some dinner and checked up on me a couple times. Betsy brought Rupert more liver soup, which he really didn't like, but I did coax him to eat some. Mom suggested she roast it with some onions. At suppertime, Rupert did actually eat all of it, which I took as a good sign of his recovery. His appetite was returning. That evening, with the help of dad and some others, Rupert was finally taken to his own house. I'm sure he really appreciated sleeping in his own bed. Of course, I had to check up on him several times a day.

The next day, Ellen woke and was more talkative, but her head was still hurting badly if she tried to get up and move around. In addition, the three wounds in her chest made even simple motions, like sitting up, painful. Yet, after supper that night, dad came to visit her. He looked very worried. "Beth tells me you are able to talk some, and I really *do* need to talk to you just as soon as you are able, Ellen. It is vital."

She smiled, and from the look in her eyes, I could tell she had a very good idea what this was all about. I was clueless. "Yes, Helmut, bring up a chair and sit close to my head. I still can't sit up, but I sure can listen. I just hate being bedridden like this. I feel like an aged woman!" Dad did as he was told.

"You listen too, Beth. This concerns you too. Where to begin?" dad fumbled about.

"Well, why not start at the beginning," Ellen offered.

"Okay. Did you hear what Simon said when the others agreed to King Randolf's offer?"

"Yes, Helmut. Just don't ask how, but I did observe it all," she said using her serious voice. I knew this must be very important indeed.

"Then you know I refused to agree to the terms. Several of us who are opposed to this agreement were intimidated into not saying 'No.' Had we voiced our negative opinions, we feel we would have been singled out as traitors or spies for the Galts. Not only by Simon, but also many of our neighbors here in Uru! I've been talking to those I know who are against this agreement. Fred has called it quits; he left today, taking what he could carry on his back. He told me he was going to seek his fortunes down south. Well, he's not married and has no family to worry about, so it's okay if he just wants to leave. But, Ellen, what about me? I've got a growing family to consider."

"I thought long and hard about just giving in and going along with the rest here in Uru — just forgetting about it — make the best of it. I think all the others who were opposed to this alliance are doing just that. Yet, Ellen, me thinks your wisdom is rubbing off on me," dad joked playfully. Ellen smiled. I didn't get the joke, but dared not interrupt the adults. I listened carefully to see if I could figure out what he meant.

"I wouldn't be true to my own self if I just ignored it and went along with something with which I didn't agree. I may be just a simple farmer — a grounder, but I still have my own personal integrity. I'm not blind or stupid just because I love growing things. I couldn't live with myself if I just pretended to go along with this agreement. Only ill can come from doing that," he explained. Now I was beginning to see what he meant. Ellen's wisdom and clear thinking was not wasted on dad. I began to understand the situation. If we stayed here in Uru and did not openly agree to swear allegiance to the King, we would be in for real trouble.

"Helmut, you have my full support and the support of the Guardians. You're being true to your own ideals, something that's in short supply these days. I agree with you. It's not going to be safe for you or your family to continue to live in Uru much longer. I don't think anyone will do anything rash so soon, however. But in a month, who knows?" Ellen replied using her serious voice.

"Sarah and I have talked it out. We must move, Ellen. But where? That's the real question, and there is also Beth to consider. She is your apprentice, but we cannot just leave her here," dad said. Now, I grasped his dilemma. We had to move to a new village, and I would get separated from Ellen! Oh no! I panicked.

"Yes, you must move and move soon," Ellen confirmed my worst fear. "Where? Well, I know Karka hasn't agreed, and the folks there will probably never agree to be anyone's vassals. Karka folks are a strong willed lot. I'm sure you would fit in with them nicely. As you know, there's land available for farming nearly everywhere you go in all directions, but the safety of a town is much to be desired for your family. Now Blankford has not yet signed on to King Randolf, but they might. The situation in Blankford could go either way. Petersville will undoubtedly agree to the King's terms in a short while. Garth and Undel have already signed on before Uru did. So if you want to stay in this general area, Karka is the only place I would recommend. Further, if by chance I'm wrong and Karka too decides to become a vassal of King Randolf, then it would be easy for you to pick up and move further westward, far out of reach of this King." We were moving to Karka! I could see no other option. My panic grew; the absolute last thing I wanted to do was to end my training!

"Now as far as Beth is concerned, she'll not be safe if she stays behind, even if we proclaim her my assistant. However, Beth," she looked straight at me, "I'm sure Willow would be more than happy to have two apprentices under her care! It's unusual to switch mentors, but it has and can be done, especially with your chosen specialty."

My nightmare evaporated into utter joy! I was going to still be a Guardian in training; I was going to have Willow as my mentor; I would be with one of my new friends; I would perhaps get the chance to learn how to do telepathy. So rapid was my emotional curve that I could not withhold yelling, "Hurray!" I started jumping up and down. I was that excited by the sudden reversal of my fate! "Oh thank you! Thank you! Thank you!" I exclaimed jubilantly.

Both dad and Ellen laughed at my wild reaction. "Calm down, Beth," Ellen finally coaxed me to sit back down. "Now, I will be visiting you, Beth, from time to time, and I can teach you other things you need to know during those visits. So it will almost be like you have two mentors, and don't worry about me, either of you. It's still safe for me to be in Uru. I'll not swear allegiance to the King, for I have already sworn allegiance to the Guardians. The King knows this, and he also knows it would be suicide for him to drive the Guardians away. He still needs us. So for the time being, I'll be safe even in Uru, but I do foresee the day my welcome might not be tolerated any longer."

"No, how could the people never not need and appreciate you, Ellen," I protested. "They'd have to be utterly blind!"

"Blindness has a habit of sneaking up on people who cannot observe," Ellen cautioned. "It comes in small steps. However, enough of that. Helmut, I'll make the arrangements tonight. Again, don't ask how. No, I'd better do it right now. You two stay put. Beth, make us some tea and don't interrupt me for a while."

My dad watched her closely, but had no inkling of what she was doing. I did. I whispered to him, "She's talking to Willow most likely and maybe some of the other guardians as well. I do hope Willow can teach me how to do that!" My dad's eyes opened wide in utter amazement. This was one aspect of Ellen he had not known, but now that he saw it with his own eyes, many hither to unexplainable events he'd witnessed about Ellen began falling into place. She could mentally communicate with other guardians far away.

I fixed the tea. While making it, I realized I really had no clue about how to cook a real meal. I still had much to learn even from my mom! I made a resolution to do so soon. By the time I brought the cups and honey and put them on another chair close by her bed, Ellen had finished. "Okay, it is indeed all arraigned. Willow is more than happy to accept you as her apprentice, Beth. Helmut, I might add that Sandy, her current apprentice, had a similar reaction to Beth's. Whoopee! I think that's what she exclaimed." Both adults chuckled.

"Willow Windsong said she'll look for a suitable home for you and have one waiting for your family. She said another farmer would be most welcome in Karka. There are plenty of fields to tend. However, she said you should insist on your rights to some remuneration for this year's work. I'll see to that detail. She contacted the Judger about all this as well. Helmut, the Judger seemed to think it wouldn't be safe for you to move. 'There is danger afoot' were his exact words. Therefore, I'm going to go along with you. I would enjoy seeing Karka again. It's been over a year since I was last there. I know; I'm not supposed to move about, so I'm commandeering the Uru wagon for the trip. I'll bring it back with me when I return. I'll make up some plausible excuse to take the wagon. I think we should leave as soon as possible, say in three days' time?"

Dad actually kissed Ellen on her cheek. "How can we ever thank you, Ellen? You're a lifesaver! Yes, we'll be packed and ready to go in three days. But will you be able to travel that soon?"

"I believe so. Make a bed in the back of the wagon; Beth can sit by my side watching over me. So I'll still technically be in bed," she smiled thinking of Clyde's admonition to stay in bed for over a week. "Beth, will you please stay the night again tonight? I really am having a hard time standing. Tomorrow, I'll let you go home to help with the packing. You can come back meal times to help me."

I was flying in the clouds with happiness that night. It was very late before I finally fell asleep, dreaming of Willow and using telepathy to talk to everyone in sight!

Chapter 4 Disaster Strikes

The next few days flashed by in a whirl. My family's meager possessions needed to be packed in sacks. We were taking our chickens and other animals — all that could fit in the wagon. Between helping mom and dad gather our stuff and pack along with helping Ellen, I was too busy to worry about anything. At first, Anne and Ben, my little sister and brother, were upset with the idea of moving and losing all their friends. But dad and I convinced them it would be too dangerous to stay in Uru. "The bad men are coming" was all it took really to convince them. However, within twenty-four hours, everyone in Uru knew we were leaving. At the time, I did not think much about this fact. I should have, in hindsight. We all should have.

Ellen convinced the villagers she was going to Karka to purchase some new corn seed that promised to be more worm resistant and thus needed the wagon to bring the seed back with her. It seemed reasonable. However, by the third day, I could see resentment and perhaps even anger directed towards my dad and even me. I firmly believe some villagers now thought we were a family of traitors and spies! Mom and dad took it hard when some of their friends turned on them. I guess they really weren't their friends after all.

I know Ellen had a hard time convincing the villagers to give Helmut his fair share. But in the end, she managed to acquire four fifty-pound sacks of seed for the next year's planting. I guessed even if things went poorly in Karka, that much seed would allow us to survive a year. What I didn't know was the seed was going to be traded for our food for this year.

Finally the moving day came. The sky was dark and ominous. A storm was brewing. Ordinarily, I would have taken this as an ill omen, but today, I only saw sunshine. I was moving to Karka to be with Willow and Sandy! Thomas brought the wagon to our house, hitched and ready to go just after breakfast. I heard him mutter under his breath, "Good riddance; we don't need no traitors in Uru!" It was a sobering thought.

It took us over an hour to load up the wagon properly, what with all the sacks and livestock, plus having to make a bed for Ellen. We had two dozen chickens in carrying crates. The goats were tied to the sides of the wagon. They would have to walk. By ten, we were finally ready to go, and dad drove the wagon up to Ellen's door. I went in to get her.

"My, you have your leather outfit on, Beth. Looks good," she said. She also wore her leather traveling clothes and her druwid cloak as I did. We looked a pair. With my help, she managed to stand and slowly walk out to the wagon, but it took dad's strength to get her up and into it. She quickly lay down in the make-shift bed. Finally, dad climbed aboard sitting beside mom. My brother and sister sat behind them on the chicken crates so they could see where we were going. As we left Uru, we had the canvas tarp covering rolled up so we could see, but it was in a position that, when the rains came suddenly, we could quickly roll them down and be protected from the rain. That was going to be my job, to help dad and mom roll the cover down. As we rode solemnly out of Uru, many of the women peered out their doors, staring at us with distinctively unfriendly looks. No children were allowed out to play, which I found very curious indeed. My family and I were now evidently considered nasty, evil people by the folks in Uru. I found myself glad to be rid of them as well.

As we slowly moved north out of Uru, I asked Ellen, "I don't see how come they think we are so bad. Haven't we and I always helped them — treated them fairly. I've even helped heal some of them. How can they feel we are so bad?" I didn't see dad strain his ears to hear Ellen's answer.

She answered slowly, "Yes, Simon only spoke a few words, but he uttered just the right words, Beth. You see, the folks in Uru are afraid; they are scared, and yet they will not admit they are in fear. People in fear latch on to anything that offers some faint possibility of hope. Simon gave them that by suggesting a traitor lived among them. Since you and your dad did not go along with their decision to become vassals of the King, they immediately assume that by being different from them, you are the guilty party. With you all gone, they incorrectly assume all will be well. Mark my words, one day Uru will deeply regret their decision. But by then, it'll be too late. I don't think even all us Guardians will be able to help them out of their plight when it comes. You see Beth, fear blinds one to the truth of a situation. Fear is your worst enemy. Always remember that. No matter how grim, how desperate a situation may be, your own fear is far worse, because it blinds your correct thinking ability, your ability to observe. Fear causes you to make all the wrong choices. You must learn to conquer your fear, rise above it. I know; we have to work on that. It sometimes is very hard to do." With that, we rode on in silence, as the sky grew steadily darker.

We were in for a storm that was certain, perhaps a gully-washer, as we called the heavy downpours that Uru sometimes got. It was a somber ride; we said little. After going only an hour, we stopped to pull the canvas top down; rain seemed imminent. We were just in time too, as the rain began pouring down. However, we stayed fairly dry in the wagon. All around us, thunder and lightning echoed across the green hills, as our wagon inched its way northward. Soon, we reached the crossroad to Karka and turned westward directly into the storm. Mom and dad, though, were drenched from the pelting rains, but in the back, Ellen and I stayed mostly dry, thankfully.

With the thunderous noise about us, Anne and Ben became frightened and began crying. Yes, even I was a bit anxious about the fierce weather. Ellen soothed our fears with some calm words, explaining how the lightning and thunder worked. Just then, a deafening crack of thunder followed a lightning strike on a nearby pine tree. An explosion followed, along with a shower of sparks. We children screamed in alarm. Ellen said, "Don't worry kids; the lightning will not strike us."

Anne wanted to know why it wouldn't, and I thought that was a good question. "Lightning tends to strike what is sticking up the highest into the sky. All around us are tall trees, so it is going to hit them long before it hits this low wagon." That seemed to satisfy them.

I felt sorry for the goats tied to the side of the wagon, for they were being pelted by the downpour and ambled along, looking forlornly at the soggy ground. Still, in spite of Ellen's attempts to lull our fears, being out here in the violent storm with nothing but a thin piece of canvas covering us, unnerved us kids. I suspect mom didn't like it either, nor dad for that matter, but really we had no choice.

Ellen spoke softly to me so that we could not be overheard. "This is a good time for you to learn about bringing down lightning from the skies. We always begin such training out in storms such as this. Can you feel the tremendous amount of power in the skies above us? Close your eyes, reach out, and see if you can feel or sense the great black masses of energy all around and above us." Suddenly, the frightening storm became my friend. I was about to learn how to bring down lightning bolts! But it was hard. I had never tried to sense the energy in the skies before. Yet, I did as she said, closed my eyes and concentrated or tried to feel, anyway. In a half hour, I really was beginning to "feel" the charges and the discharging bolts.

When Ellen was convinced I at least rather sensed the energy masses, she said, "Now I want you to concentrate, and see if you can feel the next bolt arcing to the ground." I waited and, when it came, I missed it. We tried another five times before I could actually sense the terrifying arc. Ellen helped me by saying, "Notice that the actual bolt is a tiny thin line going from the target up into the mass of energy. The line appears first and then the huge flow of energy we see as lightning arcs its way downward. The thunder follows the lightning."

After a while, I began to see what she was talking about. "Now see if you can string a line much like a piece of string up from a tree into the mass of energy in the sky." I tried and tried, and then suddenly it worked! I had made a line from a treetop up, and suddenly the lightning bolt arced from the sky down hitting the tree. Still, I wasn't certain I had actually caused that to occur. I told myself I would have to practice this a whole lot before I was sure I was the cause and not just nature.

"Now here's another interesting thing that we can do. If you count the seconds from the time you see the lightning bolt until you hear the sound of its thunder, you can tell how far away the lightning actually is. We have observed that five seconds elapse for each mile the lightning is distant from us. It's just one of those things we have observed. I don't know why this should be, but go ahead and try it."

Now this was also great! So I dutifully counted, and I watched a distant one. I counted ten, so that made it about two miles off. I smiled at her. Then, I went back to practicing forcing the lightning to strike where I wanted it to strike, still not really believing I was actually doing it. I wondered if Ellen wasn't just giving me something to do to occupy my mind. However, I was having fun as time slowly edged along.

We had finally reached the bottom of the Valley of Uru. Here we crossed the stream, which was now a raging creek. Fortunately, the Guardians had constructed a wooden bridge wide enough to allow wagons to cross. Dad went extra slowly as we crossed, making sure the goats did not fall over the very low sides. I looked down at the foaming, frothing waters. I commented, "We are getting a lot of rain, that's for sure." Ellen, as expected, stated it was good for the crops.

Here in the middle of the width of the Valley of Uru, the Crooked Creek swerved first to the right and then left as it ambled down the fifty-five mile length of the valley. The ground was low undulating hills covered with grass and groves of trees, often of ash, maple, and oak. However, on either side of the creek, the hills always rose just slightly higher than they descended. So overall, as one went either east or west from the creek, the elevation rose five hundred feet cresting at Aran Ridge on the western side and Blankford Hills on the eastern side. Karka was located on the crest of Aran Ridge.

Aran Ridge got its name from the early Guardian explorer Karka Aran who first traversed its length and founded the town of Karka. On the other side, Melvin Blankford, a companion of Karka's simultaneously hiked the length of the Blankford Hills and founded the town of Blankford. During that same time, Peter Smythe followed the Crooked Creek but chose to name the valley Uru after the name given to it by a tribe of natives who he found living there. Later, he founded the town now called Petersville at the northern edge of the valley.

Generally, the farming fields were located within a mile of each village. Once beyond that limit, it was wild, open country, largely uninhabited. Though we crossed a bridge over the creek, we were about equally far from any inhabited town or village. Still the storm raged. Our wagon had gone perhaps another mile due west from the bridge, when dense groves of trees appeared on either side of the track, as we slowly climbed the hill, meaning we couldn't see what lay beyond the hilltop. Due to the heavy rain and very dark sky, we couldn't see very far anyway. I got hungry and bent over searching the food sack, intending to make my siblings and myself a snack. Perhaps that action saved my life; everything happened so quickly after that.

Some say that in every being's existence, there are events that shape or impact the being for all time, even from lifetime to lifetime. I do not know if this is true for others, but I know it has been so with me. The events in the next few minutes changed me forever. Okay, forever is a powerful word, but I've never been the same since then, not for the last thousand years. I'll do my best to describe it to you fully, but know this: parts of what happened next are still blank or confused in my memory, even after all these centuries.

We slowly climbed towards the top of the hill with the groves of dense trees on either side of the track. I bent over searching through the food sack. The day was very dark and being under the canvas made it even darker. Peering into the food sack required my full attention as I bent low looking. I heard some horses neighing; the sounds came from up ahead of us. I heard twanging sounds and shortly afterwards a sickening thumping sound and the panicked cries of intense pain from mom and dad. I felt the wagon come to a halt. Ellen tried to sit up to see what was going on and in doing so, her left hand pushed on my back for support so I couldn't rise up. I heard more twanging sounds and more thumping sounds. Something whizzed over my head. I heard it hit Ellen, heard her groan in pain, and felt the sudden loss of pressure from her hand on my back, as she collapsed back into the crude bed. I looked back at Ellen only to see a quarrel protruding from her chest! She was unconscious or so it appeared to me. We were under attack! *There is no one to protect us!* I finally rose up to look forward, only to see both mom and dad slumped over, several quarrels protruding from their bodies. Neither was moving!

Out in front of our wagon were two dozen cavalrymen. Though it was hard to see through the heavy rain and dark sky, I later would swear these were the very same cavalry that had visited Uru and swore to protect us all from the Galts and Axemen! They carried light crossbows, a fact that I learned later. Many had already fired their first round into us and were awkwardly trying to reload while still mounted. Some others were moving their horses in and around the front ones so they could get a clear shot at us. My brother and sister began screaming in stark utter terror. Never had I heard such loud, violent screams! I watched as two riders got into position and pointed their weapons at my brother and sister!

I screamed at the top of my voice over and over, "No! No! No! No!" It was as if my intense protests would somehow stop these men from killing all of us. Lightning flashed all around, casting ghastly shadows, but illuminating their faces. They were smiling! I continued to scream in protest. Nothing could save us. I watched utterly helpless, as they fired at them, heard them cry out in pain, and slump backwards, quarrels protruding from their chests. "No! No! No! No!"

I have been asked hundreds of times what happened next, but it remains a blur, a confusion. Suddenly, the entire world went black, as if my eyes ceased to function. I saw only the massive black energy clouds in the sky. In my mind, I saw the faces of all six of my new friends, saw them for what I assumed would be for the last time. I recall my body relentlessly crying out "No! No! No! No!" It seemed like my right arm reached out to the storm clouds and grabbed a mass and threw it down onto the nearest rider; the lightning bolt killed him outright, knocking him from the saddle, sending him flying through the air. Then, my left arm latched a hold of another and cast it down on the next rider. And then the right, and then the left once more. Bolt after frenzied bolt I cast down on these beasts that had killed us all. I became blind to everything in the universe. The only thing that was real were the black energy masses in the clouds above me.

I know my arms aren't that long, but it seemed to me that my arms had become hundreds of feet long. That cannot be, but as I said it's a blur. Bolt after bolt I shot. I heard screams of terror from my six new friends echoing between lightning blasts. I would see Sandy's face with a look of absolute horror just before I let loose another bolt. Next, it might be Sarah Jane's face I saw just before another bolt fired downward. On and on it went, time did not move for me, there was only me, the lightning bolts, and the accursed men who killed my entire family, everyone I loved. Though the men and horses were long since dead, so it was explained to me much later, I kept on smashing their bodies with bolt after bolt after bolt. Hundreds of bolts, I lost total count. I could see nothing, hear nothing, just the unstoppable urge to smash these terrible men, smash them with all my might. Over and over and over and over, relentlessly.

Yes, I would have to call my behavior just then crazy, insane, but I just could not stop it. Nothing else was real in the world, save that black energy and those terrible men! Time had no meaning for me, so I cannot say how long this lasted. Others have speculated it went on relentlessly for half an hour. Over and over, I heard the screams of my brother and sister, my mother and father, Ellen, and even the imaginary screams of my six friends. Over and over. Only by letting loose yet another volley of lightning with the resounding massive peal of thunder could I silence all these screams in my mind! I could not stop! I did not **want** to stop, and that I suspect is the real reason it went on and on.

Somewhere in the middle of this hellish nightmare, I heard the weak voice of Ellen begging, pleading, ordering me to stop — that all would be well. I couldn't. She was dead. I saw her die. It only drove me to pull down even more bolts to drown out those false words!

Then, the gentle sounds of a woman singing soft and gentle began to echo throughout my mind. I believe sincerely that her tune, her words, and her calm, tranquil song actually soothed my fury somewhat. I believe I pulled fewer bolts down so as not to block out such beautiful music. Words or a command formed in my mind. *Get the wagon moving.* Repeatedly, these words appeared, perhaps within the song. Somehow, I moved myself, not my body of that I'm certain, just ahead of the horses that were wild with fright and pulled on them making them move. Only then did I notice the wagon was violently rocking from side to side from all of the chaotic, wild motions the horses were making. How the wagon actually stayed hitched to the horses no one can say.

Now vaguely I felt my body moving within the wagon. I assumed that it was dead, but could not figure out how I could still feel motion through a dead body. If I'm totally honest, my thinking was virtually non-existent at this point. As I said, the only things that were really real to me now were the black energy masses above me and this beautiful music swelling somewhere in my mind. My body's eyes did not appear to be operational, that's the best way to describe it. However, the screaming of the others subsided and finally disappeared; at least I know longer heard them over and over.

The words *find the emergency cabin* now seemed to echo repeatedly in my mind. It was definitely not my thought. I had none, save to pull down more bolts and "No!" The world was black; everything was black. I was alone, adrift in all this powerful black energy. Alone except for this beautiful song that kept going in my mind. I have been told that this portion lasted for three hours. To me it was both an eternity and but a fleeting moment. Time was also non-existent for me. All was just black energy masses and this gentle music.

I do recall the feeling of motion finally stopping. In addition, the music subsided, or rather became so faint I could barely hear it. I had the sensation that my arms were exhausted from throwing all those bolts, and so I relaxed them and stopped casting them downward. I drifted quietly among the black energy masses. Now it was peaceful, but more importantly, it was quiet. I felt a complete and total silence the likes of which I have never before or since experienced, and that was what I desperately desired. Peace. Quiet. Absolute quiet. I felt I actually relaxed into that magnificent silence, hanging onto the energy of the sky all around me.

Sometime later, I heard disembodied voices speaking. It was surreal, voices, sentences, disconnected from their speaker, disconnected from everything in my universe of black energy. They floated in and out of my mind connected to nothing that was real to me, just voices.

"My god! They are all dead!"

"They are not even recognizable as men anymore!"

"She's gone rogue."

"She's alive."

"This one is too. Quick, get them inside."

I heard crying sounds of children.

"How can we explain this to the King?"

"My god! The utter devastation!"

"We must get them to Karka immediately."

"Is she alive?"

"How could this have happened?"

"Who did all this?"

"She may never recover."

"She may not want to ever recover."

"Wash her off and dress those wounds."

"I've got this one, you take that one."

"It takes a thing called money to trade for things here in Karka."

"Will she be all right?"

"You know that if she doesn't recover, we'll have to kill her?"

In this manner, the disembodied voices occasionally appeared in my mind breaking my joyous, total silence, but I didn't fight against those voices, for they only occasionally appeared and were quickly gone, leaving me in my enchanting, loving, comforting silence.

I noticed now, though I still retained my utter silence, the energy masses were dissolving. I think I cried, "No! No! No! No!" I didn't want to lose the only thing that was real to me! I pulled on the masses and forced them together so they were solid once again, but it was only temporary. Something else was pulling them apart and that something was far stronger than I was. "No! No! No! No!" I cried in utter protest, but in vain. I felt my loving masses become thinner and thinner. Now that beautiful song began to appear in my mind once more.

I detected words here and there, *Relax. Relax. Relax.* Somehow I did, though I still tried to hold onto the last remaining vestiges of my energy masses. Now I heard, *Listen to my song.* Since there was nothing else that was real, I clung on to the voice, the sounds, for dear life!

After a while, the words changed to, *Sleep now. Sleep now.* They were followed by *You will awake feeling refreshed. Sleep now.* Suddenly, I was tired, more tired than I ever could imagine possible! Footnote: much later, I tried to stay awake for an entire week to see if that would be similar to the depths of exhaustion that I felt at this moment. It did not even remotely compare! Sleep. I wanted that now more than anything else — just to sleep — to forget everything, and at long, long last, I slept.

I smelled roses, violets, and daisies. I was sure of it. I sensed the brightness of daylight. I smelled light perfume drifting over the strong odor of freshly baked bread. I opened my eyes and blinked. I woke up into what I thought was fantasy land. I was in a light yellow room. Sunlight beamed in from large windows covered with thin gauze drapes. I was in a soft bed covered with warm covers. Sitting beside me were my dear friends, Sarah Jane and Sandy. I looked at Sarah Jane. She looked so lovely, so beautiful. I could see why all the boys desired her affections. So being in fantasy land, I spoke up, "Sarah Jane, you are positively beautiful. I wish I could have even half of your good looks."

Both girls were tending to the freshly picked flowers, and nearly dropped the vases as they turned to face me directly. Their faces lit up when their eyes met mine. Sarah Jane called out joyously, "Willow, come quick! She's awake!"

Sandy exclaimed, "Boy, are we ever glad to see you awake, Beth!" Tears of joy trickled down her cheeks. She came close to my head and hugged me. I tried to reciprocate, but an unexpected flash of pain shot up both my arms. Sandy saw me wince and said, "Don't try to move yet. You've been pretty badly shot up, but you'll be okay. Clyde says so. Oh Willow, do hurry up!"

"This isn't a dream?" I asked; my voice sounded strange to me.

"No," came the voice of Willow as she softly entered the room. She was dressed in a thin gauze of a dress, long and flowing, soft to the touch. I thought she looked like what I imagined a goddess might look like. "No, welcome to my home, Beth. You are in my bedroom, actually. Everyone is recovering just fine. None of your family has died, not even Ellen. You saved them all."

Suddenly, all those horrible memories came smashing into my mind once more. I believe I cried out, "No! No! No! No!" again. Willow's soft voice countered their impact upon me. "There, there, you have a very bad set of memories, Beth. But that is all they are, just memories. In time, you'll learn to live with them. All of your family members are on the mend. Would you like to see them? I know they are dying to see you. I've only allowed the six to sit by your side all these days. You know, Sarah Jane, Sandy, Roy, Raphael, Simon, and Thomas. In fact, I haven't been able to keep Sandy and Sarah Jane out of this room!"

"I love you all," I gushed, and they responded with joyful tears flowing down their cheeks. "Mom, dad? They are not dead? I saw them shot, slumped over. Dead. Ellen too."

"No, they took several quarrel hits, but you were very lucky. The men used light crossbows, Herbert and Roy explained to me. According to them, these only produce light wounds. Had they been heavy crossbows, it most likely would be a different story altogether. You got hit in each shoulder, so expect them to be a bit painful for the next few days," she explained. At last, I understood why my arms ached so. "I'll fetch your family now." She quickly and gracefully stood and left the room, all in one motion, like that of a practiced dancer.

I think mom and dad must have been in the adjoining room, for both came in very soon. Both had large bandages about their chests and moved as if even walking were somewhat painful. Yet the smiles of relief and joy were unmistakable. Mom uttered, "Oh Beth!" and they both hugged me for a long time, saying nothing more. I couldn't speak either. It was beyond my wildest imaginations that they were alive.

Finally, I muttered, "I thought you were both dead! Oh, I love you both so much." That was all I could say, as my own tears prevented me from saying more.

I heard the pitter patter of Anne and Ben as they come into the room. Anne said, "Let us see, mommy; let us see her!" Mom and dad got up and moved aside. Anne hugged me and said, "I'm *so* glad you are awake. We were awfully scared you would never wake up! It's been days and days." Ben just held onto my hand as if he would never, ever let it go again.

Willow softly said, "Okay. Now that's enough for now. She has only just awakened. We need to feed her and dress her wounds again. So you all go back and play."

Anne did not want to leave, "But Sarah Jane gets to stay. How come she gets to stay and I don't?"

"Cause she and Sandy are being Elizabeth's nurses, taking care of her. Someday, if you want, you may also become a nurse and take care of people when they are sick or hurt. Now go, play, and enjoy the day. Your sister will get stronger each day. Soon she can play with you again." That satisfied her and they all left. Willow then said, "Beth, I'll go get you some breakfast. You two check those wounds and make sure they aren't bleeding anymore and get her sitting up in bed, ready to eat."

I watched and observed that I had two small puncture wounds in each shoulder. Both hurt, but now that I knew they were there, I managed to overcome the pain substantially, but my arms did not work quite right. They needed to help me sit up. I told them I was not hungry, but they both laughed and said I was being silly.

Soon, Willow came in with a tray. Suddenly, I remembered the liver soup we had been giving Rupert. I hoped I didn't have to eat soup as he did. I was more than relieved to see bread covered in honey sitting on a plate beside a bowl of chicken soup. "I'm not really hungry, Willow," I tried to explain.

I tried to use my arms to get a hold of the spoon, but they wouldn't work quite right. "Don't worry. In no time, your arms will return to normal, Beth. Meantime, the girls can feed you. Remember; feed her slowly. She can have all she wants." Sandy gave me a spoonful of the soup. It tasted delicious. All at once, I felt utterly ravenous, as if I hadn't eaten in weeks. Frantically, I gulped each spoonful down and bid her feed me faster.

Both girls laughed, "I thought you said you weren't hungry," teased Sarah Jane.

Between gulps, I replied, "I wasn't then, but I sure am now!"

Sandy added, "Remember, slowly, slowly, Beth. We don't want to rush it. You haven't had anything to eat for about a week, I think."

"A week?" I exclaimed. "I've been asleep for an entire week?"

"Yes, you have given us a terrible fright," Sarah Jane answered. "We haven't left your side in all that time, except to eat and go to the bath room. We took turns so one of us would always be here when you woke up. The boys helped too, but they got bored just sitting here. It was Willow's orders. 'You six must be the first people that she sees when she wakes up.' Those were her exact words. We don't know why, though. Of course, we saw everything through you and were asleep for over a day ourselves."

I choked, "You saw the attack, the storm, and all the lightning bolts?" I gushed out.

Sarah Jane looked like someone who had just revealed something that she shouldn't have. She recovered a bit by saying, "Yes, didn't you know? You made a solid telepathic contact with all of us. We saw everything. It was horrible. None of us could break free from your hold on us — not until Willow intervened."

I cried. Finally, I said, "I'm so sorry, Sarah Jane, Sandy. I didn't know what I was doing. I didn't mean to terrify you. You are my dearest friends. I think I held on to your images until I blacked out!"

"There, there, Beth, it's okay now. We think we understand what happened. It's not your fault," Sandy added. "Now here, see if you can chew this bread." I chomped greedily at it. In a couple minutes, I had eaten everything and asked for more.

"Not just yet," Sarah Jane said using her serious voice of a healer. "We must make sure that all that stays down. Clyde says you probably will now feel tired and need to sleep some."

"No, I have to go to the bathroom," I countered. They helped me with the bedpan. Once that exertion was finished, I yawned, "Now I'm tired. I was asleep before they got me laid back down!" I slept a peacefully and soundly. The world had become beautiful to me once more.

Chapter 5 Explanations, Decisions and Conclusions

I awoke just after supper. I could tell that at once because the odor of roasted lamb permeated the room. My nursemaids were right there feeding me my share. I was hungry, just as famished as before. I wondered if I would ever get full again. After I had eaten and rested a bit, Willow asked me to see if I could get up and walk into her front room. She said all the others were there, and they all wanted to go over what had actually happened. Sandy and Sarah Jane helped me get up. I noticed I was wearing one of Willow's long robes. It felt soft on my skin. Using them for support, I wobbled unsteadily out into the larger front room.

Indeed, everyone was there. That is, all of us Guardians. All seven of Ellen's Circle were sitting on chairs on one side of the table, while all six of my new friends were sitting on the opposite side. I took my place facing Willow and Mary Ann. Sandy and Sarah Jane sat on either side of me. Mary Ann said formally, "This meeting of the two Circles is now officially in session." What two circles, I wondered. I only saw Ellen's.

Mary Ann was their Wid, so I assumed she must be their leader, if a Circle has a leader. "Elizabeth, let me begin by apologizing to you. I'm deeply sorry I didn't draw the proper conclusions from all the observations presented to me. In short, I goofed; and it nearly cost your life, your family's, and Ellen's. For that, I'm deeply sorry."

I must have looked incredibly dumb at that moment. An apology from Mary Ann was the last thing I would have ever expected. I had no idea of what to say and so said nothing.

She probably knew what I was thinking, and continued. "First, we all need a full and complete explanation of what actually happened. Beth, it is now eight days after the day you left Uru for Karka. Ellen has filled us in on what happened during the wagon ride here — that is, up to the point where she rose up, was shot, and passed out. It seems the two dozen cavalrymen who were supposed to be patrolling the Uru area for Galts attacked you, intending to kill all of you and even Ellen. Until now, we Guardians assumed we would never be harmed by those we seek to aid. That has obviously changed."

"So from Ellen, we know what happened up to that point in time. Your parents were both shot by quarrels in the opening round, as was Ellen shortly after that. We also know what happened to your circle friends, but as Willow has said, you probably do not. So let us begin by telling you what we know about what happened." That sounded fine to me. I couldn't account for the missing seven days of my life. In fact, my birthday had come and gone. I was now eleven.

Here, without a word from the others, Willow took up the tale, for this was her area of expertise. "We know that something dreadful had happened to you during the attack. Something occurred that unlocked your native abilities far, far beyond your training level and skills. Somehow, you established mental contact with each of your circle friends here. You solidly locked onto their minds, rather like a Mind Join. Thus, they actually saw what you saw. Yes, they watched in complete horror as your brother and sister were shot and as you were shot twice. They also saw you, or sensed you would be a better description, move out of your body up into the sky, and then throw bolts of lightning down on the cavalrymen. Let me just say that all six were traumatized by the horror of all this. None of them could break your intense grip upon their minds. They were literally forced to view the whole thing."

I began sobbing uncontrollably. "I didn't mean too. I didn't want to hurt you all!"

Willow's soothing voice reached me, "We know that, Beth. They know that too now, Beth. It was far, far, far beyond your control. It just happened. We all believe that this is the true measure of your bond to them — that they mean more to you than any other living beings."

Still crying, I said, "Yes, I love them. Their faces nearly saved me, but in the end, even their faces were not enough."

"We know, Beth. Next, Ellen regained consciousness only to observe hundreds of lightning bolts smashing everything in sight all around the wagon. Your horses were spooked, and it took all Ellen's remaining strength to keep them from bolting and taking the wagon off on a headlong rush. We know Ellen did her best to try to get you under control, but your power was so much greater than hers was, and she failed utterly. Only then did she send a frantic message to me. It took me only minutes to find out that your circle members were in dire peril as were Ellen and your family. Another minute and I had notified all the other members of my Circle; they immediately went to their apprentices and found them in a traumatic trance."

"I can honestly say, Beth, a situation like this has never occurred before. We all held a conference for at least a half hour trying in vain to free our apprentices and figure out what to do. We had to get to you as fast as possible, and yet we had to aid our apprentices. I finally was able to enter your mind from here. I must say that at first I was shocked by your situation. I've never heard of such a thing occurring before, and I didn't know how to deal with it. I finally tried singing to you, and that began to have an effect. Somehow, Beth, together, we got the horses moving forward. That was a terrifically positive step. We had to get you out of that horrible area where the devastation was unbelievable. Once you were moving away, I then managed to get you to look for the nearest emergency cabin. Between the two of us, Beth, we did it. It took a couple hours though, and I finally managed to get you to regain some control. The trail of shattered trees and smashed boulders left in the wagon's wake was unreal."

"Once you had calmed down, I was able to extricate your six friends from your telepathic clamp on their minds. Then, the rest of us went into action. From our various villages, all rode like the wind, as Roy described it, dragging your friends with us. Mary Ann had me stay here and continue to assist you; Sandy began preparations for housing and caring for everyone."

"Clyde and Sarah Jane from Undel were actually the first to reach you, and they found you all shot up, unconscious, and still in the wagon, which had halted beside the cabin. They had their work cut out for them. Somehow, they managed to get everyone inside the cabin and began tending to your wounds. We got a terrific break, because no one's wounds was seriously life threatening. It could have been far worse had they been using heavy crossbows. Herbert and Roy arrived shortly after they had gotten you inside; those two had cut across country to get to you faster. The healing went faster with the four of them working. Mary Ann and Raphael got to the scene next. She insisted that Herbert and Roy head back down the way you had come to see what had happened. Clyde, who had already passed through the devastation area on his way to the cabin, would only say that the site was unreal. We did not press him further because he was working feverishly on healing everyone."

"When they reached the ambush location, Frank and Thomas had just arrived there from Redun. All four said that they were speechless for quite some time. They counted twenty-four dead cavalrymen's bodies, or rather the pieces that remained, along with the smoldering carcasses of their horses. Shattered trees covered the entire track as if a giant had trampled the forest. As they headed back toward the cabin, the number of shattered trees diminished and finally ended."

"When the four had returned to the cabin, Jason and Simon had finally arrived from Petersville. We held a conference about what to do about the carnage site. Many ideas were put forth. In the end, we decided to leave the site as it was and let other patrols from the King discover it. The devastation is so great that no one would ever believe a Guardian could possibly have caused it, not in a million years. However, we now have a weapon to use against the King should he get too far out of line. We can say, remember your cavalry operation to destroy that family from Uru and Ellen? Well, you can guess the rest. That should strike terror into the King's mind. However, we will save that for a last possible option. There are other ways of handling this upstart of a King."

"About this time, Clyde pronounced that everyone was in a stable condition, and Ellen came to and told us what she knew. Now, all this began to make more sense to us, and Mary Ann realized just how badly she had erred. Under the cover of night, we brought you here in the wagon. However, try as I might, I could not free you, Beth, from the tentacles of your storm clouds. I tried and tried. Every time I started to get the clouds to dissipate, you would cry out No! and reform the clouds! My, but you are one very strong willed person! However, as I had hoped, time was on my side, and I finally got you to let go, relax, and rejoin with your body."

"Wow!" I exclaimed. "Honestly, I did not know any of that happened! Thank you all so much! I thought I had died or something, maybe gone insane," I added sheepishly.

"Now, then," Mary Ann said quietly, "can you tell us what happened as far as you can tell? If the memories are too bad, Willow can help you out, but we *must* know. It's very important to us all. It's okay if you feel like crying or anything. We just have to know what happened with you. Just do the best you can, please."

"But it was so strange," I protested. "I don't even know what I did."

"That is very understandable, Beth. That was one horrific situation you endured. No one should ever have to go through what you did. Just describe it to us any way you can. If we can't figure something out, why, we'll just ask you questions until we do," she replied.

I began at the beginning. I could easily recall bending down to find lunch in the dark food sack, followed by the noises and the pressure of Ellen's arm holding me down as she tried to get up. I related all that I could remember. They asked many questions as I went along. I hoped sincerely I didn't sound like a complete idiot, because none of it made much sense to me at all. Some parts were just black; I couldn't see or remember anything during those times. I finished about an hour later, half expecting them to chide me for having goofed in some way, that I ought to have known better. Instead, I found both the adults as well as my friends listening spellbound.

Mary Ann finally broke the silence, "Beth, I don't ordinarily evaluate for someone — that is, tell them what they should think about something that happened to them or that they did. It's best for them to draw their own conclusions. However, I do owe you some wisdom, which may help you understand what happened to you. As you are aware, we are all spiritual beings and inhabit or use a body. We Guardians are seldom, if ever, stuck inside body heads. Consider this. Would there be any real difference in what spiritual and mental things one could do, if said immortal spirit had a young girl's body or an adult's body?"

I thought about that one. I'm not as strong as mom nor can I do all the things she does, but those are properties of the size and age of the body. That was not what she was asking me to consider.

"I haven't seen spirits grow in size," I ventured to say. "I mean mom's been the way she is as long as I can remember; dad, too. So if beings do not grow like a body grows, then I think I understand what you are saying. I'll still be me when I'm all grown up."

"Yes, that is what I mean. You are you and will always be you. Now, it is only natural for a person to want to stop something really bad from happening, like having one's family slain before one's eyes. I sure would. Honestly, in all the world, the family is most crucial for us all. Without families raising new children, we would run out of bodies to use, but I digress. You haven't been trained as a fighter nor as I recall do you even like such." I shook my head; that was the absolute truth. Now, I hated it even more. "So wouldn't it be natural for someone in such a predicament to try to stop it using any means that they could?"

"I suppose so," I replied not quite seeing where she was going with this.

"So you have seen Ellen pull lightning from the sky on previous occasions. Only minutes before that attack, you had been learning to exercise some small control over lightning, right?" Again, I nodded. Suddenly, I saw what she was implying.

"So I tried to control the storm, the masses of energies, without knowing what or how to do it?" I blurted out.

"It would certainly seem so to us," Mary Ann smiled at me, giving me confidence. "Normally, we teach you how to do that in your last two years of training. One must learn many things, including self-discipline in order to control that much energy without yourself falling victim to it as well. It's exceedingly rare for an apprentice only beginning their fifth year to be able to control the lightning. I've never actually seen such, but I have been told it has occurred. However, and this is a very big however, those that did all went rogue on us."

"What do you mean, rogue?" I asked, suddenly feeling that they might want to get rid of me — that I would lose all my friends.

"There is the case of Erline Herbiscus, the priest-warrior of the fortified town of Urkut about fifty miles to the east of here. In her sixth year and on her own, she learned to grasp hold of lightning, but it took control of her life. She abandoned the Guardians and went her own way. She is highly renowned as a fierce fighter and leader of her town. She is merciless and brings down the bolts to slay all enemies before her. Hence, we call her rogue, and she calls us spineless swine. She is continually making war on the Galts, attacking them whenever she gets the chance, even provoking them. That is one reason the Galts are venturing this far from their own lands, they are trying to get around her area of control."

"So you see our greatest fear, Beth, is that since you have tasted the ultimate power to destroy and slay, it will draw you back to it. Slowly, you may succumb to using that power more and more. And each time you do, it takes more and more control over you." I looked horror-struck.

"Is there no way out for me?" I was almost crying. There just had to be!

"If we can get you successfully through all your training, I believe you'll have the power to master it and not the other way around."

I sighed in relief. "I'll do anything!" I promised hastily.

"I know you will, don't worry. We aren't abandoning you. However, our biggest fear is that another attack or circumstance similar to the last one might appear *before* you are fully ready and that could be the undoing of everything. So Beth, it is our obligation to you to see to it that you are not put into that kind of danger until you are prepared to handle it." I wondered what she meant by that.

She continued, "We are very worried about what might also happen when the next storm comes — whether you may be tempted to reach out for the storm's energy. If you do, there is nothing we can do to save you. We have not that kind of power, I'm afraid."

That was a terribly sobering statement. I wanted to scream "I won't," but inwardly, I wondered, which, I realized, was exactly her point. She added, "Additionally, we feel you're going to need some special training we can't provide you. So in your tenth year, we have agreed to send your Circle to Calgary for that very special training at our expense, since it was my blunder that brought all this about in the first place."

What did she mean "my Circle," and I'd never heard of Calgary. I guess I must have looked very stupid, for Mary Ann added, "Let me explain. The other apprentices already know about Calgary. We Guardians are organized into Circles, as you know. What you don't know is that each circle itself is but one member in an even larger Circle. We call ourselves the Circle of Blankford because that's where I, their Wid, reside. We choose one of us to represent our Circle in the greater Circle, which is called the Circle of Central Greenway. I'm also our representative in that larger Circle. So if something arises that our Circle cannot handle or has wider impact than our area of protection, we take it to the larger Circle. Make sense so far?"

I nodded, though still not grasping what Calgary had to do with this. She continued, "Further, the Circle of Central Greenway elects one of its members to be in an even larger Circle called the Circle of All Greenway. Only the wisest, most powerful of all druwids may serve on that high Circle for they oversee our entire land! That Circle has its headquarters in the largest city in Greenway, Calgary."

I began to image a large, grand city, but all I'd ever seen was the tiny village of Uru. It sounded impressive and most interesting. She continued, "So you see Beth, I needed guidance. Thus, I took this matter up to the higher Circle of Central Greenway for their opinion. However, they took it all the way up to the top, to the Circle of All Greenway! Now that gives you some idea of the importance of all this. You, Beth, have attracted the attention of some of the most powerful of all druwids! Quite an honor indeed. They personally want to finish off your last year of training! Pretty amazing."

"Wow!" was all I could say. Somehow, I felt this was going to be a very good thing to do. The nightmare had only just ended and was still fresh in my mind. That someone really powerful was going to help me greatly reassured me, and I did need all the reassuring I could get at the moment. It had been an awfully scary experience.

"You do not need to worry about your parents. I have already spoken with them. They were frantically worried about you, as you can well imagine. So when you are ready to go to the big city, you have their full support."

It seems while I had been sleeping, Mary Ann had been quite busy on my behalf. "Thank you, I don't know what to say except thanks," I exclaimed relieved. She was always one step ahead of me.

"You are more than welcome, dear child, but there is more to come." Now I was even more curious; how could there be anything better than this? "Ordinarily, the tenth year students attempt to form their own Circle. Sometimes, they are not successful for some years after that, should a position remain unfilled. Often a Wid is hard to find. However, in this case, because of the shared experience, you seven have already bonded as a Circle should. At this point, it would be devastating to all of you to separate you! I doubt very much if it could even successfully be done. Thus, it is my privilege to announce that sitting opposite us is the newest Circle of the Guardians!" She paused allowing us time to come to grips with the fact that we already were a Circle — that we had done it on our own.

"Holy grasshopper! We did it!" exclaimed Roy. "I knew it! I told you all it would be so, didn't I?"

We all looked at each other, grinning from ear to ear; then, we all let out a war hoop and cheered. Even the quiet, unassuming Thomas was cheering along with the rest of us.

"Don't let all this go to your heads, children. I've only known of one other Circle that formed in their eighth year. So as far as I know, you are the youngest Circle on record, and that means all of your training will be accelerated in the area of Circle operations. You'll be learning much of what you would ordinarily be discovering in your tenth year, but I'm afraid you will have to work doubly hard at your lessons." I caught Sarah Jane's immediate pout. I knew she felt that she was already working as hard as she wanted to work on learning things. Of all of us, she wanted time to do other things, like flirt with boys.

But Roy's enthusiasm spoke for all of us, "We can do it! I know we can!"

She continued, "We will hold the formal dedication ceremony in, oh say, a week from now. Between now and then, you must choose a name for your Circle. Choose wisely, for it will follow you through all time."

Sandy asked, "You mean that if we decide we don't like it, we can't change it later?"

"Right, Sandy. Your Circle's name will be taught to many other Circles. We cannot go around learning one name only to change it later. That only causes confusion. So pick wisely."

"We *will*, Sandy assured her.

"One more thing, children," Mary Ann added, "since you are now an official Circle in training, you all must live and stay together. So from now on, all of you will live here in Karka. Part of each day, you'll be training as a Circle."

We all let out even more cries of happiness. I know that no birthday present could never been finer to me. When we quieted down, she went on, "I have already arraigned this with your families. But don't worry; we'll take you to back to visit them just as often as you desire. Besides, you need to gain more experience in traveling across the countryside." Thomas, our Loremaster, really appreciated this statement. For he loved being outdoors even more than I did.

Up to this point, Mary Ann had been doing all of the speaking for her Circle. Now, however, their Judger, Frank Williams, took over. "Last on the agenda is what do we do about the attack? Here we have many choices. It is known that Ellen took the wagon to come to Karka under the pretext of returning with new seed. It is now known by the King that his entire cavalry band has been utterly annihilated by forces beyond imagination. At this point, he knows nothing about what happened to your family or Ellen. We have carefully erased all traces of the wagon having ever left the site of the carnage. Thus, he doesn't know if the wagon's occupants are dead or alive."

"One choice we have is to let them know that all those in the wagon also perished. Ellen is certainly not well enough to return to Uru yet. Clyde is staunchly insisting that she spend three weeks here recovering at the very least. However, it is not fair to those in Uru to keep their wagon, so if we adopt this choice, we can return the wagon along with some seed. If we choose this option, then your parents would likely be safe from any retribution for the rest of their lives, as long as they don't return to Uru or tell stories to others that could get back to the King. However, Ellen is pledged to serve the villagers and would have to break her vows to them."

"Another approach would be to have Ellen return with the feed when she is able and let others know that your family is safe. All would know you have settled in Karka, but that was never a secret. However, the King may seek revenge on you and your family here. Or at the least, seek them out to try to find out what really happened to his men. That the Guardians were somehow involved would certainly come out. That could be both good and bad. Good in that the King would think very long and hard before he tried any treachery on any of us again. Bad, in that the Guardians are supposed to be helping people. He might very well change his mind about keeping us around."

"Another approach would be to have Ellen return with the seed and then seek an audience with the King. Then, she could lie to him and say something like 'We saw a huge lightning display behind us on our way to Karka. Later, I learned that your cavalry patrol was ambushed. Do you know anything about who was behind it?' and so on, pretending that we have no idea what had happened and are seeking any information he might have — this would leave him in mystery, but, as you all should know, lies have a way of backfiring. Truth eventually wins over lies. One day the King may learn the truth. Besides, Ellen is not a practiced liar and would find that deceit most difficult to implement skillfully or believably."

So far, I didn't like any of the choices. "Please, don't make Ellen lie to them. Isn't there any way to make sure mom and dad are not hurt by that nasty King?" I interrupted him.

Frank looked sadly at me, as if to imply none of the choices were all that good. Surprising all of us, Ellen spoke up, "There is another way I believe, Frank, that might work. Suppose I return with the seed when Clyde gives me permission to travel. I could report to the King that we were attacked by his cavalry, which we were. I can insist on an apology, recompense, and a sworn statement that he will never try to harm a Guardian again. I can also tell him of our miraculous rescue by an unseen 'rogue warrior.' After all, none of us *saw* who actually brought down the lightning bolts, did we? We were all unconscious at the time. And that is the truth, though only partially. I know he has heard of Erline Herbiscus and her escapades. We can say that we're searching for the rouge warrior-priest who came to our timely rescue. We just don't ever have to say that we found her. This way, the King knows that we know what he did. We make him pay for having done it. The blame goes onto an unknown rogue druwid, which at that very time is close to the truth of the matter. The only flaw is that the King knows that your family is here in Karka and may yet harm them."

Until her last sentence, I really liked her plan. It made sense and really was only slightly stretching the truth of the matter. None actually saw me doing it. I spoke up, "I like it Ellen. I don't want you to have to lie. I always feel bad when I do, so I don't want you to. Isn't there some way we can make it safe for mom and dad? I suppose they could move to another town."

"Well, yes, they could move on, but I think that would be hard for them just now. Remember they have been through a lot too," Ellen reminded me. "Frank, couldn't we say that we have taken them under our protection, and that if any harm befalls them, we will take a similar retribution out on the King personally? Is that valid?"

"Yes, there is precedence for that, Ellen. He did unprovokedly attack you. By all codes, he is the offender, so we're well within our rights to proclaim that Beth and her entire family are now under our protection. Once so announced, then any harm that befalls them gives us the right to retaliate in kind. I'm sure he knows this, but we can remind him of this detail. I think he values his own skin. Ellen, I think you have a brilliant solution here. Well done."

"It's amazing I can think at all the way my head and chest hurts so," Ellen replied. "I think I've sat up for about as long as I dare, Mary Ann."

"Thank you for being here and helping Ellen. I know how much pain your body is in at the moment. We appreciate your sitting with us. Unless I hear any objections, then I move that we adopt Ellen's plan. Hearing none, so be it. Now, let's adjourn, and let the wounded heal. Children, we'll talk more tomorrow."

To Sandy and Sarah Jane, she said, "Will you help Beth back to her bed please?" She didn't need to ask, for both were beside me the instant I made the slightest motion to get up. I still could not move my arms very much and felt rather helpless just now.

As they helped steady me walking, Sandy exclaimed, "We are a real Circle! Isn't that positively amazing?"

"We owe it all to you, Beth!" Sarah Jane added, giving me a little hug. Then, she said, "But I'm not so sure about all this extra studying thing."

Sandy and I smiled at each other and said in unison, "We know."

Sarah Jane blushed and said, "You two will think about boys pretty soon too. I'm thirteen and a woman now. Some get married when they are fourteen! My mom got married to my dad when she was sixteen."

The boys followed us into the room and waited patiently while the girls got me back lying down. "Thanks," I said, "I'm still so very weak. Being up just that little bit has made me feel really wobbly. This is much better."

Roy finally spoke up, "Beth, we know you're over a year behind us all, so we've all promised to help you just as much as you need. I expect they are going to accelerate all of our learning. Whenever you need any kind of help, why, just say something. We have all probably already been through whatever you are trying to master."

Raphael added, "And don't be afraid of goofing up, Beth. We have all goofed many times. Also, remember each of us has already begun our specialized training. So if you need help with figures or designs, let me know. If you have trouble with herbs, just ask Thomas. Speaking of herbs, I think that topic has given me more trouble than anything has! Plants, they all look the same to me," he added, and the others laughed along with him.

Not wanting to be left out, Simon said, "Remember, I'm the Judger in training. I ought to apologize for mostly ignoring you at the solstice party, Beth. I'm afraid I was too caught up in trying to hear all of the adult news. If you need history lessons, I'm your man, and I'm learning simple conjuring skills. Frank says he thinks I've a real knack for the conjuring arts, but I've a huge amount to learn yet."

"Thanks, all of you. I sure will lean on you all, that's for sure," I answered most gratefully. "I think it is going to be just fantastic to be around all of you!"

"Yes, but what do we want to call our Circle?" Sarah Jane turned our thoughts onto the first thing on which we had to decide. "I don't like the idea that we can't change it, though. So I guess we had better come up with something we like."

"My area," broke in Simon. He spoke solemnly trying to imitate the adults. "Most Circles that are protecting a town, that is to say, the lowest level Circles, incorporate the geographic area they are protecting into their name."

"Honestly, Simon, we all know that now, even Beth," Sarah Jane interrupted him. "We don't have any area to protect yet."

"I was coming to that, my pretty healer," Simon teased. "Not all Circles are locked down to protecting a single town like our mentor's Circle. I know one is called the Bear Circle; I think they look after bears, but I'm not sure."

"Oh, now that you mention it," Sandy added, "I've heard of a Money Circle and a Navigation Circle and even a Sailing Circle."

Simon then said, "So, think about it. I think we should adopt some kind of name like that, not one that uses a geographical area." We all agreed with him completely.

Thomas suggested, "How about the Circle of Rats? I love rats. Or the Snake Circle?"

"Oh icko!" exclaimed Sandy and Sarah Jane in unison. I smiled; their reaction was predictable.

"How about the Building Circle?" suggested Raphael. "I hope one day we can be behind some really important constructions." At least no one said icko. Soon proposed names were flying left and right. Some were so funny that we all laughed.

Sandy was the first to mention the name we all liked. "Say, I have an idea. How about calling ourselves the Lightning Circle? You see, all the other Circles are very likely going to hear about us anyway. So this way, it becomes easier for them to remember us in particular. Besides, lightning can also mean a really quick and fast acting group; it doesn't always have to refer to the lightning bolts." The more we all chatted about this name, the more we all thought it was appropriate.

I finally added, "You know if we call ourselves the Lightning Circle, then we give ourselves a great flexibility in the future. What I mean is we may become a Circle known for really fast actions, so it would suit us. We may become a group of fast thinkers or problem resolvers or fast builders or fast travelers or fast conjurers or a fast finder of the truth or a fast who knows what. But the name would still be fitting." Everyone cheered.

Sandy said, "Brilliant, positively brilliant. All those in favor of calling ourselves the Lightning Circle, say 'Yes.'" We all said yes. She didn't bother asking for "No's." So she declared, "The motion carries unanimously. I'll tell Willow our new name. Yes!" I think that we were all excited; we were becoming a team.

My mind began imagining us all grown up and going around doing all sorts of things really, really fast. Then I was asleep. I didn't hear Sarah Jane suddenly say, "Sh! She's fallen asleep. Now we had all better leave her alone. Quietly, guys."

Chapter 6 The Karka Years

Karka in 555 AH was a town, not a village. That is, the population was roughly fifteen hundred, a thriving metropolis from my point of view. Incidentally, Garth, Undel and Petersville also were comparable in size, but Blankford was home to nearly two thousand folks, and the fortified town of Redun boasted five thousand members. Only a hundred lived in Uru. So not only did I have some major adjusting to do, but also my family did.

Karka was a sprawling town in transition between a hunter-gatherer culture and a farmer-tradesman culture. Sprawling along the top of Aran Ridge, the town was a half mile wide but one and a half long! Positively huge. First, there were approximately four hundred family homes compared to the two dozen in Uru. New dwellings were being built almost weekly. However, Karka boasted a hundred stores or business establishments, something we had never seen. Everything from clothing to food, from metal tools to leather goods, from weapons to planting supplies could be found in the local shops.

Several iron mines lay just beyond the northern edge of town, providing employment for over fifty men. A nearby stinky smelter bellowed black smoke daily and provided the needed metals for the blacksmiths and craftsmen to forge into useful products. I grew to admire these hardy men for they all had some of the largest arm muscles I'd ever seen. Clanking of hammers on anvils became a familiar sound as one strolled about the town.

Karka boasted some of the largest herds of sheep, goats, and cattle that I had ever seen. Daily, dozens of men would usher them out of their holds at the western edge of town at first light only to herd them back into the safety of the town just before dark. The eastern slopes were divided into some fifty fields, acres and acres, each one separated from its neighbor by a small foot high wall of stones that had been removed from the field. My dad had no trouble at all finding a field for which to tend and care. In Karka, work was plentiful. The real problem was deciding what work you really wanted to do, so great were the choices!

However, the first lesson my family and I had to learn was what money was. Until now, we always used the barter system. While one could still barter with nearly all the shops, exchanging money was vastly simpler and much faster. Willow explained it to us. "Money is Karka's means of exchange. Because there are so many different jobs to be performed here, everyone does one task and in return is paid coin tokens. These tokens are then traded at the various establishments for what goods, services, and food you desire. You see, money is just a convenient means of exchange. Helmut, as a full-time farmer, you should make more than enough money in a year to provide for all your family's needs. Many save what money they do not use for a rainy day, a very wise idea. To get you settled and started, Ellen has brought along four sacks of seed that I'll help you trade for an initial stake of token coins. The exchange should give you plenty to get by until the fall harvest. However, the field manager will, at the end of each week, be giving you your weekly pay in coins for that week's labor; that should more than cover your family's needs for the next week. It is a simple system and very workable. The coins are small and made of lightweight copper. We even have a money changer shop where you can trade about a hundred copper coins in for a coin made from gold!"

Dad, slightly confused, asked, "You mean at fall harvest, I don't keep a share of the harvest and give the rest to others in the town?"

"Oh, I see. Actually, you can do it either way. Some farmers prefer to clear their own fields east of town and tend them on their own. Come harvest, all they get is totally theirs to use or barter as they see fit. However, most prefer to tend the communal fields and get a weekly salary. At harvest time, the local shops get the goods and in turn sell it to all the other families who work in other trades, like the blacksmiths who buy their food with token coins. You can do it either way, Helmut. Personally, I believe that working in the communal fields benefits the entire town far more, since there are over fifteen hundred mouths to feed and only a few hundred farmers in total. We always seem to need more people who have a green thumb, so to speak." Since it was so late in the season, dad had little choice this year. Besides, he would get time to see just how this new system worked.

Next, we needed a home, well actually two homes: one for my family and one for us seven of the Lightning Circle. Unfortunately, we were really too young to live alone and too many to fit comfortably in Willow's small home. Her house, which was made of stone, had four rooms: a bedroom, a study, a kitchen, and a living room. Compared to my old long house home in Uru, hers was positively tiny. The arrangement that Willow engineered was perfect from my point of view.

Behind Willow's house was an old warehouse and next to it was a new wooden long house nearing completion. It seems that termites had dined on the previous one, so this summer a replacement was being built. Willow acquired both buildings. My family moved into the new replacement home almost at once ,and they assisted the final finishing work. It was a long house very similar to their old home. The warehouse got converted into a dormitory for our Circle. I would be living right next door to my family!

However, we couldn't live by ourselves, and Willow couldn't manage to live in two places at the same time. In the small home on the other side of the warehouse lived an elderly couple, Kos Aran and his wife, Yanna; both were in their late fifties. In fact, Kos was the grandson of Karka Aran, the druwid who first founded the town! Kos was a burly man standing about six feet and weighed at least two hundred pounds. Long ago, he was a Protector, but a severe leg wound and old age had ended his career. He tired easily, though his mind was bright. Yanna, though not a druwid, had nevertheless spent most of her adult life surrounded with them. She was portly, very friendly, always tried to be helpful, but was somewhat forgetful in her old age. Yanna might volunteer to make some cookies, but then forget about them completely if she got distracted. Kos loved to sit and tell stories about his "good old days." We discovered he was an endless source of historical information about the area.

By the time I had recovered, the warehouse had been converted into our Circle's new home with the Aran's acting as our live-in chaperones. The second story, western section became the girl's sleeping quarters, while the eastern, the men's. Walls gave each side some privacy from the others. The main floor had the kitchen, food pantry, dining area, and a spacious main living room-study area where we spent our time together. In case you are wondering, Sandy's family lived four blocks away, and we did see them occasionally as well.

In the couple of weeks that I remained mostly bedridden, the others industriously fixed up our new home. Though I really wanted to help, without the use of my sore arms, there was little I could actually do except watch and make suggestions. So in just three short weeks, our Circle moved into our new living quarters, and we settled into a training pattern dictated by Willow.

During that time, Willow spent many hours with me helping me to learn to master the impulse to latch onto the energy masses in storm clouds. When the next big thunderstorm came, I had not the slightest impulse to want to latch onto it. By the time the three weeks had passed, I could even selectively reach out and touch that deadly energy. In fact, once I grasped the concept of what she actually did with me and the storm clouds, in later years, I adapted the approach to many other things. In essence, she had me reach out and contact the energy masses and then knowingly withdraw from them, over and over. I found that at first, once I had contacted them, it was hard to let go. By doing it repeatedly, any compulsion I had to latch onto the masses vanished. I was finally pronounced free of its grip, for which everyone was truly thankful. I was not going to become a rogue!

In true Wid fashion, I concluded Willow's method worked by making me reach out and contact or touch the thing and then withdraw from it, over and over. When Roy was having a rough time mastering his newly acquired weapon, a curved scimitar, I had him first reach out, touch it, and then let it go, repeatedly. In no time, all his considerations vanished, and he quickly became skillful with his new weapon. Later on, Sandy had a hard time embroidering; she was always sticking the needle into her finger by accident. I did the same process with her and her needle with similar results. She actually became far better at it than I ever did. Within a few months, everyone in my Circle began to come to me, their Wid, for help when they ran into difficulties with some object.

After the three weeks of my recovery were finally done, we all settled into our new routine. In the early morning, both Sandy and I helped our parents with our routine chores, while the others helped the Arans and Willow with theirs. As soon as we finished, the seven of us and the Arans all ate breakfast together. Then, the remainder of the morning each of us worked on learning homemaking skills; we girls learned to sew, cook, and weave. Even my mom was pressed into service, sharing her skills with us. Protesting all the way, the guys also had to learn the rudiments of these skills, for there likely would be times when they were off on their own missions and would have to cook and mend their own clothes. Roy's protest was common, "But I don't want to be domesticated! I'm a fighter." The boys' protests were ignored, of course.

After lunch, we each worked on our specialized skills as best we could. Roy and Sandy had appropriate mentors in Willow and Kos, and they did their best with the rest of us. True, quite frequently, the others in Willow's Circle came to visit for an afternoon. We all took part in that specialized training, some more than others. It was especially hard for me being a Wid in training, because I had to know a lot about everything. However, the arrangement worked out fairly well for all of us.

After the late afternoon chores were done and dinner finished, the early evening hours were spent mostly with Kos and his history lessons. Frank Williams, the Judger, had been quite insistent that we learn all the history we could and learn it fast. He said the events were now moving quite rapidly in the whole area. If we were to understand what was happening, we absolutely had to know the past; and Kos was a great storyteller. Once he began, we listened intently to his tales. Because many of his dealt with places beyond our greater valley area, we also got geography lessons. In fact, we got so much information so fast, that I found myself drawing up sketches of Tarra on parchment pages. This rudimentary mapmaking of mine eventually turned out to be vital.

Some of this history I must relate to you at this point so you, too, can understand the rapidly changing events that are about to occur. It began some hundred twenty years before, around 435 AH when Karka Aran and his Circle first entered this valley. They met many local tribes who were primarily extended families living off the land by hunting the plentiful game and gathering nuts and berries and the like. They lived in crude homes made of wood and animal hides, primitive by our current standards. Karka and his companions explored the area and befriended the locals. Soon they began sharing their wisdom and aiding the people by getting them to build more permanent homes and to start growing food to supplement their hunting. The result was rapidly expanding villages, because the harsh way of life became far easier for these hardy locals. Within twenty years, the major towns in the area formed and began growing.

The Guardians taught the villagers basic skills and even more advanced ones, such as how to mine, smelt, and work with metals. The introduction of sturdy metal tools along with abundant crops made a drastic improvement in their way of life especially during the winter months. Before, during the cold wintertime, the death rate soared and many went days without any food. The death rate of their children dropped, and their numbers grew quite rapidly. In fact, according to Kos, many craftsmen now knew more than their Guardians, who now found themselves learning from those they once taught!

However, the Greenway was not a paradise, only relatively so. North of the Greenway is a land of immense pine forests and bitter cold winters, the Volksholm. This was a land of mighty hunters and powerful fighters. The Axemen, as we call them, are a proud, fiercely independent people who occasionally venture south into the Greenway wreaking havoc as they go in search of useful plunder. According to Kos, when a Volksholm man wants to prove that he is ready to become the leader of his tribe, he is required to demonstrate his fighting skill by conducting a successful raid down into Greenway. Fortunately for us, the Valley of Uru lies nearly two hundred miles south and west of Volksholm so their raids on us are seldom.

More critical to us are the Galts who live in the Northern Steppes just to the east of the Greenway. According to Kos, these lands are enormous semi-arid, sparse grasslands with rolling hills and few trees. The central and eastern portions are home to clans of horsemen, but those on the western side adjacent to the forests and rolling green hills are more warlike. They cannot effectively ride their horses into battles because of the dense forests that separate our two lands and so come mostly on foot. It is Kos's opinion that the Galts are jealous of our prosperity or easy way of life.

Kos explained that there is a symbiotic relationship between the Galts and the Volksholm. Gold. The Galts have many gold mines across the Northern Steppes. There is little to none in Volksholm although it has rich iron deposits. Thus, for as long as any can remember, the Galts trade the useless gold to the Volksholm people in return for highly useful metal weapons and such. In fact, the finest weapons to be found anywhere in all the northern lands above the Appian Way mountain range come from Volksholm. However, Kos calls both peoples simply the "barbarians," which I think is quite apropos.

Some twenty years ago, one druwid went rogue: Erline Herbiscus, the priest-warrior of the fortified town of Urkut, which lies about a hundred miles east from Karka. She tired of all the endless Galt raids and put a complete stop to it in Urkut. Now, the Galts bypass her area completely. However, she is continually expanding her zone of control, taking over neighboring villages. This is what has been forcing the Galts to attack in our area more frequently.

King Randolf, on the other hand, had an even better way of stopping the Galts. He built the first fortified wall around his hilltop town of Redun. We learned that he actually got the idea from Frank Williams, some ten years ago. Frank now rues the day he ever made that suggestion to King Randolf! When Frank comes to visit, he keeps telling us, "Be careful what you suggest to others; it may come back to haunt you!" Of course, we do not find his advice particularly useful just yet.

We all thought Kos was now finished with his history lessons, since we were now up to the present, but he had only just begun. South of the Appian Way lies the land of the Seven Sea Princes. There really were not seven men but rather seven extended families of the original founders. Each of the seven clans had their own city on the northern shore of the Med Sea. These powerful families controlled their own city-states, as well as a huge merchant fleet of boats. They traded with all lands from as far north as Calgary, Greenway, all the way down to the huge city of Galantas, Megalos. Over the years, these seven families became fabulously wealthy.

Each city attempts to outdo the others in grandeur. Some even say that their streets are paved with gold, but Kos discounts that rumor saying that gold is way too soft to withstand foot traffic. Yet all this wealth has only brought them petty in-fighting amongst themselves. Indeed, Kos claims that deceit and treachery have taken to new heights by these seven families. Assassinations are commonplace.

On the positive side, Kos did say that some of the finest music in Tarra comes from the musicians of the Princes. To our delight, he said that nearly once a year, a roving band of musicians from the land of the Seven Sea Princes comes to Karka for a week. During that time, the whole town takes part in a week-long festival called the Carnival. Sandy, who has always lived here, has been to four, so we drilled her for details. To the rest of us, it sounded like the Carnival was a week-long party of immense proportions. Unfortunately, no one knew just when the band would make their next appearance in Karka; they had no fixed itinerary.

At the eastern shores of the Med Sea lie the arid lands called Juda Arad, home to poor nomads who are barely able to survive these harsh hills. Water is scarce there, but sheep are plentiful. Grass is not. So the extended tribal families are forced to constantly move to find food for their sheep. Kos says they have lived there for as long as anyone can recall. He even said that the land boasts many ancient ruins of cities now long forgotten. No one even knows who they were. That I found fascinating, an entire people vanished; how could that happen?

However, the real power in Tarra lies on the island of Megalos whose largest city is called Galantas. He described it as a city of tall, marble pillars supporting great vaulted stone roofs. Yes, the area was very hot and dry. Winters as we know them do not come to Megalos, only slightly cooler days. Hence, they build many great stone buildings with only widely spaced columns for walls, allowing the sea breezes to cool them.

According to Kos, Megalos is home to Tarra's greatest thinkers and crafters of stone. Wood is scarce, so all buildings are made from stone, either craved limestone or marble if you are wealthy. Megalos also has the most powerful, well organized army on Tarra. They are called the Centurions. Since Kos used to be a Protector, he described their fighters at length. Each soldier is armored with leather and patches of metal. They use short swords and spears predominately. All Megalos is organized in units of ten. Nothing can be done unless there is a group of ten, claims Kos. Ten soldiers make a squad. Ten squads, a company, ten companies a regiment. He claimed that there are hundreds of regiments! Here, Raphael, our Planner who was good with figures, protested, "But Kos, that means their army numbers in the tens of thousands! Who do they fight?"

Kos explained that they use the army to take over neighboring lands, build cobblestone roadways, irrigation systems, and stone fortresses along the way. The people of Megalos are Sun worshipers. As they move their zone of control outwards, any land whose people are not Sun worshipers, are labeled heathens and barbarians, and promptly attacked and subjugated. According to Kos, they have total control over the rich farmlands of the South Lands. Some years ago, they conquered Juda Arad, and rumor has it that they are now moving up into the Sea Princes. To me, it seemed that someday, we in the Greenway would have to deal with these Megalos centurions, if they kept on moving northward. Little did I know that I would have a hand in that.

"So you see, kids, Karka is only a very tiny part of the vast world of Tarra," Kos drolled on. "Our peaceful world is threatened on all sides by men of war. The Cosmic Balance is out of order, but you had better let Willow explain that to you." Naturally, the very next time we saw Willow, we asked her what this Cosmic Balance thing was all about.

Her initial comment only roused our curiosity even more, "Kos! He knows that these matters are not taught until the tenth year!"

"But Willow, can't you at least explain it a little bit? We are all dying to know," I used my best pleading facial expressions and voice tones. She laughed and agreed, "Okay, just a brief explanation. You are all really going to have to study all this in depth, but in good time. So here is the first question for you all: what do we believe in? In what do we have faith? We are touching upon religion here." I just hate it when someone volunteers to tell me something and then immediately asks me a leading question instead! The only difference is this time I had plenty of company. All seven of us had rather blank looks upon our faces.

Since the others did not volunteer and answer, I suggested, "Perhaps it is Nature."

To my surprise, Willow said, "Well done, Beth. Yes, Nature. We do not believe in fictitious Sun Gods, Storm Gods, Fertility Gods, Hunting Gods, War Gods, or Pestilence Gods. We believe all men are in control over their own lives, not some unseen, everywhere at all times, omniscient being. Why? If there is an overseeing God behind all our fates, then we forsake our own personal responsibility for our lives, placing all that into his or her hands. We are tremendously lessened if we do such. No, for us, it is the beauty and balance of Nature that we worship. Life and Harmony. True, there is violence in Nature. Bears kill and eat other creatures, but they do not wantonly kill others and leave them to the carrion birds. No, they kill what they need to eat. A rat snake eats mice, but they do not go off on campaigns to exterminate all mice. If they did so, what would they then eat? No, in Nature there is the principle of Cosmic Balance at work."

"We cut down trees to build our homes. That is as it should be. We also replant new trees. What would happen if we cut down all trees? Nature would go wildly out of balance. Chaos ensues. So we believe in the balance of Nature herself. For you, this means that men and women are both equal in stature and importance. And this is a very vital point I'm making children. Yes, both sexes are quite different. Yes, you boys are much stronger than we women are — you make good fighters, protectors, and hunters, but it is we women that bring the new life into the world and nurture it. Both of these aspects must be in balance with each other."

"What happens if men become more dominant and defile and make women second-class citizens? We get a society bent on war, fighting, greed, and a spiritual degradation of all who live in it. Similarly, if women were dominant and forced men into the position of merely slaves to do their bidding, then that society would be equally out of balance, though I must admit I'd prefer that scenario to the other."

I suddenly began to understand, "So that is what is happening here, the Galts, King Randolf, the land of the Seven Sea Princes, even the Megalos civilization — they are out of balance. Men control more than they should."

"Keen observation, Beth. Yes, that's exactly what has happened. We know in Redun, the men are now treating their women as they do their cattle. We know Galt women are basically slaves to their men. We really do not know much about the Volksholm people, though. The men in the land of the Seven Sea Princes have traded love of woman for love of gold. And at this time in Megalos, we've heard women are bought and sold as mere slaves; they are no better than a cow. So man has upset the inherent balance of Nature and is now paying the price. We, the druwids, are the sole people on Tarra that understands this, and one of our goals is to undo this disastrous imbalance before the world is consumed in destruction of all peoples."

"Heavy!" exclaimed Simon, our Judger.

"Wow, that's a tall order," put in Sarah Jane. "I'm sure glad I don't live down there in Megalos!"

"Where do the druwids come from?" asked Sandy. "Are there any that live in those lands? If so, can't they do something about it?"

Willow smiled, "We come from all over, but I have to admit that those few, if any, that live in Megalos are facing terrible odds at correcting the imbalance. Likewise, if any are in the Sea Princes, they face an uphill battle against greed and promiscuity. And there are none that I've ever heard of in the other lands. So children, we have our work cut out for us. Somehow, we must hold the world together, until we can set things to right and restore the balance of Nature."

We did not get to discuss this further because Frank and Ellen arrived unexpectedly. After Ellen had recovered from her wounds, Frank insisted on accompanying her back to Uru and adjudicating with King Randolf. So just as we were all moving into our new home, they were loading the wagon with some seed and heading out for Uru and then on to Redun. Together, they planned to put their case before the King: that his cavalrymen wrongfully attacked Ellen and my family and that some rogue warrior came to our miraculous rescue. When they left, Frank was confident he would also be able to gain some monetary recompense for us. That was over a week ago, and we fully expected Ellen would resume her protection duties in Uru. So neither was expected to return to Karka for some time.

"Oh! You're back, so soon?" Willow interrupted her discussion of religion. We turned to look at them. I've never seen two faces as somber as theirs! Something was terribly wrong. We sat breathless waiting to hear their report to Willow. I noticed even Willow was very concerned about their appearance. Instinctively, I just observed during those few seconds before they spoke. I noticed a darker coloration oval around the seat of their leather pants and noticed a good deal of dust or dirt on their pant legs. I concluded they had ridden horseback to Karka and not in the wagon. Willow, evidently also seeing these details, added quietly, "Should I dismiss the children?"

Frank finally spoke, his jaw clenched in anger, fighting his raw emotions, and said, "No. This concerns them as much as the rest of us. Willow, call the others. We need a conference *now*! King Randolf has kicked the Guardians out of Redun and all the other towns under his control!" Willow gasped; this was not the reaction from the King we had expected.

"He, they, they didn't harm you did they?" asked Willow.

"I quote King Randolf, 'If you ever set foot in Redun again, you'll be shot on sight as a traitor.' Those were his exact words," Frank said, barely restraining himself from an explosion of temper. Probably us kids being present helped him master his emotions.

Ellen added in the softest of voice I ever heard her use, "We never even got to say so much as one word to him. The depths of his treachery run far deeper than we've imagined."

One tear quickly followed another as I suddenly realized that I had a hand in bringing about this horrible state of affairs. "It's all my fault," I blurted out, "if only I hadn't lost control and killed all those men, destroyed everything." Now I really was crying; I couldn't help myself. In my mind, I saw my action as bringing down the terrible wrath of the King upon all my friends.

Unfortunately, my sudden outburst put Willow in a predicament. She needed to contact the others, but now had to handle me. She turned to me, took my hand, and said, "Beth. Beth. It was *not* your fault. Never. You were *only* trying to protect Ellen and your family. King Randolf is the one to blame. Beth, the full responsibility of that calamity lies *solely* on his head, and he knows it! Beth, men, not necessarily women, but men greatly fear what they do not understand, and men, not necessarily women, have a great tendency to lash out at it, to attempt to smash it. Someone in fear can be counted upon to completely miss the actual target, the source."

I stopped crying. No one was going to hold me responsible. Deep down inside, I knew I bore some for my actions that day. However, Sarah Jane, her curiosity pricked, immediately asked, "If men try to destroy what they fear and women usually do not, then what do women do?" Now that she had said it, my curiosity swelled up. I forgot about feeling I was to blame. *Yes, what do we do*? I wondered.

Willow threw her head back and actually laughed. Even Ellen's stern face now grinned. "Surely you, Sarah Jane, know the answer to that one," teased Willow, bringing just a bit of brevity to the serious situation. It was her way of easing the sudden shock of this disturbing news.

Sarah Jane's face flushed, but Willow spared her further embarrassment by saying, "It reminds me of the Lady Helena episode many, many years ago. Lady Helena was reputedly very beautiful and married her town's leader. Then, one day while visiting the neighboring village, she met the handsome Vlad. She tried to seduce him, but Vlad would have nothing to do with that. He knew who she was. So Lady Helena went home and spread vile lies about how Vlad had insulted her, how he was no good, and how he tried to rape her. Her tales grew wilder and wilder. Finally, one winter's day, the men in her town could stand this insult to their good Lady no longer. A mob of them went and hanged poor Vlad without even a trial. That's what we women do; we are masters of using others to achieve our ends."

"But what happened to Lady Helena?" Roy wanted to know. "Surely, she didn't get away with that, did she?"

"She did for a time, but I suspect it wore on her conscience. They found her later that winter floating in the nearly frozen river. She had apparently thrown herself into the cold waters," Willow ended her lesson. "Now, excuse me. I need quiet for a bit. I must contact the others." We all hushed and watched, though still I found nothing actually to see, save that she had a distinctive "not there" look in her eyes.

A few minutes later, Willow spoke, "It's done. Clyde and Herbert are getting their family together, packing what they can carry on horseback. Tonight when it is dark, the two families will secretly leave, rendezvous at the Standing Stones, and then will come here across country, staying off the well-traveled tracks. Mary Ann and Jason are going to talk to their town's leaders about this before they come here. Both hope to convince them not to join up with the treacherous King. In the meantime, kids, we're going to have to house the others of my Circle in your dormitory. We'll have to get two more homes ready for the two families as well. So, let' see, here, we need materials for six more beds and six more chairs. Sandy, get a couple dozen coppers from my chest and take the others with you. Go to Elmo's store on Elm Street."

Quickly, we did as instructed, though I wondered if this was an excuse for the adults to speak privately. My mom and dad had done this sort of thing with me before. However, later events convinced me Willow was not trying to get rid of us for a few minutes.

As the seven of us fast-walked down the streets of Karka, Roy exclaimed, "Wow. I can't imagine the King doing this! Do you suppose they're going to have to get rid of the King?"

"Just because King Randolf tries to kill people to get his way," Sarah Jane protested, "doesn't mean we should do likewise, Roy. We are civilized; he is nothing but a barbarian."

Soft-spoken Thomas added, "This does spell major trouble; there is no getting around that fact, major trouble. What I cannot understand is why would the townsfolk go along with his treachery? Every person I've ever met seems to like the Guardians, even approve, and want our help. I guess I just don't understand." He shuffled his feet.

Simon answered him, "Cheer up Thomas. It's obvious the King has been spreading lies about the Guardians for quite some time now. My guess is he has been at it for over a year. A bad word here, a nasty observation there — you know, poisoning men's minds in subtle ways. Only now it's come to a head, and the seeds Randolf has sown are bearing the fruit of his desire."

"Well, I certainly hope he chokes to death on his fruit!" declared Sandy with a passion.

"Same here," Raphael added, "All these years the Guardians have been helping them, healing them, helping them settling their disputes, and now they turn on the hand that feeds them. Heck, we even helped design their own fortress! I'll bet Jason, who helped in its construction, is really mad — probably regrets he ever offered his assistance to Randolf. When I get to designing things, I'll be more careful about whom I aid!"

"But where will they live, I mean Ellen and the others now that they are kicked out of their own homes," I asked.

"I don't think they were even able to retrieve their own possessions!" declared Roy. "Both came by horseback. Frank and Ellen must have lost all their stuff!"

That was a sobering thought for us all. I imagined suddenly losing everything I possessed, which was not much actually. Still, I would be devastated if I lost my knife or my beautiful leather outfit. Surely, these adults had much more, perhaps even coins or money as it is called.

Roy went on, "I'll wager they'll sneak back into their towns and get their stuff from their houses. I know I would try."

"That would be awfully dangerous," put in Simon. "Remember, they were told they'd be shot if seen in town."

That gave me an idea. "Hey, guys, what if *we* volunteered to sneak into the towns, go to their houses, and sneak off with their stuff? There is no price on our heads!"

"Ooh, I *like* that idea, Beth. Way to go!" Roy instantly seconded the idea. "That's perfect. We can do it at, say, midnight when everyone is asleep. No one would even know."

"Oh yes they would. Those towns have guards on duty during the night, in case you hadn't noticed, Roy," counseled Simon. "However, I also like your idea, Beth. It's only just and fair that these people be allowed to retrieve their own personal belongings. Yet, I do fear that is just what Randolf expects. I certainly would expect them to return in the dead of night to get their stuff, and I would be waiting my chance to kill them." His words sobered us all but did not dampen our resolve to help Ellen and the others. We walked in silence a bit.

Thomas spoke softly, "Beth, you know the inside of Ellen's house better than any of us, and I know the inside of Frank's house really well. Suppose we have them make a list of what they want retrieved along with where it is. Then, we all go and get it. While Beth and I are inside getting the stuff, the rest of you stand guard, protect us, and let us know if someone is coming." Instantly, I liked the way Thomas' mind was working, very similar to mine.

"Well, I know for sure the adults aren't going to let us go by ourselves. If they give us permission to do this, I'm sure one or more of them will be with us. After all, just how much protection can we provide? Only Beth can bring down lightning, and she's only done it once in a storm," advised Simon. I could really see why he was a Judger; he always saw all sides of a situation at once, whereas I saw them only after the other side was pointed out to me.

"Well, they might not allow us to do this," I concluded, "but at least we have to offer them our plan. I'll be the one to do the explaining at the right time, but I may need you to back me up if I forget a point that needs making." We entered the store feeling like a group of plotters about to embark on a secret mission.

An hour later, we had all the new bedding supplies and chairs carried back to our dormitory. We found the adults hadn't been idle. They had made a space for all six to sleep, the men with the boys and the women with the girls, naturally. More dishes had been procured, and, more importantly, our pantry had been enlarged two-fold. We pitched in to help make the six new beds comfortable, and then we sat around the large oak table for a snack and some herb tea laced with honey.

I thought this was the right time, so I said, "Ellen, we know you didn't have the chance to get your belongings from your house before you were run out of Uru. You too, Frank. Our Circle doesn't have a price on our heads. We want to help you both and have thought up a way." Ellen raised her eyebrows, so I knew I hit a chord with her. I explained what we had cooked up, and Simon added a few details I forgot. As the plan unfolded, I watched the tiniest trace of a grin appear on Ellen's face, as with Frank's. Slowly, the grins enlarged, so I assumed they liked our idea.

"Well, children," Frank spoke first, "I like the sound of that! Yes, I have many things I'd like to recover from my house, including some very secret things. As Simon suggests, they'll most likely be watching my house to see if I return to collect my possessions. That makes it a very dangerous business, particularly for children." I felt my heart sink. Surely, this was a prelude to denying us the opportunity to help him. He went on, "However, Simon, as you suggest, some of us adults must go along with you and remain hidden. I'll take care of the guards personally. No, not kill them," he added hastily, as he saw us girls cringe a bit in reaction. "There is another side to a Judger, one you haven't yet seen."

"The Conjurer!" exclaimed Simon! "I forgot all about that!"

"Right. I'll just conjure up a little sleepiness on the part of any guards we find waiting for us," Frank continued. Looking at Willow, he asked, "Did Clyde and Herbert manage to leave with their possessions?"

"Yes, I'm checking with them on an hourly basis. As you might expect, their wives and children are rather scared about the whole affair, but they're all packing away right now. They'll leave probably around ten. It doesn't get dark until late this time of year. I would expect them to make the Standing Stones and stop for the remainder of the night. They should be able to travel safely during the daytime after that. My guess that with their families in tow, they'll get here in two days, probably by suppertime day after tomorrow," Willow suggested.

"I doubt that Mary Ann or Jason will be here any sooner," Frank said half thinking aloud. "Ellen, if we ride hard starting now, we should make Uru before dawn, if we push the horses, right?" She nodded, starting to grasp his plan. So did I; what the others didn't know wouldn't hurt them. "We get your belongings in the wee hours and head to the emergency cabin on South Kappa Ridge and spend the day. We ride to Redun that night, fetch my stuff in the wee hours, and get back to the cabin. One more good long ride and we are safely back here. I like it. Kids, it's high time you got serious horse riding lessons!" We cheered!

Willow protested, "Frank, you can't take the children. They are only children! This could be very dangerous."

"Relax, Willow. You'll be in constant communication with us at all times. There's no real danger to the children. Most are not even known in Uru or Redun anyway. Besides, what harm can come to them as long as Ellen and I are with them? You heard their plan. It must be they who actually retrieve our belongings, not us," Frank explained. In a way, his pleadings with Willow were quite similar to the way I pleaded with my parents. I smiled at the similarity. Willow, as expected, gave in to his plans. "Now, not a word of this to Mary Ann, until we're well on our way, Willow!" He was insistent on this for obvious reasons; she was their leader and could order him not to do this.

At once, the place was a hive of activity. First, the seven of us changed into our leather outfits, gathered necessary items, like my knife. Then, we filled our backpacks with enough food for a couple days and took along some water too. By the time we seven were ready to go, Frank and Ellen returned with fresh horses. It took them only a couple minutes to get their food supplies replenished, and then we mounted up.

Now that was an experience. It was the first time I ever sat upon a horse. I think it was the first time for most of us, except for Roy. Ellen and Frank were excellent teachers, and in no time, we felt familiar riding along. We left Karka mid-afternoon walking the horses for a few miles so we could get accustomed to riding. Once beyond the cultivated fields, Frank picked up the pace, trotting he called it. I called it bouncing! From the get go, I hated trotting! Then, he went even faster, a slow gallop, he yelled back at us. This I liked! The warm, rushing air flowing past my face blowing my long hair back of me was a wonderful sensation. All loved the gallops. Roy's face was beaming all the while. I could tell he really loved riding horses.

All afternoon, we slow galloped along for a time and then slowed to a walk to cool the horses down. Ellen had us sensing the horses so we could tell when they needed to slow down and when they were rested enough to continue the faster pace. In short, in no time, we seven learned to become one with our mount, the Balance of Nature. I found riding exhilarating and vowed to do this as much as I could.

The only pause was at suppertime. Frank stopped at the bridge over the creek so water was plentiful for the horses and us. Since it was summertime, it did not get dark until late. Thus, I could easily estimate just how far we had to go and how long it would take. I figured we'd be in Uru easily by ten. Once we had eaten, Ellen took me aside and began instructing me on what to retrieve and where it was located. It took me an hour to commit her instructions to memory.

Meanwhile, Frank outlined the plan to the others. Essentially, we would ride as close as we dared to Uru. Raphael would stay behind guarding the horses, for if anything happened to them, we would be in big trouble. Next, the rest of us would sneak into Uru, but Ellen would stay on the edge of town; Frank would enter along with the rest of us. Once he pronounced it safe to enter Ellen's house, we would form a human snake with me at the head. As I found the things and packed them into the big sacks, I would hand them to the person closest to me who would relay them onto the next person and so on, a relay team going all the way back to Ellen at the edge of town.

We were off once more. My estimations were precisely correct. By ten, we dismounted in a grove of trees just northeast of Uru. Honestly, I couldn't imagine there'd be any guards around. In all the years I lived there, there had been none. Raphael took all the reins in hand and tied them securely to branches, while we snuck quietly forward. This part we were highly skilled at doing. We were druwids after all, and forests were our homes. Not a sound did any of us make, not even Sarah Jane. We reached the edge of town where Ellen would remain safely hidden. Frank paused for quite some time sensing the area. Then, he led the rest of us into town heading towards Ellen's home. One by one, the others stopped taking up their relay position. Finally, it was just Frank and me standing on the front porch of her home. We listened for any sounds from within. Hearing none, Frank and I snuck quietly inside. Once the door was shut, he lit a small oil lantern, which produced only a narrow beam in one direction, just enough to allow me to do my work. First, he thoroughly searched the house; it was indeed empty. Frank then whispered for me to go to it; he stepped outside, and Roy came in, taking his place as the first relay person.

It was hard to find things with such a tiny light, but I managed to go methodically down her list, reciting it repeatedly to myself. I didn't want to forget something of hers, not after all the trouble we were going through to retrieve her possessions. When I had a sack filled, I handed it to Roy who then took it outside and handed it to the next person in the relay. It took me nearly a hour to find everything. Finally, I handed the last sack to Roy, and we both left this time.

We stole silently up the street of the town I grew up in; I was on the very street where we played every afternoon. I felt sickened that now all this was ended. *How could all these people allow this to happen to Ellen? She's looked after them all her life. It just isn't fair!* Then, I had an idea. I grabbed a stick and went into the middle of the dusty street. There I drew a triangle and then a second triangle upside down to the first and overlapping slightly. It looked like a five-pointed star. Finally, I drew a circle around the star, touching each point. Roy looked down at it and whispered, "What?"

"I'm leaving them something to think about tomorrow," I whispered back. "Nature's Harmony. This triangle is for you, you know your thing between your pants. And this one that is upside down is me, my thing. Both overlay uniformly, and the circle of life encompasses both."

Roy was very impressed. When we reached the others, had quietly stolen back to Raphael, and had ridden away, Roy told the others what I had drawn. Everyone loved the symbolism. Sandy suggested we adopt it as our own personal Circle's symbol, and thus thereafter that was the symbol of our group.

The very late night ride down to the cabin was exceedingly pleasant. I almost enjoyed the moonlight ride more than the daylight galloping. The cool night air, the dew on the breeze, the wet smell of grass, all combined to make it just magnificent to the senses, well at least to mine. I don't think that the boys thought of it quite the same was as we girls did. By the time we reached the emergency cabin, the very one in which Ellen had given me my cape and knife and staff just before the solstice festival night, we were all nearly falling asleep on our horses. I was very thankful Ellen and Frank took care of the horses so we could go inside and make a bed and sleep. I only vaguely remember throwing down my blanket before I was sound asleep.

We all rose late the next day, probably around ten. Ellen had a hot breakfast waiting, which was what finally got me up, food. I noticed Ellen's sacks were now neatly stowed in one corner. She intended to leave them here until our return. Once the breakfast was finished and the cabin cleaned up, we went outside to get the horses ready. Roy had me draw our symbol on the ground for the others. All loved it and complimented me about having thought it up. Our symbol discussion was ended by Frank, who proceeded to give us lessons on how to saddle, bridle our horses, and prepare them for the journey. Both he and Ellen inspected everything we did. They were taking no chances with our safety. I was glad of that, for I really knew very little about these magnificent, large animals and wanted to know everything I could about them, now that I found out I loved to ride them.

Finally, we were off once again on a fast trip toward Redun. As we rode, I began to get more excited. I'd never seen a fortified city and had only my own imagined picture made from what the others had said about it. Now I was going to see it for myself. However, Redun was certain to have guards everywhere. This was going to be dangerous indeed, and that idea kept growing in my stomach all that day, keeping me from enjoying the ride as much as I had yesterday. I felt like I was riding toward some doom. I guess the others felt something similar, for we said very little all that long ride.

Now the normal track that leads to Redun goes south from Uru until a few miles north of Undel where it finally snaked eastward, bypassing the ridge line called Blackford Hills. Frank, on the other hand, led us straight east and up the rugged, rocky side of hills, and then partway down the other. By dusk, we were still on the eastern slopes of the hills about four miles from the fortified town. Here we halted until full dark. From this elevated vantage point, we could clearly see the far off town. I must admit, it looked spectacular and not at all what I had imagined.

Redun was circular about a mile in diameter centered on the top of the largest hill in the valley below. Surrounding the town was a wooden wall of wooden tree trunks whose tops had been purposely pointed. I said it looked like hundreds of beavers had been at work here. The others laughed softly. Frank pointed out the four entrance gates now securely locked. Thomas whispered, "Wait til you see how we get inside." I surmised that he and his mentor, Frank, had snuck in and out of the fortified town before, but I liked a puzzle and resolved to see if I could figure it out before they showed us.

Observation, that was the key. Since we still had some time to wait until it was very dark, I spent it wisely just observing from this distance. I spied several whips of smoke rising from several buildings. I detected some faint motions, a play of greys against darker greys, and concluded I was seeing people, perhaps guards, moving about — impossible to say more from this great distance. It struck me that these walls definitely would keep Galts out, but they just as well kept the townsfolk *in*, interesting detail I thought. Still I kept looking.

I spied a small creek trickling water. Tracing its route back, I saw that it came from a dark spot under the hill. That had to be it, so I ventured a whisper to Frank. "Are we going to enter there where the creek goes under the hill?" My friends had me point out what I spied, all except Thomas who had been in and out through this secret way many times before.

"Very good, Beth!" Frank whispered back. "Ellen has taught you well. Yes, that's the drainage exit, foul smelling, but it offers us a safe entrance. Okay, I think it's dark enough. Let's risk walking the horses closer, but try to stay under the cover of the trees as much as possible. We'll make for that last close glen there about a half mile from the creek entrance." One by one, we followed Frank's lead and walked our horses ever closer to Redun. I could see his reasoning, if the horses were close, we could make a fast get away if things went wrongly for us. It was well after midnight when we reached the glen and tied up the horses.

Once more, Raphael stayed with the horses. His job was to keep them quiet at all costs. Frank handed him a grain sack, "Feed them a handful if they get noisy." Like silent specters, we eight crept forward along the bank of the creek. The nearly full moon greatly aided us, for we could see where to place our feet without causing telltale sounds. Soon we reached the cover of the dark tunnel. From here, we couldn't be seen from the walls. Dimly I could see some kind of iron grate work covering the exit tunnel. The gaps in the bars were sufficiently large that we managed to squeeze between them easily, though it was a tight fit for the adults. Once we were all safely inside, the stench was positively nauseating! "Sandy, this is your post. When the sacks come to you, you get them through the grate." She nodded that she understood, still holding her nose.

I wondered how we were going to be able to see our way. Would Frank light a lantern? What he did surprised me and the others, except for Thomas and Simon, who was our Judger. "Okay Simon, conjuring time. I want you to make a small light globe appear in your hand facing on down the tunnel. Think you can manage that?" Here in a perilous situation, Frank was still teaching! I thought poor Simon; he was going to be put on the spot!

I heard him whisper a chant very carefully. Eureka! A small bluish light shone from his hand dimly illuminating the tunnel ahead. It was only four feet tall so all of us were bent over, the adults more so. "Well done. Follow me," Frank whispered as another blue light appeared in his palm as he led the way. The tunnel was slippery and slimy. I believe we were walking in human feces! I avoided looking down at my feet! Slipping and sliding, we cautiously made our way down the long tunnel. Finally, the tunnel ended; we were at the bottom of the town latrine! Cautiously, Frank removed the grate over our heads, and he climbed out. Simon followed, while we waited for the all clear signal.

They were gone what seemed an eternity. My heart was thumping loudly, but it was so dark down here in the tunnel that no one could see me, or I them, for that matter. With his blue light in hand, Simon finally appeared above us. "Okay, it's now safe; we have the guards sleeping. I'll stay here and use my light to carry the sacks down the tunnel. If I'm not here when one of you brings the next sack, just leave it here by the hole. Now climb up quietly; Frank's waiting just outside the door."

One by one, we climbed out and made for the door. Ellen remained at the door to act as a rear guard. The one thing Frank was most worried about was being cut off from our exit. The rest of us were strung out along the streets, until at last Frank and Thomas stood just outside one small wooden building. I could barely see them ahead of me. Thomas was the one who actually went inside. I waited, scarcely able to breathe, fearing any sound might bring down the wrath of unseen guards upon us.

Then, I spied the shadowy form of Frank heading my way carrying a sack. Without a word, he handed it to me. Just as quietly as I could, I headed back down the street until I reached Roy and handed it to him. In the moon light, we both saw each other smiling broadly at each other. I quickly retraced my steps to get ready for the next sack. All went according to plan for about a half hour.

Suddenly, I heard two male voices and the heavy thumping of boots on the dirt coming my way. For the briefest of seconds, I felt a surge of panic in my stomach, but willed it away. I slunk back into the darkest shadows I could find, hoping they didn't have a bright lantern. I saw Frank heading my way with another sack! If he didn't see them coming, they would likely meet face to face. Without thinking about it, in my mind, I pictured Frank and thought to him, *Two men coming; take cover now!* Almost as if Frank had read my mind, I saw him duck into the shadows.

Now, the two men appeared around the corner. They looked like guards to me; each carried a crossbow and a spear; a sword was fastened around their waist. They were nearly in front of me, when both stopped mid-stride, yawned heavily, and laid down in the middle of the street. Soon, I heard them snoring like pigs! Frank quietly appeared beside me, "Good work, Beth. I got your message. Thanks." He handed me another sack and was gone almost as fast as he had appeared. *Got my message? What did he mean by that?*

I mulled that over in my mind as I crept towards Roy and handed him the sack. I was still pondering it when I got back to my waiting position. *Could I have possibly have contacted him telepathically? I really had wanted to alert him! Could I have done it somehow?* Somewhere a cock crowed. The dark skies began to show the first faint hint of dawn.

This time, both Simon and Frank came to me. I concluded we were done. Quietly, I fell into line behind them as we headed for Roy. As we joined him and he fell in line behind me, Roy pointed to the dirt in the middle of the road. He had drawn our symbol very clearly. We both smiled at each other.

Another few minutes passed before we were finally free of the smelly tunnel. Sandy had all of the sacks neatly stacked on the bank of the creek. We each picked up one sack; the adults took three, and we headed toward the glen. None too soon, for now the rosy pink dawn had come. It had taken longer than we expected. By the time we reached Raphael in the glen. The sun was just rising in the east. Poor Raphael, with almost nothing to do, he had nearly fallen asleep many times!

We tied the sacks onto the horses. However, when I tried to lift one sack, something jingled in it, and it was so heavy that I couldn't lift it. "Here, let me help you with that one, Beth," Frank whispered. "It is your family's recompense for the attack by the King." I wondered what he meant, but now was not the time to ask. Even he struggled with it as he tied it to his horse.

"Okay, slight change of plans," Frank said as we mounted. "If we cut back up the hillside, we'll be clearly visible in the morning light. So our best bet is to follow the road until we're around the side of the ridge a bit, and then cut up and over, riding like the wind to the cabin." He led the way. Though we had been up all night, none of us, except Raphael, was the least bit tired, not yet anyway. The excitement gave us a rush of alertness, of aliveness.

A half hour later, we were far enough away, and a ridge hid us from the town. Hence, Frank risked climbing the ridge to cut many miles of our path. Upward we climbed, winding this way and that, around huge boulders and thickets of trees too dense for horses to pass. Finally, we crested the Blankford Hills. Here Frank and Ellen both paused and looked back at the way we came. Neither could sense any pursuit, and Frank led us on down the other side. Soon, we reached the rolling green grasses of the Valley of Uru; here Frank turned the horses loose. Off we went galloping faster than we had ever run the horses. Wow, the air rushed by, keenly waking all our senses. Afterwards, I decided Frank did that purposefully just to keep us awake and alert.

Before long, the cabin appeared, and we made camp. I think it took me about two minutes to fix my bed and fall asleep. I found I could think of nothing else but sleep! Near sunset, I smelled food cooking and woke up. There was Ellen fixing us our breakfast or supper, I didn't know which. None of us said much, just ate, packed, and headed down to the Standing Stones. Only when we reached them did Frank halt and relax. "Kids, I do believe we are now totally safe and out of the King's reach. From here, it should be a nice cross-country ride to Karka. We should make it by dawn. So let's go single file and walk the horses. Let them pick their route."

"Wait a minute, Frank," Ellen called out. "Beth, Thomas, both of you dismount and come here." We did as we were told. "Tell me what you see and what conclusions you may draw from them." Oh no, it was test time once again! We both studied the ground, but this time the signs were easy. I let Thomas speak first.

"Well, Loremaster Ellen, from the signs, two wagons have passed through here. Some were walking on foot. Ah, adults and children," he added.

"And how long ago? What direction are they heading?" came her reply.

"I see, yes, they're heading north as we. How long, well, possibly a few hours," he ventured.

"Anything you want to add, Beth?" she asked me.

I agreed with everything Thomas had said. I looked hard to see if there was anything he had missed. "Oh, I think that one wagon or group had to wait some hours for the other wagon; see there is a chaotic trampling here by the stones."

"Very good, both of you," Ellen praised us. "Frank, the others are only a few hours ahead of us. I suggest we catch up with them, and all ride into Karka together. Safety in numbers," she added. Thanking us as well, Frank changed his route to follow the wagons. Off we went. I hoped we didn't scare them by our unexpected arrival from their rear. Of course, then I wondered how soon we would catch the wagons.

After a while, I decided I should be able to figure that out for myself and so set my mind to estimating speeds. The bright silver moon soon came to my aid. I couldn't very well stop and dismount to get a close look at the tracks the wagons left, so I did the best from horseback. After an hour, I thought I could tell some differences in the tracks. Perhaps, it was less moisture in the ruts left by the heavily laden wagons. We were drawing closer, closing the distance. I whispered to Thomas who was just ahead of me, "I think we are now very close to the wagons." I watched him look toward the ground, turn in the saddle, and nod his agreement.

Not more than a couple minutes later, the wagons appeared on the top of the rise in front of us. They saw us and halted waiting for us to join them. Clyde, Herbert, and their large families were all smiles, as we reined in beside them. Even though we were in the wilderness and off any path, Frank kept our voices low. "We got our stuff out of our houses right from under their very noses," he explained to Clyde and Herbert. "Made a clean get away. The kids are a real asset. Everyone did really well. So how's it going back in Garth and Undel?"

Clyde's reply was sobering, "Not good, I'm afraid. Too many were too quick to side with the King over us. Just before we left, even our kids were being picked on, teased, and made fun of — just amazing how fast they can turn against the hand that has helped them."

"Not really," Ellen butted in, "they are just afraid, terribly so. It's our fault we didn't recognize that sooner and do something about it. I just hope we get the chance to do so in Karka, Petersville and Blankford before it's too late there as well."

"Yah, you are probably right," Clyde drawled. "We got complacent. I concentrated on healing the sick, when I should have been healing their fears. But, tis water over the bridge, as they say."

"By the way, Mary Ann is furious with you two, running off like that and endangering the children," spoke up Herbert. "But we understand. It wasn't her stuff that was abandoned. She might be singing another tune if it was her that had to flee and leave everything behind. Fortunately, we got nearly everything of value from our places, but the kids rather dislike moving and losing all their friends."

"Thanks for the warning about Mary Ann," Frank said. "Guess we had better move out. If any of you get too tired, let us know. The kids slept all day so they should be alert most of the night." Off the wagons rumbled; half of us fell in on their right flank, and the other half, on their left. It was a long night's ride.

At dawn, we rode up the long green valley entrance to Karka. In minutes, we pulled up in front of our dormitory. Mary Ann was there along with Willow. I assumed they had been in mental contact with the others. She certainly had a fierce-some look on her face, but spoke softly, holding back her anger. "Willow will take you to your new homes. They are close by here. Children, inside now, eat some breakfast, and get to bed. We'll discuss things after supper. You two take care of the horses and meet me at Willow's at once!" She gave them a stern glare; I noticed Frank did look a bit sheepishly at the ground, and he dismounted. I hoped she wouldn't be too hard on them.

All of us were too tired to talk. We ate mechanically and climbed up into our beds. The next thing I knew, Willow was banging a pot or something, announcing supper was served. So we all got up, cleaned up, and joined the others at the table. I glanced at Mary Ann. She was smiling, so I hoped she had gotten over her anger. Apparently, Frank had appeased her.

No one said much while eating. I felt just a bit uncomfortable. After all, we had gone along with Frank's plan. Once we were done and the dishes cleared away, the fourteen of us sat on opposite sides of the table, the two Circles facing each other. Mary Ann began, as I suspected she would. "We owe a debt of thanks to the Lightning Circle for helping Frank and Ellen retrieve their belongings. You performed admirably. As you suspect, had I known about this plan, I would have vetoed it. But you were successful and did a fine job. Thank you. I believe Frank has an announcement."

I spied a twinkle in his eye as he began. "As you know, in the matter of the unjust and unprovoked attack on Ellen and Beth's family, I had intended to seek recompense from King Randolf. However, I was expelled before I could demand such, but I have extracted said recompense from the King's treasury in spite of his actions. Beth, that heavy sack contained about five hundred gold coins I was holding for the King, which now, by my official judgment, belongs equally to Ellen and your family. It's my decision that all five of you should have an equal share. Money cannot make up for the treachery, pain, and suffering that you endured. Perhaps, it will ease your life's burdens in the future." He presented Ellen and me with a small sack containing our share. At the time, I had no idea of the value of the coins. I guess Frank probably guessed as much, though the others in my Circle obviously did have from all their "oh's" of exclamations. He added, "Beth, with this you could purchase perhaps a herd of horses, a house, or live without doing any work for several years. Use it wisely." Wow, was all I could say, and of course, several thank you's.

"The next order of business," Mary Ann resumed control of her meeting, "is what to do at this point. I feel we need to make every effort to secure these last three remaining towns, Karka, Petersville and Blankford. We need to see to their total security, which is now complicated by needing to defend from King Randolf's cavalry. In this matter, the higher Circle has promised to recruit and train a defensive cavalry to serve not only our area here, but also the surrounding lands. Their plan is to encircle the King and prevent any further aggression on his part. However, that will take time, and time is what we may lack. I erred once in underestimating this upstart of a King. I shall not do so again. The higher Council has promised the new cavalry will be on patrol by the first snowfall. Our task is to see to these three town's defense for the next four months. I am open to any and all suggestions."

To everyone's complete surprise, Raphael, our Planner, the boy with the incredibly blue eyes, spoke up in his quiet, unassuming voice. "I have a design that ought to help. While I was tending the horses, I got to thinking and designing. I believe that it would stop cavalry. How do I go about getting it made and tested? I've got some sketches if you want to see them."

Wow! I was impressed. Actually, looking back, I'm sure everyone was. Of course, we wanted to know what he called it, but he hadn't thought of a name. It would throw a feathered spear into the horse and rider. This was the realm of their Planner, Jason, who immediately began looking over Raphael's charcoal sketches. "This looks promising, Raphael. Tomorrow, we'll take it to some wood workers I know and see about getting a prototype built." The excitement in those big blue eyes was impossible to miss! We, our Circle, really were helping, and that meant a great deal to all of us. Children we may still be, but we were no dummies; we could actually help. That is a terrific feeling, actually to be able to help others.

Raphael explained his ideas further. "There's only one practical entrance to Karka from the east for cavalry, up the long, sloping green way. It is too rocky for horses any other place, save from the western side. Thus, if we have a number of these in positions here on the hill crest shooting down, any charge of theirs up can be at least blunted by the feathered spear throwers. That was my idea anyway." We all cheered him and patted him on the back.

Ellen offered another idea. She suggested we recruit and pay a number of horsemen to act as long distant lookouts for oncoming cavalry raids. By positioning them at key points miles east of Karka, if they spotted the King's men coming, they were to ride back and give us plenty of advance warning. We discounted a sneak attack coming at night; such was not honorable by our way of thinking. Herbert agreed to train up a voluntary local militia force to be pressed into service should an attack come. And so the plans were made.

I should tell you a brief account of Raphael's device. When he showed the drawings to the craftsmen the next day, all grumbled about following a boy's design. Only at the insistence of the respected Planner Jason did they actually agree to do the work. Two days later, the giant crossbow was done and ready to be tested. It took two men turning the side ratchet cranks to draw the bowstring. A short spear with feathers attached was placed in the firing groove. Jason had placed a pumpkin about a hundred yards distant for Raphael to attempt to hit. We all held our breaths as Raphael sighted carefully and pulled the firing leather cord. The twang of the string was really loud, and my eyes could scarcely follow the flight of the spear. For an instant, I thought he had missed the pumpkin. Then, the top half fell off onto the ground. However, what impressed all onlookers was the spear. It had kept right on going for another two hundred feet, stopped only when it hit a maple tree! However, the spear point was now embedded nearly six inches into the tree! The amount of cheering by everyone was rewarding.

Jason could not stop talking about how great this invention was, how good a weapon this would make. Several more tests were made to determine its range, which was formidable indeed. If we had enough of these, defenders could cut down the oncoming cavalry long before they could close to combat range! The city leader ordered two dozen to be built at once. For the next three days, test firings were done for the representatives of Petersville and Blankford. The Spear Thrower became the talk of the town for nearly a week after that.

After that excitement, the days passed routinely, as we all learned much, not only from our adult mentors, but also from others. Mom continued giving us sewing, weaving, and cooking lessons that were long overdue. Our days were spent in study from morning to night. All of us had completely forgotten about playtime. There was just too much to learn, and we felt an urgency to learn it.

A month later, it was time for the six of us, though not Roy our Protector, to learn hand-to-hand combat skills. This I dreaded; I think Sandy and Sarah Jane also hated the whole idea, but Ellen explained that we had to be able to stand on our own. Thus, we went along with it, if half-heartedly at first. Roy and Herbert explained we needed to be skilled with the long knife, a staff, and a bow. However, the boys also needed to be skilled with a short, curved sword they called a scimitar. We girls were given the option of also learning how to use a scimitar, but we three declined politely. To this day, I have never regretted that decision. Well, that is not entirely true, but more on that much later.

The bow was useful for hunting game such as rabbits and squirrels, but I preferred to use the simple snares that Ellen had taught me long ago. The passing standard was to be able consistently to hit a pumpkin a hundred feet away. We spent an hour every day target shooting and eventually all passed.

The staff was another matter. First, we had to dress up in thick padding that dulled the blows. Still, I had many black and blue spots for the next month because of learning. The passing standard was to be able to knock Roy, who was also using a staff, off a log footbridge, which had been erected a foot off of the ground for our practice. At first, we thought this was unfair, for Roy was already highly skilled with the staff. Herbert insisted, especially for us girls, that the staff would be our primary means of defense against attacking men. Thus, we had to be really good at it. Roy was obviously enjoying this, as we whacked and whacked at him. I think he had a perverse pleasure in knocking us off the bridge, but I was being too harsh on him. He really wanted us to be able to protect ourselves against Galts. Two months later, the last of us finally passed; Sandy was able to consistently knock him off the bridge.

The concurrent long knife training was far more dangerous, though we actually spent much less time with it. Essentially, we needed to be able to stab a dummy in the marked heart area by using a sudden, completely unannounced, upthrust motion. This we all mastered rapidly. I found this easy; stare completely into the dummy's eyes and insert knife. Yet, I knew this would be far, far more difficult if I were really to face a Galt and have to kill him. We girls took comfort in knowing that using the long knife would be our absolute last resort when everything else failed.

After we had all passed basic weapon's training, Willow announced, "Now it is time for your sex education." Boy, talk about instant embarrassment! Even Sarah Jane blushed. While we had all been around our parents — in a long house, it is impossible not to at least hear them — it was not something we talked openly and freely about on a regular basis. I believe we all thought this was a very private matter. She continued anyway, "You all recall the Seven Aspects of Existence. Your own body is your personal holy temple and second only to that is your family. Joining with a member of the opposite sex is Nature's mystical way of creating new life, babies in our case. This is perhaps Nature's greatest mystery and greatest gift to us all, the creation and birth of a new life form. Thus, you should embrace and enjoy this, the greatest of wonders; it is nothing to be ashamed of or made less of. On the contrary, the joining should be celebrated with the highest of honor, for its product is often the beginning of new birth. It should never be done lightly or from lust or abused."

"Take dogs, for example, you have all seen the nearly uncontrolled animal lust between sires and bitches. Our normal docile pets go almost berserk. Thus, Nature has provided for this by having only two opportunities for the bitches to breed in a year. But man is not an animal; we should be able to control our animal instincts." She then discussed some intimate details, which I will not relate here. "Now, as druwids, in our roles as healers, we are frequently called upon to assist in the birth. So for the next year, whenever any of my Circle are called upon to aid, we'll bring along one of your Circle's members so you can gain firsthand knowledge. Yes, you men may very likely find yourselves having to help a villager under your protection give birth. So you must be trained and skillful at it." Of course, the guys all moaned in protest but knew she spoke truth. We girls giggled; for once, they were cowering from training as we did when forced to learn how to fight with weapons. Circumstances were reversed.

She also explained about finding the love of our life. She said to trust to our hearts in this matter. Marrying within a Circle was permitted, though by observation, the union of two druwids did not produce a child that was druwid material. That is, they bore just as many *headers* as the normal population. "So as you assist in child birth, please note whether the newborn is a *header* or is staying outside its head as we do. Be on the lookout for new potential druwids." This I found most interesting.

She also pointed out that three of my Circle were now of age, that is fourteen, and could legally do as they pleased. She urged us all not to marry and start our families until we had finished our tenth and last year of training. We all had to go to Calgary that year and toting along a family would make it more difficult.

Thus, our training continued unabated and at full steam. The only break in the intensive training occurred around the Autumnal Equinox. Here, we all took three full days off. Piled into wagons and on horseback, both Circles, their spouses, and children headed south to the Standing Stones. Though we left at dawn the day before, we did not arrive until late that night. The next day we spent in relaxation while the children played games. My Circle joined the games, I might add. As the sun set, Mary Ann once again performed the ceremony marking equal days and nights. When she finished, music and songs filled the night air. This time, I really enjoyed all the dancing. Though it was a bit on the cool side, we slept out under the vast panorama of the distant stars. By dark the next day, we were back at home and our heady training continued unabated.

The next break from training came at harvest time. At this time of year, all available hands were needed to retrieve and store the bountiful harvest. Instead of training from Circle members, we received a crash course from the townsfolk on harvesting techniques, food preservation, and storage, as well as teamwork. After a week of this, my body was aching; every muscle I had seemed to hurt. I had blisters on my hands. Now, I was more than ready to go back to our druwid training!

Just as the harvest actions were finished, the weather turned stormy. Much to everyone in my Circle's great surprise, we were beginning our training in bringing down lightning bolts from the sky. Mary Ann, an expert at this, explained that once we had mastered the relatively easy lightning, we were then ready for fire and ice conjuring. This was what I had been waiting for all these years! I applied myself with a renewed passion. Besides, I still had nightmares from that last encounter during the storm in which I had gotten swept away. The passing standard was during a storm to be able to pull or direct a bolt to a specific target on the ground, in our case, some dummy bodies. By the time the thunderstorms gave way to our first snowfall, we had all passed, though Roy and I far exceeded the others with this skill.

He and I actually loved to play a game called "Can you hit this?" I would say something like, "Okay, see that bolder over there; hit it in less than minute." Then, I would slowly count out the minute. I won if he couldn't do it; he won if he hit it. Then, we'd switch, and he'd call out the target. We finally had to give up the game when each of us consistently hit anything after only a few seconds!

To my surprise, though thinking back on it now, it should have been obvious to me then, when the snows came, Mary Ann switched us over to bringing down sheets or walls of ice. This was much harder to accomplish, and it took us the rest of winter to master it. What we didn't know but found out in the spring was that this was only the first step. With the snows gone and in a clear sky, we had to bring down bolts and ice sheets! Without the aid of Nature's storms, this was drastically more difficult. It took us all summer to master this trick, and only then did we finally begin to tackle the most difficult one of all, bringing down fires from the sky!

Without the crutch of having a storm at hand, we all struggled, all except Simon who got the hang of it in no time! He was our Judger and conjuring was part of his training. He was a natural at this. None of us ever came close to his skill at bringing down any of these without the aid of Nature's weather. The sole exception was Thomas; he excelled at creation of fires, even surpassing Simon's skill!

During the long winter, we were mostly indoors. During much of this period, we were taught basic conjuring. Frank taught us the most basic and useful trick of creating a pale blue light in the palm of our hand. As he said, "There'll be times when it is dark and yet you must be able to see, so the creation of a blue light is a vital skill to have at your command." Of course, Simon was already a master of this, and he helped the rest of us try to get the hang of it. Personally, I found this one perhaps the hardest lesson to learn of them all. In fact, Frank had almost given up on me when I finally produced a flickering light; at least it was some light.

Other times, Frank would have us sit in a Circle, and he would bring in some stranger. The stranger would tell us a tale. When he finished, Frank would ask us whether the stranger spoke the truth. The very first time he did this without so much as a warning that it was coming; only Simon got it right. After all, he had been learning how to do this for quite some time already. After our first dismal failure, Frank told us to observe and hinted at the eyes, facial expressions, the person's color, and demeanor. At least, we had a clue for the next time.

After some dozen attempts, I finally saw with my own eyes that a person who is lying displays certain telltale physical manifestations that he is indeed fibbing. One only had to observe these tiny details. After that, I was nearly unbeatable; only Simon was better than I was in the detection of a lie.

Our crash course next took up mental telepathy. Everyone needed some rudimentary skills at it, if at all possible. Sarah Jane often got things confused and picked up what she thought instead of the other person's thoughts. I had a distinct advantage here, because Sandy and I often communicated this way. Remember, she had originally asked me to help her practice because the others grew tired of it. I never did. Once I had a little instruction on how to do it, I became almost as good at it as Sandy was, but not quite, of course, for this was her specialty.

Spring passed into summer and into autumn. While there were a few Galt raids, they were easily repelled. King Randolf wisely stayed away from Karka. Word was secretly spread among the towns under the King's control that anyone who wanted out from under his yoke would be welcome in the free towns. Eventually, the extended families of Roy, Thomas, and Sarah Jane also moved to Karka along with about another hundred.

We spent two and a half years training in Karka. Looking back upon them, I think that these were the happiest years of my life.

Chapter 7 The Flight to Calgary

In the summer of 558 AH, we were entering our tenth year of druwid training. I, the youngest, just turned fourteen and am now of age. Roy, Raphael, and Sandy are fifteen, while Sarah Jane, Simon, and Thomas are sixteen. For the last week, we have been preparing for our long journey to Calgary, which lies many leagues to the west on the shores of the great ocean. It's been exciting and yet sorrowful, because we will be leaving behind our families and our mentors.

Thus, we chose to spend some time with our families, knowing we'd not be seeing them for probably a long time. In preparation for our journey, we each had readied two large sacks with our gear. All that remained would be to stow perishable foods and some water. Actually, we purposely delayed our departure for a few days because of the strange reports that were coming into Karka.

For weeks now, the Guardians had suspicions that King Randolf was planning to attack Karka or Blankford or Petersville. The Karka Defense Force, as the cavalry sponsored by the higher Circle of Central Greenway called them, daily spied upon the lands under the King's control. They reported a significant buildup of forces in the area of Redun. Since Petersville lay north and beyond the other two towns, Mary Ann felt that Blankford or Karka would be the intended target. Thus, Herbert and Frank had gone to Blankford to support Mary Ann, while Clyde and Ellen stayed in Karka with Willow. Yes, it was a gamble that Petersville was not the target.

On a more sobering note, Ellen's body was definitely showing signs of advanced aging. Three years ago, I first noticed her huffing and puffing just to get up Kappa Ridge, when we were on our way to my first druwid celebration at the Standing Stones. Now, she slept much of the day and seemed tired after even a small walk. I worried about her constantly and spent a good deal of my personal time looking out for her, helping her do the little things of life.

Of course, Ellen's frailty was more than compensated by my Circle. The seven of us could now offer significant protection for Karka. We were almost full Guardians. In these past three years, a local militia had been created and trained. Combined with this and the Karka Defense, the local residents felt safe and secure, but that was all to change in just one day.

The day before we finally agreed to leave for Calgary, a report came in from the advanced scouts that a large force had begun to move out from Redun, heading west by north. Willow quickly called for a conference between the Guardians, Captain John Smythe of the local militia, and Captain Red Stonegate of the cavalry. She began using the serious voice that only a druwid can muster, "So it has come to this, battle. Initial force estimates suggests one hundred fifty cavalry and three hundred foot soldiers. Our cavalry is fifty strong, but spread out over twenty miles on patrols that we must continue so we can have as much advance warning as possible. Our militia numbers only two hundred." Hers was a somber estimation. "We cannot hope to face them in open combat without first significantly reducing their numbers. Suggestions?"

Red, a tall, thin man with long flaming red hair and a cheery smile, was a shrewd judge of tactics and strategies, which was the reason for his success in the cavalry. His was the type of personality that others followed into battle without question. "Honored Ma'am," he began, "we still don't know their actual target; it could be any of the three towns. We can't afford to bunch all our cavalry in one place until we definitely know where that place is to be. The optimum placement of the riders probably should be in two key groups located say centrally about five miles apart — one closer to Karka and one closer to Blankford. Let scouts fan out forward of these two concentrations. Once the battle is committed, the two can join fairly rapidly into one strong group, more than likely attacking from their rear, rushing through them to our side." It sounded logical to me at least. I glanced at Roy, our Protector; his nodding indicated he thought it a sound move.

Red continued, "If they choose Karka and with the assumed forces and their types, my hunch is he intends to use his cavalry to punch a gigantic hole in our front lines through which his much larger ground forces can push on through with little resistance. That would be a prudent use of his cavalry. To attack first with his ground troops means massive losses on his part before a breach in our lines can be made. Now, therein lies our strength. There are only two ways for a cavalry charge into Karka. From the east is the likely direction; otherwise his army must spend a couple more days traveling to circle around to come at us from the western slopes, which are wider, broader, and more difficult to defend. If that's his choice, we should know before the day is out; he'll have to turn westward soon for easy passage over Kappa Ridge."

"Either way, the only way we stand any chance at all is if you Guardians and the thirty Feathered Spear Thrower engines can significantly reduce their numbers, as they charge up the long narrow path onto Kappa Ridge here. The ridge is too rugged for cavalry at any other point from the east, except the gangway road into Karka. Of necessity, the cavalry will have to bunch into a tight formation to charge up the gangway road, so those few minutes will be your only point in time in which to stop them. It's imperative you drastically reduce the cavalry before they can engage our militia here at the top by the edge of town. If the cavalry reach the militia in sufficient numbers, you're defeated before you start. The same is true if they do circle around and hit from the west; only there is no narrow confining valley so they will be spread out covering a much larger area, making it more difficult to stop them in quantity quickly."

"So if I was their commander, I certainly would flank the town and hit it from the west, but I would also certainly count on your knowing that fact at least a day before I actually could muster the forces there to launch the attack. No, had I been commanding them, you wouldn't even had known of our gathering forces, let alone the day we moved out, but then I'm not their commander. All this is assuming Karka is the intended town."

"Blankford is another story. It sits high on a peninsula of the Blankford Hills, and green, sloping hills lead up to it on all sides, save the narrow ridge behind it. To attack it, there is no choice but a widely spread-out charge up the long hill. Hence, the large number of cavalry would be best suited for an assault on Blankford, not Karka. Then again, they did not ask me my opinion," he chuckled grimly.

"However, all this is assuming they intend to attack as soon as they arrive. Mind you, have you given any consideration to another possibility — that of encirclement?" From the grimace on Willow's face, I could tell she hadn't thought of that. Red spied her reaction too. "My Lady, an even better use of this large amount of cavalry would be to entirely encircle Karka rapidly, with the foot soldiers eventually linking up and holding the circle. With that kind of strength, they could attempt to starve you into submission and take the town without an actual battle." Now that was a grim, sobering thought indeed!

To my surprise, Roy replied, "Ah, but from the initial reports, I think we may possibly rule out any initial encirclement plan." Of course, "How?" came into my mind. From the puzzled looks on nearly everyone else's face, I wasn't alone. How could Roy have deduced this fact?

Even more surprising was Red's counter, "Protector Roy, you do have a point. However, we shouldn't discount this as a secondary possibility should their initial assault fail."

Exasperated, I broke in, "Okay, I give up, Roy. How? How can we rule that one out, at least as their initial plan?" Several others in our Circle added their sentiments to mine.

Smiling his big teasing grin, Roy answered, "Supply wagons. If you intend a siege and have such a large army to feed, you need a whole lot of food wagons, a large number. The initial reports only suggested a half dozen at most. You've got nearly five hundred men to feed. My guess is they're bringing only about six days' worth of rations with them. Assuming two days are wasted getting here with the ground forces marching all the way and two back, they intend for this whole attack to be finished in two days' worth of fighting at most." He leaned back in his chair, a confident grin on his face. It was *so* logical that I chided myself for having missed such a critical detail. I mentally sent him a "Very Well Done," and I detected a slight flush in his face when he received it. I smiled back at him.

"Gentlemen, encirclement is one thing we can ill afford," Willow commented. "For one, your Circle, Beth, would be entrapped with us when we desperately need you to get on your way to Calgary. Getting you there is of the utmost importance, far more than the defense of this single town. Further, if they do that, our forces will be spread exceedingly thin trying to defend the town from all sides. Yet, that works both ways. Given time, our cavalry, which are going to be outside that circle, could attack and punch holes in their lines quite easily. It would turn into a cat and mouse game. I'm sure that sooner or later reinforcements would come to our aid from Blankford and Petersville.

Eventually, we ought to be able to break any encirclement. However, I can't risk delaying the start of your vital journey to Calgary, but it doesn't seem likely that encirclement is their current plan. Thank you Red, for your concise analysis. Oh, one moment, please, Mary Ann is telling me something."

It was Red and Captain Smythe who now looked in awe on Willow. Both had heard stories about the mystical means that the Guardians used to communicate with each other over long distances. Now, they were witnessing it; just as I did only a few years ago; both stared at Willow hoping for some clue as to how she did this. Now that I knew the secret of telepathy, I simply relaxed and waited for Willow to relay Mary Ann's words.

"Gentlemen, Mary Ann has said the moment the attack is committed on whichever town, the militias of the other two towns will begin marching to that town's defense. If we are attacked, Petersville's forces of some two hundred strong will arrive within a day, while Blankford's two hundred will arrive within two. Captain Smythe, can I tell her you'll do the same if they are the chosen victims? That is, send two hundred at once?"

Captain Smythe was a large, heavyset man, solid muscle, with long black hair and fierce black eyes. He had become Captain by combat skill and working his way up the command ladder. He was definitely a hands-on type of commander, one that would be in the front of any attack, leading the way. His deep bass voice replied, "Absolutely!" Willow quickly sent his reply to Mary Ann.

"All right, gentlemen. I assume you've much to do, so I won't take any more of your valuable time. Keep us posted. If there's anything you need, let me know at once." Both men stood, bowed to her and then to the rest of us, and took their leave.

As soon as they were gone, Willow said to us, "You may not realize just how vital, how critical, it is that you get safely to Calgary. This I can understand. Roy, as their Protector, this is my last charge to you: I hereby charge you to get the Lightning Circle to Calgary as soon as possible, despite any obstacles placed in your path. Do not fail in this charge; son, this is the most important thing I have ever asked of any of you. Do not fail us; get them to Calgary. Promise me." She was actually pleading! I'd never ever heard Willow plead before. Sandy shrieked much the same opinion into my mind! *Gosh, Willow never begs!* she sent me.

Roy always had a penchant for gallantry. He immediately got down on one knee. "I do hereby so pledge, Lady Willow, to get the Lightning Circle to Calgary without fail, upon my life." He bowed. I thought it was all just a little bit too dramatic, but Roy loved it. Mark it up as a symptom of the exuberance of youth.

However, I added, "Willow, we are packed except for food and water. We can be ready to go in less than an hour. Please don't send us away until after the battle. We can and want to help. Some of our families are here; we cannot desert them in their hour of need, any more than we can desert the town or you. You know we are strong enough to help."

Willow sighed. I knew she was not going to force us to leave now, and I relaxed. She said, "Beth, I want you to know that this has been the hardest decision I have ever been called upon to make in my entire life. I'm sworn to get you to Calgary as soon as possible, but I'm also sworn to protect Karka. I know I'm desperate for your help in blunting the cavalry charge or all is lost. I know you're powerful enough really to make a difference. I know you'd never forgive me if I ordered you to leave and harm came to your families, harm that you might have prevented. What swayed me most is the human side. I know I'd never be able to live with myself if I had deserted my family when they were under attack and they suffered because of my abandoning them. That would make an indelible mark on my psyche forever. I can't be the cause of that." I know my Circle was greatly relieved to hear her say we could stay and aid in the defense of Karka.

"However, you must all promise me that you'll leave the instant that one of two things should occur: if Karka is overrun and the enemy forces close to close quarters combat or if Karka is threatened with encirclement. Either way, you must promise me you'll leave the absolute instant that either of these occurs. Swear it to me, all of you, right now!" I've never seen her this insistent, this worried, this serious. We all swore.

She then made us go pack food and water, and get our horses at the ready. We tried to protest the battle was yet a day off, but she wouldn't hear a word. Instead, she bade us explain the situation to our families in advance so they wouldn't worry about any sudden departure. We made a hasty exit from her house back to our barracks to make the final arrangements and visit our families. I can speak for the others, saying goodbye to our families was emotionally hard for everyone. None of us had been away from them for extended periods of time.

Late that afternoon, with everything at the ready, we joined the others near the many Feathered Spear Throwers to help with any last minute preparations for the coming battle. Roy and Raphael checked and rechecked the throwers and made sure that each had a good supply of the feathered spears. We women helped Willow convert a vacant nearby building into a healing ward. We spent several hours tearing up cloths into various sized bandages. We check and rechecked the supplies of healing herbs and got several large pots of water ready to be heated up. In short, we tried to keep busy doing something to avoid stewing in fear of what might be.

Later that evening, when it was full dark, the reports began coming in more frequently; the enemy army was drawing near. Beyond any doubt Karka was to be the intended target of the King's might. Riders reported the enemy was encamped only about six miles south and east of us. Good estimates suggested the attack would be joined around ten the next morning. Our easternmost cavalry was ordered to move another five miles due south, roughly due east of Karka some ten miles. Captain Red took his half and positioned them five miles northeast of Karka, intending to hit them on their flank once they committed to a battle plan. Some of our militiamen took up guard duty and could be seen patrolling the streets, particularly those on the eastern edge of town. Finally, Willow ordered us to bed; there was nothing more we could do until morning's light. While we did as she asked, none of us could sleep much. The combination of impending attack, fear and concern for our families and friends, and worry, kept sleep from coming until the wee hours of the night.

At the crack of dawn, we arose, glad the long night of waiting was over. After breakfast and once more making sure our horses were ready for a fast getaway should the need arise, we joined Willow and Ellen at the edge of town, high upon Kappa Ridge looking down upon the green ramparts that lead up into the town from the east. Already, she had sent word to the town leaders that the attack was eminent. As we stood waiting, the trained militiamen arrived to take up their positions beside the thrower machines, three men per device. It took two to cock it and one to load, aim, and fire them. Soon those whose task was hand-to-hand combat arrived and formed into ranks behind us. I believe that all Guardians shared the same thought: if these men had to enter the fray, we would be in very bad shape indeed.

I looked at these brave defenders of Karka, ordinary townsfolk they were. Some were just in their teens as we were. I spied two blacksmiths and a metalworker. The stalwart looks on their faces could not hide their inherent fear of what was to come. Everything seemed to confirm my hatred of fighting, of senseless attacks.

The day was grey and overcast though a storm did not seem to be in the offing. For us druwids, this was in our favor, for we could more easily call upon Nature for our attack strengths. However, one unexpected action heartened us all. Three dozen men and women who were not in the militia came marching up to Willow. All carried bows and several quivers of arrows. A hunter named Max was their official spokesman. "Guardian Windsong, can you make use of more archers? We want to volunteer to let fly all the arrows we can before the enemy get close. We are basically hunters, not fighters, but we want to help defend our town. We promise to get out of the way just as soon as the enemy gets too close. I know you don't want to have to deal with untrained fighters in the middle of a battle, but we figure we can take a fair number of the enemy out before they can get that close."

Using her gracious voice, she replied, "Max, your help is most welcome indeed. Yes, our main plan now is to do just that, eliminate as many as we can before they can get close. If they get close, we don't have the strength to fend them off. So please, eliminate all you can. Thank you one and all for your assistance. Roy, can you get them into reasonable positions?" Roy eagerly set about the task of adding these new recruits to the line of the throwing engines. The rest of us waited; I've said it before, but I'll say it again, I hate waiting! Each passing minute seemed like hours to me.

Finally, we spied the King's army about two miles down the green path leading to the top of our ridge. Like tiny ants, they moved into ranks. We could see the hundreds of cavalry taking up the leading positions ahead of the foot soldiers. Willow ordered us to our positions. I stood beside Ellen to help her. Roy was the farthest from me, being down at the farthest end of the throwing engines. Willow was at the southernmost edge of town, far to my right. Between these two the rest of us were evenly spaced covering five hundred feet. This way, we all had room to bring down the wrath of Nature upon the charging cavalry. Again, we waited. Again, I hated waiting!

When the enemy cavalry were about a mile distant, Willow placed into our minds, *Begin summoning the forces of Nature. As soon as you feel they are in range of your powers, let loose. May Nature protect us all.* I took a deep breath. I could bring down fire, ice, or lightning bolts now. I must choose one and naturally, as you probably have guessed, I chose lightning. I closed my eyes and felt for the black energy masses floating high overhead. The volume of the dense clouds provided more than enough mass for my needs. Once again, I felt the crackle of energy far above me, ready to answer my pull, my direction. I waited. While I might be able to strike them this far off, accuracy wouldn't be that great. Patience, I told myself. At no point, did I feel as if I was about to lose myself as I had done four years before when we were attacked that stormy day on our way to Karka.

Now they started charging, galloping up the long valley towards us standing at the top of Kappa Ridge. I let fly my first bolt. Others did as well. Fire and lightning from the skies rained down upon the charging cavalry like the wrath of the gods. I heard the twangs from the spear engines adding to the rain of death. After the first volley from these large machines, I heard the softer twangs from the archers; they fired and fired in rapid succession. My full attention was on forming and firing massive bolts, aiming them at oncoming riders. The noise level became utterly deafening. Though I couldn't see the militiamen behind me, I later learned they were forced to cover their ears to dampen the noise.

In five minutes, it was all over. Two thirds of the cavalry were lying in a path up the long entryway — a line of dead or wounded men and horses. Those horses that were yet alive had bolted, veering off to the left or right. Smoke clouds rose from some burning men, horses, and trees; some of us chose to rain down fire. Behind us, the militia began cheering us, but their voices sounded so faint; my ears were momentarily deadened from the noise of our onslaught.

Then, I glanced over to Ellen, and my heart nearly stopped. Ellen lay on the ground gasping for breath. I knelt down beside her to do what I could. I picked up her head and held it in my lap. Vaguely, I heard my own distant voice screaming, "Ellen's in trouble! Willow, help!" Ellen looked directly into my eyes and whispered, "It's all right, Beth." There in my arms, Ellen died. A short exhale and her breathing stopped; her body went limp; her eyes took on a vacant stare and then closed slowly. "No! No! No!" I cried, a wall of tears flowing down my face.

Willow knelt down beside me and examined her lifelong friend. "Save her! Save her!" I pleaded, crying all the while. I glimpsed my other friends gathering around us.

Willow whispered to me, "Ellen's body has died, Beth. There is nothing I can do to bring it back to life. You must let her go, Beth."

Later on, Sandy told me that I was practically hysterical. I believe her. Willow put both her arms solidly on my shoulders and forced me to look into her eyes. "Beth, Ellen knew this day was coming. She planned for it, Beth. She has already located a mother about to give birth up in Petersville, a mother whom she likes. So her new body is awaiting her to pick it up." I stopped my hysterical crying, though still sobbing. "Beth, I want you to see this for yourself. Look at Ellen's body. Really look at it. Do you see Ellen in or around it? Look, observe."

Though I was crying, feeling the horrible loss of my mentor, my grandmom, I did as I was ordered. No matter how hard I looked, I could not see the being I knew as Ellen anywhere around her lifeless body. "See, I told you Ellen was prepared for this. She knew her time had come. I believe she is now off checking on her new body that is not yet born, Beth. Now, dry your eyes. We still have much to do here." She got up, motioning for Sarah Jane and Sandy to help me up and look after me. As I stood shakily on my feet and leaned upon them, I could see they had been crying as well. I looked at the faces of the four fellows in my Circle; their eyes were also quite wet. We were deeply shaken by Ellen's body death.

Roy took my hand and said softly, "Come on Beth; we have to keep an eye on what the enemy is doing. They aren't stopping their attack just because Ellen has died. Come on; look around." I tried to look, but with my eyes still flowing tears, I really couldn't see much. I relied for the moment on what I was hearing from the others. People were shouting.

"Look, their remaining cavalry is regrouping outside our engine's range."

"What are they planning?"

"The foot soldiers are moving to the left and right. What are they planning now? They aren't getting any closer."

Then, I heard the words that I secretly dreaded. "Flanking us! They are trying to fan out all around us down there!" Encirclement!

"Look their cavalry has formed into two groups and are riding hard north and south. The soldiers are running north and south too."

Then, I heard the determined voice of Willow rise above all the others, "We have stopped their direct assault on us for the time being. They have changed tactics. They are attempting to encircle the town!"

Not now! Please not now! I have to look after Ellen! My mind raced in reaction as our promises to Willow reached my conscious thought level. We'd all promised her.

Just as I fully realized what was going on, Willow gave us a direct order; her tone left nothing further to be said. "Lightning Circle, mount up and ride west out of here just as fast as you can. I'm sure we can now handle the situation here ourselves. So go now. All along, I had hoped that one from my

Circle could accompany you, but this is not now possible. I'll stay in touch with you during your trip. Go now before their cavalry blocks off your only escape route. Go and may Nature be your guide and assist you. Go!"

Roy was the first to react and started pulling the others back toward where we had left our horses. Somehow, my feet would not move; I stood motionless, utterly unable to comply. I didn't want to comply. Roy gently grabbed my arm, pulled me forward one step, and then another step. Slowly, he led me to the horses. The others were already mounted, but they were still crying. I felt the strong arms of Roy lift me into my saddle. He placed my reins in my hand and mounted himself. "Okay, Circle, it's time. Ride, ride like the wind! We must not get caught by their cavalry!" He leaned over and pulled on my horse, and we started off at a gallop. The others surrounded my horse, forcing it to follow the pace set by Roy. I heard the clopping of hooves on the town streets change to a dull thud as we hit the rolling slopes at the western edge of town.

Now, we were going downhill, and I was forced to pay some attention to keep from falling forward off my horse. Trees whizzed passed me, as we veered to the right and then left. I heard Roy call out, "Look out!" Cavalry closing on the left side, we veered more to the right. Down the long rolling hills we went, seven flying horses bearing riders whose druwid cloaks fluttered behind them. I heard something fly by my head and saw the quarrel thud into a tree as I flashed by the oak. We thundered down into a gorge and veered right and then straight up the other side and then down again and veer left and up and then down and veer more left. Roy was purposely taking a path designed to elude the enemy cavalry. I heard Thomas behind me yell that the enemy wasn't following us. That meant only one thing; we had broken through safely.

Roy didn't slow his pace until the horses absolutely had to slow down. All seven were lathered and panting, so we dismounted and walked them for quite some time to cool them down. Walking was just what I needed; a private time to collect my wits, my thoughts. None of us said a word. I think we were all thinking of the tragic loss of Ellen. This woman had touched our lives, filling them with kindness, love, and respect. Our loss was deep.

Two hours after we had fled the encirclement of Karka and with our horses cooled down, Roy ordered us to mount up. It was time to put some distance between Karka and us. "Well, we sure are on our own, gang," he said. "We have no real solid directions on how to find Calgary, except that it's on the edge of the Greenway by the great ocean west of here. I guess we just go west until we hit the water."

Sarah Jane added, "I remember Ellen saying we should avoid the towns whenever possible — camp out in the open wilderness. She said it was both cheaper and safer."

"Okay, will do," Roy answered. "I'll lead us around any towns in our path. Thomas, you be on the lookout for any shelter cabins we might use. This is our first night out, and it'll be getting dark in a few more hours, at least when we are within the forested sections. I say we stop while we have plenty of light left. We should forage for food. I think we should conserve what little we brought along, just in case."

We rode on once more. The traveling order was simple. Roy took the point. As our Protector, it was his task to lead us safely to Calgary — besides he had promised Willow as much. Sarah Jane and Thomas rode behind him. Simon and I came next, while Sandy and Raphael brought up the rear. We wore our nearly matching leather clothes with our druwid cloaks fastened about our necks. Each cloak had a hood, which could be raised to ward off the weather if needed. Our long knives were secured about our waists. We each had our bow and quiver of sixteen arrows tied to our saddle, along with a pair of very large saddle bags stuffed to the brim with sacks of personal items and our meager food supply.

Our horses were all brown mares. Three bearing we girls were nearly the same height, but smaller than those of the boys. We had previously discussed the possibility of bringing along a packhorse but had ruled it out. None of us was an expert horseman just yet. We agreed we'd have our hands full with one horse. As we rode along, I began to wonder if perhaps we shouldn't have brought along a couple of spares. Then, I remembered Roy's argument, "If we need another, we can always purchase one at the nearest town."

As we rode along now at a civilized pace, being the children of Nature that we were, it was hard not to begin to observe the magnificent lands about us. Essentially, the Greenway was one vast land of rolling hills covered with patches of forests and open swaths of grasslands. Towns and villages were wide spread; it was not a densely populated land. Much of it was still virgin countryside. We could easily tell as we neared a settlement for this was a land of growers of crops. As we rode out of a thicket of trees, before us would lay a crop field often marked with a low stone wall made from the rocks that had been removed from the field. This was an instant signal that we were approaching habitations, though we could not tell their size. Roy steered us around the fields, bypassing the settlement. Occasionally, we would meet someone working that field, and we both exchanged greetings.

By dusk, the others had cheered up; the loss of Ellen was replaced by the thrill of the great adventure we had embarked upon, along with the magnificent lands through which we were traveling. However, I had not. Ellen was my grandmom, well, not actually a blood relation, but in all ways except that. I hadn't even observed that Thomas had put us on a tiny track that led to a druwid shelter cabin. In fact, I didn't realize we were there until we stopped by its door. Roy praised Thomas, "Well done, Thomas. You are certainly earning your position as Loremaster."

Now normally as the Wid, it was my responsibility to lead, to issue the orders for what needed to be accomplished next. I was so morose that I didn't even make the attempt. Sandy said, "Beth is really taking this hard, gang. Let's give her time to recover. Sarah Jane and I'll do the cooking, if you guys take care of the horses, fetch some wood, and get some fresh meat for us to cook."

"Excellent plan," Raphael commented. He hated cooking and was still not good at it. "I'll take care of the horses, guys. You get the wood and the game." He preferred to handle horses to scrounging in the woods for kindling or for hunting. Thomas, who loved the woods as much as I, perhaps even more so, volunteered at once to hunt or snare some rabbits. Simon went in search of firewood. As our Protector, Roy was obligated to stay near us girls, just in case of danger, and he helped Raphael with the horses and carried our gear into the small cabin.

Sandy and Sarah Jane found a broom and did a quick cleaning; this cabin had not been occupied for quite some time. Me, I just sat in a corner on the floor and leaned back against the wall, trying to make myself invisible, as I reflected and reviewed all the mental images I had of this eventful day. It certainly had not gone as I had wanted, dreamed, or planned. *Ellen's gone; lost to me forever. I'm so alone without her. I depended on her; she was always there for me.* I yawned and yawned, but was not really tired. All of a sudden, I realized something. *Silly me, I haven't lost Ellen. Her body has died, true, but she still exists! She is just getting a new body. There is no reason why I can't go and find her in her new body. All I have lost is her immediate companionship.* I finally brightened up with that realization and looked around the small one room cabin.

"Ah, you are back into the land of the living," Roy jested. "Here, make yourself useful. I'm a lousy bed maker. You can fix up the seven beds. Raphael's found a small creek nearby and is fetching a skin of water so we can wash up before dinner. Thomas is out cleaning a bunch of rabbits. Simon's watering the horses; they are stabled in the adjoining open air shelter."

"And we got the veggies about done," chimed in Sandy and Sarah Jane together. The table would only set two, so it was being used as the central serving location. After doing up the bed rolls, I moved over to the table to see if there was anything left that I could do to help out there. Sarah Jane spied me and added, "Beth, you get to clean up our mess." She and Sandy giggled. I noticed they had cooking stuff all over the far side of the small cabin. I agreed, nevertheless.

Just then, the others came it. "Rabbits are ready," Thomas announced, handing seven to Sandy. Thomas saw me and added, "Ah, Beth, you are looking much better. That's good. We missed you." I managed a smile, my first since the attack.

"Here, Beth, wash up, I've brought a bucket of water. Stream's really close by," Raphael suggested. "It's good to see you smiling again, Beth."

"I'll second that," added Simon, "but hurry up on the washing. I need to wash the horse off me or you ladies won't let me near the supper table." We all laughed. While the rabbits were cooking, we sat around and talked about the momentous day's events. Raphael got many compliments on how well his invention worked. He was rightly proud of his achievement. Of course, the guys insisted on talking about the battle and how well it went. We girls just listened. We were not proud of the senseless slaughter of men and horses. I think all three of us fully realized our role in Nature's Grand Balance Between the Sexes at play. Without women to act as a counter balance, men, left to their own devices, would turn the world into one enormous battlefield just to see who was the more powerful.

Before the guys got too carried away with all the battle talk, I interrupted them and put the actual result of the battle into perspective. A hundred or so noble horses, which could have been put to a far greater use, were dead, to say nothing of the wasted lives of the men. I told them to think about the wives and children of the slain who no longer had a father to provide for them. That sobered their enthusiasm for "glorious combat." Sandy swore to me later that she thought all four of them looked rather sheepish after my little speech. Plus, she thanked me for having done it.

As we were sitting on the floor and eating, talk centered around what would happen to Karka after it was surrounded by the remainder of the King's forces. The consensus was that with our cavalry now outnumbering theirs and with the other two towns sending some of their militia, the siege of Karka would indeed be very short lived.

Once we had eaten, I did the cleanup duties, and then we laid down on our makeshift beds, girls on one side, guys on the other. Sleep came early and quickly to us all. Only Roy remembered that one of us should stand guard. After about four hours, he wakened Simon and then slept himself. Nothing ill happened that night. We all got much needed rest.

In the morning, our activities began to resemble some kind of a routine. We girls fixed the meal and cleaned up afterwards. The guys got more firewood to replenish the emergency cabin's supply, fetched clean water, and fed and saddled the horses. Actually, within a few days, we had the duties down to a very efficient routine indeed. After a week, we just knew what needed to be done and did it; no orders had to be issued. We were a self-sufficient group indeed.

As we left the cabin and mounted up, something singular happened, one that none of us expected, but one that haunted and drove my research in years to come. Just as we were all mounted, I heard the voice of Ellen in my head. *Fine morning for a ride, Beth. Do you mind if I tag along? First though, I'd better say hello to the others.* So unexpected was her voice in my mind that I shrieked. The others reacted in various startled manners; Sarah Jane nearly fell off her horse. Simultaneously, we all heard in our minds, *Yes, I'm here with all of you. The new birth is not due for a couple weeks yet, so I have some time on my hands — oops, no hands, ah well, you know what I mean anyway.* Her mood was jovial and carefree, not at all what I expected. *All along, my Circle had intended that one of us should accompany you to Calgary, but matters have taken a rather different turn. So I'm it. I'll be sitting on Beth's shoulders, if that is fine with her. I'm afraid I need a body to sort of hold on to if I'm to follow you.*

Everyone turned to stare at me. I rather twisted around trying futilely to see my backside. *Yes, it is a good time to practice your skills. Make sure that you all can perceive me.* I saw six gaping mouths staring at me searching for Ellen.

Sarah Jane exclaimed, "You really are there! I thought you were dead." She realized her blunder immediately and amended her statement, "We really *are* spiritual beings, then! I only half-heartedly believed all that stuff about not being bodies. Can you move around? Can you touch me?" All turned to look at Sarah Jane. I think that she vocalized what some in my Circle also felt. We watched her involuntarily jerk in recognition of Ellen's touch on her shoulder. Her face turned beet red, and she muttered, "Oh my! It's very real." The teacher in Ellen rose to the occasion. In turn, she touched all the others who displayed similar reactions to Sarah Jane's. Then she resumed her perch on my shoulder.

By the way, Beth, I was around the cabin last night checking up on all of you. I overheard your speech about the Nature's Balance between men and women. You did well in your explanation, altogether suiting your position as their Wid. My compliments. Now it was my turn to flush but I did not let on to the others why. *Now we best be on our way. Tell Roy to head slightly south of west.* I did as instructed, and we were off on the day's ride.

As we rode into the early morning across the splendid countryside, I thought to Ellen, *I promise to come look for you in your new body just as soon as I can. I felt so awful when your body died, but finally I realized I never really lost you. I'll come and find you.*

Dear child, none of us knows what lies in the future, but I'd be honored if you can do that say in six years. Meantime, find out as much as you can about what is happening to all the others that are stuck in their heads. They cannot do as we. I know that now. I followed one of those cavalrymen whose body died during the attack. Most strange. When he left his lifeless body, he shot high into the air. I lost track of him as he passed in front of the sun. It seemed like he was following some preordained command or something. Beth, something is definitely very wrong with this behavior. If you ever can spare the time, please try to find out. I promised her that I would.

We rode on in silence for the most part, enjoying the ride. It was early autumn but the leaves had not yet begun to turn. Occasional fog mists rose from the deeper more secluded basins we passed through. Near midmorning, we crested a hill crowned with oaken thickets only to spy what has to be the most beautiful pond in the world. Green grasslands flowed seamlessly to the still waters pale green with algae. Floating in the middle were six white swans; tiny wakes marked their silent glide across the still fog shrouded waters. We paused, daring not a sound to break the quiet of Nature's elegance. I felt as if we were bearing witness to the Grace of Nature herself. We sat watching for several minutes; none of us said a word. I did see what could only be a tear trickle down Thomas's cheek; this was a Loremaster's most prized scene.

Then, Roy did something that I would never have predicted a man would do. He motioned us to turn around, and he led us around the hill, bypassing the pond, leaving it in its unspoiled beauty. When he glanced behind to see if we were following him, I blew him a thank you kiss. He smiled back and winked at me. I was in a dreamy mood all the rest of the day.

By late afternoon, it became obvious we weren't going to find an emergency shelter before dark. Hence, we made camp in a cozy oak thicket near the crest of another ridge. That night, we slept out under the stars. Because the nights were getting chilly, even though we had blankets, we snuggled up to each other for added warmth. I slept between Thomas and Roy, and this was the first time I was this close to men. I must admit I felt a bond between us, and I felt completely safe and secure. I felt as if nothing in the world could harm me while I slept. As I drifted into sleep, I wondered if this was how I would feel when I slept next to my mate when I finally got married. Was this what Sarah Jane was actually seeking? My questions never were answered, for the next thing I was aware of was the rising of the sun and seeing my breath as I exhaled. Morning came altogether too soon for me.

On the sixth day of our journey, around midday, Roy signaled us that we were approaching a band of men. As we closed the distance, I could see that these men looked rough. Their clothes were worn and tattered and positively filthy. We were about to detour around them, when six of them drew swords, which they had hidden behind their bodies. Immediately, six others who had been in hiding rushed out on our right, while another half dozen came at us from the left side. Roy called out the obvious, "Ambush!" I was thankful they didn't have bows or crossbows or it might have been deadlier for us. The boys drew their swords, while we girls pulled our staves from their positions behind us. In a quick motion, we also moved within the protective circle of the boys. Roy was in front, Raphael, the rear, with Simon and Thomas moving off to either side of us.

One who seemed to be their leader cautiously approached us, wary of us; we were mounted. As he got close, a singular thing occurred. I saw him eyeing our cloaks and the embroidered oak leaves. Finally, he spoke, "Thee be Guardians?" It was a question.

"Aye, we are the Lightning Circle of Guardians," Roy replied. "What do you want of us?"

One of the others muttered, "They be only kids."

The leader answered back, "Still, they be Guardians." He looked at Roy and said, "You may pass. We've no quarrel with you, only with the Galts. Been a raiding party near here."

Roy sheathed his sword, and the rest of us did the same. "We've no quarrel with you either. If we come across any Galts ahead, we'll do our best to eliminate all of them, on that you can count!" That brought a broad smile to their leader's face.

"I recon you'll do just that," he motioned for us to pass, and we rode on past them and soon left them behind us. None of us said a word until we were well beyond them.

"I wonder who they were," Sarah Jane commented, "Rough looking bunch."

"Yes, but did you see the way he spied that we were Guardians?" I put in. "He must be familiar with our cloaks of office. Further, he has respect for us. That's an encouraging sign." We discussed the matter further as we rode onwards. Roy, however, now was alert for signs of Galt raiders. However, we saw none.

By late afternoon, as we rode down a long grassy valley, we spied the smoke from a campfire. Considering that the area was open for miles around us, we decided to risk riding past whoever was there. The alternative was to backtrack to get around them, which would cost us many miles. As we cautiously approached the campsite, we spied several covered wagons painted in gay colors of the rainbow. Sarah Jane called out to us, "Traveling musicians! We are in luck!" None of the rest of us had ever seen traveling musicians. "They came through Undel two years ago. I don't know if these are the same ones, but it doesn't matter." Sarah Jane suddenly bubbled with enthusiasm.

As we approached, I spied a half dozen younger men with crossbows hastily running to form a defensive line protecting the wagons. Many women were hustling their children into the wagons for protection. We had more or less taken them by surprise. Soon, we were close enough to see their faces, and they, ours. One older man, evidently their leader, put down his crossbow and smiled at us. The others followed suit. He said something, but we were still too far to hear; the women began emerging from the wagons along with the children. Roy rode us right up to their campfire and dismounted before the presumed leader.

This man was dressed in unusual clothes, nothing actually matched color-wise. His pants were brown leather, his shirt, red. His belt sash was yellow. A black bandana scarf kept his long black hair out of his face. He had a long moustache and a wiry frame, tall and thin. "Hail Guardians. Welcome to the camp of the Traveling Rainbow Musicians. I'm bard Wendell, the Great. Tonight, our camp is your camp. We'd be pleased if you would spend the night with us." Finally, I thought to myself, genuine hospitality. He went on, "Please accept my apologies for raising arms against you. We've heard there's a roving band of Galts in the area. We're being cautious."

It is customary for the Wid of a Circle to act as the wise spokesperson for the Circle except either in dangerous situations when that duty falls to the Protector or in a dispute when that duty falls to the Judger. It was expected of me to speak for us. I caught his eyes glancing at each of us in turn obviously looking for the leader of our Circle. I stepped forward, "Greetings Bard Wendell. I'm Guardian Bethany of the Lightning Circle. Yes, we too have heard that there may be Galts in the area, though we haven't seen them yet, so no offense taken; it's prudent to prepare yourselves in these times. Yes, the hour is getting late, and we do need a place to camp. We'd be most grateful to join your group for the night. Your hospitality is most generous; it is therefore fitting that we in turn offer you the protection of the Guardians for this night so you may rest in peace." I felt confident I had said it all properly. Ellen even whispered a "very nicely said" in my mind.

Bard Wendell look at me rather curiously; I detected a bit of surprise in his eyes. "You are all so young, and you, their leader, the youngest. Interesting."

"True, I'm the youngest, only fourteen actually and of age, but I'm their leader. Don't worry about our youthfulness. We have just come from a battle several days ago in which we brought down the fire and lightning from the sky." I hoped that would settle his worries. It certainly did for his eyes blinked in amazement.

Bard Wendell spoke formally for his troupe, "We share our camp with the Lightning Circle of Guardians. Tonight, we're fully under their watchful protection. Let us prove to be worthy hosts!" And with the formalities out of the way, his troupe now swarmed up close to us. I counted over two dozen in all, men, women, and children. I assumed correctly that the troupe traveled with their families, and probably most of them took part in their performances. One lovely woman dressed in a multicolored dress came up beside the bard. "Allow me to introduce my wife, Emily, musician and dancer extra-ordinaire!"

She smiled and shook my hand, "Bethany, can I call you that?" I nodded. "Come wash your face and hands. You must be tired from riding all day." She motioned with her arms for Sandy and Sarah Jane to come too. We handed our reins to the guys who followed the bard to the tethering line, where they had their dozen horses tied in a long line for the night. I was thankful they enjoyed looking after the horses. As we approached one of the wagons most likely belonging to the bard and Emily, the other women and children swarmed around us. Sarah Jane began chatting with them at once. It turned out this was the very same troupe she had seen in Undel two years before. She promptly told them how much she enjoyed their show, and how great she thought they were. I watched, as they loved the good reviews from a Guardian; I think it meant more than normal to them.

Something about these simple folk stirred a chord deep within me. Carefree, lovers of life, music and dance, they cared not for hostilities, politics or wealth. These were people driven to make music, to entertain, and to fill lives with a richness barely found here in the Greenway. I took an immediate liking to them all. I soon found myself chatting with them just as carefree as they were with us. Shortly, we sat around the campfire eating dinner with our hosts. It seems they always cook more than they need for one meal, just in case of visitors. Emily explained that her son, Jake, had shot a deer earlier, so now they had plenty to share. "Venison for the next several days, actually," she commented, and they all laughed.

"It sure is good," I complimented between mouthfuls; I discovered I really was hungry.

"You hear that, Marge, she likes your cooking," teased Emily. "Honestly, there is no finer cook in all Greenway than Marge. She has the knack, the gift, you know." I did not doubt that for a moment. I overheard Sandy asking a girl about her age how she liked traveling around the country in a wagon. I caught part of her reply "nothing could ever beat it." Sarah Jane kept asking about their music and dancing. I heard Roy explaining to some of the men that Galts attacked rarely, if ever, at night, preferring daylight raids, often early-morning.

To my delight and amazement, once dinner was finished and the site cleaned up, Wendell proclaimed, "Tonight, we share our practice session with our guests." Everyone cheered. Evidentially, they felt it was a high honor to play for a Circle of Guardians. Turning to me, he said formally, "Let tonight's merrymaking be dedicated to the Guardians who selfishly dedicate their lives to help and protect others just as we do so to spread music and dance to all." Immediately, I saw several men pickup what appeared to be short logs. One began to thump his upon the ground in a rhythmic pattern thump-thump pause-pause, thump-thump pause-pause. Then another began just slightly intertwining his beats within the pauses of the others. Then a third joined in, and at last, several other musicians began playing. Bard Wendell played what he later called a fiddle, a stringed instrument that he held against his chest and played with a stick with horsetail hairs rubbing against the strings. His wife played what she called a flute. It had a mouthpiece that she blew into and many finger holes she covered and uncovered in rapid-fire succession. Another had a reedy sounding instrument he called a fiphe that produced haunting nasally sounding mellow tones. Others began clapping in time with the music.

Then, to my surprise, all the others got up, moved into the large open area around the campfire, and began to dance. They uniformly placed their arms on their waists and by jumping up and down did the most fascinating movements with their feet and toes. I can only say it was the most beautiful dance I had seen. All moved in unison to the music; they slowly moved in various patterns, a circle that turned into an X, which turned into a W, and so on. Soon, Sarah Jane grabbed Raphael's hand and pulled him into the dance area. Before I knew it, Roy had me there as well, and Sandy and Simon joined us. A young lass brought Thomas into the fun as well. Several of the dancers came over to us and helped show us how to do it. It did take us about an hour to get the knack of this style of dancing, but we were quick learners. Song after song echoed into the clear night sky. It was ecstasy. More and more, I found myself wanting to learn how to play such music!

After several hours flew by, at last the music was coming to an end. Everyone sat down on logs. Emily's daughter whispered to me, "Mom's solo; you *have* to hear this." Indeed, everyone listened with their eyes closed. It was a lament, so moving that I had tears streaming down my face when the last faint notes faded into the cricket-chirping silence. I quickly glanced around; I think everyone was deeply moved by her song.

One by one, they all quietly and without saying so much as a word, headed into their respective wagons. We bedded ourselves down near the still warm campfire; none of us spoke either; none wanted to break that captivating spell she'd woven upon us. It was a spell that deeply moved me, telling me that there was more to life than I ever suspected. I *had* to learn how to make music like this! I fell asleep dreaming of playing half as good as Emily plays.

I awoke to an altogether different kind of music. Roy was carefully nudging each of us awake. "Galts sneaking up on the camp. No sudden movements until I get everyone awake." I swore under my breath as I slowly got up, pretending nothing was going on. However, I began summoning the energies in the billowing white clouds that bedecked the blue sky this early morning. A fog lay low over the campsite. I didn't even feel the chill in my bones so intent was I on harnessing the energies above me. Now Sandy was in my mind.

Roy says here's the plan. He will address them sudden like, and one of you launch a warning shot toward them. He wants to see if we can scare them off without a fight. I sent back that I had a lightning bolt at the ready.

Roy suddenly turned to face the men sneaking towards us. They really were not good sneakers, I thought. You could see the tall grass waving this way and that, as they crawled through it towards us. "This camp is protected by seven Guardians. Leave immediately, and we'll not harm you." I took that as the sign to launch my first bolt. I picked a spot on the ground just before where the lead man was sneaking and formed a thin line upwards to the clouds. When contact was made, a huge jolt of energy, a bolt, came arcing to the ground, sending a small cloud of debris flying and making a small pothole in the dirt. The resounding peal of thunder followed. Twenty ill-clad men waving swords got up and fled from us just as fast as their legs could take them. Following this, all the troupe came rushing out of their wagons, gaping at the fleeing Galts. Carefully, I let go of my strong contact with the clouds.

"Well done, Beth!" exclaimed Roy. "That showed them who is the boss." I smiled; I greatly preferred not to harm people. This time we got away without actually having to hurt anyone. It took a minute for the poor musicians to realize just what had happened. As they watched the fleeing raiders, they began to cheer us.

"Thank you Guardians!" exclaimed Bard Wendell above the chatter of the others.

I could tell he was about to elaborate but I interrupted him. "Just earning our keep. We scared them away. How about some breakfast?" I deftly attempted to change the topic. It worked.

While we were eating, the bard asked, "Say where are you headed if it is not impolite to ask?"

"Calgary," I replied, "though we are not too sure of our directions just yet." Then, I felt a compulsion to ask, "Say, is it hard to learn how to play the music from last night? I would really love to learn how. Emily, your solo touched my heart. It was *so* beautiful, so sad. I had tears in my eyes when you were done. Could I learn to play like that?" Her eyes sparkled. Suddenly, I knew I wouldn't need to beg and plead. She looked at her husband, so I did too.

"It takes talent, a feel for music, and years and years of practice to be as good as Emily. However, anyone can learn if they set their mind to it," he replied. "Say, I have an idea, Bethany. Why don't you ride along with us for a couple weeks? We are headed to the large town of Brownsville to play for their autumn festival. It is usually profitable for us to play there; we make enough coins to help us get by through the long winters. Brownsville is directly on your route to Calgary, probably getting you halfway there from here, I think. We'll be stopping one night here and there at some of the smaller villages along the way. They are only one-night stands and a chance for us to replenish our food supplies, like salt. We'd be honored if you would accompany us to Brownsville. What say you?"

"I'd better consult with the others; give me a minute," I answered, barely able to contain my excitement. I gathered the others, some of whom had overheard my discussion with Wendell.

"Oh let's do!" exclaimed Sarah Jane. "I want to learn how to dance and play that fiddle thing. Please, let's do!"

Quiet Thomas added, "I agree. I want to learn how to make that thumping rhythm. Imagine all that from a mere log!" To everyone's happiness, we had a hundred percent consensus. I gladly announced we'd accompany them to Brownsville and provide protection all the way. I secretly guessed this troupe would have no further trouble from that band of Galts after this morning's episode. We also agreed to help provide fresh meat and other staples that Nature had to offer in the wild this late in the season. I think Emily and the other women really liked this even better.

Finally, I remembered Ellen and asked her opinion. *Congratulations Wid Beth, you have turned a journey into a learning session for you all. Very well done indeed. You'll be safe for weeks. I'll go back and check on my new mother. I'll be in contact with you later on, if I can. Of course, you can contact me if you need anything or have Sandy do so.* I bid her bye and good luck. Then, I told the others about Ellen's departure. No one worried much about it, considering our good fortune at having run into this troupe.

However, Sandy said, "Hey, what's all this about being Bethany? I thought Beth is short for Elizabeth." The others added their 'yehs' to hers.

"I like Bethany better because it has three syllables and is more musical, that's all. You can still call me Beth if you like," I answered.

"Well, I think Bethany sounds much more grownup, if you ask me," put in Sarah Jane. The guys just rolled their eyes in mock protest. Then, it was time to eat and be on our way. Interestingly, those of us that wanted to learn to play music, namely Sarah Jane, Sandy, Thomas, and me, all were asked to ride along in the wagons for music lessons.

As I rode along with Emily and her family, she presented me with my first flute, an old one of hers. She explained Wendell made all the troupe's instruments. He promised to make a special one for me during the days that followed. Thus, it was that I first learned how to make music, the traditional songs of the Greenway as I later learned. Those were three intensely happy weeks!

By the time we got to the last village before Brownsville, we were joining the Traveling Rainbow Troupe during their performance for the village folks. Many of us had even learned some of the simpler dance routines as well. Of course, we were merely amateurs, beginners, but we seven were truly happy.

As we left that little hamlet, the countryside began to change noticeably. The forested areas diminished, replaced by many working fields. Roy became a bit uneasy about our going into such a large town. Bard Wendell apparently sensed this, as Roy moved his horse closer to the bard's wagon. "Yes, I know, Brownsville is large — thousands and thousands of people. You know human nature better than we. One can find just about anything there, good or evil. If you do go into town, be alert for pickpockets, thieves, and those who would price-gouge you."

"That's just it," Roy replied seriously, "we aren't. I was specifically advised to steer clear of towns on this trip."

"Ah, you have been wisely counseled," Wendell pointed out reassuringly. "In that case, you probably should depart from our path now. Ride due south until you finally get to the denser forests, then circle westward for half a day before angling west by north. You should intersect the well-traveled track to Calgary. Much trading goes on between Brownsville and Calgary. The path is impossible to miss. I've heard cavalry patrols the route to keep down would-be highway men, so it ought to be fairly safe for you to travel." Roy thanked him, and relayed his decision and the information to us.

Naturally, we stopped to say good-bye to our new friends. The bard told me, "Guardian Bethany, it has been our pleasure to have you as our guests. May our paths cross again and soon." He bowed to me.

"Oh no, I think you have it backwards, Bard Wendell," I replied. "It is we who have been blessed with your company and your gifts of music and dance. I will do all I can to cross paths with you as soon as I can, though I have no idea when that may be." One by one, each of us said farewell and gave them our thanks. Emily and I hugged each other. I promised to continue to practice so when we next met, she would be able to see major improvement in my skill.

We remounted and rode off to the south. Several times, I glanced back over my shoulder to see the gaily-colored wagons as they moved into the distance. I knew Roy had made the correct decision. We weren't up to entering a large town and dealing with pickpockets and thieves, not just yet anyway. Within two hours, we were back into the forested areas and beyond the cultivated fields that lay for miles around Brownsville. For us, that meant relative safety. Now I wondered what lay ahead of us in Calgary? Would we get some training that would assist us in dealing with life in these giant towns? Why would the highest Circle want to train us personally in Calgary? I just had too many questions with no answers. I sighed and watched the forest beauty slowly move by.

By late afternoon, we estimated we were about halfway around the outlying areas of Brownsville. Thomas, our Loremaster, suddenly pointed out a side track that lead up what appeared to be a high ridge. "I'd say there's an emergency cabin up there somewhere. Shall we detour and see? Might make a nice place to camp," he said. Roy agreed, and we turned now south by west climbing steadily higher and higher, weaving in and out among the tall trees. Not quite an hour later, we reached the crest of the ridge. The cabin sat concealed nicely in a dense stand of oak trees, but just beyond the trees was the bare ridge top.

Naturally, we rode to the top for a view. Spectacular was an understatement. To the north, we could see for many miles. Neatly arranged fields of crops could be seen outlined by the faint grey rock walls so commonly found around their edge. It was like a patchwork quilt. We could also see Brownsville far to the north. It looked positively huge, given the size and the distance we knew we were from the town. This cultivated crop land valley must have been at least fifteen miles across! I couldn't even estimate the sheer volume of food that must be harvested! Raphael, our Planner, of course, could and did, "You are looking at fields that would support somewhere between five and ten thousand people — given fresh meat supplements, perhaps more. Incredible."

In the other direction, a vast vista of forested hills and open valleys beckoned. Roy even spotted several small hamlets by the smoke from their rising cooking fires. He said, "Look there, we can't possibly lose the path to Calgary from here. You can see the wide winding trail from here, and we're miles from it!" I was about to ask whether this meant that we would be likely meeting more travelers when Sandy interrupted us.

"Quiet for a moment, Willow is sending us a message!" We all sat spellbound waiting for Sandy to tell us Willow's news. I had forgotten all about their dire situation when we left so abruptly almost a month ago. Sandy concentrated hard, but I could see the news must be good because her face looked happy. Finally, she broke her concentration and looked up at us. "Good news, the siege of Karka is completely over. She said that there was a week of hit and run tactics employed by our cavalry, which not only cut off the King Randolf's supply lines to his troops, but also reduced their cavalry numbers even further. Petersville and Blankford did send ground forces, which were positioned between Karka and the main path to Redun. Willow said they decided to let hunger end the siege and not take more lives. That's why it took so long. The last of the King's men has now passed Uru heading back to Redun. The retreating soldiers even abandoned their weapons along the way. Our cavalry retrieved them, intending to use them in our future defense. Interesting turn of events. Not one additional person has died on our side since that first day. Willow thinks it's a complete, total victory on our part. However, Mary Ann has cautioned that King Randolf may be angrier with us than before and be seeking revenge later on. So all's well in Karka at last!"

The news raised our spirits even higher, and we chatted about this good news as we rode the short distance to the cabin. It was getting dark now, so speed was of the essence. By now, we had our individual tasks down pat. Without any words or orders, each did their part. Within a half hour, the cabin, exactly like all the other emergency cabins, was filled with the aroma of supper and warmth. Simon was the last one to come inside, "Hey, gang, it's snowing! First snowfall, come out and take a peek!" He had several white spots on his hair. Naturally, we all dashed out for a peek. Snow was falling, large moist flakes.

"I'm glad we aren't camping out in the open tonight," I pronounced. "I'll bet it gets colder tonight." It did. In the morning, about a half inch of the white stuff covered the ground. The trees, now in full fall foliage, had a new dimension, a layer of white. The sun was out, and we knew within a few hours all traces of the light snow would be gone. It was a somber harbinger that winter was not far off. Roy resolved we should hasten our pace to Calgary. Our destination was still two to three weeks away, but we did not know the exact distance.

As usual, we left the emergency cabin well restocked with firewood before we mounted up. Roy still kept our pace on the slow side until we actually reached the west road to Calgary. He was being careful not to be surprised by bandits or such this close to the large town. Once we reached the road in the early afternoon, Roy picked up our pace considerably. Periods of slow gallops were followed by a walking cool down period for the horses. I noted they were a bit friskier in the cooler weather; I think they enjoyed the racing.

Once on the main road, I use the word road, for that is what it seemed to us, well-worn wagon ruts clearly outlined the trail. Not even a blind man could fail to follow the track. Indeed, we passed by two sometimes three wagons each day, once even five. However, the air turned chillier, and Thomas always kept a wary eye out for emergency cabin side trails, beginning by the middle of the afternoon. Thanks to his eagle eyes, only once in the two weeks we took getting to Calgary did we have to sleep in the open — I froze my fanny off that night. It grew steadily more difficult to bypass the smaller towns and villages the closer we drew to Calgary, until at last, from ridges where we could get the lay of the lands before us, they seemed to "dot" the landscape! There was almost no place we could go to ride around them without trampling some farmer's field.

Then one day I knew we must have been getting close, because I spied a flock of birds that I could not identify. Strange white birds with long beaks, they soared high in the sky. Our best guess is they were some kind of sea dwelling birds. Later, we learned they were sea gulls. This was the day that we passed five wagons on the road. By late that afternoon, we crested yet another ridge and abruptly halted. There spread out before us was the most incredible sight any of us had ever seen. We were about ten miles from the ocean. Its endless blue hue stretched of into the distance as far as the eye could see. We spotted several wooden boats with white sails at various locations along the coastline, small shapes far off in the distance, but the real sight was Calgary. This was a city, immense in size from our point of view. It stretched for miles all along the coastline. Later, we learned it was home to well over thirty thousand people, the largest city in all the Greenway and positively huge.

"Gang, I don't think we're likely to find another emergency shelter between here and there," Thomas moaned. "We've only got a few hours of daylight left."

Roy calculated, "If we really pushed it — it's all downhill — I think we can make the city by dark. Then where do we go?"

"I don't want to sound like a pessimist," Thomas interrupted, "but I think a storm is coming too — probably going to snow, maybe heavily."

"Okay, okay, I get the message," Roy teased him. "We have to make the city tonight. Where do we go once we get there? It is huge! Where are we supposed to go anyway, Beth?"

None of us had any idea where we were supposed to go when we actually got to Calgary. Willow had never been there. We realized we hadn't been given that piece of information. I, as Wid, was supposed to know; I had to say something; all were looking to me for guidance. "I — I suppose we could ask someone when we get closer." I had no idea what or who to ask for, though.

At that moment, a voice spoke inside my head, a cold, uncaring tone, *The Circle of All Greenway maintains a training compound at the eastern edge of the city about a mile south of the Brownsville road. Go there.* I repeated those exact words to the others. They were flabbergasted! Looks of "how on earth do you know" greeted my eyes. I enjoyed my slight tease for a second before I told them of the voice. "I guess they already know of our arrival, but don't ask me how." If we were going to make it before total darkness fell and the snow began, we had to ride and ride hard. Hence, a discussion of this interesting occurrence had to wait until later. We headed off at a fast gallop.

Since the end of the journey was at hand, Roy pushed the horses harder than normal. We reached the edge of the city just as the sky turned rosy with the sun setting behind billowing storm clouds. We spied a well-worn road heading due south and took it. It was nearly full dark when we finally halted before a large walled complex. Stones had been carefully stacked about three feet high forming a wall around a wide area nearly the size of Uru. We could see many trees evidently planted by human hands for they formed great circles. Seven circles to be exact. This had to be the place; seven was our sacred symbol. We rode slowly along looking for an entrance.

We found a wooden gate, and Roy dismounted, fumbling in the failing light to open it for us. We dismounted and led our horses inside the complex. Roy carefully shut the gate and joined us. Ahead, there seemed to be a stone building with light coming from cracks in the boarded windows. I decided that would make a reasonable destination and led us among the trees towards it. No one was around outside that we could see. It seemed unusually silent, I thought.

We got to within a hundred feet of the inviting building when a man dressed in a white robe stepped out from behind a tree to challenge us. "Halt. Who are you? State your business here." His voice sounded cold and harsh, completely unlike any other Guardian I knew. Most unfriendly, I thought.

It was my place to answer, so I said, "We are the Lightning Circle. I'm Bethany, the Wid. We're reporting as we were instructed by Guardian Mary Ann of Blankford."

"Prove you are who you say you are. Call down a lightning bolt and strike this tree," he challenged me.

We expected a warm, friendly greeting here at the end of our long solo journey, which was something of an accomplishment for such a young, inexperienced group. I was speechless for a moment — dumbfounded actually. I finally managed to say, "What?"

Coldness turned to vehement anger; he screamed at me, "Do it now! Call down a bolt and strike this tree now!"

For a moment, I lost my confront. My universe shrank down to a dot within my head. I was overwhelmed by his voluminous anger, insisting I do this deed. Temptation was there, utterly to annihilate the tree and this man. I remembered the tiny voice of Willow penetrating the blackness and confusion when I had gone insane wiping out all of the cavalrymen who I thought had just killed Ellen and my family. *I fear she's gone rogue.* That pulled me out of it. My peanut-sized awareness expanded outward once more. "I will not," I said, defiantly placing my hands on my hips staring back at this outrageous man. "That is a perfectly good oak tree. Besides, I sense the loving care with which it was planted and in just the right location. That tree has been very well cared for — so no, I'll not destroy that tree!"

Now. his robes began to tremble as if only some supernatural power could hold his rage in check. He spat on the ground toward me. "Alright then, if you won't blast that tree, then bring that bolt down onto me. You can't do it! I told them so. Come on, you little bitch; hit me with your best shot. Do it now before I blast you!" he screamed at me in an utter rage.

I could have gotten very flustered and done what he asked — he certainly was asking for it. However, he hadn't harmed us in any way, yet, at least. Trying very hard to keep my shaking knees from showing or my voice from squeaking, I replied, "Sorry sir, I'm not a dog nor am I in heat. Whatever *is* your problem? Are you ill? Has there been a Galt attack here recently? What *is* the matter? Why are you so angry with us? We've never met." There, I had done it in spite of everything! Inside of me, I felt elated with myself. I had managed to be civil in the face of this raving madman and even to offer to be of some help, if only I could find out what was his problem. I felt Sandy speaking inside my mind. Her voice was shaky; she too was badly upset by this unexpected uncivil challenge. *We're with you. Don't give in to his insane demands. He has to be a crazy man.*

At that moment, Roy and Simon flew into action, our Protector and our Judger. Roy darted out in front of me, his scimitar drawn almost in the same motion. I didn't realize it could be drawn so fast. Roy's intention was very clear to all: he would protect his Wid at all costs. He said not a word; his actions spoke loud and clear. Instead, Simon spoke, "Sir, I'm Simon, the Judger. And you sir have just broken the Code Number Twenty-three, which states that at no time will a druwid threaten another druwid without just provocation, of which I see none. You have violated Code Number Thirty-seven, which states that at no time will a Guardian use insulting or offensive language to taunt a fellow Guardian. Also Code Sixteen, at no time will a druwid attempt to use threat of bodily harm to force another person to do something that they feel is a wrong action. Clearly, Bethany has demonstrated that it would be entirely wrong to destroy said tree. You leave me with no other recourse than to bring this matter to the attention of the Judger within your Circle for binding arbitration. I shall seek nothing less than a full, complete, and sincere apology for your actions this evening."

All the while Simon spoke so eloquently, Sarah Jane and Sandy had unobtrusively collected the reins and backed the horses up a safe distance behind us. Thomas and Raphael had drawn their scimitars and moved to flank both Roy and Simon. If this came to blows, I knew the four wouldn't hesitate to charge this crazy man. I sent to Simon, *Thanks. I never knew you were such eloquent a speaker! Very nicely done. Did he actually break all those rules?*

He sent back via Sandy, *This is the first time I've really had to wear my Judger's hat for us. Kind of scary, if you ask me. By the way, good show for not losing your cool under his insane pressure!* I smiled, though no one could see it.

I held my breath wondering what would happen next. Would this crazy man attack us? Why? Suddenly, I realized two things. What if he should call a lightning bolt down on me? I'd be fried. I had no way to protect myself from it! The other was that for an instant, I had shrunk down to the size of a pea and was fully inside my head. However, the latter idea immediately went on my back burner, naturally.

What happened next was nearly as surprising as the angry man was. After a full minute's dead silence, the man's voice spoke slowly and softly, albeit a little wearily. No trace of that psychotic rage could be heard; it was as if it had never occurred. "Well-spoken indeed, Simon — I believe that is your name. Good protective move, Roy. Wid Bethany, please forgive my nasty, violent outburst. I had to be certain you wouldn't go rogue on us. Willow swore you wouldn't, but in this matter, I had to be certain. I am now. If *I* can't get you to go rogue, you can rest assured no one else can. Forgive me. I haven't introduced myself. I'm Alabaster Benjamin Crowley, the Wid of the Circle of All Greenway and founder of the Guardians." He removed his hooded cloak to reveal an elderly man with long white hair, which flowed into his beard that reached his waist. He was about as tall as I was and as thin. In the near dark, I couldn't guess his age nor could I when we were inside.

"Oh yes, Wid Bethany, I'm very glad you didn't harm that stately oak tree. There are seven groves, one for each of the Aspects of Existence. Each grove is arranged in a perfect circle and has seven trees, one for each of the members of a Circle. Many a novice has lovingly tended them over these many years. Don't worry. I wouldn't have let you harm one, but I'm forgetting my manners. You have come a long way, are tired, and hungry, and it is getting quite cold out here. Yes, winter is nearly upon us once again. Please, bring your horses and follow me to the stables." He motioned and quickly each of us retrieved our reins from Sandy and Sarah Jane and followed him across the grounds among the tall trees.

We approached a long building whose back side adjoined the wall around the complex. In the fading light, we could see over a dozen wide doors, all shut. This was the largest stable any of us had ever seen. As if right on cue, when Alabaster approached a door, it opened pouring lantern light out upon us all. A silhouetted, tall man came out. "Big Jim will look after your horses. Just get your things and leave them in his care. There is no finer horseman that Big Jim Thompson to be found anywhere in the Greenway." One by one, we did as he bade, fetching our two large sacks and the saddlebags, handing the reins to Big Jim who stood at least six-six. When we all had our things, Alabaster led us back the way we had come and over to the large stone building that we had first seen. On the way, large snowflakes descended upon us. Alabaster commented mostly to himself, "Martha was right; it is going to snow tonight." Thus, we arrived at long last in Calgary.

Chapter 8 The Short Calgary Year

This main building was built of stone; none of us had seen such a finely crafted building before. We entered a well-lit hallway with many pegs for hanging cloaks and such. Alabaster hung his cloak and bade us hang ours too. We also deposited our sacks and bags there as well. Numerous doors opened off this long hall entranceway. Standing by the nearest one was a middle aged woman, rather portly with long black hair with streaks of grey showing. She had an eternal smile on her face, Martha.

Her voice was matronly, "Al, are these the ones?" He nodded and she quickly added, "Come right this way. I have a late supper prepared for you. We've been expecting you. I'm Martha Lindwood, Loremaster." We followed Alabaster and Martha into the spacious dining room. A huge long table dominated the room. It could seat two dozen at one time. Places for us had been neatly arranged near one end. Along the side wall to our right as we entered were a number of wash basins. Martha added, "You may like to wash up first. Help yourselves." Turning to face Alabaster, she said, "Come here and sit a spell. That has surely tired you out." Quietly, he sat down, rather heavily I thought." We washed and took our seats.

Martha rang a small hand bell, and quickly three young women came bustling into the room. All wore similar clothes, the house servants, we discovered. In minutes, we had a large steaming meal spread before us. While we ate, Martha dismissed the servants but noticed Al was nearly asleep. She said gently to him, "Al, why don't you go to bed now. I can handle it from here. You know your body is quite tired."

He stirred and looked up at her, "Why, you don't say? Tired is it?" I noticed a playful twinkle in his eyes. "If you don't mind looking after the children, I believe I'll call it a day, Martha." To us he said, "I shall see you tomorrow morning. Until then, I leave you in the most capable hands of Martha here." He nodded and we did likewise. Slowly, he got up and shuffled out of the room.

When he was gone, Martha began talking rapidly. "Do you know who that was?" We obviously didn't, and she didn't wait for any of us to reply. "That," emphasizing the *that*, "was Alabaster Benjamin Crowley, the Wid of the Circle of All Greenway. But more importantly, he is the *founder* of the Guardians!" She paused briefly to let that sink into our consciousness. "Yes, he is very old indeed; he recently celebrated his two hundred thirty-eight birthday! It was Alabaster who created the entire Guardian group and the druwids."

I nearly choked on a piece of meat! I had been challenged to strike *him* with a lightning bolt! My companions looked at me with similar reactions. Before we could say anything, she continued along. "Dear children, don't worry. Nothing you could do could possibly have harmed old Alabaster. He was just testing you, so don't fret about that. He was terribly worried Bethany here might be another rogue. He has had quite a time dealing with Erline Herbiscus. You have heard about her?" We nodded; I had been terrified I'd become another like her until I gained control over the black energies. "Of course, Alabaster could have put an end to her at any time, but he always says 'Martha, she, like every other being on Tarra, has their place in life, their role to play. It's not our place to play Nature and say who shall live and who shall die.' Be that as it may, he had to be sure of you, Bethany. I'm sure you did just fine or he wouldn't have brought you all inside, so put such thoughts out of your minds."

She continued right along, "You see, we have been following your journey here ever since Willow notified Mary Ann of your hasty departure. You were never in any real danger that you couldn't handle. Should any have showed up, why, another Guardian was always nearby, keeping out of sight."

"You mean someone was following us all the way here?" blurted out Roy rather perplexed. I know he hadn't detected anyone following us. He had been very careful.

"Following you is not the right word, more like shadowing your progress. No one druwid could spare the time actually to follow you. We had planned for an adult to accompany you here, but that didn't work out, as you well know. As you passed from one Guardian zone into another, various Circle members checked up on you and reported the news eventually back to Alabaster. There is very little of importance happening anywhere in the Greenway that Alabaster does not know about fully. And I might add, Bethany, that your decision to tag along with the musicians was a brilliant one. He even chuckled when he heard about that. He said to me, 'A true Wid that Bethany! A true Wid.' You see, you turned the otherwise dull journey into a three week course in learning the traditional music and dance of Greenway. I think it pleased him very much."

"So anyway, where was I? Oh yes, so we knew just when you would arrive. He walked out to meet you about a minute before you got here. I was spying on him from a window, but don't tell him that. He takes a good deal of looking after these days. Anyhow, you are here now, safe and sound. Mind you, this is the very first time that we've ever had such a young complete Circle here. It's quite an honor for you all. Now I expect you are all tired. I have separate rooms for each of you. Yes, as you might expect, the seven sleeping rooms are small and have an adjoining common room where you can all meet together, and even a restroom with a bath and an indoor latrine. Alabaster has made this one fine complex indeed."

"Oh yes, if you need anything at all, just pull on the bell rope dangling from the ceiling contraption. It rings a bell in the servant's quarters, and someone will be there directly." She rang her hand bell, and a young girl not much older than me came at once. "Suzie will lead you to your rooms. Breakfast is at seven; follow your noses here. After breakfast, you'll meet with Alabaster and the rest of our Circle of All Greenway." She frowned and muttered to herself, "After all these years, I still don't like our name. Surely, we could have picked something better!"

None of us dared to ask any questions for fear of having to listen for another hour. Besides, now that we were stuffed, weariness seeped over us. Dutifully, we followed Suzie back to the entrance hall, gathered our gear, and walked on down the long corridor. At the very end, she opened a door and led us into a grand living room nearly forty feet square. Couches, tables, chairs, lanterns, and a crackling fire — more than the comforts of home. This was to be our common room for the coming year. One door from the room led to a large bathroom and the other seven led to small adjoining bedrooms. We each took one, piled our stuff into a corner intending to leave the unpacking for the morning. The bed was a luxury I had never before experienced. Made of wood, it had a soft straw-stuffed mattress and clean sheets with many covers. As I snuggled into bed, I felt as if I was in heaven; such luxury. I slept like a log.

We were up at the crack of dawn, refreshed and full of curiosity about our new quarters. While the small bedrooms had no heat, the warmth of the common room's fire provided some, especially if we left our doors open at night. In each room, we had a small, hand-carved dresser in which to store our few belongings. It didn't take us long to unpack. Soon, we were all exploring the bathroom. An indoor bathroom was a novelty to us all; we'd never heard of one. Against one side was a latrine and in the center was a huge barrel in which to bathe. A cabinet on the other side held towels, soap, and a washbasin.

However, the huge barrel contraption baffled us. A pipe hung down above it with a nozzle on its end. Raphael pointed out that there apparently was a fireplace, albeit a small one located directly beneath the barrel. A rock layer between the two would keep the barrel from burning. He pointed out the small stack of wood piled in a corner. "I'll bet we can take a hot bath," he predicted. I rang the bell for a servant.

Shortly, Suzie came into the common room, and we asked her how the bath system worked. "It's already got clean water in it; I saw to it yesterday," she explained. When it is too dirty to use, open the drain plug in the bottom here, and the water goes down this channel into the latrine. Then, shut the plug and open this one hanging down; it brings in fresh water from the cistern, which gets filled by the rains. Once it is full enough, light the fire under it. When the water is warm enough, hop in. Actually, this is one terrific invention of Master Alabaster's. We've got one in the servant's commons, and on my day off, Saturday, I love to spend an hour just soaking in the hot water. It is fabulous! Oh yes, just leave any dirty clothes you want washed outside your bedroom doors at night. One of us will come by and collect them and see that they get clean." We thanked her and then began trying to determine who got to use it first. In the end, we girls won out. Since we had to be ready for the breakfast at seven, we bathed quickly. When I was done, my comment was, "Now that *is* great!"

So by seven, we entered the dining room freshly bathed with clean underclothes. We still wore our rather dirty leather outfits, since we had no others. This time, seven were seated around the table, Alabaster and Martha were there; the other five we assumed must be the others in this Circle. We seven sat down opposite this Circle just as we were accustomed to do back in Karka. The others had been chatting but had stopped when we entered. Silence seemed a bit daunting to me as we sat down. Fortunately, Martha rang her bell, and a flurry of servants came bringing in the food. Once we had been served and left alone once more, Alabaster began, "Hum, good toast as usual. Ah, now then, introductions are in order. Lightning Circle, this is the All Greenway Circle. I'm the Wid; Martha, the Loremaster. I'm told for reasons of future security, the other members of the Circle wish to be known to you only by aliases. The reason for the security is not yet known to you and will not be for some time yet, if all goes as planned. These are the names they've informed me that they wish to be called: Protector Finch, Planner Pete, Healer Wilma, Judger Jane, and Able Communicator." Each nodded as they were introduced.

Protector Finch was a muscular, middle aged man, strong boned, with eyes of steel. Here was a man not to be trifled with, if you valued your skin. From his countenance, we presumed he was a no-nonsense type person. Planner Pete was a younger man with red hair and bright eyes that seemed almost playful. He always wore a smile and as time went on, always was optimistic, we observed. Healer Wilma was, as expected, a practical woman also middle aged and slightly overweight. The smell of herbs was strong whenever we were in her vicinity. Her face was always stone-cold and hard to read. She never smiled, at least in our presence. Secretly, I was glad she was not our matron instead of the good-natured Martha. Judger Jane was a younger woman in her twenties with long blonde hair and fair complexion. Of all, she was the best dressed and always wore the finest clothes, we discovered. She was big on making the right first impression on everyone. Finally, Able Communicator was a very small man, perhaps barely five feet tall and very thin for his size. Of all of them, he was the least likely looking candidate for a Guardian. Nothing about his bearing or looks would lead one to suspect he held power. On the contrary, he was the type of person who could get utterly lost in even a small crowd. In fact, we almost never realized he was present.

Alabaster continued, after taking a sip of his herbal tea to wash down the toast with honey, "Now, with the formalities out of the way, let me explain why you're here. We're in a pivotal time. Change is in the air. Ten years from now, things in the Greenway will not be as they are today. I'm talking politically now. The small matter of King Randolf is but a minor event. There are much more powerful forces about to swoop down upon us all. I have waited nearly fifty years for a Circle such as yours to develop. Now that you've come, time, unfortunately, is against us. I've summoned you here for very special training that has been given to no other Circle, as it will be to yours. If you all pass, and only if all pass, then I'll entrust you with a secret mission, which may mean survival or destruction of all Guardians." We gasped in unison; we had no idea something was threatening us all.

"The training will last until spring. Protector Finch will train you to survive all obstacles that large cities and extensive traveling may present to you. Planner Pete will show you how other lands operate and how to get around in foreign lands. Judger Jane will educate you in the religions of the world, which you must know well if you are to succeed in the mission. Able Communicator will hone your telepathy skills and help you learn the rudiments of several other languages. I will show you how to defend yourselves from bolts from the sky and such. Timing has become critical. You have five months to learn all these, no more. If you all are successful, at that time, you'll be fully briefed on the mission, which I might add, will certainly be a most perilous one. It is entirely possible you will not ever return from it. However, Planner Pete has assured me that if you all can pass these subjects, then your chance of success is actually acceptable. However, as always, if you should choose of your own free will not to undertake this mission, your decision will be accepted, though not appreciated. There simply is no time left to find any other Circle that would have even half the chance of success that the Lightning Circle has, according to Planner Pete. Any questions? I keep forgetting to ask that."

We were awfully silent. All this was completely unexpected news to us. However, I ventured one, "Wid Alabaster, please, I do have one that has been bothering me for a long time now. Why us? What is so special about the Lightning Circle that other Circles don't have? I don't think any of us understands this. I'm barely of age; we're all young and frankly inexperienced. We didn't even know we were being monitored by other Guardians all during our trip here from Karka. Surely, other Circles are far more experienced, far more capable than us. We're only rushed tenth year apprentices."

To my amazement, it was Judger Jane that replied, not Alabaster, who only smiled at me. "Bethany, by the way, I like the name change, three syllables sounds more musical. Let me ask you a frank question. If you saw that Roy was about to be killed and you had but one second in which you could intervene and sacrifice your life for his so that he could live, would you do it?"

"Of course, what has that to do with it?" I answered not getting her point.

"Roy, last night, you showed you were perfectly willing to protect Bethany, no matter the cost, correct? You showed not even the slightest hesitation, right?"

"Well, yes, she *is* our Wid. That's my function," he replied also baffled. *How could we not want to protect each? What is her point?*

"How about the rest of you? Suppose Bethany was in dire trouble, would you hesitate even for a second to protect her at the risk of your own life?"

"Of course not," spoke up Sarah Jane. "Actually, I'd protect anyone in our Circle. We are all one. Like Ellen, I can always get a new body though I'd prefer not to have a male one," she added as an afterthought. We chuckled amongst ourselves; none of us could imagine pretty, flirty Sarah Jane occupying a male body.

"This is precisely the point," Judger Jane went on, "couple that sense of preservation with your intense mental bonding by Bethany, and you have a combination that has never occurred among all existing Circles. You see the rest of us have an inherent hesitation before we act — an attempt to think it through. Perhaps, we are more selfish than you seven are. While every Circle's members are usually very close friends, very, very few have bonded as you have. Even then, it usually is only a bond between a couple members of a Circle — never the entire Circle. The Lightning Circle has the tightest bonding of any Circle in existence. You seven are very special in that regard. To succeed in the upcoming mission, we feel those two features will be the key to its success or failure."

Suddenly in each of our minds, the thought appeared, *Do you often know what the other is thinking before they say or do something?* Startled, we glanced at Able Communicator, who merely smiled pleasantly back at us. We laughed and answered in unison, "Yes." He nodded his head to one side implying, "See, I told you so."

Then, surprisingly the stern Healer Wilma added dryly, "You share a bonding that is often found in sets of identical twins." Though she said no more, her words gave us something to ponder later.

Alabaster regained control of his meeting, "Where you are likely to go is well beyond my range of control. You'll be completely on your own, so do take this intensive training to heart. It's the best we can offer you. Protector Finch's task will be the hardest and longest to fulfill, so you'll spend every morning under his tutelage. In the afternoon, the rest of us will instruct you on alternate days. Finally, Martha informs me that you need more clothing and winter garb as well. This afternoon, she'll take you shopping at my expense. Sarah Jane, please do not pick out the most expensive dresses money can buy." It was a tease, but she blushed anyway.

Judger Jane interjected, "Gosh, Alabaster, I thought all three girls should only have the very finest clothes your money can buy. You want them to make a really good impression on men, right?" Everyone laughed at her parody, even Alabaster.

He winked at Sarah Jane, "A pretty woman always attracts a man's attention. It is a good way to gain some control over men." He added, "If only all men would look after their women, we wouldn't be in the mess we are in today, but I fear my body is falling asleep after this wonderful breakfast. We should adjourn. I leave you in the care of Protector Finch for the rest of the morning." With that, the meeting abruptly ended; all, save Protector Finch, left.

When we were finally alone, he explained, "Normally, I train only one person at a time, but in your case, it must be all of you at once. So let's get to it. Follow me to the training room." We did as instructed. I hoped we wouldn't have to learn more fighting skills. There waiting for us was his Protector in training, a young lad about our age, lean and skinny. "Allow me to introduce Frank, my apprentice. He is going to help with your training."

Protector Finch began by saying, "In large cities like Calgary, many unsavory people exist, such as pickpockets and outright thieves. Many others would take advantage of newcomers if given half a chance. You must know how they operate, how to nullify their attempts, and how to handle them should they steal something. Most cities have laws and regulations regarding acceptable behavior, which these folks do not follow, but which you must." As he spoke, he walked among us, "Excuse me Sarah Jane," he apologized for bumping into her, and as he backed up, he nearly stumbled over Roy and me. In an apparent attempt to break the possible fall of his mentor, Frank rushed among us jostling several more of us.

"Like taking candy sticks from babies," Frank stated, as both he and Filch move apart from us.

"Ah, I see I have managed to acquire your coin pouch, Sarah Jane," Filch pointed out her leather bag now in his hand. "And I seem to have Roy's knife, as well as Bethany's. Frank has two other daggers. You see, you've just been pickpocketed by unsavory characters and didn't even know it occurred."

Our jaws dropped in complete amazement. "I didn't see or feel anything. That was really good," I commented. Thus, began four grueling weeks of anti-theft training. Yes, we got very good at detection and ways to prevent sleight of hand tricks. It took eight weeks for us all to master the retrieval of stolen items trick. To do so, we all had to learn a bit of conjuring and mind control, which is the specialty of a Judger. Simon, of course, was already a master of many of these spell and had them down pat after only a week. He spent his time helping the rest of us learn how to do this.

That first afternoon in Calgary was particularly enjoyable for us. We went shopping for new clothes and gear we would need. What a luxury to just be able to walk into a shop and trade some coins for ready-made, quality items that we did not have to spend time making! Alabaster wanted us to have two sets of leather traveling outer clothes and several sets of undergarments. He also wanted us to have a very nice set of formal clothes, the kind that we could wear to a town dance or get-together. We three girls bought very nice dresses, nearly the same patterns, except Sarah Jane's was cut a bit too low in the front, exposing a bit more of her bosom than either Sandy or I thought prudent, but that was Sarah Jane. The boys had very proper looking black suits. Plus, we got some really warn winter parkas, boots and gloves. I suspected some of our training would be out in the snow.

During our time in Calgary, Raphael spent nearly all of his free time studying the design of Alabaster's magnificent stone complex. He carefully measured every inch of the buildings, made drawings of the way the stones fit tightly together, and even discovered several secret passageways, which Alabaster asked him to pretend he had not found. Raphael kept telling us that one day he was going to build us a stone complex every bit as good as this one. I didn't doubt that he would. He was a Planner by nature.

In contrast, the time we spent with Planner Pete was more enjoyable. He told us all that was currently known about customs of other countries of

Tarra, along with modes of transportation — pros and cons. His idea was to give us enough information that no matter where we should travel, we always would have good ideas of the available ways and means. This would later serve us well.

Able Communicator worked with us to enhance our native telepathic ability. That ability varied widely among us. The passing level was the ability to send and receive a lengthy message to another member of our Circle other than Sandy, who naturally already could do this with total ease. Poor Thomas, our Loremaster, had the greatest difficulty with this and Roy, our Protector, was only slightly better at it. In the end, they passed only because they could send and receive from me, though the more Thomas practiced it, the better he became. In fact, when Able Communicator was finished with me, he told me that I possessed the skill level of many other Circle's Communicators. I was very pleased to hear that because that was one thing I'd really wanted to learn how to do ever since I discovered some could do it.

On the other hand, what he was able to accomplish with Sandy was remarkable. Always before, Sandy had to concentrate really hard in order to connect with others. Now, she could do it while being otherwise completely occupied with other tasks! We later found out that was precisely the passing skill level needed by our Communicator! Sandy was exceedingly pleased with her increased abilities.

Next, Able Communicator began teaching us some basics of several other languages. One was the dialect most often spoken in the lands of the Seven Sea Princes. One was that which was spoken on Megalos. The third was what was spoken by the nomadic tribes of the eastern semi-desert land of Juda Arad. When we began language lessons, Able Communicator apologized, "Please realize I have never been to any of these lands. So my accent, voice inflections, and maybe even the pronunciations are incorrect. With luck, you can get by if need be. Many ships of the Sea Princes dock in Calgary, though none in wintertime. They sometimes bring travelers from these other lands, and I learn as much as I can from them. If you can learn about five hundred basic words in these languages, Alabaster feels you can manage from there. So let's get to work." Work it was. We spent the remainder of our time in Calgary on afternoon language sessions. Naturally, we speculated on why Alabaster was having us learn these languages. That we might actually go to these lands never occurred to us.

However, the training from Alabaster was nothing short of remarkable. On our very first afternoon training session with him, outside in a freezing snowstorm, he explained the passing skill level. "You each pass when I can bring down fire, ice and lightning bolts upon you, and they do you no harm." I stared dumbfounded at him; seven puffs of frosty breaths billowed from our open mouths. Sarah Jane and Sandy nearly fainted. Roy and Simon caught them just in time!

"You can't mean that," protested Roy, as he helped Sandy regain her feet, letting her lean on him for support. "That's not possible, is it?"

"What I'm about to say is for your ears and your ears alone," he spoke in a hushed, serious tone. I wondered why; we were outside in the open yard with no one else around. "Only one other druwid besides me can do this, and alas, her body passed away a good many years ago, and I have now lost track of her — my wife. So what I'm about to share with you is exceedingly special — it's something no other druwid or renegade can do." He paused in thought before continuing. One had the sense that he was far away, either in the past or possible future, we couldn't tell. "Yes, it may be that you'll one day have to face the wrath of a rogue druwid. If that happens, you mustn't be harmed." This was startling news to us all, and we immediately thought of the rogue Erline Herbiscus who dwelled to the east of our lands.

Thus began the most dangerous of all the training any of us had ever had! One goof and we would be burned, frozen, or electrocuted. Actually, I fared the best primarily because of my intense initiation into the black energy masses when I nearly went insane during the attack on us when we moved to Karka. In the case of lightning bolts, the trick was to spot the line that the other had created joining you to the energy mass and move it off you to another nearby spot. The only real problem is that you only have a tiny fraction of a second in which to move it.

None of us will ever forget his words said repeatedly to us, "Confront, face it. Do not flinch. Flinch and get hit." For me the key was just to face it, to confront it. Only then did I discover that I could easily embrace it. As soon as I could do so easily, it had no effect on me, as I could readily relocate the area of effect. Yes, I was the first to be able to stand still and let Alabaster call down great bolts from the sky trying to hit me, call down the fires of the sky upon me only to have them miss me slightly, and call down freezing ice, which ended up just to one side of my body. On that day, my six companions cheered me wildly, for they now saw this could be done! I set the example, and they followed in my steps. True, Roy was the last to pass. Even though it took all winter, but he finally did pass.

On the night we passed, Alabaster held a private celebration in our honor. The others in his own Circle were very much impressed with us. We could now do something that even they could not. The result was the Lightning Circle gained the highest respect from the other six of the All Greenway Circle. During the party, Alabaster cautioned us, "Be very, very careful to whom you teach this skill. If this fell into the wrong hands, it could be devastating to the Guardian's movement."

During the party, we played songs and performed the dances we'd learned from the traveling musicians. In fact, Alabaster treated us with mead, and it was the first time in my young life that I got drunk. All of us rather over drank; we seven regretted that the next morning! But we all had fun; we'd worked hard to learn this new and dangerous skill.

The training we received from Judger Jane was very different. No fighting, no danger, no super skill — just the religions of the lands of Tarra. We sat in the dining room sipping tea, a very nice change from the other training.

She began by asking, "What is religion?"

We shrugged, for none of us had ever given it much thought. "A belief in something?" suggested Sarah Jane.

"Ah, it's more than just that. You know you are immortal spirits, beings. Well, at least you're all aware of yourself as very different from your bodies." On that we all agreed. "Have you ever thought about where you came from originally? Who created you? Not your bodies, but you? Your bodies came from your mother's wombs, but where did you come from?"

I said, "I've tried to remember, but the earliest images I can recall are being a few years old and walking with the soft, powdery dirt coming up between my toes. Earlier than that, it is just all blackness." My companions chuckled, imagining me with fine dirt puffing up between my toes.

"I understand. Same here. Religion is belief in and worship of God or gods, a respect for what is sacred. We druwids believe that Nature is God. We see spiritual beings, and though we have looked in all directions, we can find no supreme being that is creating us. Rather we see Nature as being the sole creator of life, so it's natural that we worship Nature as God. You Bethany, when you first came here, sensed the nature of the circles of trees outside and were loathed to damage them when Alabaster ordered you to strike one with a bolt. We cannot harm Nature. We worship her and celebrate her seasons at the standing stones; we plot the course of heavenly bodies in the night sky and see Nature's patterns. Remember how you all felt when you saw the forests denuded of trees to build King Randolf's fortress? We druwids took that as a total insult to Nature." So far all this made sense to me.

"But what of the headers in Greenway, those that we have sworn to protect? They are stuck inside their body's heads and for the most part consider themselves not a spiritual being but a body. To them, the miracle of life, of birth, is most sacred. Much of what we know and understand of Nature is but a complete mystery to them. Out of ignorance, from our point of view, they elect the Sun as a god or the winds or the rains. Each of these seems to headers as the cause of all unexplained effects in their lives, and so they make sacrifices to the rain god so their fields get enough rain. They carve small idols in the rough shape of a pregnant woman's body and carefully leave it beside a sacred tree to gain favor from the goddess of fertility so they may have another child."

"So that's what mom and dad were doing with that wooden statue!" I exclaimed interrupting her. "Before mom became pregnant with my littlest brother, I saw her and dad making a little wooden statue. Later, they stole away from Uru to a stately oak tree and ceremoniously laid it on the grass beneath the tree. So they were trying to gain favor from the goddess of fertility! It now makes sense — er, there isn't such a goddess, is there?"

"You mother and father certainly believe there is. Religion is a *very* personal thing, Bethany. However, people live in communities, and they tend to find a common set of ideas on which they can all agree, right or wrong. In Greenway, a belief in a goddess of fertility is very common indeed, just as there is in a rain god. The people of Greenway believe in the sacred ability of the woman to create new life. Here women are treated as equals in all respects. In other lands, it is different. Who are we to tell them that they are wrong, that their gods and goddesses do not exist? How do we know they don't? For us, God is Nature. Bethany, your parents could no more convince you that your God, Nature, does not exist than you could convince them that their fertility goddess does not exist. Religion is a very personal thing."

"In other lands on Tarra, people believe in other gods and goddesses. Far to the distant south lies a land called Megalos. It is a land of eternal heat, I'm told. It is never cold; they have no winters as we know them, no snow, and no cold. So for them, what is real is the Sun. It is everywhere. They believe if the Sun God is angry, he burns their lands, and their crops wither. They believe that when the Sun God sleeps, the sky is dark or that rains come. They believe that there is an eternal war being played out between the Sun God and the elements. The Sun God is continually battling the elements on their behalf. Thus, if more sun is needed for the crops, they hold ceremonies for him hoping to appease him and make him work harder on their behalf. In their eyes, it is a crime for one to insult the Sun God for he may go dark for days letting torrential rains wash their crops away. You see how this could be?"

"Now just to the south of the Greenway across the Appian Range lie the lands of the Seven Sea Princes, whose ships sail the perilous oceans, trading with many peoples of Tarra. Their livelihood depends upon the sea. Thus, these people believe in the God of the Sea. They conduct elaborate ceremonies when a ship is about to depart, praying for calm seas and a fair wind to guide their ship on its journey. Should a storm come up and destroy the ship and its crew, they believe that someone connected with the ship has committed some heinous crime against the Sea God or insulted him badly. They seek out this person, and their justice is swift and violent, hoping to appease the Sea God. To us, this may seem a barbaric act indeed — a man discovered overcharging for the shipment is beheaded and thrown into the sea to appease the Sea God; we see it as Nature, not the merchant, but they are convinced they are right, just as we are."

"Judger Jane," broke in Sandy, "what do the Galts believe in or the Axemen from the far north?"

"Ah, the Galts. We really do not know. Our best guess is in some kind of Hunting God that provides for successful hunts — their food, but we just don't know for sure. Axemen, we know even less about," she answered.

"So for your own personal safety, as well as for your understanding of the people and their actions and customs, you must know about their religion before you enter their lands. Can you see why this is so?" We all agreed. Now that she had explained all this to us, it seemed rather obvious to us. She was not finished; she had one further point to make, a point that would echo down through the centuries for me personally.

"We recognize that life has seven aspects. Religion lies above all of these. Since religion is a very personal thing and is a thing, which is often used to explain that which is otherwise incomprehensible, religion can be abused and used by the unscrupulous to control and dominate whole groups of people. Can you see how this could be?"

It flashed through my mind like a hurricane, I blurted out, "Suppose I wanted a town to support me and give me money coins so I could buy anything I wanted. All I would have to do is convince the people that I had a direct connection to the Storm God. When I sense a storm coming, I go around and say to the villagers, you don't believe me, so tonight I'm asking the Storm God to strike this village. After the storm passes, the people look at me as if I'm holy and begin to give me the tokens. When the next storm is about to come, I pick out one disbeliever and say to the village, he there hasn't paid his dues to me; he has committed crimes against the Storm God. Thus, tonight, the wrath of the Storm God befalls on thee. After the storm — wow, think of the power and influence I'd command over these people!"

"I couldn't have said it better Bethany," she complimented me. "Yes, that's exactly the point. Now, Lightning Circle, it's precisely this, the abuse of religion, that the Guardians are actually fighting. That is our main enemy. While we heal and advise, our real enemy are those that use and abuse religion for their own subtle, self-centered purposes." All at once in our minds, the Guardians took on a completely different point of view.

"King Randolf is against us because he believes in a God of War, for whom the mightiest makes right and controls all. We stand for the opposite of that in which he believes. Hence, his attempt to kill Ellen and conquer the nearby towns under our protection makes sense and is predictable."

"Does that mean he will try to attack Karka again?" asked Sandy fearful for her parent's safety.

"Though he has suffered a significant setback, the answer is yes, he will try again. Our hope is it'll not be for several years, giving us time to prepare." She tried to put Sandy's mind at ease. "It'll take time for him to rebuild his might; he lost nearly one third of his entire force that day at Karka. He may not do so for another ten years, but you can be sure it's always festering in his mind."

"Why don't the women of Redun rebel against him?" I wondered. "Surely, if we are equals, why do they not stop him?"

"Ah, you presume wrongly, Bethany. King Randolf has years ago forced women into secondary roles in his kingdom. As we understand it, women are all but owned objects in Redun. I know that is hard to believe, but all evidence we have been able to gather points to this conclusion."

"Well, now that explains much about my parents," broke in Thomas, our quiet, unassuming Loremaster. "No wonder dad wanted to move us out of there and jumped at the first chance he had. He loves mom and treats her with the respect she deserves. Yet I've seen many other women that are as you said treated as if they were cows. Now it finally makes sense."

"But how did it get this way?" I wanted to know. "The King must be crazy, mad, and insane. How could a whole town let him get away with doing this?"

"We don't know exactly, Bethany. We believe it began quietly, while our attention was focused on the problem of the rogue druwid, Erline Herbiscus. In hindsight, it's our assumption now that he carefully chose the time to put his plans into action, that is, when our attention was directed elsewhere. It's now water over the beaver's dam, as we say. Ask rather, how can we restore the balance of Nature in his kingdom?" We all did, but She had no answer for us.

I don't want to leave you with the impression that all we teenagers did for the entire winter months was study from dawn to dusk. After the first few intensive weeks, we were given the Holy Day in Greenway, Saturday, off. On this day of the week, we could do anything we wanted. Three activities quickly became our usual pattern. In the mornings, we'd hitch up two horses to the big sleigh and go for a sleigh ride across the countryside. We bundled up and let the boys drive us all around the outskirts of Calgary. The snow-covered lands were a remarkable sight. In the afternoons, we usually split into three groups, exploring the shops and streets of Calgary. True, most weren't open because of the Holy Day and we really didn't have coins to spend, but we could gape, wish, and dream. None of us had ever been in a city this size; you can imagine the excitement, the thrill we had just exploring, seeing what was there and what was available.

Finally, we'd return home for dinner and to change into our dress clothes. Then by six p.m., we would head for the Blue Dance Hall. This huge building had a large wooden dance floor. On Saturday nights, you could expect to see nearly all the younger set of Calgary here. Musicians would play. Many would dance, while others sang. Courting also was commonplace. If you peeked in on a Saturday night, you'd see hundreds of teenagers thoroughly enjoying themselves, us included.

I learned some interesting things at the dances. Sarah Jane really was quite pretty, especially when she was dressed up. I quickly found out an attractive woman gains the attention of nearly every man in the place. Nearly every ten minutes, some lad would vie for her; not a night went by when some boy, often whom she had never met, would propose marriage to her. Sarah Jane was completely at ease with all this attention and cleverly knew just how to fend them off without hurting their feelings or making them feel foolish for having talked to her. While I never really thought of myself as being pretty, besides even my bosom was not yet really developed, I nevertheless soon found guys swooning over me. Sarah Jane took both Sandy and me under her wing, teaching us optimum ways to deal with all this attention. We definitely appreciated this, because we saw boys doing some of the stupidest things just to get our attention.

I also noticed Roy was jealous of me, and he always stood near to my side. Once I said, "Roy you don't have to watch over me here; go meet some of the really pretty girls."

He refused. "It's my job to protect you," he muttered, staring at the floor and shuffling his feet. He no more believed his reasoning than I did. Our eyes met and in a flash, I understood. He looked at me the same way that my dad looked at my mom. Roy was in love with me! I know my face must have been red; it felt so hot. Later, I told Sarah Jane and Sandy about it, and we had long talks late at night about love, marriage, and boys. I learned much but I won't bore you with a fourteen year olds fantasies.

I will say this. Sarah Jane was a flirt compared to Sandy and myself; we really were shy around boys. We learned her reasoning. "When you find the right one, you will know it. You will not be able to keep him out of your mind; your heart throbs and pounds when you are around him." She said a lot more but that gives you the picture. "So I am meeting as many guys as I can, hoping to meet the right one. How else can you do it?" Her method seemed a rapid way to meet many, many boys, that's for sure.

Some days later, I found myself alone in the dining room with Alabaster. We were sipping cups of herb tea. Neither of us could get to sleep that night. I asked, "You were close to your wife weren't you?" He looked up at my eyes; such tenderness was there. I sensed millions of pictures of her flying by in his mind. He nodded. I ventured, "What is 'love' anyway? Sarah Jane says that my heart will throb, and I won't be able to get him out of my mind. But that doesn't really tell me what love is. I know my mom and dad are in love. How will I know who is the one for me?"

For an instant, I saw him look at me as my father might. "Bethany, you already know what love is." For a second I felt like saying, "No I don't, or I wouldn't be asking," but I didn't. "Do you admire your mom and dad, even though they are headers, even though he is only a grower of plants and she just keeps the home running?"

"Of course, I don't care what they do in life as long as it isn't something bad," I replied.

"Do you respect them for who they are and what they are?"

"Well sure. I don't think any less of them just cause they are stuck in their heads and don't know all that I know."

"Well, child, that is love: admiration with respect. That's all there is to it. Jane, my wife, she wasn't pretty, but then neither am I. Doesn't mean I don't like to look at beauty when I see it. I used to sit by the fire at night watching her embroider. The look on her face, the way her long brown hair fell across her face — oh, did I ever admire her." His eyes were vacant for some time; I knew he was looking at cherished memories. I sensed how hard it was for him to still live without her around.

Slowly, he returned to the present, "Dear child, don't rush it. Love, respect, these things take time to develop. With Jane, when I first met her, I thought she was the most obstinate, self-serving, bossy woman I had ever come across. She was settling a dispute between two men over a hunting dog as I recall. She actually made both adults sit down in the middle of the town right in the dirt. Then, she brought out the dog and turned him loose. She demanded both stay quiet. Ownership she decided went to the man to whom the dog snuggled. At the time, I thought that was silly, but then I realized she was giving the dog, not the men, control over its life. Naturally, the dog went to the man that treated it the best. Interesting approach, earned my respect. So go slow, Bethany; you have your whole life ahead of you. I'm sure the right boy will come along in due time. Now, we both had better get some sleep or Martha will read us the riot act."

"She's a lot like Jane isn't she, Martha, I mean," I speculated aloud.

"Aye, that she is," was his soft reply as we left the dining room.

Raphael and I had another nighttime encounter with Alabaster some weeks later. Though it was the dead of winter, Raphael was still measuring and drawing his version of the layout of this huge complex. Evenings in our common room, he would discuss his findings with me. The others in our Circle were not interested in the design and the way this fine stone building was made, but I, always eager to learn, found myself fascinated by his calculations, measurements, observations on its construction, and the fine craftsmanship that went into its making. Weeks ago, we'd discussed how perfectly each stone meshed with its neighbors and had even visited a local stonemason's shop to learn how that fit was achieved.

This evening, Raphael had his measuring strings out showing me his latest discovery. Measuring strings consisted of a twig with various colored strings dangling from it. It was a basic counting and recording device. It recorded measurements by a series of knots located at integral knuckle distances down from the twig. The rightmost string stored the units. If you wanted to store nine, you measured down nine knuckle distances and tied a knot. For ten, the rightmost string had no knots and the one to its left had a knot one knuckle down from the twig. The leftmost string of the entire device held a short string, the calibration string. It had one knot located at one knuckle distance down. Raphael had many different colored strings, each one representing a different room or corridor.

"See here Bethany, the yellow is that entrance hall; the red is the dining room. The brown is the outside distance, accounting for the distance the windows are from the inside walls. Can you see anything wrong with these measurements?" He was challenging me. I knew he already had figured out something, which he considered extremely important or he wouldn't have so insistent that we talk right now.

I counted them carefully twice. I looked slightly puzzled. "They don't add up," I ventured trying not to sound completely ignorant. "Are you sure there isn't an error in these?"

"Precisely, Bethany. They don't add up. I've measured them four times now."

"There are six missing feet on the inside. How can that be?" I asked still confused. The numbers had to be wrong. According to the measurements, the outside distance was six feet larger than the inside dimensions. "Could the walls be six feet thick in here?"

"Hardly likely. That would be thicker than King Randolf's wooden fortress. No there must be another reason." He lowered his voice. "Speculation, Bethany?"

"Maybe a clothes closet or broom closet?" I whispered back. "Maybe we have just not yet seen it."

"Come on; let's take a look. I'll show you that there is no closet there." Together we slipped out of the commons and headed to the long entrance hall. We walked its length, but found no sign of any closet. He pointed out the entranceway into the dining room. Sure enough, it did seem odd, perhaps an optical illusion. Where did those six feet go? We walked into the deserted dining room over to the far wall. Together we paced the room's length, and then on out into the hall, and then into the adjoining study room.

"But that's not possible! I thought you said six feet are missing?" I exclaimed. From wall to wall we had indeed gotten the same measurements Raphael had gotten measuring the outside dimensions. He smiled and next had me measure each of the two room's internal dimensions and then that of the hallway. It was short six feet!

"I told you so," he said proud of his observations, and we went back to our commons to discuss this further.

"The only thing that can account for this is another room that we cannot see," Raphael theorized.

"If we allow some inches for the walls, that room can only be just over five feet wide. What kind of a room is only five feet wide?" I asked.

"It's most peculiar. Now look here, Bethany. I measured the upstairs rooms last week while I was helping them do some cleaning." He produced another measuring stick. Together we counted out the corresponding distances above us. "See, there is no discrepancy above, only on this floor. There's more. Here, look at this one, the basement storage areas." Again, we counted and came up six feet short once more.

"We are short below as well? Raphael how can this be? Two similar sized closets is a bit much to imagine. Everything else here is so orderly."

He whispered, "Only explanation that I can invent is some kind of secret passageway."

"Why are we whispering? Everyone else has gone to bed." I asked.

"Because we don't want the others to know, in case we're proved completely wrong. I'd rather not be embarrassed in front of Sarah Jane," he whispered back. I thought I spied a hint of red in his face. *Could he be interested in Sarah Jane?* I wondered. "What has me baffled is the narrow width of this hidden room, so small. It must be very long and covering two floors yet only enough for one person to walk, not even two abreast."

"Hey, a stairs is long and narrow," inspiration struck me. "Do you suppose that it is a hidden stairs? If so, it must go down."

"I think you have it! Yes, a stairs would be a perfect match. That would mean that it goes down to some place below the basement floor. Ah ha, an underground chamber! I think we have just discovered a secret of old Alabaster's. I wonder what is down there?"

"Well, if he wanted us to know about it, I'm sure he would have told us before now," I replied. "Gosh it's late. I'm hungry again. I'm going to go get something from the pantry off the dining room. Care to join me for some cheese and bread?"

He put his measuring sticks safely into his room, and together we walked toward the dining room. The little pantry opened off this room. Here they kept left over bread, drink, and other snacks so one didn't have to go all the way to the rear to the kitchen and main pantry.

The house was quite dark, and Raphael carried a small lantern. Everyone else was asleep in their rooms, we assumed, as we stole quietly down the long hallway. When we got to about six feet from the entrance to the dining room, we both stopped in our tracks. A crack of light shone from under the woodwork wall. We moved closer, scarcely daring to breathe. The wall itself seemed slightly broken. As we got closer, a section of the wall with pegs for cloaks was actually a secret door, and that door was slightly ajar. We stood there quietly smiling to ourselves. We were right. There was a secret door here.

"I wonder what's down there?" I whispered.

"Dunno, but let's take a peek. Maybe robbers or thieves breaking in here. That'll be our story," Raphael quickly conjured a good excuse for us to use in case we were caught. He pulled the door open wide enough for us to peer inside. Yes, there were steps leading downward. A dim light came from some side chamber far below. Raphael led the way, and we both snuck down the steps as quietly as we could. I counted forty-nine steps in all, the same number of oak trees that grew in the garden area outside the complex.

Like two mice, we peered around the open entrance to this side room. There was Alabaster studying a measuring stick similar to those of Raphael's. Without even turning around, he spoke, "Come in you two. Keeping this room a secret from you two is next to impossible. I wondered how long it would take you to discover it." We walked in sheepishly, but he turned and smiled. One smile from Alabaster put us totally at ease. Any apprehensions we had evaporated instantly. "Now that you are here, you can help me with these totals sticks." He handed us each a lengthy stick with dozens of different colored strings.

"Over here are the last ones to come in for this year. Bethany, you add these to yours, and Raphael, you add this other set here to yours." We did as we were told, carefully counting and then adding these to the totals sticks we held. "Now double check it." So we did it a second time.

Satisfied, he then had us untie all the knots in the other sticks. "These I'll be returning to their owners," he explained. "Now I suspect you both want an explanation." We nodded. The room was full of measuring sticks, all arranged neatly in some unfathomable order. What could he be counting in such numbers?

"Each year, the Guardians of the towns and villages under our protection send their yearly tallies to me. The black strings number those residents who had died. The red, the new births; the green, the number that have moved away; the brown, the number that have moved into that village during the year. It is a census of our population. Clever, if I so say so." He smiled at his invention.

"But what are the white and the yellow threads for? There seems to be only one each of them?" I asked.

"Ah, observant are we? They count the number of spiritual beings that are similar to us, those that reside outside and above their body's heads as we do. The white are new additions, the yellow are departed ones. Now you can see just how rare it is for a being here on Tarra to be not stuck in his or her head." We were both speechless. The numbers were shocking indeed. People like us were only a tiny minority at best!

"I've been keeping tabs on our population now for over a hundred and fifty years. What I'm about to share with you is not to go outside this room, do you understand?" He was using his serious voice, so there could be no doubts in our minds. We nodded, quite excited. What was going on?

"The Greenway population is most definitely growing rapidly," he said, showing us many sticks that spanned this huge time period. At first, growth was slow. About a hundred years ago, the growth rate suddenly shot way up and stayed that way, nearly constant from year to year. "Now what do you conclude, Wid Bethany?" he asked.

Suddenly, I found myself on the spot. "Well, I only really have Uru to base much on personally. At the beginning, the growth rate is what I would expect with the number of families and the number of babies we have each year. Does this mean that outside Uru families are having more than one baby a year? No, more like three or four. That's not possible. We must be getting many others moving here to the Greenway."

"Correct and yet not." Picking this year's totals stick, he showed us the total number of new people that moved in; these could have come from nearby towns like my family had done when we left Uru for Karka. We removed the number that moved out. "Yes, the only answer is that the Greenway is undergoing one terrific birth rate," Alabaster concluded. Next, he carefully got down another stick. This one with the pink strings represents the birth rate in the lands of the Sea Princes, as nearly as we can estimate based on what intelligence we have gathered and refined over the years. Our birthrate was more than four times that of our southern neighbors.

Raphael chuckled, "Well I guess that tells you if you want lots of children, why then you better marry a woman from the Greenway." I smiled, but Alabaster didn't seem amused by his comment.

"Raphael, you're completely missing the most vital point in the entire matter! Yes, the Greenway is getting many new people moving here from nearby lands. This is a much safer country in which to thrive. That is also not the point. I'll give you a hint, spiritual beings. Now then Bethany, what do you make of this?"

Once more, I was on the spot. Only this time he had given me a clue, a direction to ponder. "Well, each new arrival denotes a new spiritual being. Any way you look at it, we are getting many more spiritual beings here in Greenway than anywhere else."

"And what does that tell you?" he prodded.

My eyes lit up, I saw it! "If there are only a finite number of spiritual beings on Tarra, then for us to be gaining so many each year that can only mean the other countries and lands are losing them. They must be having huge numbers of people dying, in that case. Either that or new beings are continually arriving on Tarra from who knows where."

"Precisely Wid Bethany!" From the twinkle in his eyes, I knew I was on the right line of reasoning. He grabbed yet another stick. "Here is our best guess estimates of the death rates of the lands with which we have any contact. They show no such death rate. And the overall rates of beings like us druwids is fairly constant. We neither grow in numbers nor decrease; seems steady. Thus, my conclusion is a simple one. Spiritual beings are somehow flocking to Tarra and in record numbers these last hundred years."

Suddenly, all my myriad unanswered questions about beings came back to me. "But, but, but." I attempted to verbalize even one rather unsuccessfully, for they were flashing by in my mind so rapidly.

"Yes, one 'but' will do," teased Alabaster. "It does raise many questions. Where are all these beings coming from? Why here? Who is behind this migration of souls? Is there some unseen being that is creating us? Is this another aspect of Nature we know nothing about as yet? The list is endless. This is what I have been seeking answers to for all these many years. It is my personal quest and the main reason that I have kept this body alive far longer than it should have lived. After two hundred years, I still am no closer to the truth of the matter."

"My conclusions are many, based on the data. Tarra is gaining new beings from somewhere unknown at a rate of tens of thousands a year, maybe even in the hundreds of thousands. Jane, when she was alive, had a project going in which she sampled various people at random seeking to find their earliest memories in hopes we could get a glimpse of where all these originated. But like you, Bethany, it never got very far. People just seemed to run into a wall of blackness, forgetfulness perhaps. So either I'm on to a new aspect of Nature, the creation of beings, or someone, a god perhaps, is creating them for us, though we never see any signs of his presence, or someone else is bringing them here."

"I tend to discount some new aspect of Nature. We regard the union of a man and a woman that gives rise to a new life in the womb as a very sacred act of Nature. But even if this union somehow also created a new being for that new body, it still leaves tens of thousands of new beings wholly unaccounted for. I tend to discount that there is some god going around creating new beings by the wagon loads just for Tarra — we can detect no other signs of his existence. And for that reason, I tend to discount it. This of course leaves me with the conclusion that someone is bringing them here! While I have no direct evidence, I suspect this inflow is coming from somewhere south of

Greenway, coming up here."

Another aspect struck me, "You know, if our numbers are not growing, soon the sheer number of headers that we are looking after is going to be so huge that we cannot possible help that many."

"Not unless something happens that greatly reduces their numbers and does so in a very short time," he said seriously. "What kind of a thing can so swiftly reduce populations?"

"Oh that's easy," Raphael interjected, seeing a chance to redeem himself. "Many die in wars or in plagues or times of pestilence, which destroys our food supplies. The last two seem to be Nature at work. With wars, it is men. Are you saying that a bunch of major wars are coming?" We both grimaced at his idea.

Alabaster's face drooped; a great sadness filled his eyes. "Children, I have seen this coming for many years now. Yes, I feel strongly Tarra is soon to be embroiled in massive conflicts. We must do all we can to prevent it. Every side loses in a war; war has no real winners."

That started me thinking down an entirely different line. "You know, I think you are right about someone purposely bringing lots of new beings to Tarra. Next, they foment major wars. Many years must pass while the population rebuilds itself, only to start new wars. It'd be like some really sick game. If that is the purpose behind this great being, he sure is one really sick being!"

"Bethany, for a girl not yet fifteen, you have the insight and wisdom that many aged do not have! Yes, you have stated my worst nightmare, my worst fear. We have no proof this is what is happening here on Tarra. There could be other explanations we know nothing about. Still, if it were true, I would dedicate my entire existence to somehow putting an end to this insane game. The world would be a finer place without that sick one in control."

Solemnly, I promised, "Alabaster, I promise you that I'll devote as much of my life as I possibly can trying to seek answers to these questions!" I had really sick imaginings of some ghastly creature forcing my mom and dad here to Tarra, forcing them to have lots of children, only to force them all into some vast, senseless war in which they were all slain.

He looked at me for a minute without saying a word. "Bethany, I've been looking for someone to carry on this work for many years now. You are the one. One day in the future, all my resources will be yours to command in your search. However, again, it has gotten very late, and I'm starting to fall asleep on my feet. We had better discuss this another time. Come; let's leave these heavy matters for the day."

We climbed the forty-nine stairs; I noticed it was practically all that Alabaster could do to climb these stairs. Images of my last days with Ellen came unbidden to my mind. *I just cannot lose Alabaster too!*

Finally, in the spring of 559 AH our training was complete. During the Vernal Equinox celebrations, our Lightning Circle was formally christened. We were a full-fledged, operational unit. Our many years of study and training culminated at long last. Just outside of Calgary on a hilltop was the All Greenway Standing Stones. As the sun set marking the return of spring, we two Circles stood in reverence marking the special spot that the last rays of the setting sun illuminated. That location marked the arrival of equal days and nighttime hours. In the twilight, Alabaster spoke reverently the short speech he'd done over a hundred times before. "Nature we give unto thee yet another Circle of Guardians to serve you and mankind. Accept now the Lightning Circle. Guide them, comfort them, and protect them so they may do thy bidding for the benefit of all mankind."

Martha then presented each of us with a small ring with a delicate filigree oak cluster done in gold. "Accept now this token sealing your commitment to the Guardians." I must admit as she placed the ring on my finger, this was the proudest day of my life. My only regret was that my parents and family were not here to witness it. I think I speak for the others of the Lightning Circle when I say we were proud and honored to be accepted as full members of the Guardians.

The formalities lasted only a few minutes and then the fun began. Music and dance filled the early evening night for several hours. Once, while Roy was dancing with me he whispered, "See I told you we'd all make it — you in particular. We did it!" The happiness in his eyes demanded something from me, so I hugged him and gave him a little kiss on his cheek. He hugged me back. I found I rather liked him hugging me.

However, because of Alabaster's age and physical condition, we ended the celebration far earlier than normal. By nine that night, we were back inside the complex. He had fallen asleep on the long wagon ride back but awakened when we halted before his door. However, I heard Martha whisper to him, "I still think it is better to tell them in the morning. Let the children have this one night of happiness." Out of the corner of my eye, I distinctly saw him shake his head. Judger Jane whispered back to her, "We're running out of time. We can't delay any longer. You know that. They'll just have to understand." I knew something was afoot.

We entered the dining room and found cups of hot herb tea, warm biscuits, and cheese awaiting our arrival. As usual, the two Circles sat opposite each other. This time, care was taken to position each of us opposite our counterpart. I sat across from Alabaster, Roy from Protector Finch, and so on. I knew this formal arrangement meant something important was going to be discussed. It could only be our mission! I felt the others in my group reaching similar thoughts.

Alabaster barely tasted his food. "Lightning Circle, the time has come for me to outline your mission. We'll fully brief you on what is needed. Feel free to ask as many questions as you desire. However, you don't need to council among yourselves yet tonight. You can let us know your decision tomorrow night, whether you'll accept it or not." Here it comes, I thought. My legs felt weak, my stomach just a bit queasy, but my mind was keen to know.

"For some time now, I've known the Galts and Axemen were the least of our worries. The real threat to Greenway has yet to arrive, but it is coming as surely as the sun will rise tomorrow. Far to the south is Megalos with its relentless Centurion armies ever marching northward out of the Southlands. Years ago, they subdued the lands of Juda Arad. Since then, they have been pushing both north and westward. It is likely that their might has already invaded the southern regions of the Northern Steppes, home of the Galts. The extent of their penetration there is not known to us. Yet, we do know they have already begun conquering the eastern portions of the lands of the Seven Sea Princes. Once those two lands fall, the Greenway can't help but be next. Fortunately for us, the Appian Way range stretches along our southern border, which makes a realistic barrier for armies on foot. That has given us more time to prepare. We'll be invaded either from just south of Calgary where the mountains begin or from the east where Centurions would replace the Galts. My guess is the land of the Seven Sea Princes is a rich prize and that Megalos will conquer all of that before turning north to us. Calgary is but a few hundred miles from the border and will likely be the first major town to besieged. It is the only plan that makes military sense to me, at least."

"Thus, we desperately need to know all we can about Megalos, its plans, its army, its tactics, and its weaknesses — anything we can use to help defend our land. This, then, is your mission. To go first to the Sea Princes, find out what the situation is there, and learn all you can about these invaders. When you have gotten all that you deem likely, then you go on down into the Southlands doing the same. I want you to go all the way to Megalos and their great city of Galantas. Find out all you can. If there is anything you can do to delay their assault upon us, do so. If there is any way you can find to thwart their expansionist plans, do so. None of us expects that you alone will be able to stop their armies. Just do what you can to slow them down or even ignore us. Do your best to keep war from the Greenway or worse still from having our lands fall under the control of Megalos."

"Some years ago, I inserted two covert Circles — one into the Sea Princes and one into the Southlands. Both Circles have lost members already, particularly those in the Southlands. It is a very dangerous mission I'm asking you to perform. I believe other countries treat spies in very deadly manners. So as you go along, you may expect aid from these Circle members. To protect their identities as well as yours, we'll only send you the information on one of these operatives at a time. As you find out anything of even the slightest significance, report it at once to Able Communicator, and he'll relay it to me."

"Your cover story is that you are seven grain merchants from Calgary seeking to open up new markets for our corn and wheat. To that end, we have booked passage on the Lucky Lady, which sails from Calgary in a week on high tide, bound for the Velona, the westernmost Sea Prince city. The ship's captain, Bartoloma, is a friend of the druwids and will see you safely get into Velona and to your first contact, who now goes by the name of Luigi, the Net Maker. When you have learned all you can there, he'll assist you in gaining passage further up the coastline of the Sea Princes. Have I omitted any details?" he asked of his Circle.

Judger Jane spoke up, "Traveling money. You'll each be given a reasonable amount of coinage we hope will get you by without attracting too much attention. We'll attempt to arrange to have additional funds periodically sent to you as long as we can maintain some direct link to you. Finally, if something disastrous befalls one of you, we pledge your family will receive compensation and protection from us for as long as they live." While I was very glad to hear my family would be well taken care of I should not return from the mission, it was a scary, spooky, and ominous thought!

Martha had the last word, "Now go to your commons room and discuss the matter fully. In the morning, you may ask as many questions as you need. Only then do we expect your answer." With that, the other members somberly rose and quietly left.

Alabaster and I were the last two to leave the room. He caught my arm as I was near the door, "One more word, Wid Bethany." It seemed strange to hear him use my formal title. Our eyes met. "You have a secondary mission. Remember the secret chamber and the measuring sticks? Well, keep your eyes open for anything that may cast the light of understanding upon that critical matter. We know the influx of new beings is from the south and that is precisely where you are going. Let me know personally anything you find out; do not relay it via Able Communicator. He knows little to nothing about it. Let's keep this between us Wids." I agreed and then hurried to catch up to the others who were already in the commons.

When I arrived, Raphael was saying, "Well, Sarah Jane, it looks like I'll have to put on hold my intentions to build a magnificent stone complex like this one." He looked a bit dejected.

"It's only delayed a little while," she encouraged him. "I know I'll just love to live in it when you do get it built." Her eyes met his.

"Really?" he answered. Both saw me and fell quiet. The others turned to face me. I was on the spot once again.

"Ah, well," I began non-committal as I fell into a chair and pulled my feet up under me, tossing my hair back. I couldn't think of any more delaying actions. "I guess this mission is not exactly what I had in mind when I wanted to become a Guardian. I had always rather thought we'd get assigned some towns to protect, but it seems that view is just a bit too narrow. What do you think? Is the Greenway about to be invaded and conquered? Gosh, that would be just horrible."

Simon eagerly answered me, "Bethany, have we ever known the Guardians to be entirely wrong about anything? Mary Ann had King Randolf's intentions correctly identified; only her timing was way off. If Alabaster believes we face a powerful outside threat, I for one believe him. Who else could he send? Such a trip, while fraught with dangers, can only be done by younger druwids who have speed and agility to maneuver out of harm's way. Besides, none of us have any families of our own that would be jeopardized by our leaving for so a long time. I know we can do it!"

Sandy was watching him closely I noticed. She added, "We have to try anyway. If I can do anything that may help my family from being harmed by some crazy invaders, then I'm all for it."

Simon looked at Sandy and nodded, "Yes, I forgot about our families. Jeesh, we *have* to do something. Now that you've reminded me of that, Sandy, I have an urge to stay right here and help defend my own family like we did in Karka."

She replied, "There we knew all about the enemy and what they were likely to do, you know, their tactics and strategies. With these Centurions from Megalos, we haven't the faintest notion of how they think."

"I see your point," Simon responded, "We knew that Randolf's supply wagons were equipped for only a few days. We know nothing about these Centurions, not even how they fight. I almost get the feeling that the entire defense of the Greenway lies in our ability to find out these things firsthand, somehow."

"Hey everyone, there is another angle to all this as well," broke in Raphael who really was not interested so much in armies. "Think of all the really fancy cities, the buildings, and the people that we could meet. Why, the amount of new ideas we can bring back is staggering!"

Sarah Jane carried this idea onward, "Yes, think of all the different kinds of clothing we can see, the different customs, songs, dances — the people we may meet. This should be very exciting indeed."

Thomas, always the quiet one, catching Sarah Jane's enthusiasm, added, "Think of all the magnificent lands we'll see, the trees, the bushes, and the animals. This is what intrigues me. If nothing else, we can expand the knowledge of druwids fantastically in these areas. We gotta go on this trip!"

We chatted several more minutes exchanging similar ideas when I realized that Roy had not yet said even one word. This was not like him at all. I looked at him, and I could tell that something was troubling him. He shared none of the excitement of the others. No, he was reserved and almost in tears. "Hey everyone, hold on a minute here. Something is bothering Roy. We had better listen to what our Protector has to say." I tried to make it acceptable for him to let us know what was troubling him so deeply.

Fighting back the urge to cry, Roy said falteringly, "I — I don't know if I have the skills or ability to protect all of you. This mission has so many dangers in it, I'm almost afraid even to take the first step! I'm *only* sixteen. I've really actually been directly involved in just a handful of fights. What if I can't protect you? If something bad happened to any of you, especially Bethany, I don't think I could live with myself. Don't you realize this is not a picnic, a vacation, or a traveling sightseeing expedition? If anyone finds out we are spying on them, I guarantee you we'd be sentenced to death in short order! We're talking life and death here. I'm very afraid; heck I'm scared to death actually." His words sent our enthusiasm crashing into fear. My intuition told me that what I said next was of the utmost importance.

Speaking slowly, I backed him up, "Roy, you're absolutely right. I believe your attitude, your worries, and your fears are precisely the correct ones we should be having. We've already heard Alabaster say that several druwids he sent there years ago have been killed. We're going into hostile lands. Those people have a very different outlook on life than we do. I can't imagine a more dangerous undertaking, frankly. We *should* have a sense of fear about this. I think a little fear may sharpen our senses. However, Roy, none of us can possibly expect that you and you alone can be totally responsible for our safety. That is ridiculous; it's neigh on to impossible to expect you could or that any one Protector could do that. No, each of us must share that responsibility."

I continued, "But we do have one thing going in our favor. We're a team. We think and work together as a single unit. Haven't our mentors always told us that a team is stronger than a group of individuals? I believe that and that alone is our most powerful weapon of protection. I'm sure *that* is the one thing that offers us a good chance for survival; we're a team. Personally, I know I'm only about to be fifteen and that I lack the wisdom of most other Wids, so I'll be relying on you to help me understand things I don't get, follow, or see at first. Gee, I guess I'm already concluding that we have decided to go, to accept the mission."

That lightened the mood slightly, and everyone agreed we'd go and do our very best. That was never in doubt. Roy commented, "Yes, we have to go. There isn't any real choice in the matter as far as I'm concerned. It's just I'm scared; I'm afraid of failing you, especially you, Bethany, and not just because you are our Wid." The tone in his voice, the look in his eyes, to say nothing of his unspoken words, announced to me something that had until now just been in the back of my mind. Roy cared for me, cared for me personally, far more than just as a friend. If I weren't mistaken, I would hazard a guess that he was in love with me.

Sandy placed into my mind, *Bethany, he is in love with you! Can't you tell? Go easy on him.* My face flushed; it felt hot; my heart skipped a beat and then raced. I didn't know what to say or do. Sarah Jane did and came to my rescue.

She cleverly announced, "Well, it's settled. We're going. So why don't we all try and get some sleep? Bethany, you look a bit hot. Why don't you go for a walk, maybe get something to drink from the kitchen?" The others all got up and stretched. *Thank you Sarah Jane!* I thought.

"I'm a bit overheated. I think I will. Say Roy, want to accompany me to the dining room pantry?" I asked knowing he certainly would. Intentionally, my hand found his hand as we walked out of the commons. My whole body tingled with an excitement I had not known before.

By the time we got to the pantry and helped ourselves to some refreshing mead, I had cooled down and was back to normal. He and I sat beside each other and enjoyed chatting about the day's events. About ten minutes later, Sarah Jane and Raphael joined us. I noticed they were also holding hands. Further, shortly after they had gotten some mead and cheese,

Simon and Sandy wandered in; they were also holding onto each other. I now realized something I had not recognized before. Our Circle was becoming something more than just a Circle of close friends. A half hour later, all six of us walked slowly back and headed to bed. We all had dreams, most pleasant ones.

Chapter 9 Into the Lands of the Seven Sea Princes

The white sail billowed in the early morning breeze that came out over the water from inland. The Luck Lady slowly leaned to the left and then rolled over to the right as the combination of the outgoing tide and crosswind moved her out of the port of Calgary. We seven stood on deck, holding tightly onto the guardrail staring back at the magnificent view of the largest city in all of the Greenway. It was Monday, April 1, 559 AH, and we were on our way. All of us felt uneasy in our stomachs, we were cutting the thread that connected us to our home, the only way of life that we knew, embarking upon a vital mission.

The lean Captain Bartoloma Birtelli had been barking orders to his six crew members as they got underway. Now the hectic activity had died down. As he passed us he commented, "Homesick already? Don't worry. It'll pass in time." I tried to smile but I think I must have looked very pathetic. His cheery outlook was comforting.

These last few days since we accepted Alabaster's mission had been hectic. First, we spent time at Able Feed Company, getting to know the owner, Fergus Masters. Since we were to pretend we were his agents in the field, we needed to be seen with him a good deal. Alabaster was certain that agents from other lands were in Calgary and were watching. We had to make our cover look believable. In fact, we were actually allowed to setup new markets for his company. However, whenever we needed more coins for expenses, we only needed to relay a message to Fergus and he would send it by the next boat, in keeping with our "jobs" as his advance sales people.

In fact, Roy did manage to spot someone hiding in the shadows spying on us on three occasions. However, he never did get a good look at whoever it was. It was startling to find out that there were spies in our own city. "An eye opener," was the way Sarah Jane put it. From now on, our safety rested in our own hands, just a bit scary for me.

We each brought along three large sacks with our personal gear. We had our dress clothes, the leathers we wore and a spare set of leathers. Our weapons, for the most part, were also stored in one of the sacks. Following Alabaster's advice, we each carried two hundred coins divided into four portions and stored in various places. We girls had a terrific hiding place for two of these, a place the guys couldn't use. Additionally, I also had a small pouch of gemstones, which Alabaster assured me was worth more than all our coins together. His insurance policy, he declared. We each carried a seal from Fergus that denoted we were employees of Able Feed Company. All of us carried our long knives in their sheaths strapped to our legs just inside our boots. The guys also had their longer daggers around their waists. The larger weapons were stowed.

At Bartoloma's suggestion, we bought along a rain poncho. Our camping equipment, the tinderbox, oil lantern, and similar gear, we divided equally among our packs so one person didn't have to carry all of that. Additionally, we each had about a week's worth of dried rations to be used in an emergency. Alabaster had purchased our accommodations aboard the Luck Lady, so we had a place to stay and three meals a day provided during our voyage. Martha had also insisted on sending along a pouch of herbs that she claimed would help us recover if we came down with seasickness on the rolling ship. Fortunately, only Thomas got it; he was awfully greenish looking for a couple days and vomited quite a lot. I think Loremasters love the land not the sea.

Nevertheless, we all felt more than just a trifle sad during the hour that it took for the city to disappear behind us. It was humbling. It was scary. It was exciting. It was novel. It was forbidding. It was lonesome. It was all these and more. Yet we marveled at the new, expansive perspective of the city. From seaward, we could see it the way few others could. The great stone houses loomed large and grey as we left. Numerous chimneys curled smoke that spiraled into the clear blue April sky. Cobblestone streets ran at all angles around the hills and valleys. At first, we could see people bustling here and there going about their business, but they, too, soon shrunk into matchstick objects before disappearing altogether. Interestingly enough, we couldn't see the druwid complex that we stayed at all winter. It was always hidden behind a hill. Thomas thought he could see the tops of the forty-nine trees, though, as his hands gripped the guardrail with all the force he could muster.

Actually, we all held onto the guardrail. The swaying boat made even taking a step precarious. Bartoloma commented as he passed us, "You'll soon get your sea legs." We could not help hear the snide chuckles from several other crew members nearby. Since there wasn't anything actually for us to do, standing and watching Calgary slowly disappear seemed just the thing for us to do.

The Lucky Lady was seventy-five feet in length on the deck; Raphael measured it. She boasted two masts, each of which carried a huge square-rigged sail. To our eyes, myriad ropes ran seemingly in a chaotic pattern both fore and aft as well as to port and starboard. After a week of studying them, Raphael announced that he understood the purpose of each rope. I complimented him for they still seemed a maze to my eyes. The below deck was divided into four sections. The central cargo hold was by far the largest, but on this run, only half of the space was occupied by fifty-pound gain sacks bound for the Sea Princes. Our passage compensated Bartoloma for the loss of cargo on this run. The captain's quarters was a small room at the stern. The crew's quarters lay on either side of a narrow hall that led to the captain's room. The cooking, eating, lounging, and resting room was at the very front of the boat. Thus, we seven made our quarters in and among the cargo.

We were not sailing alone. A sister ship, the Lone Light, drafting low in the water, trailed us. She was captained by Georgio Musa. Both men worked for the same shipping company who actually owned the boats. We had met both while the ships were being loaded prior to our departure. The two men were a study in contrasts. Georgio, perhaps ten years older, seldom smiled. He constantly barked his orders in a manner that suggested his men were idiots, which they were not. He was greedy and slightly overweight. When he learned that Bartoloma was to carry passengers, Georgio took on some extra cargo. I watched him load another twenty sacks that were not on the initial loading orders. I estimated that was another thousand pounds of cargo. I should have followed my instincts when I spied that occurring, but I didn't and nearly lived to regret it.

Bartoloma, on the other hand, always seemed to find something to smile about, including us. He was slim with a large moustache and black eyes. From my point of view, he treated his crew as equals, never ordering in a domineering way; rather his orders were just a confirmation of what they expected to hear. I liked Bartoloma instantly.

Three other ships also left Calgary about the same time as we did. "Tide's up; time to go," was the explanation I got. It seems that at certain times, the offshore currents flowed more swiftly seaward. Wise sailors took advantage of this to speed their departure. The time of day also had something to do with it as I learned later. In the early mornings in the Greenway, the land was cooler than the sea; hence the winds blew out to sea — warm air rising pulling in the cold from the shore. By late afternoon, the land was the warmer, and the breezes blew landward, making it easier for these boats to dock. One ship sailed northward, while the other two also trailed us for a few days before dropping back.

One fact we learned rapidly. These ships, while they seemed huge to us, were coastal huggers. That is, they never sailed more than a few miles from sight of land. Bartoloma told us of the huge waves and immense sea monsters that lay further out to sea. "Besides, if you lose sight of land, how can you tell which direction to sail?" he explained. "Many a ship has been lost after they have lost sight of land for a lengthy time." When Thomas heard that, he urped over the side once more.

Within two hours, Calgary receded to a barely discernable dot on the rear horizon. The ship settled into its normal motions, and Bartoloma took us below to have some tea. Though cramped and very dingy below, we were grateful for the chance to chat with him and to begin giving Thomas his herbal remedy for his seasickness. We sat on barrels and talked.

"Well, yea all seem to me awfully young to go off traveling," he began. "Old Alabaster must think pretty highly of you."

"Yes, I think he does," I replied. "How long have you known him?"

"Well, I reckon about ten years now. Met him when I first landed in Calgary, fine old gentleman, honest and straight, if you take my meaning. I ne'er met a smarter fellow, I'll say that about 'em. Say, I take it you are all married? Three couples and an odd man?"

Taken completely by surprise with his assumption, I faltered, "Ah, no. None of us is married. Is that a problem?" I really didn't know what else to say and neither Sandy nor Sarah Jane jumped in to help me out. Perhaps they were as surprised as I by his question.

"Well, looks like I have one up on ol' Alabaster this time. Look, since I count him as one of my friends, I'll explain things to you. Different lands have different ways they live. Now up in the Greenway, women are as equals to men in all things, as near as I can tell. I think that's right, personally, seeing how they are the ones that bring new life into the world and nurture it. But the Sea Princes don't see it that way. Where you are headed, women are more like cattle, something a man owns. True, all land and buildings belong to the woman in theory, because many of us go out to sea for long periods and sometimes never return. In the lands of the Sea Princes, the man owns his wife just as he owns his boat or cows. She is supposed to look pretty, serve all his wishes when he is around, and look after the house and stuff while he is away. In the actually running of the towns and businesses, a woman has no voice, no say, just as a cow wouldn't. Therefore, your not being married may get you three into a lot of difficulties that you have never experienced where you come from. Customs where you are heading are very different for women."

Thank heavens Sarah Jane, the eldest of us women, came to my rescue, for I had no idea what to say. "Golly, how barbaric *are* these Sea Princes! Why do the women put up with all that? I know I would rebel instantly!" She faltered a second and added, "Except for the looking pretty part." Her huge grin defused the tenseness of the situation all around.

Bartoloma laughed. "No, Sarah Jane, I expect you are a real eye-catcher when you dress up. It's been this way forever, as far as I know. Guess they don't know any other way. Besides, what could a woman actually do to enforce such a change over the domineering men? I expect any that would try would just be beaten or worse still, just cast out and left to making a living selling her body to men. I figured Alabaster had explained all this to you, but then, maybe he doesn't know about this cultural detail. So none of you are married?"

"No, but we seven are all looking?" she teased him.

"Well, then a piece of advice from a seafaring friend: things would go a whole lot easier for you all if you were married or *seemed* that way." He stressed that word and raised his eyebrows.

I took that as a signal and asked, "Are you suggesting we could get along better if we just pretended to be married?"

"Aye, who's to know otherwise? You come from a foreign land. As long as you act like you are, then you are as far as everyone in these lands reckon it," he replied sincerely. He lowered his voice to a whisper. "Make it look good while you are onboard the Luck Lady. When we dock, while I trust all my lads, too much ale makes tongues wag, and there are plenty of ears that listen for news about strangers, if you take my meaning. I know Alabaster has sent you on some kind 'o mission, but what tis be none 'o my business. I know he means us no harm. He's the most helpful man I know of." Whether he would have said more, we did not know, for at that moment, one of his crew called for his assistance in taking a land bearing. He excused himself and left us staring at each other.

As Wid, it was my responsibility to lead. "If what he says is true about the culture in the lands of these Sea Princes, then perhaps we should heed his warning." The others, except Thomas, who hastily staggered back on deck to vomit over the side once more, nodded their concurrence. I smiled at Roy, "Well, Roy, how would you feel about you and me pretending to be married?" For some reason, my own heart skipped a beat as I held my breath anxiously waiting his reply.

His grin from ear to ear, gave his reply away even before he said a word, "Bethany, I would really love to be or pretend to be your husband!" For an instant, I suddenly saw the power that a woman had over a man.

Quickly, Sarah Jane asked, "How about you, Raphael, are you up to being my husband? We do think a lot alike, you know. We both have really big plans for the future?"

He let out a whoop, "You bet! I'm the luckiest guy around! You are the prettiest girl I've ever known, and we do think a lot alike. Beside, other than Bethany who listens only to learn, you are the only person who actually listens to all my great designs for the future. I say it is a match made in heaven for both of us." He would have continued, except that Sandy interrupted him.

"Simon, I'd be honored if you would pretend to be my husband," said Sandy rather shyly. "I've always thought you were really handsome. You are so tall, and I love the way your eyes never miss a thing."

"You got it, Sandy," he eagerly responded, "but I have to be honest with you, Sandy, I have had eyes for you, so to speak, for the last couple years. Only I never had the nerve to actually ask you outright."

Their eyes met, and she whispered, "Me too, Simon. I haven't had the guts to ask you either, though I have long wanted to."

"Hey, now that this has all worked out perfectly, I have a question. Just how far do we take this pretend business?" Roy asked bashfully. "I — I know we'll have to kiss each other and sleep beside each other. But. . ." he faltered. I picked up his intention at once.

"Right, Roy. We are on a lengthy, vital, and dangerous mission. This is no time to create and bear children. So under no circumstances do we go that far," I ordered.

"You men will just have to pay close attention to us women. We know when it's relatively safe and when it's not," Sarah Jane added.

I blushed, swallowed hard my embarrassment, and said, "I'm afraid that I don't, Sarah Jane. I'm only fifteen," I justified.

"Don't fret, Bethany. Give me five minutes with you alone in private, and you, too, will know. Guys, this is a woman thing," Sarah Jane replied so confidently that my embarrassment began to evaporate.

To my relief, Sandy added, "Can I listen too?" Hence, I knew that it was not just my own ignorance that was highlighted.

Roy, glancing at the others, answered for them, "We promise we will abide by your complete wishes in this at all times. What about poor Thomas? Won't he feel like he is being left out in the cold? Won't he become jealous of us six?"

Suddenly, I realized he had a critical point. If we six were going to be pretending to be married, that would leave him out of the "intimacy" and could lead to jealousy or worse. Sarah Jane eased our fears, "Not at all. I know he has a girlfriend back home. I don't know how serious they actually are, mind you. I do know that Thomas has never had any "eyes" for us three girls. I'm sure he's looking for someone who really loves Nature and the out-of-doors as much as he does. In fact, I don't believe he even thinks like any of the rest of us; I guess that is why he is our Loremaster."

At this point, something happened to me that I can't explain, though in quiet times, I have often reflected back upon this moment. The closest I can get to an explanation is that somehow in this brief instant, I caught a glimpse of our future. In my mind, I got an image of Thomas holding, hugging, and kissing a woman whom I had never seen. It was only a brief image, but a solid, vivid one, one that you cannot ignore or say you imagined. It was *so* real. On the other hand, I can't tell you just how startled I would become when we actually crossed paths with this woman for the first time later on.

This settled, while Sarah Jane discussed intimate matters with Sandy and me, the guys went to see about creating four separate "living areas" for us They were surprised to find the way that Bartoloma had stored the cargo had already created the basis for separate sleeping quarters. Stacks of grain bags made effective "walls," so there was very little they had to do to make our private spaces. Soon, we joined Thomas on deck.

Sarah Jane checked on his condition and found the herbal tea remedy was slowly beginning to have some effect on Thomas — either that or he had nothing left to vomit up. His voice was weak, but he did manage to say, "Look back over there. See that impressive green island? Someday, we just have to visit it. I feel drawn to it."

"That's the island of West Reach, Thomas," I explained. "I'm not sure it's even inhabited." We seven stared for quite a while at this slowly receding land mass of green. It was far greener that the Greenway. Evidently, spring somehow came sooner to that island.

Now the major problem that we faced on the long voyage was that of utter boredom. Used to high levels of training and activity, we seven had nothing to do except stare out at the sea or the coastline slowly moving by us on the port side.

Ten days into the voyage, the Lucky Lady approached the Narrows. Here, giant rocks formed a peninsula that stuck out into the ocean forming immense toadstools. Between the rocks, the sea surged wildly. Sailors had two choices, shoot the Narrows, or go around them. Bypassing them added nearly five additional days onto the already lengthy voyage and ran the risk of getting too far out to sea. If the winds failed, a ship could be forced even further off course or even lost. Thus, most captains chose to shoot the Narrows. All this Captain Bartoloma explained, as we watched the large rocks slowly appear far ahead of us.

However, April is the storm month in the Greenway ocean sector. Thus far, we had only encountered a few light squalls, but to starboard, we could see a major thunderstorm brewing. So did Bartoloma and so did Georgio. Bartoloma decreased the speed of the Lucky Lady so the Lone Light could catch up and pull alongside. The two captains held a brief conference; both had to shout just to be heard. "Big storm comin'," yelled Georgio.

"Tis a bad'un. Make Narrows darn near impossible to do. You ride'n awfully low. You okay?" Bartoloma yelled back. We could see the Lone Light was barely two feet above the waters.

"Okay for now. Big trouble if waves rise. Shores 'round here are no good for shelter."

"Sail back — ride it out or go around the Narrows?" hollered Bartoloma. I surmised if this bad storm hit us while we were going through the Narrows, the Lone Light riding so low might actually sink! Though we were a mile off shore, I could see only a rocky line marking the shore. If we tried to land, surely both boats would be crushed by the boulders or sunk by partially submerged rocks. Did he mean we could sail back the way we had come? Was he suggesting we change course ninety degrees, head out to sea, and straight into the incoming storm trying to go around the Narrows?

"No go around — takes too long. No go back. Shoot the Narrows anyway," yelled Georgio back. Evidently, Bartoloma didn't like this response. He frowned and uttered a profanity. Several of the crew, who were also watching and listening, agreed with their captain. Georgio was suggesting a foolhardy move. The two argued back and forth for a few minutes before Georgio insisted, "Shoot 'em. We'll make it. Likely beat the storm to the Narrows."

Since Georgio showed no signs of giving in, Bartoloma reluctantly did. "Okay, we'll pull out in front. Follow our wake." He turned to his crew and spoke softly, "Pull ahead a thousand yards." His crew didn't actually need to be told what to do. They had already begun making the adjustments in the sails.

Turning to us, he said, "Nothing to worry about, at least for us. We are high in the water. Storm waves won't bother us much, but the Narrows will be heaving and surging. I think Georgio made a bad call. He runs a real risk of losing his ship. When the storm hits, you all go below. I don't want any of you being washed overboard. There'll be no way to recover you." We agreed and went to starboard to watch the approaching storm.

Lightning flashed in the distance. I estimated it was still five miles off, the seas already began heaving more so than normal. Thomas immediately went below and laid down on his bed moaning something about dying at sea. Simon said to me, "Bethany, the cross winds are making forward motion slow. The storm's going to hit us long before we make the Narrows ahead. I estimate we're going to be battling the storm at least a half hour before the Narrows." I wanted to know how he figured this out; even Sarah Jane was curious. He happily explained his deductions to us, sketching a charcoal picture on the deck, pointing out the different factors. Both of us agreed with his reasoning. I seriously began to worry about our safety.

A mile away now — we druwids could easily tell just how far a storm was from us. Rain pummeled us, but thanks to Bartoloma's suggestion before we set sail, we had on our rain ponchos. We watched as one by one, each of the crew tied a heavy rope about their waists so if they were cast overboard, they would still be connected to the ship. Bartoloma lashed himself to the helm. He would personally steer the Lucky Lady through the Narrows. We needed no further indicator to head below deck to our beds. For safety, the crew had extinguished most of the lanterns. No sense fighting a fire in the middle of a storm. Couple that with the darkness of the storm, the cargo hold and our beds looked quite dim and foreboding.

For Thomas, it was pure hell. The great swells lifted the boat high into the air only to come crashing down at weird angles. We hugged our partners, as we rolled about in our beds. Frankly, I was becoming scared. I think the others were as well. The storm roared with violence around us. We were druwids and loved Nature's fury, but that was when we were on land and safe within our homes. Out here on the open sea, it was quite a different story.

Then Raphael yelled to us. "Hear that? We must be approaching the Narrows. I swear that's the sound of water smashing upon rocks!" Worse still, the Lucky Lady was now pitching wildly up and down, right and left in a chaos of motion. I felt awfully sick. "I've gotta see this!" he yelled and crawled over us to get to the stairs.

"Not without me!" yelled Sarah Jane, "I'm right behind you." Never in a million years would I have predicted that Sarah Jane would take such a risk. Clearly, she, like Raphael, didn't want to miss the chance to see what was really going on topside. Petrified, I clung hard to Roy who clung to me as we rolled first this way and then that way. Only with great difficulty did the two manage to gain the stairs and climb up enough to peer outside. They both clung solidly to each other and the railings on either side of the stairs.

The Narrows is a navigable passage through the peninsular extension of the Appian Way mountain range that separates the Greenway from the lands of the Sea Princes. Here where it meets the ocean, great mounds of rock protrude from the water like knobby knuckles on an enormous finger. Stretching out to sea some hundred miles, the knobs slowly grow smaller and less high above the surface. To go around them adds days of travel onto a journey. However, one safe passage has been learned by the mariners who sail the coastline, the Narrows. A scant passage only a hundred feet across between two enormous knobs of stone, the Narrows demands expert sailing to pass safely through during calm weather. This was anything but a calm passage!

"Oh my gods!" Sarah Jane exclaimed. "We're not going to make it! The waves are nearly sinking the Lone Light! The rocks are enormous! We are going to be smashed to bits!" Raphael did not say anything. His "wife" had said it all.

Her dire pronouncement stirred something deep within me, something I did not know I possessed. *I'm their Wid. I'm obligated to **do** something. The*

Weather — we must modify the storm. "Listen everyone, we must use our skills to lessen the storm; it's the only way. Everyone concentrate. Push the storm off us. Make the storm bypass us — go behind us!" I cried out at the top of my lungs. I didn't wait for the others to reply, but immediately began my weather chanting Ellen had long ago carefully taught me. Vaguely, I heard the others follow suit. I expanded my awareness far beyond my body and created a stillness, a peaceful tranquility around the whole area.

Ten minutes later, Roy commented, "It's working. We are not pitching so violently. The thunder is well over a mile from us now." I opened my eyes to see and feel for myself. What he said was true. The ship seemed calmer somehow. Slowly I crawled to the stairs. Raphael and Sarah Jane had returned to their beds I discovered. I climbed up, poked my head out, and could see Bartoloma gripping the tiller for dear life. His knuckles were white from the effort.

"How's this?" I yelled back to him. "Is this better? How's the Lone Light faring?"

"It's a miracle! Storm's all about us but not within a mile — keeps moving around us. We'll make it if it keeps up like this. Lone Light very nearly sunk. Now she's just able to keep pace. Think she'll make it if the weather holds like this through the Narrows."

"Okay, we'll keep it like this," I yelled back, shut the door, and crawled back to the clutches of Roy. We lay back down and continued our slight control over Nature. All we were really doing was deflecting the storm off from us for about a mile. That was just enough to remedy certain disaster.

Now the noise of the sea smashing violently on nearby rocks became deafening. Once again, Raphael and Sarah Jane just had to witness this for themselves, though while they looked out the hatchway, they maintained their storm pushing efforts. The noise went on for an hour unabated. I just clung to Roy, and he, to me. Outside, Raphael and Sarah Jane witnessed the tremendous surges of seawater over the immense boulders. It was quite a sight. Gigantic waves rose high in the air only to pause before coming crashing down upon the rocks. Finally, Raphael called out, "We're through the Narrows! So is the Lone Light. We've made it! What a sight! Fantastic! We gotta do that again sometime, right Sarah Jane?"

"You betcha! I feel *so* alive!" she exclaimed. Personally, I felt almost as sick as poor Thomas who had actually just passed out and missed the whole thing. However, the crashing noise was abating, lessening. I could hear it for myself. Now that horrible sound came from our rear, so I knew he was right. We were through the worst of it.

A half hour later, an incredible silence filled the air. Even the sea seemed to calm. The violent tossing subsided to almost an imperceptible motion. I took a deep breath and tried to stand only to find my legs most unwilling; they did not seem to be connected to my body anymore. Roy helped me to my feet, though he was faring only slightly better. One by one, we managed to pull and crawl our way topside.

The six crewmen lay sprawled on the deck, completely fatigued, resting. Bartoloma hung over the tiller like a wet blanket, beyond exhaustion. Behind our ship and trailing some thousand yards, we could see the Lone Light; she was listing badly to port at a crazy angle. Her two masts looked somehow wrongly positioned. Simon suggested she may have taken on water or perhaps her load of cargo had somehow moved out of its proper place. What caught my eyes was the sea — so calm it now was. Far to the rear, the picturesque thunderstorm raged inland, smashing its fury onto the shores of southern Greenway. All around us, the seas had calmed drastically. For a time, none of us moved; we just gazed back at what we had come through, the slowly receding Narrows.

Sarah Jane climbed out onto the deck to see if she could do any healing. "I don't think it is a good idea to just leave them lying there," she commented. The rest of us managed to get our legs operational and joined her. She first attended to Bartoloma. "Bethany, go back down, make a gallon of hot tea, and lace it heavily with honey or sugar if you can't find any. They need an energy boost. They're soaked to the skin and losing body heat. Be quick about it." I did as she asked.

Five minutes later, with Roy's help, I hoisted up a bucket steaming with the remedy and several cups. I found the others had wrapped the men in blankets and were rubbing various arms and legs, renewing circulation. Quickly, the tea was administered, and Bartoloma came back into the land of the living, teeth chattering uncontrollably for over a minute. When he could finally talk and after accepting his thanks, Raphael asked, "Should we take over for a while and steer some course while you and the others recover and warm up?"

"Aye, steer parallel to the coastline, my boy. That would be a welcome relief." He turned to see how the Lone Light was doing. He cursed. "Looks as if her masts have cracked!" He cursed once more. "Belay that last order. Raphael, can you and the others unfasten the sail lines? We need to fall back and come to her aid." Quickly, Raphael and Roy undid the lines, but only after figuring out which ones to loosen. I watched as our forward motion, slow as it was, subsided, and the Lone Light came up toward our stern.

It was now late afternoon, and the sun peeked out behind huge cumulonimbus clouds. Now, we could see she was listing, and her wooden masts were broken. Only the numerous ropes still held the two giant timbers semi-vertical. The crew was slowly coming round, amid the yelling orders of Georgio, who looked much the worst for wear. He'd nearly lost his ship and crew. The two captains yelled some ideas back and forth. In the end, both decided to put in to Tranton's Cove immediately for repairs.

"Raphael, tighten those ropes you loosened, take the tiller here, and steer toward that dark patch along the coast there." He pointed to a darkish area about five miles distant at a forty-five degree angle. "We're heading for a safe portage. We're going to have to make two new masts before we can continue." At the slow pace we were making, mostly for the sake of the Lone

Light, it was nearly dark when we rounded a bend near the coast and spied Tranton's Cove.

The cove was actually a tiny village of twenty-five people who made their living fishing and helping others repair damaged ships. Evidently, many ships needed repairs after passing the Narrows. Steep walls of green rose sharply on both sides of the sheltered cove. The ships could easily sail between them, and once inside the cove, it was safe to dock. Both ships pulled up on either side of one long wooden dock, which stretched fifty feet out into the water. Two large lanterns were lit; obviously, someone had spied us sailing here. A burly man waited patiently as both ships came to rest and mooring ropes were thrown and tied.

"Be need'n two masts, I see, Georgio," said the man, as the captain stepped off the Lone Light onto the dock.

"Hail, Franko. Well met. Yes, cracked by the storm. Can you fix us up?" he asked, now being very polite with Franko, unlike his earlier attitude toward his crew. They chatted, and we learned we were going to be stranded here nearly a week while the ship was repaired. The tiny village had more small boats moored to the docks than it had buildings! Only six dwellings comprised Tranton's Cove, and one was a fish-drying barn.

By now, it was dark, and all of us were hungry, so we relished the supper bell. Over the hastily made dinner, Bartoloma asked me, "That sure was a deadly storm, but a strange one. Forgive me if I'm out of line, but from what you said back there, did you do something to the storm? It was most peculiar, seemed to blow around us somehow."

I answered for us, "Yes, we sort of pushed it out of our way. I hope you didn't mind. It sure seemed to me that the Lone Light was about to be devoured by the waves."

"Well, bless you all, then!" he replied exuberantly. "You saved Georgio and his ship, that's for sure. He was too overloaded to deal with both the Narrows and the storm at the same time. Looks like I owe you a big favor. If you ever need anything, why, you've only got to ask." From that point on, Bartoloma held us in a higher respect than before.

The next day, Thomas went ashore and finally recovered from his seasickness. In fact, he slept ashore and even ate there, refusing to set foot back on the boat until we were ready to depart! I slipped Franko a gold coin, and he provided a bunk in one of the wooden houses for Thomas. I had no idea if I was overpaying him or not, but to give him a few good nights' sleep, I thought it well worth it.

The next few days, Simon, Raphael and Sarah Jane studied how the repairs were done to the Lone Light. The process fascinated all three. Sandy was bored and spent her time ashore chatting with the recovering Thomas and the local villagers. Roy and I, on the other hand, were fascinated with the land about us. Steep cliffs rose on all sides, save the inland side opposite the sea. Here, the land rose sharply but was climbable. The village was nestled in the valley of the cove.

Naturally, Roy and I had to go exploring, and one day we hiked up the backside of the cove. We soon found a trail that wound its way upward and followed it. Puffing, we finally made the top. The view was well worth the climb. Neither of us had ever seen the Appian Way close up, or mountains for that matter. First, we stood atop the cliffs that looked seaward. Magnificent. We could see for miles out to sea. To the northwest, the Narrows looked impressive, like a finger of a giant stretching far out to sea. We thought we could see the tiny opening that we had sailed through. We did spot six other ships sailing on either side of the Narrows.

Then, we turned our attention inland. The peaks of the Appian Way range here were only about a few thousand feet maximum. From the sea, the successive peaks rose higher and higher. Signs of spring were everywhere; new green growth dotted the peaks. Only the very tops of the highest, most distant ones still showed the white patches of snow, blending with the bluish-grey of the cold stone. We noticed one thing was missing: trees. Up and down the coast from Tranton's Cove, various trees grew tall and dense. However, once up at the level of the first foothills and from here on upward, trees were scarce. Nearer the tops of the taller mountains, only a kind of greenish bush grew. Curious, we set off inland down the next valley and up even higher to the next peak to get a closer look at these unusual plants.

Once we reached the start of the brush-covered terrain, foot passage became exceedingly difficult. The hills were quite rocky and boulder-filled with sharp, irregular edges. The twisting, gnarled shrubs fought for life by forcing their roots down tiny cracks in the granite stone. It was a harsh environment and one not easily traversed, certainly not on horseback. Upon reaching each successive crest, the panorama grew in beauty and splendor. We saw no signs of villages or habitations, just Nature in her raw, pristine condition, untouched by human hands. Both Roy and I were quite impressed and vowed to one day come back and fully explore this strange land.

It was just after lunch when we reached the crest of the sixth foothill heading inland. Puffing and panting from the exertion, we paused to catch our breaths. Just then, a young man, not much older than us, suddenly appeared from his hiding place behind a large boulder. He waived a sword menacingly at us. His unsteady, nervous voice bellowed, "Halt in the name of Count Basilica d'Grange. Identify yourselves!"

Dressed in leather pants tied loosely around his heavy boots and wearing a yellow cloth, long sleeved shirt with a red bandana holding back his long blonde hair, he didn't really look menacing to us. Hence, Roy didn't react. We both instantly recognized his dialect — that of the Sea Princes and Bartoloma. For the first time, I was thankful for the time spent learning the basics of this language. I replied as best I could, hoping my command of his language was good enough, "I'm Bethany, and this is Roy. We're passengers on the Lucky Lady back down there in the cove. They're repairing another ship; we hiked up here to see these magnificent mountains. We've never seen mountains before. The brush is very unique; we don't have plants like these back in the Greenway. We were just very curious, that's all. We didn't mean to frighten you or anyone else. The lands around here seem to be deserted. We're quite surprised to see another person. Do you live around here?" There, I calculated enough simple banter would defuse any alarm or worries this lad might have had with us, show him we meant him no harm, and that we trusted him. It worked.

"Well, you don't look like Centurions, though I will admit I've never seen one yet. My dad, the Count, says they are coming. We must be prepared; we must be vigilant; we must be always on the lookout for them." He sheathed his sword and stepped closer to us. I guessed he was about sixteen. "The Count — he's my dad. We have the biggest fortification in the whole West Rim. That's what this land is called, West Rim. He looked us over. "You do look rather like the Greenway travelers that occasionally visit dad, and your accent is pretty bad. My name is Leonardo d'Grange, eldest son of the Count. You can just call me Leo, if you like."

I smiled and wanted to say, "I figured as much," but didn't. "Say Leo, what do these nasty Centurions look like anyway?" I asked. "We've never seen any either." I thought that might be a good way to put him more at ease and give us some more information. Besides, my curiosity now was ballooning. There was a fortification out here somewhere, one that would be resisting the Centurion army. Allies. We needed allies. If Alabaster was right and the Centurions attempted to get into the Greenway, this area offered the path of least resistance. With Calgary being only perhaps a few hundred miles to the north, having allies here to bar the way would be ideal. I believe Roy also knew what I was thinking; he squeezed my hand reassuringly.

"Dad says he's heard they wear leather and metal armor and carry huge shields and spears. He says they are strong and relentless, like a swarm of ants. Already the easternmost city-state, Zargarb, has fallen, as well as the feisty city of Solamina. Rumor has it that Pieta is besieged even now, which maked Bonilla next, then Vito, Barcella and finally Velona. If Velona falls, then it's only a matter of time before they'll come after Fortress d'Grange." Leo's voice betrayed a great sadness; his face, the hopelessness of a destiny beyond his control, one he felt powerless to control.

I felt obligated to say something encouraging to Leo, "Well, Leo, when the time comes and your fortress is besieged, look for some help from the north. The Greenway should provide some needed help in fighting these barbarians." A faint smile formed on his thin lips.

Roy interjected, "Say Leo, how long ago did Zargarb fall to these invaders?"

"Oh, we think it was last spring. Solamina fell last summer. We just got word last week that Pieta is besieged, but we're not sure how outdated the information really is. Rumors tend to be exaggerated, you know — at least that's what dad says. Why?"

"For estimating, Leo. How far apart are these seven cities?" Roy continued to press for key information. I started to see where he was heading with this line of questioning.

"Oh, that's an easy one. The original Seven Sea Princes didn't trust one another, so when they founded their cities, or so legends say, they made them all about a hundred miles apart so none would be close to the others. In many ways even today, the seven cities are in competition with each other for the lucrative trade routes. Why? What has that got to do with it?"

"Well, it gives us a time line. During the good weather months, the Centurions apparently cover the distance in about three months. In the winter months, their progress is slower. So my guess is that once Pieta falls, then Bonilla is next around midsummer, with Vito falling by autumn. Barcella faces them next spring, with Velona around midsummer. Hence, that makes your fortress likely to be hit by the autumn of next year. That gives you a year and a half to make preparations. See what I mean?" Little did we know our time-line was slightly off.

"I see, so you're suggesting that we lay in provisions way ahead of time, make weapons and armor." Leo looked a bit more self-assured.

I added, "Yes, that's the idea, and if you send word now to Calgary telling them that you need a supply of grain for the coming siege, why, I bet you get it at no charge. In fact, when you send that message, relay also that Bethany suggested that there would be no charge for the supplies."

He gaped at me in surprise. "Sure! Sure thing! I will. I'll tell dad, and we'll send a message today even. Thank you both!" If I was not mistaken, the look he gave us now was that of "these are people of importance!" "Say, I do have to be heading back. I'm a long way from the fortress, and the hour is getting late. You two ought to head back down to the village. Navigating these hills in the dark is exceedingly treacherous." So we thanked him for chatting with us, and he, for our generous offer of grain from the Greenway. After an enthusiastic farewell handshake, Roy and I headed back down the slope, picking our way very carefully between the brush and the sharp protruding rocks. We both felt we'd just made a strong ally in the fight against the invasion.

When we were safely out of earshot, Roy wondered aloud, "Why would it take an army three months to march only a hundred miles? That's what has me puzzled, Bethany. If they only marched a lazy five miles a day, it is only three weeks to the next town. Why three months? Do you suppose these cities are holding out for over two months each before they are conquered?" Neither of us had any answer, but it was an interesting question, one worth answering.

The next day we lent a hand hoisting the two new masts into position on the Lone Light. The following day, at high tide, we cast off, resuming our voyage to Velona. Only now, we had even more questions. I was beginning to think this trip would net us far more questions than answers.

In contrast to the previous week at sea, the next three weeks were picture-perfect. Once we were into the Med Sea proper, the days were positively balmy for early April, warm days and nights as well. During the day, the rich blue sky contrasted with the blue-green seas, highlighted by the occasional billowing white clouds. Late afternoons often brought a short-lived squall whose fresh water was used to replenish the ship's water barrels. We spent much of the daylight hours leaning on the port railing watching the countryside slide slowly by our view.

Actually, from the sea, we had a terrific overview of the Lands of the Seven Sea Princes, at least this smaller western section. We consistently sailed about two to three miles from shore. The lands tended to rise higher and higher the further inland one went until at last reaching the nearly barren Appian Way mountains proper. True, many hills intervened blocking our total view, but still we got a good sense of the land. We spied many smaller towns and villages; Thomas, who had now recovered from his seasickness, pointed out the neatly terraced farms that dotted the country side. We learned many were olive groves and vineyards, for these lands were famous for their olives and wine, which comprised their primary exports.

Inhabited lands stretched from the shores inland approximately two hundred miles as ground slowly rose higher and higher. While many trees, some of which we had never seen before, lined the coastal areas, their density diminished the further inland one went eventually being entirely replaced by the green, tough-rooted shrubs that Roy and I had examined earlier. Slowly, I realized why these people made their living trading by sea. Without the trade, these lands would not support a large population. This was a land composed primarily of traders, merchants, and the occasional craftsman, quite unlike our Greenway, which was almost entirely agricultural. Simon speculated, "The economic impact here must of necessity enforce the usage of coins as the underlying means of exchange, not like home where barter is our means. Conclusion: I'll bet anything in this land greed has taken a foothold in a major way."

Bartoloma concurred with Simon's observation and cautioned us to be wary of those charging high prices to "foreigners." Such was commonplace in the bazaars of Velona. I didn't quite grasp the full meaning Simon conveyed and had him elaborate. "Amassing a huge amount of gold coins means wealth here. With the real objects that sustain life removed and replaced by trading coins, some may easily lose track of what is important and become obsessed with gaining as many coins as possible. For example, back home, if a man had an extra couple cows, he has emergency food if needed and milk for breakfast each morning. However, would you then try to accumulate a hundred cows? Certainly not, for there would be no real use in having and caring for that many, unless they were the "town's cows," as is done in Karka. If one removes the cows and substituted small gold coins in their place, it is altogether too easy to lose sight of the purpose of money as a means of exchange and become obsessed with collecting as many as possible. There is no downside to having a hundred or thousand coins as there is with having a thousand cows. So expect men to fall victim to avarice here."

Again, Bartoloma overheard him and concurred, adding, "And also expect that women, who have not the rights of men here, to sell their bodies for money. It is a very lucrative business in some parts of town." I shuttered at that idea; so did Sandy and Sarah Jane. We each had many other avenues available to us to make a living, but I realized we were actually special in this regard. Take my mother, for example, she did not have as many possibilities, especially in a large city setting. I suspected she could barter her sewing skills for copper coins. He continued, "Also be alert for outright thievery in our towns. Watch your money pouches. Many unsavory characters, both men and women, find lifting another's money pouch to be an easy way to make a good living. I've been robbed three times! I never even saw who did it!" Boy, were we thankful for all of the training Alabaster had given us during the winter. This promised to be most interesting.

The Lucky Lady made several stops at small port towns along the way to Velona, mostly to take on fresh water and food. On other trips, Bartoloma explained they would take on cargo to trade and leave bags of coins in return. Since this was a mostly a charter trip, compliments of Alabaster, he took on very little, only a few cases of wine.

However, he did make one stop at San Puerto for pure pleasure. He explained as we drew close, "San Puerto is a small fishing village, but it also has the finest white sandy beaches in all the Lands of the Sea Princes! There are no finer swimming beaches to be found anywhere that I have ever sailed. No trip to our lands is complete without taking a swim here. So tonight, my friends, we lay anchor just off San Puerto. We'll take the dingy to shore, supper on the beach, and swim in the Med Sea. As we neared San Puerto, the white sandy beaches became the most prominent feature along the coastline, stretching for miles. The Lucky Lady pulled into a sheltered area about five hundred feet from the beach. We took two dingy boats and paddled to shore. Five minutes later, we had a small bonfire going and soon supper was roasting.

We all stripped down to our underclothes and headed into the water for a swim, while Bartoloma watched the cooking supper. He was right. The waters of the Med Sea were warm and refreshing as well as salty, which made us lighter in the water than we were used to, making swimming and floating a breeze. This was truly paradise. After a swim and dinner, Roy and I lay on the beach with our feet in the warm waters. Neither of us spoke; we just felt with all our senses. Later, I fell asleep with my head resting on his arm and shoulder. We both had the most contented, restful sleep that we could ever recall having had. Sandy and Sarah Jane did likewise. When I awoke, I had to give Roy a loving kiss and said softly, "Roy, we should spend our honeymoon here sometime." He smiled and returned my kiss. I began to feel our pretended marriage was not all that pretended. I think Roy did too.

Chapter 10 Velona, Seven Sea Princes

It was May 1, 559 AH, when we glimpsed Velona, the first city on our agenda. Midmorning, we rounded a bend, and the immense city came into view. Breathtaking is a good way to describe it, at least to our eyes; Calgary, the largest city we'd ever seen, was positively dwarfed by Velona! Neither the largest nor smallest of the Sea Prince cities, Velona stretched inland for miles. Its docks could handle over three dozen ships simultaneously. Population estimates suggested nearly a hundred thousand folks called Velona home.

Red tile roofs added color to the larger blue-grey stone buildings and brown adobe smaller homes. Very few buildings were actually constructed from wood, since all available wood was used to build and maintain their immense fleet of ships. We learned well over a hundred ships called Velona home. A dozen were docked as we entered the sheltered harbor; a half dozen were tacking out to sea, while another five, including the Lucky Lady and the Lone Light, were slowly entering. Yes, it was a grand sight. We seven stood on deck watching the city grow larger as we approached. People seemed to be scampering about everywhere — so many people!

However, Bartoloma's countenance suddenly changed from cheerfulness to fear, and he whispered to me, "When we dock, you can find Luigi, the Net Maker, on Water Street down by the Old Docks. Be careful, to get there you have to go through the slums." I noted his directions, but also noted he grew more and more uneasy the closer we drew to land. I strained my eyes to observe what was causing his alarm. I could make out several men, some armed, standing by a portage, evidently the one for which we were making. Two of the men caught my attention. One wore an elaborate set of purple robes, which seemed awfully out of place. The other wore expensive clothes, at least that would be my guess from this distance, but a glint of reflected light around his head suggested he wore some kind of crown or jewels. I also observed some kind of large wooden device just behind them.

As I turned to face Bartoloma, I saw he was seeing what I had. "Who are those men and what is that wooden thing?" I asked in a hushed voice, trying not to alarm him further.

"That'd be none other than Prince Jamil Alvelardo, Velona's ruler, and the High Priest Horton Po beside him in the purple robes. All the Sea God Tur's priests wear purple robes. Something major must be afoot because the two of them only greet incoming boats when something is very wrong. I have a very bad feeling about this. Remember, Water Street by the Old Docks. Excuse me." He grimly faced his men and added, "Looks as if we have an important audience, so let's make this a perfect docking." He began issuing mostly unneeded orders to his crew, perhaps to get his mind off what lay ahead, perhaps to calm his crew. I noticed they also looked ill at ease. Quickly, they scampered to execute his orders. I glanced behind us and saw that the Lone

Light was following us and would dock immediately to our left. Both ships slowed to a crawl and eased alongside the two docks.

The crew threw out two huge rope lines, which dockworkers caught and wrapped around huge capstans. As they pulled on them, the Luck Lady slid gently up against the padded dock. The crew nodded to each other, a sign of a perfect docking, I gathered. Once the ship was moored, the greeting party walked down the long boardwalk towards us; their faces were somber at best. Captain Bartoloma climbed onto the dock to meet them; we seven hopped off and followed at a respectable distance from which we could hear everything that was said. I felt very uncomfortable. Sandy sent me mentally, *Something bad is about to happen. I can sense it.*

Prince Jamil Alvelardo spoke first, "You have arrived at last, Captain Bartoloma, but only apparently by the grace of Tur. News of the near calamity at the Narrows has already reached us. You were in charge of this return voyage, correct?" Bartoloma muttered affirmative; he held his hands tightly behind his back; his knuckles were white from the intense pressure of his grip. "Then by the powers invested as your Prince, I give you to High Priest Horton Po." The Prince was a young man, about thirty with long black hair and slender build. Indeed, he wore the finest set of clothes I'd ever seen. About his head holding his long hair in place was a small golden circlet with a large green emerald in its center.

Bartoloma's grip tightened even harder, if that were possible, as the priest took one step closer placing himself one foot closer to Bartoloma than the Prince was. Six well-armed men now moved in behind him, and the Prince stepped aside and back to make way for them. This did not look good, I thought. What kind of welcome was this anyway?

The priest I instantly disliked, and I seldom disliked anyone I had never met. Perhaps, it was his snide, self-righteous, pompous attitude with which he bore himself that triggered my instant rejection of him. He was a short man and well overweight, fat even, probably at least two hundred pounds. Gluttony immediately came to mind. When he spoke, his tone was cold, threatening and snide, "Captain Bartoloma, is it not true that the Lone Light was nearly sunk during the passage of the Narrows?" He nodded, but didn't say a word. "You know the Laws of Tur. The great Sea God must be appeased. Your blunder at the Narrows must be atoned or Tur will destroy our entire fleet. Since it was your command, it is so decreed that your head must be given to Tur." Bartoloma's face turned ghastly white, but he still did not say a word.

"Wait a minute," I interrupted, "we were there. We saw the whole thing. It was not Bartoloma's fault. Georgio intentionally overloaded his ship to make more profit on the trip. We. . ."

"Silence, woman!" screamed Prince Jamil, whose grim face now was livid and red with anger. "You are obviously a stranger to our land. Your clothes alone are proof enough. Here in our lands, a woman speaks only when she is ordered to speak. Those who speak out of turn have their tongues cut out, are stripped naked, and thrown out into the streets to make their own vile living. Open your mouth once more, and I'll ignore your status of visitor and have your tongue for dinner!"

In that brief instant, I suddenly realized why Willow had been so worried that I may become a rogue with my power over lightning. It took all my will power to keep from conjuring a lightning bolt down upon this man's head! I seethed with anger and disgust that such a man should even walk this earth and be allowed to live. I also fully realized we had indeed entered a barbaric society, despite the magnificent trappings of grandeur. I was out of my head and had grown huge in size, nearly touching a cumulus cloud overhead, which was full of the energy I needed for a bolt to this man's head before I even realized it. Just as I did, I recognized Sandy's presence in my mind trying to calm me. She too was totally upset and angry, and her attempt to calm me was feeble at best. Prince Jamil never knew just how close he was to death in that split instant before I reacted!

Instead, to Roy I sent, *Roy, speak. Say this. I saw Georgio take bribe from someone back at the Calgary Docks. In return, he loaded about two dozen extra fifty-pound sacks of grain on board the Lone Light.* He did as I ordered, though he fought against his own vehement anger as well. My words came out his mouth verbatim. He added, "I didn't think much of this encounter until we were at sea because this was the first time I've been on a ship. My estimate is Georgio intentionally overloaded his ship by something like a thousand pounds without the approval or knowledge of Captain Bartoloma here. I'm sure Tur would *not* be pleased with the head of the wrong party. I'm not learned in the ways of your Sea God, but what would he likely do if you gave him the wrong head?"

While Roy repeated what I was placing in his head, I glanced at Georgio to see his reaction. I was pleased. Priest Horton Po spoke simply, "Is this true, Captain Georgio?"

The overweight captain's face reddened; his fidgeting body language spoke volumes. Confronted as he was with the truth of the matter, looking down at the ground, he muttered, "Yes."

"Speak up" sneered the priest. "Did you secretly overload your own ship without the approval of Captain Bartoloma?"

"Yes, what of it!" he sneered back, his embarrassment of discovery gave way to that of defiant anger. "There's more profit this way. We all do it. We're trying to make money, aren't we? We won't become the number one trading city by carrying passengers now will we?"

The priest turned to Roy, "Thank you honored visitor to Velona. You've done us a great service. Had we given the wrong head to Tur, he wouldn't have been appeased, and all of our ships would have faced his anger and wrath!" Turning to Georgio he said, "Come forward Georgio. Your head must be given to Tur." I sincerely hoped this wasn't going to be literal.

Georgio marched stoically up to the priest. I spied a large moneybag change hands. The priest bowed his head. Georgio pointed out his cook, and his other crew members brought the protesting, screaming man forward to face the priest. Evidently, money allowed Georgio to pass on the punishment to one of his luckless crew members. I watched as the priest held up a goblet high in the air. "Tur, the blessed one." Quickly, he forced the liquid down the throat of the struggling man who was held secure by his fellow crew members. Now, the guards took over as the crew hastily retreated all the way back to the ship! The cook had been given a fast acting drug, I surmised, because soon he became quite limp; two guards held onto him or he would have collapsed onto the dock.

They carried him over to the wooden catapult. One guard held up an enormous scimitar while Horton said a prayer. "Tur, bless this blade that we hereby use to atone for our misdeeds." He gave a hand signal, and the man swung the scimitar down with all his might, completely severing the cook's head! Quick hands grabbed the head and placed it into the catapult's basket, while blood gushed onto the front of the machine. I gagged uncontrollably; I vaguely heard my friends doing likewise. It happened so fast that I couldn't turn away. That image is forever burned into my memory. "Tur, oh great God of the Sea, protector of Velona's ships, accept our offering of the head of the guilty. Be appeased at our wrongdoings. We atone for our guilt." Another hand signal and the catapult launched the head high overhead and far out to sea. I heard it splash in the near silence broken only by the sounds of the sea lapping onshore.

I raced back to the Luck Lady and vomited over the side. Sandy and Thomas were not far behind me doing likewise. The others joined us, but no one spoke. I felt Roy's reassuring hand on my back; Simon supported Sandy as well. In the background, I heard both the priest and the Prince laughing at us and making jokes about their visitors' squeamish stomachs. At the moment, I just tried to keep from fainting.

A few minutes later, Bartoloma joined us. He had brought a goatskin and several cups with him. "Here, sip this," he said, his voice quite shaky. I took the small cup from his trembling hand. *So it affected him too*, I thought. It was a soothing wine. I felt the sudden warmth tingling all the way down into my stomach and shortly even out to my fingers, which I'd forgotten I even had. I eagerly accepted a second cup. Soon, I was numb and could relax, leaning on Roy for support. All of us had at least one drink before Bartoloma spoke again, "Thank you all. You saved my life. I owe you. If you ever need anything that I can do for you, you only need to ask. I'm forever in your debt. Perhaps, it would be wise if you did not disembark just yet. Why not go below and help the crew unload the cargo? That'll give you time to recover. I've only seen that done once before. I was sickened then and am sickened now. Come on; let's all go below." We followed him, but Roy nearly had to carry me for I was as limp as cooked cabbage.

Sandy, Thomas, and I laid down in the galley while Sarah Jane looked after us. The others lent a hand hoisting up the grain sacks to the other crew members. Even Bartoloma hoisted up sacks. For a time not a soul spoke a word. Finally, I could hold it in no longer and began crying. "Barbarians, these people are barbarians!"

"That's okay, Bethany, go ahead and cry. That was the most disgusting thing I have ever heard of — let alone see!" soothed Sarah Jane, whose tears quickly joined ours.

Thomas fairly bawled, "Why do we even want to help these criminals? I'd just as soon leave them to the Centurions. Let them slay them all! I just want to go out into Nature and live out my life alone. I hate all of them! These people are worse than beasts — the scum of Tarra if you ask me." He cried bitter tears. Even swamped in my own despair, I could sense the intense hatred Thomas had formed for these Sea Princes. Perhaps, it was a mistake to bring a Loremaster with us; they belong out in Nature. Of all of us, Thomas was the least equipped to deal with man's inhumanity to man, but he was here; we were here; there was nothing I could do about it except cry.

An hour later, fortified with some wine, cheese, and bread, we seven toted our many sacks and bid the Lucky Lady farewell. When I stepped out on to the boardwalk pier, I saw only a bustling crowd of workers loading and unloading ships. All traces of the bloody misadventure were gone; evidently, someone had cleaned up the mess. No one seemed to pay any attention to the fact that only an hour ago a young man had been ritually murdered right before their eyes. We said goodbye to Bartoloma and joined the throngs on the busy street.

No sooner had we left the docks proper, when a priest in a purple robe moved out of the shadows of a building, where he had obviously been waiting. He had his head bowed in reverence I supposed and was a young lad not much older than we were. "Excuse me, but I'm to give you a message. His Exalted Excellence, Horton Po wishes you to come to the Church of Tur on Main Street at your earliest convenience. I believe he wishes to purchase grain from the Greenway. That is all." He bowed, spun on his heels, and moved off on down the street before us, his head still bowed.

"Swine!" muttered Thomas, "He never even made eye contact with us."

"Perhaps, he is not allowed to do so," suggested Sarah Jane. "We don't know their customs very well yet."

"I wouldn't sell that fat pig a sack of manure," Thomas added under his breath.

"Well, that attitude won't do very well," Simon chided him. "Remember our cover. We're supposed to be trying to open up new grain markets." Thomas only grunted halfheartedly.

This major street at the docks was twenty feet wide. All around us were two story, stone warehouses, which served as staging areas in the movement of all the commodities in which the Sea Princes traded. We were on Center Street. As we walked another block beyond the rows of warehouses, the street opened into a large market square, one of hundreds in Velona. Minor merchants sat on mats around the perimeter hocking wares from fresh vegetables to fruits to fresh fish and breads. For the first time, we saw many women shopping gathering supplies for their families. Children ran and played with reckless abandon darting here and there, as if the market was a vast playground. I smiled at them, for there went I only a few years ago.

The various men we passed by all carried either a short sword or a long dagger displayed prominently in elaborate sheaths strapped to their sides. Typically, most wore darkish pants of a weave that we had not seen before and a cotton-like long sleeved shirt, squarish in design with an open neck. These shirts, unlike the drab pants, were brightly colored, some red, some yellow, some blue, and some green. A stripped bandana tied around their heads just above the forehead kept their rather long hair rather from interfering with their activities. Most wore soft leather boots half hidden underneath their pants.

While the men's apparel was rather plain, it was the women's faces that really caught our eyes. Unfortunately, I believe all of us rather stared at the first few we saw up close; the guys, more like a gawk. Their faces were somehow painted; lips were red, seemingly fuller or larger than they actually were; cheeks were rouged; eyes lined in black, which made their gaze appear soul-piercing or enticing, as the men suggested. Many wore elaborate, tight necklaces that seemed to me to be more like a collar than decoration, if it were not for the fact that most were golden and bejeweled. We later learned when a woman gets married, she is presented with her collar for life. The wealthier her husband, the more expensive and larger the necklace. Those that wore none were unmarried. For the women, these served overtly as a status symbol as well as a fashion accessory.

So intent were we on observing the local people that we barely noticed that the street had narrowed. The clothing began to look more worn, the women less gaudy. We had entered the poorer part of the city. Following the directions we had been given, we turned down onto Water Street and headed to the slums of the city, the Old Docks. In the earliest days of Velona, the Old Docks were the only docks and hence the lifeline of the city. That was a hundred years or more ago. When the port had been expanded, the Old Docks had been left to rot and were now occupied by the scum of the city, the poorest of the poor. Every large city has them, we learned in time.

We saw some men and women who had lost an arm or leg. Several blind tapped their way slowly along the street sometimes counting steps aloud. Still, every few blocks the street opened into a market area, though here the quality of goods suffered. Few had the means to pay much. We observed barter in this area was more prevalent than exchange of coins. One elderly man traded three freshly caught fish for some vegetables and oil. We spied a one legged woman trading a hand-knitted, small fishing net for several fish. Among these women, only a few had the flashy face paint. None had golden collars, rather simple leather ones predominated. We weren't impressed with the generosity of the city leaders, as we continued on our way to the Net Maker, our contact.

Water Street paralleled the edge of the Med Sea, and soon we arrived at a rundown wooden building, whose front door opened onto the street, but whose rear section was built upon raised pillars. Below the floor, the land sloped sharply down to the water. The rear half of the building actually was out over the water proper. A crudely drawn sign indicated the Net Maker Shop. A small board hanging from a nail displayed a red X. We wondered what that meant.

Roy knocked on the door, unsure whether we were supposed to just enter the store or wait to be let in. He opted for formality. Almost at once, an older man opened the door. "Come on in quickly," he said, his eyes darting beyond us; obviously, he was trying to see if we were followed. We entered his damp shop; the smell of rotting wood was a bit overpowering. The dingy shop held nets of all shapes and sizes along with several tables on which lay those in various stages of construction. Luigi was clearly from the Greenway, blue eyes and blonde hair. He wore leather clothing similar to ours, however his were many times patched and with bits of cloth not leather. Luigi looked the part of a down on his luck net maker. He ushered us to the rear room adjoining what served as his kitchen. A kettle was boiling. He pointed to some crude wooden chairs and went to fetch some tea and biscuits.

"There now, I don't often have guests. Tea is about the best I have to offer," he said. "I've been away far too long now." I assumed he meant from our homeland. "I see you were not followed here. I thought you might be."

"Someone did follow us for a while," Roy explained. "When we entered the slummier part of town, he stood out from the locals and quietly dropped back. Guess he didn't want to follow us that badly."

"Could you see if he was wearing a purple head band or a red one?" asked Luigi.

"Red," Thomas answered. "I got a good look at him."

"Ah, then that would be one of Jamil's men," Luigi surmised. "The prince's men wear red bandanas around their heads, while those of Horton Po wear purple. Predictable." He sipped his tea and began more formally, "Welcome to Velona. You may call me Luigi. That's not my given name; best you don't know it. Around here, I'm old Luigi, the Net Maker. I was down at the docks to meet you personally this morning. However, when I saw both of them and their armed escorts coming, I beat a hasty retreat. They'll know you came here soon enough. Hear you got the royal initiation to Sea Prince Law. Barbaric. I still can't get used to the miserable living conditions in this land."

We agreed with him and introduced ourselves. He was most impressed with our youthful age and the fact that Alabaster had sent an entire Circle. Luigi told us his story, a painful one. Fifteen years ago, he, a Loremaster, and the rest of his Circle had come to the Land of the Sea Princes where they split up. His wife, their Healer, and he stayed in Velona, while the others moved on to other cities. Over time, he learned the others in his Circle had been discovered and murdered. Seven years ago, his wife had spoken up for some women who were being savagely beaten for "alleged offenses," which they could not possibly have committed and was herself summarily executed. He'd not known of it until the slayings were over. Luigi vowed revenge and had gone underground, adopting the guise of a poverty stricken net maker. One by one, he sought out and killed all those involved in the killings. However, at Alabaster's insistence, he stayed on here in Velona analyzing the political and military situation. He too knew that the Centurions were eventually going to besiege the city.

"Now before we say much else, I must share a vital secret with you. If trouble comes, flee. I've got a secret escape route set up. Follow me, and I'll show it to you. It might save your lives." He moved a moth eaten rug from the center of the kitchen floor revealing a trap door. Once opened, we climbed down a rickety wooden ladder and found ourselves on a very smelly bank of the seacoast. Refuse and rotting fish littered the dark, hidden beach. In the dim, late afternoon light, we also saw a "sea" of huge rotting timbers supporting a multitude of buildings as far as the eye could see. He led us up the slope to where he had hidden several small dingy boats. "You can take a dingy or two and head in any direction or you can make your way that way following the beach. It will eventually lead you to the western edge of the city where you can disappear into the countryside." We gratefully thanked him for showing us this secret escape route, but the filth and stench was more than sufficient to keep anyone from wandering down here. I even spied feces lying about. Yuck.

Next, I explained the basic idea of our mission, that we were to attempt to open new grain markets as a cover, and asked him for his ideas on how best to proceed. He was not surprised to hear we already had a summons to see His Exalted Excellence, Horton Po, and that we should expect to be asked to visit Prince Jamil Alvelardo as well. "These two men are heads of their two respective clans that have fought for control of Velona since the city's founding. Over the years, the power has shifted between these two ruling clans. Currently, the Alvelardo's were in control. "Both men are acute observers and will certainly attempt to find out why you are really here. Be careful what you say to these men; both are utterly ruthless in getting what they want. Tread carefully; your cover may already be blown if only by your clothing. I suspect, but cannot prove, that they associate leather with Greenway Protectors. Now your first order of business is to find appropriate lodging fitting with your disguise. Most traders and merchants opt for rooms at Corello's Inn; that's where I would suggest you stay. Take rooms rented on a weekly basis so as not to arouse suspicions unduly. Get settled. I'll drop by tomorrow morning, and you'll pretend to hire me as a guide about the city. Then, I can explain much about the goings on in Velona."

We asked a few more questions and then left, Roy studiously following his directions to Corello's Inn. It was located in the center of the town, which was roughly divided into four quarters: the docks, the slums, the merchants, and the rich, ruling clans, which were all located on the northern edge of Velona. As we approached the inn, Thomas spied an unusual merchant in the last market square before our inn: a flower display. "Hold on a minute! Flowers!" I realized that for Thomas, being cooped up in a city of these proportions so far removed from Nature, was tantamount to an imprisonment.

Something as simple as a flower meant much to this gentle man.

Now that he mentioned it, I realized we really hadn't come across other such stalls. We watched and waited for him. The shop or stall was nothing more than a dozen small flowerpots with water in them accompanied by two small, light trellises. Various cut flowers either were in the water pots or nicely arranged tied to the trellises. A young woman about twenty ran the outdoor shop. She had very short blonde hair, deep blue eyes, and a slender, though muscular body. She wore a plain leather outfit, similar to ours, though sewn entirely differently. Unlike ours, hers was very old and worn. Multitudes of non-matching patches lined the legs and arms. He walked up and began chatting with her. "Hi, I'm Thomas. I really appreciate your most beautiful flowers. I've never seen most of these. They don't grow where I come from, but these are really nice."

She didn't say a word, but only smiled at him. Her eyes focused intently on him. He picked out four tied bunches and asked her, "How much?" She displayed two fingers, so he handed her two gold coins. Her eyes opened wide, and she shook her head violently from side to side, indicating he had paid way too much. She fumbled with her money pouch tied to her waist along with a short sword. I also spied a dagger in each boot. She brought out a coin and held up two fingers showing him a copper coin. Finally understanding, Thomas said, "Here, you take one gold coin anyway. I don't have any coppers yet, and, for me, these flowers are worth a gold one. They remind me of home, of Nature." Graciously, she accepted his coin and explanation, though her keen eyes never left his. As he was about to leave, he got an idea and asked her, "Say, you don't have any yellow daffodils by chance do you? I think those are Bethany's favorite flowers. After what she has been through today, I'd like her to have some to remind her of home too."

The woman shook her head negatively but made numerous signs with her hands. Taken aback by this, he asked, "You cannot speak?" She nodded affirmative. "Okay. Show me the signs again, only slower. I bet I can figure out what you are trying to tell me." She did. "Ah, tomorrow. You want me to come back tomorrow. Okay. Will do. Thanks." She beamed at him, and he grinned at her and then brought his flowers over to us. He presented each of us women with a bunch and kept one for himself. We gave him a hug to show our appreciation.

However, from the corner of my eyes, I saw the flower woman still had not taken her eyes off Thomas. Roy, anxious to get to the inn, hustled us forward. Ahead was a large building two stories tall with an enormous sign out front depicting beds, tables, and food. We stepped inside and found ourselves in a large, homey room with three side corridors and a large main desk at the back of the room. A man was standing behind it and behind him was a huge board with many keys hanging from small hooks. "May I help you?" he asked politely. Roy took charge and acquired our rooms. He got us four adjacent rooms, and we overheard him discussing the eating arrangements. A large dining room lay just down the right hallway. He paid four gold coins for one week's food and lodging. Proudly, he returned to us hanging the guys a key to their room. We headed down the left hallway looking for our rooms. "Find a door with a yellow bird on them. Then, we look for vertical lines; we have rooms four through seven."

Thomas took room four; Sandy and Simon took five; Roy and I, six, leaving Sarah Jane and Raphael, seven. Roy explained that he felt safer with our Wid being surrounded by the rest of us. I smiled at his sense of my well-being. "Ah fair lady, allow me to open our door for you," Roy said gallantly though teasingly. Inside, we found a comfortable room about twenty feet square with a small desk, two chairs, and a large bed with real cloth sheets and several blankets.

"Ah, Roy, we have arrived in Paradise," I jested plopping down on the bed to check its softness. Roy carefully examined the room. It had no windows and only the one door. I watched curiously, as he carefully examined all the walls looking for secret entrances into the room. He found none, but did come up with an extra chamber pot.

"Here, put the flowers in this; we can share the other pot." I did so and then we both unpacked a few items from our sacks. Carrying all these grain samples along with our gear had worn me out. I was thankful finally to be able to let go of the three large sacks. Roy then went outside to explore our surroundings, leaving me to wash up in the large washbasin. I knew I could really get to like staying at an inn where I did not have to do all these mundane chores. Heaven, I thought.

After a half hour, Roy returned accompanied by the others. "Okay, there is a side door down at the very end of our hallway and a stairs leading up to the second floor. So there are not many ways out of here in an emergency. More importantly, these keys actually operate every other door, so in fact, there is almost no security here. Don't leave anything in our rooms that is valuable, if you follow me." We did and headed out to find some dinner. When I left the room, I was surprised to find that someone had been by lighting all the hallway lanterns. A lantern hung near each door providing dim illumination down the long hall. As we walked the long hallway, I realized just how hungry I actually was and how exhausted my body felt.

After a filling fish dinner, we returned to our rooms. Roy and I turned in almost at once. It felt very strange and somewhat exciting to be actually sharing a bed with a man, as my parents did. Though we slept apart, I did roll over and give Roy a kiss, whispering, "Thanks for looking after me today." He squeezed my hand in reply. For once, as I drifted into sleep, I felt really excited, happy, and secure — rather like the feeling I had as a child when mom tucked me in for the night. I knew I could really enjoy being a wife. I wondered how Roy felt, but did not dare peek into his mind to find out.

I awoke to find Roy beside me supporting his head on one arm gazing at me. "Morning beautiful," he said lovingly. That excitement stirred in me once more and without even thinking about it, I leaned up and we embraced. Instead of the tingling going away, it grew! It was like a burst of energy filling my whole body. I blushed. "What's up?" he whispered.

"I — I really am fond of you Roy," I managed to say awkwardly. His reply was to give me another kiss.

"Same here, Bethany," he finally said. We got up, dressed, and prepared to get some breakfast. When we reached the door, we paused and kissed each other once more. Again, I felt electrified and resolved to ask Sarah Jane what this meant, if only I could find a private time to ask her.

As we were eating, a courier came to our table. He wore fancy clothes with a red sash about his waist. "Excuse me, but are you not the group that arrived in Velona yesterday aboard the Lucky Lady?" Roy acknowledged that we were. "Good. I come from Prince Alvelardo. He commands you to visit him this afternoon." He was slightly annoyed when we told him that we first were ordered to visit Horton Po, but suggested that we come to the Royal Palace as soon as we finished with the priest. Roy carefully memorized his directions to the palace. I found it interesting that already the Prince knew where we were staying.

After he left, Roy commented, "Looks like Luigi was right on that one." We chuckled. Once we ate our fill, we went back to our rooms and packed our valuables carefully into a small sack to take with us. Also, Raphael carried one small sack that held a sample of our grains. Then, we headed for the front door. Sure enough, Luigi was there waiting for us. "I see you're new in town. May I offer my services as a guide for say a coin a day?" he asked loudly keeping in his role as a poverty-stricken man looking to earn a bit of coin.

"Sure," Roy agreed and doled out a coin. We strolled off down the street heading for Horton Po's church. As we passed the corner market, both Thomas and I looked for the flower stall, but she was not there yet. It was early morning. I detected the slightest sigh from Thomas; curious, I thought.

Nothing in my training prepared me for the sheer size of Velona. Its streets were a veritable maze. All of us were used to using the surrounding distant hilltops, trees, and such as our anchor points, for these were always visible just beyond our towns in the Greenway. However, Velona was so huge, that once deep inside the city, nothing but buildings could be seen in any direction. Compounding our confusion were the winding streets and their widths. Luigi explained there were twelve major thoroughfares: six going roughly east-west, and six, north-south. Main Street, Center Street, and Water Street were the only three of which, thus far, we had seen a tiny portion. These major arteries tended to be anywhere from twenty-five to forty feet wide. Another thirty medium streets connected to these and were never more than twenty feet wide. However, hundreds of side streets adjoined these and were only fifteen feet with a multitude of alleyways that ranged from ten feet down to a scant six feet.

In fact, Luigi told us that his late Planner had estimated that there was at least three hundred miles of streets within Velona's ten-mile radius! One did not have to try very hard to get lost! "If trouble comes your way, it's wise to duck down side alleys, because you can get lost from view very quickly. Of course, the downside to that is you also can get lost as well. Moreover, it is exceedingly dangerous going down certain alleys. There are many thieves and gangs of thugs patrolling their turf. From my own observations, the guards seldom pursue anyone down side alleys. I believe they are just as scared as the rest of us," Luigi chuckled.

He went on, "So you must learn to use buildings as your guide markers." We paid very close attention to our passage to the Church of Tur. We'd covered nearly six miles from our inn before we finally got to the church. Fortunately, it was in the well-to-do northern sector of the city, lay on the eastern side of the main artery, and was so impressive a building that it could not be mistaken. Actually, it was more like a complex, since a six-foot stone wall entirely surrounded the grounds, which occupied more than a city block. To the far north against the wall were a number of small stone, single story buildings that served as the living quarters for the priestly staff and guards. The Church of Tur proper was a three story, red stone building, squarish in design. Sarah Jane's comment that "it is rather plain" was an understatement. There was nothing gaudy about its simple design, save only the huge ten foot tall double entrance doors carved in the shape of a pair of large sea fish.

This main entrance opened directly onto the street. I could see no side entrances in the walls about the grounds and wondered if everyone had to enter through the church itself. It seemed rather a poor way to design it if that were so. Raphael later suggested this was very likely a security feature. However, I wondered if the walls were to keep people inside rather than to keep outsiders from gaining access. Just inside the door, a purple robed acolyte greeted us. "Ah, you're the newcomers. His Exalted Excellence, Horton Po, is expecting you. This way please." Luigi, acting his role of guide, stayed behind and ducked outside into the street to await our return. We were suddenly completely on our own, which I found more than a little unnerving, especially, since women could not speak freely here. It was all going to be up to Simon, our Judger, who was best trained for such dealings.

We were led down long, winding halls that echoed with our footsteps, perhaps just to confuse us, I suspected. At last, we entered a throne room, which didn't look like what I had expected. Yes, Horton Po sat on a huge raised dais covered in gold foil; light sparkled from the many gemstones embedded in various patterns and arcs, several formed a semi-circle over Horton's head as he sat regally on his throne, giving one the illusion of a god-like radiance emanating from him. I could see at once that his man thrived on appearances and that he really desired the Princedom. The room was about thirty feet square with the ceiling some fifteen feet over our heads. Hanging down were ten giant lantern groups that cast a yellowish glow over us all.

"Ah, yes. Our visitors from the Greenway, correct?" Horton Po said, with a touch of insinuation in his voice.

Simon stepped one step forward from the rest of us, a subtle gesture indicating that he was in charge and our spokesman. "My compliments, Your Excellency, on a good observation. Yes, we're from the Greenway lands above the Appian Way. We're official representatives of the Able Feed Company, one of the largest grain producers in all the Greenway. We're here searching out new trading partners, new markets for our grain. Of course, Velona must, of necessity, be our first stop for we must use your ships to transport our grain to whomever wishes to purchase it. I believe these type details are more fitting to be discussed with the Prince of the city rather than its spiritual guide. I'm sure you would be quite bored discussing grain purchases." I could see Simon was giving Po a polite way to get rid of us.

"Ah, tis so, tis so. I'm not really interested in grain markets," a slight sneer was present in his voice, as we recognized that he recognized Simon's ploy. "But you see, I'm responsible for the well-being of all the hundreds of Velona's ships and crew, so I must know the true nature of those with whom we intend to deal. Moreover, you come at a very ill time. You are aware that the Land of the Sea Princes is under invasion by the vile Centurions of Megalos?" This was a direct attempt to gather information.

"We've certainly heard an earful about it from Captain Bartoloma during our voyage here. Admittedly, I have only a vague notion of where this Megalos place is at, and none of us has ever seen one of these Centurions. For our own safety, Sir, may I ask are we in any danger here in Velona? I mean is the city facing imminent attack? Should we perhaps abandon our search for new markets? You see, we brought our wives along, thinking to combine business with pleasure." Now that, I thought, was a very clever reply by Simon, turning it around on Horton.

Horton stalled as he readied his reply. He straightened out imagined creases in his elegant purple robes. "As you should know, Velona is the westernmost city and still is far from the actual fighting. However, if we ever find out that you have sold grain to the Centurions, then I'll personally see to it that your deaths are as slow and painful as we can possibly make them."

Simon skillfully put on the appearance of having just been horribly affronted. "Oh Your Excellence! If ever I hear of anyone from the Greenway using your ships to bring our grain down here to sell it to your enemies, why I'll do it for you! That would be a treasonous act even in our simple farming land. You have our solemn word, Sir, that none of us would ever sell our grain to the Centurions, ever!" While he was speaking, I noticed that Horton chanted something to himself and then gazed sternly at Simon, concentrating his vision.

A spell of some kind, Simon, be wary, I sent mentally to Simon.

Don't let on we know he is, he sent back.

"Ah, you speak truthfully," Horton replied. I spied a strong sense of relief on his face. We evidently satisfied him. The meeting was abruptly over, "Go now then with my blessing. Make grain deals as you can. I fear we may need your grain in the future." He waved his hand, and the apprentice who had been standing by the door quickly came up to us and ushered us out. Simon bowed low as he backed up and joined us. In a few minutes, we emerged into the light of the late morning sunshine. Luigi was patiently waiting across the street, sipping a cup of tea. We crossed over and joined him.

We headed down the cross street called fittingly Po Way, Luigi in the lead. When we were a block away, Simon said, "Whew. That went better than I expected. Looks like he most feared we were going to sell our grain to the Centurions."

"He cast some kind of sooth-saying spell on you," I commented.

"Yes, I spied it too; he's not too subtle with it. Yet I was saying the truth. We have no intention of selling our grain to the Centurions — mostly because we really have none to sell!" We all chuckled over that one. So much for sooth-saying. Horton Po, for all his pompousness, was no match for us. That was encouraging.

"If I might make a suggestion," Luigi broke in on our laughter, "we should head over toward the Palace. Then, get a bite to eat for lunch before tackling the Prince." We agreed and followed dutifully behind him, marking our pathway by the surrounding buildings. I felt safe on these main roads because there always seemed to be a couple of guards within a few blocks. So if trouble came, they could stop it fairly quickly. Thus, we learned that the main streets were well patrolled, but that meant the alleys were no-man's land, if Luigi was correct.

Slowly the general layout definitely was becoming familiar. Every few blocks, the road opened into a general market place. Where the larger roads intersected, the largest of the markets were found. Interestingly enough, here on the main streets in the wealthy section, few people walked, and those were always well-dressed. Yet, back near where our inn was located in the merchant district, the streets were thronged with people. In that one brief trip into the slums to find Luigi's shop, the narrow streets were also filled with folks whose clothing and appearance was fitting their section of town. This was my first introduction into the segregation of people based solely on wealth, and I wasn't impressed. I was beginning to suspect the Prince had to rule his city with an iron hand or the populace would revolt.

Our first stop was what Luigi called a "moneychanger." The square stone building had thick iron bars over its four windows. A sign over the entrance door depicted small piles of coins. "These people seem to put an exorbitant stress on protecting their coins," I commented to Luigi. "On the whole, it seems to me to be rather a silly waste of resources. These coins are only a means of exchange."

"Aye, but it gets even more interesting. I want to stop here so you can exchange a few of your golden coins for a larger pile of coppers, which is the usual means of exchange for what we need, like lunch. These folks even charge you a fee for exchanging coins! Amazing," Luigi added and then opened the door for us to enter. Inside two armed guards stood on either side of the door. From their facial expressions, I could tell that they were exceedingly bored men. I know I would be if I had to stand by a door all day on the watch for robbers. We walked past them and up to the counter where a small, overweight little man sat on a tall chair. The trade took all of one minute; we placed four gold coins on the counter; he replaced them with twenty coppers and then removed his fee from our new pile, two coppers. I observed the great care he took carefully placing our four into one drawer, while placing his two coppers in a bottom drawer. Since the two were obviously his profit, the ritual made sense to me. At the end of the day, whatever he had in his drawer was his.

At the next market beyond the moneychanger's shop, we browsed among the food stalls purchasing bread, cheese, and a drink. Luigi picked out four large loaves of bread. The woman who operated the stall said, "Four coppers, please," in a most bored, mechanical tone.

Affronted, Luigi exclaimed, "Four? Down in the merchant's section, they charge one copper for four."

Sardonically, she replied, "Well, you aren't down in the merchant's section, now are you? Here it's a copper each. If you want four for a copper, why, I suggest you walk the five miles to the merchant's section and buy them there." That was the end of his futile protest. My next lesson in economics was a simple one: in the wealthy section, one could charge more and get it. I was beginning to dislike this coin exchange mechanism as implemented here in the Land of the Seven Sea Princes. I asked Luigi if the other cities operated similarly. He nodded affirmatively. I shook my head in disgust.

It was around one in the afternoon when we finally made our way to the Royal Palace of Prince Jamil Alvelardo. Ah, here was my idea of a royal palace! An ornate ironwork fence surrounded fully four square blocks, the tops of the fence were pointed and shaped like fish and boats in an alternating pattern. Standing at least ten feet tall, this fence allowed everyone to look onto the palace but kept visitors out. The palace was a large complex with many ornately designed stone buildings, all painted or dyed a deep sea blue to match the waters of the Med Sea. It was visually spectacular. We made our way to the South Gate where two armed men screened those who desired entrance. As before, Luigi, acting his role as street guide, took up a waiting position on the opposite side of the street. "We have an appointment to see the Prince," Simon announced to one of the guards.

I watched his eyes count our number, which evidently agreed with what he had been told to expect, and he noticed our clothing as well, which marked us as foreign visitors. "Follow me," he said sternly, though not unfriendly. We walked along a cobblestone path that led directly to the giant blue building, the largest in the complex. As we approached the two double doors covered in gold leaf, great relief murals of fish and boats adorned the front wall of the palace. These had been carved from the solid stone blocks that formed the outer walls. Raphael marveled at their design and wondered about just how such artistic stonework was actually made.

Once inside, another man dressed in richly colored, expensive clothing greeted us, took our names, rather I should say took Simon's name, dismissed the guard, and bade us follow him. As we entered, we walked on some kind of blue carpeting, which felt soft and luxurious under our feet. The walls of the hallway contained huge wall hangings depicting mariner scenes, perhaps the founding of Velona. All the lanterns that illuminated our way were made of pure gold, ornate in design, carrying the fish and boat pattern to new heights. The hall was not long, and as we entered through another pair of double doors, our arrival was announced by music! Two musicians played some kind of loud double reed instruments whose sounds were quite nasally. I liked this royal fanfare immensely, but said nothing. I resolved once again to keep quiet. This meeting was in Simon's capable hands.

A lush red carpet lay over the top of the blue one leading straight up to the immense throne, an elaborately made chair four times larger than a normal chair with gemstones and gold inlay in abundance. Sitting on his throne sat Prince Jamil looking the part of the ruler of the city. He spoke first, "Welcome to my palace, visitors from Greenway. You may approach my throne." Only Simon did; the rest of us stayed our distance adding to the impression that Simon was our leader. We knew that this man simply couldn't "have" a woman as a leader.

Simon spoke much as he had done before for Horton Po, "Greetings your Eminence. I'm Simon from Calgary, Greenway. We're traders for the largest grain company in the Greenway, the Able Seed Company. Our charge is to open up new trade routes with the Sea Princes. We've brought samples of the various grains we're empowered to market. If you would like to see a sample, we've brought some with us today."

Unlike Po, Prince Jamil was quite straightforward. He wanted to know the purpose of our visit. He explained that the entire land was at war with the Centurions from Megalos and that it would be considered an act of treason to sell any grain to their enemies. While they were discussing the situation, I observed the Prince. He was still a young man, probably around thirty, strong in muscles with no fat on his body. He obviously didn't lead a sedentary lifestyle. I spied some callouses on his hands, which matched those I'd seen on men who trained extensively with swords. His emotional tone was probably covertly hostile, and he didn't seem to react to anything Simon said, either in favor or not. However, I did detect some worry when he mentioned the ongoing war.

Simon now said something I hadn't expected, and I became alert once more to the talk. "We would like permission to visit the outlying towns and even the other six cities of your land to see what can be setup for grain trades. If, as you say, you are at war, then the more grain we can ship to you, the less you would have to rely on your own production. Unfortunately, I don't have any idea of what production of grains that might be, since this is my first time in your land. Do we need to get your permission to travel beyond Velona or to the other major cities?"

"Ah yes, you're quite right. Please make all of the grain deals you possibly can. I fear the day will come when such grain may be lifesaving, but I must extract your word that when the grain does arrive, if our city has been captured by these barbarian Centurions, then you'll dump the grain overboard, rather than delivering it into their hands. Do I have your solemn word on this? It's the only restriction I place on your dealings." Simon readily agreed, which pleased the Prince. "Now about traveling beyond the city. We have always deemed those from the Greenway welcome visitors. Our ships trade with you quite often. I accept you as friends unless your future actions suggest otherwise. You may travel to outlying towns freely. However, you cannot enter the other six cities without a visitor's pass. On your way out, I'll instruct Hamil to give you them. Guard them with your lives, but I caution you severely not to go to those cities that have fallen under Centurion rule. In Solamina and Zargarb, these passes, you may find, are likely worthless, and you may even be imprisoned by the Centurions there. Also, Pieta is besieged; even gaining entrance there is perilous. You might get captured by the enemy."

"Thank you very much. We certainly appreciate it. We didn't know there was a war going on before we left and brought our wives along to make this an enjoyable trip. I see now that was certainly a mistake on our part. I take your words to heart. None of us would want to endanger our wives," Simon replied formally.

Jamil laughed unexpectedly. "Then, you should do as I and take many wives. The loss of one is irrelevant." I tried to not show any reaction and bit my tongue. "Go now. Hamil will meet you at the entrance with the passes and instruct you in their use. Good day to you and may you form many valuable grain deals." Simon bowed and retreated to join us. Our guide then led us back the way we came.

We waited a couple minutes at the door for Hamil. The effeminate man finally arrived bearing seven sets of seven metal tokens, apologizing profusely for his delay. Using girlish mannerisms, he explained which pass went to which city. To assist us further, he gave Simon seven different bags to keep them in and bid us adieu. Yes, Hamil was a strange one, and we wondered who he was and what his position within the palace was.

Once out on the street heading back toward our inn, we asked Luigi about it. "Ha, so you met Hamil. Do you know Jamil has a dozen wives and so many children that no one seems to know their count?" Simon repeated what Jamil had told us. "What you probably don't know is Jamil has no affection for any of those wives. All of them are simply a front. His real lover is Hamil." At first, I was appalled at what Luigi was saying. I had seen no such signs at all from Jamil, but Hamil was definitely effeminate, rather like a woman wearing a man's body. Pieces of the puzzle of the society here in the Sea Princes were beginning to make a little more sense.

It was close to four in the afternoon when we finally reached the market closest to our inn. Thomas spied the flower shop woman and immediately headed her way. I trailed behind him with Roy following me. He had no intention of ever letting me beyond his sight. The others headed on into the inn. When I caught up to him, he had already spied the two tied bunches of yellow daffodils she had somehow acquired for him. "Wow. You found some! I'll take both and these two others here for Sarah Jane and Sandy. How much?" Again, she said nothing but held up two fingers. So Thomas placed two gold coins in her outstretched hand.

She looked aghast! Using hand motions, she indicated this was too much. She fumbled in her money pouch, brought out a copper, and signaled two coppers. "Oh I see, two coppers. Hum, here take one gold coin anyway. These are really beautiful. You deserve a little extra for finding these spring daffodils." He gave her one coin over her protests. She looked him squarely in his eyes and smiled.

Thomas handed me a bundle of the yellow spring flowers. "For you," he said with a big grin.

"Thanks, Thomas. It reminds me of home, that's for sure. They are beautiful," I replied.

Thomas then asked the flower woman, "Say, what is your name? I'm called Thomas. Now that I think about it, I don't believe you have ever spoken a word to me."

A frightened, scared look instantly flashed across her face. If I had not known better, I would have sworn it was the look of stark terror. She made some gurgling noises and began crying. Thomas looked at me completely upset that he had somehow upset this lovely woman. His look was "what did I say?" She hesitantly touched his shoulder, pointed to her mouth, and opened it. "Oh my god!" cried Thomas with a horrified look flooding over his face. Turning to me, he fumbled, "She's — she's had her tongue cut out! Barbarians! God this town is full of utter barbarians!" I've never ever seen Thomas this upset over something. He was positively livid with anger. At the same time, I felt pity for this poor young woman. *What could she possibly have done what would warrant such a horrid sentence for life?*

Unwittingly, I did something that set many events into motion. I mentally sent to Thomas, *Relax. Be careful what you say. We don't want to blow our cover. There are probable many spies around us.* He looked at me with the strangest look on his face. I did not know what to make of his expression. However, instantly, he suppressed his anger, an emotion he hardly ever expressed. He turned to the flower woman but said nothing. I watched wondering what was going on. I found out later.

Thomas, picking up on my mental message, realized he could communicate with her via telepathy. So he placed in her mind, *No problem. We can communicate this way. Just think what you want to say to me, and I'll hear it in my mind. I'm Thomas from the Greenway, north from here over the Appian Way. I come from a land that is always green, full of trees, and myriads of flowers. I love the out of doors, Nature, as we call her. Thank you very much for finding the daffodils. Back home, we have fields of these in the spring, a magnificent sight to behold. I hate living in cities like this one. So tell me what is your name? What should I call you?*

I saw the most surprised look suddenly appear on her face, and it didn't take me long to figure out why. Her lips feebly began moving as if she were talking, though no sounds but a gurgle came out. *How can you do this? You're talking in my head? I'm Thallia Mussio, but no one else knows my name except you.*

Thomas took her hand gently in his, but said outwardly nothing. *I'm very pleased to meet you, Thallia. I'm honored.* And he kissed her hand; she blushed, for her, his gesture was totally unexpected. *Do you mind if I use your name aloud so others may also call you by your proper name?*

No. The others just call me Tee because I have never been able to tell them my name. Does your homeland really have so many flowers? How can it be so green?

I heard nothing for ten minutes. From the two of them, obviously they were exchanging heartfelt ideas. I watched her face become delightfully enchanted. She stared wonderingly into his eyes as he did hers. I let Roy know what was going on so he would not worry, and we waited patiently on Thomas.

Roy spied another woman heavily armed approaching us rapidly, a look of concern in her eyes. *Trouble may be coming,* he sent me. I looked at the newcomer. This woman was also dressed in tattered leather that had seen better days. She was about six feet tall and all muscle. Strapped to her side were two short swords with two long daggers fastened to the outside of each leather boot. Across her back was a small crossbow.

She strode defiantly up to us, "Tee, are these people bothering you?"

Startled by her sudden appearance, Thallia looked at her and shook her head signaling an adamant "no." I could see Thallia's sudden frustration. She really wanted to explain to this woman, but had no means but clumsy hand signs, which the newcomer watched closely. She turned to us and said, "Don't be taking advantage of Tee here or there will be hell to pay. I'm Severnia Tolli, Tee's protector. She's had her tongue cut out. So don't try to take advantage of her." She placed both her hand menacingly on her two swords.

Thomas defused the situation rapidly, "Hello. I'm Thomas from the Greenway. I wouldn't dream of taking advantage of Thallia here. She is a beautiful and honorable woman. She's even found me some daffodils, for which I have gladly given her a gold coin. They remind me of home, you see. In fact, Thallia here is the nicest, neatest person I've met since I got here! We were just talking about my land, the Greenway, when you came up, and I must say I'm very pleased to find out that she has such a strong protector. You have my heartfelt thanks for looking after her."

Never had I heard Thomas speak so eloquently, so like a Judger. Perhaps, some of Simon's ways had rubbed off on our Loremaster! Situation totally defused, Severnia was now on the defensive. "A gold coin? Sir you must be crazy. A copper would be more than enough for a bunch of flowers. Wait a minute. She's Tee, not Thallia."

"No, we were just chatting when you came up. Her name is really Thallia, Thallia Mussio. She told me what had happened to her, how you rescued her from death, and helped her back to life," Thomas explained.

Severnia looked at Thallia, "Is this true, Tee? But you cannot talk. Surely, he is pulling my leg."

Thallia frantically made a flurry of signs with her hands trying to explain what he said was true, but really, there were no signs that could explain this circumstance. "Slower, Tee, slower," urged Severnia trying desperately to make sense of the hand motions. She pointed to his mouth and then her head, then her lips and his head. Severnia look mystified.

Thomas took matters into his own hands. *Like this. We talk like this. You just think what you want to me, and I'll pick it up. Doesn't anyone around here talk like this?* he placed in Severnia's mind. Now it was her turn to look startled and shocked. She put her hands involuntarily up to her lips. Her eyes opened wide.

"Then — then it really is true? Your name is Thallia, not Tee, like we all thought?" Thallia nodded vigorously yes. "Wow!" She looked at Thomas anew. "Are you a god?"

"Oh no, I'm just a man who loves the out of doors, Nature as we call her back home. Actually, all of us do, love Nature, that is, but me most of all. We're here trying to sell Greenway grain to the merchants in Velona and other cities around here," he explained.

She seemed somewhat satisfied by his reply so I interrupted them, "Thomas, the others are probably wondering where we are. They are waiting on us to go get supper. We should be heading to the inn shortly. Besides, I want to get these flowers into some water soon before they wilt."

Thomas agreed, begrudgingly, but gently took Thallia's hand, "May I see you tomorrow sometime?" She sent him, *Sure.* And her eyes were bright and eager, a fact that did not go unnoticed by Severnia either. As we left, could feel Severnia's eyes staring after us until we were out of sight.

Thomas happily trotted back to the inn, supremely happy. Roy and I followed discussing what we had seen. I was beginning to wonder about Thomas. Over dinner, Thomas told the others about his encounter with Thallia. After he had finished, I grasped better what he had done, but I was slightly worried. "Thomas, you came awfully close to blowing our cover there. Now at least two citizens of Velona know we are not just normal merchants. I hope word of this does not reach the wrong ears." Of course, I half expected Thomas to sheepishly look at the floor or something, indicating he knew he may had accidentally blown our cover, but he didn't.

"Sorry Bethany, but I believe I've learned something perhaps I wasn't supposed to find out. It bears directly on your concern. Thallia told me that, when she was assaulted, stripped, and thrown bleeding and naked into the slum's streets, she just wanted to die. For a long time, she just lay there in the street. There was a strong storm raging and water flowed all around her. After a long while, Severnia came to her aid, helped her into a house, washed her off, gave her some clothes, and even helped her to learn to eat without a tongue. Once the wound had healed, on a dark night, Severnia took her to a secret location outside of town where there was a large band of women who called themselves the Sisterhood. All are skilled at fighting and surviving in the wilderness as well as dealing with town thugs."

"Apparently, this Sisterhood is a secret society, for Severnia had neglected to tell Thallia that she was never to mention them. I think she figured that since Thallia couldn't talk there was no need. I picked up her concern that Thallia had indeed told me about it. Thallia said the Sisterhood members wear leather clothing, carry many weapons, and are highly skilled in their use. Often they wear these yellow headbands. I asked her if any had extracted revenge for her mutilation. However, Thallia said no one could ever get close to Horton Po to carry out that justice. So, Bethany, I think we may safely form an alliance with these women of the Sisterhood. What do you all think?"

Simon spoke first, "Well done Thomas! This is highly encouraging. Before we go exposing ourselves to the Sisterhood, we need to find out more about them. How large an organization are they? Ten, twenty, hundreds? Are they found only here around Velona? That sort of thing. If their numbers are large and widespread across the land, then we must enlist them as allies."

I added, "If they are not that large, we should at least offer them sanctuary in the Greenway should all of the Sea Princes fall to the Centurions. They seem, so far, to be very descent women who look out for others. In any case, Thomas, I give you the assignment to find out as much as you can about this Sisterhood." He willingly took on that task.

During the next week, Thomas always spent part of the day visiting with Thallia and occasionally with Severnia, who always seemed to be hovering nearby her, but out of sight for the most part. However, the next day when he asked her more about the Sisterhood, she replied in an embarrassed fashion that she found out she wasn't supposed to say anything about them. He left it at that, but that did not stop him; he was still a Guardian. From Luigi, he learned there was indeed such a Sisterhood, that it was an underground, secret organization of amazon women, as he called them. Beyond that, he could only discuss rumors the Sisterhood rescued those in dire need, mostly women.

Thomas kept his eyes open. From time to time, he spotted a women being hassled in one of the market areas. Often he would see a leather clad woman appear, as if from nowhere, blades drawn, setting matters right only to disappear the instant the situation ended. The Sisterhood was most definitely in operation in Velona.

The rest of us spent the week going from trader to trader attempting to establish new grain trades. Nearly half of those to whom we made our presentation seemed genuinely interested, but few could meet the payment, which was to be various weapons. The genius of Alabaster's plan slowly sunk in to my mind. If we could sell grain for weapons, we'd gain the means to defend our land better when the time came. Metalworking was rare in the Greenway, so importing them seemed like an obvious solution. Only the impending threat of war made the negotiations troublesome for the local merchants here in Velona, but those that thought they could acquire weapons did agreed to ship them to Calgary with grain in return as payment. We felt that if even some of these deals panned out, the Greenway would profit enormously. Wooden spears and arrows do little to armored Centurions, we assumed, still not having seen one.

The end of that first week in Velona brought two interesting situations our way. The first involved Thomas. A later afternoon thunderstorm rolled in over Velona while he was visiting with Thallia. The sky drew dark, lightning flashed wildly, thunder rolled over the city shaking even the ground, and the torrential rains plummeted down. Her flower shop was out in the open in the market square. As the storm first threatened, she and Thomas hastened to pack up her remaining flowers and take down her various collapsible trellises on which she displayed her flower bunches. However, when the thunder, lightning, and rains hit, Thallia panicked. She began crying uncontrollably, her body went limp and would have collapsed to the ground had he not caught her at the last instant. "What's the matter, Thallia?" he spoke aloud to her, suddenly terrified that something awful had happened to her that he had somehow missed completely.

Just then, Severnia appeared out of nowhere. "Leave her to me. She gets this way whenever a big storm hits. It's like that terrible day, if you know what I mean. I'll take her inside and care for her." She fully expected he would give Thallia to her and depart, probably never returning. After all, at the moment, Thallia was basically insane. Severnia knew no one wanted to have anything to do with a crazy person, male or female.

Thomas wasn't about to let go of her. "No. I'll help. I have her. Lead the way, please. Now that I know what is wrong, perhaps I can help her. Please, Severnia, please let me try!" He actually was begging her! Severnia looked sternly at Thomas and thought, "How can this be?" The heavy downpour had already soaked them, and the chilling effect was causing even her teeth to chatter. She had no time to argue with him. Begrudgingly, she led him down a side alley; Thomas carried Thallia, while she carried the sacks and other items that comprised the flower shop. Halfway down the dark, narrow alley, which was full of refuse and obstacles, she opened a door and motioned him to go inside. She glanced in all directions; seeing no one, she entered and shut the door. It was pitch black inside.

"Don't move. I'll light a lantern as soon as I get dry enough," Severnia whispered. Thallia was just shivering and moaning. Soon, a dim lantern illuminated a small room, about fifteen feet square. On one side was a single bed. A table with two chairs occupied the center on which the feeble lantern sat. On the other side, stacked against the wall were the equipment and sacks of flowers that was Thallia's shop. Also, on a small shelf lay the few meager clothes she owned. It was a very stark existence indeed. Severnia occupied a room that connected to Thallia's, and she left to get something with which to dry themselves off. Thomas sat down on one of the chairs and held Thallia in his lap, cradling her face to his chest. She continued to moan and shake.

Severnia returned with several towels, "Here, dry her off. I guess I must waste a little firewood. If we don't get her warm soon, she may take ill — us too, for that matter. Darn, that's a cold rain!"

"Yes, get it plenty warm in here, please, Severnia. I didn't know wood was so expensive here. I'll pay you twice what it is worth, if only you get it warm in here quickly; she's in shock. We must warm her up and fast, please." A look of complete surprise came over her face. No man had ever offered to pay for heat; none had ever cared for their well-being, for that matter. Yet here was this stranger, who only had known them for less than a week, and he was actually assuming some responsibility for their basic needs. She honestly did not understand how this could be. He looked like a man, but acted as one of the Sisterhood, but the Sisterhood only had women in it, not men. Men were the villains. Surely, this man had some devious plot in mind; perhaps, he intended to rape both of them. She, Severnia, wouldn't allow that! Still, she started the fire in the fireplace near the doorway to her room. Soon the crackling fire began to produce both light and warmth. Thomas moved his chair over to the fire.

"Darn, this'll never do it, Severnia," he said. "Our leather is soaked; we need to get her and ourselves out of these wet things and into something dry. Of course, we don't want to let the wet leather to get too close to the fire or it will become quite stiff when dry. We need to oil the leather a bit as soon as it gets slightly dry. Have you some dry garments we can use?"

Ah, now it comes. He is going to get us all naked and then have his way with us! Now it makes sense. I knew I shouldn't have let him come in here! Now how are you going to extricate yourself from this one, Severnia? She hesitated unsure of the best way to proceed.

Thomas picked up her thoughts; she was fairly screaming them. "Look, I'm not going to molest either of you. I'm here to help. I'm somewhat skilled in the healing arts. I have even helped two women give birth. Look, I'll put, no you take, all my weapons and place them anywhere you deem best. You keep all yours at hand. You're likely physically stronger than I am. So how's that? But please, let's get her out of these wet things, into something dry, and get her warmed up. Do you have a teapot? Something hot would also help warm us from the inside. Please, trust me. I know I can help her, if only you will cooperate, please Severnia, please."

At length, she yielded. She took his sword, dagger, and knife and placed them in her room under her bed where he couldn't find them. She brought out three nightgowns, thinking to herself, "No men's clothing in this house. He'll just have to wear a woman's gown. That'll teach him!"

Five minutes later, they had Thallia and themselves out of their wet clothes, dried off, and into the three nightgowns. Severnia watched Thomas closely, but he didn't stare at either woman's body and maintained a standard of dignity throughout. He didn't balk a second when putting on the nightgown. Instead, he reminded her of the tea and moved himself and Thallia closer to the fire. "It's working; she's shivering less. I'm going to reach her now. Don't interrupt me please."

Thomas expanded his mind and entered hers. He found her staring at her nightmare pictures, lying in the cold street, naked, and bleeding profusely.

I'm here, Thallia. It is okay. This is in the past. Feel my arms holding you. Yes, that's it. Feel your body touching mine. Good. Feel the warmth coming from the fire. That's it. Good girl.

She opened her eyes and stared at her surroundings, slowly coming back into the present. She clung to Thomas for dear life. He kissed her forehead, "It's all right now, Thallia. It's okay. We're here. And look, Severnia has made us a cup of hot tea. Can you sit up and take a sip?"

Severnia had placed three mugs on the table, drawing it and the other chair closer to the fire, for she was also in need of warmth. She held one cup up to Thallia's lips. "It's hot, sip slowly, Tee dear," she said. And then to Thomas, she added, "She's always embarrassed to eat or drink in public because of the way she has to do it — you know with no tongue; it's really hard."

"It's okay, Thallia; go ahead and sip," Thomas said reassuringly. "I promise I'll not laugh, if you promise not to laugh, Thallia." His remark was so out of place that she actually smiled and took a sip, throwing her head back to force it down her throat. While she sipped, Thomas and Severnia also began sipping theirs, feeling the warmth all the way down. "Ah, this is much better. Thanks, Severnia," he said and meant it.

"Severnia, I'll share a bit of healing wisdom with you. When she gets this way, all you need to do is to try to get her to feel her surroundings, like your arms about her, the floor, chair, whatever she is actually touching. Encourage her to reach out, touch, and feel what is here and now. That action often brings one back into the present and out of the past. My master once said he got a man out of a coma by having him feel the bed beneath his prone body. Admittedly, he said it took nearly an hour of doing it before the man regained consciousness, but it does work."

"I'll remember that," she said, "It seems simple enough." She though, *Now why didn't I think of that?* "I'll get our leathers set out to dry." She set about the task, glad to have something to do so she could ponder this strange man. He couldn't be a man; all men were bastards.

Presently, her strength back and warmed up, Thallia told Thomas that she was tired. He carried her over to her bed and tucked her in, making sure she was well covered. Again, he kissed her on her forehead, and she drifted off into a deep, much needed sleep. He moved back to the fire, joining Severnia. "She's asleep now. If it's all right with you, I'll stay a while longer until the rain lets up a bit and my leathers dry out a tad." She didn't object, so they both sat staring at the fire, watching it crackle, flicker, and warming their bodies. Neither said a word.

After a long time warmed by the fire, Thomas finally said dreamily, "You know Severnia, I come from the Greenway. Back home, life is so very different from here. In my land, men and women are complete equals. A village is more likely to have a woman running it than a man. The only thing that separates the sexes is that the really heavy tasks are done by men while the magic of birth is given to the woman. We believe that is the way of Nature.

I come here to this land, and I'm aghast at how perverted the beauty of Nature has become. Here, I find women, the bearers of the magical gift of life, new birth, are treated with less respect than we show our chickens! Sometimes during this past week, I have found myself wanting to kill all the men in the Sea Princes! Of course, that would never do; they have to recognize the error of their ways and remedy it themselves. I know that, but still there have been times." His voice trailed off as he stared into the flickering, warm flames.

Severnia listened with keen ears, noting his every word. When the silence came again, she added, "Then, your Greenway must indeed be a paradise." After another long pause, she commented, "Your friends or your wife must be missing you; it's been well over an hour." All her training patterns wanted this "man" out of her home. Yet, from underneath all that, her instincts suggested he should stay. She thought her comment would satisfy both urges, but she didn't anticipate his reply.

"Oh, Bethany knows where I am. We're always in touch, you know, mentally. She's said it was in Thallia's best interests that I should try to help her today. No, I have no wife. Heck, not even a girlfriend, but I did once have eyes for a girl back home." He couldn't help but glance over at the sleeping form of Thallia. *Then, again, maybe I do. She sure is pretty. I think she likes me too.*

From the back of her mind, Severnia's Sisterhood training kicked into high gear. *These people are different. They aren't what they appear to be. We must know all we can about them. Find out, Severnia.* "Are the others your friends? Can they all talk with minds as you do? That must be really wonderful if you all could."

Half asleep, warm, and dreaming, Thomas spoke without thinking, "Yes, we all do. Best friends." After a pause, he decided to ask the one question he really wanted to know but was almost afraid to ask. "Say, does Thallia have a boyfriend? Is she engaged to be married or anything?" *Boy, I sure said that badly.*

Though she was still grasping the full significance of his short reply and all that it implied, his sudden question was so silly. *Now that **is** a stupid question. Who on Tarra would want anything to do with a woman with no tongue, who cannot even talk and only barely eat? She'd be long dead if it wasn't for me and the Sisterhood.* She laughed in spite of herself, and, as he looked at her, she saw his face redden in embarrassment. "No, silly. No man will have anything to do with her. She can barely eat." *He is not all-knowing, duly noted.* "Why? Why do you ask?" *Surely, he doesn't — no, that cannot be.*

"I'm sorry if I've offended you," he apologized completely baffled at what his affront had been. *Perhaps, here men and women don't talk about relationships.*

"No, no apology needed; you've said nothing to offend me. It's just such a ridiculous question. If it weren't for me, she wouldn't even be alive any more. No, there is no one, and will *never* be a man in her life. None would want her. That's why I laughed. Nothing personal, you understand."

He brightened up; his mouth, she noticed, curved into a broad smile. "Well, since she has no family and since you seem to be her guardian protector, then I should ask you for permission. Severnia, may I court Thallia, that is, if and only if she wishes it? I have become rather fond of her." *There, I've actually said it aloud. Now, there's no turning back. It's okay if she doesn't want me too, I suppose. This is a different country, different customs. Heck, she hardly knows me.*

She stared at him for a moment and then smiled, "Ah, you're teasing me. You make a joke?"

"No, I'm serious. I really am fond of her. We share many likes. True, we barely know each other. That's why I want us to spend time together so we can explore each other. She is really a remarkable woman, beautiful too, in my eyes."

"Look, she is precious to me. No one should ever have had to endure what she has. I don't want any more hurt to befall her." Her training told her to tell him categorically to stay away from Thallia, but she found her lips saying, "But if I let you, will you promise to do nothing to hurt her in any way?" *What are you saying?* Hastily she added, "If you do, I'll have to kill you." *There, that should put him in his place. Is there such a thing as a kind, gentle, loving man?* She had a thought and voiced it, "Say, are all men similar to you in the Greenway?"

"Thank you. I promise never to hurt her, emotionally and certainly not physically. After all, I'm in part a healer not a mutilator. I take your question really to mean that you want to know more about how men treat women where I come from?" She nodded. "Yes, it is our nature. As I said, men and women are equal partners in life, sharing all the good fortune and bad. Both sexes love and respect the other, quite unlike here. I don't know how you all can tolerate life here," his voice took on a definite antagonistic tone. "I know I'd kill anyone who tried to hurt my friends: Bethany, Sandy, and Sarah Jane. They would return the favor if I were in danger." He soothed his emotions, "I'm afraid I'm just a foolish country boy; I'll never get used to this city living. I need trees, grass, flowers, birds, forests, meadows, hills, and space."

Severnia found herself repeating herself, "Then, your Greenway must be paradise."

"I don't know that it is paradise; we get attacked by the Galts and the northern Axemen. But yes, compared to what I've seen so far in the Sea Princes, yes, it's paradise. You'd be most welcome if you ever came to our lands."

The germ of an idea quietly stole into the back of Severnia's mind. Thomas, now fully awake, noticed the brunt of the storm had passed and slowly got up. "I guess I better be getting back to the inn now. I'll change into my leathers; they're almost dry. Thank you again for letting me wear these in the meantime." *So polite*, Severnia thought. She kept her back to him, fighting the urge to catch a glimpse of him. Hastily, she retrieved his weapons from under her bed. Fastening his sword, he said, "I'm sure Thallia would be too embarrassed to go out to eat at an inn, so I'll just bring dinner back with me tomorrow night, but first, I'll ask her tomorrow. Say, do you all have community dances here? I'd give anything to take her to a dance. That would be fun. She could really enjoy herself, and she wouldn't be in any position where she would have to talk and be embarrassed about it."

Gods, he is thinking of her well-being! "Well, yes, but this isn't for public notice. Come Fridays, many of us get together for music and dance. I'll ask and see if it is okay for you to join us." *How fortunate. It is a Sisterhood dance. This would be an excellent opportunity for the others in our group to meet these strangers, and I'm sure after I tell them all I've learned this afternoon, they're going to want to meet them.* "I'll let you know in plenty of time." She walked him to the door and undid the locks. He hadn't noticed them when they entered, but Severnia had her protections here with three dead bolts. In spite of the drizzle, Thomas walked light-footed back to the inn, whistling a melody from home.

When he got to his room, he found the others in it waiting for him. He looked a bit sheepishly at them. Sarah Jane teased him, "Ah, so you have been out with a woman, have you, two in fact." Even Sandy and Bethany were grinning at him.

"Is this a conspiracy? I was healing her. She was in severe shock. I got her out of it and safely asleep in her bed. Then, I had a long talk with Severnia while my leathers dried a bit. That was a cold rain." The three girls nodded in mock disbelief. "Honestly, that's all." After a pause, he confessed, "Well, I really like her. I asked for permission to date her. Severnia gave her okay. So tomorrow, I'll ask Thallia about it. Say, we may get an invitation to a dance on Friday night. That would be fun!"

Finally, the three girls relented, "Okay, let's eat, and you can tell us all about it. Honestly, Thomas, we're glad you've found someone you like. It's just that this is a rather awkward time to have found someone," explained Sarah Jane. They headed to the dining room.

Over dinner, Thomas explained all he'd learned. Simon had him repeat several things that he found most interesting or curious. "A private dance, invitation only," he said, "Don't you think that is just the least bit strange, Thomas? I sure do. I wonder if it's private because it's a Sisterhood dance? If it is, then you've done well indeed. We have a chance to meet more of them and find out what they're all about. If we get invited, we all must go, agreed?" Everyone did and not solely because the Sisterhood may be involved. All relished the idea of some carefree time. This spying business was absolutely no fun at all.

The next day, on their way to visit other merchants, Thomas stopped by Thallia's flower shop. He took her hand in his and mentally said, *Thallia, may I have your permission to court you? I already have Severnia's permission, but it's yours that matters. I promise not to do anything to hurt you in any way. Please?*

Big tears rolled down her cheeks as she replied, *But I'm a ruined woman. I can't even speak. You really don't want me, really?*

Yes, I do. Look, you are speaking to me right now. So that isn't a problem. I think you are a beautiful young woman. And so far, we have a lot in common that we can share. Let's give it a try, please?

Are you really sure you want to do this?

Only, if you care even a little for me. If you don't like me, why just say so, and I'll not bother you about it again.

Oh I do. I do care for you! You are kind and loving and gentle and honorable. She smiled, *And you like flowers. I've never met a man before that liked flowers.*

Then that's settled. Let's get to know each other better. I know you'd be embarrassed to come to dinner with me at the inn. So tonight about six, I'll bring the dinner to your house. Severnia can join us if she wants too. Your job will be to fix up the table really fancy. Decorate it with lots of flowers, okay? She nodded enthusiastically. Aloud he said, "I have to go now; they are waiting for me. See you tonight." She flushed and smiled with the largest smile she had ever made.

This was the longest day Thomas had ever endured. He couldn't keep his mind on anything but the time. Finally, carrying several large sacks, he found himself outside her door, which opened into the back alley. Thallia opened it, let him in, and quickly locked the three bolts. "Wow, you look exceptionally beautiful tonight, Thallia, and whoa, look at our table!" She beamed. She had visited the communal bathhouse and had Severnia fix her hair with many violets intertwined. She had covered the bare table with a sheet and cleverly arranged all the unsold flowers around it. A third chair had appeared, but once the three had sat down, the flower arrangement surrounded them, making a unique dining atmosphere.

Thanks, glad you like it. Our private bower, there is no inn like this, she thought to him. Severnia came into the room from her adjoining room making a last minute adjustment to her hair. Even she had washed up for the occasion. She still did not fully trust him, and, when he saw the horrible way Thallia had to eat, why, there was no telling how repulsed he might be. Above all, she did not want her charge to feel ashamed or hurt, not if she could prevent it.

Thomas helped each woman settle into their chair, but he had to rush it because neither expected such. Then, he took out the plates, utensils, and cups, which the women neatly arranged. *What did you bring?* Thallia asked mentally, barely able to contain her excitement. Even Severnia felt the tingle of a long unfelt emotion in her stomach and watched eagerly. He produced a full course meal from the sacks.

"Roast duck in almond and olive oil," he said, "I'm told it's the finest, and everything else to go with it. Plus, da ta!" he exclaimed as he produced a keg of wine. "Here, we have a keg of the finest red wine the inn had, Amore 521. Was that a good year?"

Severnia gasped. Thallia protested, *Thomas! That's an extremely expensive wine! Only the very wealthy can afford it. And the duck, yes, it's a gourmet meal; we've never had it. You shouldn't have spent so many coins for this. It — it is nearly a months earnings for me!*

"Oh, it's only a few gold coins; that's all. What good are coins anyway? It's what you can get in exchange that means anything. Besides, I wanted this to be a very special night — for both of you and for me too, for that matter. I've never done this before, so if I mess up, why let me know."

You mean you've never taken a woman out to eat? Thallia asked both in disbelief and out of feminine curiosity.

He spoke aloud so that Severnia had a chance of following the conversation. "Nope, I've never taken someone out to eat. Actually, until now, I've never known anyone I particularly wanted to take out to eat. Come on; we best start. It's already getting cold." He poured everyone a mug of the wine.

Thallia was a bit hesitant. Before now, only Severnia had ever been present when she actually ate anything or drank anything. It was so hard to do without a tongue, so utterly humiliating. She hesitated afraid to begin for fear that this romantic evening would come crashing to an end. Thomas also sensed her fears; Severnia had long known this moment would come and held her breath. *If this doesn't drive him away, then nothing else will*, she thought to herself.

Slowly, Thallia put the mug to her lips, dreading the moment. There was no way out, she was going to have to eat. He was going to have to see her in her misery. After taking a sip, she tilted her head back so the wine could ease down her throat more readily. *There, that wasn't too awfully bad.* Then, she remembered he could read her thoughts and blushed hoping he hadn't heard that thought. Instead, he said, "Good, eh? As good as it is reputed to be?"

He didn't laugh or think her funny, thought Severnia.

"Try the duck; it's really savory, though I'm not sure I like these olive things. Never had them before. Seems that you folks have them in everything around here. Still, maybe they take some getting used to," he chatted. Emboldened, she took a bit of the duck. It was every bit as delicious as stated. Of course, she had a hard time chewing it, moving her head side to side to help move it between her teeth and again, had to tilt her head back to help the swallowing action. "Good, eh?" he said, ignoring her eating methods.

Absolutely! It is the best thing I've ever had, though I wish I could taste it better.

"Oops, sorry, I forgot about the taste aspect. Still, I hope you enjoy it," he said bashfully.

Oh, I do! I do. Then, she ate in earnest. For the two women, this was indeed a royal feast.

When they had eaten until they felt like bursting, Thomas sat back and said, "Well, if we were back home now, Thallia, I'd take us out for an evening, moonlight stroll in the meadows, stop and lie down amongst the tall grass and flowers, and smell Nature at her finest. We can smell the flowers here and pretend. As I understand it, it's not safe to go for evening walks in this part of town, perhaps not in any part of the city. How can people live like this?"

Do you really have all those green meadows where you come from? asked Thallia.

"Yes, for hundreds and hundreds of miles, there is nothing but tall forests and green, rolling hills, and meadows. True, we have towns and villages, and some people have converted some nearby lands into farmsteads to grow crops, but the vast majority of the land belongs to Nature. I do wish you could see it. I know you would love it there."

"I'm going to leave you two love-birds alone for a while. I have urgent errands that must be handled yet tonight. However, Thomas, you and your six friends are most welcome to come to the dance tomorrow night. However, if you choose to come, then you *must*, I repeat, *must* abide by whatever rules I place on you. It is a secret dance, held in a secret place — one that cannot be revealed to you."

"Oh that is terrific! My friends already said they would just love to come! Whatever you say," he said.

"Okay then. Come here about seven just after full dark. Knock three times on the door. I'll take it from there, but remember, not a word of this to anyone else under pain of death. And it is secret. You cannot know where the dance is located — your safety and ours."

"Not a problem. From what little I have seen of this city, I agree wholeheartedly with you on that," he assured her. Satisfied, she took her leave, letting them have some time alone with each other, but insisting Thallia re-bolt the door after she left.

As Severnia left, she felt a slight twinge of jealously toward Thallia. *If only I could meet a Greenway man like him.*

Later that night, when Thomas finally entered his room, he knew he was in love with this marvelous woman of Velona. He related the invitation and the restrictions. Simon thought the restrictions were justified, if indeed this was a secret underground society operating in the heart of the city.

Friday night at seven sharp, the seven stood outside Thallia and Severnia's door. Thomas knocked thrice and Severnia opened it. Her eyes stared into the darkness up and down the alley. Confident no one was spying, she let them enter the nearly dark room. A single half-shuttered lantern provided the only light. Several other women were inside as well. When the door was shut, Severnia spoke sternly, "Okay, there's seven of you and seven of us. We must walk several miles through the back alleyways. We go in two's; one of us with each of you. There will come a point when we'll blindfold you for the final leg of the journey. May I have your word not to try to peek?" We agreed; Thallia doused the lantern, and Severnia opened the door cautiously peering into the dark alley. Then, Thallia took Thomas's arm and headed out the door. One by one, the other women took one of us and led us after them. Severnia took my arm, and we paused while she secured their door.

No one said a word, as we cautiously walked the length of one dirty alley to the next, pausing only to spy out the street intersections before darting across into the next alley. After an hour, I estimated we were likely nearing the northwestern edge of the city. I could smell earth faintly on the cool evening breeze. Now it was blindfold time, and I must say they did a thorough job making sure we couldn't see a thing. I do remember smelling horses just before we entered a building and heard a large door close. The blindfolds were removed; Thallia now held a lantern so we could see that we were inside a building of some kind. I assumed some form of a barn. She led the way into the rear and then down a long flight of steps to a huge underground room. Once inside, our eyes blinked from the brightness.

Here was the party, the dance. Many lanterns hung from huge rafters about eight feet above us. I estimated some hundred women were gathered here. The musicians were seated against the far wall, while tables with food and drink sat along the wall to either side of the entrance. Severnia spoke first to the other women, "Okay, here are the visitors from the Greenway. Now let's show them a dance!" The musicians struck up a lively tune, and, though hundreds of eyes stared at us, the women broke into pairs and began dancing though still eyeing us. Thallia pulled Thomas out among the dancers, but their dance form was completely different from what we knew. Awkwardly, we joined in and slowly picked up the basics.

Theirs was a close up, personal form in which each held the other's hand and also had an arm around the other's waist and shoulder. I could tell Sarah Jane was really going to like this new style of dance, once she and Raphael got into the feel of it. Roy and I fumbled a bit more than the others did, but soon we too were enjoying this very personal style. After perhaps a half hour, other women began cutting in on us all, and we found ourselves dancing with the others. As you might expect, the guys bore the brunt because all hundred wanted a turn with them!

At last, during a break, I asked if they would like to hear some of our dance music and see our style. Of course, they insisted. Roy borrowed one of their musician's lute-like instruments. I had brought my flute. Sandy, Simon, and Thomas found some heavy boards that would serve as logs, while Sarah Jane and Raphael, our two best dancers, took center stage. Everyone stared at the boards completely bewildered. I said, "We have an overabundance of trees and a distinct lack of musical instruments in the Greenway, so we compensate. Watch."

First, Thomas began thumping his board on the floor, playing long, evenly placed beats. Then, Sandy joined in playing the same long, even beats, but exactly in between his beats. This gave the illusion of a doubling of the beat. Finally, Simon came in as well, still playing the same long pattern but in between the other two. Now the rhythm seemed really fast. Then, Roy and I began playing one of our fast dances. Sarah Jane and Raphael let the music roll for a minute and then began our fanciest jumping, toe tapping dance, which predominates everywhere in Greenway. Although at first rather bewildered at this very different style, they soon began clapping and trying to emulate the vertical jumping motions. Soon, all Roy and I could see was a sea of bobbing bodies.

We played several more tunes and then Roy whispered to me, "Play your favorite lament, Bethany, please?" I agreed and he announced, "Bethany is going to play one of our traditional songs, the Lament for the Willows." The lone flute began slowly and softly, melancholic, as a breeze in the distance. As it grew louder, soft percussion joined in, and the crescendo gave way to the lament, as it seemed to float off into the distance over the hills. A large round of applause told me that they did appreciate it.

Then, their musicians took over for their next set. However, one woman took my hand and asked, "Thomas says that you are their leader, is this so?" I nodded wondering why. "I'm Rosita Bellini, the leader of this group. May we have a private word?" Again, I nodded. *Finally, maybe I can find out about them.* She led the way over to a wall and slid open a concealed door. We stepped through and she shut it behind us. Inside, I found myself in an armory. There must have been a hundred weapons nicely stacked and well maintained lying on various tables. She motioned to a chair, and we sat down facing each other.

For a moment, neither of us said a word; I felt as if Rosita was sizing me up or thinking of the best way to begin. At last, she said, "I'll be honest and frank with you and expect that you will be likewise or this discussion is ended." I nodded. "We've been watching you from the first day of your arrival in Velona. You're different from the normal travelers who come here, very different. Thallia and Severnia have also added their observations. Although none of us has ever been to your land, we aren't ignorant women. We do know something of the Greenway; don't ask how. We know within that land are small bunches of very special people who are called the Guardians. We also know these Guardians look after the well-being of the other people. The only conclusion I can draw is that you seven are indeed Guardians. Is this not so? Are you all Guardians, protectors of the common folk?"

"It is supposed to be a secret. I mean, we're supposed to be 'traveling merchants,' but this is our first such trip, and obviously, we're not doing so well at maintaining our cover. Yes, we're all Guardians back home," I answered truthfully, waiting to see what came next and also wondering that if she saw through us, then perhaps so did Horton Po and the Prince. That was a scary thought.

"May I ask one question that really has nothing to do with anything, but one which the other women out there are dying to know." Again, smiling, I nodded, but I could guess what was coming; I wasn't far off. "Are women really treated as equals in the Greenway, that is, outside of the Guardians, the ordinary men of your land, do they really see us as peers? Is this possible?"

"For the most part, absolutely, though there are a very few isolated pockets of local tyrants who do not. But yes, we're all equals, though the men do the heavy, hard labors, and we bear Nature's gift of new life. In smaller villages, the village leader is a woman, if that helps any. We're all horrified at the conditions here in Velona. It's sickening really."

"Good, the others will be pleased to hear that. Now let me tell you a bit about ourselves, before I ask anything further of you. In the Lands of the Sea Princes, women have been second-class people for as long as anyone has memory, perhaps more like objects or possessions of the men. We have virtually no rights whatsoever. Many of us at one time or another rebelled or rejected this inequity. You have seen what the men here do to any woman who even speaks out of turn. Thallia is a good example. Thus, we have banded together and gone underground, the Sisterhood. Each and every new sister we accept undergoes a rigorous training period before she is accepted. We must be able to fight and fight better than most men, if we're to survive. At this point in time, we have a reputation that has spread far and wide: mess with a Sister and you end up very dead. So we're tolerated as long as we stay in the background. Not even the Prince's guards would dare challenge one of us."

"Are there members in all the other six big cities or the more rural areas?" I asked hoping she would answer and not think I was prying.

"Absolutely, the Sisterhood is everywhere, even in the Centurion conquered lands as well. The Centurions, however, may not know we exist, and we intend to keep it that way. We travel to all the outlying villages helping women where we can, recruiting too. We often provide escort to traveling merchants, who pay royally for the total security and confidence that no one will attempt to rob them. We make a considerable amount of gold doing just that, which has financed the Sisterhood. On a couple of occasions, we have even been hired by the Prince himself, though we first had to know what it was about; we reject any assignment that in any way is harmful to women, if you follow me."

"It is no wonder that the cities are falling to the invaders. The men here have become complacent and are poor fighters, preferring bravado to actual deeds. Though we have eyes everywhere, we're invisible, unless we desire it. Only then do we don our yellow headbands. Many a highway man has accosted us only to spy our headbands and quickly run away."

"Now that I've told you a bit about us, I would like to ask you a personal question. Yes, you may think I'm prying into your affairs, but we need to know. What is your purpose here in Velona? Surely, it is not trading grain for weapons."

She was being honest with me. Though it meant really blowing our cover, I felt an alliance with the Sisterhood more than warranted it. "We Guardians know it's just a matter of time before the Centurions invade the lush Greenway. We have few metal workers in the entire land, so in part, all the weapons we can slowly acquire will be put to good use against the Centurions, but that isn't our real purpose, only our cover."

"We are trying to find out if there are any allies in other lands whom we can support to help defeat these invaders. Also, we know nothing of the style of war that they make, nothing of their strategies or tactics. Unless we can observe them first hand, we will not know their weaknesses in order to exploit them. We cannot fathom what their purpose in attacking all their neighbors can possibly be. We are to go all the way to Megalos if we have to in order to find out the real reasons behind their passion for attacking their neighbors. To that end, we already have acquired the necessary tokens to enter the other six cities."

All through my speech, I felt the stern, icy drill of her eyes on my face. I knew she was seeking signs of the truth. I gave her no reason to doubt me. Rosita then said, "Thank you. I believe you are telling the truth, for it is what I would do were I in your position in the Greenway. Knowledge is the answer that I try to drill into all our recruits. Knowledge and the force to back it up," she added. "Therefore, I offer you the services of the Sisterhood, should you ever need it."

"It's my turn to thank you," I replied. Then an idea struck me, "Say, if ever any of your women want to migrate to a new land and leave this forsaken land, the Greenway awaits. No one can cross the Appian Way. Instead, head all the way to the western coast and then go north. Not too far north is our largest city, Calgary, known to all mariners, I assume. When you get there, ask for Alabaster; say Bethany sent you. He'll look after you, on that you can count. However, I suspect most of you are like us and want to stay and protect the others as you can. If ever that becomes untenable, know that you can always seek refuge in the Greenway, a most welcome refuge, I might add."

"Thanks for the generous offer. I'll pass it along to the others. Say, we had better get back to the dance. It'll be over soon. I'll relax the blindfold rule on your way back." We shook hands and reentered the dance; both of us got what we wanted in that meeting.

By ten, the dance was over, and after thanking our hosts, we departed much as we had come, save the blindfolds. An hour later, we stood outside Thallia's home, while Thomas gave her a good night kiss. Then, we hastened on to our inn. Once safely inside, I relayed all I'd learned from Rosita. We felt a bit more secure, more confident, knowing that all around in the background were people who had values somewhat similar to ours.

The second event happened late on the Monday night. We seven had been working out the final arrangements with the last of the traders we needed to see in Velona. It was dark by the time we finished up, shaking hands to seal the deal. This night, Luigi was not with us, and we were forced to make our own way back to the inn. However, in the dark, we took a wrong turn and ended up in the slummier part of town. Slowly, we made our way through the streets, cautious of every passerby. Eventually, we recognized the general area of where Thallia'a flower shop was located and relaxed our guard just a bit. While we were discussing why we got lost, Thomas heard a woman scream from a darken side alleyway across the street from Thallia's alley.

He didn't wait for us or even listen to us. I suspect he had visions of yet another woman being brutalized, maybe even Thallia. Even I did, now that I mention it. He dashed headlong down the alley many hundreds of feet, tripping over various bits of junk along the way. He came upon a hooded man standing over a young woman. The man had already ripped most of her clothes off and was preparing to have his way with her, a dagger held to her throat. "Let her go now!" yelled Thomas, drawing his own short sword.

The man growled, "This bitch is mine to do with as I wish, and I wish to play. Get away or I'll kill you as you stand!"

Thomas ignored him and tried to reach the prone woman to drag her out of the assailant's way. However, the man lashed out with his dagger. It cut deep into his left arm. Instinctively, all Thomas's fighter training kicked in. In a flash, his sword found an opening, and one swing later, the man's throat was cut. He dropped his sword, clasped both hand to his neck in a useless attempt to stop the gushing flow which spurted all over Thomas and the young woman, who screamed uncontrollably. The man slowly sank to his knees and then collapsed onto the cold, filthy alley.

We caught up to Thomas at that instant. Sandy immediately entered the woman's mind and sang calming words. Her screaming subsided to a whine, and then she was quiet and finally passed out. Sarah Jane looked at Thomas's bleeding arm and began tending to it at once, tying her leather belt tightly around the gash. Simon and Roy went to inspect the fallen man. They pulled back the hood revealing a familiar face. We all gasped. It was Horton Po. Thomas managed to whisper, "He'll never mutilate another woman. Justice served."

Just then, Severnia and Thallia arrived, swords drawn, but on seeing us, quickly lowered them. "Oh no. You killed Horton Po. There'll be hell to pay for this one. Did anyone see you?" We looked about at the nearly black alley. "Come on; we gotta get you out of here fast! Bring the woman. She cannot be left to identify you. Come," she ordered. We were really still in shock and hesitantly followed her. Thallia, seeing that Thomas was wounded, clung to his good arm, with Sarah Jane, still holding the belt tight, on the other.

Just as fast as we could we ran back out of the alley. Simon and Raphael carried the young woman, Roy acting as read guard, Severnia leading. No sooner had we crossed the open street and ducked into their alleyway, than we heard the tell-tale thumping of many feet coming from up the alley from where we had left Po. Evidently, his guards had been close by. We heard yelling and screaming from his men. "Search, they can't have gone far! Follow the blood trail." Roy saw a number of lanterns spring to life, illuminating the street and at least a dozen guards. He watched them slowly heading down the alley toward the street we had just crossed.

Severnia cursed. She knew she could not hide them in their house; if the blood trail did not lead the guard directly to it, why, a house-to-house search may well ensue. She cursed again and whispered, "We're going to have to make a run for it. If only there was some way to distract them."

Simon responded, "Thallia, come with me. Roy, take over for me; help carry her." Roy did as he was told, but it took Thomas to convince her to leave his side.

"Here, hold my hand Thallia, as if we are on a date. I'm going to distract them. Trust me." She nodded and did so, albeit hesitantly. Simon walked them to the end of the alley where it joined the street, chanting a spell under his breath all the while. I knew what he was doing, and smiled. He timed it right. They reached the edge of the alley just as the first of the guards came from the other direction.

"Ho, what's the trouble, sir?" asked Simon innocently.

"There's been a killing back down there. Did you see a bunch of thugs running away?"

"Sure we did. Three headed on down the street that way," he said, pointing in the general direction of Thallia's market square. Of course, Thallia saw the blood trail clearly crossing the street and heading down her alley. She almost panicked. Surely, they would not believe Simon. "If you hurry, you can catch them," he added for good measure. The two completely ignored the blood trail and headed off toward the market square. Simon stood still while pairs of other guards came onto the street. He motioned them in the right direction. Finally, after the last of the guards had run off the wrong way, he pulled Thallia back into the shadows of her alley. "Now let's run and catch up with the others. You know where Severnia is likely headed, so I'll follow you."

But how come they went that way? The blood goes this way, Thallia thought in protest. Simon, senses acute, picked up her confusion.

"I cast a little spell over their minds, clouding their senses. Now come on; let's hurry. Soon they will backtrack. We want to be long gone when they come back." She needed no further urging. Quickly, they raced down the alley. Thallia was sure she knew what Severnia had in mind. Besides there was always the blood trail left by Thomas. However, the drops became fewer and fewer, more and more widely spaced until they stopped altogether.

Severnia knew that deception was their only hope. She led them down one alley and up another, in a confusing, twisted path that seemingly went nowhere in particular. Yet, she had a definite destination in mind. Meanwhile, I saw Thomas was continuing to lose blood, marking our passage. So I took off my leather top and wrapped it tightly around his arm. That did the trick: no more blood. I admit that I looked a bit unusual running through the alleyways in my undershirt, but no more so than the young woman the guys were carrying. Soon, I heard the telltale sounds of surf crashing on a beach. We neared the Med Sea.

Severnia led us down a very narrow alley full of unseen obstacles. We slowed to a walk, carefully making our way trying not to make any sounds. Then, Severnia stopped by a door, took out a key, fumbled in the darkness, and finally got the door opened. "Step inside just enough to let me shut the door. Only then will I strike a light. We don't want to be seen," she breathily whispered; we were all out of breath for that matter. We managed to get inside without stepping on too many toes in the process. It seemed like an eternity standing there in utter darkness waiting for the light.

I heard the sound of stone on steel, spied a spark, and vaguely saw her blowing. Soon, dim lantern light illuminated the squalid room in which we stood motionless. "This is a safe house. Light the other lanterns while I go out and watch for trouble."

"May I come too? That's my job in our group," Roy asked her.

She nodded, but said, "Be very still and quiet."

They swiftly stepped out into the dark alley and hid behind some boxes from where they could see the way we had come. "That way leads to the sea; no one will come from that way," she whispered.

Sarah Jane and Sandy immediately went to work on Thomas. I scrounged for water and anything that could be used for bandages. "No poison. Thomas, you are lucky," Sarah Jane commented. "Bad cut though, clean. Going to have to sew it up, and we don't have our gear. It's all back at the inn. Now what do we do?"

Raphael managed to get a small fire going in the crude stove, and I set a pot of water on to boil. We then met to try to figure out how we could sew him up without any of our equipment. Just then, the door opened, and the four others came in; Thallia brought Simon here. Sarah Jane said to Severnia, "We need to get our things from the inn so we can sew him up. Do we dare go back there? We can't just leave all our things back at the inn."

"If you all don't go back to the inn, or at least most of you, they'll be very suspicious, so we need to get you back, but not Thomas. He's going to have to stay here," Severnia thought aloud. "It won't do to have you all go back this late, leave again, and then get back even later — way too suspicious. What exactly do you need to fix him?"

"Well, at least a needle and thread," Sarah Jane explained. "If we don't close it, he'll just keep on bleeding. Tomorrow perhaps we can make some healing potions to put on it, but tonight, we at least have to close the wound."

Severnia thought fast, "Okay, here's the plan. Thallia will go back to our place, get what you need, and return here. One of you can stay the night here with him. The rest of you, I'll escort back to the inn and return here. Tomorrow, the rest of you can meet Thallia in the market, and she can bring you here, how's that?"

I spoke up, "Even better, we're done with our dealings in Velona anyway. So we will check out of the inn tomorrow morning, saying we're heading to Barcella. That way, it'll not raise any suspicions."

"I'll stay behind," Sarah Jane insisted. "After all, this is my specialty."

Thallia left to fetch the items Sarah Jane needed, and we waited patiently until she returned. Severnia refused to leave until Thallia returned. "She is a very good fighter; she knows how to defend you." Thallia returned in less than a half hour, panting heavily; I suspected she ran all the way. Raphael gave Sarah Jane a goodbye kiss and told her to be careful. Then, we took off, following Severnia. Roy really hated splitting up like this, but there really was no other way, unless we wanted to announce to the world that we did the deed. We knew, though it was self-defense, it would not matter in this city. He had killed their High Priest.

Alone with Sarah Jane and Thomas, Thallia was very worried. She longed to ask if he was going to be all right, but Sarah Jane was busily sewing him up, and he had passed out from the pain. Besides, Sarah Jane didn't grasp the hand signs she was making. Finally, Sarah Jane realized she was trying to communicate. She paused in her work and concentrated on Thallia's mind. *Ah there, that's better. Now I read you loud and clear. I cannot usually do two things at once. Yes, he is going to be fine. It's a clean wound, no poison. He'll be stiff and sore for a while though. We can chat once I have him fixed up. You had better keep an eye on the young woman we rescued.* She saw the relief on Thallia's face and watched her go over to look after the unconscious woman. Sarah Jane returned to her careful sewing. She decided not to put any bandages on it until the others brought her gear. *There is nothing worse than a dirty, makeshift bandage.* She heard moans from the other woman. *She's coming too. I'd best see to her.*

Please do. I cannot talk to her.

"Hello. I'm Sarah Jane. Are you hurt?" she asked the totally disoriented woman who immediately grasped at her torn clothes to cover up her bosom.

"Alicia. I don't think I'm hurt. Did he — did he do me?" she asked, afraid to ask what she had most feared.

"Nope, Thomas here rescued you before he did more than rip your clothes. You had a narrow escape. Your attacker knifed Thomas here. He had to defend himself, and he killed your assailant." Alicia smiled hearing the news. "The real problem is that your attacker was none other than Horton Po, the High Priest." Alicia gasped, nearly screamed, and then fainted. This was worse than she could imagine. As soon as she re-opened her eyes, she began wailing and crying. Thallia desperately wanted to talk to her, to sooth her nightmare fears, but couldn't. Instead, she tugged on Sarah Jane's arm pointing to her head.

Tell her that she's among friends. That we'll protect her. Tell her that she has nothing to fear. We'll protect her from any retaliation. Ask her if she is married, Thallia thought, hoping Sarah Jane understood her. Through the voice of Sarah Jane, Thallia comforted Alicia and brought her sobbing to an end. Together, in silence, they awaited Severnia's return.

An hour after she had left, Severnia returned with three other Sisters, all armed to the teeth. After Sarah Jane explained what she had told Alicia via Thallia, two of the new women whisked Alicia off into the night to take her to a place of total safety. Sarah Jane pondered what this poor woman must be going through — to suddenly be uprooted from her whole life. She hoped Alicia would somehow be allowed to retrieve her possessions. She sat on one side of Thomas and leaned her head on his chest intending to monitor him through the night. Thallia did likewise on the other side. Severnia and the other Sister took turns standing watch. Sarah Jane thought to herself, "Beyond any doubt, this Sister had already gotten many things into motion that we know nothing about as yet."

214

Chapter 11 Antonio Po, High Priest of Tur

It was May 10 officially, as it was just after midnight, when a bodyguard awakened the young Antonio Po. "Sire, I hate to disturb your sleep. I bring terrible news."

Lean and tall, Antonio, just twenty years old, wiped the sleep from his eyes. He hated being awakened from his fabulous dreams of sailing on the high seas and glorious combat with the infidels, all in the name of his God, Tur. "Yes, what is it? It had better be important, Jan." He knew Jan would never dream of entering his room, let alone awakening Horton Po's eldest son, his handpicked successor.

"Bad news, I'm afraid," Jan fidgeted with his pants. He knew this hot-blooded Po would likely take his wrath out on him when he heard the news. However, as Antonio's main bodyguard, he had to inform him. "You father has been killed tonight, just after ten pm." He braced himself for a fiery retribution. Sometime ago, he had brought Antonio the news that his mace had been broken and couldn't be repaired. His buttocks still echoed the severe beating he had endured, while Antonio raged at him, as if it was his fault, not Antonio's, even though it was Antonio who had misused that weapon. This time, however, Antonio reacted very differently.

"What? How can this be? Where? Who did it? Where were his guards? Come on man, spill it all?" yelled Antonio, as if the sheer volume of his voice would somehow pry this man's tongue loose.

Taken aback, Jan tried to explain, "Sire, I don't know much more. Apparently, Horton Po was down in the slum section visiting a local entertainment house." He wanted to say flophouse or pub of the wretched, but substituted a more polite wording. Everyone knew what he meant. Horton was well known as a frequenter of houses of ill repute. He enjoyed beating and maiming helpless women, who should know better than to earn a living serving wine, beer, and their bodies to men. Horton was often heard justifying his actions as "teaching them the errors of their ways."

"Sire, I'm told it was fairly dark inside the pub, and Horton slipped out the back alley with the wench. The guards didn't notice he was missing for several minutes. When they noticed he had gone, they headed out back into the alley and found him dead. It happened within just minutes. Naturally, the guards charged after the killers, but lost them. They're still searching; one came to notify us and ask for instructions. He awaits orders down at the gate."

"Well, what of the wench? Did she identify who the killers were? Why didn't the guard bring her here as is the standing law?" Antonio forgot to be harsh with Jan, because his mind was racing to accept the facts and correlate them. He had no real love of his father, considering him little more than a womanizer and a drunkard. How Horton had ever acquired the High Priest position eluded him. He, Antonio, had spent years memorizing all the rites and rituals befitting the status of High Priest. He, Antonio, should have been High Priest. Now fate had just unexpectedly thrown this coveted position into his lap! He knew he must act the part, don the role of High Priest, though the council would have formally to anoint him, and they could very well pick his cousin Flamel! He remembered that Horton had just last week sent his rival to Vito on church business. By the time word reached his cousin and he could get back here into the city, he, Antonio, would have already assumed the position. He would have to act as if he already had it. "Come, my nightgown. Help me look presentable."

Jan fumbled through the wardrobe to find the exquisite purple gown and helped Antonio to look proper. Why this young man could not even dress himself eluded him. "Sire, the wench also disappeared I'm told."

"What? All in the space of a couple minutes? Horton goes out into the alley with a wench to have some fun and gets killed, and the killer and the wench both disappear?" He was angry now. This made no sense. Either the guards were skillfully lying about the time factor or something else had gone on. But what? Satisfied that he looked presentable, Antonio charged out of his bedroom, down the staircase to the door, and out across the grounds to the front gate. He spied five of the grounds guards in their perfectly matched purple uniforms standing and talking to one of Horton's personal guardsmen whose clothes looked disheveled. He recognized the man.

"Andre, as the new High Priest of Tur, I command you to tell me what happened, all the details, leave nothing out. Be warned that I, as Priest, can tell if you are lying. So if you value your head, do not alter anything!" Andre's face paled, and he visibly shook, knowing if he erred in any way, his life would be over. Antonio inwardly chuckled. This was the one thing that his father had taught him that was worth knowing. He could no more tell whether a person was telling the truth than his father. He remembered his words, *Even though we can't tell if a person is lying, act as if we can and are, then the other person will automatically believe that we can. Works every time, but you must be convincing.*

"Well, Your Excellency, Horton took us down to the pub on Market Street in the slum section. We got there about nine. The place was smoky and not well lighted; you wouldn't expect otherwise there in the slums. Anyway, Horton struck up a conversation with the serving wench and ordered us to a back table; drinks were on him. We kept an eye on him as best we could. Somehow, around ten when the wench had a break, they both disappeared — ducked out the back, as we found out when we rushed up to the bar. We headed out the back door, which opens into a dank alley. About ten feet from the door, we found his body lying on the ground with his neck cut clean in half. His blood was everywhere. We got some lanterns and spied a fair number of bloody footprints leading back down the alley. The wench was nowhere to be seen. There were fresh tracks, so we rushed down the alley following them. Unfortunately, we lost them when they entered Center Street. I went back and inquired about the wench. She owned no weapon, and we have her address.

On my way here, I stopped by her place and broke the door down looking for her. She wasn't there, and her neighbors said she was working at the pub and wouldn't be back until the pub closed around midnight. Just in case she should show up at her house, I left an armed guard there. Then, I came here to report the devastating news."

It wouldn't do to alienate Andre just yet, so Antonio said, "Very well. Then, you swear Horton was alone for no more than a few minutes at most?"

"Aye, Your Reverence. Anymore and you would rightly call for our heads!" Antonio caught the faint glimmer of being played up to — Andre was no fool. With Horton gone and Antonio, his son, the likely heir to the throne, if he wanted to keep his position as Head Guard or even be a guard, he would have to endear himself to Antonio.

"Very well, let me think a moment." To ensure his position as the new High Priest, he knew he must act the part, starting now. Give the council no opportunity not to anoint him. "Okay, first thing Andre, collect a wagon and horse. Take three of the guards here with you and retrieve the body. Take one of the Holy Purple cloaks with you, and see that his body is honorably covered. See that he is given the proper respect on his return journey here. Jan, see to it that a visitation space in the Chapel is ready to receive him when they return. Second, Andre, on your way, send word to Prince Jamil of what has happened. Order, no make that request, request him to launch a full-scale investigation at once, starting yet tonight. These assassins mustn't be allowed to leave the city! I must visit the site and see this blood trail myself. I can't understand how you could lose so easily a defined trail!"

"But Your Reverence, these assassins are still running in the streets. It isn't safe for the new High Priest to travel them, especially at night. Perhaps, their intention is to slay you as well. Could Flamel be behind this?"

"You're right. They may be watching me even as we stand here! No, I know Flamel; he is basically a coward with chickens for a brain. He wouldn't be able to think of such a plot, but I fear I may be the next target. Okay, then, I'll go at first light when the streets are safer. Have a large mounted escort here at the crack of dawn. I must see these tracks with my own eyes before they are trampled. Go, you have your orders." Andre clicked his heels and headed out back to fetch our wagon. Two gate guards accompanied him.

Antonio and Jan headed indoors, but not until he ordered all the sleeping guards to be awakened. He wanted total security here on the church grounds until morning, just in case he was the next target. Once back in his room, he changed into his formal priestly clothes, confiscating his father's scepter and robes of office. The robes were made for an overweight man, but they would do for now. Satisfied he looked like the High Priest of Tur, he accompanied Jan to make ready the official viewing room in the Church. He would give the council not one item to criticize, leave them no choice by to anoint him and very soon. Then, he ordered breakfast and waited until Andre returned with his father's body. After ensuring the body was properly dressed and lain correctly upon the slab for people to pay their final respects, he sat down and ate a large meal.

At the crack of dawn, true to his word, Antonio walked to the front gate, half expecting to find his orders not fully complied with. To his surprise, twenty guards with their horses stood at attention awaiting him. In addition, Feliz, a Captain of Prince Jamil's Home Guard, was there.

"Ah, High Priest Antonio," Feliz, a burly fighter not prone to formalities, greeted him. That he referred to him by his new title surprised him somewhat. Evidently, Jamil also calculated that he would assume the position. After all, the two highest positions in Velona were that of the ruling Prince and the High Priest. Antonio smiled inwardly; Jamil was already appeasing him. That was a good sign. After all, this assassination occurred on Jamil's turf. "Prince Jamil sends his greatest condolences. He wants me to tell you that no expense will be spared in tracking down the assassins responsible for this despicable, unholy deed. I'm told you wish to visit the site. We await your orders." Antonio thanked him and mounted a horse. His guards formed in around him protecting him from all sides. They galloped through the mostly deserted streets, as the city slowly showed signs of life.

Once on the site, it was obvious what had happened. Horton had come out into the alley. There were numerous footprints in the now dried blood — all leading on down the alley toward the major cross street. Antonio examined them. He could easily see where his father had fallen. Apparently, the wench was also on the ground, for bits of her dress lay covered in blood. He reasoned she'd been on the ground when the killing occurred. Studying the dried footprints, he could see three different sized feet clearly marked. One of the guards pointed out this is what led them to believe at least three assassins were involved. The evidence was overwhelming. Next, the group followed the prints on down the alley. Certainly, the trail had been muddied up with the passage of the guards on their several trips back and forth. Even the wagon wheels left their mark.

At the intersection, the trail unmistakably continued into the next alley. Here, Antonio halted and summoned the guards who had chased after the assassins last night. Repeating his do not tell a lie speech, he asked them to describe what happened when they reached this spot. All said they'd thought they saw the blood trail going right into Center Street and had gone that way. All six guards repeated precisely the same story. Antonio fumed; even in lantern light, the trail was unmistakable! He railed against them in an effort to change their stories, but even though they feared for their lives, none varied it.

"Hey wait a moment. I remember now. I was in the lead when we got to this spot. I remember seeing a young couple walking out of that alleyway there where the blood trail obviously goes. I recall now. I asked them if they saw three men running away. The man said that three men just came running out of the alley and headed right onto Center Street only a moment ago, and that if we hurried, we might catch them."

Antonio breathed a sigh of relief. *Now we are getting somewhere!* "Who was this man that misdirected you? What did he look like?"

Naturally, he received six different descriptions. One said, "You know, I think it might have been one of those foreign visitors. You know — those that came in on the Lucky Lady a week ago. I've seen them around town quite a lot during the week. I'm not certain it was one of them, but it looked like one of them. Usually, those folks have been going places together, all seven of them. I can't recall seeing just one of them by themselves. The young woman was definitely not one of these visitors."

"Okay, thanks. You realize you probably were staring right into the face of the assassins or at least one of them? Guess you were lucky you weren't killed on the spot. So, on the offhand that the man you met was one of them, take some men, go check out the visitors at the inn, and also check out that local guide they hired to get them around the city. I recall seeing him outside the gates when they came to see dad. I don't know his name, but I think he is some kind of net maker down here in the slums somewhere. Check it out. The rest of you, escort me back to the church. I must officiate at the visitation ceremonies and make burial arrangements."

Around ten when the guards finally got to the inn, they found the visitors had checked out only minutes before they got there. They then went to the home of the night manager and asked him about the visitor's activities the previous night. He could only say he thought they were all there. Certainly, he had seen several coming in that night. None appeared injured in any way, and they appeared normal. Andre, though, had an idea. He went back to the inn and found the maid who looked after the rooms. From her, he discovered an interesting fact. According to her, one bed had not been slept in that night. The other three showed signs of use. It was interesting, but not conclusive, but at least he had something to offer his new liege.

Jamil's forces had not been idle. With so obvious a trail, he had ordered fifty of his guards to do a thorough search of the alleys, knocking on every door, asking if anyone had seen or heard anything that might be helpful. They did learn the visitors from the Greenway had been seen in the company of the Abominations heading out of the city early that morning. However, they also knew these visitors intended to leave shortly anyway and had been given passes to the other cities. That they should choose to hire the Abominations, while a bit strange, did make sense. They provided the best escorts that money could buy, and surely, these visitors would need their protection. After all, they were only young kids.

It took the guards two days to locate Luigi, the Net Maker. He had been out on a short trip helping the Venturesome repair her fishing nets and had not been their escort for the last two days. Luigi swore he knew nothing about these visitors other than they paid well for his navigation about the city for a few days.

For the next week, Antonio had little time to ponder the assassins. He had many priestly duties to perform, even though the council had not yet anointed him. Carefully and paying close attention to proper detail and ritual, he carried out each task including presiding over the burial of his father. He even sent word to the council asking them to anoint him soon, explaining that with these assassins still at large, the Church of Tur must have a leader at once to show the people of Velona that the assassination of their High Priest would not bring down the wrath of Tur upon all their vessels at sea. It was his incessant pressure that forced the council unanimously to agree to anoint him on Saturday.

Only on Sunday after services did Antonio finally have time to relax and consider all the evidence that had been gathered by his guards and those of Jamil. Since no sign of the assassins had been unearthed, Prince Jamil was in a tenuous position at best. Thus, he volunteered all the information, scant as it was, to the new High Priest — via, of course, one of his attendants. Antonio paced the length of his room for the twentieth time, thinking hard on all the bits of information regarding the assassination. The only fact that kept annoying him was the deliberate deflection of the guards onto Center Street by the young couple. The wench still had not appeared, and by now, most presumed she was dead as well. Likely, she had seen the faces of the assassins, and they'd disposed of her — maybe even dumping her body into the sea for Tur to deal with as he saw fit. Antonio found it most curious that the guards found a resemblance to one of these strangers from the Greenway. How convenient it was for them to leave in the early morning right after the assassination and in the company of the Abominations.

Finally, he reached a decision. An hour later, five ill-looking men were ushered into his meeting room. His father had used their services on many occasions; now Antonio would do likewise. "Gentlemen, this meeting has never taken place. I've never seen you." He said the very words he'd heard his father use with them. They nodded agreement, and their eyes brightened up knowing a lucrative assignment had just fallen into their laps.

"Two weeks ago, we had seven visitors from the Greenway here in Velona. You can recognize them by their attire; they wear leather always. Shortly after Horton was assassinated, it's possible that one of them misdirected the guards, leading them away from the assassins. It's clear that one or more of the assassins were wounded by Horton before he died. Just how seriously remains a mystery. Conveniently, they left Velona early the next day in the company of the Abominations. They were last seen riding northward from Velona. Your assignment is to find out where they have gone, what they are currently doing, and most importantly, find out if one or more of them have an injury of some kind, but under no circumstances are you to make any contact with these visitors or the Abominations. I'm not paying for your deaths. Report back to me and me alone; don't speak of this to anyone connected to Prince Jamil. How much do you require?" He hoped he had the amount of gold they wanted at hand. It wouldn't do to go dipping into the Church funds so soon after taking office.

The five muttered amongst themselves a moment before one spoke, "Mess'en with Abominations is most dangerous. If these be the assassins, it could mean our hides. We can do it, but tis gonna cost you. Say a hundred each?"

Inwardly, Antonio signed in relief. His shrewd guess was correct, and he was prepared. He recalled his father had always made a formal protest at this point in the bargaining process, so he did likewise. It was only a token, and he quickly handed them five bags. They nodded, thanked him, and abruptly left without another word. *Five hundred gold coins are well spent if they bring back what I suspect they might. However, Antonio, you must tread very carefully! It's likely Prince Jamil may be the one ultimately behind the assassination. He hated dad for years; they hardly ever agreed on anything. On the other hand, these five are the very best spies in all Velona; I don't know how many times I've heard dad proclaim that fact. If my guess about these visitors pans out, I must plan my revenge very carefully indeed.*

During the ensuing week, Antonio kept himself more than occupied with official church business. Affairs had to be straightened out and the unfinished tasks completed. Plus, he completely reorganized the church staff — out with the old and in with the new — well, younger men, and ones that he trusted. Daily, he hounded Prince Jamil about the progress the Prince was making on finding the assassins. Politically, this was his key opportunity to strengthen the hand of the Church, while weakening significantly that of the Prince.

For days, the slaying was the hottest topic of conversation among the common people of Velona. Antonio sent many of his guards out to mingle with the larger crowds, spreading rumors about how unsafe the streets of Velona had now become under Prince Jamil's weak rule, so bad that even the High Priest wasn't safe! He knew instinctively he was slowly wrestling popular favor over to the Church of Tur.

On the other hand, Prince Jamil's attention was more occupied on the upcoming war with the Centurions. His comment to one of his aides summed up his position: "I hated that old man, good riddance I say. Look, we've no clues about who is responsible, so we'll just let it be. All the fuss will die down in a few weeks anyway. Any loss of favor among the people will be more than regained when the Centurions come knocking on the city doors later this year. Probably the young upstart High Priest will come to me on his knees begging for help. So we just wait it out."

On Sunday night, exactly one week after Antonio sent his five spies abroad in search of clues, his aide, Jan, hastened to fetch Antonio from his study. "They are back, Your Excellency — those you hired. Shall I admit them to the same waiting room?"

The High Priest looked up, trying not to show outwardly the intense excitement boiling up within him. "Yes, right away. Make sure no one sees you let them in." He donned his purple robe of office and headed to this side chamber of the church. He only had time to sit in his high chair and arrange his robes to look proper before Jan came ushering in the five darkly clothed men.

Once Jan had left and closed the door, the priest commanded them to report. The same one who had spoken on the last visit replied for them. "Your Eminence, the seven did go with the Abominations to their training station in Portillio. They stayed there until the morning of the seventeenth, when they accompanied the Abominations on a protection caravan bound for Bonilla. The cargo is a fair number of ship masts bound for the city. From some of the townsfolk, we learned one of the men of that group is indeed injured. His left upper arm was heavily bandaged during his stay at the training camp. While the others took weapons practice with the other Abominations, this one did not. The injury must be a significant one. However, no one heard any talk from any of them, including the Abominations, about the assassination, other than what is common talk around here in Velona."

"You have done exceedingly well, my associates. Tell me, were the Abominations at all alerted to your presence? Do they suspect we might be on to them? Any hint that the Abominations may have played a hand in this foul deed?"

"None, Your Holiness, none in answer to all those questions. I trust we have fully complied with the original bargain?" Antonio sensed that this was the man's official attempt at closure of the deal.

"Yes, excellent. However, I may have a follow up mission for you, one that is less dangerous. Interested?" The greedy smile on the man's face plus the encouraging grunts from the other four in the background satisfied Antonio. "You say they have joined a convoy headed to Bonilla. Well, I would like to arrange a slight accident for them along the way. Wouldn't it just be too bad if a large band of bandits attacked them and killed these seven?" The five men chuckled, instantly grasping the nature of this new assignment.

"What about the Abominations?" he asked.

"Kill them all, of course; leave no one left alive," Antonio answered almost in anger.

"Even the drivers?"

"Yes."

"Your Eminence, that might not be so wise, killing the drivers, I mean. If only these visitors and the Abominations are slain, no one will say anything, save good riddance. Killing the drivers — now that is another matter."

"Ah, I see your point. It wouldn't do to get the people enraged. So, spare the drivers, unless they intervene," Antonio hastily amended his suggestion.

"The only possible inconsistency, Your Eminence, is to attack a caravan of ship masts makes no real sense. No profit. Normally, bandits strike on the return trip when the drivers are carrying their rich payments back home. That is only a small detail in an otherwise clever plan." He tipped his hat and laughed in a covert, evil manner. His companions did likewise. Antonio knew they had already agreed to execute his plan.

"So you would not by chance know of any bandits who, for a tidy sum, would do this deed without asking additional questions, would you?" Antonio held his breath. It was one thing to accept his plan, but quite another to know whom to buy to carry it out. The five put their head together consulting among themselves in whispers. Try as he might, Antonio could not hear what they were saying. *Have faith, Antonio, faith. Tur answers all.*

The leader turned to the priest, "Yes, I do believe we know one that you seek."

"Hush, not a word to me, gentlemen. This way I can honestly say I didn't even know who it was that attacked these unfortunate visitors." He grinned and they chuckled; he got the distinct impression they rather liked his style. "Perchance, might you have some idea how much funds it would take to so convince this person to do this deed?" He expected the sum to be large, but he also hoped it was affordable. He just couldn't lose this opportunity to strike back, not for his father's sake, rather for his own. He intended to show the world that he, High Priest Antonio, was a force with which to be reckoned.

"Aye, I would expect that said individual may agree if presented with twenty-five hundred. Send along say thirty-five hundred so we may bargain and get you the lowest price, returning any excess." Inwardly, Antonio breathed a sigh of relief. This was approximately what he had already set aside for just this eventuality.

"And what amount for you to tend to this affair?"

"Oh a mere hundred apiece will suffice. As you say, there is no danger to us in this matter, just using our connections, transport, and bargaining powers. It may take us some time."

"Excellent, gentlemen. I do believe we have reached another agreement. How soon can you begin?"

"In the morning, if the funds are available. You realize we're not to be held accountable if said bandits fail in their attempt?"

"Perfect timing. Yes, you can't be held accountable if they fail, but do try to pick ones that will not fail. Now about these funds. Surely, it shouldn't be in gold coins of the realm. Traceable. Correct?"

"Ah, His Eminence is most wise. Yes, gemstones would be the means; stones tell no tales, if you take my meaning."

"Okay, wait here with Jan for a moment while I fetch what is owed you, gentlemen." He got up, signaled for Jan to enter, told him to watch over them until he return, and hastened to his bedroom. There, he opened a secret compartment in his bureau and brought out a number of sacks. Already he had a sack with five hundred gold coins in it. A larger sack held a large number of gems, emeralds and diamonds mostly, each one worth about fifty coins. Carefully, he counted out seventy gems. Without thinking, he placed them into one of his church leather pouches. After replacing the rest, he shut the secret door. Satisfied, he hastily rejoined the others, and Jan once more left the room.

"You'll forgive me, but this time I have run out of money pouches. This one contains the five hundred. I assume you can divide it up equally at your leisure?" The man nodded. "This one contains seventy gems worth about fifty each. Spend it wisely. I will be awaiting the results, though you're not obliged to report back on the results. It would be wise if you were nowhere around when it happens, if you grasp my intention."

"Aye, you're right on that account. We'll be long gone, ere it happens. Once again, we thank you for your business. If ever you have need of us in the future, you've only to ask. We wish you the best of luck in the results." With that, the meeting was over. Jan came in and ushered them outside, watching them slink unseen across the church grounds. He wondered just how they managed to get inside without the guards noticing them. Jan resolved to find out. This could represent a security threat to the church.

Chapter 12 Flight Across the Lands of the Seven Sea Princes

It was May 10, 559 AH, when we checked out of the inn in Velona. Already the news of the assassination of the High Priest was on the lips of nearly everyone. Yes, it was called an assassination by parties as yet unknown. While we ate our usual breakfast in the dining room, we heard others discussing it in hushed tones. We listened but said nothing. Later, while others carried all our gear outside, Roy and I checked us out of the inn, settling the account with a few more coins. As planned, Roy casually let the manager know that we were heading for the next large city, Barcella. We suspected many other ears would soon learn of our supposed destination. I believe he was never tenser than that morning; relief only came when we finally joined the others in the street.

Casually, we strolled along, mingling with the usual morning crowds of people. Sandy stopped by several food merchants picking up supplies, especially for Sarah Jane and Thomas who probably had not eaten since yesterday noon. Slowly, we made our way along the main street and then turned onto smaller and smaller byways until at last we approached the alley. When we were certain no one was following us, we darted into the alley and rushed to the door. By daylight, the abandoned slums looked rundown. One heavy push on the door would likely break it off its hinges. We knocked three times, and Severnia opened it, glanced in all directions, and then let us in, quickly shutting the door once more.

"How's Thomas?" I asked, as soon as I was inside.

"Still sleeping," Sarah Jane whispered. "Food. I'm starving. Please tell me you brought some!"

"Right here," exclaimed Sandy, who produced what she'd acquired a few minutes ago. I inspected Thomas's arm, while the four of them dove into the food. Even Thallia forgot about her embarrassment, stuffing bread and cheese into her mouth. I could see Sarah Jane's neat handiwork; she had the knack for sewing up wounds, almost as if it were to be looked upon as a work of art.

Severnia interrupted me, "How soon can he be safely moved? We must get you out of the city and the sooner the better. There may be a house-to-house search. Po was an important man; the Prince must at least pretend to look for his assassins."

"Pretend?"

"They are — were rivals for power — their families, that is, so Jamil has no real liking for Horton Po. The deed has shifted the balance of power at least temporarily over to the Prince. I'm sure another in the Po line will soon step forward and assume the High Priest post. Since he has three brothers, I suspect they will in-fight some days before one wins out. We can't let Thomas be found," she explained.

"Well, Sarah Jane's the Healer. At the least, she needs some time to dress and bandage the wound, and he must eat something to gain his strength. I'll see to repairing his leather shirt and get the blood off of mine." I set to work first on getting the blood off, and then I sewed a patch in his left sleeve. By the time I finished, Sarah Jane had finished dressing and bandaging his arm. Roy had his spare shirt out, and we carefully pulled it on over Thomas's swollen arm and thick bandages. Sandy then tied his cloak around his neck to hide his arm further. Meanwhile, Thallia fed him, so in less than a half hour, we were ready to depart. Thomas got up and tried a few steps; he was still weak and a bit woozy. Thallia remedied that. She put her arms around him, supporting him and also giving the appearance of their "lovers," which of course they now were.

Before we actually opened the door, Severnia held a brief council. "Okay, here is the plan in case something happens and we get separated. Our first destination is the barn where the dance was held. We walk in pairs and stay close together so no one can get between us. Keep Thallia and Thomas in our middle. At this point, we don't want the Sisterhood to be seen escorting you out of the city, so I'll go some distance ahead of you but close enough in case of trouble. At some point, another Sister will fall in behind us protecting our rear, so don't be alarmed, or pretend to notice her. She'll just nod her head once as a signal. Reports are suggesting there are an unusual number of guards patrolling the streets this morning. Let's try not to raise any suspicions." We agreed, and after peeking to make sure the alley was still deserted, she boldly walked out.

When she crossed the larger street ahead, Roy and I followed; Thomas and Thallia came next; Sandy and Simon next; Sarah Jane and Raphael brought up the rear, though she was still munching on the remainder of the loaf of bread. We held each other's arms to assist in creating the illusion of four happy couples out for a morning stroll. As we crossed the street, I saw a number of guards to either side of the larger street; they were stopping passersby. Severnia cleverly kept to the alleys as much as possible to avoid them.

As they walked, Thomas sent to Thallia, *Well, my dear, you've seen justice served on the animal who inflicted all this misery upon you. I think it's ironic that he died while trying to molest and ruin another young woman's life.*

She replied, *You know, for a very long time I wished to see him dead. Now that the deed is done, I actually rather pity him. He died still never changing his ways.*

Thomas added, *He'll be back in another baby body soon, I expect. He and we all are immortal spiritual beings. I wonder what will happen to him if he ends up with a woman's body next time around?* Thallia actually laughed and smiled. *See, you laughed! This is the first time I have seen you laugh! You look positively beautiful when you laugh.* She squeezed him and leaned her head onto his shoulder. However, before they had gone too far, she felt him weakening, leaning more and more on her for support. This worried her, and again she lamented the fact that she could not easily let the others know. She resolved to carry him, if need be.

Sandy came to her rescue, "Slow down a bit; he's weakening. Say, after we get into the next alley, stop for a moment. I've a plan." While we wondered, Sandy and Simon quickly visited a shop in the market area that we'd just bypassed. She came back with a bottle of wine and proceeded to pour a large amount of it over Thomas' face, drooling it down onto the front of his spare shirt. "There, now you reek of drunkenness. Thallia, Simon is going to take over. It seems Thomas has celebrated our departure this morning with a wee bit too much to drink."

Her plan was brilliant. No matter how much Simon had to support or even carry Thomas, anyone checking could not help but smell and see the wine. I complimented her on her quick thinking. We resumed our slow passage once more, Thallia falling in beside Sandy right behind Thomas. Sandy's ploy actually worked.

At the next intersection, three guards accosted us. One asked, "What's the matter with him?" They were on the lookout for one or more wounded men.

One look at Thomas, one whiff, told them all. Simon, though he was prepared to force an illusion on the guards, didn't have to say anything further than, "He's celebrated our departure just a wee bit too much this fine morning." They motioned us onward, suggesting we get him home before we ran into any trouble.

After two harrowing hours, we finally left the edge of Velona and walked up to the small farmstead, which was adjacent to the northeast edge of the city. Severnia was already there and made sure we weren't followed. Once inside, the men carried Thomas over to a large straw pile and laid him down, Thallia and Sarah Jane at his side, examining him. "Just fatigue. Wound is fine. He's just done a bit too much too soon," the Healer officially pronounced.

Only then did we notice we weren't alone. Ten women dressed in leather and armed to the teeth with swords, daggers, and crossbows strapped across their backs were waiting patiently with a large number of horses; all were concealed in the back shadows. Severnia said, "Go change Thallia." She turned to me and said, "It's all arranged. The Sisterhood will take you north about ten miles to a small village called Portillio. There, we have a safe house and training area. You can rest up and make further plans. Is he well enough to ride? Can you all ride horses?"

"Yes to both," I said, my voice full of thanks, "and thank you for helping us out. I hope one day that we can return the favor."

One woman who I remembered seeing at the dance spoke up, "You already have!" I smiled and didn't have to guess what she meant. Thallia soon rejoined us, dressed in leather ready for action. She, too, was now well armed. She tied a yellow ribbon around her head, and I noticed all the other women had similar headbands on. I realized that from this point on, if anyone came close, they would immediately see we were under the protection of the Sisterhood. From their supposed reputation, I suspected we would not encounter any further trouble.

We mounted up and rode out into the late morning. The sun shone brightly; the sky, clear; the air, fresh. We were out in the open spaces, which we all loved, and our spirits soared. Only then did I realize how much we had all felt confined while in the city. Even Thomas perked up once we began riding. About two miles out, we crested a large hill and paused to look back down at the view. The city sprawled like an octopus below — its tentacles stretching out into the sea — its docks. "Amazing how beautiful the city can appear and yet be the home of such misguided men," I commented.

Severnia nudged her horse closer to mine and asked, "You have great wisdom. Please answer me this: can men ever change for the better? We already know that anyone, man or woman, can change for the worst. Is there any hope that they can change their ways for the better? Or do they all just have to die out? Some Sisters think that the coming of the Centurions may be a good thing — that the killing of many of our men would force them to change their attitudes toward women."

"I don't know the answer to that, Severnia. Yes, we have all seen good turn to bad. How to change bad back into good remains a mystery to me thus far. As for all the killing, nothing good will come from it. Look, have you ever seen dead men creating, building anything? No, wanton destruction is never good. It only makes it easier for the winning side to control the losers now, replacing one tyrant with another. My guess is that life here will become a good deal harder than it is, if and when Velona is conquered by the Centurions. But, Severnia, you ask a really interesting question: how can one change bad into good. I promise you that I'll try to find an answer to that one."

Thallia made a number of hand signals to Thomas, who gave up trying to figure them out and just chatted with her mentally. Then he spoke up, "Thallia wants me to tell you what I told her a while back. That is, we're all immortal spiritual beings that inhabit a body. When the body dies, we merely go find another baby body and begin once more. What Thallia wants to say is that, if Horton Po accidentally gets a female body next time, he'll get to experience what we have, so maybe he'll then see the errors of his ways."

"I don't know anything about spirits and such," bemused Severnia.

"Oh, it's easy. Can you get a picture in your mind of us walking through the alleys this morning? Okay. That picture is your mind. Now who's looking at the picture?"

"I am," she said slightly confused.

"Well, that's you, the being. You, the looker at the pictures — you are immortal and cannot ever die as we know death of these bodies. Back in the Greenway, we Guardians hold a special ceremony for anyone under our care whose body dies. During that ceremony, we help them find a new mother about to give birth. That is, we help them to get their new body. It is the least we can do for them."

Severnia thought a moment and said, "Well, if all we women could suddenly come back in male bodies in vast numbers, we could change the way our society treats women, but we'd have to resist the temptation to do as was done to us now."

"That, Sister, is an astute observation," I replied. We nudged our horses onward.

As we rode along, we noticed the countryside for the first time since we arrived in the Lands of the Sea Princes. The ground was generally arid. While we passed some grain crops, barley and wheat, groves of olive trees and enormous vineyards predominated. Small farmsteads dotted the countryside within the first few miles from Velona. The ground itself tended to be very rocky, and the hills rose and fell, but always rose higher the closer one got to the Appian Way. From the hilltops, we could just barely make out the line of the towering blue mountains, some still snow-capped in a few places at the higher elevations.

What were missing were trees. All trees in a giant semicircle around Velona had long ago been cut down and used to build their great fleet of ships. To get timber, they now had to go more than ten miles inland and so found it cheaper and easier to acquire timber from other lands bordering on the oceans. The village of Portillio stood at the very edge of the timber cutting arc. Some villagers still made their living cutting timber and hauling it down to the Velona shipwrights, but the village mainly made wine and exported olives. We arrived there just after sunset while we could still see.

At the edge of the village stood a large home and barn complex, the Sisterhood's retreat. We headed straight for the barn where several other women stood awaiting our arrival. A woman about thirty spoke first, "Welcome Sister Severnia. Safe journey? Are these the ones?"

"Greetings Sister Lucretia. Yes, no trouble. These are they. Guardians from the Greenway. Yes, one of them did slay Horton Po; good riddance." We dismounted and she introduced us one by one. "This is Sister Lucretia, the leader of the Portillio band. She will look after all your needs. My band must return to Velona in the morning. Thallia can stay as she chooses."

We shook hands in turn with Lucretia. She was a strong woman, about five-six, with short black hair and black eyes. Stern though she was, she yet made us feel welcome. She had a brownish, weathered complexion; my guess was she spent most of her time out of doors. "You are safe here as long as you are within our complex, within the fenced in area all around here. After you take care of the horses, I'll show you to the bunk house and where meals are served."

While the guys helped the Sisters with the horses, we three women carted all our large sacks up to the bunk house, a long narrow building with many doors and rooms. A quick estimate yielded close to twenty doors. Each opened into a twenty by twenty foot room that was starkly furnished with two beds, table, chairs, two wardrobes, and a washing up table with a facing metal mirror. As Lucretia showed us to four adjacent rooms, I took the opportunity to thank her. "We really appreciate all the help you are giving us. I hope we aren't a burden or bring you trouble for harboring us."

"Dear child, heavens no. We owe you. Already news of the slaying of Horton Po has reached us here. You have no idea how many times we have plotted to get him only to have him elude us. We just never could get close enough to him to kill him. We also heard that you managed to save another woman before she could be victimized by that foul man. So you have our heartfelt thanks." Her sincere voice spoke volumes. "Am I to assume that you are the leader of this group?" she asked curiously, scarcely believing the reports that had come to her about us.

"Yes, I'm the leader of this group of Guardians," I replied.

She smiled but asked, "And your men — they don't mind that a woman is leading them? They actually take orders from you?" I nodded. "Amazing. I find this so hard to believe. May we talk frankly later tonight after you've eaten and freshened up a bit?"

"Certainly, but we should look after Thomas first. He's still quite weak; Po gave him a nasty cut in his left arm before Thomas cut his throat." She smiled, and I sensed that she wanted to hear all the details of the encounter. I wasn't wrong, but that was only a prelude to what she really wanted to know.

The meals were served in the huge dining room of her home, capable of handling thirty women at one time without being overly crowded. This evening, after we had washed up, examined Thomas, and joined them, we found the room was packed. The ten of Severnia's group plus the twenty or so of Lucretia's and we seven more than filled the room. All eyes were upon us, and we heard snatches of conversation about us and the deed we'd done. Thomas became an instant celebrity, which he just hated. He had only lashed out at Po in self-defense and hardly considered himself a hero. He was only trying to help Alicia.

After dinner, Thomas continued to be the center of attention, with dozens of women hovering around him, chatting. I spied Thallia hanging onto his right arm, a gesture that announced that he was hers. I suspected that she was inwardly probably feeling bad that she could say nothing to stem the harmless flirting that many of the younger women were doing with him. Lucretia interrupted my observations. Holding a teapot and a couple of cups, she said, "Let's retire to my study so we can get acquainted." I followed her into an adjoining room.

What immediately caught my attention were her walls. All available wall space held parchment maps fastened securely to them! I spied the Narrows, Velona, and even this village, Portillio. There were many circles and dots on the map, which I assumed represented the cities and towns. Lines connected them in a dizzying array, the roads or trails, I figured. "Ah, you recognize these?"

She pointed out where we were at on one map. "I'm the coordinator of all the Eastern Sector shipping. I travel quite a lot as well. Made these maps myself." After complimenting her on a job well done, I added a circle for Calgary and explained a bit about the Greenway. We sat down and over tea; she had me relate the events leading to the slaying of the hated priest. She smiled when I tried to explain that it was all just an accident.

"What I really want to discuss with you is something else," she deftly changed the topic. "You now know quite a lot about our secret Sisterhood. I know only a very little about you, but from what I've gathered, I suspect that you and I are somewhat similar, in that we both are protectors of others. I would like to know more about your country and your customs, especially with respect to women, and just what you Guardians actually do or are capable of doing. I've heard all sorts of wild rumors. You know how unreliable those can be, how exaggerated they can become. If I'm really to be of significant help to you, I must know more about you. However, it's your rights here to refuse to answer at all. It's up to you. How is it, for example that Thallia and Tomas get along so well? I trained her some time ago. She has such a hard time communicating with others, you know."

"He reads her mind. She thinks her thoughts to him, and he hears them and thinks his thoughts back into her mind as well. We call it telepathy," I answered truthfully. Obviously, if she had trained Thallia, she really understood her situation; only the truth would satisfy her.

"This is magic?" she asked. "Can you all do this?"

"Normally only one of us can do this. In our case, we all do it to some extent. Sandy is by far the best at it; she's been extensively trained in this art," I explained hoping she would move on to other subjects. "I know Thomas and Thallia really do like each other a lot."

"You know, there is a spark of life in her eyes that I've never seen there before. I never expected to see it in her eyes, I must admit. No man here would have anything to do with her. Yet, along comes Thomas. He isn't bothered by it or her unusual eating methods?"

"Not in the slightest. They seem to have quite a lot in common, especially a love of flowers."

"Ah flowers. Yes, that is Thallia. Flowers were the one thing that saved her when she first came here. She would spend hours and hours sitting alone among them. For the longest time, she wouldn't have anything to do with any people. She felt so shamed, so mutilated, so humiliated, and so embarrassed about every little thing. It is a joy to my eyes to see her so happy now. I never dreamed that could happen. Thomas must be a very kind and gentle soul for her to let him near her. She normally avoids all men. You can understand why. Tell me more about yourselves. How is it that you are here in the Sea Princes?"

Sandy had days ago communicated with Alabaster about this secret Sisterhood. We had his full permission to explore alliances with them. Hence, I went into detail about our lengthy trip. While I did tell her that we actually formed a complete Circle, I did not specifically describe our capabilities, preferring to keep that to ourselves. We talked nearly an hour about our mission as well as what life was like back in the Greenway. I also invited her to migrate there if the need ever arose. I believe she appreciated knowing that she and the Sisterhood had a last retreat available to them. Yet, I knew that she, like we Guardians, would only use it as a last resort because our purposes were very similar: protect and assist those in need.

Confidence breeds confidence. When I had finished, she then told me much about the Sisterhood. I learned that periodically, they provided protection for commercial caravans that traveled overland between the main cities and outlying towns, and sometimes even the smaller villages. Much cargo went by ships between the seven cities; it was safer and faster to move goods by sea than overland. However, their ships were often needed to sail to other lands. If the shipment couldn't wait for the next available ship, it went by land.

The roads were generally poor, save between the seven cities, and those roads paralleled the coastline, never venturing inland more than needed to bypass rugged terrain. However, extensive goods had to be moved between the outlying towns and these seven cities. Here, caravans were heavily utilized, and these caravans of goods made excellent prey for bandits. Large numbers of bandit groups operated within the land of the Sea Princes.

She noted that many of these robbers were actually outcasts from the city or those who were unable to make a go of city living, resorting to the easy life of thievery instead. Interestingly enough, the various bands did not rob the nearby towns and villages. Rather, they would come into those towns and barter for the necessities of life. For example, the Black Eagle Band operated within twenty miles of here, Portillio. Yet never had they stolen from anyone here in Portillio. Thus, no town had any grievance about them and tolerated their presence. The seven cities were unable to stop their activities; their only recourse was to send along heavily armed escorts with the caravans or to hire the Sisterhood to protect them.

However, the Sisterhood charged the merchants of the seven cities stiff rates to guard their caravan, while charging only a modest fee for those of the outlying towns and villages. The reason for this disparity lay in the treatment of women. I learned that the further from the seven cities one traveled, the more civilized the treatment of women became. However, nowhere in the land were women treated as equals. It's just that in the smaller outlying towns, women played a far more crucial role in the overall survival of the town and so had more respect from the men as a result.

I also learned that for the Sisterhood to be able to survive, they had to be better fighters than most men — the bandits and the city guards, in particular. Thus, of necessity, the Sisterhood had the most able fighters in the entire land, a fact not lost on anyone in the Land of the Sea Princes. Over time, those acquainted with the Sisterhood gave them a wide berth, avoiding any hostilities. Thus, caravans under Sisterhood protection were only infrequently robbed, usually by upstart bandit groups that didn't know better or were very desperate.

The one fact I most desired to know, Lucretia couldn't honestly answer.

She didn't know the total number of women in the entire Sisterhood. For safety, they were organized in groups of no more than a few dozen. A varying number of groups formed a local band. Those that attended the dance that night in Velona were mostly from the Velona Band of the Sisterhood. A varying number of bands formed a regional group with a training center as its central focus. Portillio was the center for the entire western section of the Sea princes. Lucretia has been the training leader for over fifteen years now.

Those in the Sisterhood were vehemently hated by the men of the seven cities, who referred to these women as Abominations. Years ago, if a Sister were openly found alone within the city, they would commonly be attacked by at least six guards and executed. However, the reprisals from the Sisterhood were ruthless. The rule they adopted to counter this was: one Sister slain begets ten Guards slain. Thus, the cost of killing a Sister was set high enough to lessen the threat to their safety. Still, the Sisterhood found that secrecy was the best way to prevent conflicts. In contrast, here in the outlying towns, such as Portillio, the Sisterhood was accepted as a fact of life. They could openly walk the streets of the town, suffering only the stares and glares of the local men. To date, no Sister had even been killed in these outlying towns. Humiliated, spat upon, called despicable names, yes, but never attacked.

Eventually, the topic turned to our immediate plans. From her, I learned that Pieta would soon fall to the Centurions. Considering that the towns closer to the invaders would be ramping up for a war, it seemed useless to attempt even to try to setup a grain for arms trading deals with them. Besides, now that we had completely ruled out allying the Greenway with the Sea Princes, there seemed little point in actually visiting these cities. Instead, our focus now shifted to learning about the invaders. And to do that, we would have to travel half-way across the country to the next likely city to be besieged, Bonilla. We needed to observe directly the strategy and tactics used by the Centurions. Further, once that was accomplished, we also needed to understand how life was maintained under their occupation, which meant entering a conquered city, such as Solamina or Zargarb. Both activities were fraught with physical danger.

Lucretia offered us part of the answer. "In about a week, I'm leading an escort to protect a caravan of timber destined for Bonilla. You are welcome to accompany us all the way. Once there, I'll put you in contact with my counterpart, the leader of the Bonilla training sector. She should know far more about the actual current scene in Pieta as well. We can make further plans at that time."

"That sounds just perfect, Lucretia, thanks a lot. But one small detail: we want to exchange something for the hospitality. We should probably outright purchase our horses, since we may need them to continue our journey. Is there something we can do to earn our keep rather than just giving you coins, unless you really need them?"

She thought for a moment before replying, which I determined was a good thing. "Well, if you would agree to volunteer your assistance in protecting the caravan and help with the mundane trail chores, that would be more than sufficient payment, beyond paying for your horses. I have an uncanny feeling we may run into trouble this trip. We may be heading into a war zone, and I honestly don't know what to expect. Knowing that we can rely on your Circle would be an immense comfort, especially your knack for healing."

"Agreed. Splendid," I replied, much relieved that we could do something useful. "I have been involved in a number of smaller battles where the enemy numbered only several hundred. My Circle has many things we can do in such situations. However, none of us has experienced or seen a war zone. I would expect it would be one immense field of chaos."

"My hunch too," she concurred. "I fear the chaos may expand far beyond the battlefield. Opportunists. Bandits may become bolder in last ditch attempts to steal before the oncoming army. Men get desperate." Little did we know how close to the mark her hunch actually was.

The week passed quickly. The men occupied themselves by inspecting the available horses, choosing wisely for us. We decided to buy nine, one for Thallia and one as a spare/pack horse. They then worked on the necessary tack. Finally, they made sure all our weapons were in perfect condition. They also found time to practice combat techniques with the other Sisters-in-training and their instructors, an action that was mutually beneficial, especially for Roy, who was our Protector and our best fighter. He taught nearly as much as he learned, telling me at night that these women had a unique style and that some were actually much better than he was!

We girls assisted in the various domestic chores and the packing of needed supplies, helping as best we could. We often found ourselves describing life in the Greenway to the Sisters who never ran out of questions for us.

Thomas's wound healed rapidly, and he and Thallia were hardly ever separated. When he was stronger, both disappeared one afternoon. Lucretia took me aside to inform me that Thallia took Thomas to her Special Place. She explained that when Thallia was depressed, she would go off alone to her spot for hours. She had never taken any other person to her Special Place. "For security, I would have to be able to physically see her, you realize. Follow me." She led me into the barn and up into the hayloft. She pointed out the spot far in the distance.

Behind the barn, a low hill crested blocking the view. Just beyond that hill, several hills intersected and a small creek trickled fresh water down into the village. Close to the stream, vast fields of wild flowers bloomed profusely, and grass even covered the lower portions of these hills. There I spied the two lying among the flowers, gazing up at the sky. My sole comment to her was, "They both have much in common. Both value many of the same things." I couldn't say more because I fought hard to keep my tears from being overly obvious to Lucretia. We stood in silence for several minutes watching them.

On May 17, Lucretia's band of Sisters and our Circle left Portillio to join up with the caravan. She led twenty-five fighters, and we were now eight, counting Thallia, which made thirty-four in all, a strong force, I thought. As we prepared to mount up, Lucretia presented us three girls with yellow ribbon headbands. "This way, you appear to be one of us, just in case of trouble," she explained. Our guys just watched fascinated, as thirty women took a moment to tie their headbands. "We are now on official business," Lucretia pronounced. Then, we headed off eastward toward a major junction of roadways some five miles southeast of Portillio. There, we were to meet the caravan, which was hauling timber to Bonilla.

Lucretia explained that as we passed other outlying towns, additional wagons would be joining us for a total of some twenty wagon loads of heavy timbers destined for boat construction. The initial number of wagons was expected to only be four from Velona. As we rode along on the sunny morning, she explained camp protocols. "The wagon men form into an inner, close quarters circle each evening. We form four outer circles around them. Under no circumstances do they come to our circles, and we don't go to theirs, unless they specifically invite us for a conference. That is, they stick together, and we do likewise. Remember, these drivers still consider us an abomination, but a necessary one. They are paying for our services."

I thought all this was just a bit weird, so did my friends, but we fully agreed to cooperate. We rode swiftly along the narrow wagon-rutted dirt road that led southward. Groves of well-tended olive trees passed by, interspersed with sweeping vineyards whose new growth added a sea of dark green to the countryside. In the lower basins, we spied small grain fields, barley we suspected from this distance. Often, we would pass near men tending their fields; invariably, they stopped to look at us and often spat disgustingly on the ground, their sole gesture of disapproval of us. The Sisters took no note of it, but we did, and personally, I felt more than a little disgusted with these men. More and more, I wondered what could have happened to cause this enormous division between the sexes throughout the entire land.

Riding was something we all loved to do, so we thoroughly enjoyed the ride. By noon, we arrived at the appropriate crossroads, dismounted, fixed lunch, and waited beneath the shade of a small grove of trees. We chatted amongst ourselves. All of us were most impressed by the well-ordered, seemingly endless vineyards. Their neatly aligned rows flowed up and down across the hills. We'd never seen anything like this, and it did make an impression on us. While we could easily relate to the grain fields, which now sprouted green shoots that were already perhaps six inches tall, all the grapes we couldn't. The incredible volume of grapes the fall harvest would produce, just here where we could see the growing vines, was staggering. Surely, we thought, these people must produce wine for the whole world! We wondered where regular farms were located — the kinds that produce cows, pigs, sheep, and chickens with which we were accustomed to seeing. Here, Thallia, via Thomas, explained that those farms were normally beyond the ten mile radius of the big cities. It seemed that wine was their most exportable crop and hence most valuable crop, and which they kept close to the city of origin. It was not uncommon for even smaller towns to have one or two vineyards for their own use.

From this crossroads in a basin, we couldn't see Velona, but we judged we were only about five miles from its northeastern corner. Just after lunch, we heard the sounds of wagons on the move, heading our way. Lucretia made a hasty hand sign, and at once, all the Sisters gathered their gear, stowed it, and stood in a neat, orderly line, ready to greet the wagons. Presently, the creaking grew louder, and, one by one, the wagons appeared around the bend, making the eastward turn. The lead wagon halted just before Lucretia, who stood proud and tall in front of the rest of us. We seven were close enough to hear the conversation.

The wagons looked peculiar, but then that's because we'd never seen loggers, as the locals referred to these. Yes, they had the usual buckboard seats up front, but in place of the cargo box, several V-shaped supports rose with perhaps twenty large tree trunks cradled in the gap. Now, we knew how these ship builders managed to transport the giant masts of their ships. Two men drove each wagon. However, their leader was on the first one. He wore nondescript working leathers and boots. I estimated he was in his early thirties and very experienced at hauling this type of cargo. Rippling muscles spoke of the great strength needed to manhandle such heavy cargo. More importantly, he did not seem overly friendly. Gruffly, he said, "Greetings; you are the protectors of this shipment?"

"I am," came the stern reply. Lucretia stepped forward to the side of his wagon.

"Payment," the man barked between clenched teeth. I sensed it was all he could do to keep his emotions from loosening his tongue. She took the heavy money pouch from his hand. From her sudden unexpected motion, I gathered it was quite heavy. Lucretia carried the sack halfway back to us and handed it to another Sister who had come towards her. It was a well-synchronized motion that the two women displayed.

In an attempt to be civilized, Lucretia asked, "What news out of Velona, Good Sir?" This loosened his lips.

"Assassins, that's what. They've killed His Excellency, High Priest Horton Po that's what! There'll be hell to pay now," his face grew animated, which is exactly what Lucretia desired.

"Golly, that is news. Have they caught the assassins yet? Were they from the Centurions or just our usual bandits?" she prodded. I detected she was asking also for our benefit.

"Nay. Soon they'll have them. Going door-to-door. Seems they know that old Horton did not go down without a fight. They say he critically wounded one of his attackers. T'was blood all through the streets! My money is on the Centurions; I'll wager anything that the culprits are an advance party of the invaders — come here to soften us up before their main strike. You reckon that we'll make it to Bonilla without running into them?" I detected this is what most concerned him.

Lucretia spoke cautiously, "Well, based on the length of time our other cities held out, I believe we should make Bonilla safely without running into the Centurions. However, I need to know your wishes. If we run into the invasion army, do we return or somehow try to get into the city with the cargo? Or do you wish to just abandon the timber and run to safety?"

"Hey, Abom — I mean Protector, you are the fighters. My men and I work for a living. We are carters and don't want no part of no war. If we run into the Centurions, your first order is to help us cut our horses free of the wagons. Second, get us out of there as fast as possible. We'll just claim we lost the load to the Centurions. No one will ask any questions about that. We've already said this is going to be a risky run, but those shipwrights in Bonilla apparently really need these timbers. Probably planning a mass evacuation or something. So, first sign of trouble, you get us out of there, understand? That's what we're paying you for."

"Agreed. We don't want to fight either, so flee it will be. I'm told up to fifteen more wagons will join in; is that still the correct count?" she asked.

"Yes, unless some others chicken out of the deal," he replied, implying that he and his crew were somehow braver than others we had yet to meet. This, after he just ordered us to flee at the first sign of the invaders.

So without further conversation, Lucretia gave us the hand sign to mount up and form a defensive line. Roy sent to me, *I wonder what her order of march will be? Like we'd do it?* We watched waiting for some sign indicating where Lucretia wanted us positioned. Three Sisters fell back to guard the very rear. Two foursomes headed off on either flank, scouting the hills from about a half mile away. Six more moved some distance in front of the lead wagon. Five more dashed off ahead of us ranging anywhere from a quarter to a half mile before the convoy. Lucretia finally motioned for the eight of us to join her leading the way. We fell into pairs behind her, Roy and I immediately behind her. We were far enough in front of the wagons that we could talk freely and not be overheard. I smiled, realizing that was her intention.

As we began the slow march, she leaned back and said to Roy, "Do you approve of my force placement?" Roy knew she was really asking him if this would be how he would have deployed the guards. From long experience, she knew this was the safest for the job at hand, but I calculated she was probably testing us. After all, we were very young and new at this.

"Weakest spot is the rear and that is the least likely avenue of attack, so yes, I think this is a sound deployment. We'll not be taken by surprise from the front or flanks. With us here in the front, we can move to meet any attack." She smiled, evidently pleased with his confirmation.

Perhaps, they know what they are doing after all, she thought to herself. *I can't afford to overestimate them. They're after all barely of age, and Bethany only just, if I know women's ages. Yet, if they weren't capable, I'm sure they wouldn't have been sent on such a dangerous mission so far from home and any help. Damn, I sure wouldn't want to be in their boots!*

They're likely riding to their deaths.

The wagons rolled along at two miles an hour at best, slowing at the steeper upgrades. This was very different from the galloping rides we had done last fall. I smiled, as I remembered flying along with my long hair billowing behind me. That was exciting and invigorating. This was incredibly boring. Three hours later, we finally rolled into a small village, Porti, I was told, home to perhaps three hundred. We rode straight through the town without stopping. Still, that didn't stop the passersby from issuing derogatory catcalls at us as we passed. Lucretia and the others rode straight in the saddle, seeming not even hearing these exclamations. I knew it must hurt them deeply. Here these women were providing a very great service at the risk of their own lives and yet not even that earned them the slightest respect. I wished with all my might that I could just move all of these women straight into the Greenway! Though, if I did, who'd be there to rescue the next victims from this disgusting country?

However, Thomas just could not stand to hear these women being degraded. So he began cursing the cursers, but in our tongue. He was certain no one here knew the Greenway dialect. It was so funny that I almost laughed. He was smiling and waving at them while cussing them out. If Lucretia understood anything that he was saying, she didn't let on, but kept us moving through the town. Midway, another wagon carrying more timbers pulled in behind the line. The rear guard pulled back a little to let that one into line. Soon, we left the town behind us. Lucretia commented, "No other way. Had to pick up that wagon. Loaded as they are, they can't go across country. Sometimes not even on the road — if it rains too much, they get stuck. There is nothing worse than a stuck wagon. They expect us to get them unstuck. Drivers!"

We pressed on until sunset when we made camp beside a narrow creek that flowed on down to the Med Sea, some five miles south of us. We could smell the sea breeze on the night air and even saw soaring white gulls high in the sky. Just as Lucretia told us earlier, the wagons took a central position pulling three abreast and parking close. The men set to making their own campfire and did their own cooking. The Sisters formed into four groups making an outer ring around the wagons. We camped upstream from the wagons. Roy said he did not want to drink from the creek after it had been fouled by these men. A quick glance showed me that none of the other groups was exactly downstream either. We smiled knowingly at each other.

While the rest of us setup our campsite, Thomas and Thallia worked their way northward, scavenging for firewood. When they returned heavily laden, he exclaimed, "Hey you guys, come see what Thallia has found. It's beautiful!" So we followed them back up the gully a ways. Thallia made a broad gesture as if to say "There!" Nestled on either side of the bubbling creek were blooming buttercups, hundreds of yellow cups closing for the night. The aroma was intoxicating. We found this impressive, and the next morning we came to view it in the daylight. Thallia put a half-dozen in her hair that morning.

Let me say a word about the weather here. It was only mid-May but the high sun already warmed the afternoons into the upper eighties. We could only guess how hot it got here in mid-summer! Every couple of days, a rain shower came in from the sea. Usually, it was just a light rain, and the caravan didn't stop. However, every couple of weeks, a heavy thunderstorm with massive lightning bolts swept inland. On those days, we camped and waited it out. The days passed by slowly and monotonous otherwise. So I found myself praying for the next big thunderstorm out of sheer boredom! Each long day brought us another twenty miles closer to our destination.

From my discussions with Lucretia, the wagons weren't expected to be attacked by bandits on this leg of the journey. After all, what would bandits do with hundreds of logs? No, the threat of attack was really on the return trip when these same drivers would be carrying back the payment for the logs. Nevertheless, the Sisters continued their defensive measures.

Midway through our journey, on the fifteenth day, June 2, I finally got to see some bandits. We were told the outriders had spooked several raiding bands, but those bandits never got close enough for us to spy them. However, this day, a fast moving thunderstorm swept inland mid-day, forcing us temporarily to halt in the basin of a valley to wait it out. Lucretia hated stopping at such a low point, but to continue would only mean a worse situation — stuck wagons. The road was still just a well-worn dirt rut. The wagoners took cover beneath their cargo and stayed mostly dry for the most part. The rest of us donned our rain ponchos and waited it out.

In hindsight, it did make a perfect time for an ambush. Of necessity, our outriders were here with us and could give no advance warning. Suddenly, some fifty men came charging down at us from both the left and right hilltops, waving their swords menacingly in the air. Another two dozen closed from the front. Outnumbered three to one, we had perhaps less than a minute to react. Roy issued orders for us to split into three groups to attack each wing of the bandits. All seven of us chose the same defensive action: lightning; after all, it was all around us anyway. As I prepared to begin, I noticed the Sisters were all arming their crossbows so I assumed they would let loose a volley before closing to hand-to-hand combat. Lucretia seemed to be everywhere in that minute, issuing orders and arranging a hasty defense.

Our first volley of lightning bolts occurred first, with seven riders and horses fly wildly in all directions ending with a hard smash onto the ground. Roy ordered, "Girls, keep it up. Guys, out in front, protect them." On our side, he and Raphael moved about six feet in front of Sarah Jane and me.

Lucretia said a single word, "Now!" Suddenly, twenty-five quarrels flew in unison outward; most hit either man or beast. About half of those who were hit by the quarrels halted their attack; the others roughed it out, continuing the charge. I sensed Sarah Jane and Sandy were being cautious in their command of lightning, only getting off another set to my two. The odds were still at least two to one, so I escalated my rate of fire, much as I had done when

I had gone temporarily insane during the surprise attack on my family and Ellen, when we were moving to Karka. After another five bolts, I knew the bandits were now too close to hazard a bolt without risking striking one of our people. I halted and took hold of my wooded staff hoping I wouldn't need it.

Somewhat fewer than fifty men, some with smaller wounds, charged through our positions, but we simply dodged out of their way. This defensive action forced them to dismount to attack us on foot, which was what Lucretia desired. In all our many practice sessions, combat between two opponents lasted a long time, with slashes here and there, parries, feints, and thrusts. This was real combat, not practice. I watched as several closed to attack the Sisters nearby Thallia. Uniformly, the men charged forward attempting to swing their weapons down hard onto the women, slicing or crushing or breaking bones — it didn't matter which. The women's fighting style, which we had observed back at Portilla, countered this nicely. They lifted one leg and whirled around bringing the airborne leg into a position to deflect the sword swing. On the follow through of their circular pivoting motion, they thrust their swords up into the now exposed chests of the bandits. Thus, an actual combat lasted but mere seconds. Once stabbed in the chest, invariably the Sister would follow through with a clean neck slice, ending life. I spied Thallia doing just these actions twice. She was impressive, another side of her that I only now saw.

Of course, if the circular kick failed to deflect the blade, then the Sister bore the brunt, often with a leg cut, which was far better than the gut rips that they delivered. My sole conclusion from firsthand experience was that to survive close quarters combat, one had to have lightning fast actions and reactions. There was simply no time to think about moves. This battle was over in less than a minute after the bandits had dismounted!

I blinked; bodies lay all around us, men and women. Systematically, the unharmed Sisters visited each bandit body. Without even checking whether he was alive or not, they thrust their short sword into each heart. Forcing myself to move, I joined Sarah Jane and Sandy who had already begun to attend to the wounded Sisters. Five had taken sword cuts to their legs, and one had nearly lost her arm. None in my Circle were wounded, so in spite of the pouring rain, we assisted in bringing the six women together in one smaller area. Sandy and the guys began working on the leg wounds. Sarah Jane and I tackled the woman in critical condition. "Stop the blood flow," ordered Sarah Jane. I put my hands into the bloody remains of her arm and pinched the artery with both hands. It was slippery because of the vast amount of blood mixed with the heavy rain falling on us. I managed to halt it significantly, while Sarah Jane began examining the depth of the wound. Lucretia came over to check on how badly her fighters were wounded.

The wounded woman was called Luzzi, and as soon as she saw Lucretia near her, she cried out in pain, "Please, I don't want to lose my arm. Please!" From Lucretia's dour expression, Luzzi knew that Lucretia saw no hope. "Please, please." Then, shock set in and she passed out.

I really need boiling water! thought Sarah Jane, but I picked up her thought. With my full attention required to keep Luzzi from bleeding to death, I relayed to Thomas, *We must have a pot of boiling water. Start a fire quickly.* Unfortunately, I wasn't as accurate as I usually am when sending ideas to others, and I placed it in Thallia's mind as well.

She grabbed Thomas's arm and gestured, so he began to read her furious thoughts. He nodded, but I knew that they exchanged ideas. She ran off to gather some firewood, but from her face, I knew she thought it would be impossible to light a fire in this downpour with completely soaked branches. Two other women saw what Thallia was doing and pitched in to help — they too wondering if this was not a futile effort. Soon, the three had stacked up enough wet wood for a reasonable bonfire. Thomas then showed her how to hold the wad of cloth tightly over the leg wound on which he was working. Thallia took over keeping that woman's blood loss to a minimum, all the while she watched Thomas.

Lucretia came over to him and said, "I know that hot water would help, but in this downpour, it isn't possible to light a fire or keep it burning. We'll just have to wait the storm out." Thomas shook his head no and began his chant. When he finished, a great ball of fire appeared in the sky above the huge stack of firewood. Slowly, he lowered it onto the wood. A great cloud of steam arose, accompanied by massive sizzling. After a couple minutes, the wood had dried and began to blaze. He did not cancel his flames until he was satisfied the wood had fully caught. When he looked up, he found absolutely everyone, except us of course, staring open mouthed at him. From their point of view, a miracle had just occurred. Thomas must be a god in disguise! "Okay, someone get a large pot of water on the fire. We need lots of boiling water," he said and went back to a gaping Thallia, her mouth wagging, though making no sounds. She stopped and stared at him, so I knew he was explaining things to her, though he said nothing.

"Okay, Bethany, you are doing fine. I need to check quickly on the other five. Be right back." She rapidly examined each of the other five and gave them all orders to wash the wounds clean and sew them up the usual way. Then, she sighed and returned to the unconscious Luzzi. *This is going to be tricky,* she sent to me. *How are your hands holding out? Can you hold on for another ten minutes or so? I need quite a bit of time if we're to attempt to save her arm.*

If I cannot, I'll get Roy to come over, once he is done. Go for it. What are you going to try? The artery is severed isn't it?

I'm going to try to sew the artery back together. Got to overlap the ends slightly. I think I can stretch it a bit. The bone's not cut, so that's in our favor. If my patch on the artery holds, there's a good chance we can save the arm. Tricky. I've never done this before. If it doesn't work, why, we can always take the arm off later on once she's recovered a bit, I hope.

She got out of her bag the tiniest needle she had and some thread. Laying her knife at her side, she motioned for the hot water. Once she had dipped everything including the thread into the steaming water and counted to fifty, she pulled them out and set to work. In the dim light, I watched her execute the absolutely tiniest needle strokes I have ever seen. Her stitches were very, very small. My arms were weakening, but, if I let go even for a moment while someone else took over, the gush of blood might ruin all her work. I grimaced and forced my hands tighter. Finally, she began stitching the muscle tissue back together; her patch was done in layers. These bits of string would remain forever inside the woman's arm, if she were successful. Finally, she sewed the outermost skin back using her trademark X stitches. She bound the whole area in several layers of ripped up cloth and tied it tightly. *Okay, Bethany, slowly let loose. Keep your fingers crossed. Be ready to clamp down hard if it doesn't hold.*

My arms almost refused to work; they had long ago gone numb on me. I tried my best to release them slowly. Sarah Jane had to tell me that I had actually fully let go and could move my arms around. Seeing that we were nearly done, Roy came over and began massaging the circulation back into my arms. I gave him a quick thank you kiss and he smiled. For another five minutes, Sarah Jane stared at the bandages, feeling the lower portion of the arm, testing to see if the circulation was actually returning. She saw a bit of color reappear in the otherwise pale fingertips. Seeing no profuse bleeding, she finally got up, stretched briefly, and then quickly made the rounds of her other five patients to inspect the others' handiwork.

At last, she addressed an anxious Lucretia. "Well, I think the five leg wounds are going to recover just fine. I'm hoping I've managed to save Luzzi's arm. It's too soon to tell. Might be a week before we know for sure. If I have failed, we'll have to remove it."

Lucretia simply hugged her tightly before speaking. "Sarah Jane, I just don't know how to thank you. I have seen miracles here today. Even if it doesn't work, you have tried something we could never do. If you weren't here, we'd have just cut it off and hoped that the patient didn't die from it. They often do, you know."

"Well, we're not out of the woods yet. All these bandages are rain soaked. They need to be dry bandages, and I need to put various healing herbs on them. That must wait until things dry out. Everything is soaked. Gosh, I'm starving. Anything to eat?"

After the fire had been used to heat the necessary water, several other Sisters began to cook up some lunch and hot tea. Thus, we all joined them; hot tea never tasted so warm and refreshing, even as the rain poured down upon us. While sipping my tea, I noticed that the other women had not been idle. Nearby, was a neatly tied string of some fifty horses. Saddles and other gear lay in a large pile some distance from the fire, drying out. Obviously, they had rounded up what horses they could and brought them back here. All the dead bandit bodies had been moved some distance away from the camping area, and from the large pile of personal effects; they had been thoroughly searched. Several women were organizing the captured goods, sorting out the coins and few gemstones. Others were examining the weapons, casting the ruined ones into yet another pile. They intended to keep all those that were salvageable.

While I was watching, the leader of the wagons came walking over to Lucretia. "Say, may we use the fire to warm ourselves and perhaps heat some food?" I observed a change in the man's demeanor toward Lucretia. There wasn't the slightest hint of degradation in his voice, no covert or cynical put downs, just a genuine request among equals. He added, "Are your warriors going to be all right?"

"They will live," she replied sternly. I could tell she too observed a change in him. "You can share our fire if you will help us dig a hole to bury the dead once the rains let up. They may have been bandits, but we're not savage beasts. They deserve at least to be buried."

"Thank you, Sister. We'll lend a hand. I must say, I've never seen fighting like this before. You and your people were . . . well, let's just say I wouldn't have believed it unless I'd seen it with my own eyes. I think I speak for the other drivers too. Thank you." She nodded graciously; he returned to his wagon to tell the others and to get their food and gear. Shortly, the men crowed around the fire warming themselves, cooking a bit of food, and heating several pots for tea. Interestingly enough, the Sisters moved back a good distance.

The rain showed signs of easing off. Meanwhile, one Sister brought Lucretia a large, heavy sack. "You need to have a look at this. We found about a thousand gold scattered amongst the bandits. We also found this on one of them, probably their leader." She handed the sack to Lucretia.

"Thanks. That means about thirty more gold coins for each of you on this trip. We are making a tidy profit this time!" The Sister grinned and left. She explained that she would also give each of my group the same portion that her women received. "Of course, the horses are likely worth half of that and the arms, perhaps an equal amount. I'll make it square with you at journey's end."

"Thanks, Lucretia, but we just wanted to help out. You don't have to do that," I offered.

"I insist. You took the same risks as we, did nearly as much damage as we did, and to top it off, are healing our wounded. I wouldn't feel right if I didn't compensate you for your assistance," she answered. So I agreed; a little more coins would help our meager supply. We might need the money later in our journey. At this point, Lucretia opened the sack inside the other large sack. "Oh my. What is this?" We looked on, as she poured dozens of shiny gemstones out into her hand. "Rosita, over here please," she barked an order to another Sister.

A young, bright-eyed woman with short blonde hair and deep blue eyes rushed up. "Yes, ma'am. You wanted me?" She was completely unsure why she had been singled out and was just a bit uneasy about the attention.

"A task for you. Sit down," she said, spreading a piece of cloth over the woman's lap. "Examine these." She dumped the contents of the sack onto the cloth. Our eyes blinked to see so many beautiful gems in one large pile. She explained, "Rosita is very knowledgeable in gems. Meanwhile, let's have a look at this bag; it's unusually well made," she said, turning it over in her hands. "What have we here? Bethany, have a look at this." She pointed out an embossed mark on one side of the fine leather bag. I'd seen that symbol somewhere before. "That's the official seal of the Church of Tur. This bag came from the church. I wonder how it got in the hands of bandits?"

"Could they have robbed a priest?" I asked.

"What priest would be carrying this valuable a pouch with him? If stolen, this is a fortune, I'll wager. A mighty hue and cry would go out if this had been stolen. Strange, very strange. I don't know what to make of it."

"Seventy stones, ma'am, all worth about the same, fifty each. So all total, there is about thirty-five hundred worth here. Can I tell the others that instead of getting about thirty coins we are going to get more like a hundred fifty? That will sure cheer them up!" Rosita asked grinning from ear to ear.

"Absolutely!" Lucretia said, and we watched the young woman eagerly spread the word to the others. "Bethany, what do you make of this find?"

I thought a moment, piecing together the few suppositions we had at hand. "First, as you said days ago, it's nearly pointless for bandits to attack us just now; there is little to no profit, save the funds you were paid, and what little traveling money the drivers carry. Not all the wagons have joined us. Secondly, if a church lost this valuable pouch to some bandits, severe repercussions would befall the bandits. If they can slay an innocent seaman for next to no real offense, then stealing this much would more than warrant a full-scale retaliation. Perhaps that hasn't occurred. Or perhaps the bag was stolen on another date and filled by this bandit with their group's total wealth for easier carrying."

Lucretia countered, "But if bandits had this much money, they could afford to purchase a home in town or even start up a business. For the poor, this is a fortune, even if it should have been divided up among the other bandits." We both were silent for a while.

Roy spoke up, "Look, ladies, if it wasn't stolen from the church and doesn't represent the total wealth of the bandits collected over years of thievery, then there is only one other possibility that I can see." We both looked at him as if saying, so "What?"

"They were given that pouch with the money. Look, that pouch is not even dirty. Have you noticed that all the other bags and gear of these dead bandits all look the worst for wear? All except this bag, that is. I'd wager these bandits only recently came into possession of the bag and its contents," Roy commented.

"But Roy, are you saying that the Church of Tur hired these bandits and paid for the service in gemstones?" I asked, making sure that I wasn't misunderstanding him.

"Yes, that seems to me to be the most plausible explanation for how a bunch of grubby, low life bandits suddenly possess a church bag full of gems."

"I wonder what the Church of Tur hired these bandits for?" I mused aloud. Suddenly, Roy looked at me. I looked at Roy, and Lucretia gasped. "Us! The bandits were after us? How could they know it was us? We've told no one except the Sisters."

"That's why I gasped," Lucretia interjected. "Could one of the Sisters have told the Church priests about what you did to Po? Do I have a traitor amongst us?" I could tell that she was more than a little concerned. The thought frightened her, casting heavy doubts on her entire group.

I could see the uncertainty, the doubt she had, even if false, would completely undermine her entire group. I had to do something and so called Simon over, quickly explaining everything to him. He grasped even better than I the mess that this created for Lucretia. Wisely, for he is a Judger, he said, "Lucretia, before you panic over this, let's consider it further. First, it's only an assumption on our part that one member or several members of the Church of Tur have hired these bandits to attack us. True, nothing suggests that your Sisters were the intended target. It's just an assumption so far that we are the target, not your group. I admit the facts as we see them just now do tend to suggest that fairly strongly, though. Second, the facts suggest that every one of your Sisters here is totally loyal; all fought bravely and killed many bandits. Had one of them been a traitor, I would have expected that coward to have somehow slunk from battle, to hide out, and await the intended result so as not to be slain themselves. None of yours backed off or retreated in any way whatsoever. So if you have a traitor in your ranks, she can't be here with us now; she must be back in Portilla."

He made sense. Simon wasn't done, "Third, if there was a traitor that had spilled the beans on our involvement in the killing of Po, then the Church would have been totally justified in seeking our arrests *legally*." He emphasized legally. "The Church would have proudly put us on public display, including our execution, to show the people they're in charge and have meted out justice as they see it. Hence, I'd have expected to see a large contingent of guards come after us, formally demanding that you turn us over to them. Instead, a band of thieves attacks us. Hence, Lucretia, it's my opinion at this time that there is no traitor within your ranks. Rather, I suspect that somehow the Church has suspicions, but not outright proof, of our involvement in the affair and is seeking revenge, not justice."

Lucretia listened carefully to his every word. When he finished his conclusion, she spontaneously leaned over and gave him a hug and kiss. "Thank you. Simon you're positively brilliant. If Sandy doesn't want you, let me know. I would love to get to know you much better, if you wouldn't mind an older woman." Simon blushed and he took her praise in stride. Judgers are often held in the highest esteem by those they serve because of their uncanny ability to get at the truth of a matter. From this day forward, Lucretia seemed always to be watching him, every chance she could muster. That night, I couldn't help but tease Sandy about it, telling her that she had competition for Simon's favor. She laughed good-naturedly. However, we seven knew we had a new enemy, and it was likely whoever was now the High Priest back in Velona.

An hour later the sun came out. Because the six injured couldn't be expected to ride for many days, Lucretia sent six women into the nearby village under orders to purchase a wagon. Two hours later, we were on the road once more. Each of the wounded was helped into the wagon and covered up. With sopping bandages and no healing herbs on the wounds, we didn't want to chance ripping open the stitches. Besides, Luzzi was still unconscious. One sister drove the wagon, while another sat in the wagon bed looking after the needs of the wounded. Five others rode at the rear leading along strings of ten horses each. With only twelve others available for outriding guard duty, Roy, Simon, and Raphael volunteered to join with three women each and ride our flanks and out in front. The rest of my Circle and Thallia rode next to the six wounded women, while I rode up front with Lucretia and the remaining three Sisters.

Finally, with some distance between us and the wagons, she could speak openly. "Bethany, I have many questions for you. Let's see. First, why did so many bolts of lightning hit the bandits? Was that just because they were out in the open?"

"No, that was our doing, I'm afraid," I acknowledged, hoping she wouldn't ask how we could do that. She didn't.

"You can — you can command the lightning?" she asked almost in disbelief.

"Yes, when needed. We don't do it often because the results are nearly always a violent death," I replied truthfully.

"And the fire that Thomas made — I swore the fire appeared out of nowhere just above the wood and floated down onto the wood. Did my eyes deceive me or did that really happen?"

"Yes, of all of us, Thomas actually is the best at doing that trick. Really, it was necessary to have the boiling water. Without it, wounds grow infected rapidly. I just hope and pray that with all the rain falling and everything, that it has not undone the effects of the hot water. Time will tell. I sure hope we don't have to deal with six infected wounds. That can be very painful and messy."

"Thank you for being so honest with me about all this. I had no idea of your skills. I just thought you were so young. You're only barely of age, am I not correct?"

"Yes, just barely," I replied.

"Can I ask one more question of you?" I nodded yes. "These things that you can do — do all the people in the Greenway, can they do them too, or are these unique to you Guardians?"

"Just us, I'm afraid, and we're so few," I replied. However, left like this, Lucretia would undoubtedly think we were godlike or superhuman. Thus, I said, "Now, I would like to compliment you and your women on their terrific fighting skills! They were just amazing. I think they're the best fighters I've ever seen. I think it's a testimonial to your skills that, at three to one odds, you suffered only six non-life threatening wounds and slew all opponents. That alone is an accomplishment of which to be very proud! Is that circle kick thing of yours hard to learn? I think it's very effective in the hands of a woman. Honestly, I'm scared to death when a man comes at me with a sword! Your women acted, whereas I would panic and think instead."

"Unlike your magic, ours is just a skill, which practiced hard and often enough, becomes second nature. Yes, if you care to devote the time and effort, you can learn it. We teach it to nearly every new recruit we get. It just takes time and lots of practice."

Suddenly, I saw my opening. "Ah, time and practice, a skill. Lucretia, we don't practice much magic. All that we do I swear to you we can do only because of time, and practice. Do you realize it took each of us nearly ten years of constant study and practice to be able to do these things? I've been studying since I was six. With us, it's mostly just the same as with you, time and practice." I wondered if I had done anything to defuse the ideas of magic.

She turned in her saddle and stared at me, repeating, "Just time and practice?" I nodded. "Well, then perhaps you and I aren't so very different after all." She smiled; I smiled back. To my great relief, she said, "I'll not ask you to teach me how to make storms do my bidding. I haven't ten years to spend at it. Gosh, that must have been a grueling training period. I doubt I could have had the patience to see it through."

That night, around the campfire, we put herbal salves and dry bandages on all the wounds. Luzzi regained consciousness, and Sandy prepared some light soup for her. Thus far, Sarah Jane's handiwork held. We all knew it was too soon to tell, and we carefully explained this to Luzzi. She did have sensation in her left fingers, so that was a very good sign. She was so grateful to find she still had her arm intact that she didn't complain about the pain. I think Sarah Jane fully realized how devastating it would be for Luzzi to lose her arm. A one-armed Sister would make for a grim existence in this land.

After a week had passed and all wounds showed no signs of infection, Sarah Jane finally permitted those with leg wounds to ride once more, only if they were extra careful. They all swore to be, naturally, for these women, it was embarrassing to be forced to ride on a wagon not to mention awfully bumpy. With Luzzi, it took a week for her to regain her strength; she had lost a good deal of blood during her ordeal. With her arm in a splint so she couldn't jostle the stitches, she, too, was permitted to ride once more.

June 9 thus found all the Sisters now riding their horses once more, as we began to approach the region controlled by the Sea Prince city of Vito. Here the last of the wagonloads of timber joined us. For the next four days, all continued to be quiet and rather routine or boring. The dirt road we traveled continued to parallel the coastline. The Med Sea lay to our right varying between five and ten miles away. By now, the road or track system in use here became obvious to me. Each of the seven cities was a focal point from which all the larger roads originated. We traveled along a ring road that connected each of these, going east-west. Perhaps every five miles or so, a cross road headed off usually to our left heading deeper into the outlying lands, rising toward the distant Appian Way.

Occasionally, we'd meet another convoy heading either north or south going to or coming from the outer towns and villages. Twice, we met another group being escorted by the Sisterhood. They exchanged greetings and smiles, but we never stopped to chat; these were strictly working assignments, which the Sisterhood observed quite arduously. However, all this changed as we began to enter the region controlled by the city of Bonilla.

By June 16 as we spied the large city from a hilltop some three miles from its edge, the road traffic was noticeably quite different. We saw dozens of small wagons carrying whole families and their belongings heading our way, abandoning the city. Sometimes, the family walked on foot, pushing or pulling handcarts overloaded with their personal belongings. One look at their grim faces told me much: fear. These people uniformly were quite scared. The terror of the invading army was far greater than that of up and moving their entire life to some other city! Some of these headed northward to outlying towns and villages, while others headed back the way we had come, evidently making for one of the cities that had not yet fallen. I felt pity for these poor folks; in the end, after the entire country had fallen, there would be no place of safety left to which to migrate. All their current hardships were doomed to futility in only a few more months. Grim indeed.

When we finally approached the last crossroad and were about to turn right or south to head into the outskirts of Bonilla, the lead wagoner got Lucretia's attention. She slowed her horse and dropped back beside his wagon. "About a mile and a half to the edge of Bonilla, sir," she said the obvious. I suspected she had a good idea of what he wanted.

"Ma'am, considering the situation, as usual, you may cease your escort duties at the edge of the city. We'll take our loads on down to the docks. However, I'll do our utmost to get the cargo off-loaded yet today so we may be back here by nightfall or tomorrow morning at the latest. Can you be re-supplied and ready by that time?"

"Certainly by tomorrow morning we can be ready to head back. So far, we've seen no signs of the invading army, so you should be safe enough for now. Considering the likely situation in Bonilla, I doubt you're going to find enough hands to accomplish the unloading so quickly. Nevertheless, we'll be camped just outside the city and be ready to depart say midmorning tomorrow. Agreed?" He nodded but looked very worried. She rode back to the front, pulled in alongside of me, and briefly repeated what he had said.

"So Bethany, it looks likely that tomorrow we shall be parting company for a while. I certainly will miss all of you. In the short time that I've known you, I've come to regard you as good friends. I hope we can meet again under better circumstances."

"Same with us, you, all of you, are just terrific people," I replied. Suddenly a million thoughts entered my mind, not the least of which was what do we do now, head out on our own? Lucretia picked up on my thoughts. I guess they were obvious.

"Tonight, I'll take you into Bonilla and introduce you to the head of the

Sisterhood here. Together, you two can then make intelligent plans. Besides, I'm dying to hear the latest news. It appears the war is about to come to Bonilla." I thanked her and we rode on, jostling off the road a bit for several families who were fleeing the city with small wagons heavily loaded.

As we neared the edge of Bonilla, I found little differences from Velona, at least to my eyes. It was a vast, sprawling hilly city with a magnificent, well-protected harbor. From our height advantage, I could see dozens of ships docked and a dozen more sailing either in or out of the harbor. I spied what must be the Prince's Palace, clearly the tallest building in the city. What got our immediate attention were the thundering sounds of approaching cavalry.

Perhaps fifty guards came up across country from the east, passed us without a word, and entered the city. Just as we halted outside the city, another batch of cavalry trotted out of the city and veered east also going across country. Activity was everywhere this late afternoon. The lead driver actually waved and smiled at Lucretia as we halted, watching the wagons pass by us and enter the city. "Now that is a good sign, Lucretia," I suggested. "He was actually civil to you. I'd say he may be a changed man, perhaps."

"Aye, most pleasant for a change, I'll admit," she replied, "but the real test comes once we have him safely returned to Velona. Will he go back to his old ways then, when he doesn't desperately need our protection?" Neither of us had any idea. Once the last wagon disappeared into the twisting streets, Lucretia gathered the Sisters about her. "Okay, we camp nearby. I saw a little creek just to the west of this road about a half mile back. Let's camp there; it's off the road. It seems there is a lot of traffic heading east; we want to stay away from all that cavalry. Luzzi, pick ten to come into town with me and get provisions for the return trip. The rest of you, make camp. Once they have returned, take turns heading into town to the public bath. I think we all are long overdue for a bath." Cheers went up from all sides! A month without a bath was pushing hygiene, especially for us women.

"Oh yes," she added, "it's time to say goodbye to our new friends from the Greenway. I'm taking them into town to meet Jan." We spent five minutes making the rounds. Every one of the Sisters thanked us personally, especially the six whom we had helped heal.

Luzzi was overflowing in her gratitude, tears streaming down her face. She said to Sarah Jane, "Thank you once again for saving my arm. You saved me from death. No one wants a one-armed woman around; it's a horrible liability, you understand. Sarah Jane, I owe you my life. If ever I can repay you in any way, please just ask. Really, I sincerely mean this. I have a life-debt to you." Sarah Jane gave her a big hug in reply.

Then, we were off, trotting toward the edge of Bonilla. Instead of heading directly into the city, she cut across country just beyond the last rows of homes. After about two miles, we spied a large farmstead located about a half mile from the northwestern edge of the city, our destination. As we approached, I spied dozens of Sisters doing various tasks within the fenced in main courtyard. Here was a large barn, a long set of row houses, and one main farm house, much the same as Lucretia's back in Portilla. As we rode into the complex, six armed Sisters appeared from seemingly nowhere to challenge us, particularly we seven.

"Halt! This is Sisterhood land. We recognize you Lucretia, but you bring strangers unbidden," challenged one large woman with blonde hair and blue eyes. She was in very good physical shape and quite strong.

"Greeting Sister. These are our allies from the Greenway, visitors of great importance. We must see Sister Jan at once. We'll wait here at the entrance for admittance. Please get Jan at once." One of the other women hastened back toward the main home, but the others remained on guard, though no weapons were drawn. As we waited, other Sisters began filing out from wherever they had been working to watch this exciting event unfold. I assumed it was a very rare event indeed to have outside visitors here. Perhaps fifty women slowly gathered about us, looking each of us over carefully, especially the men.

Presently, Jan came out of her house, apron still tied about her waist. She had been cooking. Similar to the other women of this land, she also had blue eyes but her short hair was more of a dirty brown. Her face was tanned with weather-worn lines that indicated an outdoors person. I guessed she must be in her late twenties and was about five feet-eight but weighed more like a hundred fifty pounds. She wore a short-sleeve lightweight blouse, which revealed strong, well-toned muscles. Jan was a fighter as well as a leader.

"Allow me to present Janisseko Bottellio, the Bonilla Master Trainer," Lucretia did the introductions. "Jan, these are very powerful allies of the Sisterhood from the Greenway up north beyond the Appian Way. In their land, they are called Protectors of the common folk as we are here. This is their leader, Bethany Stanton. This is Sarah Jane Greenleaf, Sandy Gaston, Roy Ron Randell, Raphael Penton, Simon Donegal, and Thomas Wilkins. And this is Thallia Mussio, one of my Sisters who has had the misfortune of having her tongue cut out. She is accompanying Thomas; they are bonded, though not yet formally. It has become impossible to separate those two!" Thallia blushed, but Thomas sat taller in his saddle, immensely proud of Thallia. I heard a number of hushed voices commenting upon Thallia's situation, but could not make out either the words or their intentions.

Jan eyed us carefully, noting that we were dressed differently. Evidently satisfied that we were visitors from another land, she said, "Welcome to Ranchierro Presto. Put up your horses in the barn and come up to the house for some mead or tea." To Lucretia, she said, "We have much to discuss, Sister." We complied. Soon, we nine found ourselves sitting around a large mahogany table in Jan's dining room. Hot tea and mead were aplenty along with biscuits and cheese. Jan sat at the head of the table while Lucretia took a position opposite her. We divided on either side.

Lucretia said, "Jan, thank you for your hospitality. I owe you an explanation for bringing these outsiders into your safe house without your advanced permission. Permit me to explain the situation." Jan nodded. So

Lucretia began relating all the events beginning with Thomas's befriending of Thallia. When she told of Thomas's accidental slaying of the High Priest Horton Po in order to protect a woman he was attacking, she gasped and stared at him.

"We had heard that some assassins had killed him and that they made a clean getaway. This puts everything in a very different light! Please continue," Jan said, still eyeing Thomas closely.

Lucretia then told of the trip here and of the surprise attack by a large band of bandits during a heavy thunderstorm. She described how we had pulled down lightning bolts onto the charging horsemen, how we had healed her six wounded women, how Sarah Jane, a great healer, had actually saved Luzzi's arm, and how Thomas had brought down fire from the sky in order to light a bonfire in the pouring rain. This, of course, I had to acknowledge as truthful for Jan was nearly in total disbelief. Finally, she told of our suspicions about who may be behind the bandit's assault.

"Well, I do have some news for you. We've heard that Horton's son, Antonio, has been elected the new High Priest of Tur. So it was probably Antonio who set the bandits onto you. Men! Around here, it has only been reported that Horton was assassinated and that the culprits got away. I'll bet Antonio is fuming." She chuckled.

"Now about the situation here in Bonilla — as you can tell, war is about to arrive; people are scared; many are fleeing, as you probably have seen. Pieta fell some weeks ago. My spies have reported the Centurions are now marching slowly our way. It's anyone's guess when they'll actually arrive, but mine is within the week, based upon their progress. Actually, for once, our estimates and that of the Prince's cavalry agree. I have already sent word to all the outlying Sisters to rendezvous here within five days."

"Are you going to stay and fight?" asked Lucretia in near disbelief of what she was hearing.

"No. Absolutely no. The Sisters in Zargarb tried that and all were slaughtered. The Centurions show no mercy to any fighter, man or woman. No, directly fighting the Centurions is not in our best interests. We have now had time to study their methods, their intentions, their new laws and demands, and their actions." I perked up, for this was just the information we needed to find out!

"I'll relay all that we've found out, Lucretia. On your return trip, please let the other leaders in the other cities know about all this as well. While I can't order them to follow our lead, I think you'll find that it makes sense." Lucretia completely agreed to relay the news.

"Only now is information coming out of Zargarb regularly. There, everyone fought the Centurions to the last fighter. It was a total butchery. Thousands of lives were lost in the attempt to save the city. All the fighters who surrendered were shipped off far down south somewhere to work in the slave salt mines until they die. The conquered city held mostly women, children, and old men. The women, the soldiers routinely raped, declaring it a way to rebuild the city's population. Each conquered city now has a Megalos governor who now represents the law in the city. He makes all the laws and sees that they are enforced to the letter. Any disobedience and the culprit is sent off as a slave, if a man, or sent back to Galantas as a concubine if a woman." We all gasped at the horror of their treatment.

"But what do they want of your cities?" I asked. "Don't the Sea Prince's ships trade with Megalos? Aren't they cutting the hand that is serving them?"

"Oh, sea trading is unaffected by all this, or so the governors' claim. Each city is forced to pay a royal tax to Megalos each year. The ruling Sea Prince is free to determine how much each citizen is to pay, as long as the total amount is paid on time; it's about one-tenth the entire gross income of the city as near as I can determine. What I find weird is that they have decreed that the official religion in the Sea Princes is now that of their god, Sol. Each city's population has been ordered to go to the Sol Church every Saturday. However, we are allowed to also worship Tur on Sunday. I guess with a seafaring people, you can't just abolish Tur."

"What of the Sisterhood?" wondered Lucretia, as this concerned her the most.

"Ah, just coming to that. We've heard that in the battle for Zargarb, the only real opponents of the Centurions were the Sisterhood fighters. Though every one of them perished in the battle, the Sisterhood fighters gained the respect of the invaders. We have a truce of sorts now with the governors. We don't attack the invaders, and we're left alone to do as we wish, as long as we follow the new laws and pay our taxes as the Sea Prince dictates. Personally, I believe that this is a great victory for the Sisterhood. Because all this had not yet become known, the Sisters in Solamina and Pieta took a different approach. They only knew that the Sisters of Zargarb were slain to the last woman. Thus, their approach was to abandon the cities. Every one of them left for the outlying towns before each city became encircled and besieged. Those of Solamina rode to the far north up to the last villages before the Appian Way to wait out the war. Only now is word starting to reach their scattered forces of the new treaty we've reached with the governors."

"Closer to hand, the Sisters of Pieta stayed bunched together at their training base just outside the city and the encirclement. The Centurions honored the treaty and did not harm them or bother them, just bypassing them altogether. However, the conquering soldiers passed through the city, looting, pillaging, and raping. The Sisters there have asked for our aid, and that is why I have summoned all Bonilla's forces here. I plan to ride to Pieta within three days to help them rescue what women we can from the ravages of these invaders. It's strange imagining these big cities without many able-bodied men in them. All were slain defending the city or are deported to the slave mines."

"What of the outlying towns and villages?" I asked.

"So far, they have shown no interest in them, unless they are in their path toward the next city. I suppose that once they have conquered all the seven, then they will comeback for the rest. I just don't know. Maybe they'll not even bother with the outlying towns. We can only hope so, anyway."

Lucretia breathed a great sigh of relief. "You have done a tremendous job for us all. I'll do as those in Pieta have done — let the war pass by us, but be ready to rescue as many women as we can."

Jan smiled, "Don't thank me; thank Rosita Rosario of Pieta. She was the one who worked out the treaty. I just hope we can do some good by the time that we get there. Of course, I hope to see as many of your fighters as you can spare come here and help us out, once Bonilla falls."

"You have my word on that. Just let us know when. Send a rider; have her use the northern route; it's lots safer," Lucretia said.

"This is why we are here," I piped in at this point. It seemed a fitting time. "We're here to learn all we can about the Centurions, their purposes, their strategies, and their tactics. For we know the Greenway is very likely the next target, once Velona falls. We need to gather as much information as we can and get it back to the Greenway. By the way, Jan, I have made Lucretia a standing offer. If you ever need a place to which to retreat, come to the Greenway. We'll give you sanctuary and a very decent life, unlike here. In our country, women and men are truly equals in all matters, save the two obvious ones, strength and bearing of new life."

She looked at me in utter and complete disbelief, "Equals?"

"Absolutely. I can't tell you how much all seven of us have been appalled at the horrible treatment of women in this land. How can Nature get so completely unbalanced? Yes, you can have a far better life in the Greenway. If you come, go first to Calgary and ask for Alabaster. He'll see to your needs. In our land, men love and respect women."

Jan looked at Thomas and Thallia. I could see her mind correlating facts at a mad pace. Now the young couple's growing relationship began to make some sense to her. "You know, Bethany, from time to time, we rescue women who really don't want to join the Sisterhood but just want to get away to somewhere safe where they might possibly start a new life. Could these perhaps be sent to the Greenway?"

"I don't see why not, but let us check with Alabaster first," I replied. "I'll let you know tomorrow. I wonder, since you are heading toward Pieta in a few days, might we tag along with you so we may get a closer look at these invaders? We can pay our way."

"No pay is needed; we'd be honored if you'd accompany us," Jan said. I could tell she meant it from her heart. "However, if we run into trouble, you would lend us a hand, right?"

"Certainly, without hesitation," I replied with no lag. "And we might be able to help you all in Pieta with the rescue operations."

"Terrific," she glanced at our men, and added, "only one slight problem — your men." She grinned. "The Sisterhood has the treaty. Men are not included in it. My only concern is if we run into Centurions, we women are covered, but your men could very well be snatched up and sent off as slaves in their mines, wherever that is. We don't yet have any agreement for our usual role of caravan protectors or mercenaries for hire. I fear for their safety."

We discussed lighter subjects for a while. My mind continually raced over the sole problem: the four men. True, this new treaty was still tenuous at best. If the men were challenged by the Centurions, the Sisterhood couldn't afford to come to our aid, for that would likely be viewed as a deliberate break in the treaty.

Simon intruded into my thoughts, *Bethany, don't worry about Centurions challenging us. I believe I can control their minds, if need be, without violence. I know that the other guys are not as skilled in illusions as I am, but we have a few days. I say, let me work with them on this very thing. Then, when we're ready to go, we'll conduct a little experiment and see how effective we can be at it. If we aren't successful, then there is always disguise: we could disguise ourselves as women. We all wear approximately the same outer leathers; our hair is not much shorter than the Sisters hair. Though we would find it a bit embarrassing, I think we could pull that off as well. What say you?*

I sent, *Terrific.*

Finally, I asked about perhaps getting an escort into the city. We needed to purchase some supplies for the next leg of the journey. "Based upon what I've learned today," Jan answered thoughtfully, twisting strands of her hair idly, "it isn't wise for the seven or eight of you to be seen together in town as a group. Could perhaps just a couple of you women go, if I send along, say, six Sisters for protection? Would that work?"

I agreed. Sarah Jane and Sandy insisted on going. Sarah Jane needed to find any means to replenish our supply of healing gear, and Sandy was in charge of our daily food supplies. Besides, Roy let me know that he'd insist our leader not expose herself so unprotected. I relented; he had a valid point. Later, I said farewell to Lucretia and thanked her for all she had done for us.

The rest of the afternoon, I contented myself by helping setup our rooms for the few days that we would here and helping the other Sisters with their chores and dinner preparations. The guys took the opportunity to inspect all the horses, trim their toes, and oil all the tack. That didn't take them too long, so after that, they set to work on some construction repair jobs. Several sections of the barn's roof needed new shingles. The heavily used barn doors needed some boards replaced and the hinges reset. By dinner, they had worked up a good sweat, but their volunteer work brought them many compliments and thank you's from the Sisters.

Over dinner, Sarah Jane just had to tell us about their shopping experiences. "I almost got my tongue cut out," she began. "It is so hard to remember to shut up whenever a man enters your vicinity! Imagine this, you are in the middle of saying something important, and a man walks up. If you don't instantly stop talking, why, the man at first glares at you and then threatens you. This is just so utterly incredible that you would just have to be there and experience it." When she calmed down, she told us she had doubled our original bandage supply. However, she was only able barely to acquire a few healing herbs. "Gang, if any of you spot anything useful growing by the wayside, please stop, and let's pick them. I fear we're going to desperately need all the healing herbs we can find." We all agreed.

After supper, the guys disappeared into Thomas's room to practice their illusion creation. I later learned Simon had them all casting the exact same illusion in the hopes that their joint forces would overcome all resistance to it. Sandy and I contacted Alabaster and got permission for anyone who wanted to immigrate to the Greenway. He said that anyone who was not a thief or threat was more than welcome. He agreed with our plans to go onward to Pieta to get a closer look at the chaos and disruption caused by the invaders. Sandy relayed our dangerous shortage of healing herbs. Alabaster sent, *I've already calculated this might be the case. Martha has put together a large bundle of what you need. I'll arrange for its shipping tomorrow. If I send it to you at Pieta, it will never get there in time, and besides with the current chaotic mess there, I don't think it would be wise. Probably the best place I can have it delivered to you would be Zargarb, for that city is likely now the most settled in to its new occupied status. Certainly, the package should be there before you can get there, that is if you intend to go to Zargarb.*

I replied, *Yes, I believe we must go to Zargarb for two reasons. One, it is the jumping off point if we are to travel beyond the Sea Princes and, two, we can observe firsthand how the city copes or has adjusted to occupation.*

Alabaster also sent, *Bethany, Sandy. Some bad news. I have completely lost contact with the remaining two members of the Circle that were stationed in the Sea Princes. One was Sandra Smythe, their Communicator, and the other was Planner, Isabel Ironhand. When I last had contact with Sandra, she and Isabel were in Zargarb before the city fell. I've not heard from them for a very long time now. Luigi has been unable to locate them and believes they're dead. So when you get there, can you please see if you can find them? I'd really appreciate it.* We told him that finding them would be our top priority when we got there.

Later, Sarah Jane was delighted to hear that a good supply of healing herbs was on its way to us, but she was rather taken aback that she would have to wait nearly two months before they got to us. She pointed out that an awful lot could happen in that time, especially in a war zone.

The next morning, more and more Sisters arrived. Space became a premium. So we doubled up, the women sharing one room and the guys, another. Finally, by the day of the planned departure, June 19, well over a hundred Sisters had gathered here at the training camp. During the early morning, the six wagons that they decided to take along were loaded with supplies. On the return trip, they could be used to carry passengers. A string of ten extra horses was tied to the trailing wagon. These would serve as backup as well as horses for those rescued who had not the means of transport. I estimated probably twenty wounded could be brought back in the wagons without sacrificing the food and water.

At departure time, Jan had all the Sisters form into lines. Our group of eight was positioned in the middle. Jan commented, "Say, where are your men? Aren't they coming? Say, you four Sisters belong over there," she said pointing to our men. My eyes opened wide; surely, she could see them. They were as plain as the nose on my face. Apparently, none of the other Sisters in our immediate vicinity could see them either. Their heads glanced all around trying to find the four men. Simon finally spoke, "Cancel, fellows. It works, Jan. You did not see us, right?" Jan's mouth moved, but no sound came out. She blinked and rubbed her eyes. Simon said, "I think we can handle any Centurion challenges, if they come."

"How, how did you do that?" asked Jan.

"Power of suggestion," Simon replied truthfully. "We four have worked out an agreed illusion, and it appears to be working."

"Amazing, simply amazing. I can see how this could be very useful indeed. Can you make others believe what you want them to see and hear?" asked Jan, dying to know more about this skill.

"I'll explain more while we ride," offered Simon, always eager to discuss the creation of illusions. I smiled. She would really get an earful.

Then we were off. Unlike the earlier trip with Lucretia, Jan was not protecting any convoy. We rode together as one large unit. There was no chance any bandits would attack so large a force of the Sisterhood, especially when they weren't escorting any lucrative cargo. As before, she kept to the main dirt track that paralleled the Med Sea. We covered some twenty-five miles each day. On this first day, we met two galloping cavalry groups, one headed out ahead of us and one returning. Not a single cavalryman said even one word to us as they passed us by. In fact, I swore they tried to ignore us completely, as if we weren't even there! Yet, I couldn't avoid feeling a little pity for these men. Soon, very soon, they would be either dead or slaves themselves in the salt mines, wherever those were. For these young men, fate would certainly be cruel. I know, for generations they had committed atrocities on women or had countenanced them. Still, no person deserved the fate I sensed lay before them.

Chapter 13 Pieta and the Centurions

On June 20, barely thirty miles from Bonilla, we encountered the front lines of the advancing army of Centurions from Megalos. What we found was so utterly, so vastly different from anything that I had imagined we would find that it was a good thing we had come in the first place. As we crested a tall hill, we spied a very large force of the Centurions only a mile south of our position.

Immediately, a force of some twenty-five mounted men rode hard toward us. Jan called a halt to await this challenge. The scene was totally unexpected. Below, hundreds of brown-skinned men were hammering and chiseling limestone blocks from a newly established stone quarry in the side of the hill we had just crested. Other men drove horse-drawn sleds transporting loads of these neatly stacked "bricks" further down the hill. I call them bricks, because from this distance, a quarter of a mile, that's what they looked like. Even further down the hill, another group of workers were either digging away at the roadbed or laying the stones to form an actual road. Stretching off as far as we could see was a red brick road heading straight as an arrow for Pieta! The road was about ten feet wide, I estimated, and perfectly flat! Back beyond all this construction crew were fields of tents flapping in the gentle sea breeze. If each tent housed say ten Centurions, there must be well over a thousand here alone! I also saw many neatly stacked weapon piles not too far from these work crews. Armor lay there as well. So the soldiers were In fact building a paved road between the cities. No wonder they needed three months between attacks on the cities!

The small greeting party reined in before Jan, who had nudged her horse slightly out in front, signaling she was the leader. Uniformly, these mounted men had brown skin, brown hair, and black eyes. All were tall and robust and well-muscled, prime examples of virile manhood. All wore leather armor with metal plates at crucial points, such as their chests. All carried long spears and sheathed swords. Even their horses had bits of metal protecting their fore-chests from puncture wounds. One man rode forward to meet with Jan. He spoke first, "I'm Major Hercules Thesis, Commander of the First Phalanx, Forward Assault Group. State your name and association please?"

"I'm Janisseko Bottellio, the Bonilla Master Trainer of the Sisterhood. These are my Sisters," she replied attempting to match his solemn, serious tones. Clearly, though, she was just as surprised as we were with what we had just discovered. I detected a slight wavering in her tone.

"Ah, I thought as much, Sisterhood, that is. You all dress similarly, quite unlike the norm. You are entering our territory. You must state your business and destination."

"We are headed to Pieta in answer to our fellow Sister's call for assistance in helping the women there recover and get settled under the new Governor's ways," she replied. Her voice wavered slightly; she was very nervous and tense, unsure of what to best to say to him.

"Very well, Sister Janisseko, you may pass. You are aware of the primary directive: do not attack or challenge any Centurion on pain of deportation?"

"By the treaty, we do understand that your people represent the new Law of the land, if that is what you mean. We haven't come to challenge you or your men in any way. We come in peace on humanitarian grounds," Jan answered with newfound strength of conviction. She had finally found her pace.

He smiled, "That is good. It is always good to find sensible people, especially those of the fairer sex. There is still a good deal of disorder in Pieta; there always is when a city is conquered. We welcome your assistance. If you'd like to get there faster, why, circle around the construction zone and catch the new road into Pieta. It cuts miles off of the distance; horses and wagons can shave days off of the travel time." He was going out of his way to be nice and polite to Jan. This was definitely not what I expected from a conquering army. He was even smiling at her!

Jan returned his smile, "Why, thank you for your suggestion and hospitality. I do believe we'll accept your offer. The sooner we can get to Pieta, the sooner we may be of assistance in helping the folks there return to normalcy. Thanks."

"My pleasure, ma'am. Here's a safe passage token. Just show it to the various guards you may find ahead." After handing her a copper token, he added, "Oh yes, and if any of your women want some company, you know what I mean, why just let them know." He winked at her. "Of all the women in this land, we find ourselves most attracted to those in the Sisterhood. You all are real women." Now he really grinned. She smiled back and thanked him for the compliment. He then turned and the cavalry rode back down the hillside to their duty position.

I heard more than one Sister commenting in hushed tones among themselves: "These are really attractive men! So bronzed. Did you see their muscles? Such bodies, gorgeous. And these are their fighters! Wow. I wouldn't mind bedding that one there, or that one, or that one!" The Centurions had had quite an unexpected effect upon the Sisters. Okay, I'll admit it: we women of my Circle thought that these were positively the sexiest men that we had ever seen. Perhaps, it was their exposed bronzed skin; we had not seen a brown-skinned man before, and so well-built, so tall. All right, they had an effect upon us, okay?

Jan led us on a wide arc around this construction zone. About a mile further along, we turned south and shortly came upon the newly paved road. Raphael, our Planner, had to dismount for a closer inspection. "This is a magnificent piece of construction! Look, the road goes straight as an arrow. They've removed part of hilltops and used it to fill in the lower valleys, leveling the grades somewhat. This is really going to be a speedway between the cities! How did they actually engineer all this? How can they cut across country in a straight line? Look how the stones interlock. This is simply amazing!"

Roy commented, "Ah ha. We all know that an army cannot move faster than its stomach, that is, its food supply. So building the road is actually an offensive action. I'll bet anything that we'll encounter their supply wagons rolling along as we head into Pieta. No wonder they take their time. With a road constructed, they are guaranteed fast supplies and fast communications. Now things are making more sense."

"Look, did you notice that it's the fighting men who're doing the construction?" Sarah Jane pointed out. "So that makes their fighters *skilled* men, not just a war machine. Interesting indeed."

"I find it fascinating in that the conquering army is actually creating something lasting, enduring, and valuable in the lands they conquer," commented Simon. "This I wouldn't have expected from invaders. Typically, they plunder, rape, pillage, and then move on, leaving the conquered towns destitute. Apparently, not so with these Centurions. Conclusion: they intend to be here for the long term. Could they be trying to annex this land, make it part of Megalos?"

"We won't find those answers here," I replied, sensing Jan's impatience to get moving once more. "The sooner we get to Pieta, the sooner we may find some answers." Once more, the band of Bonilla Sisters moved out, spreading out onto the paved road, now riding only three abreast. We formed a long column. We had not gone but a few miles, when we had to move off the road to allow a couple supply wagons coming from Pieta to pass through us. Each wagon had a driver and two Centurions guards, each with the familiar long spears and metal armor bits. They nodded at the women and even smiled as they passed. Some winked. We heard numerous catcalls and whistles as they moved past the end of our line. More than one Sister smiled back; several turned in their saddles to watch the wagons disappear behind us.

About five miles further down the road, we spied a small stone guardhouse beside the road on the north side. Four Centurions were on guard, sitting on the ground leaning against the building. Their horses were tied near the rear of the approximately twenty-foot square blockhouse. As we approached, the men rapidly got up, moved out onto the road to block our passage and set their spears.

As we reined in before them, Jan dismounted and presented the copper token. The one in charge briefly glanced at the token and said at once, "You may pass." I noticed he never took his eyes off Jan, watching her every body movement as she remounted. They stepped aside, but I could feel their eyes staring hungrily at us women. Perhaps, thousands of miles from their homes and families, these men obviously were lonely and probably quite bored, save for those doing the actual construction work.

That night, we camped several miles north of the road. Jan didn't want to be taken by surprise by overly friendly Centurions looking for a good time. She also posted guards throughout the night but nothing occurred. During the dinnertime, these bronze-skinned invaders were the prime topic, not only among the Sisters, but also among my Circle.

Midday the following day, we noted our progress toward Pieta was more rapid than expected, as we encountered another phalanx of Centurions. Their leader identified themselves as the Second Phalanx, Forward Assault Group. As we watched nearly a thousand men march past us, it struck me that these men each carried a rather heavy load. In addition to their armor and weapons, picks, shovels, and other construction tools were strapped across their backs. This was more like a worker-fighter army, totally unlike anything we had ever expected. This we dutifully relayed to Alabaster back in Calgary. He also thought this was highly unusual and wanted to ponder its significance some more.

Finally, on June 23, we approached the western edge of Pieta itself. This city had fallen to the invaders two weeks before, yet signs of destruction lay all around the outskirts of the large city. Just north of our position here on the western edge, a flock of carrion birds circled over one of the many skirmish battlefields. Unfortunately, we were downwind; the stench of decaying flesh was nauseating. Jan sent three outriders to check it out. They returned hurriedly in just a few minutes; all held cloths over their faces. Some fifty unburied Pieta men with nearly as many horses lay rotting on the field of battle. Many had their bones picked clean; it was a sickening sight even for the Sisters, who had grudges in general with the men of this land. Why they weren't buried haunted us as we rode on to the edge of town.

Where the road finally entered the town proper, a new red brick stone gatehouse now stood, and four guards stepped out to greet us. Jan flashed the token and we were waved entrance to the city. As we rode on past the sentries, Jan explained to us, "The Sisterhood shelter house is near the Slums. I thought we should go there first. The training camp is on the opposite side of the city." We entered the city and stared in all directions as we rode. None of us expected the sights that our eyes perceived.

Here and there, smoky wisps trailed into the clear blue sky from the burned out shells that once had been buildings. A rough estimate was one in twenty buildings had been burned down. In stark contrast to Velona, few people walked the streets. Centurion soldiers stood guard at nearly every street intersection. The usual market places were almost completely deserted. Those that walked the streets were mostly older women and some children. Pieta appeared to be a ghost of its former self. Many shops had been looted, doors lying at cock-eyed angles, ripped from their hinges. Children ran out of some, carrying food or other survival things, such as pants that were way too large for themselves.

On the way to the safe house, we had to pass by the Church of Tur in Pieta. Its ornate iron gate doors that opened onto the walled complex had been ripped off and lay at the side of the wall. It was plain that even the church had not been spared from the looting. We spied two purple robed priests working on restoring the front doors of the church proper. Their work was only half-hearted and almost done in slow motion. Apathy was everywhere.

By the time we finally arrived at the safe house, all of us were in apathy as well as sickened by what we were seeing. The worst we had yet to see. A bedraggled sister met us at the door; her face told of seeing horrors upon horrors with the ability to do little to nothing about them. However, seeing the hundred of us lining up down the block brought the first glimmer of hope to her eyes. Jan dismounted and greeted her. "I'm Sister Jan from Bonilla. I've brought a hundred with me to help. Where can I find Sister Rosita?"

"She is at the training camp where we've setup emergency headquarters. You'll find her there. Please, can you spare any food? We've got nearly a hundred sick and injured women inside and almost no food. Anything you can spare, please?" she pleaded with every ounce of begging she could muster.

Jan considered the situation before replying. If food were this scarce, then surely we would need our meager supplies. In the end, she left one supply wagon on the doorstep along with six of her women to help unload and spell the overworked Sisters here. The rest of our party headed across town to the eastern side and the training camp. A couple hours later, we finally left the city behind us and rode up to a farmstead, familiar in its layout to the other training camps we had seen. During the trip, I counted only ten Pieta men, who were between our ages and say thirty, on the streets!

Normally, the training camps could house fifty women comfortably or a hundred for a short duration, if everyone doubled up. However, the entire grounds lay covered with makeshift shelters and beds, if you call a few blankets laying on the open ground a bed. Soft moaning and out-right crying greeted our ears from all sides. The thirty Sisters of Pieta who remained here attempted to service the several hundred refugee women who came to them for help. You could tell they were Sisters only because they were afoot and moving from prone woman to woman.

Rosita, a woman of thirty, came hastily out of her house to greet us. She was a short woman, tanned, slightly overweight, though strong. In no way could she be called pretty or fair, but she had the kind of smile that made you feel quite welcome and fully at ease — that you were important to her. "Ah Jan, so good of you to come. So glad to see you. What a mess we have here!" She also had an effervescent personality, one that could be cheery in spite of the forlorn situation about her.

"Greetings, Rosita, I brought all I could gather in so short a time. I wish you had told us you were in dire need of food and supplies."

"Didn't know how bad it really was until we got involved here, sorry. I do hope you brought enough for yourselves. I trust things will get back to normal real soon," she said cheerily. What an optimist, I thought.

Jan added, "I've also brought some help from our Greenway neighbors, an entire group of their Guardians. They are all healers. Can you make use of their talents?"

"Well, doesn't that beat all? Really? Healers? We have hundreds in need. The worse off we have put in the normal bunk houses so we can attend to them better, but we need help with just about everything. Every day we get more and more coming here for aid. I just cannot turn them away, but I just do not know where to put any more! The Centurions have been good enough to bring us a wagon load of blankets and some food each day, but it is not nearly enough."

Jan introduced us to Rosita. "Oh dear me, four men! I'm afraid that their presence here may really upset some of the women. They have been horribly mistreated by the soldiers, you see."

Roy said softly, "Why don't you spread the word that we four are healers from the Greenway who have come to help them. That might go a long way to avoiding panic. We can treat those who can still tolerate the sight of a man. Our women can deal with the others. Besides, Sarah Jane is the best healer among us by a mile."

"Yes, that is a good suggestion. Racine, you go start spreading the news. Help has finally arrived." One of her Sisters grinned and began dashing from group to group announcing our arrival. Rosita continued, "Jan, can you help bring order here? Set your group to work on just about any project you can think of. Healers, let's get to work on the worst cases now. Tonight over dinner, as meager as it is, we can discuss things and formulate a real battle plan. With so many of you, we can now begin to make a big difference here in Pieta." I wondered if her scale was slightly off — a hundred versus a city that once boasted of at least a hundred thousand people!

A Sister led us to the long narrow bunkhouses, explaining that the worst off were closest to Rosita's house. Sarah Jane decided we should make a quick examination of all those that were housed in the buildings, then meet, compare notes, and make a battle plan for healing so many at once. "I need to know how many have life threatening problems, how many have serious troubles, and how many could wait for another day for our assistance. I'm worried we'll have so many critical patients that we can't handle all of them in time." We agreed and quickly began the survey, going from room to room. A Sister accompanied each of the men, explaining to the occupants that these were healers from the Greenway come to help.

An hour later, we seven met outside the first bunkhouse to compare observations. We had one hundred patients indoors, ignoring completely what was outside on the grounds. Two Sarah Jane declared were hopeless; all that we could do for them was to make them as comfortable as possible before their bodies expired. Thallia volunteered to sit beside these two here in the first bunkhouse. I must say that she did an excellent job even though she couldn't speak a word. She held each of their hands, moped their foreheads, brushed their hair, and somehow made each woman feel more relaxed during their last hours.

The other eight critical ones, we attended to first, with Sarah Jane tackling the worst ones. Somehow, she still found time to visit each of us offering us guidance as well. My first patient was a woman in her twenties whose left arm had been so badly broken that the bones were protruding from her flesh, and gangrene had already set in. To save her life, I had to amputate it above the elbow. Had I not had those ten years of druwid training, I could never have confronted doing such a ghastly task. Under Sarah Jane's guidance, I managed to accomplish the task in a couple hours and actually saved the woman's life. My next patient had a horrible sword gash in her leg, and she pleaded with me not to cut it off. I didn't need to, though. Mixing up a mud and herb compress, I was able to sew it up and suck out the infection into the mud, but it took her several days to get to the point where she only needed a bandage on the wound and could be moved outdoors.

I later learned Sandy had a really bloody mess with her first patient, a once attractive young woman who had been brutally raped and beaten near to death. Her womb was a mass of bleeding flesh. No one knew how she had come by such disfigurement. Sandy worked on her for nearly four hours before she pronounced the woman had a good chance of a full recovery. I guess there is no other word for all this except gruesome. The eight of us worked as fast as possible all that day and managed to get to all hundred patients. Admittedly, the last fifty went quickly, for they had mostly knife cuts that needed sewing up and proper bandaging.

When the dinner gong sounded around five, we eight, bloody from head to foot, dragged our tired bodies over to Rosita's house. Several Sisters had a huge water barrel waiting for us, and we let them wash us off and clean us up. I think the guys really appreciated the attention being bestowed on them. From this day on, these Sisters here looked upon our men as near gods. They'd already classified us three women as goddesses.

Jan and Rosita made sure we had plenty of nourishing food for dinner, and rightly so, for we were now their official healers, perhaps the most important people here at the moment. It's amazing how a good, relaxing meal can raise one's spirits. By the time we finished eating, we felt the energy of life flooding back into our bodies, and we were ready to hear all the details about what had happened here and to assist in making plans for the immediate future.

Much of what Rosita said she had learned from those that remained in Pieta when the invaders came, for she and her sisters had carefully stayed far outside of the city proper. At first, Pieta's army of volunteers under the leadership of Prince Vasilli attempted to engage the Centurions on the hills around the city. We had passed the outcome of one such foray on our way into the city earlier this morning. When that tactic failed, the Prince drew his forces back into the city and street fighting began in earnest. If a building were too heavily defended, the Centurions simply burned it down, capturing or killing those that fled the flames. It had taken three days to capture the large city. The Prince finally capitulated to the Centurions and their demands.

The surviving fighters were rounded up, taken prisoner, and marched out of the city toward the east to work in their salt mines; no one knew where those were. Next, the Centurions literally went door to door, seeking out other men to arrest, stealing what was particularly valuable, mostly gold and jewels, and raping women that they desired. We learned some men adapted to this by going underground and hiding. Many a family hid their male members; many tried to sneak away as the search closed upon their homes. Some were successful, others not.

The affluent Fish Market Square block had been confiscated to house Pieta's new governor, one Lexus Thebes. Since the fall of Pieta, the Prince had not set foot outside his pillaged palace. Now the Centurions themselves brought the only law and order. While the majority of the army had moved on westward, some five hundred remained to secure the town. Ten days later, all resistance had ended, for people were beginning to run out of food, and hunger dictated harsher survival methods. Pieta's residents began looting other shops that had once sold food or clothing. The Centurions mostly turned ignored this.

Rosita had re-entered the city once Lexus had arrived and most of the fighting had subsided. She immediately went to see the new governor, finding him to be a reasonable man who spoke her language fairly well. It was easy to work out arrangements with him. The Sisterhood of Zargarb had already won the total respect of these invaders. She and her fifty Sisters slowly collected the women most in need of help and brought them here to the training grounds. Those that just needed living arrangements were kept at the safe house, which was now overflowing well beyond capacity. Rosita estimated for every one they helped there were likely a dozen more they had not yet reached. It was a grim situation indeed, one that grew steadily worse with each passing day.

I asked but one single question, "What has the Prince been doing to help his people or the Church of Tur? Any help from either of these two?"

A wry smile formed on Rosita's face as she answered, "Nothing at all. He is now the Prince in name only. He barely has any servants to do his bidding. The Church leaders are mostly wiped out. Why?"

Suddenly, a gem of an idea began forming in my thoughts. I knew I had to talk in private with Simon, our Judger. "Would you excuse Simon and me for a few minutes please?" I asked. While everyone expressed wonderment, including Simon, they didn't object, and he and I went for a walk outside behind the buildings where we could be alone.

"Okay, Wid, what's up? You've got some wild idea I'll wager or you wouldn't need me," he teased.

I laughed, "You are right on that one. Look, seriously, I really need your input. You heard the situation, the Prince, who is the usual leader here, is nearly powerless because of a severe manpower shortage, and the church has been likewise nullified to a large extent. Who's running the town? Who's going to get things relatively back to normal? Not Governor Thebes. He's letting Pieta find its own way back into a livable situation. So who is doing anything about it? No one except Rosita and the Sisterhood. So my idea is: what would happen if, with Thebes' backing, the Sisterhood was put in charge, given the real Pieta authority? Suddenly, we start to get the women here back into some semblance of balance. Brilliant, eh?"

"Oh, you are a devious one, Wid Bethany!" Simon half teased and half complimented me. "You want to know if this would be a wise course to take, right?"

It was my turn to tease him back, "Spoken like a true Judger! Yes, that is it precisely."

"There are lots of things to also consider, Bethany. First, many of the younger men have fled the city. They're likely to return when things settle down. Eventually, the church and the Prince will have their followers and assistants back to run things, not to mention the countless ship crews that are at sea waiting it out. When these all return to find the Abominations now in power, they could cause enormous trouble. The Sisterhood here number at most, say, a hundred; yet the city once was home to a hundred thousand. They're stretched thin as it is already. Then, you need to consider the Sisterhood members. These are all women who have suffered badly at the hands of men. Should they gain the upper hand, wouldn't their hatred of men be merely replacing one tyranny with another? I'm not saying that all of them would seek retribution on men, but some may very well do so, that is, treat men as second-class citizens."

"Then, too, should they succeed and bring back normalcy to Pieta, later on, wouldn't many who lost loved ones in the defense of Pieta feel that these Sisters were just puppets of the new governor and consider them traitors to the Lands of the Sea Princes? You know, aiding and abetting the goals of the invaders? If the governor supported them openly, this would certainly create just such an apparency to many who live here. If so, they would attempt to sabotage anything the Sisterhood created or just plain act as terrorists toward the Sisterhood."

"Further, are the Sisters well enough educated in shipping and trade that they could even make educated guesses at what needs to be done? I doubt it. The men here never included them in such matters. Politics can be very nasty, Bethany, convoluted and embroiled in distrust."

I looked downcast and actually felt that way. "I know you thought that here is a golden opportunity for the women to change their condition, but politically, I think there are too many possibilities for them actually to worsen their tenuous position in this society if you go this route. However, I wonder if we can inveigle a way for them to gain from providing this crucial humanitarian aid in a time of crisis?" I brightened up; he sounded hopeful.

"It is a golden opportunity for them. We need to find a way for them to come out ahead. What we need is an agreement between the Prince, the Church, the Governor, and the Sisterhood, and I think I know just the way to pull it off. Come on, Wid. We need to arrange a meeting!" We quickly rejoined the others who were pondering how to get more food delivered into the city from the outlying towns and villages.

I interrupted them, but they were half expecting me to do so. "Excuse us again. It is vitally important that we arrange a meeting tomorrow morning with all of us and the Prince, the church's High Priest, and the new Governor

Thebes. Based on what you have said, if Thebes orders the Prince and the Priest to attend at a meeting, they have no choice but to come, right?" Rosita nodded and I continued, "So we need to see Thebes and let him arrange it."

"But why?" Rosita exclaimed. I could see that everyone else, save Simon, echoed her intense curiosity.

"Pieta is effectively leaderless at the moment. I believe the time is ripe for the women of Pieta to gain a more equitable balance of power, to gain the respect they deserve. In short, the tyranny and suppression of women here in Pieta is going to drastically lessen," I declared solemnly.

"That isn't possible," interjected Jan. "How can you change the treatment of women that dates back over a hundred years?"

I replied, "I agree with you Jan; it is not going to be easy or painless for men or women for that matter. We can make a positive start, that is, if you are willing."

Rosita looked me squarely in my eyes, "You think this is possible?" I realized that she was actually closely observing my body language, and she wasn't druwid trained!   I also knew instinctively that my reply was going to be pivotal. "Rosita, honestly I can't say until we have discussed a number of things with Thebes. I'll not jeopardize your Sisterhood until I'm certain it truly is possible. In fact, as you listen to the discussion, I think you'll know just what to say and when to offer it. I do believe there is a very good chance the Sisterhood can make a positive change in the way women are treated here. Shall we at least try? I promise I'll not bring up the Sisterhood until we are convinced that Simon's and my idea will indeed work."

"So you're saying we just talk first and if and only if positive change can be had will the Sisterhood become involved?" she replied.

"You have my word on it," I declared.

"And my word as well," Simon added. "Arrange a meeting to discuss the current situation in Pieta. I'll run the meeting personally; that is, after all what I do best, arbitrate between warring parties."

"Well, I guess there actually is no harm in talking to these men," Rosita said rubbing her face with her hands. "Alright, I'll see to it. Will midmorning be acceptable?" We agreed and Rosita went to find a Sister to act as a messenger.

After that, the eight of us made our rounds with our hundred patients, making sure they were doing as well as could be expected under these pitiful circumstances. Then, we turned in as well to get some sleep; it had been a trying day tending to so many wounds. However, I found I couldn't really fall asleep, worrying about whether I was doing the right thing, whether I was going to actually help or bring more trouble to these valiant, caring women. Would the talks go as Simon suggested? An endless sea of doubts and questions poured through my mind until at last I was asleep or rather awakened by a distant crowing cock.

We ate a small breakfast and then prepared to ride into the city to the new Governor's Office. Jan and a dozen of her Sisters accompanied Rosita and us along with a few of Rosita's Sister, those few who could be spared. Riding through the nearly deserted streets looked little different from the previous day. Some smoke still twisted upwards into the clear blue sky. Centurions still patrolled nearly every major intersection. Virtually no market owners were operating their stalls. This had to change and change rapidly.

Around midday, we arrived at what had once been a wealthy man's estate, now confiscated by the Centurions as their central headquarters in Pieta. Two guards stood at the door, their bronze skin in sharp contrast to the reddish stone of the building and the blue sky. We dismounted, and two Sisters took charge of the horses, remaining outside with them. I had no doubts that they would strike up a conversation with these handsome guards once we had gone inside. "This way please ladies," the taller guard commanded, leading us inside the elegant wooden doors whose inlay carvings depicted scenes of ships at sea.

Jan and Rosita both gave me a sideways glance as if to say, "Doesn't he see that four men are with us?" I winked at them. The entrance hall was huge and elegant; tapestries hung on the walls illuminated by golden lanterns hung ten feet over our heads. We were led into what used to be a study. Again, two more guards stood at attention just outside the doors, which were shut. When we reached the doors, the man who led us in promptly turned and left us to return to his outside post. One of these new guards asked, "How many of you women will be entering? We must have enough seats."

"Ten, I replied. The others can wait out here with you, if that is permissible, kind sir." I replied. I knew Thallia wouldn't stand to be separated from Thomas, so I included her. In a way, she represented the atrocities perpetrated on the women of Pieta that we were about to attempt to change. Once more Rosita and Jan gave me a glance. "How could these guards not see our four men?" Again, I smiled knowingly at them. One guard quickly entered and returned shortly, presumably making sure that there were sufficient chairs present.

We then were allowed into the room. Opulence was everywhere. Three tall windows let in the morning sunlight, which illuminated the mahogany table around which sat three men. Lexus Thebes was obviously sitting at the head of the table. He stood recognizing Rosita, "Welcome Sister Rosita. Good to see you again. Please have a seat. So many of you this morning."

The Prince was perhaps thirty years old; yet he looked pale and thin probably because of having just lost his war. His animosity had not diminished; he stood up and yelled, "I'll not be in the same room with these Abom—" he didn't finish his word, for he had a stern look from Lexus. He quickly continued, "with these women!"

Lexus, a slightly overweight man also in his early thirties, rose to his full height and fumed, "Prince Pietro, you can and you will! Now sit down and be civil, or I'll send you off to the Salt Mines to live out the rest of your years. I probably should have already done just that!" The Prince, visibly shaken, paled even paler than he was, hastily sat back down and kept his eyes from looking at the women. During this brief interlude, Simon had sent a mental message to the rest of us. Only Rosita, Jan, Simon, and I sat down at the table. The others moved the chairs back against the wall. This gave the impression that these were observers and not the actual participants.

Simon began the meeting by saying, "Hello to all of you. My name is Sister Simone, and these are Sisters Jan and Bethany. I don't believe we have met," he directed his statement to Lexus Thebes.

"Ah, welcome Sister Simone. I'm Governor Lexus Thebes of Galantas, Megalos. This is Prince Pietro Almarino and His Holiness Alfredo, the newly appointed leader of the Church of Tur here in Pieta. How can we be of service this fine day?" *Good, a true diplomat*, thought Simon.

"Well, I assume that you're here in Pieta for the long term, your Centurions, that is. I couldn't help noticing the magnificent new roads you have built and are constructing. A marvel of engineering I should say. They certainly will cut down the overland travel time between all the cities," Simon began.

"Ah Sister Simone, you've noticed! Splendid indeed. Why yes, very observant of you, yes indeed. We're bringing civilization to these barbarian lands. First come roads. I can't believe there isn't a single paved road in all this uncivilized land called the Sea Princes, but that is to be expected, I'm told, when dealing with barbarians." He winked at Simone, as if to gain the favors of a woman. "Just you wait a few months until the aqueducts that will bring vast amounts of fresh water into the city are built. Then, will come the new public bathhouses with hot and cold running water. Oh, what a joy it will be to have a good hot bath once again. It has been over a year since I left them behind in Megalos. I'm sure you women will be most appreciative of them. Our women certainly do so back home."

Barbarians. So that is what he thinks these people actually are. These Centurions actually think that they are bringing civilization to the world. That is highly illuminating, I thought.

Simon acting impressed replied, "Hot baths, now that will truly be something! Surely that will cost a fortune to build."

"Well yes, it is expensive. That is what part of your yearly taxes will be paying for, you see. We charge each city-province ten thousand gold coins each year. Part of that will go for bringing civilization to the city. In years to come, we'll extend civilization to the smaller towns up north. It's your Prince's task to make sure the revenues are collected on time." The Prince grimaced visibly, but there was nothing he could do about it and he knew it. So he sulked in silence.

Simon went on, "As we came here, I couldn't help noticing the city is barely alive. No shops are open. People are starving, some even driven to thievery just to get food to eat. People are wounded, and there is no one looking after their needs. Ships aren't docking. Food isn't entering the city. Surely, this isn't optimum, not what you have in mind, Governor Thebes."

"Oh no, certainly not. You must understand. I have all the Centurions I can out patrolling the streets. Surely, you saw many of them on your way here." Simon nodded he had. "I'm sure the city will return to normal fairly soon now. It took over a month for Zargarb to begin to thrive once more. I do believe ships are now docking there. Solamina, though, has still not fully recovered. You see, our policy with the barbarians is just let nature take its course. In time, they will find the means to recover and rebuild. Conquered people always do, you know."

"Shouldn't the Prince and or the Church be helping their people get back to some semblance of normalcy?" asked Simon. I knew that this was the key question, the point of this visit.

"With what?" antagonistically spoke the Prince, glaring at Thebes, who represented the victorious army, though Thebes probably never wielded a sword or spear in his entire life. "I've got no men left alive. The few I had are all shipped off to the Salt Mines. I cannot do anything about it if I wanted to." Under his breath, I caught the rest of his sentence, "which I don't, not for these invaders." If Thebes heard it, he didn't let on; he probably expected resistance from the Prince.

Alfredo, a man in his forties, portly though partially concealed by his royal purple robes, spoke for the first time. "Yes, the Church would like to come to the aid of our parishioners, but sadly, we lack the means as well. There are so few of us, and we have no authority in these ruling matters." I caught the subtle dig at the Prince. Here too, the two warring clans still fought for control over the city. Simon had them setup. I almost could guess Simon's reply.

"Gentlemen, we've just reached the first point on which we all agree, for the Sisterhood as well wants the city to recover rapidly. His Holiness Alfredo has just said the Church does, and I'm sure the Prince also wants the situation vastly improved as quickly as possible in order that he may set about the task of collecting the taxes." Prince Pietro glared at Simon, as if to say let them rot and maybe these invaders will leave, but with the reminder of the taxes he had to pay, he ceased. "After all, Prince Pietro, though Governor Lexus hasn't actually said so, I expect he holds you personally responsible for the funds. I assume he'll insist that you make up any difference from your own treasury?" From his grimace, Simon knew that he struck a nerve. Yes, the Prince would have to pay the funds from his own pocket should he not get it from the citizens of Pieta. "And I'm sure, Governor Lexus, you too would really like to have Pieta back to normal really soon. After all, wouldn't it be a great source of pride, if under your stewardship, Pieta became thriving far faster than did Zargarb or Solamina?"

Lexus puffed up, straightened his shirt, and replied, "Oh my yes. This is an aspect of the Sisterhood that we hadn't yet discovered! Not only are you amazingly good fighters, but now you have shown that you also have political savvy. I would never have predicted such. I must say I'm most impressed with you all. We find the Sisterhood represents the first true civilizing force among these barbarians. It is a shame that you are not in control, for perhaps all this loss of life could have been completely avoided."

What happened next I couldn't have choreographed better! Rosita chose this moment to speak, "Well, Governor Thebes, we're doing what we can, though our numbers are small. As we speak, hundreds of women, some gravely wounded, some nearly dying of hunger, are at our complex. We could do more for the ill and injured if only we had more space, more supplies."

"That is most admirable, Sister Rosita, most. Don't you think so Alfredo, Prince Pietro?"

"Oh most," the priest replied, seeing his chance to get on better terms with the governor, "they're doing what we should be doing, if only we had the man-power, finances, and *authority* to do." That last was obvious dig at his rival, the Prince.

This put the Prince on the spot. He could hardly say that what Rosita was doing was bad. In fact, he knew as the ruler he should be doing at least as much. He'd watched all his plans for a glorious defense of the city dissolve, watched all his army destroyed to the last man, watched over half of the city's population depart for the north, and finally found himself a vassal of this Governor. He, once the proud ruler of Pieta, was now at the beck and call of this Centurion, forced to be in the same room with these Abominations. What made matters worse, these women were doing what he ought to be doing. It was as if they were slapping him in the face, and he was powerless to stop it. These women had the utter audacity to speak openly and frankly without his consent. Suddenly, the Prince realized the room was utterly silent and that everyone was staring at him, waiting his reply.

In the Prince's mind appeared the thought, *What you say and do next is going to make or break your position in Pieta. Choose wisely, putting prejudice aside.* It was Simon's nudge. At once, the Prince realized the significance of his newfound circumstances. He hadn't gained the rulership of Pieta by doing nothing. No, his was a long hard fought battle with shrewd deals solidifying his position. He wasn't about to step down now. He spoke, "Yes, the Sisterhood is doing what I should be doing, had I the means." He even managed to look at Rosita and say, "Thank you, Rosita."

The governor breathed a sigh of relief. He'd finally gotten from the Prince exactly what he most wanted to hear — that he, the Prince of Pieta, should be working toward getting the city operational once more. Again, Governor Thebes was most impressed with the political actions taken by these very intelligent women of the Sisterhood.

Now Simon spoke, "The Prince has the authority to get things straightened out; the Church greatly desires to do what they can in their capacity. The Sisterhood has the means, but not the authority, and you, Governor Thebes, have the command authority to enforce it. May I make a proposal?"

Most impressive, Simone, most! thought Thebes, wondering if she was married. He decided that didn't matter. "Oh please do so!" he replied. If she had half the brains he now thought she had, he knew just what Simone was about to propose. She didn't let him down.

"Let us all work together. Give the Sisterhood the full and complete support of you three — give them the opportunity and means to greatly expand their relief aid; let the Sisters become the temporary aides of the Prince and the Church in carrying out the Prince's orders and the church's humane assistance. Work together and the job can get done in short order. All here must contribute toward achieving that goal."

"Let me see if I grasp what you're implying," the Prince spoke up. "You're saying that I still run the daily operations of Pieta and that the Sisterhood would act as my aides in seeing it gets done?"

"Correct, Prince Pietro. Look, the Sisters don't know how to run a large city, nor do they want to do so. That is your specialty. You and Alfredo both know very well how much animosity the men of Pieta have toward the Sisterhood, due in some part to your own actions. Thus, you must publically announce this change in policy toward the Sisterhood, ensure the men here know they are now your aides for the time being, and are accompanied by some Centurions to enforce your orders. It would be even better if a representative of both the Church and you, Prince Pietro, also accompanied them. It would demonstrate to everyone that all four groups were truly working toward restoring this city."

"Now that is a most reasonable plan, Simone — positively brilliant, I might add, very well done indeed." He grinned at her. "You have my full support. The sooner things get back to normal around here, the sooner my Centurions on the streets can leave." He didn't say they would then be free to join in the conquering of yet another city, nor did he say that his own political clout would be enormously higher than the other six governors. His would be an example to follow; his policies would be taught to new aspirants back in Galantas. He, Lexus Thebes, would be famous.

Prince Pietro thought fast; he prided himself on the speed with which he grasped the political ramifications of situations. That was what had kept him in power these many years. *It's clear that my enemy intends to back this plan of the Abominations. One second, Pietro, remember, these women are the only trustworthy people to be found. I've had to use their services on the quiet many times, when I couldn't trust even my own people. I'd have them fully on my side, carrying out my orders. No one would dare countermand them, not even Alfredo's clan who has been trying for twenty years to get the throne back from us. An alliance directly with these women may yet keep me in full command here.* "Yes, I agree; it's quite a worthy one. I would welcome the opportunity to work with the Sisterhood, don't you agree Alfredo?"

Alfredo saw his opportunity to wrestle the throne from Pietro evaporating rapidly. His plan — allowing the Prince to fail to salvage the wounded city and then his stepping in with the reserves of the Church — would have endeared the populace to him. With the Prince in disgrace, the throne would have been his. He watched his carefully thought out plan evaporate. Now the Abominations were stepping in to provide humanitarian aid — aid he intended the Church to provide later on. He knew he had only seconds to devise a new strategy or all was lost. "This is a noble, honorable thing that you Sisters propose. Of course, the Church of Tur wants to help in any way we can, and we must do so, even without the support of either the Prince or the Governor or even you women. However, before I commit the Church, can I be assured that any support and aid that the Church can provide to the people of Pieta will be widely known and acknowledged by all parties?"

"Oh absolutely, absolutely," Governor Thebes enthusiastically replied. "We must acknowledge the parts that all play in the reconstruction of Pieta."

"That is most generous, sir. I do so commit the entire reserves of the Church of Tur to this relief effort," Alfredo promised. *Little do they know just how vast it actually is. If they hold to their word, then the Church stands to gain much respect from the citizens of Pieta, far more than the Prince would ever have allowed. In fact, if he really knew, I doubt he would even agree to this plan.*

Lexus then asked the final question, "Simone, I hate to ask this, but if we all go along with this plan, what price is the Sisterhood asking for their services in this endeavor? I know there is a long-standing hatred between you and these men here. While I don't doubt that behind your offer lies some compassion for the people of Pieta, never have I found such to be the true motivating force behind either men's or women's actions. So what is the real price for this bargain?"

Simon noted that Lexus was a shrewd judge of character, of men, and their motivations. "Governor Thebes, all we ask is for a change in the tyranny and mistreatment of women by the men of Pieta. No more mutilations. Let women speak their minds freely without restraint."

"Surely that doesn't occur, does it?" asked Lexus. He'd heard rumors of the treatment of women, but hadn't really believed it.

Simon looked over at Thallia. "Thallia, open your mouth. Show the governor just how women who dare to speak their minds have been treated." All eyes turned to her. She was humiliated by her mutilation, but she trusted Thomas who held onto her hand. Hesitantly, she did as asked.

"Oh my god!" exclaimed Lexus. "It's true then — all I've heard. Oh you poor thing, that must have been awful. Who did this to you?" Instantly, he regretted his words. "Forgive me; you cannot speak any more. I'm not used to such atrocities. You'll forgive me, ma'am?" He looked quite sincere, and Thallia nodded, trying to hold back her tears.

"What barbarians you all are here!" he exclaimed almost in anger. Lexus Thebes seldom, if ever, was actually angry, though he often feigned it to make a point. "Thank goodness we've come to bring civilization to these lands!" In his mind, the invasion of his people was now more than justified. "Gentlemen," he pronounced staring straight at both Alfredo and Pietro, "let it be known that from this day forward that women in Pieta will be treated fairly and justly as men. There'll be no more tyranny against your women. If I ever find out or hear a report that even one more woman has been mutilated or harmed like this, you both will suffer the same mutilations and then be sent to the Salt Mines for the rest of your lives. Do I make myself perfectly clear in this matter?" *This is fun. I should practice being livid with righteous anger more often. Look at their faces. Oh, I'm so enjoying this chat.*

Both men's jaws open in shock, which turned rapidly into dismay. "But, but," the Prince struggled for words. "But it is our tradition here. How can I be held responsible for what other men in the city may do of their own volition?" He desperately wanted to put the responsibility elsewhere than himself.

"Your barbarism has ended, Prince Pietro. You're the Prince, are you not? Then, set a good example; enforce your will. It is *your* tongues, gentlemen. If I were you, I would work very hard to keep my tongue, if you follow my meaning. You see, if I were unilaterally to order this change from your barbaric tradition, then no one would really follow it. Things would just happen in the night, so to speak, with no witnesses. I've seen it many times before. No, for me to keep my side of the bargain with these honorable Sisters, I must see that this barbarism changes. No, gentlemen, my ruling stands. Who better to carry out this doctrinal change but the two city rulers? No, if you wish to keep your tongues or whatever's, why, you make sure the men under your jurisdiction here in Pieta obey. *Absolutely brilliant, Lexus. If more atrocities occur, and they are likely too, traditions and habits, however foul, take time to die out; it'll not be on my head, rather these two. Brilliant, if I do say so myself.*

Fear, true fear, outlined both men's faces. Both knew it would be next to impossible totally to change this overnight. Eventually, someone would slip up, and they would have to pay the price. Lexus continued, "So gentlemen, you had better take strong measures in this matter and immediately."

Turning to Simone, he said, "Okay, do we now have a deal?" He felt supremely confident that he did.

"Oh, it isn't my position to say. It is Sister Rosita's. This is her council," Simon adeptly transferred full authority over to her. Rosita and Jan had listened in complete disbelief at this postulated change in the treatment of women. That Thebes was holding these two personally responsible made all the difference. This was all Simon's doing, but she managed to find her voice and state, "Yes, this is completely acceptable to us. We agree to the terms."

"Great! Let's all shake hands on it. I always say that a handshake seals the bargain, so to speak. Come gentlemen," and he vigorously shook her hand. It took all the strength that Alfredo could muster to make actual physical contact with her hand. She noticed his grip was weak, and his palm was wet with nervous sweat. The Prince's likewise. Inwardly, she smiled. *They are getting a taste of their own medicine, like little boys.* "I assume you want some time to fully communicate these momentous discussions among your staffs, so let's say that we adjourn until mid-afternoon. Let's meet then and begin to get some relief to the deserving people of Pieta. I declare this meeting adjourned until then." With that, everyone rose, and the two men left as quickly as they could.

Lexus offered to host Rosita and the rest of us for lunch, but she graciously declined for another day. She too had much to do before their next meeting. As we were leaving, Lexus whispered to Simon, "Simone, if you are not too busy this evening, please come and join me for an evening stroll and tea. I would like to get to know you much better. I admire the way you handled yourself today, yes, most impressive, my dear. A talent such as yours could go far, if you take my meaning."

"Why thank you, your excellency, I'll come if I can," Simon replied modestly and politely. We all hastened out just as fast as we could, trying not to laugh.

No one said a word during the hour's ride back to Rosita's complex for fear of being overheard. Besides, Rosita and Jan's minds were attempting to grasp the incredible meeting that they had just witnessed. This kind of responsibility, this kind of authority, respect for themselves and for the other women of Pieta — this was all happening way too fast. The Sisters definitely appreciated the silent ride home, giving them time to think, to reflect, and to ponder. Each had many unanswered questions, not the least of which was this in fact the beginning of a new era for women?

As the party reached the training area, the stark realities of the current situation hit home once more. Hundreds of women crowded into all the open area within the fenced in area that marked this safe haven. Quickly, Rosita issued orders to the Sisters who came over to greet her arrival, "Please take care of the horses. Jan, you eight, follow me inside please. I've got so many questions to ask that need asking and quickly." We dutifully followed the two leaders inside, taking seats at her table.

"I can scarcely believe what we have just witnessed. Tell me, is it really true? Should we trust these men? Are we being set up? Or have we somehow accomplished a miracle here?" Rosita blurted out the first of her questions.

Simon replied for us, "Yes, Rosita, you have done it. I do believe that congratulations are in order." He bowed his head toward her.

"But I, but I," she faltered, and then quickly regained her composure. "No, Simon, it was your doing. I don't know how you did it, but you got the situation set up for me. I had actually very little to do with it. Can we trust them to hold to their part?"

"Look, I have no doubt each of those men, including the governor, got what they most wanted out of the deal. If all goes well, Lexus gains immense prestige at having found the means to secure a conquered city in record time. After all, it's in his best interests to have a safe, stable, and thriving city under his jurisdiction. The Prince has found a way to continue to be the figurehead leader of the city and not lose any more face. The Priest has a way to keep his Church in power and prominence. You have put the Sisterhood into a strong, respected position in the town, as well as helping all the women of Pieta gain a more equitable life. Will they hold to their agreements? Yes, they actually have little choice in the near future, though the abuse of women isn't likely to end overnight. I seriously doubt either man will suffer directly Lexus's promise of retaliation in kind. I suspect that at the moment of justice, they'll hand Lexus a large sack of gold so that another member of their group may suffer the consequences, just as we witnessed when we arrived in Velona. Lexus is no fool; he needs to keep the power structure intact. It would reflect badly on his work if he were forced to bring in hundreds of Centurions to maintain order. So yes, they'll keep their word for now. Trust them not; I suspect they'll seek to undermine you at any opportunity. Your task is to not provide them that chance."

Jan exclaimed, "Then, this is indeed a miracle, and we have you to thank for it! All praise shall go to our friends from the Greenway! We'll make songs and tell our children and their children how we were led out of bondage by the Guardians of Greenway!"

Rosita seconded it enthusiastically, adding, "We can never ever thank you enough. We owe you a debt that we can never repay!"

"Whoa just a minute here, Sisters," Simon halted their celebration. "No word of our involvement in this affair should ever be known beyond the two of you or your other leaders. Think for a moment. If those three men should ever hear that we were behind it, they could claim trickery and deceit on your part, and instantly cancel the whole pact. No, our part in this must forever remain unknown to others. Besides, our safety would be completely compromised should these three learn that it was us. This, you must swear to us, that you'll never tell our part save to other leaders who must know."

"Never?" questioned Rosita. "But you have more than earned the gratitude of every woman in Pieta."

I added my viewpoint, "Never is a long time, Rosita. Let's just say that never means for say something like ten years until the situation has long passed from the thoughts of these men. How's that?"

"I so swear," Rosita said sincerely, adding, "I don't want to bring harm to you because of my desire for the truth to be known and for you to gain the admiration and respect that you're due for giving us this opportunity to change things in Pieta. I'll see that it isn't broadly known until there is no chance for any reprisals of any kind, though that may take a dozen or more years. Guardians, know this: one day, all women in Pieta will know the truth of this day, and songs praising you shall then be sung throughout this land."

I smiled and Simon added, "Thank you. Jan, you should be able to secure the same arrangement in Bonilla as well without our direct help. By the time Bonilla falls, the word of Lexus's incredible results will have spread to all the right ears. You only need to repeat what we did here, though I suspect the new governor who takes charge of Bonilla may likely seek you out to try to arrange a similar agreement, of course, taking all the credit upon himself."

"Simon, I'm way ahead of you on this one. I've committed the meeting to memory, and I've already been working out how I can follow this lead. If it works, I'll spread the word back to the remaining leaders in Vito, Barcilla, and Velona. However, Simon, I do have one burning question for you. How is it that those men saw you as a woman, a Sister? I saw you plainly as you are now?"

Rosita added, "Yes, I've been wondering that since we met the first of the guards. I do believe Lexus was flirting with you." We all laughed.

Simon explained, "I'll share a little secret with you two. People often see what they want or think they see, not what actually is. You see, they believed they were meeting members of the Sisterhood. Everyone knows there are no men in your organization, so they expected to see only women. We all dress similarly in leather pants and tops; our hair actually is somewhat longer than yours is. With just the tiniest help from us men, they saw what they expected to see. Yes, Lexus most definitely is going to be seeking out Simone. You're going to have to concoct some story that she had to go to Bonilla on an urgent protection mission or some such. Simone can't ever be seen in Pieta again."

Rosita and Jan only half-believed his words. "I suspect there is more to this deception than you're admitting, but Bethany has told me that you have trained for over ten years and that sort of thing is your specialty. So while your words bear some merit, I suspect there is more, but I have not the years to spend learning it. Still, we thank you," Jan said.

Rosita interjected, "Is there anything we can do for you to show our deepest thanks to you? If you need anything that we can give or do, please let us honor you with it."

Here I spoke up as Wid, "Thank you Rosita. There are two things actually, Rosita that either you or Jan might be able to help us with: one, we still need to observe the actual combat style and tactics of these Centurions and after that, we need to get safely into Zargarb, though we don't know the way."

Jan replied without hesitation, "I can see that you get into a position to observe the battles around Bonilla. It'll be dangerous. If we surround you with say fifty Sisters, the Centurions may see those numbers as a hostile force, as the Sisters did in Zargarb. Instead, what if I lend you one of my best scouts to act as your guide there and back? How's that?"

"Perfect!" I replied cheerily, for this was exactly what I had in mind. "You're right; fifty could be viewed as a threat; nine not likely."

"Ah, and I may be able to give you something that you may find very useful if you intend to spy on the battles from afar. One moment." She left the room, leaving us all wondering what she meant. She returned with a long brass tube with glass at either end. She proudly held up her treasure. "This I got in trade for services rendered some time ago. It is an invention of the Centurions. They call it a far-seeing-eye, I believe. See, it slides open, and when you look through it this way, it makes far-away things appear much closer. I don't know how it works, but it does. Here, take it with my blessings." She handed it to me. Naturally, we all thanked her for her precious gift.

Rosita went on, "I suspect you must leave soon if you are to witness the battle. Ride fast and hard. By the time you return, I'll have arranged some means for you to get into Zargarb. I'll try to get as much advanced information about their situation as I can in the meantime."

"Terrific, Rosita, that really does help us out a lot. Now, we had better let you two begin your planning for this afternoon's meeting. We want to go check up on the hundred patients we have before we head back to Bonilla."

We did just that, re-examined each of the wounded women we had tended to the previous long day. While thus occupied, we heard Rosita announce the incredible news to all the Sisters and other women. You wouldn't believe the cheers and praises that were sung to Rosita and Jan. Yet, we each knew how they must feel, accepting this intense gratitude themselves, when they knew it should have been us that were the recipients of the praise and adulation, but it had to be this way. We spent the rest of the day assisting the wounded women, changing bandages and such.

That evening around the dinner table, Rosita excitedly told us all that had gone on during the meeting that afternoon. It seems the priests, foreseeing the current situation with respect to food shortages, had secretly been stockpiling non-perishable food in rather large quantities, such as dried fish. She guessed their plan was to have been to have the Church of Tur miraculously come to the aid of the citizens of Pieta, gaining the Church much more respect and power. Now, however, it was the Sisterhood that began to disperse the much-needed food with the Church still acknowledged as the true source of the assistance. Thus, within days, this food shortage crisis would be over. The Prince issued orders to signal the ships lying just off the coast to begin to dock and resume normal trading. I had no doubts that the situation here was on the mend.

As we were getting ready for bed, Thomas brought Thallia into the men's room. "Simon, Thallia has something she wants to say to you." She walked up to him and spoke the first words that she had ever tried to utter since that horrible day years ago. Though garbled, her meaning was clear. She said, "Thank you," kissed his cheek, and hugged him. Simon actually blushed.

"Thallia," Simon replied to her, taking hold of both her hands, "Today you have done two very brave things. First, you publically showed the governor what was done to you. That took incredible guts. Second, you just spoke. I know it was barely understandable, but it was understandable. If you want my opinion, I think you should talk more. Don't be embarrassed by it. We know you're not your body. Just accept your body as it is and work with what you can do. Mind you," he teased her, "keep your speeches short, though, at least at first."

His joviality rubbed off on her. Yes, it had taken her all day to work up the courage just to utter those two words, but she felt that she absolutely had to thank Simon. Carefully, she said her next words, "Yes Sir." While difficult to make out, we understood and laughed along with her. Her face aglow, she tenderly kissed Thomas goodnight and went back to the women's room, radiant.

We, of course, saw this huge change in her and plied her with questions about why she was so happy. She then slowly said, "I talked." We girls gasped, for none of us had heard her make a sound before, other than crying or moaning. She took us by surprise, and unfortunately, we had to ask her to repeat it once more, listening carefully. I cried out, "You talked!" She nodded visibly excited that we actually did understand her. We three jumped up and down, grabbed a hold of her and danced gaily around the room for several minutes. This was worth celebrating. Albeit her sounds were very hard to understand or make out, still it was understandable and a giant step forward for her. Sarah Jane sent to me, *She has finally accepted her life as it is. Now she can heal all the way! This is a miracle indeed!* I now understood just how big this step for her actually was.

Chapter 14 The Battle at Bonilla

The cock crowed at the crack of dawn, and someone was knocking on our door. I got up wiping the sleep from my eyes and opened it. A Sister stood outlined in the doorway, ready to hit the trail. She introduced herself, "I'm Sister Florencia Bugatti, but you can just call me Flo. I'm to guide you to the battle at Bonilla. We must leave at once; we all suspect the battle rages even as we speak. How soon can you be ready to depart?"

"We'll be ready in say a half hour," I replied, springing into action. I put the guys in charge of getting our horses ready, while we women hastily put together some necessary supplies for the journey. We found that Jan had already seen to most of our needs and had eight food sacks ready to go. The men found that the Sisters had already saddled our horses. I found Flo with the horses. The Sisters are a model of efficiency!

She explained, "We're going to have to push the horses hard if we are to cover the hundred miles to Bonilla in just a couple days. We'll have to really watch their needs closely and not stress them too much. With luck, we should be there in two or three days at most. I do hope you're used to some hard riding."

Florencia had the usual short blonde hair and blue eyes so common in the Sea Prince lands. Her face was worn with lines; her age was hard to guess, but we found out that she was thirty years old. She was short and of a wiry build, only just barely five feet tall. Flo's alto voice had a rough quality to it, somewhat similar to a man's. Her hands were calloused from constant riding. Flo was an expert with horses and knew the land like the back of her palms. Often others accused her of being able to navigate across the Lands of the Sea Princes with her eyes closed. In fact, as we discovered, this woman knew more about the land and its terrain than any other person in the whole country did. From the southern Med Sea to the northern Appian Way, from Juda Arad in the east to the ocean in the west, this woman was a walking encyclopedia.

While we packed our sacks and gear onto our horses, Jan appeared to see us off. Sleep was still in her eyes as well. "Florencia is our best guide. Trust her completely in all matters while on the trail. If possible, I would like her back in two weeks. She is a most valuable woman. Please, do not under any circumstances put her well-being into jeopardy." We promised her what we wouldn't put her into any danger with our mission. She added, "Flo, if you ever feel threatened by circumstances, I hereby order you to do your disappearing act." Flo nodded, though the look on her face said those orders were not needed. We looked blankly at Jan, so she explained. "Flo isn't a fighter. Instead, she has the uncanny ability to disappear without a trace, even when inside a town! If you ever need to 'vanish,' why just let her know. I don't know how she does it, but it is nothing short of miraculous." Flo looked a bit embarrassed by this compliment.

We thanked her, said our good-byes, mounted up, and carefully rode out of the complex, avoiding all the sleeping people on the grounds. Once clear of the gate, Flo headed due west across country. She waited until we fell into our usual line, two abreast before she turned and spoke, "Please, let's go single file. I'm going to take all the shortcuts there are, and many places aren't wide enough for two's. Please stay close together and follow each other and my lead. Some places we'll canter for an extended period because I know what's ahead and where we must go slow. The horses will get rested during those spots where it's best not to canter." We acknowledged her orders, and she added with a grin, "I just love these trips; we ride like the wind! Come on," and she nudged her horse into a canter.

When we last rode this fast, we were attempting to break through the encirclement of Karka. There, however, we had some familiarity with the land. Here, Flo was leading us across barely discernable tracks of which only she and animals knew. I found it just a bit scary riding this fast. Flo was correct; all the while that we cantered at full speed, the land was smooth though hilly. Up one hill and down we went, my hair flying, flapping behind my head. Still, I loved every minute of it. After ten miles, she slowed to a walk, allowing the horses to cool down, as they carefully placed each hoof on the rocky slope. Two miles later, we left the stony ground behind, and off we went once more. Thomas sent his observation to me, *I think she's going in nearly a straight line.*

We cut across country; we wove around small farmsteads, skirted the edges of vineyards and olive groves. However, Flo never cut across a tilled field out of respect for those that worked the land. Since we weren't on any "road," we met no fellow travelers, only the occasional field hand working in the hot sun.

We halted for lunch beside a small stream with thick grass on either side. Once the horses had cooled and drank from the fresh, cool water, they happily dined on the grass. We, on the other hand, lay back on the soft turf and relaxed. On another day, this little glen would have been a very romantic spot, but today, our thoughts were on what lay ahead. That is, all of us except Thallia and Thomas who lay in each other's arms. Unfortunately, Flo only let us rest up for a half hour before we were back on the trail once more. Five hours later with only one fifteen minute rest stop, we stopped for dinner. She gave us only an hour before we mounted up once more.

The moon rose nearly full and gave her sufficient light to press onward until nearly ten that night. By then, I was exhausted and saddle sore. This was more riding that any of us were used to doing. When she finally halted for the night, she led us into a sheltered grove of trees far from any settlement. After seeing to the horses, hobbling, and tying them to a line where they could graze on the sparse grass, we bedded down, stiff and sore. I lay beside Roy and Flo, and we stared up at the stars, which shone like thousands of jewels in the clear night sky.

Flo said, "Well, you've been able to keep up. That's very good. I set a fast clip today, in part to make sure you could. You did well, actually better than I would have predicted."

"We love riding like the wind," I idly replied. "I just love my hair flying behind my head, the breeze rushing past my cheeks, but I admit, I'm not used to this much hard riding. My legs ache a bit."

"It's freedom that you feel," Flo waxed philosophical. "When riding like this, I feel completely free — one with nature about me. Sometimes when I get too many problems in my mind, why I just go for a long, fast ride until my problems and worries have vanished."

"I can appreciate that," I answered. "Say, how long have you been in the Sisterhood? You don't have to answer anything personal if you don't want to talk about it," I added, suddenly realizing that she probably had a horror story in her past.

Florencia was observant and sensed my intent, "It's okay. Been in it for fifteen years. Grew up on a farm north of Bonilla. Raised horses, my father did. He taught me much before I left there in the middle of night." Her voice took on a very sad tone by the end of her last sentence.

"Good God! Not your father!" I exclaimed, suddenly realizing what she hadn't said.

"Yes, I was fifteen and of age. He got drunk one Saturday night, came home, beat me up, and raped me. All thanks be to Tur that I did not become with child. That is the only good thing about the whole affair. For weeks, that was all I feared. It was sickening to me and always on my mind, fearing I would bear a child from that awful night. For six weeks, I kept telling myself it was the wine that made him do it. During that time, he kept doing little things for me that seemed awfully like flirting. Then, one Saturday night, he went into town to drink with his buddies once again. I knew he would come home and start in on me again, so I packed up, took a horse, some food, and rode out on my own. Of course, it's not safe for women to ride the roads alone, unaccompanied. They're fair game for any man that comes along. Hence, I stayed off all the main roads. I soon found that I really loved traveling around all by myself. No one ordering me around, no duties, save to me and my horse. For months, I wandered the byways between Bonilla, Vito, and Pieta, living off the land."

"Then, one night, way out in sticks, I came across a band of women, Janisseko Bottellio, the Bonilla Master Trainer, and about two dozen of her trainees. Since they were all women, I ventured into their camp to find out what was going on. I found out they had gotten lost, and I offered to guide them back to the main roads. The rest is history. Janisseko has always urged me to ride as often as I desire. She has given me so many opportunities to travel all over this land that I can never thank her enough. She, alone, understands my soul."

"Now, I believe that I do understand you a bit," I replied. "I'll bet anything right at this moment you feel completely at peace, like you were in a paradise. Am I not right?"

Flo rolled over onto her side so she could stare at my face in the moonlight. She didn't have to answer me; her face told all. After a long pause, she said, "You're a lot like Janisseko in many ways." I took that as a compliment.

Roy asked, "Have you never found a man worthy of you? I really love being around Bethany. She's become a part of my life." He squeezed my hand slightly; I returned the squeeze.

"What man would have me as I am? I can't live without riding and traveling about the land. I would surely wither and die if I were forced to spend all my time in a house somewhere doing wifely duties. Besides, until you came, I would never have considered being with a man. Why on Tarra would I want to propagate this woman servitude status? A man would just confine me — force me not to say what I want and when I want. None would listen to me anyway. If I did have children, I'd live in daily fear that he would do to my daughters what my father did to me. How could I live like that? I'd go mad. No thanks, but I would rather have the love and respect of Janisseko than that of tyrant men, but now maybe things will change."

Roy replied, "Good solid reasoning, Flo. I concur with you choice of abstention. All I can say is that if you lived in our land, the Greenway, why, you would be highly sought after by many men of good heart. You would have many suitors from which you could choose just the right person for you. Maybe in time that may happen here. There is always hope."

"Until yesterday, there certainly was very little of that here," she added. "We'd best get some sleep. We're riding at the crack of dawn again."

True to her word, she was up with the rising of the sun, and we were on the road once more barely a half hour later. We had just enough time to take care of personal needs and eat. As we were mounting, she said, "We covered about forty miles yesterday. If we do the same today, we should arrive just outside Bonilla around ten tomorrow morning." This was very encouraging news indeed.

Once more, the cool morning wind rushed through my hair, chilling my face, as we cantered off again. I, like Flo, felt the refreshing sense of freedom as we raced across the countryside. This scout certainly knew her terrain as she unerringly knew just when to slow down and when it was safe to speed up once more. Around farmsteads, around vineyards, we sped, diverting little from the straight line path to Bonilla. The only real diversions were made to bypass actual settlements. However, the closer we got to the big city, the more scattered farms and ranches we encountered and the more men working in their fields as well. Only now, we also met a few wagons loaded to capacity moving northwards from Bonilla. These families had deserted the city perhaps as much as a week ago and had taken little used paths to avoid detection and bandits. These, too, we gave way to and bypassed.

However, by afternoon, the constant riding began to become both long and tiresome. I no longer felt the enthusiasm of the morning. It was hot by late afternoon; both my horse and I were sweating. My legs were cramped, and I know my horse was approaching exhaustion. The others in my Circle also felt miserable, but we kept our attention focused on just riding the horses, leaving all else to Florencia. Indeed, she thoroughly enjoyed this ride. Of all of us, only she was all smiles when we finally halted for supper. Admittedly I felt grumpy; we all did. Flo's comment was, "You'll sleep soundly tonight. Rest up while you can; we still have more riding ahead of us tonight." In unison, we groaned in mock protest teasing her. Yet, it wasn't all in jest. We were tired and sore, but not enough to chance taking another day to get there, perhaps missing the battles.

When we finally stopped for the night, I was so exhausted that I cared little where I laid down to sleep. No matter how or where I lay, the ground seemed to be continuously moving around me. I drifted into sleep still swaying in a saddle! I even forgot to take care of my horse, a fact that Roy reminded be about the next morning. Boy, was I ever embarrassed. "You were out like a zombie," exclaimed Sarah Jane playfully.

"Leaving me to rub down her horse, as if I weren't tired too," Roy playfully added.

"Me thinks our Wid messed up," joked Simon.

"Yes, all right, I goofed up," I owned up. "I guess no damage was done because all of you weren't tired after that ride," I jested back.

"Well, I wasn't," Flo joined in the fun, but we saw she was serious and broke out in laughter.

"Seriously, gang, we can't go so fast today. We are just about ten miles east and just north of Bonilla. The Centurions are likely to have patrols some miles out from the city. I assume we don't want to be spotted by them, correct?" asked Flo.

"Absolutely," I replied. "Get us in close enough so we can see the action and yet stealthily so we aren't seen by those on either side. We just want to observe the battle. Under no circumstances are we to get actively involved with either side, no matter what happens. If threatened, mount up and ride like the wind north out of here. Understood?"

"If we can position ourselves, Flo, on the far side of some hill or ridge overlooking the battle, then we can use Rosita's gift to spy on them," Roy suggested. "You, Thallia, and Thomas can stay well back with the horses. If anything goes wrong, we'll dash to the horses and ride off."

"That's fine with me," Flo answered. "Remember, I'm not a fighter. Yes, I have had some basic training, but about all I can do is fend off the shallowest of attacks. I just never did get the hang of sword play."

"Hey, don't fret it," Sarah Jane consoled, "neither did Sandy or me or Bethany. We all only barely passed that training. We're with you; let's get the heck out of here if we can." Flo smiled, realizing she wasn't the only person who didn't like to partake of combat.

Again, we saddled up, but this time we moved slowly and very cautiously. Roy now rode on Flo's left, and both were constantly alert for trouble well ahead of us. We knew the land to our left or west was under the control of the Centurions. Their road to Bonilla was likely finished, and the thousands of men had now donned their combat gear heading for a fight to conquer the city. None of us said a word; only the occasional horse snorting broke the stillness. Yes, we still passed farmsteads, even more frequently this close to the city. Many looked deserted. Evidently, those who lived here had gone into hiding or had temporarily abandoned them for the safety of northern towns.

The sun had climbed halfway to its zenith when Flo halted and whispered to us. "I have an idea of a really good vantage point. Let's go north a bit and circle around, follow me. Vitorrio's Ridge may be just perfect. It's the highest hill around Bonilla and is about four miles from the city's edge. Several smaller hills lay between it and the city, so we might miss some of the action, but it should be relatively safe, since it's so rocky that nothing can grow there save stunted trees." It sounded perfect to me, and we now veered due north for a couple miles before going west once more. Around eleven, the ground rose sharply in front of us, and as we pressed on, the ground became littered with small rocks, which steadily grew in size the closer to the top we came. We halted about a hundred-fifty feet from the crest at the last stand of trees. Here we handed the horses to Thomas and Thallia, and made our way on foot the rest of the way, moving in and around the boulders, which were between three and four feet in diameter.

Carefully, we lay on our stomachs, crept to the crest, and peered down. On another day, the view would have been spectacular. Lower hills lay between us and the northern edge of the huge city, which lay spread out in a hemisphere over the land. The Med Sea shimmed and sparkled in the distance. I spied several sets of sails far out to sea and wondered if our friend on the Lucky Lady was out there watching and waiting. Coming from due east, the newly built red brick road cut through the land itself, like an arrow through Nature. It ran right up to within perhaps a quarter mile of the city. The construction workers were nowhere in sight. Instead, well-armed Centurions laid siege, taking up strategic positions in a semi-circle around the city.

Instead of making a line of men entirely surrounding the city, they had placed their forces in good defensive positions, such as the top of a hill or along a ridge line. Each clump held hundreds of soldiers. Sunlight reflected off their protective armor. Each held their typical huge rectangular shield with their left arms while holding a spear on their right. Carrion birds circled high overhead way down by the eastern edge of the city where it met the sea. Evidently, we'd missed some battles in which the defenders of the city had tried to out flank their opponents.

Since this was a perfect spot, I sent Flo back to the horses, got out the far-seeing-eye that Rosita gave us, and began to systematically scan the scene before us. I noticed they had three groups of cavalry, each numbering well over a hundred men, positioned well outside the encirclement. Obviously, if the line were breached, the cavalry would rise fast to close it. Then, I noticed something odd, handed the instrument to Roy, and let him view the scene.

"What are those things down over there, just on top of the next hill from us, there to the right of the city?"

Roy looked long and hard at them before passing the instrument on to the others. "I don't know," he said. "There appears to be a team of horses attached to broken wagons or wagons with no rear wheels. What can those things be?"

Raphael had the answer once he got his turn to view them in the far-seeing-eye. "Those are chariots. I've heard about their design. Yes, they are like a front wheeled wagon — no rear wheels. Or you can call it a box on two wheels. As I understand the principle, one man drives the contraption, while several others stand in the box part and fight from there. I suppose they shoot arrows or throw spears. That's about all I've heard. I wonder if we'll get to see them in action?"

Roy added, "They must be awfully unstable with only two wheels. Pulled by two horses, why, they must go really fast. If they use spears, they probably only have a few available to throw before they run out. It doesn't look big enough to carry much else beyond the three people."

"Well, we've got a good idea of their overall strategy," I mused. "They take their time and build terrific supply roads right up to the proposed battle area. They encircle the target. All this takes time and must scare the heck out of the defenders who can only watch as the noose tightens around their city. I'd hazard a guess that each new battle is well planned in advance, down to the precise positioning of their attacking forces. It would appear their cavalry is held in reserve to thwart any weakening of their main ground forces."

"Add to that their formations," Roy commented, "are all well-formed. With those big shields, they don't have to worry much about a devastating rain of arrows. One only has to duck behind it to be almost impervious, unless the arrow came down on them with a very high arc. They appear to be highly trained and well-led men. So far, I don't see any weakness that can be exploited. If they line up with shields forward forming a defensive wall, any attacker is going to be very hard pressed to get to the individual soldier. These guys are good."

"Cut their supply lines?" I suggested. "That might be one thing we could use against them."

"They are vulnerable to a massive cavalry charge of heavy horses," Roy observed. "If they were attacked by say a thousand heavy cavalry, they could be defeated, but who has that many cavalry, let alone heavy ones, you know, that use the large draft horses?"

"Well, how they respond when their leader is taken out remains to be seen," Simon commented. "Sometimes, when the one in command is slain, the common soldier doesn't know what to do on his own initiative and so becomes exceedingly vulnerable. Somehow, with all these men also being skilled workers, I'd expect they'd manage to survive with the loss of their immediate commander. If they weren't, then we could systematically take out their leaders with lightning bolts and the rest would succumb easily. Yet, I don't think that will be the case with these Centurions."

Sandy whispered, "I've relayed all this to Alabaster. He sends his compliments. He wants to use me to look through this far-seeing-eye instrument. Is that okay with you all? Can I borrow them for a while?"

"Great!" exclaimed Roy, handing her the bronze instrument. I still thought that looking through someone else's eyes was a darn powerful skill, which I still hadn't a clue how it was done. I hoped Alabaster could see some weakness that we had missed. So far it didn't look good for the Greenway should these Centurions invade us. From Governor Lexus's talk of bringing civilization to the barbarian, uncivilized lands, I knew it was just a matter of time before they turned their attention towards us.

Some ten minutes later, Sandy whispered, "Alabaster wants to talk to all of us through me." One by one, she connected with our minds. When she had all six of us at one time, Alabaster began speaking to us all.

You've done very well indeed. Yes, these Centurions look amazingly powerful. I highly doubt the meager forces the Greenway can muster will be able to stop them. I think that if they are to be defeated, we must look elsewhere for the means. You must travel all the way to Megalos and see if you can find some other means by which to halt their advance. Perhaps dissension at home; perhaps there are some there that are opposed to this conquering of their neighbors with whom we can ally ourselves. You must find a way somehow. Yes, Bethany, I'll give some thought to ways and means of cutting their supply lines. Yet, I now see why they want to take over the Lands of the Sea Princes. If they can control the seas and all major shipping, then they aren't so dependent upon their overland road system. Brilliant strategy, I must admit. We aren't dealing with dummies. Go first to Zargarb and see if you can find out what happened to our two druwids there. Then, head on east through Juda Arad. I suspect that their supply road goes through that land. Maintaining this strong a telepathic contact has tired me. So I think I'll take a little nap. Again, I thank you from the bottom of my heart!

Then the contact was broken. I felt so excited while he was in my mind. Now, sadness came over me, as if I had lost a close friend. I know that's silly, but that's the way I felt. When Alabaster broke his bond with my mind, it felt like I had lost something, something I loved and treasured. No one spoke; we waited and watched.

Around noon, Roy sounded the alert, "Hey, something's happening. Look there on the northwest side of the city. It looks like a large force is coming out to do battle." We peered at the spectacle before us. Probably five hundred men came marching in long rows out of the city, heading toward the hill defended by only about a hundred Centurions. The defenders quickly formed into a solid line stretching across the hilltop, awaiting the approach of the city forces that outnumbered them five to one. From this distance, it looked more like ants crawling along the ground after discarded picnic food.

When the city guards were just about to close upon the defending

Centurions, the chariots began moving. At top speed, the chariots rushed from their position on a neighboring hill, angled around and headed straight for the left flank of the city forces. Roy watched them closely with the magnifying tube. "Hey, there is some kind of thing protruding out from the wheels of the chariots." We watched as the chariots ran into the city guards who attempted to move out of the way of the charging horses. However, the things that protruded were in fact similar to metal blades. We watched in horror as the blades hit the men diving out of the way. Arms, legs, and other severed body parts went flying in all directions, creating massive havoc among the city attackers. After the first pass, the chariots swung round and headed back the way they came, carving another bloody path through the heart of the forces. Then again, they turned and cut a third path though the city guards whose nicely arrayed lines were now in complete chaos.

At this point, the hundred Centurions on the hilltop began to move down the hill into the confusion of the guards. It was a total slaughter. Within just a few minutes, five hundred city defenders lay dead or dying on the battlefield. Only a very few Centurions were wounded. I counted possibly ten were severely wounded at most with maybe two dozen just slightly wounded. The victorious Centurion soldiers systematically visited each fallen city guard, killing any that remained alive. Satisfied that none lived, they marched in perfect order back to the top of the hill from which they'd come. I felt very sick. In fact, I had to back away from the hill to puke. Sandy did likewise.

I felt Roy's reassuring arm steading me. "Thanks," I feebly replied and tried to regain control over my stomach.

When we rejoined the others, Sarah Jane, used to witnessing death by virtue of having spent ten years learning the healing arts, commented, "The real tragedy here is that all at once some five hundred spiritual beings are unexpectedly without a body. Does this imply a sudden baby boom next year in Bonilla? If the city loses so many men and assuming there is an equal birthrate between males and females babies, this city is going to have far more women in it than men in the next generation, interesting idea." Her comment suddenly reminded me of my secondary mission given to me in secret by Alabaster: to find out what is happening with the spiritual beings. I had completely forgotten about it until now. I chided myself for this lapse.

"Say, can any of you spot what the spiritual beings are doing right after their body dies?" We all observed as carefully as we could. Spotting the being is much harder to do than spotting a physical body. I tried shutting my eyes to dull the overpowering visual stimulus of my normal vision. For the longest time, I saw just blackness.

Sarah Jane was the first to spot one. "Say, I picked up one there. Weird. They rise up into the sky a bit, stare at some whitish image in their minds, and then shoot like a rocket up that-a-way," she exclaimed pointing generally north and west toward the Appian Way. Now I picked up one and watched him float off there as well. Soon the others began sensing the spiritual beings. We all concurred. They all, to the last man, headed in the identical direction!

Weird, to say the very least.

"This doesn't make any sense," protested Sarah Jane. "They should be heading back into town looking for a pregnant woman."

"I know," I replied, "strange indeed. Yet, we know from the Sisterhood that the Centurions go on a raping rampage once they take a city. That has got to create any number of pregnancies, doesn't it?" My education here was sorely lacking. Thankfully, Sarah Jane was older and more informed; as a healer, she often dealt with such matters.

"We are only fertile for a short period each month. I would hazard a rough guess that one out of every four women raped might be at the right time to become pregnant. Even if the actual numbers are smaller, given the number of rapes the Sisterhood has reported occurring, there has to be hundreds of babies coming as a result. So why don't these beings stick around to get a new one? Where are they going and why? Have we stumbled onto a new aspect of Nature that has not been known before?" she asked me. "You know, this has roused my curiosity."

I thought a moment before I decided to share Alabaster's findings. Quickly, I outlined the long study he had made. Raphael backed me up on this, as he was involved in finding the secret room in which Alabaster kept all of his records, the counting sticks with colored strings.

Sarah Jane looked a bit bewildered, "Are you saying all these vile men are taking new bodies in the Greenway? We are inheriting them and their awful ways?" She looked positively disgusted.

"No, he has not observed sudden spikes in the number of new beings, only a slow growth over time and has been wondering where they're coming from, that's all. Let's say that ten thousand men are killed during the conquering of one of these cities. We have not seen ten thousand new babies in all the Greenway. That is way too large a number. Besides, if they all went to our land, then who is taking over the new babies born down here? No, they must be coming back some time to get new baby bodies here. Then again, maybe some of them don't and go further north to the Greenway. We should study this when we get the chance."

Left out of this discussion for the most part, Roy took this opportunity to add, "Sometime, we are going to have to try to follow them up into the Appian Way and see exactly where they go and what they are doing up there. Sounds like a mystery to me."

Simon brought us all back to reality. "First, we have to find a way to defeat the Centurions or there'll not be a Greenway to go back to. I believe we've seen enough here," he said. "Shall we head back to Pieta?" I nodded. There certainly was nothing more to be learned here.

That night, Sandy relayed the battle scene to Alabaster along with our observations of what happened to be beings afterwards. She reported he was just as confused about it as we were. However, he did offer us some comfort: *In the Greenway, there is not much space for chariots to operate, if we pick the battlefields.* I felt somewhat encouraged that he had found a way to nullify those machines of destruction. After what I had witnessed today, I wondered just which side were actually the barbarians. We were a somber group as made our way back to Pieta, arriving there in the early evening of June 27.

We had been gone less than a week, but the changes at Rosita's Sisterhood training complex were huge. Gone were the hundreds of women camping out in the open areas of the ranch. Only the most critically wounded women were still in the bunkhouses, and they only numbered a little over a dozen. As we entered the complex, we watched a stream of supply wagons passing by, heading into the city from the northeast road; several Sisters were escorting them accompanied by a priest in purple robes and another younger man barely in his teens who wore the colors of the Prince. As the Sisters rode past us, all four waved at us; we returned the gesture.

As we rode up to the barn, two Sisters came out to greet us. One said, "Hi, back so soon? I think Rosita will be surprised to see you. I think she thought you might be gone a couple weeks. Boy, have things sure changed around here. Rosita's in the house. I know she'll want to see you all immediately. We'll take care of your horses for you."

"Hey, thanks, we appreciate it," Roy relied. We dismounted, grabbed our sacks and saddlebags, and headed to Rosita's home. Thallia and Flo stayed behind to help with the nine horses. We were just in time for a late dinner; Rosita, Jan and several others were just finishing up.

"Well, this is a surprise," exclaimed Rosita. "Come on in and have something to eat. For once we have plenty." She motioned for us to have a seat. One of the other women got up to go bring in more table settings and the remains of their dinner. We quickly washed the trail dirt off and sat down with them.

"Set two more places. Thallia and Flo will be here shortly," I advised. "They are helping bed down our horses."

"Well, I've much to report and much to ask you," Rosita began, "but I'll be a good host and let you eat first. You must be starved with only trail food for nearly a week."

While we ate, Rosita described the significant developments of the past week. It seems the Church had stored up a vast amount of food, blankets, and similar necessities. Now, they were dolling them out to anyone that needed assistance. The Sisters were the delivery personnel, and a priest initiate accompanied them to make sure the recipients knew it was from the Church of Tur. Respect for the Church grew enormously everywhere that the aid came. Already, six ships had docked and had unloaded vital cargo. However, there was a drastic shortage of dockworkers, because many had been pressed into service in the defense of the city and were now lost. Others had deserted the city. As of yesterday, word had spread that it was safe to return, and the Sisters reported spying several dozen making their way back into the city from the northern towns and villages.

The fires were out now. The representatives of the Prince, accompanied by pairs of Sisters, were now going door-to-door, assessing what rebuilding assistance would be needed. True, the Sisters were still not well received, but the climate had noticeably improved for them. People were now seen on the streets, and some of the market shops had reopened. More were opening each day when their supplies reached them from the outlying areas.

We spent an hour trying to answer the myriad questions that Rosita had. She had never attempted to manage such a huge operation. Her biggest problem was the small number of Sisters who had to be a part of every action. Already, her profits in this week alone doubled all she had made in the previous year. A large percentage was given to the Sisters who more than earned their reward. Though overworked, their morale was high. Several temporarily vacant warehouses were donated to house the homeless. One had been designated the infirmary where the wounded and ill were now being watched over by the best physicians that remained in Bonilla. I say physicians, but these were not much more than mid-wives, really, nothing like we druwids.

"Where normally we might get one new recruit in a week, already this week three dozen had expressed a desire to join us. How can I train so many so fast?" Rosita asked.

"That is good news," I answered. She was obviously looking for something more tangible. "Well, whatever you do, don't lower your standards."

Simon, as expected, gave a more helpful answer, "Delegate, Rosita; that is the answer. My guess is that you have been run ragged trying to oversee everything."

"You can sure say that again!" Rosita heaved a huge sigh of relief sensing that he understood her position accurately. "If it hadn't been for Jan's help, why, I wouldn't have accomplished a fraction of what needed to be done!" Still, both women looked worn out.

Simon elaborated, "Find your most trusted Sisters and delegate a portion of the overseeing responsibility to them. I know you have section leaders, and that, for security, the individual members often don't know those Sisters beyond their immediate section. Without sacrificing that aspect, delegate complete responsibility for an action to one section leader and let her figure out how to handle it best with her available workforce. Then, you only have to oversee these to make sure things are going along well. When an organization is small, you can run all aspects, but as it grows, you have to give others the full responsibility to carry out some operations independent of you. Mind you, you need to monitor such and perhaps smooth out any problems that arise. You simply scale it up by adding responsible persons in positions of authority and responsibility, that is, between you and the lowest echelon. We, ourselves, like to go in units of seven. That is, one at the top, seven below him; seven below each of those seven; and so on down. You may find it more practical to go in larger groups because of your fewer numbers."

"Simon, what you say makes perfect sense! I don't know why I didn't think of that already." Rosita exclaimed. "You make it sound so simple!"

"If you see it as simple, then you have indeed grasped what I'm trying to explain," he complimented her. "If you get the chance to examine the management structure that the Prince uses to control and direct the shipping operations, I suspect you'll find he does it similarly."

Jan added, "When I came here, I expected to work hard. Instead, I find that I'm learning vast amounts of terrifically useable skills that will be most valuable when I try to do the same thing back home. Amazing."

"What of your quest?" Rosita changed the subject. She realized that she had dominated the conversation with her troubles since we arrived. "Were you successful?"

"Aye, we were," Roy answered. "The Centurions are a formidable army; defeating them is going to be a really hard thing to accomplish. On the battlefield, they have many strengths and almost no weaknesses that we could see. Just how we can stop them remains a complete mystery to us." This, of course, made both leaders feel more confident. It wasn't that they and the Prince-led armies were no good — rather they faced a quite superior opponent. "We are similar to you in many ways. Our people are mostly farmers who spend their lives raising crops, as your people are skilled in shipping and trading. Neither of our peoples is trained in the arts of war. It appears that these invaders are skilled only in making roads and fighting. On the battlefield, they aren't likely to be defeated except by another army at least as equally skilled. Any ideas where we might find such an army for hire, say ten thousand fighters? You wouldn't have some ten thousand Sisters around that we could hire, would you?" Simon playfully teased, and we all laughed. In all the Lands of the Sea Princes, there probably were no more than a thousand of these women and not all those were skilled fighters.

"Seriously, Rosita, we now need to travel to Zargarb for several reasons, one of which is to see if we can find out what happened to two of our colleagues there before the city fell," I broke into the discussion. "Any suggestions? Should we go by boat or overland? I suppose we could just travel down the new Centurion roadway."

"Jan and I have been thinking a lot about Zargarb in the last couple days. We both have reached the same conclusion, and that is surely not all the Sisters may have perished in the defense of the city. For one thing, all the Sisters aren't necessarily good fighters. Flo is a prime example. Neither of us would ever place Flo into a combative situation, if it could be avoided. We think that what more than likely happened in Zargarb is that the fighters were killed as reported, but the other Sisters fled into the night, probably towards the northernmost villages and towns."

"Actually, that makes good sense to me," I replied, beginning to see where she was headed with this line of thinking.

Rosita continued, "Right now, the future of the entire Sisterhood in the Sea Princes lies in our hands, and we desperately need all the help we can get. Thus, we think a wise move would be to send a small scouting party into the Zargarb sector, see if we can find any remaining Sisters, and bring them back here to help and get trained. Once we get ourselves firmly established here and the other governors see what we have done, perhaps we can then go to the aid of Zargarb."

"And I bet you know just who you want to lead this scouting party," I grinned, looking straight at Flo. She also just figured it out and smiled back.

"Yes, Flo, this is your next assignment. Lead our friends safely to Zargarb by the back roads to avoid any possible confrontation. Once they are safely where they want to be, scour that sector for Sisters. It is probable that you may find small, isolated groups of the women now residing in the northernmost towns and villages. Any that you find, explain to them what has happened here. I'm sure they'll be more than eager to come here and lend us a hand. It's in their best interest to do so." Flo saluted her acceptance of this new action. "We can spare only two fighters and one other Sister. So you'll be traveling very lightly armed."

Flo thought a moment before replying, "Well, since I must take our friends to Zargarb and since the only real likelihood of challenge lies in the vicinity of that city, let's take advantage of their skills to protect us. Send only one fighter; you need them all here. Send along two others to help me. If those two can ride well, then my approach will be to just out run any hostilities."

Rosita looked at me, "Are you willing to accept the responsibility of protecting my scouts on this trip?" I wholeheartedly agreed. "Okay, then that works out the best for us. Take Cherie; she's a good fighter. Take Louisa, she has some knowledge of the Zargarb area; some of her relatives originally came from there. Also, we have a new recruit, Leonia, she appears to be really good with horses, at least that is her background. If possible, work on her Sisterhood training some during your journey. Four weeks ago, during the first counter attack that the Prince made, her husband was killed. She went out onto the battlefield to retrieve his body. Instead, she was badly beaten up by the Centurions because she resisted being raped. Her left wrist was mangled so badly that their intervening physicians had to cut it off. Physically, we believe she is healing just fine. Perhaps, you healers might want to verify this is so. We've discovered she is very frightened in the presence of men now. Hence, being in the company of you fellows may help her over this barrier."

"The long days of riding will not cause a problem for her arm?" asked Flo. "Won't we have to help her do a lot of routine things, since she has only one hand? Are you sure this is wise? We're going to be roughing it quite a lot." She knew better than to come right out and say that she did not want a cripple on this trip. All the Sisters were "crippled" in some way, physically or mentally.

Sarah Jane spoke up, "Let me check her over in the morning. If I think she is up to it, then we can bring her along. If I think for her well-being that bringing her along is not a good idea, perhaps we should leave her here."

This brought complete agreement. We chatted on lighter matters for a while and then went to bed. It was to be the last night in a bed we would have for quite some time.

The next morning, Sandy and Raphael accompanied by Flo set about the task putting together the supplies we would need. It was essential that we had enough provisions for the twelve of us for perhaps a month. Of necessity, this meant we would have to bring a packhorse along with us. Even so, some of the load would have to be divided equally among us as well. Flo totally ruled out taking a supply wagon, for she knew that they were now critically needed to bring in food and supplies to Pieta. In another month, we could safely borrow a wagon, but we didn't have that month to wait.

Sarah Jane and I went to the stables to check on the recovery of Leonia. Thallia accompanied us as well. As we walked to the barn, Sarah Jane said, "Look, this one is my call. If I think she can physically do it, she comes. However, let's all chip in and lend her a helping hand as she needs it." I agreed, but still had some reservations. "Bethany, she has lost her husband and a hand. Mentally, she has to be really suffering, maybe even depressed. If she is going to survive, she has to regain her own self-worth, self-pride. Going on a scouting mission like this might just give her the break she needs." We stopped chatting; we neared the barn doors. Inside, we found that the Sisters had already begun the preparations. Our horses were bridled and standing in a long line waiting to be saddled.

Two women were brushing down the thirteen horses as we approached. They stopped as we entered. "Hi there. I'm Cherie Leggio, and I must say I'm deeply honored to get the opportunity to accompany you on this long journey." She was twenty-one with the typical short blonde hair and blue eyes. Standing at a commanding six feet, she was well built and muscular, fitting for her role as a Sisterhood fighter.

"Hi, I'm Bethany, and this is Sarah Jane. I think you already know Thallia," I replied. "But it is we who are thankful for your presence on this trip," I added, attempting to put her more at ease and reduce the obvious "awe" factor these Sisters displayed toward us.

"I'm Louisa Bertronelli," the other woman added, "I can't figure out why I'm along, though, but like Cherie, I'm most honored to accompany you." With long brown hair and hazel eyes, she looked quite different from Cherie. Her skin was darker than Cherie's, almost as if she had a permanent tan. Moreover, she was observant, for she noticed me noticing her and added, "I come originally from Zargarb. Most of the locals are darker skinned there and none of this bleached colored hair," she ribbed her fellow sister. I could tell at once Louisa had a good sense of humor and permitted everything to be as it is. "I expect you'll want to see Leonia. She's back in that dark corner. After helping us bridle these horses, she got to fearing that you would be coming soon and headed over there. Please, go gentle with her; she's been crying some."

We had no choice; we had to inspect her arm. As we walked toward the darkened corner, we saw her sitting on a straw bale. Sarah Jane took charge at once. "Hi, I'm Sarah Jane from the Greenway. Back home, I'm called a Healer. As you can probably guess, I'm here to take a good look at how your arm is healing up." How she would be able to see much of anything in this corner I couldn't guess. "Bale got room for two?" she cleverly said, and Leonia moved over a bit so she could sit down. Gingerly, Sarah Jane took the handless arm in her hands. Actually, I realized she was actually sensing Leonia's emotions and reactions to this attention. "I'll bet you are rather embarrassed and humiliated by all this." She nodded, and even in this dim light, I could see tears trickling down the young woman's cheeks. "Well, this will never do. A Healer and her patient have to have some privacy."

Sarah Jane asked the other women to take a break so only we and Leonia were present. Then, she moved the woman out into the light near the horses. "Ah, this is much better. Now I can actually see how it is healing." Leonia was nineteen, tall and wiry with the typical blonde hair, now recently shortened, and sky blue eyes. Her face was comely; I suspected she once was admired by many men. Now, of course, none would even look her in the eyes. Her husband was dead, and she, a cripple. So undoubtedly, she felt like her entire world had been ripped from her. Carefully, Sarah Jane unwrapped the extensive bandage, wrapping her stump. Indeed, her hand had been removed just at the wrist. The recovering skin was quite pinkish and tender still, but Sarah Jane saw no signs of infection. "Does this hurt?" she asked, as she gently touched various places around the healing wound.

She mumbled "No. It just feels funny."

"That is a very good sign. You can feel my fingers touching it, right?"

"Oh yes, is that important?" she asked becoming slightly curious.

"Most definitely. If you had no feeling in it, that would be a sure sign that something isn't right. No, it looks like it's healing well indeed. So I can't see any reason to keep you from going on this mission, do you?"

"But I'm a cripple! I'm nearly useless. I can't even put on my own clothes or easily go to the bathroom without help. Why me? I don't even know much about being a Sister. I'm about the most useless thing around here," and she began crying.

Thallia picked this moment to speak. She put her hand on Leonia's shoulder, looked her in the eyes, and said in her garbled voice, "I worse."

Leonia looked up at Thallia and stopped crying. It was obvious she didn't quite understand what Thallia had said. "Huh?" she responded, now looking at Thallia.

"I worse," she repeated, trying as hard as she could to make the words sound like human speech.

"Oh my god! You've no tongue! God, what did they do to you?" Immediately she regretted her surprised outburst. Obviously, Thallia couldn't really answer her. Slowly, we all watched Leonia realizing just how bad it would be to lose one's tongue. Leonia tried to swallow and realized she needed her tongue to do that. "How can you even eat?" She regretted saying that just as soon as the words left her mouth.

"Like this," Thallia managed to utter and rocked her head from side to side, trying to show her how she managed even the simplest thing as eating. "Me worse," she added. Leonia could only nod her agreement.

"Look," I said in an attempt to put rational thought back into Leonia's mind, "the real question we have is: are you any good with horses? We are going on a long trip and must have someone that really knows horses. So it's not about whether you have one, two, or three hands. It's all about horses and your skill with them."

Leonia was definitely over her crying spell; Thallia's action had brought her attention outward into the world instead of vegetating on her own misfortunes. "Sure, I was anyway. I was riding horses before I could walk, actually. Raised on a farm just west of here. I used to be good with them before I lost my hand. Now, I don't know anymore; I don't know anything anymore."

I sensed she was heading back into her victim's shell rapidly. I said, "Well, your knowledge wasn't in your hand, I hope. Losing a hand doesn't make you lose your horse sense."

"Well, no," she moved from being a tad bit griefy to slightly hostile, "No, don't be silly. I mean, can I even handle them now, with only one hand?"

"Did you ever ride with no hands at all, controlling the horse with your legs and weight?" I asked. I remembered Roy telling me how expert riders could do just that, though I never felt confident enough to let go of the reins.

"Oh sure, all the time," she replied slightly interested, "I'd be hanging on to ropes and things, helping around the farm. Oh, I see what you mean now. Yes, that part is okay. No, I mean I, well, I don't know what I mean. I just may not be able to do things anymore."

"That's no problem," I said, "it just means you're going to have to make some alterations in the way you do things — a trifle relearning how best to accomplish a task. That's all. I've no problem with that at all. I'm still learning myself. Say, can you teach me how to ride using no hands? Can one learn that easily or is it really a hard thing to do?"

Immediately, she began explaining to me just how to do it before she caught herself. "Are you teasing me or do you really want to know how?"

"Really I want to know how. I just love riding fast in the wind, but I'm still afraid to let go of the reins!"

She brightened up at once. "Say, I substituted Fredio here for the other pack horse, Luzzia. The mare can be a bit skittish at times, while the gelding is impossible to spook. Since he is carrying our supplies, we cannot afford a skittish packhorse."

"Excellent, this is just one of the many reasons why we need you along on this journey. You may have already saved our food!" We all chuckled, and the other Sisters returned to finish saddling up the horses. Sarah Jane, Thallia, and I pitched in to help out.

I noticed the other two watching, as Leonia managed to throw a saddle on one horse and experiment with how to tighten the cinch with only one hand. Cherie, standing next to me, whispered to me, "She's never tried to put on a saddle since she's been here. Interesting." It took her about five times as long as it took us with two hands, but she did it to her total satisfaction, and that is what counted in my book.

Everyone else walked into the barn, carrying numerous bags and sacks containing our gear and provisions. Rosita and Jan were with them, also carrying sacks. Rosita asked Sarah Jane, "Well, is she healing well enough to travel?"

"Oh most definitely. She is an excellent choice to come with us; she really knows horses. Thanks." Rosita heaved a quiet sigh of relief; so far so good was her obvious conclusion.

"Sisters, I've given Flo a hundred coins for emergencies. Each of you will also get a pouch of twenty-five gold coins. That way, if you get separated, you'll have some means of quick exchange that will be honored nearly everywhere. I can't stress just how important this mission really is. You must find the remaining Sisters from Zargarb and get them back here so they can be trained on how to bring about the same kind of change in their city as we have here. I expect you to be gone at least a month. If you find you need more time, send back a message to me. May the blessings of Tur be upon you all."

She handed each Sister a small money pouch. Normally, Leonia would have accepted it but waited for someone to attach it to her waist belt for her. Instead, she fumbled about doing it herself. Thallia cleverly inserted her hand at the opportune time to help her out. She turned to Thallia and smiled. A comradery had formed between these two victims.

We thanked Rosita and Jan for everything they'd done for us, and they, likewise. Waving goodbye, we mounted up and rode out into the mid-morning daylight. Once past the entrance gates, Flo headed us due north. "We'll ride north for ten miles before cutting across country and disappearing from the usual roads." For any prying eyes, it would appear we headed north and vanished. None of us wanted our true destination to be common knowledge just yet.

Chapter 15 The Road to Zargarb

Large white clouds slowly moved inland from the Med Sea. Louisa commented, "Storm's a'comin later this afternoon." I asked how she knew and got a thirty-minute discussion of the weather patterns here in the Sea Princes. We were following a well-established track northward. The passage of many wagon wheels had cut four-inch deep ruts into the earth. Thus, with a wide trail to follow, we rode two abreast. Thomas and Thallia brought up the rear. In front of them rode Louisa who led the packhorse. Sarah Jane and Raphael came next then Roy and me. Cherie and Leonia were next, closest to Flo who led us down the track. This way, Cherie was in a good position to help defend either Flo or Leonia, whoever needed it.

Flo set a leisurely pace. While she was familiar with our skills, she was not of her fellow Sisters. Thus, she set a pace with which to let us all adapt. She wanted to make very sure that Leonia would be able to handle the riding. She kept turning in her saddle to look back upon our line, though she more often kept Leonia in view, I noticed. She needn't have worried about her, though, for once Leonia was in the saddle, she felt at home and totally comfortable. If she had forgotten anything, it had come back to her instantly. I knew that any problems with Leonia wouldn't come from the horses but from more mundane things, like going to the bathroom.

It was June 27 and the noon sun burned down upon us. The air stirred little and was stiflingly hot. The summer had officially come last week, if you go by the stars, and the temperature began to cooperate with the season. Already, my leather pants were sticky with sweat, but I knew it would only get worse. Finally satisfied that we were all doing okay, Flo picked up the pace until we were finally trotting at a good clip. "We want to make Bonita Pass before the rains come. That's where we will head out cross-country. Rain will help hide our passage." This made good sense to me, at least.

Twice we had to move off the road to allow wagon caravans that we met to pass through us on their way to Pieta behind us. Each time, the small convoys were led by two Sisters, accompanied by a representative of the Prince and the Church. While we didn't hear any conversations between the four, at least they were working together, a very good sign.

We didn't stop for lunch until two when we reached a steep-sided pass, Bonita Pass. Two great hills had smashed together, leaving a narrow gao between them. Further northward lay the village of Hamilla. Flo halted us before we entered this interesting pass. "Lunchtime," she announced. "We await the rains before proceeding. Say, who's in charge of the food this trip? Not me!" We all laughed.

Leonia laughed as well and added, "Certainly not me, that's obvious."

"I make a mean rabbit stew, only I haven't seen many rabbits around these lands," Thomas jested. "Nor herbs, for that matter. How can you have rabbit stew without the herbs?"

What happened next surprised us all. Thallia grabbed Leonia by the hand and pulled her along to the packhorse. She signed for her to help her. Together they fixed the lunch, with Leonia doing much of the stirring and simpler tasks. Indeed, from this point on, Thallia and Leonia became the cooks. Now normally, none of us would have minded sharing that duty, but it was instantly clear to all that this was really good therapy for Leonia. It was one of those unspoken truths that the rest of us readily observed and did not need to vocalize. However, we insisted on taking turns cleaning up the dirty dishes afterwards. For one thing, Sarah Jane didn't want Leonia getting her bandage wet.

With full bellies, we sat back against the rocks beside the little stream that ran nearby to await the coming storm. The sky grew darker even while we ate. We had our rain ponchos out and at the ready. I found it exceedingly peaceful sitting out here listening to the babble of the trickling water, and I wondered if ever would come a day when I could just do this without having to worry about anything, just to snuggle onto Roy's chest and lay here completely at peace.

Kaboom! Lightning flashed and the thunder came loud. Sandy's horse spooked and broke its tether. In a flash, Leonia was at the mare's side, not holding on to the bridle, but with her good arm around its neck, talking soothing words to her. In a moment, with her arm still around the mare's neck, she moved the horse back into its place, and Sandy took hold of the reins. "Thanks!" Sandy exclaimed. "I think the storm just got here."

"Good move, Leonia," Flo complimented her. She smiled. If Flo had any doubts about Leonia's horse skills, they were gone now. "Okay, mount up. Time to disappear." We angled around the easternmost hill and angled east by northeast following a line of valleys between the hills. The rain pelted down in sheets making the going a bit of a challenge. By staying close and not going fast, we managed to make some ten miles before the fury of the early summer's storm passed us by, rolling on northwards. Flo turned to us and said loudly, "We must cross the Po Creek before the hour is up or we'll have to wait there a day. The creek swells to a torrent when we get rains like this. So let's pick up the pace." Trotting it was, for nearly an hour. All afternoon, we saw no one and no signs of civilization, just the semi-arid hills and valleys. Finally, we rounded the base of yet another hill, and here a wide valley opened before us. The Po Creek trickled pretty much down its center.

The rocky ground slowly sloped down to its edge. However, already, the water level had risen eight inches, and muddy water swirled and thrashed this way and that around its stony channel. Bits of twigs and bric-a-brac appeared and disappeared as they were swept rapidly downstream. Normally eight feet across, Po Creek had expanded to twelve so far. Flo went first, letting her mount pick the safest path. Once she made it to the other side, one by one, we followed her approximate crossing. Flo explained, "A half hour from now, we'd be stranded on the other side. These creeks carry water from the Appian

Way all the way down to the Med Sea. It's quite a sight to see when it floods like this. Come on; we can spare a little time. Let's ride to the hilltop and watch it swell in size for a while. Besides, I can also make sure we aren't being followed. Once the creek has risen a bit more, anyone following us will be delayed at least a day." I didn't like the sound of being followed. I had no idea who that might be or why. We followed her on up the side of the hill. Near the top, we found a grassy area and tethered the horses there, allowing them to graze on the sparse grass while we hiked on up to the top.

Sure enough, we had a grand view of the creek. Even during the short time it took us to get into position, I swear it had risen some more. The noise of the thrashing water definitely was louder. I'd never seen such a raging creek before and found it fascinating, as long as I was safely on this side of it. Flo pointed out part of a tree coming wildly down the creek, smashing into rocks and ground, only to bounce off and rebuild its forward speed once more. If that had hit one of the horses, the damage would have been great indeed. Flo saw no one attempting to cross following us. Since several big branches had now passed by, she said it was time to get moving once more.

Now, she angled us north by northeast. After another ten miles, as the sun was sinking after it finally broke through the heavy rain clouds, we entered a long narrow valley. On either side the hills rose steeply, forming a very sharp angle, exposing the red limestone rock that lay under the hills. Once we entered the valley, there was no way to climb out except to retrace our steps. The further we traveled, the higher and steeper the side rose. Yes, there was a small creek running down the middle but it was not fed by the uplands, only this valley complex, so it was not a raging torrent, just a bubbling brook. Flo pointed to the right side, "Been mined for limestone rock some time ago." We could see the rectangular cuts that the miners made as they lifted layer after layer out of the cliff face.

A little further, rounding a bend in the growing darkness, I could see we were reaching a dead-end. Instead of turning to follow the bend, Flo led us to the right, past a small grove of trees, which seemed to be at the very edge of the cliff face. She dismounted. "Why are we stopping here?" I asked. This seemed a most inhospitable place to camp. We would be sleeping in a boulder field.

Flo loved to tease, "Lead your horse, and follow me through the trees. You'll see." There was a hint of excitement in her voice. Leonia followed her, then Roy and me. One by one, the others followed us. With the sun long set and only twilight to illuminate our way and with the steep canyon sides blocking most of that, I was only barely able to see where I was going. Suddenly, I felt a coolness blowing on my face, and a near total darkness surrounded me. Flo's voice was my guide. "Keep coming toward me, make room for the others. I'm lighting a lantern as fast as I can with everything being so wet."

Light. She said the magic word. I'd forgotten all about our ability to create a bluish light upon need. I muttered its simple chant, and presto, a dim blue light glowed upon my hand, which I held aloft so I could see where I was at and so others could see me. I didn't want to be bumped by a horse from behind. We were in a large cavern, but the look on Flo's face as she looked back at me glowing in this bluish aura was that of a child watching a magician pull a rabbit out of his hat. "Just casting a little light on the scene," I teased. "Hurry up and get that lantern going. My light is not so bright." As the others entered, they also cast their blue light; when all seven of us were inside, we actually could see fairly well. It was Thomas to the rescue, lighting her lantern by creating a flame from the sky settling it on the wick. Quickly, eight other lanterns were lit from this one, and finally we examined our location.

"This is my secret cave," Flo explained. "I found it many years ago before I ran into the Sisterhood. I've stayed here many nights. It's almost like my home away from home. Back that way is a good place to tie up the horses, and there should be some hay still back there as well. I usually try to keep a little reserve here for horses and people. Over there hanging from the ceiling is a dry food sack. Emergency rations. The last time I was here, I brought in two loads of firewood, so we should be able to make a hot dinner."

The limestone cavern was huge with several side caverns attached to this main one. The ceiling was about eight feet over head, on the average. We put the horses into one of these side chambers, rubbed them down, fed them a bit of grain, and left them to munch on a flake of hay. Soon the fire was going; Thallia and Leonia began to fix our meal, while the rest of us dried off and explored the cavern. Roy estimated that at least thirty riders could easily be housed in here with room to spare. As we all were wandering about, I noticed that every time one of the men drew near to Leonia, she would flinch, back away from her cooking area, and look at some other part of the cave, only coming back to her place when the man moved away. Flo also saw me observing her. We both knew that Leonia was very leery of being physically close to a man, even those she must count as her friends. Once more I was reminded that all these Sisters had been mistreated by men or they would never have joined the Sisterhood in the first place. I knew Leonia didn't actually hate Roy, Raphael, Simon, or Thomas; it was just an uncontrollable reaction on her part, to put what she considered a safe distance between them and herself.

Finally, Leonia called, "Supper's ready. Help yourselves." Everyone headed for the cooking area, picking up a plate on the way. She moved back against the wall out of the way.

"Ah, I might have guessed," Roy commented as he began serving himself and also me. "Dried fish and pasta. They sure do eat a lot of pasta and fish in this land. Guess it comes from being a maritime country."

"Dried food is far lighter to carry," Leonia explained, speaking very softly, "and it doesn't spoil readily."

"Very true," he commented. We chatted lightly while we ate, thanking Flo for bringing us to this terrific spot to spend the night. The guys did the cleanup chores this evening, while we got out the blankets and arranged the bedding. To save on lantern oil, just as soon as the dishes were done, we lay down for the night. While there was no need for us seven to pretend to be married here, still, Roy and I lay beside each other, as did Sarah Jane and Raphael, and Sandy and Simon. However, Thomas and Thallia, using the dying campfire as light, walked around the cavern for a private moment together. From the corner of my eye, I spied Leonia, who lay between Flo and Cherie, staring at the two. I know she saw them kissing, and I wondered what was going on in her mind. Though I could have asked Sandy to probe and find out, there was no need to be so rude and invade her private thoughts just to satisfy my curiosity. So instead, I rolled my head onto Roy's chest, closed my eyes, and drifted into sleep.

The ruddy sun cast reddish hues into this red limestone cavern as it rose in the east, reflecting off the western sides of the canyon and straight into my eyes. Uniformly, we all rose together and began to share the morning duties. The guys went to fetch more wood. In part, they intended to leave more here than was here when we came. There was nothing we could do to replace the hay, though. I must say we made an efficient team. No one had to issue any orders, and everything was done nearly automatically. We ate, were out of the cavern, and back on the trail in less than an hour after sunrise. I think this made a positive impression on Flo that we all could work together without the need of orders or guidance. I didn't tell her that we seven had much practice before.

As we rode back down the canyon, Flo said, "By tonight, you should get a really good view of the Appian Way. Though we'll still likely be some fifty miles from them, their peaks are going to be clearly visible."

This sounded most interesting to me. So I asked her, "Are we going to get even closer to them at some point on the trip?"

"Yes, my orders are to sneak you into the Zargarb sector. As you know, most of the towns and villages lie in a radius of some fifty miles of the cities. The further out you go, the fewer there are. Of course, there are some nomadic shepherds up near the foothills; it's good grazing land for sheep. Not much good for anything else though. The bandits mostly hide out in the middle sections, not too distant from outlying towns and villages. They have to get supplies too, and they need to be close enough to the main tracks they desire to raid. Right now, we're in the prime position to run across isolated bandit groups. So actually, the next couple of days are going to be the most dangerous for us. We must be very careful to avoid them and not let them find us. Think of it this way, we are entering their homeland. They know all the nooks and crannies, and places to ambush us. However, so do I. That is why I was asked to lead you. If anyone can get you across bandit territory without them finding you, it is me."

"However, I'm going to need your cooperation. We're a small party. I can't be looking in all directions at once. I need you to be constantly on the lookout for any signs of people. If you spot anything at all, give a low whistle."

I heard Thallia making some noises and realized she might not be able to whistle any longer. Then we all heard her voice say, "I ithel." She found she could make a whistling noise by inhaling, not exhaling. I glanced back at her and saw her smiling proudly at her minor achievement. With that, Flo led us around the hill, which formed this enclosed valley and then headed once more north by northeast. She kept the horses at a walk, giving us the opportunity to watch the distant areas for signs of riders, campfires, or any signs that people were about. We rode along in silence all that morning.

At our noon lunch break, the guys stood guard while we ate, and then we stood watch while they ate. By late afternoon, I could tell we had been steadily gaining elevation with each passing hour. Even the sparse vegetation began to change. The trees didn't seem quite as tall, and actually, there appeared to be more grassy areas, though the grass was of a stiffer, hardier variety. We camped for the night in a small side valley. Flo pointed out we were at least seven miles from the nearest known inhabitation. By being in this small side valley, we could risk a small cooking fire. However, Flo insisted on posting guards all night long. Though we all volunteered, Flo decided that she, Cherie, and our four men would take two hour shifts, which would be more than enough to cover the night. I vaguely remember Roy separating his body from mine when he left to take his turn around midnight.

The morning of the next day passed just as this one had, totally uneventful. In all this time, we saw no other living person, which in our case, was desirable. Flo said about midmorning that we had just entered the Solamina Sector, but I could see no real difference in the land about us, the same arid hills with sparse vegetation. I wondered just how she knew that, but then realized she'd obviously spent a lot of time roaming the countryside.

At noon, we stopped for lunch, to stretch our legs, and to rest the horses. While we were eating, Thomas asked, "Say, Flo, should we be seeing a thin smoke trail over that way to the east, the way we've been more or less going?" Instantly alert for trouble, we looked where he was pointing. Sure enough, there was a thin tendril of smoke twisting into the sky. A good guess was that it was just over the next hill.

"Excellent eyes, Thomas. Okay, party's over everyone. This far out, it's most likely a bandit encampment. Cherie, you go sneak a look. We'll ride northward, following the valley line. Catchup with us when you can." Still holding a biscuit in her mouth, Cherie grabbed her sack, stowed her saddlebags, and hopped onto her horse. She disappeared back the way we had come. The rest of us hastily got our things together and headed on up this valley, trying not to make any undue noise.

Roy whispered to me that Cherie was circling around to come upon the encampment from the south. If anything went astray, she would be laying down a false trail, giving us more time to put some distance between them and ourselves. I hoped that nothing would go astray. Cherie was now on her own, and I was more than a little worried about her safety. Flo probably sensed my concern and whispered, "Don't worry about Cherie. She knows how to take care of herself. She's done this many times before. She's only going to get close enough to see who is there. She'll probably join us in an hour.

We continued following the valleys that led northward or in that general direction. However, I noticed that the elevation rose higher with each passing valley. Time seemed to drag on, as I waited impatiently for Cherie. Finally, Thomas placed into my mind, *One rider coming up on our rear fast.* I relayed the message to Flo. She took no chances. Quickly, she had us turn to face the rider. We drew our swords and waited for about a half-minute until Cherie came galloping into view. She raised her hand and made a pointing gesture for us to ride fast. Flo didn't hesitate; she didn't need to issue any orders either. We all grasped the meaning of her gesture and rapidly fell into a gallop behind Flo, as Cherie pulled alongside her.

"Bandits. About fifty. Not spotted. One of their patrols was heading to where we had lunch. They can't help but find our tracks. Let's put some distance between us and them."

"Fall back to the rear. I'll go out front and ride point. This settles it. We make for the Paese di Dio," called out Flo, as she cantered out ahead of us. The time for silent riding was past. Hooves thundered on the valley floor; the hot valley air rushed past my face. We twisted to the left around obstacles, and then right in a dizzying dance on up this valley over ridge and into the next. It was a wild ride over rough ground, especially for the horses. Ever we seemed to be gaining altitude, as the heat of the day seared these valley floors. After an hour, Flo lessened the pace, for the horses were heaving from the strenuous exercise. Still, she pressed onward at a trot, but there was no sign of pursuit. Wisely, whoever these men were, they chose not to follow us.

The late afternoon sun sank low in the western crystal clear blue sky, as we climbed up out of this last deep valley. We had put close to fifteen miles between us and the bandit encampment. I wasn't prepared for the view when we climbed up out of this valley! Now clear of the gorge, the terrain that stretched out before us was unlike anything that I had ever seen before. The red limestone gave way to a grey sedimentary rock. Here was a sea of low, gracefully undulating hills filled with large patches of green grass and moss as far as the eye could see. Flo called a halt, as we stared at the vast panorama before us. Just a hint of reverence in her voice, Flo said quietly, "Paese di Dio, God's Country, the foothills of the Appian Way."

Paese di Dio, some thirty miles deep, led slowly up to the actual mountains, whose towering, intensely rugged, angular peaks we could see far off in the distance, like a set of giant's teeth ready to crush anything into crumbs. Awesome? Yes. Spectacular? Yes. Magnificent? Yes.

Flo explained that the Paese di Dio, who's average elevation was short of two miles high, stretched the entire length of the Lands of the Sea Princes. For its entire length, it looked exactly like this, a barrier that separated the red arid hills that ran down to the Med Sea from the impassable, craggy peaks of the Appian Way. Flo said, "The only inhabitants up here are nomadic shepherds with their flocks of sheep. Come winter, no one is here; this entire plateau is covered in snow. No towns, no villages. Some shallow basins act like reservoirs and hold some of the finest drinking water you'll ever taste. Up here, we should be totally safe. Even the nomads are friendly to everyone. I think they're glad for any human company. Look, there is a flock way over there," she pointed out some greyish forms about a mile to the west of our location.

For nearly fifteen minutes, Flo had to listen to all our exclamations of the sheer beauty of the Paese di Dio. "I know, I know," she said at last. "I come up here as often as I can. Spend a day riding in any direction, and your problems simply vanish. That's why it's called God's Country. You're going to get to see quite a bit of it; we'll cover about a hundred-fifty miles straight east into the middle of the Zargarb Sector before we head back down. It does get quite chilly up here at night, and there is nothing we can use for firewood. However, we can always duck back down a ways into the red hills to get enough dry wood with which to cook a meal. Speaking of which, Cherie, how about you taking Thomas and Thallia back down, and fetch up enough firewood for tonight and tomorrow morning? We'll head a little more east and find a good spot to camp." With only a brief acknowledgment, the three retraced our path and soon disappeared below the horizon.

If all this land was the same, I wondered what she meant about a good camping spot. I soon found out. She halted about a quarter mile further east. Here the land dipped slightly forming a basin or bowl. In its center was a fair sized pool of crystal clear water, and there was plenty of grass growing on all sides. Here we set about making camp. We unloaded the horses, and while some rubbed them down, the others set up a campsite including forming a small fire pit. The ground was soft, but as one dug into the earth, various sized stones appeared almost at once, just beneath the shallow layer of dirt. By the time the other three returned carrying three armfuls of deadwood, we had a fire pit dug and camp setup.

While Thallia and Leonia prepared the food, the rest of us relaxed and chatted. This was also Leonia and Louisa's first time up here in the Paese di Dio, and they were just as impressed as we were. Cherie had been up here once before, she explained. I mused, "Sometime, I'd like to come up here and ride the entire length, from one end to the other."

"Did that once, took over a month," said Flo, remembering that time long ago. Obviously, she felt moved to talk about it to us. "Was a month after my father beat and raped me. For weeks, I had wandered around down below. Then on a whim, I came up here or maybe it was something that pulled me up here, I don't know. Rode to the western edge, turned around and rode to the eastern edge, and then back to where I started. Healed me, you know. I entered this land a miserable victim and left with my mind whole once again, at peace with myself. The Paese di Dio healed me, still does. It's a magical land."

"Your father actually did that to you?" exclaimed Leonia, staring wide-eyed at Flo in disbelief. "If that had happened to me, I don't know how I could live with myself — so utterly humiliating — your own father!" I noticed Cherie and Louisa were also listening intently to Flo. While they had heard rumors of what had happened to Flo, the most renowned scout in the Sisterhood, Flo had never openly spoken of it before.

"Yes, well he was drunk. At first, I blamed myself. Maybe it was because my breasts were becoming full. Maybe I was flirting with him in some way that I did not quite see how. You know, until then, dad mostly treated me as the son he never had, teaching me all about horses. So I assumed that somehow I had brought it all upon myself. Once up here for that month, I realized it was most likely just too much wine. Drunken men do incredibly stupid things. Drunken women do too, for that matter," she joked.

"If that happened to me," exclaimed Louisa, "why I'd feel so utterly dirty, so soiled, so rotten. Why, I'd. . ." her voice trailed off, and she didn't finish her sentence.

"Yes, I did too," Flo admitted. Laughing slightly, she added, "I spent a week sitting in a deep creek pool trying to get clean. I washed and washed and washed. No matter how much I bathed, I still felt utterly filthy." She remembered something else, chuckled to herself, and then added, "I even washed so hard that I began bleeding in places. What an idiot I was back then. But after a month up here, life fell back into place, so to speak. Don't know how it did, it just did. Wait until you see the stars tonight. You will see too."

"Was that your first time?" asked Leonia, just a bit hesitant, but her curiosity was roused. "I mean, well you know."

Flo sighed, "Yes, first and last time. I swore I'd never let a man violate me again, ever! Then, I joined the Sisterhood, and that took care of all my man problems; none will now even get near me. That suits me just fine. Problem solved."

"But don't you want to eventually have a family, to have some children, a house, and all that goes with it?" wondered Leonia. We knew she must have lost all this when her husband was killed and herself maimed.

Flo became animated, "Absolutely not! If I ever became pregnant, why, I would go stark raving mad worrying about whether it would be a girl or not! There's no way I want to have a daughter and watch her become another victim like me. There isn't a man in the Sea Princes I trust!" Her vehemence suddenly gave way to a flush of red; she added quickly, "That is, except for you men. But you guys are different — you aren't from here." Her outburst rather quieted the conversation for some time.

A meteor streaked across the nighttime sky, instantly attracting everyone's attention. I'd forgotten that Flo had told us the stars were terrific up here. Suddenly looking up at the heavens above literally astounded me. Several of us gasped in total surprise. Never had we seen the stars so brilliant, so clear. I reached upwards with my hands thinking I might touch them. I know it sounds completely silly, but that was my reaction. The stars seemed to reach down and touch me. As long as I live, I shall never forget how the stars looked to me that night and all the nights we spent up here on the Paese di Dio. I felt a peace flow through my very beingness that night, a peace unlike any I had ever known since.

After a long silence, I muttered, "This is incredible." My words seemed so utterly insignificant compared to the sky above.

Raphael summed up everything very astutely, "You know, we could learn a tremendous amount more about the stars if we could come here and study them. Back home, the sky is never this close, this clear, this brilliant. It is a natural wonder of the world. Ah, this is the best-kept secret on Tarra, I'll wager. Incredible. Thanks Flo for sharing this with us."

After a time, Louisa felt like talking. "I was born in Zargarb, right in the heart of the city. My dad was a moneychanger. All through my teens, my mother kept instructing me in the ways of being a good woman. You know, the usual, 'Do everything you can to please your man. Speak only when asked. Your life is not important. Your man is all that matters. A happy man takes care of you. A man always knows best.' All that sort of tripe. Now I'm ashamed I actually bought into it, but I did. I had my eye on a close friend; we played together when we were kids; we grew up more or less together. He talked about getting married one day. Then one day my dad ordered me to marry this ugly, older fat man. He said this would be an advantageous marriage for us. He even brought the slovenly pig home to meet me so he could ask for my hand formally. Of course, whether or not I agreed to his proposal was completely irrelevant. It had already been completely arranged beforehand. I was supposed to say 'Yes' and show my utter obedience to my father and this pig of a man. They sprung it on me and when he proposed formally at the dinner table, I gagged and actually vomited onto my plate. Boy did that cause a row!"

"I had several violent arguments with my dad over this. He accused me of all sorts of nasty things, none of which were true. I tried everything I knew to convince him not to make me do this, but he wouldn't listen. Mother tried to make me see reason, that I was making dad lose face and worse. That night, I realized there was no place for me in their home any longer. When they finally fell asleep, I packed the few things I owned into a sack, skipped out the door, and never looked back. He had called me 'One of those Abominations.' So, naturally, I sought them out to see for the first time what the Sisterhood was actually all about. Two days after I ran away, my father called out the guards, and the hue and cry was on to find me. The Sisterhood quietly snuck me out of the city. In the end, I ended up here in Pieta, two hundred miles away from home. Here, I've been safe for the last ten years. Sometimes, I wonder what might have been if Fredolio and I had gotten married. Would we have been happy? But always I keep coming back to the basic fact that I really don't want to be an object of a man, like a plate, to look pretty and to give him pleasure. I'm a person. Not the greatest person, mind you, but I can never be like my mom, never."

Louisa continued, "I heard about your offer to immigrate to the Greenway. I have actually given it serious thought. After the Sisterhood no longer really needs my help, I hope to travel there somehow and see for myself if life can be any better there than here. In the meantime, I do know most of the Zargarb sector, so I can get you around, only if things have not changed too much under this occupation force."

"I'm glad you stuck up for your own ideals," Flo commented. "Was he really a fat pig?" She giggled. Louisa outlined his shape with her hands and everyone laughed.

The next day we rode mostly eastward going around any flocks of sheep that we came across. That way, we avoided any contact with the shepherds. None of them would be able to describe us to the wrong ears, should anyone be following us. Thankfully, we did not detect any signs that we were followed up onto the Paese di Dio. In four days travel, we covered about one hundred-twenty miles, or thirty miles a day. Occasionally, a light rain fell, often in the late afternoon, but it was never sufficient for us to take shelter. For one thing, there was no place to take shelter, save in a shallow basin.

On our last night sleeping out here under the embracing stars, as we laid on our backs staring up at the shining beacons, Leonia opened up for the first time. "My husband was young and good looking. I knew I couldn't do any better than him. We got along fairly well. He only beat me when I went against him or didn't agree with him. We had just gotten a nice place, and I became with child, when this damn war broke out. He kept telling me he was going to help win the survival of Pieta from these invading Centurions and by doing so bring great fame to our house. He looked so handsome parading around the city with all the new recruits. He was tall and proud. Then, one day, he got his orders to join a regiment, which was going to break the siege on our city. That night, when he came to bed, he sounded frightened and scared. He made me pledge to him that if anything bad happened to him, I wouldn't let the vultures devour his body. Instead, I had to swear to him that I would place his body in the Med Sea as an offering to Tur. That was the last thing I ever promised him." Tears trickled down her cheeks and a knot welled in her throat. None of us said a word, but waited for her to finish her story when she felt able to do so.

After a few minutes, she continued. "They all were slaughtered like pigs or cattle. Some were even gutted like a fish by those terrible machines of the Centurions. I waited until the night for them to bring the bodies home, but no one made any attempt to retrieve the fallen. I went to the guards to ask them when they would be bringing them back. I nearly got my tongue cut out for talking to them about it! I resolved to do it myself. It was my last promise to him. I had to keep it. Next morning, I finally found a handcart, you know, one of the two-wheelers. I pulled it out onto the battlefield."

"Carrion birds were everywhere. Bodies cut and mangled, ripped open — it was the most horrible thing I have ever seen. I vomited twice, as I went from body to body looking for him. Just as my strength and resolve nearly failed, I found him or rather what was left of him. Half of his chest was gone, chariot gouge I think. His magnificent uniform was torn and shredded. Parts of his insides lay beside him on the ground. The frozen, terror on his face caused me to vomit right there. Finally, I began to try to lift his body onto the cart. That's when some Centurions came galloping up to me. 'What have we here? A wench stealing a body. Let's have our way with her.' They dismounted and grabbed at me, ripping my dress off. I screamed, kicked, and bit at them. One tried to force himself onto me, and I kicked him in his tender spot. He yelled, cried, and cursed me. Another swung his sword at me, and I put up my left hand to defend my head from his blow. I felt a huge surge of pain and passed out. I remember coming too inside a physician's tent. My private parts hurt intensely. I was told I had lost my baby, and my hand had been crushed beyond repair. At least that Centurion physician was kind to me. I gagged and vomited again and passed out. When I awoke, it was night, and I was in a wagon being carried to the edge of the city. Strong arms lifted me out of the wagon and laid me on the deserted street there at the northwestern edge of Pieta."

"I just laid there in the street too weak to move, too much in pain to even try. I wanted to die. I'd lost my husband, my baby, and my hand. There was nothing left to live for, and I hurt — hurt so badly that all I could do was sob to myself. I think I fell asleep there in the street or passed out. I don't remember which — it is all such a painful blur. I woke feeling the warm sun on my face. I opened my eyes and saw faces looking down at me as they passed me by. Staring, gaping faces. After a time, a Sister in leather came to me, lifted me up, and carried me some distance. I hurt so badly that I passed out again."

"When I came to, I was in a room, in a clean bed. I had been washed and had on some clean clothes that didn't quite fit me. She looked after me day and night, feeding me, and helping me stand to use the chamber pot. Finally, when I regained some strength, under the cover of night, she led me to their safe house. I cried and cried for days. I begged them just to kill me. What use was I anymore? I'm a cripple. I can't even go to the bathroom without help. That's when Sister Rosita came to me and asked me to tell her what had happened to me. Later, she asked me what I used to do. I told her about how I was raised in Fidelio, a small town just outside the city. Those were pleasant memories. I figured she was trying to get me to remember pleasant things, the good times. I found them much easier to face, and I told her about my love of horses, how I used to work with them and all that, before I got married and moved into the city six months ago."

She paused once more, fondly remembering her childhood. "You know, being up here is kind of magical. My husband was not that great, just good looking. Besides, I hated being beaten when I suggested to him that he might be wrong. The man just plain had no common sense, I swear! Even an idiot could see that. I was beaten for trying to help him. I guess I should admit to you all: I really didn't love him. He was just my ticket into the big city, a family, and nice house — you know the good life. I think I thought his star was rising, and I wanted to be riding it too. Now that I look back on it, it does seem a bit foolish of me."

"But hey, I really am not a cripple. I can still do things for myself; it's just harder. Thallia showed me that I can. Flo, I promise not to let you down on this trip. I know you probably didn't want to bring me along; you know, no hand and all, but I'm glad you did. Somehow, I'm able at least to accept myself as I am now. I too, think one day I might like to visit your Greenway and see for myself."

Thallia glowed and Flo said, "Leonia, thanks for telling us. You've had a horrible time of it all. I just cannot imagine the horrors you endured and yet are still alive and doing well. You have great courage and strength. I'm honored to have you ride with me." She also felt that a little joviality was in order, "I promise not to try to make you climb a rope on this trip." At that, everyone, including Leonia laughed loudly. We all felt relieved by laughing. Somehow laughing at life's travails made them seem in their proper perspective, simply a minor obstacle to be overcome.

As I fell asleep that night, I realized each and every one of these Sisters had a horror story behind them. I could only imagine the thousands of other women who simply bore their burden and went on with life. I hoped and prayed that Simon's agreement might yield a better future for the women of the Sea Princes. Then my thoughts strayed to the Greenway. Was this what was in store for us in another year or two? We just had to find a way to avoid the invasion from the south.

By noon, we'd reached our desired location. Directly south, some hundred-fifty miles lay Zargarb. Flo kindly paused for lunch just at the edge of this magnificent high country, allowing us one last, long, lingering view of Paese di Dio. I hoped I'd get the chance to ride up here once more, if only to renew my spirituality. Yes, I agree with Flo, this is God's country. While we ate, she shared her plan, which was altogether a simple one. First, we would head down the middle of this sector, angling east and west a bit to pass through the major towns and villages. In each, we would spend a little time checking to see if we could find any of the Sisterhood who might be lying low. Also, we would try to find out any information about how this sector was now being governed by the Centurions. That way when we entered Zargarb, we might be better prepared for the city. She also pointed out that our greatest threat from bandit groups likely still lay when we would be within a hundred miles of Zargarb. None operated out this far; there was nothing out here worth robbing.

In fact, Flo suggested we might even find enough hospitality in some of the most isolated communities out here near the Paese di Dio that we could spend a night at an inn and use the public bath. That last sounded very good to us. Personally, I felt quite grubby after so many days on the trail. We mounted up and began our slow descent into the Zargarb sector.

At once, the abrupt land transformation occurred, with the familiar red limestone rock making its appearance as we entered the first valley. Smaller trees appeared along with the sparse, tough grasses. Also, the temperature rose noticeably the further down we descended. I had forgotten just how hot this land actually was; the high country was so different. After about five miles, we came across the first village, which had perhaps fifty residents. As we rode into the village from the north, the villagers stopped and stared at us, for they rarely got visitors from the north. One man, the elder in his fifties, with dark skin and brown hair walked up to greet us. "Hail, travelers. A Sister's party?" he asked, though we all knew that he knew the answer. It was just his formal way of beginning a strained conversation.

"Yes, from Pieta actually. We are looking for any other Sisters who might have come here last year after the fall of Zargarb," Flo spoke honestly and openly.

"None here," came the terse reply, though not unfriendly. "You are the first we've seen since the fall of Zargarb. What news do you bring us? Have the other cities managed to stop these invaders?" One glance at the others, who had stopped their chores and paused to listen, told me that everyone here was starved for news.

Flo decided to relay as much news as possible, telling of the fall of Solamina, that of Pieta, and the eminent fall of Bonilla. While everyone cursed and wailed cries of dismay, the response was only half-hearted. In their minds, they knew that this was inevitable. Just that hearing it confirmed made them upset — the old hoping against all hope syndrome. She described the destruction of Pieta and the carnage as best she could. Then, she told them how the Sisterhood had come to the rescue of the common man in Pieta, spreading food, clothing, and housing for those in need.

For the first time, I saw the average person actually speak kindly of the Sisterhood. The elder said, "Well, that is indeed a good change. You know, we have long said, to ourselves mind you, the only people in all this land that we can trust to do the right thing are the Sisters. I'm sure that many are most grateful for your timely aid. We heard about the fight the Sisterhood put up during the fall of Zargarb. It's said that every one of them were killed on the battlefield, but not before taking hundreds of Centurions with them! From what we've heard not even one of the enemy were killed by all the Prince's overrated guards. In my book that says a whole lot about you folk."

Flo graciously accepted the totally unexpected compliment. Never had she been thanked or even remotely admired before. In response, she asked, "Say, how goes it for your village under the rule of these invaders? Is it safe to even travel the main roads?"

"Aye, tis safe, except for the occasional bandits. Not even the Centurions can stop them. In fact, I think they have become bolder with the absence of you Sisters. Life's pretty much the same, actually, except for that darn new tax. Every fall now, the Prince's tax collectors come by, and our village must give him fifty gold pieces — that's half of our profits for the entire year."

One woman whispered cautiously in his ear, "Tell'em about what Romero told us, you know, about the last Sister on the battlefield."

"Oh yes, there is one other thing. I don't know if it's true or not, taking into account its source is the trader Romero, who often embellishes his stories, which grow wilder and wilder with each new town he enters. He says that on that last day of battle when the Sisterhood rode out to defend the city and were slain, one Sister, the last one standing, singlehandedly killed a dozen Centurions before they physically tackled her. According to him, they took her alive, cut off her arms so she could never attack them again, and left her dying on the battlefield, but Tur must have intervened, says Romero, because when morning came, her body, and hers alone, had vanished without a trace from that bloody field. He says she is now a bodyguard for Tur in his underwater realm. I don't believe it, well not all of it anyway."

"Yes, these invaders are incredibly vicious, I've seen them slaughter men without flinching. Maybe one day they will meet their match. I hope so anyway," Flo defiantly added. "Say, do the Centurions bother travelers on the road? I mean will we have any trouble riding into Zargarb?"

"Aye, that you will. They like to control things, but usually only near the city. If you have a token, you can pass," he said.

"How do you get a token?" Flo inquired, seeing an advantage in getting one.

"Oh, they are handed out to all the drovers and merchants. I have some here that I give to those that are carting our produce into the city," he replied.

An idea formed in Flo's mind. Certainly, it would be advantageous for us to have one of these tokens. She already knew what the elder actually needed. She asked, "How about a trade, kind sir. I give you some gold pieces, and you give me a couple of the tokens, that is, if you can spare them and not get into trouble over it." His eyes opened wide in surprise. She had just mentioned the magic word, gold. We all knew that now it was just a matter of the amount.

"How many do you want?" he asked scarcely able to contain his excitement. This stroke of good luck would lower the amount he needed to collect for the taxes. Indeed, that very same idea formed in everyone else's minds as well!

Flo had no idea of how much they were worth, so she suggested, "Well, how about I give you five gold pieces for two of them. That's a tenth of your yearly taxes."

"Done deal!" he exclaimed. "Thank you, dear Sister!" Before Flo could get her coin pouch opened, I dashed forward and handed him six instead.

"Just a little extra because you have been so nice to us," I added as he handed me the tokens. I gave Flo one and kept one for my Circle. Since there was little else to learn here, we mounted back up and rode on south out of the village. Looking back, I saw several villagers waving farewell, genuine smiles on their faces.

"How come you paid for them?" asked Flo, as soon as we were out of hearing from the village.

"Because you wouldn't really need them if you weren't taking us into Zargarb. If there are any Sisters to be found, they are likely to be found outside of the city. So it is only fair that I cover the expense. Okay?"

"Sure thing, thanks," she replied.

"Are these villagers always so friendly to the Sisters who pass through?" I asked the real question I wanted answered.

"Actually, no. In the past, about all we get is polite conversation with subtle hints to keep on moving out of town as soon as possible. No, a real change has or is occurring here, an unexpected change." She added as an afterthought, "Evidently, the last stand of the Zargarb Sisters may not have been entirely in vain. Now that is something to ponder."

A little later on, Flo said, "Next stop is a town actually, Cicillia. Last time I was through there, it had maybe three hundred people in it, maybe more. They have an inn and a bathhouse — well they used to have. Who knows what we will find now. We should get there around suppertime. If we are as welcome there as we were back at that village, why, maybe we can chance staying at the inn and use the bathhouse. God, I would love a bath right about now! I don't know about the rest of you, but I am getting pretty smelly."

"Go for it," I teasingly replied. We both laughed.

As we rode deeper into the Zargarb sector, I noticed subtle differences in both the terrain and the vegetation. True, red limestone predominated, but here it seemed more weathered. The hills were not as rough, and sandy pockets occasionally appeared in the valleys. More arid than the other sectors, I spotted prickly cactus plants thriving in the sandy places. Here the climate was definitely changing toward that of a desert region. Of course, Thomas enjoyed this part of the trip, constantly noting each new plant he'd never seen before. For a wilderness Loremaster, this was a heaven-sent trip. I knew he would've loved to stop and examine each plant if we had the time.

We met one empty wagon caravan partway to Cicillia. As we rounded a bend, three wagons lumbered our way, pulled by a pair of draft horses each. Two men sat on the bench. We moved off to the side of the track to let them pass. As they met us, the lead driver said to Flo, "G'day Sister." Shocked, Flo mechanically returned the greeting.

Once they were out of ear shot, Flo exclaimed to me, "Drivers have never said hello to me before. Boy things sure have changed here!"

Around four-thirty, we rounded another bend in the track, which was dutifully following the lowest portion of the valley system, and saw the town of Cicillia ahead. Centrally located within the current valley and surrounded by hills on all sides, the town sat close to a very small stream, which carried only a tiny trickle of water in it. Flo said in another month the creek would dry up entirely. The town depended on two deep wells for its water supply. The track opened onto the main street of the town, some thirty feet wide with single story adobe buildings on either side. However about one in ten were made from the red limestone instead of mud bricks. Cooking fires curled into the sky from many homes off main street, and some twenty people were walking down the street or milling around as we entered from the north.

Just as soon as the townsfolk spied us, the air filled with excitement. Here and there, people whispered to each other. Some ran indoors and came back out with others. Evidently, we were a sight worth seeing or of note, but we didn't know why. We'd gone partway down main street when we saw what most definitely had to be a Centurion! He took one look at us, ran further down the street to one of the stone buildings, and ran inside. Curious, I thought. No sooner had he entered than he came out accompanied by two other Centurions! All three moved into the middle of the street to block our passage. More alarming, they carried their huge shields in their left hands and spears in their right. I saw the flash of steel at their sides.

Everyone sensed trouble, and Cherie rode out in front of our group; it was her job to protect us. We certainly didn't need protecting, but the other Sisters, save Thallia, were not fighters, and depended upon her. Horses at a walk, we slowly approached the three men. Their leader stood out in front of the other two. As we drew close, all three looked very nervous, which I thought totally unexpected as well. My obvious conclusion was in this sector, the Governor had dispatched guards to maintain order or enforce his laws into these outlying towns and villages.

When we were about fifty feet from them, we halted and dismounted in unison, spooking the three men further. The two in the rear had muscle twitches or else they liked to vibrate their spears. Flo spoke first, "Greetings Centurions." She hoped a civil greeting would start things in a satisfactory mode.

"State your business here in Cicillia. I'd prefer it if you'd just mount up and ride on out of town," said the leader.

I didn't like the sound of this. Flo replied, "We're on our way to Zargarb and intend to spend the night at the inn, if it still is open, and we want a bath. We've been on the trail many days now."

Sandy placed into my mind, *These Centurions are afraid of the Sisters! Scared even!* I'd already surmised that much, however.

Cherie spoke before their leader could reply, making a hand sign behind her back for Flo to see. "Boss, can I *please* kill these three men? I haven't killed any men for over a week, and it's making me terribly grumpy! The rest of you Sisters, you stay back. These three are *mine!* It'll only take me *two* minutes. Time me. If I take longer, supper is on *me.*"

What is she doing? Sandy fairly screamed into my mind. I had no time to answer, but then I had no idea anyway had I had the time to answer her. Flo spoke up immediately, watching the three men really get nervous. Now their shields were vibrating slightly, as if they were too heavy to hold still. "Cherie, *hold*. I know you're grumpy! Gods, you've been grumpy all week, but we're on a *peaceful* mission. We're not here to *kill* Centurions, so hold." Flo appeared to be chastising Cherie. She turned to look the leader in his eyes. "Forgive Cherie. She's just over-enthusiastic about slaying men. We aren't here to bother you three in any way. We have important business down south in the city with the new Governor. Here is our pass." She flashed the just purchased token of passage. "Surely, we can stay at the inn, spend our money there, and at the public bathhouse. We've not heard that the Centurions are uncivilized."

"Ah, er, well, no we are civilized. I see. Yes, of course — of course, you can stay overnight at the inn, but only if they'll have you. But — but you must promise to keep her restrained!" he exclaimed pointing to Cherie. "We — we don't want any men in this town killed on our watch. If you cause any trouble, I'm — I'm afraid we'll have to arrest you." This last was said so feebly, so hesitantly, that we knew that would be the last thing they would try to do to us. The scene was almost comical, except that it was deadly serious. I surmised Cherie and Flo were playing out a routine they often used to intimidate others into getting their way.

"Thank you, sir," Flo replied. "We want no trouble either. We'll not bother you three. Well," she added after a pause, "as long as you three haven't been bullying, harassing, or harming these fine townsfolk! But then, I'm sure you've done *no* such thing. Yes, a good hot bath will put Cherie here in a better mood, a kinder one — that is, unless later on she finds out that you have hurt any of these good people here. Is the inn still down at the other end of town?"

"Good, good," he replied, still not taking his eyes off of Cherie. "Yes, inn's still there. May Sol guide you on your journey," he added.

It took Flo a bit of time to figure out what or who Sol was; me too, for that matter. Suddenly, I remembered that was the name of their God, Sol, the Sun God. These people worshiped the Sun. "Thank you kind Centurion," Flo said after she figured it out. She turned to remount; we followed suit. The three guards made a hasty retreat back into their stone building, which they had confiscated as their local office and home. As we rode on down the street, we saw over seventy-five people had come out to watch this confrontation. From the smiles and whispers behind our backs, they were quite impressed with the way it had gone. Flo had made it seem that we were on the side of the townsfolk. Undoubtedly, there must be a great deal of ill will between these people and their new overlords.

As Cherie fell back into line, she whispered, "They were quaking in their sandals! I just couldn't help myself from having a little fun at their expense. Sorry about that, Flo."

"Actually, it worked out rather beneficial to us. Perhaps, we'll learn more information from these people now that they believe we're on their side. Say, could you really have killed all three by yourself?" asked Flo curiously.

"Probably not. One or two, yes, but they were afraid of me, so maybe I might've, dunno for sure. I'd probably get hurt doing it though," Cherie answered honestly.

I whispered to her, "Don't worry, Cherie, if there had been a fight, Roy would have taken one on instantly. Shortly after that, the other guys would've gotten there as well. What I can't believe is that these men are actually afraid of you!"

"I don't understand that either," said Cherie, "Here we are." We stopped by a huge building with many windows and a large stable behind it. Smoke rose from several chimneys; evidently dinner was cooking.

Flo took charge. Accompanied by Cherie, she went in to make the arrangements. In a couple minutes, they came back out. "No problem. For once, we're 'most welcome' here. Normally, I get a begrudging 'you can stay.' This time, we're 'most welcome.' I don't get it. But heck, I'm not going to worry about it. Some of you take care of the horses; the rest of you, come with me and bring all the gear. I've got us six rooms in a row, and they start serving supper in about a half hour."

The rooms were small, just large enough to sleep two people. Quickly, we stowed our gear, washed up in the washbasins in the rooms, and together we all went down a long hall to the dining room. We sat in a back corner next to the hall in case we needed to make a hasty exit. This was standard Sisterhood policy when eating at an inn. It was segregation, actually. They kept themselves apart from the locals, who ordinarily took offense to their presence. There were only about twenty others in this large room already eating; only a quarter of the seats were occupied. I figured business must be down, probably because the new taxes were making everyone tighten their purses.

As we sat down, two men across the room actually waved hello to us! Flo whispered, "That never happens. Trust me, never!" She was rapidly getting uneasy about all this sudden friendship with the Sisterhood. Soon, she forgot about it as a waitress brought our dinner. However, as we ate, I noticed more and more people coming into the dining room. Some merely glanced in our direction; some were very covert about actually staring at us; even two smiled and waved as they went by us. One even ventured to say, "Good evening, Sisters." Flo about choked on her food as did Cherie.

She whispered to Louisa, "You didn't tell us that the people of your sector are this friendly towards us." Poor Louisa, the look of dismay on her face spoke a thousand words."

Louisa managed to say, "This isn't the way it used to be, believe me. I don't know what is going on here either."

By the time we were finished eating, every seat in the dining room was taken, and the innkeeper was rushing about to find more chairs and trying to squeeze in more people. Both women and men were here, but more men, as might be expected. Just as we were finished and thinking we should leave so that our dozen chairs and large table could be used by those still waiting to get inside, the innkeeper came rushing over to our table carrying four bottles of wine and his best metal cups!

"Ah, Fidelio's my name, innkeeper. Permit me to give you four bottles of my finest wine" Before we could even reply, he began ceremoniously pouring.

Flo, Cherie, Thallia, Leonia, and Louisa sat there utterly speechless, though shocked actually would be a better description. As Wid, I stepped in at once, "Thank you very much. Might I ask to what do we owe this gift?"

"Why, just look about you? This place is packed! Normally, I get about twenty-five in here for dinner. It's all because of your presence. Everyone's already heard how you put those Centurion bullies into their proper place! They've been riding roughshod over all of us for months. Serves them right to get back what they've been dishing out. And we've you to thank for that! Can't talk more just now, though. I have to call in all my off-duty helpers. I'm going to make more money tonight than in an entire two weeks and all because of you. Please, stay here at the table as long as you like!" With that, he hastily ran off to try to handle five things at once. He was exceedingly busy, and he thoroughly enjoyed every minute of it.

Flo sipped some wine and declared, "By Tur, this is a good wine! He's not kidding, but I still don't get it. Okay, so we hustled the Centurions a little. Surely, that isn't enough to dissolve all the hatred and disdain for us women. There must be more to all this; there has to be."

Also, we were now very obviously the center of attention. Many were not even trying to make it look as if they were not staring at us! All twelve of us felt more than a little uneasy with all this attention. It was not the kind of attention the Sisters were used to getting. Suddenly, the Abominations were looked upon as saviors — a complete reversal of roles; this is what actually caused Flo and the others so much worry. Further, they didn't know how to handle it. Since every one of these women had suffered grievously at the hands of men, suddenly being at the center of attention was beginning to make all the Sisters extremely nervous.

"Say, I have a plan. Let's announce we really need a bath before the bathhouse closes for the night, and that we'll drop back in to finish our wine once we've gotten cleaned up. That'll get us out of here fast. Later, some of my Circle can come back if you all don't feel up to it. This is sure strange," I proposed.

"Fabulous idea, Bethany," Flo said greatly relieved, adding, "Can you make the announcement? I'm shaking so badly I might even faint."

"Relax, Flo, we'll be out of here in no time." I stood up and waved my hands. That, of course, got everyone's attention. The din quieted down instantly, as if a bomb had gone off. "Just a brief announcement for you. We have been on the trail for quite some time now and are badly in need of a bath. Probably you can smell us all the way in the back there." That brought a few chuckles. I continued, "We are off to use your bath house. I promise we'll come back to finish this fine wine once we have gotten cleaned up some. Meantime, enjoy yourselves." Several cheers and whistles came in reply, and the talk of well over a hundred people resumed. Hastily, we got up and made a fast exit. On the way out, I handed the unused bottles back to Fidelio and explained our intentions. He was overjoyed that we would return; this guaranteed him a steady business for hours!

As we got our gear and headed down the street toward the bathhouse, Flo wondered, "Gosh, I hope they don't decide that now is the ideal time to come and take a bath with us!" One glance at all five Sister's faces told me they were in a near panic over such an eventuality.

"I don't think we'll be bothered that way. I think they're more interested in talking about us than actually *being* with us, if you take my meaning." That calmed their fears a little, as we entered the bathhouse. The man in charge was just about to close up shop as we entered. Startled, he looked up at us, very surprised. "This is a surprise. Welcome Sisters, welcome! I was just about to close up shop and go over to the inn." His face turned beet red. He didn't finish his sentence, which I figured would have been, "to see the Sisters."

I spoke hastily, "Well, we told the crowd there that we're in dire need of a bath and that we'd be back to finish our wine once we got cleaned up. I do hope you can remain open just a little longer, please?"

"Oh absolutely, absolutely. Anything you need, you've only to ask," he face returned to its normal dark brown color. "Say, haven't you been here before?" he said to Flo.

"Yes, but it was before the invasion, been well more than a year," she replied. "Will a gold piece cover the bath for all twelve of us?"

"Oh yes, more than enough. Thank you for your generosity. I'll fetch the towels now. Take all the time you want. The place is empty, like I said. I was about to close up for the night." He made a hasty exit, and while we entered the steaming room and rummaged through our sacks for clean clothes, he returned with an armful of towels and washrags. After dropping them off, he left us alone, returning to his front desk, closing the door behind him to help keep the warmth inside. We noted the charcoal fire had already been put out, so the water was slowly cooling off. I had not the heart to ask him to relight it, though I knew in his frame of mind, he'd do so without any hesitation.

Without any request, Thallia helped Leonia remove her clothes. With only her one hand, this was too challenging for her to do unaided. Sarah Jane slowly unwrapped the bandages and cautioned her, "The new skin here is likely to be very sensitive to the heat, so you might not want to immerse it too much. Let me wash it for you when you are ready for it. You're my only patient at the moment, so you get my full attention." Leonia chuckled at that; obviously she wasn't really a patient.

Ah, there's nothing more relaxing than a long warm bath! Finally, I could wash my grungy long hair! We took turns scrubbing each other's backs and in general had fun. I did notice that Thallia was always keeping an eye on Leonia. Any time she needed any kind of assistance, Thallia immediately gave it before Leonia had to ask someone for help. Now I began to understand. It is embarrassing and humiliating for someone with a disability to have to ask for help. A true friend observes and provides that help thereby relieving the person's feeling of degradation. Yes, I learned a valuable lesson from Thallia this evening.

An hour later, pink-skinned and in clean clothes, we finally say goodbye to the owner and headed back to the inn, refreshed, though with still dripping-wet hair. My long hair wouldn't be completely dry until morning, but I love long hair and am more than willing to put up with the inconvenience. As we walked back, I asked about who should go back into the dining room and who preferred to go straight for our rooms. Cherie, who had actually done the deed, said that she felt obligated to go back into the dinner. "Everyone's probably talking about me," Cherie declared. In the end, everyone decided to go finish off the wine. The bath had eased their fears somewhat. I took that as a good omen.

When we entered, we found our table was just as we had left it, only cleaned up with fresh cups. However, the rest of the place was now standing room only, probably one hundred-fifty people had crowed in here. Fidelio spied us entering and rushed our bottles over to us, exclaiming, "Table is just as you left it." He rushed off still trying to take care of five things at the same time. We took our time, sipping the wine, and chatting.

As the night wore on, slowly the crowd began to disperse. One woman, as she passed by our table, whispered to us, "Thank you." We nodded. Later on, one man actually said "Thank you" as he passed by our table. For the Sisters, this was almost unbelievable. However, seeing the crowd slowly leaving spelled relief for them.

Finally, when most all had left, Fidelio came over to the table, drew up a chair, and sat down beside us. "Well, this has been the biggest night in well over a year, maybe more. Thanks again."

Simon spoke up, "My name is Simone. Why is everyone here so friendly to us Sisters? Last time we came through here, we were the Abominations. It's quite a change."

"Oh, haven't you heard about — no I expect you haven't. You're the first actual Sisters we've seen since the battle for Zargarb was lost. Being an innkeeper, I hear all the news travelers bring. Last year, the Prince threw his entire army against these Centurions. Thousands of them, I hear, he sent out to do battle with the invaders. Yet, not one lived or returned to the city! Things looked mighty bad for the city then. Just as the Centurions were about to enter the city, why, out rides the entire Sisterhood to do battle! Very unexpectedly, mind you. Whoever would have thought they would want to defend the city? Well, they were outnumbered probably a hundred to one; some say it was higher than that. Then, all heck broke loose. I've heard tell a huge thunderstorm came up, that lightning from Tur came down upon the invaders. That's probably an exaggeration, mind you. The Sisters punched through the front lines of the Centurions. Some say bolts of lightning smashed the charging chariots of destruction, but like I said, it's probably an exaggeration. Well, then they say that thousands of the Centurions poured down on the hundred Sisters in wave after wave, finally killing all of them but one. The tales people tell of the last Sister are hard to believe. They say that she stood alone and felled Centurion after Centurion, until finally they had to physically tackle her to knock her out of commission. Now here comes the queer part. I don't know whether any of this is true or not, mind you. I've heard different versions of this from all sorts, and they rather agree, sort of. After they tackled her to the ground, they bound her and refused to kill her. Instead, the bastards cut off her hands proclaiming she'd never again slay Centurions. They left her to bleed to death on the field of battle, along with all the other dead women."

"But when the morning came, she was gone. I mean all the other dead were right there where they fell. This last warrior, she was gone, no body, no nothing! Everyone keeps saying that in the night Tur himself came down upon the field of battle, took her in his arms, carried her into his realm, and healed her. She is now his personal guard-woman! Now I don't know whether this is true or not, mind you, but traveler after traveler has told me pretty much the same thing. They all agree. This last warrior just vanished without a trace. That alone put the fear of the wrath of Tur into the minds of these Centurions. Well, also, the fact that one hundred Sisters killed or wounded over five hundred Centurions. After that day, why, people's opinions toward you rather changed. You see, the score was our Prince: zero Centurions; Sisterhood: five hundred. Ever since, these Centurions seem to be afraid of the Sisterhood. Didn't you see how scared those three here were when you came into town this evening? They haven't shown their faces all night, highly unusual. I don't think they'll come outside until you've left town! So yes, you've given folks here something to talk about, something to think about, and let the invaders know you aren't all slain."

I think innkeepers the world over have one thing in common: they love to talk. Finally, he finished, and we could ask some questions. After we asked the usual follow up questions, I carefully phrased the key one I knew Flo desperately wanted to have an answer to, "Say, sometime after that fateful battle, have you ever seen any of the remaining Sisters around town? They weren't all at the battle; some were off on business and running errands. They all weren't killed that day. We'd like to get in touch with any that survived. We suspect for their own safety that they might have moved to these northern villages." I spied a grateful look of thanks on Flo's face.

"Well, you know that was an awfully confusing time there for several months. Some could have come through, and I might not have noticed, actually. Let me sleep on it, and see if I can remember anything that might be useful. I can ask around and see if anyone else might have some news. I'll do it on the quiet. We don't want to let the Centurions know about this." He winked slyly at me.

"Perfect," I replied, giving him a knowing wink back. For once, a man realized that it was in his best interests to keep the Centurions in the dark. Since the hour was now getting late, at least for us weary travelers, we thanked him again for the wine and headed to our rooms. We had much to ponder.

My Circle gathered in my room, the guys sitting on the floor and us girls on the bed. Simon spoke first, "Well, change, it had to come. Looks like this sector is now ready to welcome the Sisterhood, but for all the wrong reasons. Even if they wanted to drive the invaders out of the Sea Princes, they haven't the numbers to do it. I sure hope these people here are not counting on the Sisterhood to come and wipe out the Centurions. If so, they're in for a surprise, which could again alter their opinion of the Sisterhood for the worse."

Sandy commented, "Well, maybe they're only hoping the Sisterhood will help keep the Centurions off the common man's back. Do you suppose that might be the case? Everyone here seemed quite happy to see Cherie strike a little fear into those three."

He answered, "Could be. I was only thinking worst case scenario. We probably ought to relay a message to Rosita, telling her that Zargarb needs fighters to help keep the Centurions from bullying the locals, so she can emphasize that point when she expands to deal with this sector." We all agreed with his point.

"But what do you make of the Last Warrior and the Tur god intervention?" mused Sarah Jane. "I think this is really weird, supernatural even. Can it be this Tur may actually exist and took the Warrior from the battlefield?" We chatted about this for a bit.

At last, Thomas spoke up, "Sounds more like something one of us might do. The sudden appearance of a big storm, lightning bolts destroying chariots, and all that. Sounds like a Guardian at work to me, not the Sisterhood."

"Well, two Guardians were in Zargarb when it was under siege," I replied. "Alabaster wants us to find out what happened to Sandra Smythe and Isabel Ironhand. Both are or were women, and this was a women's battle. You don't suppose they joined up with the Sisterhood to help defend them do you?"

Roy chuckled, "I wouldn't try to put anything past you women, especially in women's matters!" We roared with laughter.

"I'm not that bossy am I?" I teased back.

"Seriously, though," Simon brought us back to the present problem, "it certainly sounds like those two were on that battlefield or sure had a hand in it. While men tend to go for direct hand-to-hand combats, you women prefer to stand back and let loose with the lightning bolts. Perhaps, they weren't directly on the battlefield and later beat a hasty retreat."

Sandy observed, "But that wouldn't account for their Communicator, Sandra, not getting any word back to Alabaster for over a year now. I hate to be the one to say it, but surely Sandra's body has been killed or she would've tried to get a hold of Alabaster. I know I surely would have or even sent a message via the next ship sailing to Calgary."

"One thing is certain: we can rule out their being captured by the Centurions. They just don't take prisoners," added Raphael, "Oops, I forgot about their salt mines. I guess they could have been taken there."

"No, only the men," Sandy reminded him. "Besides, prisoner or not, a Communicator can always make contact with others. Minds aren't as limited as bodies. No, if they had been captured, Alabaster would know about it. Remember, he has been trying to reach Sandra. If she were alive, she would respond."

Getting us back on the right track, I broke in, "So the real question is how do we go about locating these two women or finding out what happened to them? They were here clandestinely so they wouldn't openly advertise that they were from the Greenway."

"It's like looking for a needle in a haystack," moaned Sandy. Sarah Jane and most of the guys also echoed her, except for Roy.

He said, "Well, probably we should try to interview a number of witnesses of that last battle. True, we don't even know what these women looked like. From eye witness accounts and descriptions, perhaps we can tell if the evidence suggests Guardians were involved. If we can locate some surviving Sisters who witnessed it, we might also gain valuable clues."

"Excellent Roy," I validated him. "It looks like we ought to assist Flo in finding any surviving Sisters as our first action." On this suggestion we found complete agreement. With our immediate plans decided, we turned in for the night.

Early the next morning while we were washing up for breakfast, Flo heard a knock on her door. Quickly grabbing her sword and knife, Cherie asked, "Who is it?" Through the door, she heard a man's voice say that he had some news for the Sister leader. Flo decided to let them in, while Cherie stood back on guard in case this was a trap.

Flo opened the door and said, "Morning, I'm Sister Flo. Come in." She added that last because she saw both a man and a shy looking woman peering inside. As the man walked in, he had a distinctive limp in his left leg, which made walking troublesome at best. He was perhaps fifty years old with greying beard and hair. His face looked kindly enough, Flo thought, though weather worn from spending days outdoors under the hot sun. The much younger woman, who was about thirty, shyly followed him into the room. She had the typical brownish skin found in the people who lived in this sector and long hair with brown eyes that looked fearfully around the small room, darting from Flo to Cherie and back again, as if uncertain who was in charge.

"The innkeeper said you wanted information on any Sisters who may have survived the great battle in Zargarb," the man began.

"This is true," Flo answered. "We want to help them if we can and help the people of Zargarb to better survive this infernal occupation. Why?"

"My name is Aldorado, and this is my wife who I call Onie. She can't speak; her tongue was cut out a long time ago. I call her Onie because that's the best I can make out from her attempts to tell me her name. She wanted to come to see you when she heard that you were looking for the lost Sisters."

Flo smiled, eager to hear what information these two could provide. She signaled for Cherie to sheath her weapons, and she offered her bed for the two to sit, while she sat on the floor before them. These rooms were meant for sleeping and little else.

"Well, I guess I'll tell you all I know. Maybe it'll help you, maybe not. I've had this bad leg since I broke it when I was sixteen. Life's been hard on me because of it. I'm a simple farmer growing grapes for wine. Until last year, I'd resigned myself to living alone, for no woman ever wanted anything to do with a crippled old man. About two weeks after the city fell to the invaders, Onie here showed up in town, dirty and starving. Since she can't talk, no one would help her out. My house is on the very northern edge of Cicillia, and my fields lay just beyond and to the east. Well, finding no help in the city, she walked north until she came by my place. I was sitting on my porch squishing a batch of grapes when she staggers along. Mind you, she looked pitiful. I asked her if she was hungry and tried to get her to come inside so I could heat up my leftovers. But I think she was afraid to be inside with men, probably has something to do with losing her tongue. I fixed her some food and brought it outside, along with a bowl of water and soap. I think she saw my horrible limp and helped me carry the heavy bucket."

"After she washed a little and ate, the poor thing fell asleep — exhausted she was. I figured I'd best not carry her inside. I fixed up some blankets on the porch and tucked her in. Next morning, she was still there, so I fixed breakfast for us, and we both ate out on the porch. She was so embarrassed about eating, you know, no tongue and all that, but I says, 'It's all right with me, dear woman. Tur knows how I suffer because of my leg.' That seemed to put her more at ease. After that, I asked her if she wanted to use the bathhouse and get some clean clothes. I think she was indicating she had no money, but I says, who cares. I took her to the bathhouse, but she discovered that I walk very slowly, and she had to slow her pace down to stay with me. While she was bathing, I bought some loose-fitting clothes I thought might fit her. When she was clean, she had clean clothes to wear. That's when she first began to try to talk to me. I think she was saying thank you."

"When we got back to my house, I told her I had to go work my fields, but I would be back in time to fix us supper. When I got back, I found she had done all my dirty laundry. That's how we started out. After a few days, she found more and more things she could do for me and finally was brave enough to enter my house when I was there to eat and sleep. Funny how things go. Here I was a lonely old man, and this woman with a heart of gold enters my life. Well, about a month after that we got married. A man could not have a better wife, no sir. Onie here is a fabulous, wonderful woman. We've been very happy together."

"Anyways, I think she may have been with the Sisterhood before she came here because your leather clothes are very similar to the tattered ones she wore when she came into my life. I don't know how much you can really learn from her, since she can't talk, but she and I wanted to at least try."

"Thank you both for coming. Onie, were you in the Sisterhood before you came here? Just nod yes or no," asked Flo. Onie nodded excitedly yes. "Great! Now don't worry about talking. I think I know just the answer. We also have a Sister with us who has no tongue, but her boyfriend can somehow communicate with her. Let me get them. Cherie, go get Thallia and Thomas at once! Say, we were about ready to go get breakfast. Do you want to join us or would you rather finish this? I know Thallia hates to eat in public."

Both had already eaten and didn't want to be seen in a public place. In a couple minutes, Cherie arrived back with Thomas and Thallia in tow. Thallia broke the ice by going up to Onie and attempting to utter "Hi," which was mostly understandable, given the circumstances. It allowed Onie to see that Thallia was like her. Thallia also shook Aldorado's hand and said "Good man," but this wasn't really understood.

Thomas spoke up, "She says you are a Good Man." We can communicate mentally. We can read each other's thoughts. Actually works faster than speech, really. So if you want me to, I can help you tell Flo here what you want to tell her." Onie nodded, so he continued. "You just think what you want to say. I'll hear it and tell them. If I get it wrong, why, you just tap me on the shoulder and shake your head no. Okay?" Thus, the woman's tale became known to all.

"Ah, her full name before marrying was Lonnia Frescobaldi." Her face radiated intense happiness now that Aldorado could finally know her name! Once the thank you's for that gift had ended, she continued with her brief story. "She was a seamstress by trade."

Aldorado interrupted, "So that's why you were able to mend all my worn clothes. Now that makes sense!" She nodded enthusiastically.

She and a fighter named Paulia had been on a mercy mission to a small village to the northwest of Zargarb when they received the news to return to the city as fast as possible. That had been their undoing. As they galloped as fast as they could, some bandits, who were lying in wait for a caravan, waylaid them. Their horses stumbled into the trap set by the bandits, and both riders were thrown clear. Since Lonnia wasn't a fighter, as the bandits closed in on the two, Paulia ordered Lonnia to flee on foot. She did as she was told and heard the clash of swords behind her as she ran for dear life.

Sometime later on, she heard the bandits riding in pursuit of her, and she figured that they had slain Paulia. Lonnia was clever and managed to hide from her pursuers. Knowing that the bandits lay between here and the city, she headed north. Slinking around some towns, she learned that the city had fallen to the invaders and all the Sisters were killed. Dismayed, lost, and alone, she tried to find somewhere to live. But those in each town she walked to would have nothing to do with her. Unable to speak, she could not even beg. She was just about dead when she finally ran into Adorado, who saved her life.

"She also wants you to know, Aldorado, that she loves you very much," Thomas whispered to him with Lonnia nodding in an exaggerated confirmation. To Flo, he said, "When we are finished questioning her, may I have a few minutes alone with these two? Lonnia wants me to tell him some personal things that she hasn't been able to tell him before now. This is sort of like a golden opportunity for her, you see." Flo not only agreed, but insisted that he do so, Thallia nodding her agreement as well.

Flo said to Lonnia, "First, Lonnia, it looks as though you no longer need to be in the Sisterhood. I'd say you have made a successful new start in life. So you are released from any obligations to the Sisterhood." Lonnia breathed a huge sigh of relief. Flo figured that detail was probably what was troubling the woman most — that she would be forced to abandon her new husband. "If you should ever have need of us in the future, let us know. You should be seeing more of Sisters in this sector in the not too distant future. That's partly why we are here."

She went on, "I assume you don't have any direct knowledge of what happened at the Great Battle by the city, right?" She nodded. "But you are living proof that not all the Sisters perished that day. We are seeking others who somehow survived. Do you know of any others who may have gotten away somehow? Any clues you can give us?"

No one spoke for several minutes as she tried to remember anything useful. At last, Thomas began speaking for her once more. "She says that when she and Aldorado have traveled by wagon to deliver his wine to other villages, she thinks she has seen some other Sisters, though they weren't wearing their usual leathers. She can't be certain, though. She is certain she did recognize one Sister who is living in a village near the border with Juda Arad. That's the only one of which she is certain. She thinks there are others around some of these northern towns and villages. She has never gone back to within fifty miles of the city, however. Does this help?"

Flo replied, "Yes, it sure does. Thank you very much!" Next, she got directions on how to find this village, which Aldorado called Florintine Junction, home to about a hundred-fifty people. Then, she and Cherie left the four alone and came to inform me what she had just found out. Over breakfast, Louisa explained she actually knew where this village was located and could direct us there, which was a relief to Flo who didn't have to try to remember the shaky directions that Aldorado had attempted to relay to her, for his were based on familiar landmarks such as trees and hills.

A short while later, Thallia and Thomas joined us, both were extremely cheerful, especially Thallia. Thomas explained that Thallia had convinced Lonnia to try to talk to Aldorado and not to be embarrassed about how garbled the sounds came out. He could always ask her to repeat something when he couldn't make it out. About what private things he relayed between them, Thomas never said a word.

While we ate, the discussion centered on whether we should continue to head directly to Zargarb or to follow this tenuous lead that Lonnia had given us. I explained that we needed to try to locate two of our missing kinswomen and that they might have been at or in that the fateful last battle. Thus, it was also in our interests to help Flo find other Sisters who survived. Actually, Flo was quite pleased that we would be assisting her for the present. Hers was a tough assignment. Flo, using various cups for towns and forks for tracks, laid out the major towns in this sector. While we could cut overland in a wide arc to get to this town on the very eastern edge, the main tracks would be quicker.

The seven cities are the focal point in this land. Thus, all tracks angle out from Zargarb like the spokes of a wheel. At various distances from the city, cross tracks meander east-west. Florintine Junction lay about one hundred miles northeast of Zargarb on one of the major spokes. However, Cicillia, where we were now at, lay on a different spoke some hundred-fifty miles from Zargarb. Thus, to get there we would have to continue southward for fifty miles before taking an east-west track another hundred miles to the town. Cutting overland would shorten the total distance by something approaching fifty miles, depending on the terrain.

Flo's original idea was to head straight down this spoke delivering us as soon as possible to Zargarb. Then, she would begin a zig-zag east-west course, visiting all the other towns starting with those closest to Zargarb first, ending back out here on the rim of the sector ready to head home. However, bandits presented an additional consideration. Prime bandit country lay roughly in an arc from about thirty miles out from Zargarb to about ninety miles. Beyond that range, such as out here in Cicillia, there was no profit to be gained. The lucrative shipments lay far closer to the city. Naturally, the immediate area surrounding the city was more heavily patrolled. If we traveled the main track toward Zargarb and then took the cross-track to Florintine Junction, we would be entering bandit country. On the other hand, if we cut across country, we would not likely run into thieves. In the end, Flo opted for safety and speed.

We finished eating, stowed our sacks onto our horses and rode south out of town. As we rode down the last stretches of the main street, several men waved goodbye. We waved back, no longer so surprised at how the Sisters were being accepted here. Incidentally, Roy spied the Centurions watching us, discretely partially hidden behind the side of a building.

Once clear of the town and any prying eyes, Flo headed off to the left, leaving the track behind. I must say, Flo certainly does have a remarkable sense of direction. For two days, we rode up one valley and down the next, sometimes going eastward, others southward. With each new valley, she always knew whether to head east or south. These two days, while hot, were peaceful. We encountered no towns or villages. However, we did encounter several hermits and a couple of small stone mining operations, but we did not stop.

Chapter 16 Florintine Junction

Finally, midmorning of the third day, Flo headed due south and continued taking every southerly valley. When I asked her about it, she replied, "I'm making for the east-west track that leads into Florintine Junction. This way we won't miss it." Her logic made perfect sense. I should have thought of that. Around noon, we spied the town ahead of us, cradled in the middle of the next valley. Here, the hills were weather-worn with red, sandy soil, very arid with sparse vegetation. A few trees grew near the almost dry, small stream that trickled down the middle of the valley. The town was on the southern side consisting of a hundred or so red adobe, single story buildings.

The sounds of hammers on anvils echoed in the hot air; the town sported five blacksmith shops. Louisa told us that out here near Juda Arad, little food was locally grown. In contrast, the area was rich in minerals, and a thriving metalworking industry was formed. Periodically, the town would trade metal equipment for food. There were some vineyards, but since they also exported a great deal of wine to their neighbors in Juda Arad, they had to import wine from many other outlying towns, such as Cicillia. Louisa estimated that the town had grown, since she had last been here and now had something like five hundred people living here. Slowly, we rode into town, each of us wondering what kind of a reception we'd get here and if there were Centurion guards stationed here as well. Nevertheless, I was still not prepared for the sights I saw next. Neither were any of the others, save Flo.

The streets were very wide over fifty feet. We passed by three groups of camels — caravan traders from Juda Arad, Flo informed us. Their drivers from Juda Arad wore light colored, very loose-fitting clothes that gave the appearance of bagginess. Their heads were wrapped in colorful turbans, reds and yellows predominated. Flo explained that the red turban fellows came from the northern part of Juda Arad, while those with yellow lived just across the ill-defined border with Zargarb Sector of the Sea Princes. As we rode by one group, a camel made a strange grunting noise and actually spit toward my horse! This particular group of camels was being loaded with crates of wine, one on either side of its hump. All the while, the heavy clanking of hammer upon anvil echoed up and down this main street.

Yes, we stared at the camels and their drivers. Interestingly enough, they and the locals stared at us as well. Women doing various chores and children playing a tag game were also in the street. Street life was a well-orchestrated chaos, befitting a town called Florintine Junction. Here two different cultures met at the crossroad. Flo commented, "Look for an inn." However, she quickly stopped and asked a woman carrying a load of clean laundry.

The dark skinned woman with long brown hair and deep blue eyes replied, "You are from the Sisterhood aren't you?" Flo nodded. "I thought so.

326

We haven't seen any of you since the city fell last year; figured you all died. Guess not. Well, there are two inns; one's over there," she pointed to a large red adobe building sporting a wooden sign with a camel on it. "Lonzo's Inn serves mostly those from out of town. I don't think you would like the company there; men, you know, rough and tumble, kind of harsh on women to stay there, if you know what I mean. Then there's Romeo's Inn way down at the other end of the town. He doesn't take in foreigners, like the Arad folk. You would get along better there." Flo thanked her, and as we began to walk out horses toward Romeo's Inn, she called out to us, "It's good to see Sisters around once more." We smiled at her as we rode past her.

I wondered what kind of a welcome we would receive in this town. The front of Romeo's Inn, a sprawling structure that showed signs that it had been expanded in all directions several times, all except out into the street, had a desert rose flower on its sign. I wondered if this was meant to appeal to the romantic nature of women or that the innkeeper enjoyed romance. This time, I accompanied Flo and Cherie as they went inside to get us some rooms. Once inside the entrance, I grasped at once its layout. Essentially, the inn was a series of separate one room buildings that all opened onto a large central plaza or courtyard. The only entrance to the rooms was past this check-in desk. Thus, the occupants had a deal of safety and the innkeeper was assured that you couldn't leave without his knowledge. Cherie thought it was more like a prison than an inn.

As we walked in, the innkeeper, Romeo was bawling out one of his young female maids. "Can't you ever do anything right? How many times must I order you to put the dirty sheets in this pile over here not over there?" The maid was perhaps thirty years old and said not a word, but stared at her shoes the whole time that he chastised her. In fact, I'd swear she was not even listening to a word he said; she was daydreaming. I could tell by her eyes and body language. Another maid walked in with several chamber pots and stood quietly nearby awaiting his orders. "Amilia, go dump them in the street now." Like a robot, she walked past us without as much as a glance at us and went on outside.

Romeo saw us and immediately turned on his charm. He was probably forty or so, short for a man, only about five feet tall, slightly overweight, but his clothes looked expensive. He had a well-tended moustache. "Ah, ladies, you must forgive my ignorant maids. I have to tell them every little thing to do. Welcome to Romeo's Inn, the finest establishment in the Junction. You appear to be from the Sisterhood, if my eyes don't deceive me. How may I be of service to you? One moment, please." He spied Amilia walking back through the front doors. "No Amilia, you bring the empty pots back inside — don't leave them on the street! Imbecile!"

Turning back to us, he apologized by saying, "You just can't get competent help these days! I've been running this inn for twenty-five years now, and I swear the help just gets dumber by the day. I try so very hard to help women find work here. I give them a job when no one else will, but I have to give them directions on how to do every little thing, and I repeat those same directions every day. You'd think that after five years on the job, Amilia would finally know the routine? But no, everyday it is the same thing. I have to tell them each thing to do, and if I don't watch them like a hawk, why, they would just stand there all day doing absolutely nothing." Amilia walked in with the pots. "Good Amilia, now go wash them out. No! No, not from the drinking water vat! Use the dirty water barrel, you fool!" Turning back to us he explained, "See there, if I hadn't issued that order, she would have washed out the bed pots in your drinking water! Can you imagine what I have to put up with here? She has been here for five years, and every day I have to order her to do the same things, over and over. I swear she hasn't any brains at all, but she does have a pretty face, and I sure wouldn't want her to not have a job, because I know she has three children at home to feed. Ah me. Now where was I? Ah yes. You are Sisters. I haven't seen you before, have I? No I never forget a pretty face ever."

Flo explained that we wanted six adjacent rooms for several days if possible. "Six, well that is quite a few. Adjacent, well it just so happens I do have them. They would be the six along the courtyard opposite us here. That will cost you a gold coin a day. Oh yes, and it includes three meals each day. I do have enclosed stables out back that are locked at night — security you know. We do have a lot of riffraff coming and going. You know, those strange Arad foreigners. They simply can't be trusted. I swear every one of them is a born thief! You beautiful ladies should watch your money pouches very carefully whenever you are around one of them. Now where was I? Oh yes, if you want us to feed your horses a bit of grain instead of dried grasses — how many horses did you say? Well, that would be another gold piece a day in that case, so a total of two. My, but you have a large party. All Sisters?"

"No, we've four men with us," Flo replied.

He raised his eyebrows, "Isn't that just a bit unusual? I don't mean to pry so just tell me it's none of my business. I've always thought that the women in the Sisterhood, well you know, didn't get along too well with men." Before Flo could answer, Amilia returned and stood quietly at his side awaiting instructions. "Now go put clean sheets on the bed in Number 4. No Amilia, you idiot, not dirty sheets! Clean sheets go on the bed. Remember to take the dirty sheets off before you put the clean sheets on." Turning back to us, he said, "Honestly, yesterday she put the clean sheets on over the dirty ones in four rooms! Can you believe that?" Flo handed him two coins for today. He thanked her profusely and gave her six keys, each with a metal tag that had a different number of holes drilled in it, which matched a tag on the door to the room. "See, this one has seven holes, so this one is for Room 7."

Flo commented, "Clever idea; this way you can even find your room in the dark by feel alone.

He beamed with satisfaction that someone had seen the utter brilliance of his idea without his having to explain it fully. "Ah, thank you for the compliment. It was just a little invention of my own. It is so refreshing to meet a woman who not only has good looks but also has a bright mind." He was trying to compliment Flo, but Flo never thought of herself as having good looks and so it was wasted.

We then went outside to our waiting companions. Once outside, I finally said a word, "That guy sure is weird. Either he is hiring the stupidest people he can possibly find, or," I didn't get to finish my sentence.

Flo explained with a sigh, "No, that is normal domestic life here in the Sea Princes. He treats women just as the men in the city do. Those poor women are not allowed to speak unless he Okays it first. Thus, they just dutifully follow his orders. Their 'goofs' are just their own way of protesting his treatment, though he obviously hasn't a clue about it. Men! Come on; let's check out this secure stable; it's costing us as much as our room and board."

We led the horses around to the rear. Sure enough, there was a stable built onto the back side. It was obviously a more recent addition, for its adobe bricks were not as weathered as those of the back walls of the inn itself. We led them inside where a young lad only twelve took charge. "Hello. You can lead them this way. I'll put them all in adjoining stalls if that's okay. You have some fine horses there. Name's Piazza. I love horses and promise to take good care of them. Stable is locked after dark so if you need them at night, you have to get the innkeeper Romeo to open the doors. We've never had a horse stolen since he built this stable five years ago."

We chatted with this lad while we unsaddled the horses and rubbed them down. The boy was cheerful and did appear to know how to handle them. He spied Cherie's many weapons and asked, "You're one of them warrior Sisters aren't you? I've never met one before, but I've heard all about you. Have you really killed Centurions?"

"Piazza, I hate to kill anything except perhaps a viper, but I've been forced to kill before, lost count actually how many men I've downed. Regretted everyone, but they left me no other choice. Kill or be killed. Not much of a life, is it?" Cherie replied hoping to take some of the "glory" off her position as a Sisterhood fighter. Nevertheless, the boy ogled over her weapons asking if he could just touch them. He was impressed with Cherie.

Later, we walked around to the entrance and out into the courtyard, which actually was refreshingly romantic. Vining flowers grew on trellises while many others grew tall in various pots strategically located around this forty by eighty foot yard, whose floor was red limestone bricks. Benches and the occasional table and chairs were perfectly placed beside the flowers, giving one the illusion of isolation for a romantic interlude. I had to admit that in spite of the owner's attitude, he had a very nice inn. As we decided who got which rooms, Amilia came out of one room and said, "Hello. I'm Amilia. Don't pay any attention to old Romeo. He never beats or hurts us. I put some fresh flowers in your rooms for you. Don't tell Romeo though. Aren't these flowering vines just great? They flower all summer long. I just love walking out here in the courtyard." Then, she spied our men, who had brought up the rear carrying most of our sacks. She instantly stopped speaking.

"It's okay. You can talk freely and whenever you want around our men here. They aren't like your boss," I tried to explain. She was so thoroughly trained, that she still refused to speak while they were around. I just thanked her for her kind gesture, and we checked out our rooms. Later, we met together to decide upon our next move: how to go about finding Sisters who were "in hiding."

In the end, Flo's idea won out; after all, she was the leader here. Her plan was to make ourselves highly visible as Sisters. Then, let those that may be in hiding contact us. For safety, she and Cherie would walk around town together. Likewise, Leonia and Louisa would do some shopping. Because this was actually the first chance we'd had to witness male-female interactions, Flo thought it best if we girls did not go walking around town alone. If we were to keep up the appearance of being Sisters, we would very likely blow it, when we encountered any males. So we three and Thallia decided to do everyone's laundry. The guys, with Flo's hesitant agreement, also went for a walk around the town, familiarizing themselves with our new location.

Hence, I went to find Romeo to ask him where we could find a washtub and soap. I walked up to him calculating that I ought to await his permission to speak, but as soon as I drew near, he said, "Ah, such beautiful long hair you have. So different from the others."

"Yes, well, I do have a passion for it," I replied wondering if he was sincere or just flirting with me.

"Ah, so do I. Permit me," and he picked a flower and inserted it into my hair. "There, you look as pretty as a flower. Now, how can I be of service?" So I asked about laundry barrels, rather non-romantic. As I went into the next room to see the setup, I felt his eyes following my every move. It was just a bit unnerving, and I was very glad to have the other three join me.

While we were washing, Thallia tried to say, "I like that once." Since none of us could really understand her, Sandy just read her mind.

"Really?" I asked in surprise once Sandy had relayed her words.

Shaking her head dolefully, she said "Yes."

"Well, I'm sure glad you aren't like that anymore!" We had a good laugh.

Pair by pair, the others checked in later that afternoon. None had seen any signs of any Sisters here in town. This was going to be harder that we thought.

After dinner, we took our teacups out into the courtyard. Several other guests were strolling about here was well. I sat on a bench with Roy chatting about how nice this courtyard as and how it could double as a dance floor when Amilia came by. "Hi again," she said to me but then noticed Roy and shut up.

"Hello Amilia, isn't it?" Roy said, "You can talk freely around me. I'm not like Romeo." She was still a bit hesitant, but continued by looking at me.

"I'm going home for the night. I thought I'd see if there is anything you need before I go?"

"No, not really. Wait, say, we're looking for any women who may have moved into the Junction sometime shortly after the city fell to the invaders. By chance, do you know of any women who may have arrived here about then? We want to chat with them is all. We are trying to find out more about that last battle." It was a gamble, and I didn't reveal that these women may have been Sisters or that they may have been forced to go underground for their own safety.

"Gee, there are always people coming and going around here, but I guess you'd want to know only about those who've stayed. Let's see." She thought about it for a while. "Well, as a matter of fact, yes, there are two really poor women who came here late last year. Usually people come and people go; you know Junction is a stepping off place. Not much of an economy here, except trading with the Arads. These two are really destitute and live in the most rundown house in the town, over on the northwest side at the very edge. The owner was going to tear it down and build a new one, but that was before the city fell. Now everyone is counting their coins to pay the darn tribute taxes. I think he's glad to get some tiny amount of rent for it. These two women often come here to the inn and do the laundry once a week. They collect the dirty linens in an old rickety two-wheeled pushcart. They bring the finished, nicely folded sheets back a couple days later. Sometimes, I don't see them when they come, so just let old Romeo know that you want to talk to them when one of them comes for the laundry sometime this week."

"Thanks, we will."

"Well, I best be going then. I've three kids awaiting their dinner. See you tomorrow." She left and I went to tell the others about our lucky possibility.

Waiting is not a fun game. Since we didn't want to arouse anyone's attention to these two poor women, we continued strolling the town and relaxing in the courtyard. The next day late in the afternoon, Romeo sent Amilia to find us; the laundry woman was here. Flo and I decided that we should be the ones to confront the woman rather than all of us; we might frighten her away. We found her loading the last of a large pile of sheets onto a small pushcart that had seen better days.

She was a young woman, tall and thin, perhaps in her early twenties. Her long brown hair was carefully tied into a ponytail. Her deep blue eyes reminded me of the Med Sea, and she had thick lips. She also looked worn out and very haggard, as if she was carrying the weight of some immense unspoken burden on her shoulders. We walked up, and Flo said, "Hello. Might we have a word with you, please?"

Flo startled her; she look up and nearly dropped the armful of sheets onto the ground, as she gasped and put her hand over her mouth. "You, you are Sisters?" she asked, nearly choking on her words. Flo could not tell if this was a positive or negative reaction, so she just nodded and said that we were.

"Oh, all thanks be to Tur! Please, please come with me. It is almost too late. Come now!" she pleaded, pulling hard on Flo's arm.

"Good heavens, what's the matter? Too late for what?" Flo tried to understand this startling change in her demeanor. I guessed Flo immediately thought that she would need Cherie's fighting skills and ours too.

"We have a very ill woman with us. Please, please come now, I beg you." So insistent, so pleading she was that we could hardly refuse.

"Wait a minute. We have a healer with us. If she is ill, Sarah Jane would be far better equipped to heal than I am," I explained. She agreed, and I went to fetch Sarah Jane who, hearing that she had a new patient, grabbed her healing gear sack, which was exceedingly empty, for we had already used nearly everything we had brought. Hopefully, Alabaster's resupply would be waiting for us when we got to Zargarb.

As we followed the pushcart through the busy streets, we introduced ourselves. She was called Alicia Bortolo and her friend, which we had not yet met, was Angelina Torquoras. That was all Alicia would say out here in the open. Five minutes later, we neared the edge of town. There was only one dilapidated building left with rags covering the windows, a door hanging by one hinge, and a roof badly sagging. This had to be the place, I thought.

Alicia left the cart outside and told us to follow her inside. There were only three rooms, a kitchen, a living room, which had been converted into a bedroom, and another room, which had a heavy blanket serving as a door. Angelina looked up startled by the three of us. Alicia quickly said, "I bring Sisters. This is Angelina." We quickly introduced ourselves. Angelina also looked immensely relieved that we'd come.

"This way. Please don't be shocked by what you are going to see. She is dying; we are sure of it. We've tried our very best for more than a year. Lately, she is fading away from us. Please save her," begged Angelina.

However, what struck me was some horrible stench, as if something had died in the living room. Sarah Jane said, "I'll do my best, where is the patient? In here?" she said pointing to the blanket over the doorway. Angelina pulled back the blanket, and Sarah Jane stepped into the dimly lit room; one blackened lantern burned on a side table. The window to the outside was covered with another blanket. The stench of decaying flesh nearly caused her to gag. I did gag. I don't know how Sarah Jane could endure that awful smell, but she did. I heard her say, "Oh my god!" And she came quickly back out into the living room.

"Okay, we need to open this place wide open to let in tons of fresh air. I need hot water, lots of it. I need light, lots of light in there," she expected the two women to hop to it, but they didn't.

"We're out of oil; that's the last of it," Angelina began to cry. She blurted out, "We have only a little charcoal left to cook dinner tonight. It won't make much hot water. We are doomed. Now that we finally have found a healer, we have failed her." She cried so hard that she could not speak much else. Alicia looked crestfallen and near tears as well.

"Alicia," I addressed her since she still retained her wits, "we are new to the town and don't know where one might get oil, lamps, or charcoal. Come, you lead me, and we'll go get them at once."

"But we have no coins," she looked forlornly at the dirt floor. Angelina bawled even harder.

"I've got lots of coins. I'm buying. Now let's get going before Sarah Jane kicks us in our butts. She is the healer." I literally pulled her out of the front door.

"Oh thank you, thank you. How can we ever repay you?" she said, as we walked as fast as we could down the street.

"You don't need to," I replied. "Only let's get the stuff really quickly." We did. However, I sent word to Sandy back at the inn. *Hey, we have a very sick person here, and the two women have virtually nothing. We need food, charcoal, and more lanterns. You guys see if you can purchase some, and I'll direct you to where we're at.* Sandy replied that they would do so at once, glad to have something useful to do. She hated the waiting as much as I did. A half hour later, loaded with two oil skins and three heavy sacks of charcoal, Alicia and I reentered her home.

Sarah Jane and Flo had not been idle. The blankets were off the windows, and the light breeze had begun to blow some of the smell outside, fortunately off to the north were there were no other homes. They had filled several cooking pots with fresh water and were waiting our return. Sarah Jane had gotten Angelina calmed down with Flo's help, and the two residents set quickly to lighting the charcoal. As you know, charcoal takes a long time to get fully burning. Sarah Jane muttered, "Where's Thomas when you need him? Oh stand back you two. I'm not very good at this." I knew at once that she was calling down fire from the sky to get the charcoal fired up rapidly. When the flames appeared in the air above the fireplace, you should have seen the women gawk in complete astonishment, including Flo. All three women stared at Sarah Jane, as if she was a goddess. For Sarah Jane to take this drastic a step in front of strangers, I knew that it had to be a life and death situation in the other room.

Curiosity got the better of me. I slipped into the room to get a quick peek at the situation. "Oh my god!" I could not stop myself from blurting out. An emaciated woman lay naked on the bed. She had no hands. Bandages covered the ends of her two arms, though I saw no blood. She had long red hair, green eyes, and a very pale skin color. There was absolutely no doubt she came originally from the Greenway and probably from the western area! Further, from the various bits of healing herbs that remained in the room, she had to have once been a Guardian! She was one of us! Hence, my sudden outburst, and now I realized Sarah Jane's too. Could she be one of the missing women we were searching for?

As if reading my mind, Sarah Jane entered the room and said, "Yes, you are looking at what's left of Isabel Ironhand. Sandra Smythe died on the field of battle. Angelina told me while you were out."

"What's happened to her? That awful smell?" I asked. Sarah Jane pointed to Isabel's womb. I saw greenish puss oozing out of it. "My god, she has a horrible infection," I whispered.

"I've never seen one this bad — actually never heard of one this bad. We may already be too late to save her. She is almost in a coma now, dying. I think her body is shutting down. Where there is yet life, there is hope. Bring in the hot water just as soon as it is boiling. Get word to Thomas. We are going to need his skills in tracking down some local herbs and roots, if I am going to have half a chance of saving her."

I did so at once. As soon as I had contact with Thomas and Sandy, she helped me connect all three of us to Sarah Jane. *Ooh, this is great*, Sarah Jane thought to us. Then, she relayed to him what types of remedies she needed. If we were back home in the Greenway, Thomas could have brought just what she wanted in less than a half hour, such was the knowledge and skill of a Loremaster. Here, we were in a strange land with its very different plants. Thomas would have to use every ounce of his skill and training. He and Thallia went roaming about the nearby countryside, accompanied by Cherie who acted as their protector so they could concentrate wholly on their search.

I brought the first of the hot water into Sarah Jane. She had been tearing some old bits of cloth into strips. "Get a pan for me to put the used strips into and, when it gets full, take them out, wash, boil them, and bring them back to me. I'm going to have to get inside of her and clear out as much of the infection as I can. I just hope that Thomas can find us something we can use to help kill it." I left her to do her work and went to fetch another pot.

"Is she going to die?" asked Alicia when I come out for the pot. "We're too late aren't we?"

"She is still alive, and we've got our best healer caring for her," I answered. "I've sent some of my companions out into the countryside looking for plants, which might help heal her. Flo, can you go back to the inn and lead Sandy, Roy, Simon, and Raphael back here? They have purchased a bunch of necessary supplies we need."

"Sure you got it," I could tell that Flo was greatly relieved finally to have something she could do.

"Alicia, why don't you come with me to keep us all from getting lost?" asked Flo. She knew one couldn't get lost in so small a town. Once she had been led here, she could easily find it again, but she knew Alicia also needed something with to occupy herself, and she wanted to get her used to being around these men.

A half hour later, they returned laden with more supplies than these two women had seen in a month! Sandy and Alicia set to cooking up a large dinner for everyone. Even Louisa and Leonia had come, not wanting to be left out completely. The two poor residents had no idea how they could feed so many and were completely surprised that Sandy had already thought of this detail. Forks, cups, and plates were also in one of the sacks they brought.

For my part, I spent the next four hours bringing out the green ooze saturated cloth strips, washing them, boiling them, and taking them back to Sarah Jane. I did point out one encouraging sign, with each trip, there was less and less of the smelly green ooze.

Just as Sandy announced supper was ready, Thomas arrived along with the others. "Where's Sarah Jane? She owes me a big one this time!" He proudly held a large sack stuffed with various plants. I led him into the room and watched his present his finds to her.

"How on Tarra did you find all this stuff?" she exclaimed obviously delighted with his finds. "Bitter root! Just what we need. Bethany, go get this diced up and boiled down in about a cup of water. Bring it to me as soon as the tuber gets squishy. That liquid is very precious!"

"I know, I know," I answered. "Very well done, Thomas!" He beamed satisfied that we properly acknowledged his efforts. *Men*, I thought to myself.

We had all finished eating and were sitting around on the dirt floor chatting, when Sarah Jane finally came out, and washed her hands carefully in some very hot water. She looked very exhausted; her hair was completely disheveled, and her eyes watered from the strain she had forced them to endure. She had a satisfied look on her face. Turning to the two women, she said, "Well, I've done all I can do just now. We'll leave her rest tonight. In the morning, we shall see. Either she'll begin to recover or her condition will worsen — could go either way. I've never seen such a massive infection like that one." She spied the food. "Food! Famished!" She helped herself.

Unfortunately, this prognosis caused Angelina to begin to wail again, "Oh, it's all our fault. If we only had coins or gone somewhere else or," she began crying and couldn't finish her regrets.

Simon, ever the Judger, took charge, "Angelina, Isabel Ironhand is one of our people, one of us. She was sent here to help you. I believe we have an idea what happened to her. If so, then you are blameless. In fact, we owe you for saving her life. So stop the crying; it certainly isn't your fault. I suspect you've gone far beyond the call of duty to save Isabel. What we really must know now is the full story — what happened, all of the details. Can either of you tell us, please?" He knew they were trained to obey males, though he didn't know how much their Sisterhood lifestyle had compensated for this cultural suppression. He hoped it was enough to get them speaking.

"Let me," Alicia spoke hesitantly to Angelina, who sniffled and nodded her consent. "You've heard of the battle the Sisterhood put up in the defense of Zargarb?" We nodded, so she continued. "Both of us are Sisters, but not fighters. I'm a translator because I speak fluent Juda Arad. Angelina is actually a seamstress and a good one, though she has no more sewing gear; we had to sell all our possessions to feed and provide for Isabel. It all began late last year when we were on an assignment in a small town about fifty miles north of the city. One day, word arrived that all Sisters who could fight were to meet in the city in two days' time. The rest of us were to finish our business and come when we could. It was very important, the message bearer said. So the two fighters who had been with us, our protectors, left at once. We hurried as fast as we could, and we arrived on a distant hill overlooking the last battlefield. We stopped and took shelter as best we could, for never have we seen such a ferocious thunderstorm raging over the field of battle. We watched as our dear friends attacked the invaders. For a few minutes, we thought our Sisters would be victorious, but the Centurions kept pouring more and more men into the battle, so many we couldn't even count them."

"No one can imagine our horror as we sat there on the hilltop watching all our dearest friends being brutally slain, one by one. We felt so utterly helpless, so alone. I wanted to charge down the hill and join our Sisters in death, but Angelina held me back. Finally, all were slain save the last two, Isabel and her friend, Sandra, who now fought back to back. The lightning was terrifying. Great blasts blew Centurions into the sky like flightless birds. Finally, an arrow pierced Sandra's forehead. Angelina said she probably died instantly. Still Isabel fought on, the lone Sister on the field. The bodies of hundreds of fallen Centurions and our Sisters littered the field, which flowed red in the pouring rain. They could not kill her. Over and over, they charged only to be added to the mound of the dead before her. Finally, they tried a new tactic. Hundreds of them charged her and literally fell on top of her as if she was a pillow! I felt sure this was the end, but it was only the beginning."

"When the giant pile of men arose, the men held onto Isabel, pinning her arms behind her. The Centurion general, I assume that is what he is called, rode up before her, and stared at her. Then he said, "We must show these women a lesson. Do not slay this one. Cut off her hands that she might never raise a sword to a Centurion ever again, but leave her alive. All of you may rape her to your heart's content. Show her and all women who is the boss. Set an example that no one will ever dare challenge us again."

"She screamed in rage at him, calling him horrible names before someone hit her over the head knocking her out. They strung her up and hacked off her hands, then stanched the wounds so she wouldn't bleed to death very quickly. They ripped off her clothes, tearing them into shreds that she might go naked from the field, should she live. Then, we watched the most disgusting sight we've ever seen, as man after man had their way with her while she was unconscious and slowly bleeding to death. Still the storm raged, and finally, the men left the battlefield, leaving her naked and alone to bleed to death slowly over time, surrounded by hundreds of dead women. Naturally, the invaders carried their own fallen comrades from the field and dug a deep burial pit. We watched them far into the night."

"When it became totally dark and quiet, Angelina said we must rescue Isabel somehow. We knew we couldn't transport her by horseback. I snuck into town and stole an old pushcart. Together, we carried and dragged her unconscious body from the hill, all the while the torrential rains fell upon us. Angelina said the rain would wash away our tracks. Both of us feared for our lives if it didn't. Finally, we were able to get her into the cart, and together we pushed her down the valley and up the hill to where we left our horses."

"With the Centurions taking over Zargarb, we knew we couldn't take her there; we had to secret her away so these vicious men could never find her. Angelina suggested we head north and east — all the way to Arad if necessary.

But how? Neither of us had anything of value except a handful of coins. We took turns pulling the cart, slipping, and sliding on the wet, muddy ground while the other led our two horses. When we saw the morning twilight, we had gone a fair distance, and we found a rocky cave in which to hide out during the day light hours. Besides, we were now completely exhausted. We got her inside though still lying in the cart and we collapsed into a deep sleep."

"When we awoke, it was dark again, and Isabel was semi-conscious, moaning in great pain. By the moonlight — we dare not light a fire — we examined her arms. Neither of us knew anything about healing, but they weren't bleeding anymore, just looked frightful. I vomited. We had only a little food with us, having expected to go to the Sisterhood's complex once we arrived. We ate a little, rationing what we had. Then, we continued our journey, taking turns pulling, pushing the cart. When daylight began to appear, we were close to a town. We found another place to hide. Angelina said one of us should go into the town and barter our horse for food, supplies, and bandages, anything that we could use to help Isabel. I was so scared that she offered to do it while I stayed with Isabel. She had me promise her that if she didn't return by nightfall, I was to go on alone without her — do anything to save Isabel and get her far, far away and in total secrecy. I did so, but not without crying like a baby. If Angelina didn't come back, I don't know what I could have done."

"But she did. Around midday, she came back on foot carrying several heavy sacks. She said, 'I got all sorts of stuff, Alicia, but I just don't know what to do. I don't know anything about wounds.' Just then, the most miraculous thing occurred. Isabel spoke ever so quietly. "I do. I'll tell you what to do before I pass out.' We both cried like babies, and then listened to her every word, memorizing the sequence of things to do. Whether Isabel had finished or not, we never knew, because her feeble strength gave out, and she fell unconscious once more. Angelina and I began to do the things we were told. I vomited again, just looking at her arms. Thank Tur for Angelina. She went ahead and did all the things with me helping. When we ran out of the list to do, we both were so emotionally exhausted that we collapsed into sleep right there on the bare ground."

"We awoke with the chill of the night air upon us. Again, we gathered our things, put as much of it as we could on the remaining horse, and began our secret travel. Angelina decided we should head out across country to avoid the risk of meeting any late night travelers on the main tracks. Neither of us is experienced in doing this, even in the daytime. I think we got more than a little lost, but we did put distance between us and the city."

"We hiked for at least a week before our supplies began to run out. Each day, Isabel seemed to regain some of her strength, but never enough actually to walk on her own for any distance. When she was conscious, she kept telling us what to do, and we did it as best we could. Finally, we did run out of food, and Angelina spied a town a couple miles away down in the valley and traded our last horse for more supplies."

"Now we had a new problem; winter was coming on, and the nights were getting colder and colder; we had no winter clothing or blankets. We had to find somewhere to hold up. We talked about what to do for a couple days. Isabel finally convinced us to try the next town we encountered, which was the Junction. Never have more pitiful women ever arrived into a town than we two. Coinless, possessionless, somehow we had to find somewhere to live through the cold winter months. Thanks to the great sense of Angelina, she found this rundown place. She figured we could live here for next to nothing, which was more than we could afford. She was the one who made the deal with the owner, one gold coin per month. We moved Isabel in late at night so no one would see her. To this day, people only think we two live here. At first, I tried to get a job as a local translator, but without the Sisterhood backing, no men would listen to me, and there was no way we were going to let on we were from the Sisterhood. Isabel made us promise never to mention that we were Sisters. Besides our clothes were tattered and torn beyond repair by the time we made it here."

"Eventually, we found odd jobs about town, and it has provided only enough for the barest necessities. Every extra coin we could manage to get we spent on Isabel and her needs. After a month of bed rest, she grew stronger, though as you can imagine, she is utterly helpless and begged us more than once to just cut her throat and put her out of her misery, but we refused. On those days when Isabel felt better, she began to teach us many things. I must say that in the last year I have learned more useful things from her than I have during my whole childhood. We've decided that she must be some kind of goddess, for there seems to be no limit on what she knows."

"Well, things seemed to get better during the winter. Then, we began to notice that greenish ooze. When we asked her about it, she said it was nothing to worry about. We now know she was lying to us. Even so, had we known just how bad it would get — we have no idea what to do about it. Angelina began to stay by her bedside day and night, instead of our normal routine of taking turns. Someone has to be with her at all times; she can't do anything for herself. We were at our wit's end when you ran into me. That's about it. Right Angelina? Did I leave anything important out?"

"No, but she just has to live! After all she has been through, she just has to make it!" sobbed Angelina.

I've never been as humbled by a story as I was theirs. I think we all were, for no one said a word for a minute. Finally, Simon spoke softly and sincerely, "Words cannot express our gratitude for all that you have sacrificed and done for our Isabel. We can never ever thank you enough. You are both goddesses of mercy in our eyes. I can tell you that your sacrifice, all your care for her, has not been in vain. No, quite the contrary. From your small act of compassion has caused a tremendous change for all women in the entire Lands of the Sea Princes! Let me tell you what has come about from your actions. It is pretty unbelievable."

Slowly, he related what the Centurion reaction had been on the disappearance of Isabel's body and the rumors circulating that Tur himself came upon the battlefield that night, stole her away, healed her, and made her his personal bodyguard. "The actions of the Sisterhood that day with the help of Isabel and Sandra along with your actions that night broke the center post of a long house. Slowly but surely, the rest of the building sagged, gave way, and fell into rubble." He explained what happened in the neighboring cities that were attacked and conquered, finally getting to the latest sudden rise to prominence and authority of the Sisterhood in Pieta. They, of course, found it hard to believe and asked him to repeat it several times. Then, they asked what happened to Simone who had brokered the deal. Both women laughed when he said meekly, "You are looking at him, er her." He explained that he had the power of persuasion and that people often see only what they want to see, not what actually is there to see.

At last, Flo spoke up. "You two are welcome to come with us eventually back to Pieta. There you will be given the highest honors we can possibly bestow on anyone. I personally guarantee you both all the help you need to get your lives going again." She looked at Simon and asked, "What will you do with Isabel? Can you get her back to the Greenway?" Both Alicia and Angelina looked crestfallen at the prospect of losing her.

"If she lives, it's her call. She has made terrific sacrifices. We'll help her in any way we can, but right now, the main thing is to keep her presence here a secret and to heal her infection if it can be," he replied solemnly. "I sure hope it can be healed. Sarah Jane is the best healer we have." His voice trailed off into his own personal thoughts. We sat in silence for a minute.

Leonia broke the silence, quite unexpectedly. "I lost my hand a while back and I thought my life had ended. I was a hopeless cripple who couldn't do anything for herself. I wanted to die. Then Thallia here, who has lost her tongue, came into my life, and she has shown me that I still can do most everything, just differently. I recovered from my depression, thanks to her. Isabel has lost both hands. Even if she recovers from her infection and her body regains its strength, she can't ever do anything for herself. How can she ever recover in her own mind? She can't even pick up a knife to cut her own throat to end it. I can see why she let the infection fester; it was the only way she had left to her to end her suffering and misery. How then can you heal her mind?"

We all sat in utter silence. We all knew that she was right. It was depressing. Sarah Jane, ever the optimist, spoke up, "Well, first things first, you know. We have to heal her body first. Then, we can tackle the next problem." We nodded but still felt miserable. "Come on; we had better get some of us back to the inn so we don't draw undue attention to this house. Raphael and I will stay the night." Cherie also volunteered to stay in case a warrior was needed. The rest of our somber group headed back to the inn.

From the quiet of her room, Sandy contacted Alabaster and relayed all of the news. She reported she sensed that he was crying as she relayed the grim details. He told her to keep him informed and that he would see if there was anything that he could do. If she ever regained consciousness, he asked Sandy to let him view through her eyes and mind. Sandy knew Alabaster wanted at least one chance to talk directly to Isabel.

Roy and Simon kept me company in my room. That I was upset was an understatement. "These Centurions are the most vile, evil men I've ever heard of — they make the evil bastards of the Sea Princes look godlike. I wish I could slay every one of them! They are evil incarnate!"

"Whoa, Bethany. I too feel outrage and anger, but let's watch our terms here. Evil is not the right word, for really, we know there's no such thing as good and evil. Both are agreed upon actions of conduct between men. What one people consider evil may be considered good in another people. From the Centurion's point of view, defiling Isabel as they did may be considered a good action if it prevents other women, other Sisters, from fighting back against them. This way, they may have prevented untold thousands of deaths. So one example versus thousands would make this a good action to take."

"You're saying that it is perfectly okay for them to defile Isabel — that is good?" I protested, knowing he was right, though.

"The life of one versus the lives of thousands? Yes, I can see their reasoning, but that doesn't mean I condone it or support it, mind you. I think what they did to her is an atrocity of immense magnitude. Look, rather, at what it has actually brought about: a change in the treatment of all women in this entire land. I'm sure the invaders didn't have that in mind when they martyred Isabel! Yet, it did happen as a direct result of it. The real truth is that men can do actions that benefit more people than those actions harm or they can do or fail to do what is needed, which in turn harms more broadly than it helps."

"Take our own personal case at hand. We're here to try to find any weaknesses we can exploit to defeat these invaders. Back home, this would be considered an action that helps the Greenway. Should these invaders get wise to our true purposes here, they would consider that treasonous at best, posing a threat to their survival or chances of success. It is just a matter of viewpoint. That's all I'm saying. It's not good versus evil, but rather survival actions versus contra-survival actions."

I heard his words, knew he was right. The inequity, the injustice, the inhumanity, the bestiality, okay, the contra-survival nature of this atrocity allowed me to understand something I had been wrestling with since that day I nearly went insane. In a flash, I understood now the passion of Erline Herbiscus, our renegade druwid — why she felt and acted as she did. Even though I had never met her, I knew her mind, and it scared me. I sobbed quietly in Roy's arms. He helped me into bed, and I was grateful for both his compassion and understanding on this of all nights. I knew for me, there was just the finest of lines separating me from Erline. Had I been on that battlefield instead of Isabel, I know I would have easily overstepped that line, gone into an insane rage, killing every single living man anywhere for miles around; even after they had slain my body, my rage would have killed and killed and killed until there were no more men left to slay. I know I have that power, and it scares me deeply. What I mean is, if I had been there, lost it, and done just that, then the thousands upon thousands of women in the Sea Princes would still be being treated as objects little better than dogs. Even if I had the foresight to know the outcome, I wondered if I could have controlled my rage. I fell asleep reliving the frightening memories of that night so long ago when we were attacked and I thought that Ellen had been killed.

Next morning, I still felt rather in the dumps. Over breakfast at the inn, Roy asked, "Simon, I still don't get it. You mean there is no such thing as good and evil — that these are just labels men make up for their own motivations or for controlling others? It would seem that just about everyone knows what is good and what is evil."

Simon, who always loves a good political discussion, grew animated, "Yes, you have hit upon the crux of the matter. What you and I deem good and evil, say here in the Land of the Sea Princes, is altogether a different thing than what the Princes' deem to be good and evil. You will never get two people to agree completely on these two terms, because they are *relative* to one's point of view. However, in contrast to this, we know there are Seven Aspects of Life. If an action helps broadly across all seven of these, such as helping the family, the group, the animal kingdom, spirits, then it is undeniably a correct action, a right action. However, if that action harms more broadly than it helps, it is a wrong action to take. On this basis alone can one make intelligent decisions."

He was on a lecture roll, "With most people, the words good and evil have also a gut emotional reaction. All the Prince has to do to get men to fight for him is to convince them that the Centurions are totally evil, and men will flock to his army. The High Priest convinces his flock that the Church of Tur is good, and then no one doubts his decisions. A shopkeeper convinces you it is good for you to buy something, so you buy it. Someone has convinced the Centurions that the people of the Sea Princes are barbarians and evil, hence it is perfectly acceptable to slaughter the barbarians; after all, they are evil. No, people use good and evil to justify their actions, particularly if their actions have caused more harm than good to the Seven Aspects of Life."

"Well that is something to ponder," Roy commented. "I wonder if that distinction will be made by Isabel who has been terribly wronged by these invaders?" In my heart, I sincerely doubted that it would.

After eating, we wandered over to Alicia's to see how Isabel was doing. We knew Sarah Jane would send word if her condition changed drastically, for good or ill. We found them cleaning and fixing up their home. Raphael had already done a bit of carpentry. The front door was now operational, and he was working on the windows when we approached. "No change," he filled us in.

Indeed, no significant change occurred for two more days. Then, finally, Isabel awoke somewhat stronger than before we came, but she was still very weak. Sarah Jane related her first conversation with Isabel. "She awoke and I told her who I was and that a whole Circle was here. She moaned and begged me to let her die. I told her no way and forced her to eat some healthy broth with chicken bits in it. Once she had eaten, she fell asleep once more. Now this is a very good sign she might just recover!"

For the rest of the day, we camped out here waiting for her to wake up and hoping for a brief bit of conversation. Late that afternoon, she awoke, and before Sarah Jane would let us into the room, she covered her with a light sheet. Meanwhile, Sandy contacted Alabaster who began viewing through Sandy. Sarah Jane introduced us, "You are looking at the Lightning Circle." She introduced each of us by name and title as befitting another druwid.

"Please," she apathetically moaned in a very feeble voice, "please give me the Passing Ceremony, put the body out of its misery, and help me find my way home so I can get a new body. I'm totally lost and know I can't find Greenway anymore; I'm so disoriented. Please, I beg of you, do this for me." Giant tears dripped down the faces of Alicia and Angelina, who just knew we would help her die, and they would lose her, whom they had so devoted their lives to help live.

Sandy's voice took on a deeper tone. Alabaster spoke through her. "My dearest Isabel, Sandy has kindly loaned me her body. Alabaster is here with you now. I'm so deeply sorry that you had to go through all this torture on my account. I guarantee you we shall not let you down ever again. Please answer me this one question: why didn't you contact me? I tried so many times to reach you, but our minds couldn't connect. I feared you were dead or worse."

From the sheepish look on her face, the slight hesitancy in her feeble voice, I knew what she was about to say. "I'm sorry Alabaster. I disobeyed your direct orders not to get involved here. I just couldn't face you like this. It's my fault Sandra is dead. If I had not forced her to come to their aid. . ."

"No, Isabel, there is no fault on your part. It was very silly of me to order you not to get involved. How could you stand by and watch your new friends get slaughtered without attempting to help them? No, it was my mistake, not yours. If I had been in your boots, I would have done just as you have done, Isabel."

"Really?" she asked in disbelief. Alabaster would have done what I did? This she could scarcely believe. He had to repeat it several times before it sunk into her mind — that he wasn't just saying the words, that he truly meant it. Small tears glazed over her eyes when she finally understood.

She then whispered, "Alabaster, please tell them to give me the Passing Ceremony and to go ahead and put this body out of its misery and guide me home, please Alabaster. I cannot live like this; I'm so useless to myself and everyone around me. I'm now nothing but a horrible burden to everyone. Please, Alabaster?"

We held our breath; certainly, he would grant her wishes and let her body pass quietly away. "If your illness cannot be cured, yes, they may speed you on your way. However, it would appear to my eyes that you may in fact be recovering. In that case, I offer this bit of wisdom, Isabel. One, don't be so hasty to take life if you yourself can't create new life. Two, let the Lightning

Circle tell you just what your sacrifice has caused, for you may think better of your actions after that. Three, the Centurions are certainly going to get to the Greenway, and then I'll need every druwid who can bring down lightning to fight them off. As you know, it doesn't take any hands to bring down fire and lightning. Instead, I offer you a second chance to meet these Centurions on the field of battle. After you hear from the Lightning Circle, ponder just what the significance of your reappearing upon the field of battle may do to these Centurions and their morale. I'm nearly spent; forgive me, Isabel, but I'm very old and frail. I must sleep now. I'll touch your mind tomorrow for your decision. Until then, accept my loving kiss." As we watched, the skin on her forehead depressed slightly in the form of a pair of lips gently pressing on her skin. Naturally, I wondered how he managed to do that. Tears drowned out her vision for a silent moment. Then, he was gone from Sandy's mind, and she nearly fell upon Simon who supported her.

As the Wid, I knew what Alabaster desired of me. I began a very lengthy explanation of all that had happened. It took me nearly a half hour to put everything into its proper sequence and order of magnitude. "You see, Isabel, your action that day was like a falling of the first domino. Like a wind, it has swept across all the Sea Princes bringing larger and larger changes as it grows. You and the Sisters of Zargarb have finally brought a tremendous positive change in attitude and treatment of women to this entire land! That is one tremendous achievement. I personally bow to you." And I did; we all did, out of tremendous respect for what this woman had achieved by her actions.

Hearing all of this and verified by Flo, her mind relaxed, content in that it hadn't been utterly in vain and fruitless. "Nonetheless, it does nothing for me now. I'm a totally useless shell that must be tended to night and day. I'm so completely helpless. It's so utterly demeaning, so humiliating, so degrading, so horrible," and she began to cry once more.

However, I wasn't finished. I knew if I left it here, she would feel satisfied that her sacrifice wasn't worthless and could now pass away with respect. No, I had to do more. "I'm not done yet, Isabel. Thallia here, she lost her tongue. Besides not being able to speak anymore, she can barely eat. Yet, she has overcome her handicap and even found someone who loves her as she is."

Thallia crept forward. Never before in front of so many people had she tried to speak, but she knew she had to for Isabel's sake. "That's true," she uttered several times trying to make it as clear as she could. She reached out and held onto Isabel's right arm comfortingly.

I continued, "Here is Leonia who lost but one hand. She felt much as you do now too, but she has discovered she's not really helpless either. She just has to do many things slightly differently, that's all. Yes, there are some things that are almost impossible to do with only one hand, but she has her caring friends to help her, and she, in turn, has helped them so that it isn't humiliating or degrading. Yes, if all you get is help from others and cannot give back anything, and then degradation can occur."

"But I have no hands," she sobbed. "I can't even go to the bathroom or feed myself or even get a drink of water. I cannot do anything. I'm completely, utterly, and totally useless to myself and to everyone else about me. I do not and will not be such a burden on other people. I can't live with myself if I do that. I just can't. Don't you understand that?" she pleaded. I saw she was tiring fast and decided to hurry this up a bit.

"Now you're lying or deceiving yourself. Have you forgotten the first lesson we're taught? To observe? You need no hands to bring down fire and lightning upon the enemy, destroying their chariots of death. How many people do you know in Zargarb who can do that besides you? You can give back something that they attribute to a god, not mortal man. And if that isn't enough, then I ask you to look at Alicia and Angelina, who have so long looked after you. Ask them if you haven't given back to them something that they consider so far more important than just helping you eat and pee. Go ahead; ask them right now. Do it!" I was so insistent that she couldn't help but look their way and see them standing behind us, trying to be invisible while in the company of this group of giant beings. "Go ahead, Angelina, tell her what you told me."

In a faltering voice, Angelina said, "It's true, Isabel. During this past year we've looked after you, you have taught us so many things, so much knowledge — it's more than I ever learned in all my childhood. I know you probably don't think that Alicia and I are worth teaching; we aren't like you from the Greenway, but what you have been doing for us we think is more precious than all the gold coins in the Prince's treasury. You must believe us."

Alicia echoed her friend's words. "Please don't die on us. We need you; we love you; we respect you; we want to be with you," Alicia added. "Please don't go away. Take us with you."

I watched something snap in Isabel's mind. After feeling only grief and sorrow for herself all this time, I'd forced her to observe what was around her. And she saw. Nothing could ever remove what she now saw so clearly. She could wallow in self-pity, but in her mind, she knew that was a lie. It's very hard to live with a lie of this magnitude, pretending it's the truth when you know that it isn't.

She looked at the two young women, tears streaming down all three faces. Isabel gestured them to come to her. As they bent close over her bed, Isabel reached up with her arms and hugged them both, the first time she had used her handless arms to touch and embrace another person. They hugged her back, and we stepped quietly out of the room. As my mind raced over everything I had said looking for any idea left untouched that might help persuade Isabel, I spied Roy's face. It was wet with his own tears, and when he saw me looking at him, he gave me a loving hug, whispering in my ear, "I love you, Bethany. Thank you."

Then, I noticed that there wasn't a dry eye in the entire Circle or among the Sisters. Thallia took my hand and said, "Thank you." Garbled as it was, her intention was clear. I hugged her back. I knew I had earned my "Wid-hood" this day.

None of us knew whether or not her body would recover or if it did, if she would desire to continue to live. Only time would tell. Shortly the two women came out, saying that she was asleep once more. I knew we'd really tired Isabel out, but it had to be done; now it was in her hands. Okay, her arms. Silly expression anyway.

During supper, we discussed what our next actions should be. Flo needed to get on with her task of getting us to Zargarb so she could devote her full attention on locating any other remaining Sisters. We needed to get to the city to retrieve the shipment of herbs that Alabaster had sent for us. Yet, we needed to be here helping Isabel with her recovery. Sandy pointed out that Sarah Jane had to stay here and that both Sandy and I, the two best telepaths, couldn't go to Zargarb. If anything bad happened, one of us had to act as the communicator for the rest of the Circle. Sarah Jane pointed out that if Isabel still wanted us to perform her Passing Ceremony and guide her as a being without a body safely back to the Greenway, that task belonged to a Wid, me in other words. That was my responsibility. I had to stay here. Raphael wouldn't be parted from Sarah Jane, insisting that he stay behind as well. From the forlorn look in Roy's eyes, I knew that he, too, wanted to stay with me, but he also knew his duty lay in protecting the Circle. There was nothing that we needed protecting from here in Junction, but huge unknowns lay on the journey to and from Zargarb. He knew he had to go.

They decided to leave first thing in the morning. The next day, the three of us moved out of the inn and brought our horses here to the house keeping them in a crude corral, which Raphael built. After getting us safely back to the house with our gear and horses, the others said farewell. Roy took me aside and gave me one powerful kiss, I felt tingles of energy all throughout my body; my knees nearly gave way from a sudden unexplained weakness. Then they mounted up and rode off, with all of us waving farewell. I felt an emptiness rising inside as I watched them ride off out of sight. Until now, we had not been parted since we began our advanced training so many years ago.

"That was some kiss," Sarah Jane teased me, bringing me back to the present. "He loves you, you know. I can tell when a man really loves a woman, and boy does he ever. In fact, I think that he idolizes you." My face felt suddenly very hot and crimson.

My voice seemed high and squeaky, "I know. I love him too. Does love do this to you? I mean, I almost fainted there. I can hardly stand even now. I feel so lost." Was that really my voice speaking just now I wondered?

She only teased me further, "Our pretend marriages might not be so pretended after all." Suddenly I wondered if she felt this way about Raphael and he, her, but I did not ask. Duty called; Isabel was awake and asking for me.

I found the two women tending Isabel; some pillows propped her up, the first time she had sat up in months. When I entered the room, she angrily said, "Damn you Bethany, you won't let me die, will you? What does a druwid have to do to finally be killed around here? Even the damn Centurions wouldn't do the deed!" In spite of her anger, both Alicia and Angelina were smiling; their beloved Isabel was alive and recovering.

I replied using a little antagonism, "Oh it's Alabaster's fault. You see, he wants to use you when the Centurions invade the Greenway. He wants you to rise from the dead, scare the heck out of them, and send them running all the way back to Megalos. He just wants to keep on using you, that's all." I said it trying to keep a serious tone, but she broke into a laugh, her first laugh in over a year.

After a couple minutes, I said in a quieter tone, "The real question is what are we going to do with you?"

"Yes, what are you going to do with a handless old maid who always orders you about?" It felt good for her to tease another in a friendly manner. She had forgotten when she last jested lightheartedly; it had been so long ago, longer than even her stay in the Sea Princes.

"Well, you can't stay in the Lands of the Sea Princes, that's for sure. Soon the whole country will be under the control of the Centurions. If they ever get wind you are alive and here, I'm sure they'll spare no expense to hunt you down like a rabid dog. You can't come with us. Our journey is likely to take us much further south into the lion's mouth, so you can't come with us for the same reason. It looks like your only option to go back home and pester Alabaster."

Her voice grew serious for a moment, "I wondered what you were really doing down here. I didn't think it was just to find me."

"No, you are, were, just one small item in our lengthy assignment. We had to come here anyway to get re-supplied with healing herbs and stuff. We used our entire supply helping wounded Sisters and other women."

"Well, I'm not going home without taking my two assistants with me," she said defiantly, looking at Angelina and Alicia, who were terrified that Isabel would soon be leaving them.

"Of course, I wouldn't dream of separating you from your two assistants. That is, unless they don't want to leave this land and go live in the Greenway with you," I added.

"You mean you'll let us come along with you — all the way to your homeland?" asked Alicia in complete disbelief, yet full of an intense longing to go with Isabel.

"Yes, you've both more than earned safe passage to a better life. If you want to come with Isabel, we would dearly love to have you. If you want to stay here, I'll understand that too, but I'll likely try to persuade you to come anyway," I teased them.

"Where Isabel goes, we go," triumphantly declared Angelina.

"Then that's terrific; I won't have to try to persuade you, will I?" and we laughed. It was so good to hear Isabel laugh.

"But how will we ever pay for our passage there?" asked Alicia, ever the practical one of the pair.

"Dear Sisters, you have already earned your passage, earned your right to be with Isabel wherever she may go. Indeed, in our small group of druwids, you two will be highly honored and revered for what you have done. You shall never want for the necessities of everyday survival ever again. You may even find some of the young men in the Greenway to your fancy. You'll find our men love and treasure women, for you are their equals in life. It is quite different from anything you have ever seen before. In my opinion, it's the way it should be. First, we have to get you some traveling clothes, preferably leather-made so they are durable to last the long journey. I suspect you can't buy them around here." They explained that leather was available and Angelina was an excellent seamstress, but that they had long ago sold all her stuff to buy food. Naturally, that very afternoon, I took them shopping. We returned laden with piles of leather and sewing equipment. Angelina was back in business.

During the quiet times, the three of us, Sarah Jane, Raphael and I, discussed how best to get Isabel safely back to the Greenway, handicapped as she was, without alerting the Centurions of her presence. I suggested the safest path would be to head up to the Paese di Dio, travel its length to perhaps Velona, and then by boat to Calgary. Sarah Jane pointed out there might very well be other Sisters who might also desire to move to the Greenway along with Isabel. Along the way, the party might grow in size. One thing, however, was obvious; one of us would have to go with them all the way to Calgary. Our Circle would be broken; there wasn't much chance that whoever went would be able to rejoin us. Who should go? This we discussed for days. One of us had to go with them to continue the lengthy healing of Isabel.

In the end, I knew that this decision would rest upon my head as Wid, for good or ill; the others trusted me. I had to make the call. After pondering for several days, I decided that Thomas would be entrusted to get Isabel safely back to Calgary. Any of us could likely handle the follow up healing care, so that factor didn't enter my decision. Of all of us, our Loremaster felt the most out of place, the most disoriented so far from his beloved grass-forest lands he knew so well. We were about to head into even more unknown lands; his lost feelings might grow even worse. If he went, I knew Thallia would follow and likely Leonia. Both women deserved the opportunity for a better life, even if it were only for a few years before the Centurions attacked the Greenway. Further, as Loremaster, should they be forced to detour because of bandits or Centurions, he best could chart a new route home. He could fight when needed, where as we girls were not much good at combat. Further, picking any of the other guys in our Circle would break up our disguise of being "married couples." So far the deception had worked in our favor. I just hoped that Thomas would not be terribly upset with my decision.

Once the weight of reaching that decision lifted, I relaxed and enjoyed the next few weeks learning something new. Alicia who spoke fluent Arad gave us three a crash course in the language spoken in Juda Arad. It felt good to have nothing to do but learn new things once again, though ever in the back of my mind, strange, fabricated, ghostly images of the looming unknowns, which would come our way very shortly poked their way into my conscious thoughts, casting doubts about our preparations, our skills, and our supplies.

Raphael hated to be idle. He continued repairing the house, though he knew that shortly we would abandon it. Though you might think this was a waste of time, Raphael experimented with a number of construction techniques he had observed during our time here in the Sea Princes. He said there was a great similarity of technique between laying of adobe bricks and those of stone. Raphael intended to become a great designer of magnificent stone buildings; what better way than to experiment here on a run-down home that would likely be torn down and replaced fairly soon anyway? When he finished some two weeks later, the home boasted a domed and arched roofed entryway, reminiscent of the great stone churches of Tur. He had mastered a technique he called the keystone that allowed him to create curved ceilings. Sarah Jane and I were impressed, particularly because the whole thing didn't fall down on his head. Actually, it was quite solid; he climbed onto the domed roof and jumped up and down on it to prove its structural soundness.

Daily, Isabel regained her strength, much to the happiness of her two close friends. I suspect knowing she was going home to the Greenway helped motivate her. Alicia and Angelina, when they were not doting on Isabel, lent a hand. Alicia taught us a much of the Arad language as we could master in the time we had. Angelina turned the leather hides into much needed sets of clothing for themselves and Isabel. However, she displayed an immense creative ability as well as skill on Isabel's new clothes. First, the top was designed as a pull over so that in a pinch, Isabel could wiggle into it without the use of hands. The pants were loose fitting about the waist and had two straps that went up over her shoulders. Without much trouble, Isabel could, using her stubs, slide the straps off, which would lower her pants with ease. If she had to go to the bathroom, she could at least mange this. Getting them back up and on was more of a challenge and awkward, but it was doable. All this was assuming that she wore no undergarments.

When Angelina finished them and had Isabel try them on, explaining how the two halves worked together to grant her some freedom, Isabel just had to see if she could manage it. After being unable to go to the bathroom without the assistance of another for over a year now, the incredible joy, the satisfaction, and the regained self-worthiness that Isabel showed after successfully going to the bathroom unassisted brought tears to all our eyes, to say nothing of the mountains of praise upon Angelina's handiwork. Isabel's spirits soared after that day.

On the fifteenth day since the others left for Zargarb, they returned. Raphael, who was outside experimenting on the house, called out, "Riders are coming. I think they are back. Yes, it's them." We rushed outside to greet them. Of course, their coming didn't surprise me, for Sandy had stayed in daily touch with me, mentally. The first thing I noticed was that they returned with more riders than with which they left! Flo had picked up four Sisters who survived the great battle because they could not get there in time. It was hard to say who was happier finding the other. The four were ecstatic that the

Sisterhood had not been destroyed, and Flo was quite pleased that she had found these remnants of the Zargarb Sisterhood; it was a good start.

Roy's comment echoed the others as he dismounted and spied the ornate, fancy domed entryway. "What had *you* been up to, Raphael? Building a church?"

"Ah you noticed! Good man, no, just tinkering waiting for you to get back. Been fairly dull here," Raphael replied. "Good to see you too."

Flo came up to me and said, "Mission accomplished. How's Isabel?" It was obvious to me that her welfare had been on Flo's mind the whole time.

"Doing better than expected. Looks like you added some more to your ranks," I replied with a smile, nodding toward the four Sisters who stood shyly at the back of the group. Introductions were made all around. One of the new Sisters was missing several fingers on both hands. She was jokingly introduced as Miss Three Fingers, Felicia. She was a proud woman who had a good sense of humor. She had started everyone calling her Miss Three Fingers. I later learned that her husband had cut them off merely because she had smiled at other men. When she had recovered physically and he then threatened to cut out her tongue, she removed his head while he was sleeping and then fled to join the Sisterhood. Another Sister, Jolline, was missing her left eye; a leather patch covered it. Her drunken husband tried to shoot an apple off her head with a crossbow, and had obviously missed. Jolline was lucky even to be alive. She left him and took her daughter with her to the Sisterhood. One night, he broke in and killed their daughter; the Sisters killed him before he got to her. The other two, Jamia and Illia, appeared normal; their scars were mental, I assumed. I was reminded once again, that for a woman to be in the Sisterhood meant she had faced significant abuse from men — scary, pathetic, disgusting and revolting.

Once we were all introduced, Sarah Jane permitted the others, but only two at a time, to visit with Isabel, while the rest of us exchanged tales. Our tale was pretty uneventful, and I finished bringing them up-to-date in about four minutes. Their tale lasted an hour, but was relatively uneventful as well.

The biggest event turned out to be a non-event. About twenty miles from the Junction, a group of twenty-five bandits attempted to rob them. However, as soon as they closed to five hundred feet and saw this was a band of Sisters, they hastily turned around and galloped off into the distance, wanting no part of any action with them. When they got to Zargarb, it was a different story altogether. Here Simon took over, pointing out that if they appeared to be a Sisterhood party, the Centurions might conclude their arrival as a serious threat. The guys used their illusion skills to make the entire party appear as men, with Sandy taking directions mentally from the Sisters and relaying them mentally to Simon, who appeared to be their leader. Of course, the women thought this was hilarious. Everywhere they went in the city, they were accepted as men even though they looked not the part. It was as Simon suggested; people see what they desire to see, not what actually is.

Our supplies were waiting at a storage facility at the docks. There was no trouble getting them. We now had seven large sacks brimming with healing herbs, salves, needles, thread, and bandages. In fact, we now had somewhat more supplies than when we left home.

Because of the unsafe nature of being in the city, they didn't stay there overnight. Indeed, the city was still a shambles, a ghost of its former glory, according to Louisa, who had been there many times before. They learned the Governor ruled with an iron hand, and no one was entirely cooperating. While they were at the docks getting our supplies, they watched some men unloading a ship, which carried cargo from Megalos. Several men bumped into each other, lost their footing, and dropped their boxes conveniently into the water, ruining the foodstuffs they contained. "Accidents" such as this was a daily occurrence that the Governor faced. We could now see just how significant the deal that Simon had made in Pieta actually was. Indeed, Governor Lexus would become famous and gain significant political influence back home.

Their return trip was delayed in two outlying towns. Pairs of the newly found Sisters were hiding out in them. Though they saw Flo's party passing through the towns, they didn't believe their eyes. On their return trip, seeing that Flo was still alive after going into the city, they stopped Flo and introduced themselves. Flo convinced them to come along with her and help rebuild the Sisterhood by returning to Pieta and learning all they could before re-establishing their presence in this sector.

When it came time for dinner, we decided to eat outdoors, mostly because there wasn't enough room inside for all of us, even if we sat on the floor. To everyone's surprise, Isabel walked out of the house to join us, braving it at last, and showing her utter dependence on others to the world. She would have to be fed as if she were a baby, utterly humiliating, and degrading. She knew she had to face it, and it was better to do it among her close friends than total strangers.

Miss Three Fingers shrieked and dropped her plate of food on the ground as she saw Isabel appear. "My god! It's you! You're alive! You're not Tur's bodyguard!" Her three companions had similar exclamations of surprise — shock and joy at seeing the woman they knew as Sister Betellini. All four grabbed her and hugged her tightly, crying and speaking at once, which was mostly unintelligible.

After the joyous reunion subsided and everyone resumed their places, Isabel explained in a quiet voice, "No, I'm not dead yet, though I came perilously close on several occasions. No, Sisters Angelina and Alicia rescued me in the dead of night from the battlefield and secreted me away. At great expense to themselves, they had kept me alive and in hiding ever since then. Now, it was Alicia and Angelina who became the objects of adoration from their fellow Sisters who heaped mountains of praise and thanks upon them until both turned quite red, embarrassed by all this unexpected attention. I knew in the days to come that these two women would go down in the local history for what they had accomplished, for what they had done.

However, I felt it was my obligation to fill these four newcomers in on the actual situation. No word of Isabel's existence must be revealed or her life would be likely forfeited, as the Centurions would spare no expense to hunt her down like an animal. No it was far better to let the rumor of her now being elevated to Tur's personal bodyguard. Wisely all four agreed completely, once they understood the bigger picture. Still they insisted on sitting near their Sister Betellini and even awkwardly helping to feed her, trying not to show their uneasiness and unfamiliarity around a person with no hands. Actually, I think if the truth were known, none save Alicia and Angelina, were comfortable. However, Isabel chatted with the Sisters, asking about how they had gotten along this past year.

When the after-dinner tea was served, Flo took command once more. "I'll be blunt. I think all of us should leave here tonight. I don't feel entirely safe; we could have been followed or spotted. Certainly, such a large group of Sisters meeting here in the Junction can't have gone unnoticed. It is imperative we get Isabel to a place of safety."

"It's going to rain," added Isabel, taking us all by surprise. "Yes, I've studied the weather patterns around here. True, when rain comes to the Junction, it's not very much, but it may help hide our tracks. I believe I can sit on a horse for a while." I noticed she didn't say "ride," because with no hands she could probably only sit. Then I wondered: does necessity causes one to be creative?

Now it was my turn, "Okay, I agree with Flo. One from my Circle must go with Isabel. We intend to take her back to the Greenway until it is safe for her to return. Considering her situation and recovering illness, there can only be one safe route, and that is to cross the Sea Princes via the high country, the Paese di Dio, which is largely uninhabited. Whether it's safe to take a boat to Calgary from Velona or whether they should go overland I leave up to them, when they get that far. One of us must go with her to tend to her continuing recovery."

"I volunteer," Thomas interrupted me cheerfully. "Who best to lead a party across the wilderness than a Loremaster? I'll get her safely home and then somehow rejoin you much later on." I wondered if he read my mind. Did he already know I'd chosen him? Or was the choice this obvious to all in my Circle? Had I worried myself for three days over nothing?

"Thank you Thomas. You were my choice. Of course, Thallia should go with you, if the Sisterhood agrees and Leonia too, if she so desires, and Alicia and Angelina naturally. We have often told the Sisters that any who want to immigrate to the Greenway are more than welcome. I think this would be an excellent opportunity for those who wish to do so. Thus, as you go across the high country, you may find others joining you." The Sisters hollered "Yes!" for they were more than willing to go. Indeed, Thallia had an awful look on her face when Thomas volunteered to go. I knew there could be no parting them; she'd go even if she had to do it in secret.

"I guess I'm the official voice of the Sisterhood here," Flo looked around at her friends. "I give my permission for all those who want to go with Thomas and Isabel to go with our fondest blessings. Bethany, your plan to go via the Paese di Dio is a perfect one! In fact, you can angle north by northwest from here and bypass all the inhabited Zargarb sector and make the high country in perhaps less than a hundred miles. I'm sending Laura with you until you reach the high country. Once there, she is to ride swiftly on ahead to Pieta and let Rosita know the news. I'm sure she'll in turn let Jan know and so on back to Velona. The Sisters there can meet you up on the Paese di Dio, and let you know whether or not they feel it's safe enough for you to ride into town and board a ship for Calgary."

She continued, "As for me and the rest of us, we are going to now begin the methodical search for other Sisters who may be in hiding. We will ride back towards Zargarb and then begin the east-west spiral search pattern, hitting all the outlying towns and villages. May I ask where you are your people are heading?"

"Juda Arad," I answered. "Our quest is to find out more about these invaders and what and how they treat their conquered lands. Thus, it is east for us. We've picked up a bit of the local dialect so I hope we can get by acceptably."

Worried looks appeared on Flo's and several other faces. She said, "I fear for your safety. None of us has traveled into that semi-desert land. I can't offer you any guidance. Please be extra careful; you have become dear to me and many others. We owe you such a debt for all that you have done. I guess I can say we all look forward to your return." She gave me a big hug and I returned it.

The next half hour saw people hustling about making preparations. All the supplies Thomas' group would need to see them at least to Pieta had to be loaded onto two packhorses. We in turn had to load up one packhorse with all our supplies as well. Flo's group had little to do, save run into the town and pick up some extra rations for their journey. The yard outside looked like organized chaos with three sets of horses in three locations being visited by men and women hurriedly moving sacks to and fro. Since it was approaching mid-summer, the sun wouldn't set for another three hours. We hoped to be on the trail with two hours of light left, as the sky grew steadily darker with storm clouds moving in from the coast.

One interesting side note: as Isabel approached the horse she'd been given to ride, Leonia came up to her and said, "No, not this one, Isabel. Here, you are to take my horse. I have him well trained to follow directions by the way you lean in the saddle. You almost don't need reins with him. Here, I'm tying the reins into a knot. Now you can stick your arm through here and hold it in the crook of your elbow, like this." She inserted her left arm stub through the loop and bending her arm, secured it. "You can then neck rein him fairly easily, except for very tight turns. That's the only problem I've been having, sharp turns."

"Thank you, thank you!" exclaimed Isabel, catching on and realizing that she might not be completely useless after all. "How am I to mount with no hands?"

"Oh just put your stubs up here to balance and mount as you normally do. Try it; I'll hold him from moving." Isabel, using her arms mostly for balance, inserted her foot into the stirrup, and using mostly her feet and knees, rose up, swung her other leg over, and proudly sat on her horse, no small accomplishment. "See I told you. Now practice with the reins. If I can do it with my stub, so can you." We all watched as she managed to get the reins loop into her joint at the elbow. It was and looked very awkward, but it worked. Isabel had some control over her horse and with that came self-pride; she was not completely a helpless invalid. Indeed, she was smiling!

I took Thomas aside, "You know where we are headed. By the time you get her back to Calgary, there's not much chance you could catch back up with us. I relieve you of even having to try. Gosh, think of the incredible distance you'd have to come, and besides, you wouldn't even know where we are for that matter. You keep the home fort protected and take good care of Thallia; she loves you very much."

"I know, I will. As I said, I'll try to catch back up if it is possible and if Alabaster will allow it," he replied and gave me a farewell hug.

Thallia, came up and gave me one too, uttering "Thank you." I returned her hug too. Then, everyone got into the act saying goodbye to all.

Isabel asked me to come over for a private word with her. When I was beside her horse, she leaned down and asked me, "Bethany, how old are you anyway?"

"Golly, I think I had a birthday pass while I've been down here in the Sea Princess. I think I'm now fifteen, why?"

She smiled and answered, "I can see why you are their Wid. I can't imagine you are so wise and yet so young! It's amazing. Usually wisdom comes with age and experience. Fifteen, amazing," she repeated. "Well, I owe you much, Wid Bethany. Good luck on your quest and for heaven's sake don't do anything foolhardy like I did. I wouldn't wish this mess I've undergone on anyone, male or female. So do be careful." I told her I'd be extra cautious, which made her feel better. I had no intention of telling her what all I had already been through, that I had almost become a renegade druwid.

Then, we watched Thomas lead his group almost due north heading for the high country by the most direct route. Thallia and Leonia rode point with Alicia and Angelina on either side of Isabel. Louisa and Laura brought up the rear leading their packhorses. My eyes watered more than a little to see them go; our Circle was broken. I didn't expect to see Thomas again until we returned from our lengthy quest, if we ever returned. A quick glance at my friends told me they shared similar thoughts.

We mounted up as did Flo's small party. Waving a last farewell, our two groups rode in opposite directions. Flo headed southward, while we rode around the northern edge of town before striking out nearly due east into the lands called Juda Arad. An hour later, a gentle rain began falling and continued the rest of the night, completely washing out the tracks we left in the sandy soil. Thus, if anyone was spying on us, they might not know that we had split up into three groups nor which way we went.

Chapter 17 The Lands of Juda Arad

The end of autumn of 559 AH was rapidly approaching; we'd been on the trail for nearly a week now, heading due east following a well-marked track hoping it led to a larger town or perhaps city. The intense heat and shortage of water had now become pronounced. Juda Arad was a strange land, hot and dry, though not quite a desert, although there was sand enough in some valleys. Soft reddish-brown sedimentary rock formed the geological backbone of hills with steep cliffs and wide valleys between them. Generally, the cliffs rose a hundred feet to the top of the hill, which itself was relatively flat. Sandy described the terrain best by liking it to a chocolate cake in which the hand of God came down and gouged out great sections here and there, like a holey cheese. Yes, it was spectacular to view, but incredibly hot and dry. Sparse grasses grew in the more sheltered areas. We rapidly discovered that a traveler had either to bring a large supply of water with them or know the local watering holes. We, unfortunately, did neither, hence our growing concern, bordering on panic after only a couple days. This is why we hired a local guide in the first inhabitation we encountered, a small hamlet of an extended family.

Our guide, Ahmid el'Zeil, a young man about our age, who had a wife and small baby, agreed to guide us to Jerilum, a large town about a hundred miles further east. When we offered him a couple gold coins for his services, all his resistance to doing it evaporated. He kept saying that you had to know the water holes along the way and that these were not spaced uniformly along the route. Some days we only made ten miles, while others, nearly twenty. We couldn't afford to outdistance our source of water, for the horses drank considerably each day, even though we never even trotted them. Camels would have worked better, but we had none.

He, like all the inhabitants of Juda Arad, wore loose-fitting robes and a turban like cloth over his head with a cloth that dropped down covering the neck. One could also pull it completely across one's face for additional protection from the scorching sun. As we rode along, we chatted with our guide about life here in this land, practicing our new language skills and increasing our vocabulary. These people grew very little of their own crops, depending heavily upon their numerous flocks of sheep for wool, milk, and meat. Indeed, a man's worth was measured by the size of his flock. With the money Ahmid was making from us, he could nearly double his herd, increasing the survival potential for his new family. The land also produced thickly scented oil from a type of tree-like bush that we had never seen. This oil was used to light lanterns and to anoint one's body. Hence, they bargained much oil to neighboring lands. The other major activity was copper and iron working. Further north, rich ore bearing strata lay exposed on the surface. There, miners gathered as well as craftsmen, who forged blades and copper utensils, again, most of which were exported.

With the coming of the Centurions some thirty years ago, they found their overlords keenly interesting in purchasing all the spear points and blades they could forge. Thus, in Arad, one was a shepherd, an oil manufacturer, a miner, a smelterer, a weapons smith, or a copper craftsman. Oh, yes, or a merchant trader or wagoner, who bought, sold, and transported said goods.

We also learned that when the Centurions came, they built a marvelous paved road that led from the southern border with the Southlands all the way up the middle of Juda Arad to the mines and smelters of Amurdin, the largest city in the far north, not too far from the Northern Steppes. Now, some thirty years later, almost all major traffic traveled this road. We would hit this north-south road in Jerilum, which was a major crossroads town. The westward track led to the Sea Princes, which was the track we were following. The eastward track led to several other larger towns cradled up against the tall, impassible mountains, Kathas, beyond which lay the Desert of Despair, a land totally devoid of water.

Jerilum was also a religious center, for these people were highly religious. Each morning when he arose and each night before he lay down to sleep, Ahmid unrolled his woolen prayer mat, sat facing toward Jerilum, and prayed silently for several minutes. When we inquired, he told us he prays to the One God, Jehosa. He explained that Jehosa created the world and everything in it, including all men. Everyone in Juda Arad worshiped only the One God, though the Centurions had brought their worship of Sol or Helios, the Sun God, and had built temples to their god. However, their attempts to convert the Arad people or force them to worship the Sun God failed utterly.

Ahmid told of the Great Desecration some twenty-eight years ago. It seems that the Centurion Governor attempted to force everyone to worship only the Sun God. He forced people off the street and into the new Sun God Temple. He ordered them to pray, at which point, they all sat down on their mats, faced Jerilum, and prayed to Jehosa. In a rage, he threatened them with death if they did not pray to the Sun God. None did. He then tried beheading those that refused. Many lost their lives, but Jehosa is merciful, Ahmid explained. After hundreds were slain with no effect at all, he then tried painful crucifixion upon wooden crosses, leaving them to slowly die, and the carrion birds to eat upon their flesh. Even this had no lasting result. Finally, he sent the able men that refused off to the Salt Mines, there to slave until death came. But Jehosa is merciful, Ahmid explained; even that didn't work, for soon there were too many slaves, and they could only use so much salt. In the end, the Governor gave in and now only beats up those who openly and defiantly refuse to worship his Sun God.

We were amazed at just how vital their religion was to these people. I would never have guessed that it would be this intense. As Ahmid put it, "Jehosa is with us every moment of our life; he makes the air we breathe, the food we eat, the ground we walk upon, our bodies, and all life. We are entirely a part of his creation. It is only fitting we give him our thanks."

Since religion is such a touchy subject, we dropped it and asked about bandits. In the Land of the Seven Sea Princes, banditry was rampant. We wondered if we had to be concerned about being waylaid in Juda Arad. He looked at us with a funny look upon his face, a look that suggested he was not telling the complete truth when he answered, "Oh no. No bandits here in Arad, oh no. Not Jehosa's way. No bandits, only prophets and messiahs." At least that was the literal translation of what he said, we believed. Since our language skills were wonting in this area, we had him explain more fully.

"We have a number of great men who hear the word of the One God in their minds. These Prophets walk the breadth of the Arad spreading His Word broadly among our people. In turn, we give them a little food and water and an occasional robe or pair of sandal when theirs are worn out. They are very great men who hear the Word of our Lord, oh yes." His animated face shone brightly as he described these holy men, the Prophets. Then, that strange look appeared again as he tried to explain the messiahs. His word, which we translated as messiah, actually described something more like a warrior king. "The messiahs will lead us to total freedom. It is said that one day the Great Messiah, who will be the Son of God it is said, shall come among us, and at that time, the Centurions will be driven from our land forever." We were confused over exactly what these messiahs actually were and what this Great Messiah's real purpose would be — that is, spiritual freedom was suggested, yet perhaps also freedom from the Centurion overlords. We found it completely confusing.

After two weeks of travel, we rounded a bend in the valley and saw Jerilum ahead. The town was large, spreading out over a mile covering the entire valley floor. Great mud walls entirely surrounded the town, but four great gates allowed passage into the city, one at each of the four cardinal compass points. As we neared the Western Gate, Ahmid bid us farewell, "I don't go into the town. I leave you here. The road you want goes south from Jerilum. You can't miss it." We sensed there was something more to his unwillingness to enter the city than what he was saying. Instead, we asked him if he could recommend an inn for us to stay. "Most humbly sorry. Do not know. Never been inside the walls. You ask the Gatekeeper; he'll tell you. I go now. Thank you for gold coins, will buy many sheep." He turned his horse around and trotted off back the way we had come — most unusual, since we had not trotted our horses all the while he had led us here.

"I don't like his behavior — more than a bit strange," Simon spoke up. "Be doubly on your guard, everyone. I smell trouble of some kind." None of us knew what to expect; we just felt that something was amiss here. Slowly we walked our horses closer to the Gatehouse. As we neared, other people, some on foot, some pulling wagons, and a few riding as we were, moved in closer to us from both sides, all funneling in toward this one entrance point. The Gatehouse was actually two buildings standing twenty feet apart with the roadway passing between them. About fifteen feet above the roadway as it entered the town, the two buildings were joined by an additional connecting building, giving us the impression that we were entering the side of a box.

Drawing very close, we saw two guards with long halberds standing on either side of the entrance, while a toll collector moved among those wishing to enter collecting coins. He kept saying repeatedly in a monotonous voice, "One copper." Apparently, this was the entrance fee.

As we pulled up, I said that I was paying for the six of us and handed him a gold coin. "You may keep the change, if you can direct us to an inn where we may find food and lodging." I thought that about summed up our desires, hoping the little extra would give us the information we needed.

Carefully, he counted out my change and pocketed that portion into his own money pouch, whisking it away under his robes. "Take Hadid — third street on your right as you enter. Go fifteen blocks — look for Amin's Inn with a picture of a lamb's head on it. Good place. Next: one copper." He didn't even look at me, but went right on with the man carrying a large sack on foot next to me. So we rode on through the gate and dismounted.

We couldn't easily ride inside the city; the streets were thronged with people moving pushcarts or walking or shopping at the many stalls along the street. Young boys ran through the street carrying water urns, yelling "Water, one copper," over and over. Women out shopping wore long robes and sandals with a head scarf hiding their heads protecting them from the sun, I assumed. So crowded were the streets that we had to go single file. Thankfully, Roy, who had overheard the directions, took the lead and I followed. We stayed very close together for fear of beibg inadvertently separated. It was a maze. Obviously, the town had long outgrown its size, but with the outer wall surrounding it, there was no way to expand, so it grew in internal density.

About a half hour later, I was sweating like a pig. This was nerve wracking trying to jostle our way through the throng. We felt we must have been getting close to the inn when we entered into a large market square with a central water well. Occupying the entire eastern side was a large church. On the opposite side, two buildings with bars over the windows could only mean the moneychangers. A line of women with copper urns waited their turn to draw from the well. What really caught our attention was a man standing on the steps of the church speaking loudly to all that would listen. Perhaps twenty stood riveted, enthralled by his words. Naturally, we paused to hear a bit of what was going on here. He was an eloquent speaker; unfortunately, he talked so fast that we had to concentrate on grasping his words; we were ill prepared in the Arad language.

"And God has told me that each of you is an immortal being fit for his holy Kingdom. Do not believe that your mere flesh and its appearance has any value in the eyes of God. Fat or short or ugly or beautiful, it is only an earthly body that will perish in time and turn back into the dust from which God created it. You are not of flesh but of the Holy Spirit. Prepare yourselves to enter his Kingdom. Do not lust after another's mate. Honor thy neighbor and help him. Avoid the deadly sins of greed, avarice, and lust. Throw off the infidel's yoke of oppression, for yea are not of flesh but of the Holy Spirit. I say unto you, do not follow the infidel's pagan worship of the Sun, for the Sun is but one of God's many creations. Worship it not; worship the Supreme Creator as we have done since the beginning of all time. Be worthy to enter God's Kingdom when it is your time, for surely your time shall come. As I stand here talking to you, God has already chosen another of his flock to leave their flesh behind and soar into His Kingdom, eternally free at long last, free of the earthy labors and toils, free of the intoxicating temptations of life. Fear not to join with God. Only those whose sins have buried them are afraid to meet the Supreme Creator, for what would they say, 'Oh Lord, I have forsaken thee for the golden metals, for wine and drunkenness, for lust of a woman?' Nay, now is the time to repent, change your sinning ways, prepare yourself for that day when your fleshly body fails and you go to meet the one Supreme God. Do not follow the sinning ways of the infidels, for you may find your way into the Kingdom of God blocked by your own sins. Be prepared to throw off this yoke of suppression the infidels have placed around our necks, for remember it is said that one day soon the Great Messiah, the son of Jehosa, shall walk our land destroying all of the infidels, showing no mercy. And God has told me that that day draws neigh upon us. When that time comes, do not fail to rise to join the Great Messiah and help destroy all the oppressive infidels."

Suddenly, he was interrupted by a loud bellowing voice coming from the southern section of the square. "Hey you, stop this at once. You are under arrest for disturbing the peace and for preaching sedition against the Centurions. Stop at once and come with us." All eyes turned to see who was speaking. Six Centurions, well-armed and with their familiar metal body armor and huge shields, had come into the square from the south. Five stood in a line in front of their leader who'd issued the ultimatum. Mass pandemonium broke out almost simultaneously with his arrest orders. As they tried to move forward through the crowd to arrest the speaker, people began throwing eggs, tomatoes, and other squishy foods into the faces of the Centurions. They ducked behind their shields to avoid getting plastered. Each time they tried to move or peek around the shields, someone would throw more at them. After a moment, their leader ordered them to lock shields and charge into the crowd, arresting all that stood in their way.

As they shoved their way forward, there was no place for the crowd to retreat to without falling over each other. That's what happened; people fell back onto those behind them and landed on the ground. However, no one could be successfully arrested because as a Centurion attempted to grab a hold of person, they would be plummeted with volleys of fruit and eggs, which allowed the intended target to scoot along the ground out of the way, only to get back to their feet and prepare to throw stuff once more. During the ensuing chaos, I glanced back at where the speaker had been — only he was gone. I thought I saw him darting down a side street followed by one or two assistants. He'd made a clean get-away, thanks to the townsfolk.

Now we had more serious problems. With our horses, we couldn't move in any direction easily, and the Centurions moved closer to us. The locals dove underneath and between our horse's legs, getting out of the way of the advancing Centurions. As the wall of five shields reached where Roy and I were standing, they shouted in their own tongue, which we did not understand. I tried to explain we were just bystanders, but they didn't understand a word I was saying and shoved into me, grabbing my arm. This was unfortunate for him, for my horse, spooked and reared up. His forelegs came smashing down splintering his shield and smashing into his left arm, badly breaking it in several places. Roy tried to turn to help me, but his horse then kicked another Centurion with similar results. The other three now hastily backed off because all the horses began rearing and jumping about, just as startled and confused as we were. It was pandemonium.

A soft voice whispered into my ear, "Fair Lady, if you value your life, you'll follow me at once without the slightest delay. I implore you; follow now! You'll not get a second chance to save your life and the lives of your companions." I turned to see a man dressed in nondescript robes, with his head piece completely covering his face so only his eyes showed, black and piercing. One hand held the cloth over his face. With his other, he gently pulled on my free arm, indicating for me to follow him. I had to make a split second decision. I moved with him, pulling my horse behind me, knowing the others would fall in line behind me. He headed into the crowd, which miraculously opened up to allow us through. Glancing behind me, I saw the others following and watched as the crowed flowed back into place, blocking the Centurions from pursuing us. Instinctively, I knew the others would follow their Wid without question in an emergency, and this had rather become just such.

Once clear of the square, he broke into a jog. At each street corner, he made what seemed to me to be a random turn, to the left, to the right, never straight on ahead down that street. Not until all sounds of the near riot had faded into the normal bustle of the town noise did we slow down. Finally, he turned and spoke softly, "Just a little further. We must get you off the street, especially the horses. You are easily spotted and not just because of your mounts, My Lady. This way." He led on, only this time we ducked down a quiet alleyway. Halfway down it, he whistled, and someone opened a large door. One by one, we headed inside wondering what we had gotten ourselves into.

Once we were all inside, two men in similar robes hastily closed the doors and bolted them in an interesting way. One ducked outside with a lock, fastened the lock on the outside of the door, and then came back inside through a secret doorway that looked like a wall. We were in a dimly lit blacksmith shop as near as I could tell. In one corner, a fire still glowed red-hot. A well-muscled man continued working there, pounding upon an anvil. He took no notice of the six of us and seven horses suddenly entering his shop, rather weird, I thought.

Now, our benefactor removed the cloth from his face, revealing himself as a handsome man perhaps in his mid-twenties with black hair protruding from his head wrapping and very black, piercing eyes and a moustache to match. Something about his countenance, his manner, his bearing, caused me to trust him. He spoke, "Permit me to introduce myself. I am the Messiah Jackal, the Accursed, leader of the Hessainite Movement. We are dedicated to the removal of the invading infidels. You have just done us a tremendous service; you have inflicted pain and damage upon the infidels. Indeed, your deed will spread like wildfire throughout this holy city of Jerilum tonight. My compliments, I could not have orchestrated it better. Who do I have the pleasure of addressing?"

It was my place as Wid to take charge. "I'm Bethany, our leader. We're from the Greenway. And these are my companions." I introduced them one by one. "Please, can you speak just a little slower? We aren't as fluent in Arad as we should be. I — we're having a difficult time catching all the words, though I believe we caught most of the meaning. Thank you for rescuing us back there. We were on our way to find the inn when we stopped to listen to that man by the church."

"That was the Prophet Emil Tamil, a great religious teacher," he answered mechanically. With keen interest he exclaimed, "Ah, a woman leader, interesting and from the Greenway no less. Now this is something. We don't get many visitors from your homeland. In fact, you're the first I've ever met from there. This gets even more interesting. All praise to Jehosa, whose long hand touches everyone. You're so far from home. My spies reported your arrival at the West Gate and overheard the gateman give you directions to the inn. It was not a chance meeting in the square. I was following you trying to catch up with you and find out who you were. We don't often get strangers entering the town's gates. Pray, how did you get to Juda Arad, if you don't mind my asking?"

"It's a long story and we are tired and hungry. We came across the entire length of the Sea Princes. Will it be safe for us to go to the inn now?" I replied.

He laughed, "Heavens no dear child. All of you are now marked for Centurion wrath. Dressed as you are and with horses — no, if you go to the inn this way, why, you will find yourselves being roused during the night by the infidels, taken off to some mock trial, and summarily executed, likely crucified on a cross as a warning to others who defy them. No, you aren't safe openly in this town any longer, at least until this incident has been forgotten." Perhaps he spied our sudden worry, perhaps not. "But the very least Messiah Jackal can do is offer you a safe place to stay tonight and safe passage out of the town on the morrow. We can leave the horses here for now. Come join me for some refreshments; my band is staying in the empty storage building adjoining this blacksmith shop. Stable your horses over there out of the way." He pointed out makeshift stalls on the far end of this large room opposite the blacksmith, who still did not even let on that he noticed us. I assumed that in this manner, he could truthfully say that he "saw" no one.

We spent fifteen minutes caring for our horses and grabbed a few things we would need from the many bags. Then, we followed our host to another concealed door. Here he knocked a unique pattern, the password I assumed, and we heard a deadbolt sliding and the door opened. Total darkness greeted our peering eyes. Jackal muttered a word, which we could not quite hear, and suddenly, several lanterns were unshielded, illuminating the room and the faces of a couple of robed men by the door. We followed Jackal inside.

This was a warehouse consisting now of a vast empty space. Two large double doors to the outside were locked from the inside and there were no windows. The room was hot and stuffy, smelling of horses, leather, and smoke. A number of bedrolls lay at one end; on the opposite side was a series of converted workbenches, which now served as tables. Over twenty people, all dressed in similar robes, sat around the table and called out a welcome greeting to Messiah Jackal as we entered. All eyes really were upon us. A woman's voice called out, "What have you brought us this time Jackal, serving wenches? Why are they dressed so strangely? They must be melting in all that hot leather. Was the Prophet's speech successful?"

"Missa, gang, let me introduce to you our new — allies, all the way from the Greenway. They have just managed to break a number of the infidel's arms by the clever use of their horses! Yes, it went far better than anything we could have imagined — a total, complete success. Our new friends were there at just the right time to inflict some major casualties on the infidels." Spontaneously, cheering and hollering broke out in response to his brief report.

"This is their leader, Bethany," he presented me, and I gave a courteous nod of my head. "I'm sorry, but I've already forgotten who's who. Would you be so kind to introduce the others in your band, Bethany?" I smiled and did so. I heard numerous whispers among his band and caught the distinct phrase, "woman leader." Evidently, women were not known for being leaders here, I surmised. Somehow, I wasn't too surprised by this.

Next, he introduced his band, beginning with Missa, his wife. She nodded towards me, and I could tell she felt rather embarrassed about having called us serving wenches. I could tell that she was biting her tongue. Undoubtedly, she would later on be teased no end for her comments. Next followed a whirlwind of names of which I was unable to keep up with who was who. "Tonight they are under my protection and care. Missa, will you see to some dinner for us all please?" Turning to us, he said, "Lay your gear down over there in that unused corner. Over there is the washing basin; I suspect that you may want to wash. I must apologize for the crude living conditions, but here you will be safe, though maybe not as clean as you might like. It would be suicide for you to visit the local wash-houses; the infidels are sure to search there after the inns, looking for you." We did as he suggested. We found a large barrel of clean water and a half-empty barrel containing the dirty water. Obviously, around here, water was a precious commodity not to be wasted. We took turns washing our faces and hands attempting to use as little water as possible.

By the time we had freshened up and looked as presentable as possible, Missa had returned with several other women carrying with trays of steaming hot food and drink. All took off their headgear, unwinding yards of cloth, revealing themselves more fully. We were surprised to find that half of the band was indeed women, wives and girlfriends of the men. Jackal motioned for us to take the place of honor at his and Missa's side, and we all sat down. Then, they all lowered their heads and placed their arms across their chests forming an 'X' pattern.

Jackal spoke; it was their evening prayer, we discovered. "Jehosa, we are gathered here this evening to partake of the bounty that you have provided us. We thank you for seeing to our fleshly needs. We pray that no Arad goes hungry this evening and, if any are, please see to their needs. We give thanks to those who have labored to prepare this meal. Also tonight, we give you a very special thanks for having chosen to send Bethany and her people to help our cause. As you already know, they defied the infidels and caused them great pain in your name. Thus, we continue to let the infidels know that they are not wanted in this land. We pray that they will take themselves and their heathen religion back to their own land and leave us to be free so that we may concentrate fully on being worthy of entrance into your realm. Once again, oh great Jehosa, we give thanks for your having brought these people into our cause. We pledge to get them safely out of the hands of the infidels. Amen." One by one, all of the others echoed the "amen."

"I hope you like lamb and yams," Missa said as she passed us one large tray. "We've got honey mead or water; take your pleasure."

"Thanks, we have lamb in the Greenway also, though not as often as we might like. We raise them more for their milk and wool. Is the honey mead strong like the Sea Princes' wine?" I asked.

Several men chuckled, and she replied, "Heavens no. Don't give these men wine or they will be no good for the rest of the day." Several catcalled her some names in response. "You'd have to drink at least four cups to get as blasted as you do from one cup of their red wine. We don't often have wine for it is terribly expensive. Besides, much of our food is provided by our local hosts." She saw that we had no idea what she was talking about and Jackal interceded on our behalf.

"Is this your first trip to Juda Arad?" he asked. I nodded. "You are perhaps ignorant of our ways?" Again I nodded. He smiled, "I thought so. You see, some Arads are blacksmiths, some tend flocks of sheep, some are miners, some are merchants, some are traders, but I am a Messiah." We must have looked very dumb, so he explained further. "A local freedom fighter — it is my task to take the battle to the infidels to convince them to leave Juda Arad. Although none of us really expects to achieve that, the prophets all say that one day the Great Messiah, the fleshly son of Jehosa, will come and walk among us. It shall be he that drives them out of Juda Arad once and for all time. In the meantime, I do what I can to hasten their departure and to prepare the way for the coming of the Great Messiah, though I do not know if he shall come in my lifetime or not. Everywhere we go, our people provide the messiahs and their followers with the necessities of life. Otherwise, we would not be able to carry the battle to the infidels. We are appreciated amongst the people of Arad."

After we had eaten and chatted a bit, over tea served in copper mugs with long handles, Missa asked a leading question. "We have heard rumors from the Sea Princes that an outside group was helping the Sisterhood there. By any chance, do you know anything about that? Or in your passage across that land, have you heard anything about that?"

Before I could decide how best to answer her, Jackal sensed that this could be a touchy subject and put in rapidly, "You don't have to answer my prying wife. But I should explain further," after taking a glaring glance from his wife. "You see, Missa is our planner and I the messiah executioner. She plans all our major attacks upon the infidels. She is a genius at strategies and has worked out some amazing plans, which I then executed, causing the infidels great difficulties. I owe her my gratitude for myself being so well known here in the central part of Arad." That satisfied her, in part; she felt she gained some respect for her earlier hasty verbal blunder.

"You know of the Sisterhood?" I asked. "You see, we wouldn't want to violate or compromise them in any way." I looked at Simon and sent, *How far should we trust them?* I spied Missa watching me closely, as my eyes met Simons. He sent back, *We fight a common foe. It seems we have fallen in with the local rebels. So go as far as you think appropriate. Perhaps you should not mention specific names.*

"We know of them and have had some contacts with them, but that was before Zargarb fell, before the great slaughter of those fine women," Missa replied. "They even helped us sometimes, again before the infidels invaded their land."

"Okay, yes, those that you have heard who were helping the Sisterhood are indeed us, my band here. In our own land, we're called the Guardians, the protectors of the local people who depend upon us for their protection and well-being. We're certain the infidels will be attacking the Greenway once they have finished off the rest of the Sea Princes. We're trying to find out all we can about them and how best to defeat them. We traveled with the Sisterhood across the entire land of the Sea Princes and helped them as we could in return for their aid," I answered truthfully, though wondering if this would only open the door to many questions. From the hushed whispers and exclamations from the others, I assumed it would.

"Ah, Jehosa works in mysterious, unforeseen ways," Missa replied. "If the rumors be true, then you must have been exceedingly helpful to the Sisterhood, for your men are the only men we've ever heard tell that were accepted into their group as equals. It is a Sisterhood, after all. Is it true that all of them have been brutalized by men? We've heard that, but is it true?"

"I don't know how women are treated and viewed here, but in the Sea Princes, Nature is or was totally out of balance. Yes, the horror stories are almost unbelievable, unless you actually are there and see those women."

"Do they actually cut out their tongues and hack off arms?" asked Missa. From her expression, I could tell this was something that had long worried her, concerned her, yet filled her with curiosity.

"We traveled with a young woman whose tongue was cut out merely because she spoke out of turn. We've met women whose hands have been cut off; women whose own fathers have raped them. As I said, I've never seen the Great Balance of Nature so distorted, so unbalanced as in that land. Yes, probably all the rumors you've heard about the brutal, inhuman treatment of women in that land are true. In fact, it's probably worse than you can imagine," I replied solemnly.

She held her hand over her mouth in shock; her mind was an open book at this instant. *Then, it really is true!* Aghast and shock and pity simultaneously formed on her face. Even the men here were silent and ashamed that other men would treat women so badly. Missa finally managed to utter, "Oh those poor women. We should have tried to do more to help them when we had the chance. Now they are no more. We have failed those who really needed our aid in their time of need. Oh Jackal, how could we have been so, so stupid, so ignorant?"

"Don't blame yourself," I counseled, "for they would never want your sympathy or pity. That is not their way. They must regain their own self-respect, their own sense of self-worth and that cannot be done by living off the sympathy and pity of others. No, if you gave them assistance or let them assist you, then you did more than your part to help them recover their dignity." Again, much muttering occurred among his entire band when I finished speaking.

Jackal looked at me with a surprised look on his face, "Are you a priestess or a prophet in your land? For you speak wisely, and thus it would seem so to me. If you were of our land, you most certainly would be so considered, though there are no women prophets here. You are very wise, yet so youthful."

"Thank you for the compliment, but no, we are not priests, though you will find all of us Guardians of the same mind and thought. We are entrusted with the well-being of our people and thus must know a great deal and be as wise as possible. We all have studied since we were six years old in order to be prepared to handle our appointed tasks as Guardians." This explanation seemed to satisfy them.

"Have no fear, the Sisterhood is not dead. True, a great many lost their lives in that last Great Battle, but some around Zargarb still live. In the other sectors, the Sisterhood has taken a different approach to the invaders. However, I can report that change is occurring for women in the Sea Princes." I briefly outlined the current status in Pieta and its ramifications, though I didn't mention how it all came about, that would be potentially placing too much at risk. I knew Missa and the other women would really appreciate hearing that the long abuse of women was perhaps ending.

"Permit me one last question," Missa begged. "Do you know anything about what happened during the last Great Battle? We have heard that a storm of storms occurred all during that battle, and yet they fought on in such poor weather. Here it actually rained! Well further west from here, I should say. Normally, rain is just a heavy mist; only rarely does water fall from the sky. But this time, it came down in huge quantities, so much so that trails were washed out and low lying areas became streams. Earth eroded in many places, tumbling down the steep sides of the valleys. After the rains quite, oh, the flowers that grew. Tremendous fields of flowers sprang up everywhere. Magnificent indeed was the Arad for a brief time. Some said it was perhaps announcing the coming of the Great Messiah, but we have seen no signs of him as yet."

"Yes, we talked with some that were there that day. A great storm indeed raged during the entire battle, letting up only after the last woman fell to her doom. They said that the lightning was ferocious, destroying all the invader's mighty chariots, which is a good thing from the battle we saw outside of Bonilla." I purposely didn't mention that the storm was caused by Isabel who pulled down all that intense lightning. "I don't think that it was a signal from Jehosa that the promised Messiah had come," I added as an afterthought.

"Well, we had best get down to the business at hand," Jackal interrupted. "If we're going to get you safely out of the town, you're going to have to look like natives. Missa, we'll need six sets of robes, head scarves, and sandals." A couple other women left to get them for us. "Also, we must get your horses out separately. They'll be watching for a band of six horses. I can have my men lead one horse out at a time from different gates. We can rendezvous later on just outside the town. How does that sound? We do this all the time, so it won't be a problem for us to secret your horses out; we have to get ours out as well."

"Thanks that would be great," I replied. We went to get our things from the horses. Some things we wanted to carry personally. By the time we had gotten the horses ready for the clandestine operation, the women had returned with arms full of clothing. I insisted on paying for them and finally got Missa to accept two gold coins. "Er, what do we wear under them?" I asked her wondering if they were naked inside the robes.

She laughed, "You think we've nothing on under these?" She lifted her robe up to reveal some long undergarments. I breathed a sigh of relief. We could keep our under clothing on. Quickly, we changed out of our sweat soaked leather and into the loose-fitting robes. That part was easy enough. None of us had a clue how to wrap the long scarves into the turban-like head coverings. "Tomorrow, we'll show you and help you with them," she said. I smiled my thanks.

Missa now gave her plan to Jackal and the others. "We meet at the Crooked Cross at midmorning. We've some thirty horses to sneak out between now and then. Follow the usual procedure. Get the entrance coins from Emil before you leave." Four men got up, wrapped their turbans in place, took a few copper coins, and took one horse. Missa explained that they would each walk through town to the four gates and leave, meeting up south of town where one would spend the night guarding the horses. The other three would return, but enter by a different gate. When they returned, another four would repeat the pattern. By midmorning, all horses would be there awaiting our arrival. The Centurions wouldn't have a clue how we had vanished right under their watchful eyes, for certainly they would have men at each gate looking for a party of six with horses. I complimented her on her plan, ingenious.

With the details handled, there wasn't much else to do but talk before going to bed. Jackal took me aside and asked, "Today in the square, you were listening intently to our prophet, Emil Tamil. You found it enlightening?"

Ah, religion, I knew at once where this conversation was headed. "Yes, I found that he and we share many ideas and beliefs in common. Until now, I had not met other people who shared such beliefs. I found it most encouraging, even enlightening."

"Ah, that is indeed good," he replied with a smile. "May I ask what beliefs we share in common? You also believe in Jehosa?"

"We know that we are immortal spiritual beings and that we merely inhabit a fleshly body. Most of the people in the Greenway are ignorant of their own selves, believing that they are the body. Actually, I think that everyone in the Lands of the Sea Princes feels likewise — that the body is all that there is. At least, we met no one who felt otherwise. Rather disheartening, really."

"Most intriguing. Here, our prophets find that they must continually remind our people of their true spiritual nature. It is so easy to become consumed in the day-to-day living of the mortal flesh. They always remind us of our true nature, though sometimes I think it falls on deaf ears," he replied.

"Oh yes, I liked the part about avoiding greed, avarice, and lust. We feel the same way," I added.

"Then you too believe in Jehosa?"

"Er, not as such. We believe in the Great Balance of Nature. Perhaps, they are one and the same thing," I replied diplomatically. He seemed to accept this.

"But do you not believe that one day you will join Jehosa or the Nature? To be in spiritual form in his realm, his Great Kingdom?" he asked.

Simon, who had overheard our conversation, placed into my mind, *Be careful, Bethany.* This was dangerous ground. "I guess that you could call us shortsighted, Jackal. We never look that far ahead, rather concentrating upon trying to get everything in total harmony with Nature. We try to make the Greenway as close to what we feel Nature intended it to be. So we deal with the here and now, leaving the future to be what it will be. Shortsighted, as I said."

"Ah, I see. Yes, shortsighted. You may think us long-sighted then, but we agree; we must make our lands as close to what Jehosa and Nature intend, for that is the path to follow to prepare oneself to enter His Kingdom. We certainly agree on this. And the Centurions, the infidels, are completely against all this. We fight a common foe," he concluded, rightly so for many reasons.

"Well, you won't get any fighting done if you stay up any longer," Missa interrupted. "You need to let them get some sleep." We smiled at each other and all turned in for the night, my Circle sleeping in one corner, his in another. However, I heard men quietly coming and going all night, until I fell soundly asleep.

Next morning, after a light breakfast of cheese and bread, the women helped us wrap our heads. Soon, one couldn't tell us from the locals, unless you saw our whiter faces, which the head scarves could conveniently cover. "Will it be a problem if we split you up, taking each one of you to a separate gate to leave the town?" asked Missa.

"Not at all, we can keep in constant communication with each other," I replied, and then bit my tongue, hoping she wouldn't ask how that was possible. I didn't want to discuss telepathy with her at the moment. She gave me a rather funny look, though. I suspect had there been more time, she would have asked just that.

Quickly, my Circle was paired with six of Jackal's group. Naturally, Jackal took me as a courtesy, leader to leader I presumed. Missa took Roy, probably for the same reason. The first four pairs left the storage room, entering into the blacksmith's workroom. Our horses were gone. For a fleeting second, I panicked: what if we had just lost all our horses? Quickly, he guided me through a door that opened into the blacksmith's storefront and then out onto the street we went. Again, the town was alive with people going about their normal early morning routines, a cacophony of sounds and smells. I wished we had more time to absorb the sights and sounds of this new town. Jackal held onto my arm while I held the headscarf over my face with only my eyes showing. He said we were heading to the western gate, but I soon lost my bearings with the many side streets and turns that he took, trying intentionally to be devious in case we were being followed. Yes, he was just a little paranoid, I thought.

Finally, I spied the gate and it was busy with traffic coming and going. Several wagons were out-bound, their cargo covered by canvas. Standing at the gate were six Centurions, who weren't there yesterday when we entered the town. As the wagons rolled up to the gate, the Centurions ordered them to stop and proceeded to uncover and search the contents. This held up the line of folks leaving on foot or on horseback. I could hear others ahead of us grumbling about the unneeded delay. The Centurions paid no heed to the locals, intent on their thorough search.

Finally, it was our turn to pass by these men. As we approached, one said, "Halt. We must see who you are. Please reveal your faces." Slowly Jackal removed his covering and the Centurion nodded. I refused saying, "Oh please sir. I have contracted the plague. I have these horrible black pussy splotches all over my face. If I undo my scarf, I'll likely be infecting you. That's why I'm leaving the town. I don't want to infect anyone else. It's just too horrible, but I'll undo it and risk giving this plague to you, if you insist, because in that case, it wouldn't be my fault if you catch it." Testing him, I made a slight motion to undo it.

"Oh no! That is *not* necessary. Yes, please leave the town. Wise move,

move along now," he hastily said, motioning us to get going rapidly. He wanted no part of the plague.

Once we were well clear of the gate and could not be overheard, Jackal chuckled, "Now that was very good thinking. You think impressively in a crisis. Are you sure you don't want to join up with my band? We could use more like you, especially if you can also hold your own in a fight."

Meanwhile, I sent to the others mentally what had just happened with me. I found out that Roy had to convince the guards that he was Missa's younger sister, which only confused her, so Roy had to explain that people tend to see what they think or want to see, not necessarily what actually is there to see. She didn't like his explanation, though. I suspected she would be asking me about it later on when we camped for the night. Sandy used my trick, for she was just getting into the line by the southern gate when I contacted her. Simon responded that his Centurions saw a dark-skinned Simone. We both chuckled; he was quite good at illusions.

Sarah Jane, who was poor at illusions and disguises, chose a different method since she wasn't to leave until the first four pairs had made good our escape. She found an old rotten blanket, covered it in horse manure, and pretended to be very sick. Raphael just cast an illusion and had the Centurion say, "You are not the ones we are seeking. You may go." He thought it was nice and simple to enforce his will over these invaders. He reported they were very susceptible to mental suggestions. I filed that bit of useful information for later use.

By midmorning, we had all finally rendezvoused by a dry creek bed completely out of sight of the town and the roads — a place where no one normally travels. The rest of Jackal's men were already here as were our horses, which they had saddled and gotten ready for the day's trip.

"Thank you for helping us escape the town and the wrath of the infidels, Jackal," I said sincerely, "We didn't realize just how serious the situation actually was. We owe you one." He seemed very pleased with our gratitude.

"So what plans do you have now that you have escaped the clutches of the infidels?" he asked curiously.

"To be quite honest with you, Jackal, we hadn't gotten that far. I think we were more concerned with getting out of there. Let's see. We ought to head south I believe. Is it safe to travel upon their paved roadway? Do many locals use it or is it limited to the Centurion's usage?"

Missa answered instead, "Yes and no. It is heavily traveled by infidel supply caravans. Our people generally avoid it; we prefer to have as little to do with them as possible. If you traveled on it, undoubtedly around here suspicions would be raised, especially as a party of six strangers similar to those who caused the trouble in Jerilum."

Jackal took over from his wife, "Further, the open road is the primary zone of action for the messiah's actions, if you take my meaning. We attack their convoys, disrupt their supplies, and harry them as we can. As strangers, you might be mistakenly attacked by other messiahs."

"Makes sense," I replied. "That brings up another question we have had for some time now. We thought perhaps an effective strategy might be to disrupt their long supply lines as a way to slow them down and so on. How effective are your attacks? Have you seen any significant results?" I figured I might not get the straight truth here because it would be human nature for them to say they were being effective.

Surprisingly, Missa answered this one, "We have spies with big ears in all the towns. Consistently, we get reports that the infidel governors consider these raids a major problem. However, they are afraid to report the true situation back to their homeland, saying instead that they need these additional soldiers and supplies to help put down local rebellions up north near Galt territory. In fact, they have nearly as many soldiers currently in Juda Arad as they had when they originally invaded. So yes, in a way, we are being effective, for those infidels cannot move on to other lands and attack there. We are indeed making the Arad a costly land to occupy in hopes that they'll decide it isn't worth the trouble and leave."

"That brings up another question," I asked. "Seems as if I've a lot of them this morning," I teased playfully, hoping they didn't mind my asking so many. "The Galts. The Greenway has been plagued with more and more Galt raiding parties in the last ten years. Their attacks are going deeper and deeper into our land. At first, they were content to raid only the border towns and villages, but now they are penetrating sometimes a hundred miles on their raids into our land. Have they been raiding Arad too?"

Jackal replied, "Ever have the Galts raided northern Arad, but there's nothing worth their time and effort this far south. They've always been content to raid our mines and weapon smiths that border upon their vast open steppes. I'll say this, though, since the infidels arrived, they have positioned a large number of troops up north to protect the area from the Galts, because they want all the spearheads and swords that we can make. Thus far, the Galts have been no match for the infidels, and their constant raids have nearly come to a halt. Perhaps that is why they are reaching deeper into your land. If so, I'm sorry we've been unable to do more to stop these infidels." He was genuinely serious in his feelings; I could tell he really meant it. I found it refreshing to speak with someone who spoke from his heart and found myself liking this messiah.

Simon commented, "It's fascinating to see what appear to be dis-related facts and actions suddenly making perfect sense. Now if we only knew whether the infidels intended to attack the Greenway via the Northern Steppes of the Galts or via the Sea Princes, we could begin to create reasonable defenses. Perhaps they have yet to make that long range decision."

Missa answered, "They've yet to build up the proper forces for attacking the Galts. That land is a sea of steppes with wave after wave of hills. The Galts are superb horsemen. If they attack on foot as they did here in Arad or in the Sea Princes, their forces could easily be defeated. In my opinion, they would need a large number of cavalrymen, which they don't have anywhere in Arad right now, as far as we have heard. At least no spies have reported seeing any great numbers. Maybe they have not the cavalry or maybe they wish to finish off the Sea Princes before making their next move. Who knows the minds of infidels? Only Jehosa, all praise to him. Say, we tarry here too long. We went into Jerilum to resupply and find out the infidel's current convoy schedule. If possible, we need to intercept the next one yet today, while they are still a long way from Jerilum. Over the course of the next month, Bethany, we'll be slowly working our way south to the border, harassing their convoys along the way. You are welcome to join us, as long as you lend a hand in the attacks, but you must agree to follow my plans. We tolerate no deviations from the plan, except when the unexpected occurs. No plan that is good doesn't allow for the unexpected."

"I sincerely thank you for your hospitality. There are very little alternatives. We already tried to journey through Arad on our own when we began and soon found a severe water problem just following the track and had to hire a guide to get us safely to Jerilum. Your offer of a safe way to the southern border is most welcome. Certainly, we can help in fighting the infidels, but realize that we are also known as healers in the Greenway. Much of our skill lies in tending the wounds and illnesses of others. Perhaps that will be of more value than our combat skills." I hoped to avoid the risk of sending my people into direct battles with the Centurions.

The other men and women who overheard our conversation began intensely whispering among themselves. Jackal replied for them all, "All praise be to Jehosa, who once again has answered our reverent prayers. Healers! Oh such is a rare gift from Jehosa. Be it known that only a very few prophets in all of the Arad have that gift from Jehosa, the Almighty. Welcome, be thee in our band of the Hessainites!"

Missa asked, "Are you saying that all six of you have this gift of Jehosa and are healers, even the men?"

"Yes, we all do. Sarah Jane is about twice as good as the rest of us. It is her specialty, and she has studied long and hard, and has had much experience in healing, though her young years might lead you to conclude otherwise," I answered diplomatically. They obviously believed that their God bestowed the gift of healing, but we learned the craft just as one would learn blacksmithing. Then again, Arad was a deeply religious society.

Jackal issued the marching orders, "Okay, mount up. We ride south and must get several miles beyond El Adid before the sun sets so we can setup our morning surprise attack on the infidel convoy." We mounted and headed out across the dry arroyo, following the winding hot and dry canyon floors.

As the day drew on, it grew hotter and hotter. However, I was delighted to find that these robes kept us far cooler than our leather had. I wasn't swimming in sweat, though still awfully hot. During one short break, I commented to Missa just how much cooler these robes were, and she smiled back. By late afternoon, from the ground signs, I spied a well-worn track leading eastward that we didn't take. Jackal noticed that I noticed it and said,

"Leads to El Adid, which is just over yonder hill, but to get there you have to go around this hill; the sides are too steep for man or beast. We are going around the village. Good messiahs plan their attacks well, so they don't bring the wrath of the infidels down on innocent villages. We attack well beyond the village and will ride on south so the infidels will know the El Adid had nothing to do with the raid." It made sense to me, and we continued our ride.

A half hour later, we veered due east and soon came upon the stone paved road of the Centurions. It was deserted, a long, thin red line stretching north and south as far as the eye could see, which was not too far because of the intervening ridges. He sent riders up and down the road, while we waited for their return. Missa explained, "They are looking for the ideal ambush location. We lie in a concealed ambush and attack them from their sides, as they march forward with their huge shields facing forward. That way, the first shots hit their targets. While so confused, others rush in and hack at them before they can form into a solid rank. If they ever do manage to form a line, we depart at once. We have neither the skill nor the numbers to attack them openly when they are in their defensive formation. You could call our methods a 'hit and run' sort of thing. It has proven effective, but only if we can take them by complete surprise. You will see."

Soon, Jackal saw a hand signal from the southerly rider, and we mounted up and headed further south. About a half mile further, we dismounted on the road. Here the roadway was built slightly higher than the surrounding valley. On one side, steep cliffs rose some hundred feet above the roadway. On the other side, the land sloped downward before leveling out. A series of large boulders lay scattered about some hundred feet from the road. Jackal issued orders, "Okay this is an ideal spot. After we have our dinner, we'll prepare the ambush."

Mostly for our benefit, he elaborated, though his men didn't need to hear his explanation. "A few will stay with the horses in two groups, one behind the boulders there, and one behind that tall hill. The women, our bowmen, will scale that hill and take their position high atop there, where they have a clean shot at the infidels as they march along the road. We fighters will bury ourselves in the sand over on this side in the sand. As usual, if Missa decides we should proceed with the attack, the bowmen will open fire. Once the first volley hits, that is our signal to rise up out of the dirt and spring upon them as their backs are turned toward us. After inflicting our damage, we then rush behind the boulders, mount up, and ride off to the south. The bowmen slide down the hill, mount up, and also ride off to the south, circling across the road to join us. If Missa decides that this convoy is too risky to attack, we do nothing, and the Centurions march on by without ever catching sight of us."

Simon's comment was simply, "Brilliant plan! Commendable, I might add. Can I fight alongside you? I'm not that good with a bow."

"Hey, me too," Roy hastily added. "I'm the best fighter in our group. I want to see some close action, er if that's all right with Bethany?" Both he and Simon looked my way; I smiled and nodded my consent.

"I'm good with bows, so I'll go topside," Raphael volunteered. We all remembered his gigantic bows that he designed for use back in the defense of Karka. Too bad he didn't have time to build another one here. We mounted up again, rode around the hill from which we intended to shoot bows, and made camp. The women prepared dinner, while the men walked back to their site and excavated small holes in which they would later be buried. Then it was time for relaxation, food, and prayer.

As the sun sunk ruddy red in the distant horizon, spelling relief from the heat of the day, the Arad was quiet and beautiful. Only the sounds of distant animals could be heard in the stillness. Overhead a pair of hawks circled for prey. I laid my head back on my saddle as a pillow and gazed out over the land. Arad had a peculiar beauty about it and, just now, it was very peaceful indeed. We all fell asleep early and woke at dawn.

Quickly, the men with their swords went to their pits and laid down in them, while the women covered them lightly with sand, leaving only their faces slightly visible so they could see and breathe. At any instant, they could rise up from the ground and attack. Next, the women carefully raked brushes over the ground to hide all our footprints, leaving the land appearing as virgin as it was before we came. At last, the women returned to our camp, packed up everything, got out their crossbows, and a handful of quarrels each. Then came the difficult climb up the steep side of the hill. The soft, crumbly rock made climbing difficult and treacherous. Several times, I managed to slide down more than I had just climbed up. The others fared little better. After a half hour, and breathing heavily from the exertion of the hundred foot climb, we made it to the top.

Now, we crawled across the nearly smooth, flat hilltop to our shooting positions on the other side, several hundred feet away. Up here, there were many deserted bird nests; the ground was crawling with insects; flies buzzed around us. We ended up close to the edge from where we had a clear view of the red stone road below us. Each readied their crossbow and then began the wait. From here, we should be able to see them coming from over a mile away around a far distant hill. Again, Missa reminded us of our orders, "Don't shoot until I give the word." I think she said that mostly for our benefit. We girls did not have a crossbow, for we did not know how to use one. I explained we could do some other actions if needed, and Missa did not question us further.

We waited, as the sun rose into the morning sky, heating us up as we lay watching. I hate waiting, but I think I've said that before. For hours we waited, and I found myself dozing off several times. Inactivity will do that to me. Then just when I thought I'd have to retreat to go to the bathroom, one woman hissed a warning sound. We all looked and became instantly alert. Far off, just rounding the bend around the distant hill came what appeared to be a small army of ants — the infidel convoy marching along the road.

Minutes passed as they drew ever closer to our hill. Now I could clearly see their handsome brown-skinned bodies glistening with sweat, carrying their heavy shields in front of them. They marched three abreast stepping in unison, much like a well-choreographed dance, but this was no dance. I counted nine men in front of six wagons, which were being pulled by two horses each. Another nine men marched behind them. Then, I spied what was bringing up the rear — a chariot with a driver and two spear-men!

Missa saw it and cursed. "Do not fire. The chariot will trample and smash our men as they attack! These infidels are getting smarter. They know we haven't the means to stop their war chariots. Curse them!"

On a whim, I looked up at the clear blue sky. I spied one large billowing white cloud. *It's enough.* I sent my idea to Sarah Jane and Sandy. Then, I whispered to Missa. "Let my people destroy the chariot, while you shoot those on foot. We need about a minute's notice before you want to fire so we can coordinate our actions. Trust me, that chariot will be in pieces when we're done with it." She looked at me sternly and hesitantly.

"If you fail, it'll mean certain death for those below," she added extremely seriously. She was debating whether to trust us. She had no idea what we could do. I thought about trying to explain my plan to her, but decided against it; she wouldn't believe me unless she actually saw it occur. Better to let her witness it. We were, after all, the Lightning Circle.

"Yes, we'll not fail. Roy and Simon are down there. I can't lose them," I replied. She agreed and I reminded her to give us a minute's notice. Meanwhile, the three of us began chanting softly to ourselves. My mind went blank as I reached out for the cloud that now lazily floated overhead. I made contact, felt the tingling of energy, and began congealing it. Then, I waited. Out of my body as I was, I had a wide view of the action. She timed her minute so the wagons would be in front of the hidden men. That way, they could charge both the two groups of infidels.

Finally, Missa whispered, "Fire now. Don't miss." Nearly simultaneously, the telltale twangs of a dozen crossbows firing their deadly missiles reached my ears down there. I let lose my ball of energy I had been handling. A pair of lightning bolts struck the wheels of the chariot, while mine hit the driver. The wheels splinted crashing the chariot into the ground; the driver was thrown completely off the remains of the chariot. The other two fell off onto the ground, as the horse bolted and the body of the chariot disintegrated into splinters of wood. The quarrels found their marks, though none was fatal. As predicted, the infidels, taken by complete surprise, rushed to form a line facing us on top of the hill so that our next volley would only hit their massive shields. They didn't see death rising up from the sand behind them until it was too late. I watched Roy and Simon as they quickly dispatched their two men. The entire attack was over in less than a minute. The three drivers raised their hands in a gesture of surrender.

With scarves covering their faces, I heard Jackal order them to climb down and begin walking towards El Adid and not look back unless they wanted a quarrel in their eye. They began running as fast as they could northward up the road. Missa stared up at the sky wondering where the freak storm that had come was at. She saw only a dark cloud overhead. She looked at me, and I merely smiled and said, "I told you we would take care of that chariot." Her mouth made some motions but nothing came out. Jackal yelled for us to come down. We quickly slide back down the hillside. Going down took less than a minute. A few minutes later, leading the horses, we joined the others who were going through the spoils. Several men were examining the fallen infidels.

I found one aspect quite interesting. When they finished their search, Jackal was handed a sack that contained approximately a hundred gold coins. He proclaimed, "Fifty of these we will spend on our supplies, and the other fifty we will deposit with the village elder in El Adid to help them meet the infidel's yearly tax. How fitting they should help pay their own tax." His band got a good laugh at his comment. I thought this was very interesting. Here, the messiahs were helping the local towns and villages raise the yearly taxes. Amusing and ironic. Later, he told me that they would melt the gold down so that its origin would be unknown to the infidels.

The three wagons contained great urns of scented oils, reams of fine cloth for clothing, a good deal of rations, and a few weapons. The urns were smashed spilling their contents upon the roadway. The cloth was shredded by swords into a useless mass. No Arad would ever have any use for infidel material. The weapons, mostly spear points, were collected, and buried in the sandy soil where no one would find them. The rations, no Arad would eat. Jackal and his men spread out all the rations across the sandy ground to feed the animals and birds. Finally, a great pit was dug, and the twenty-one dead were buried in a shallow grave, well-marked so the infidels could find it. An hour after the battle, we were once again riding southwest out into the deserted hills of Arad, mission accomplished.

Once we were on our way, Missa asked me the inevitable question that I knew eventually would be coming. "Back there, how did you or did you — I mean, how is it that lightning came? There was no storm, only one little white cloud in the entire sky?"

"Missa, we can bring down the lightning from the sky when we absolutely have no other way. And yes, we all can do this. It is part of our training; it took me ten years to master it, so it is no easy thing to do." I hoped this simple explanation would suffice to quell her deepening curiosity. It didn't completely.

"Well it was very impressive to say the very least, and it totally wiped out that war chariot. If we had hundreds of you, why, we could begin to drive all of the infidels from our land. Would you consider joining up with us in the cause of God doing His Will?"

"That's just the problem, Missa, there are not hundreds of us, only a handful, and it takes such a long time to master this skill. Besides, even if we started training hundreds right now, we would be invaded and subjugated just as Arad has been, long before the first trainees were ready to call down lightning. No, I'm afraid we're on a quest to find some other more workable method. As yet, though, we haven't a clue what that might be."

"So few? What a shame, for you have the power to stop them, just not the numbers. Jehosa works in very strange ways sometimes. I think this is one of them. I know that I speak for all Hessainites, in saying we are both proud to have met you and honored to have had you fight along with us. Truly, Jehosa is attempting to open our eyes that we may see."

Simon added one comment, "However, I would caution you, Bethany, not to bring down lightning in the future. Remember, at that last Great Battle of Zargarb, the Sisterhood fought them and tremendous amounts of lightning devastated the infidels. It does not take much imagination to conclude that the Sisterhood may have been behind the use of lightning here in Arad, and that might undermine all the progress the Sisterhood had made recently. I caution against using lightning anymore."

"I'm sorry, Simon; I just didn't think. I saw the chariots, and Missa said that we could not attack because that chariot would wipe all you out. I see your point now, and I wish I'd not acted so impulsively, Simon. We won't do it again," I answered him and felt rather foolish that I hadn't thought about this aspect before I acted. Missa, who had probably been hoping we would repeat our strikes in future battles, looked dejected knowing that in all likelihood there would be no more fantastical gifts from Jehosa to help them.

"It's probably okay, we only did it once. If it doesn't happen anymore, why they might think it an isolated freak occurrence," Simon attempted to put my mind at ease, but it didn't. All the rest of the day, I worried and fretted that my foolish action might have now jeopardized all that the Sisterhood had gained. I hoped and prayed that it didn't!

That night we camped out of doors under the crystal clear, starry sky not too far from a watering hole. The further south that we rode, the less steep the sides of the hills became. This night we camped on top of a hill, which offered us more protection. Far off in the distance to the east we could see the outline of a village, and before the sun set, the red ribbon of the Centurion's road was also quite visible to the east as well. We ate well before the sun went down so when darkness came, our camp would emit no light, which also meant that we went to bed early.

During the twilight, Missa and Jackal discussed their next move, and I could hear clearly their discussion about this new twist: the infidels were now sending along a war chariot for protection. This definitely made their raids more complex, because they really didn't have the means by which to put them out of commission. On the other hand, by bringing along a war chariot, the Centurions fully expected their caravans to reach their destinations successfully. I asked Raphael, "What can stop a war chariot? These people desperately need some way to prevent their use or nullify them in some way. Can you dream up some clever device or plan that could put one out of commission, besides our lightning bolts?"

"Ah, love a challenge," he teased me, "and it has got to be portable." Sarah Jane immediately began listening closely. She loved the way Raphael looked when he was totally engrossed in some construction project. Sarah

Jane, who was lying on a blanket, rolled onto her side so she could watch every detail on his face. "It has got to be usable by mostly untrained hands. It has to be foolproof, and you have only have one shot at it. Further, the chariot will not be charging, but rather moving at a wagon's slow pace. That hinders the design as well, you see. If it were charging, one well-placed metal spear or rod between the spokes of the fast moving wheels would disintegrate the wheel, disabling the chariot. However, moving slowly, nothing much would happen. Ah, Bethany, my dear, you certainly have given me an interesting problem. Say, what are you staring at?" he just spied Sarah Jane staring at him, watching his every motion.

"You, silly. When you are working on a problem, you get the cutest expressions on your face," she replied. He blushed slightly and tried to concentrate on the task I had given him.

"You could catapult a large boulder onto it, but they would likely see it coming and get out of the way. You could dig a deep pit and conceal it so that when the chariot drove over it, it would fall in, but them so would the wagons, which were ahead of the chariot. You could kill the driver, but that would take a very lucky shot from the distance you were at today. No, we cannot rely on luck." His fingers pulled at his chin as he thought. "I must make use of the Arad strategy and the Centurion's likely responses. That is the key. They don't attack chariots in open combat but only from a surprise ambush. We don't need to destroy it so much as temporarily disable it right?" I nodded and he thought some more. Finally, he muttered to himself, "Yes, now that might work." Then to me, he looked up and said, "I have an idea. I'll look into it tomorrow." That's all he would say no matter how much I prodded him, teased him. I even tried to tickle him to get his idea out of him. Nothing worked; I'd have to wait and see like everyone else.

After breakfast the next morning, Raphael took everyone east to the deserted red stone road. "Now the idea is to disable the chariot by making it do what the infidels want to do in the battle. Here, this rock represents the chariot; these represent the rear guards. What we do is dig a three foot deep narrow trench say about this wide," he explained holding his hands about two feet apart. "We put a thin mat layer over the top and cover it with sand and then place several small stones here and there so that it looks just like the normal side of the road. Next, you divide your forces into three groups, not just two. First divide into halves as you normally do, half for the front guards and half for the rear. Then divide the rear into halves again. Put half of them here just beyond the end of the hidden ditch and the other half way over on the other side. Those stay hidden until the chariot is dispatched. You'll see why in a minute. Now the positioning of the initial strike is critical. We must have them seeing the attack while the chariot is still back where it is now by that rock there. Okay. Once the quarrels fly, all turn to face the bowmen up on the hill. As usual, the men on this side all come out of hiding to attack the backs of the infidels. But not this second smaller group here at the rear. No, it's their job to look startled, scared, and afraid of the looming chariot. Perhaps take a step back or two as if perhaps retreating — anything, just to goad the chariot driver to kick into action and begin to gallop his war machine off the road here to come straight at you. Once it comes off the road, the chariot's left wheel cannot help but ride over the thin matting and smash, down goes the left side, and the chariot should tip over, disabling it for a while. Of course, all the rear guards are now going to be facing the semi-retreating men, so finally the hidden men on the far side rise up and attack the rear guard from the rear once more. What do you all think?"

"All praise to Jehosa! I do believe this might just work!" exclaimed Jackal. Raphael grinned, as did Sarah Jane, who was proud of Raphael. I saw her watching him much as I had sometimes spied my mother watching dad, when he wasn't looking. It dawned on me right there amidst this discussion, that Sarah Jane really was in love with Raphael; they were not "play acting" either. It had become the real thing. I wondered if she knew it.

Raphael, very excited and enthused, went over it all again, "Normally, I would want to make a complete test of the concept. You know, get a real chariot, some play actors, and actually act it all out and see if it works in practice. You know theory is one thing and practice is sometimes quite another, but we have no chariot on which to experiment." Some men shook his hand to congratulate him, while others patted him on his back and shoulders.

Simon added, "You know, proper positioning and timing are everything in this plan, Raphael. If something should go wrong, the chariot may well carve up Jackal's men. I'll tell you what, the first time we try this out, if anything goes wrong, I'll handle it by the proper illusion. There won't be very many minds to have to influence, mainly the driver. So if the plan goes astray, I'll see to it that the chariot is ineffective at hurting the rest of us."

"Excellent!" exclaimed Raphael. "That will make up for not having any practice sessions to work out all the details. Now the first thing we need is to build about thirty feet of mats using the low growing brush around here. Once made, the mats can be reused each time."

The rest of that morning was spent in building the mats. Yucca grew here and there in these arid valleys. Its long, narrow leaves were easily woven into the mats, which we reinforced with twigs so they would hold the weight of some sand without any telltale bowing in the middle. Over lunch, we discussed where the trap should be laid, which meant that we needed to know when the next supply caravan was due to pass by this general vicinity.

According to Missa, the infidels sent weekly caravans to each major town in Arad. However, because of all the messiah raids, the exact times were kept secret, but spies have big ears, and infidels, big mouths. She estimated that another would pass along here sometime in the next couple of days, vague, but hopeful. Jackal ordered a few scouts to fan out along the road and give us advanced warning of any approaching caravans. He pointed out that we would have to be careful when we were doing the actual excavation work because the infidels often sent riders carrying orders to and fro along the road, which connected all the major central towns together with their homeland far to the south. It wouldn't do to have the pit half-dug when a rider came along on other business. Raphael suggested a couple of lookouts could be placed on top of the higher, nearby hills; from that vantage point, advanced warnings could be made. Even so, we'd only get a few minutes warning that a rider was approaching. Thus, he suggested using a canvas covering, which could be quickly thrown over the pit, propped up, and sand hastily spread lightly over it. A fast riding horseman might not even notice it. Another rider was sent to a nearby village to purchase enough canvas to make the covering.

That afternoon we hid ourselves behind a gully and some boulders waiting for the canvas to arrive. We did hear several riders during that time, so it was not a deserted roadway. Raphael also suggested that the major portion of the digging be done at night when there was little chance of discovery. At dawn, the mats could be placed and prepared; that step could be done quickly, as long as the landscape could be made to look "natural" and unaltered.

While we waited baking in the hot sun, Jackal and Raphael scouted further south along the road for the ideal location for the first attempt. The rider returned with the canvas before they got back. The women took charge, and hastily cut and sewed it into a long strip some five feet wide and forty long. They also inserted reinforcing cross pieces so that, when covering the ditch, it wouldn't sag too noticeably. Yet, the entire canvas could be rolled up into something like a bedroll and carried on horseback. When they finished, Jackal and Raphael returned having decided upon a spot some three miles further south. Late that afternoon, we packed up and rode south.

The location they chose turned out to be ideal. On the eastern side, a steep cliff rose more than a hundred feet to the hilltop. There was enough clearance between the cliff and the edge of the road for a few men to dig shallow hiding holes. However, on the western side, beyond the road bed the land sloped gently down into a dry wash, which was boulder filled. Thus, any chariot attempting to drive off the road to attack Jackal's men, wouldn't go far off the road for fear of rolling over. On the other side of the wash, a series of undulations in the land would serve as an excellent place to conceal the horses and make our camp.

After setting up camp and setting several lookouts on several hilltops, using the last of the sun, Raphael, Missa, and Jackal laid out the plans on the road proper and on the western side. First, Raphael placed a series of boulders to outline the dimensions and general layout of the trench that would be dug. He angled it askew from the red brick road so that no matter at what angle the chariot left the road, its left wheel was sure to hit it. Next, he carefully paced out the exact locations for the three groups of hidden men, based upon there being three wagons in the convoy. Again, he used stones to mark the spots. "Timing is critical, Missa. You must get them to stop at the precise spot. Too short or too long of the mark and the chariot could miss the trap completely."

"But how am I to know this exact spot from way up there?" her voice full of concern as she pointed to high atop the nearly dark hilltop. She was well aware that if she failed, she'd bring doom upon all of them.

"You are used to firing at the lead man, but the location of the chariot is what is really important. I want you only to fire at the chariot driver. Let the others aim for the foot soldiers. Now let's see if I cannot make it foolproof for you. I have another idea but it will have to wait til daylight. It should work perfectly." Once more, he wouldn't say what that idea actually was.

Once satisfied all was laid out according to his plans, they returned to dinner, which the others had waiting. After the meal, the men went to dig the pit. The women and Raphael stood by with the canvas should it be needed in a hurry, but no night riders came. They discovered that it took about two hours to actually dig the long trench and scatter the sand and rocks. Mostly it took so long because it was dark. Then, it was covered with the canvas until morning.

Just as the sun appeared, the canvas was removed and the mats installed. A light covering of sand made them nearly invisible. When a few stones of various sizes were randomly placed around and on top, why, it did look like the normal roadside. Next, the men dug their shallow pits in which they would conceal themselves. While the others were doing this, Raphael had Missa climb to the hilltop and take the position from which she would fire her first quarrel. He then sighted her and a stone on the road where he wanted the chariot to be position. Next, he hiked some distance off the road following the line from her atop the hill and the rock on the road. There, he arranged a number of stones into a long arrow formation whose form would only be visible from atop the hill. All she had to do was point toward the stone arrow and when the chariot crossed her line of sight, fire. When she rejoined him on the roadway, she exclaimed, "Brilliant! I can't miss this way!" She gave him a hug. He felt just a bit embarrassed by her sudden show of emotion.

Raphael's last action was to train all of Jackal's men on the exact positioning of each component. He had them pace off the distances to each feature and commit that number to memory. After a half hour, every one of his men could recite the exact layout of all elements of the trap. Now it was waiting time once more. The women took their horses around the hilltop, hiding them, and leaving two to guard them. The rest of us scrambled up the steep cliff to the top, which was no easy climb on this slippery, crumbly rock slope. We got into position. Down below, we watched the men burrow into their holes and cover themselves up with sand, leaving only the front part of their faces showing. Two men rode off to act as distant lookouts. They would give us as much warning as possible.

We waited. Oh how I hate waiting, especially in the hot, burning sun, unable to stand for fear of giving away our position, unable to find shade for there was none on the barren hilltop. Finally, I dozed off and lost track of time.

Next thing I knew, Sarah Jane was poking me in the side, whispering, "It's coming." I noticed the sun had moved a considerable distance across the blue cloudless sky since I last was aware of it. Hours must have passed, I reasoned. I peered towards the south. Sure enough, another infidel caravan was slowly approaching. "Boy these guys are methodical," I whispered. I counted three by three foot soldiers in the lead, followed by three wagons, followed by another nine on foot, and the chariot bringing up the rear with its driver standing tall and two others slumped over half dozing as I had been moments ago. They were about a half mile away. We waited some more, only now it was not too boring; action was eminent.

Missa whispered, "Remember, ladies, do not fire until you hear my signal." None of us really needed to hear that, but she felt better having said it. As they finally drew close, I could see the wisdom of Raphael's marking arrow. From up here, I could easily see it, aim for it, and fire just as soon as the chariot crossed the line of sight. Indeed, brilliant. Finally, Missa whispered, "Now." Her crossbow twanged, followed in a split second by the twangs of another fifteen bows. Missa hit her target, the driver, but it bounced off his metal chest plate. Over half of the foot soldiers were not so lucky; they took quarrels in their right arms, sides, or legs. Now I could see Missa's wisdom about always having the bowmen on the eastern side of the caravan. Those hit were hit in their right side. Their left arms carried their heavy shields. Thus, their sword or spear arms, that is, their right sides, would be wounded, lessening their overall fighting capability. I assumed if the caravan were traveling south, she would position herself on the western hilltop.

As expected, the caravan halted instantly; those on foot repositioned their shields to face the hilltop, effectively shielding themselves from any further quarrels. Right on cue, those on the western slopes quietly got up out of their concealed prone positions and stabbed at the backs of the infidels. However, four moved toward the nine in the rear and halted abruptly, staring and pointing fearfully at the chariot, as if its appearance was totally unexpected and about to be devastating to them. Slowly they backed up a step, while the nine on foot in unison did an about face to face the fighters, glad that they had not been stabbed in the back like those in the front.

Just as Raphael had calculated, the chariot driver, seeing the men look terrified of his war machine, seeing them falter and not attack but retreat slightly, hollered and whipped his two horses into a gallop, pulling off the road heading straight for the four men and behind them, the other men who were finishing off the nine in front. No sooner had he moved off the roadway, when the chariot's left wheel rolled over the mat covered pit. Instantly, the wheel fell down three feet tipping the entire chariot over onto its side. Still being pulled by galloping horses, the chariot was actually smashed; wheel, axle, and sides splintered. The three occupants were thrown hard upon the ground, and quickly slain before they could even get to their feet. While the rear nine were watching in horror, the remaining men climbed out of their concealed positions and attacked them from the rear.

So once again, it was over two minutes after the attack began. As before, the three wagon drivers were forced to hike on north up the road on foot, if they wanted to live, which they certainly did. Once they were out of sight, the searching and cleanup work began. Jackal found Raphael and shook his hand, "It worked just perfectly! Amazing indeed. Well done Greenway Guardian!" Others added their cheers and congratulations, too. Jackal pointed out another benefit of the trap: the graves for the fallen infidels had already been dug. The bodies were dumped into the pit, after the women carefully retrieved all the mats. Actually, in less than a half hour this time, everyone headed to their horses to leave. "Most efficient indeed," muttered Jackal. This time, he had acquired seventy-five gold coins for the neighboring towns and an equal amount for his band.

We then rode south and a little west to put significant distance between us and the road, and then between the ambush and ourselves. As we rode, he explained the nearest watering hole was twenty miles south, and that we would have to spend the night there at El al Bol, a small village, which had formed around that source of water. "Don't worry. We'll be more than safe there. The infidels don't know of its existence, and the extended family that lives there are friends. Missa comes from here. If we are lucky, we'll make it by nightfall." Hence, we rode hard. Still, I loved the air rushing past my face, and I could feel the breeze through the robes. Finally, I felt somewhat cooler even though it was still very hot.

With all the twists and turns of the tangled web of valleys that we followed, I would never have been able to find this watering hole on my own. The sun was just going down when I spied green in the distance — green of trees! I rejoiced; I hadn't realized just how much I was missing good old trees. Back home they were everywhere. In the Sea Princes and in Juda Arad they were scarce. I wondered what kind of trees could grow in this arid land.

El al Bor was a very small village of some twenty small, red adobe mud homes ringing a large ten foot in diameter watering hole. Crystal clear, underground water filled the deep pond here in the middle of nowhere. All around and out to a distance of several hundred feet strange trees grew tall. I learned that these were date trees in the main. A small corral housed perhaps fifty sheep and goats for the might. Predictably, as our large group rode up to the village, heads began appearing at the doorways. By the time we rode up to the water hole, the entire village had come out to greet us. They numbered perhaps a hundred, old men and women, younger families, and some twenty children of various ages.

One face I recognized instantly — the face of the prophet who had stood on the steps in Jerilum preaching to the crowd and who started the riot that day when all our adventures in this land had actually begun: the Prophet Emil Tamil. He spoke to Jackal as he dismounted, "Welcome Messiah Jackal the Accursed. Welcome. I trust Jehosa has shown his light upon you. What took you so long to get here? We were expecting you yesterday."

Jackal and Emil hugged each other with their arms tightly around each other's shoulders. "Ah, Emil, Jehosa has done more than shine upon us. He has sent us powerful allies from the far north — allies who have shown us the way to defeat the war chariots! It has been most profitable. Here, you have two bags to give to the towns," and he gave Emil the two sacks of gold coins to be melted down and given to the towns to help pay the infidel's taxes.

"Everyone, listen up. I want you to meet our new allies all the way from the Greenway," Jackal proudly announced and then introduced us all. He added, "But we need water. We've ridden all afternoon without water or supper. We need a drink and dinner, and then let the tales begin!"

One village woman handed him a small sack. He opened it and put something from it into his mouth. Then he explained, "Salt. Here take a bit of salt first before you drink. Out here, salt is almost as valuable as water." I took a bit in my fingers and put the raw salt into my mouth. Suddenly, I knew my body now craved salt! I took a large amount and passed it on to Sandy. Then, I drank three cups of water from the hole. Ah, cold, clear, refreshing was that water, but then I felt a bit dizzy and had a bit more salt. I didn't realize how much salt my body had lost during the heat of these past few days. Once we all were properly salted and watered, we shared the hastily prepared dinner that some of the village women gathered from their leftovers. Several villagers saw to the care of our horses. We had a lot of bread, cheese, and dates from the many trees around us.

One little girl, who was about six, pulled on Jackal's sleeve. "Can we hear the stories now? Mommy's going to make us go to bed soon, and we don't want to miss them. You tell the best stories, Uncle Jackal." He smiled and agreed. Holding her on his knee, he began telling them about what had happened, beginning with his sudden rescue of us, after our horses had severely injured two of the infidels who were after Emil that day. For an hour, the entire village sat on the ground entirely enthralled with his tales. Uncle Jackal was a gifted storyteller who consistently managed to demonstrate in his story how faith in the Lord Jehosa led him on the proper course of action to do the right thing. He ended by saying, "So you see, Jehosa expects us to help our fellow man in their times of need without thought for our own selves. See how he has rewarded us for helping these six visitors out that day? Lord Jehosa works in mysterious ways that we sometimes cannot see. Do not doubt for a minute that he is working with us."

The Prophet Emil then rose and said quietly, "Amen. Now let us bow our heads in evening prayer before we put the young ones to bed." Instantly, everyone became totally quiet and bowed their heads. We followed suit, not wanting to offend our hosts. Solemnly, he prayed, "Lord Jehosa, once again we thank you for all that you have done on our behalf this day. Our fleshly bodies remain alive and strong, and we have followed your ideals this day. If any have strayed from your golden path, we pray that you will enlighten them so that they may once again see the way. We thank you for providing us with all our fleshly needs this past day. We especially thank you for having blessed and guided your Messiah Jackal these last few days. We recognize and affirm once again that we are immortal spiritual beings. We continue to strive to meet your standards so that we may be fit to one day enter your Holy Realm and dwell at your side. And Lord Jehosa, bless and guide our honored guests from so far away, that they may see your divine light, that they may understand and that they may seek your golden path as well. Lord Jehosa, watch over us and protect us while we rest our fleshly bodies yet another night. Amen." A chorus of amen's echoed his.

Without a word, the younger women hustled the unusually quiet children into their homes and put them to bed. Most of the other villagers returned to their homes and beds as well. Jackal's party quickly spread their bedrolls around the water hole, so we followed suit. As I lay down, I saw Jackal and Emil moving off a distance to speak private words, so Roy and I snuggled into each other's arms for the night. I noticed almost no one spoke a word after the prayer was finished. Actually, I felt rather mellow and rather serene and didn't need to say anything. Neither did Roy, who lay for a time on his side looking at me, and I, him. Then, he gave me a loving night kiss and we both laid back. I was asleep almost at once and slept a very peaceful sleep.

At dawn, the village came to life once more. Over breakfast, Missa introduced us to her mother and other relatives; her father had been killed some time ago by the infidels. Most of the villagers were part of her extended family, aunts, uncles, cousins too numerous to mention. In fact, the Prophet Emil was her uncle on her father's side. These people led an austere life but wanted for nothing, seeking to be worthy of Jehosa's realm. Once everyone had finished and was sipping the traditional café, a brew we'd never had before and rather like a strong coffee, Jackal, Missa, and Emil took us aside for a brief word.

"Here, our paths diverge," Jackal said, though I detected just a bit of sadness in his tone. "We've heard the infidels are now going to try to send their supplies via Harun, a town far to the east of Jerilum, thinking to bypass the ambushes. We must ride in haste to show them the error of their ways. I know you wish to continue on south to the edge of Juda Arad. So my cousin, Emil has volunteered to guide you. If you wish some protection, I can spare a couple of men to accompany you. I'm truly sorry that we must part company here. You have become a true friend of all the Arad people."

"Good luck and may Jehosa guide you on your quest," I replied getting into the mannerisms of these people. "No, you need your fighters; we can take care of ourselves, but we do appreciate the guide. Water and salt spell life in this land, and we don't know where either lies on the route south. Thanks for volunteering, Emil." He bowed low acknowledging me.

The goodbyes were quickly said, and Jackal's party rode off at a gallop heading northeast. I wondered if we would ever see him and his wife again. I felt just a bit sad at their departure, but we had our own mission to perform, and our next step was to get to the southern edge of this arid land. After we thanked the folks for their hospitality, we prepared our horses and our gear for the next leg of the journey. Emil handed each of us a small pouch containing salt. Additionally, we each got a goatskin water bag. He explained that the next stretch held little water, unless one wanted to stop at the water hole beside the infidel's new roadway, which neither he nor we did. Then we were off. Emil and Roy rode on either side of me, Sandy and Simon came next, followed by Sarah Jane and Raphael leading our packhorse.

This was a leisurely journey, for nothing it seemed could cause the

Prophet to hurry along. He constantly pointed out the magnificent landscape; here was a man who could be content just wandering about the land. Of course, he told us many stories concerning the history of his people. It seemed that hundreds of years ago, they had lived far to the south. There they had been oppressed and taken as slaves. Many escaped and fled to the Arad. Here in this arid land they, with their holy and austere viewpoint of life, thrived where others might not. Then came the infidels. For many, many years, the prophets all spoke of the coming of the Great Messiah, the son of Jehosa, who would free them from the infidels. I certainly hoped that would happen, for it would benefit all lands conquered by these Centurions.

Roy asked, "Are there any expected signs that might foreshadow the coming of the Great Messiah? Does anyone have any idea how soon he may come?"

"Strange that you ask this," Emil answered. "Each prophet has his own special bond with Jehosa. When you listen to each, at first you may be baffled by the apparent differences between the predictions. If you study each, you find that we all have received the same basic message. The signs are said to be three. The first two have already occurred. It is said and predicted by all prophets that first shall come a great thunderous rain, rain in great quantity unlike any rain we have ever seen before. That occurred some time ago, when Zargarb fell to the infidels. The second sign has also appeared. Great fields of desert flowers shall bring forth massive blossoms where before only stark grasses grew. We only await the last sign of the birth of our savior, the Great Messiah, son of Jehosa. It is said that on the night of his birth, a new bright star will appear in the heavens where none shone before. It shall shine for seven days and then fade away, marking the cycle of fleshly life. Our bodies are born, grow to adulthood, then gradually fade, and then die out. The star marks the passage of the son of Jehosa as he is born, grows to maturity and then fades and dies, as do all of our fleshly bodies. So, Roy, we nightly observe the heavens above looking for that new star. So far we have not seen it, but surely as I am here now, the star will come, but who can say just when. However, I have an intense feeling that we have not long to wait."

I felt rather awful. The first two signs were entirely the doing of us druwids calling forth immense lightning to try to defeat the Centurions at Zargarb, specifically Isabel and her friend. After such an intensification of the storm, of necessity, it had to dump its vast amounts of rain over the land just beyond Zargarb, here in the western section of the Arad. Nature, suddenly blessed with such massive rainfall, seized the opportunity to germinate its many seeds, which had lain dormant all this time, waiting for just such a chance rain. I felt embarrassed that the first two signs foretelling the coming of their Great Messiah were entirely man-made, or druwid-made I should say. I was thus reminded of the druwid saying: "Our actions here and now often have an impact far beyond what we see here and now." Never have I thought it more apropos than with Isabel's summoning of that storm. However, I took consolation in that we druwids certainly couldn't create the third sign, the new star in the sky. I just hoped these people didn't lose hope if that star did not appear for a long time after the first two signs.

Roy then cleverly changed the topic, because he too felt rather embarrassed about the signs. We all did. "How far do we have to travel to get to the southern border?"

"Ah, as we ride, perhaps three or four days unless you want to take the direct route over the infidel's road, in which case it may be but two days," he replied.

"Ah, four will do quite nicely," Roy commented quickly, "besides, we all enjoy looking at this land. It has a particular charm about it — bit hot and harsh and unforgiving, but still, it has an attraction to us."

He laughed, "Bit harsh, eh? Well, yes, if you don't have salt and water, deadly, not harsh. At first when the infidels first came into the Arad, we hoped the lack of both would drive them away. Alas, they soon found salt mines and slaves to work them. They built their roadway to go from water hole to water hole. We learned that these infidels are not dummies; they learn from their mistakes."

There is little to tell of the next four days. We got an earful of religious teachings but nothing out of the ordinary occurred. The salt and water got us through without any difficulties. On the evening of the fourth day, we climbed a small rise and stopped to gaze at the panorama below us. There was the Med Sea once again. Further, here lay the only port city in Arad, as well as the southernmost city, Al Barq, whose population had now swelled with occupation forces. Indeed, Al Barq was at pivotal location in the Centurion supply line. From here, boats took supplies and men over to the cities of the Sea Princes. Caravans and marching reinforcement foot soldiers constantly arrived from way down south, stopping here to refresh and await deployment. Emil explained that over half of the local Arads had abandoned the city, fleeing to more remote and distant towns and villages. The actual population had grown two-fold due to the large numbers of infidels who were here at various times. Since night was nearly upon us, after gazing our fill, we retreated into the hills to camp for the night. The next day, we would venture into the city and see about our next step.

That night, after we ate supper and had lain down for the night, we were gazing up at the stars, thinking about Emil's omen. Suddenly, Roy cried out, "Look there — in Drago, by his head. That star was never there before now!" Seven sets of eyes turned northward to gaze at the constellation we call Drago, the Dragon.

"Oh my," said an almost speechless Emil. He stared long at this new star, "All praise be to Jehosa! For tonight, he has created a fleshly form for his son so that he may come among us and free us from the infidels! Oh glory beyond all words!"

It was a new star, smack dead center in the head of Drago! None of us could now sleep. As time passed, we all swore that it grew steadily brighter! It was not moving, so it could not be a "falling star." By midnight, the new star was the brightest star in the entire northern sky and growing still brighter. We speculated that we might even be able to see it in the daytime sky if it got much brighter!

Never have I seen a man be so devoutly religious, so humble and yet so excited. His God had sent him the long foretold sign. I began to wonder about this religion. All these prophets predicted the same three signs. This one certainly could not be of druwid origin. Had Nature somehow spoken to these prophets? If so, when and how? Was there a Jehosa? Was Jehosa and Nature one and the same being? Was he a being, perhaps with no need of a body to create effects? Certainly, it took godlike powers to create a new star! Then a completely new line of thoughts flew through my mind. Had Jehosa known about Isabel and used her storm as his portent? Had he somehow influenced Isabel into doing what she did? Was Isabel acting with her own determinism or had she been controlled or used by Jehosa in some way? Were we, the Guardians, somehow connected to this religion and Jehosa? Were all of our actions, our decisions, part of some larger scheme? Could we, I, be being used by some god, without my even knowing it? Or could Isabel have been so influenced? How had this Jehosa known when Isabel would call forth that storm? These prophets had known of those two signs many, many years before Isabel ever set foot in Zargarb!

Sarah Jane, ever the practical one, asked, "Emil, just where in Arad is this new baby being born tonight? Does anyone know? Could we ride there to help in the birthing? We are, after all, experienced in birthing and healing."

Emil looked torn between oaths and friendship. "I — I know the place, that is, the town. That knowledge is something that is shared only among us prophets. You understand, for the safety of the newborn child, the Great Messiah, the son of Lord Jehosa. He must have time to grow safely to adulthood. I dare not name the place, though of all people, you, who have given unselfishly to all Arads, should know. I'm sworn to never say the name of the birthplace. Yet, if you will all swear to me never to reveal this information, even on threat of fleshly death, I'll give you a sign that you may interpret as you will. That is the most I can do for you."

Instantly and with no hesitation, we all swore never to reveal this information.

The Prophet Emil Tamir said only, "We first met in that town."

It had to be Jerilum, their holy town!

"I must ride yet tonight," concluded Emil. "I have seen you safely to the southern town as you have requested. This event naturally changes my life. I must ride north yet tonight. I bid you all farewell."

We thanked him profusely for all he had done for us and watched him gallop off on his northerly journey. I wondered if he would take the infidel's road this time because it would cut days off his journey back to Jerilum. I never found out, though.

We finally fell asleep sometime after midnight, still staring at the new star, which continued to grow in brilliance. The last thought I recall having before sleep took me into its embrace was "I wonder how many people are watching this new star right now?" I had no answer for that question.

The next day, the star was so bright that we could see it even at noon. Over the next two days, it grew steadily brighter. Thereafter, it began to fade. And a week from this night, it was gone, as suddenly as it had come. Drago's head was back to the same faint stars outlining its head. We relayed the news to Alabaster. He, too, had noticed the star, and was curious to hear our interpretation of its significance. I suspected he didn't believe in Jehosa and the Great Messiah. In some twenty years, maybe something would happen. I swore always to keep an eye on what was happening in Juda Arad, somehow.

Chapter 18 Al Barq, Juda Arad

The dog days of the summer of 559 AH baked us when we first entered the southern city of Al Barq — hot and dry even with the Med Sea at hand. At night, some relief came from the sea breezes. The days were still sweltering as we rode into the bustling city, even as we did early that first morning. Centurions seemed to be literally everywhere; they had taken over a large percentage of the city for themselves. Yes, here and there, we spied a dark-skinned Arad local, but the bronzed skin of the Centurions predominated. Al Barq served as a major nexus for their broad field of activities in the northern part of Tarra.

Our initial plan was simple: find an inn and a public bathhouse. My long hair felt incredibly dirty having been balled up in the turban cloth for so many days. I relished a good long bath. This city was not walled, or if it had been, Al Barq had long ago outgrown its walls. Sprawling across several miles of hills and valleys, this was the largest city we'd seen in Juda Arad. In fact, according to Jackal, it was twice as big as any other Arad city — that is, it was before the infidels took the city as theirs.

Just because there were no walls surrounding the city didn't mean it wasn't guarded. As we approached, we spied three Centurions on guard duty near the large street that we were headed for, as we rode down from the hills overlooking the city. As we approached, one said dryly, "Arad sector is down by the docks. Stay out of the Centurion sectors, please. Just ride on through them if you don't have business with us." We nodded and rode on past them. Roy looked at me, and I, him. We both smiled; we were thinking the same thought. We were taken for locals. Wearing their traditional robes and turbans plus our tanned faces, why, we looked the part.

As we rode down this large street heading for the Med Sea and the docks, I observed the type of shops we passed. Soon it became impossible to remember them all. Just about everything imaginable was represented at least once. However, the Centurion's new bathhouse caught our eye. It was huge and boasted hot and cold running water, but there was a guard on duty at the front door — safe assumption, Arad locals were not welcome here. Finally, we entered the slummier section of town, the warehouse district. Here, huge three story buildings, which at one time long ago had held goods, either inbound or outbound, temporarily until their ship docked, had been converted to hold those Arads who had been displaced by the infidels.

We found an inn called the Boar's Head because of the huge stuffed pig's head over the main entrance. Simon and Raphael did the honors of making inquiries and getting us three rooms. Shortly, they reappeared waving keys and smiling, so we knew this was the right inn. We led the horses around to the rear to where the inn's stables were located, paid a gold coin to have them well fed and looked after, and then headed for our rooms, lugging all our saddlebags and sacks. Simon already had the location for their public bathhouse, so once we unloaded our gear in our rooms, got some clean items to wear, we headed off to take a much needed bath!

At this early hour in the morning, only a few women were bathing so we had the huge bath mostly to ourselves. It consisted of a huge stone basin some twenty feet across with stone steps leading down into it along all four sides. Its depth was three feet and the fires in the corner ovens kept the air warm and moist. Why is a bath so utterly relaxing? I find I can't properly "live" without spending hours soaking at least once a week. Naturally, the guys didn't want to soak for an hour or more. When they began to get restless, I sent them out to do our laundry. Just around the back of a bathhouse is a laundry facility. They grumbled but did it for us. Incidentally, it cost me a gold coin to pay for six baths and all the laundry, darn cheap if you ask me.

When we three women finally emerged an hour and a half later with pink skin but feeling human once more, Simon presented us with a little present. "Here, I took the liberty of purchasing us another set of robes and turban scarves. Change into these and we'll get the old ones washed too. I assumed we would want to continue to look like the locals." Sandy gave him a big hug and thank you kiss. We quickly changed into the new clothing, thanking him several times.

Next, I decided we should hang out in the inn's dining room, taking a long lunch break. I hoped we would hear the local gossip. Besides, we needed time to plan the next leg of our journey. Over lunch, we discussed our next move; the consensus was that we should go all the way south to Megalos and see what their homeland was like, what their rulers' thought and had planned. Simon pointed out all we really needed to do was follow the brick road and we would eventually find Megalos. I pointed out we didn't know how far away it was or the availability of towns for re-supplying or whether travel by non-Centurions was allowed.

"Perhaps, once we leave here, we should go back to using our old disguise, that of seeking grain trade routes," Simon suggested. "That should give us sufficient reason to be on their roadway." We thought this was a wise move. Just then, a number of local workers came in to eat their lunch. We shut up and began to listen to their talk.

The sudden appearance of the new star was the sole topic of their conversation! One insisted he could even see it right now at noon. There was much speculation in just what town their Great Messiah had chosen to be born. Equally, speculation was rampant on just how soon the Great Messiah would begin to act to drive these infidels out of their land. The optimists claimed that, since he was the son of Jehosa, he could do it by the time he was six years old. The pessimists suggested that perhaps when he was twenty-five, he would take action. Next, came the speed with which the Great Messiah would drive them out of Arad. Some thought that it might take weeks, while others thought it would be more like years. The only point of agreement amongst these people was that nothing was likely to happen for close to a decade.

Since the local gossip was mostly pointless, we left the inn, deciding to explore the city and observe all we could firsthand. Thus, we split up into three pairs, each taking a different section of the city. We planned to meet back at the inn at dinnertime. Roy and I strolled around the docks. We counted six vessels loading, two unloading. Far off in the distance, another pair would make port later today. Of the eight we could see up close, five flew the Sea Princes' flags and looked similar to those we had seen before when we had sailed to Velona. The other three we learned were Arad designs, good for short coastal hauls, principally to Zargarb.

On the humanitarian side, from chats with various locals, we learned that over the years, the infidels had slowly pushed the Arads out of the more prosperous sections of the city. Many chose to leave for more distant towns. Those that remained either could not afford to leave or stubbornly refused to depart, choosing instead to harry the infidels every chance they could. Everywhere we walked, the whispered conversations all centered on the "new star" and what exactly it meant both in short term and long term.

At one market square, we met the Prophet Rama Sama Hama, a middle aged, skinny man with a long, fuzzy, black beard and moustache to match. Today, locals flocked to hear his words, for the appearance of the star made believers out of even the most skeptical. During a break in his preaching, we introduced ourselves explaining that we had journeyed here, guided by the Prophet Emil Tamil. "Ah yes, Emil. Good man. Why would Emil guide you here to Al Barq? Surely you must know the way?"

We explained where we came from and how we got here, just the basics, mind you. I felt we ought to be relatively open and straightforward with their holy men. As it turned out, this would turn out to be exceedingly fortuitous in many ways in just a few hours. When he learned that we, along with Emil, had first spotted the new star when it was very faint, he insisted that we tell him all about it. He didn't ask, nor probably needed to ask, why Emil had left us so suddenly in the middle of the night. Then he was besieged with a new group of women demanding to know if this was the foretold "new star" that would bring them deliverance. We left him as he began to explain the prophesy he had long memorized from his teachers and they from theirs.

About the only other useful fact we uncovered was that there remained about forty thousand Arads in the city. Finally, we decided to give it up and headed back to the inn; we had walked a fair number of miles around and around the dock sector. That's when we both got an emergency mental message from a highly upset and distraught Sandy. *Bethany, Roy — it's horrible! We have to do something really fast!*

Slow down. Tell us what's the matter. Are you and Simon in danger? Where are you? You want us to come at once? I sent back, imagining all sorts of dire situations those two could have gotten themselves into on their walk.

No, we are safe. She took a breath, and tried to relay calmly. *We've been exploring the sector in which the Governor lives and rules the city. Quite by accident and using our special skills, we've overheard a discussion between the Governor and his commanders and councilors. They are exceedingly afraid of this prophesy of the Great Messiah, mostly because such rumors are disrupting their control over the Arad peoples. Since no one knows in what city this new supposed savior has been born, in anger, the Governor has just ordered the execution of all newborn babies throughout this entire city!*

You are kidding?

No! One commander even pointed out that his wife just gave birth to his second son last week and did his orders include the Governor's own son? He said absolutely every newborn child must die, even those of the Centurions. He reasoned who knows what physical form this supposed savior would take? He can't risk any baby being left alive.

The Barbarian! How can he get away with this mass murder?

Simon says with enough might, you can do anything you want. They control the town. Bethany, we have to do something!

Calm down. We will. When is he planning to go on this murder spree?

Tonight, late after everyone is in bed. The soldiers are to go door-to-door, rousing, and searching. All newborns are to be taken from their mothers, killed, and thrown into the Med Sea. What are we going to do? What can we do to stop this? We have to do something!

Get back to the inn as fast as you can. Let Raphael and Sarah Jane know. We'll be along as soon as we can.

"Come on Roy; we have to find Prophet Hama and fast!" I declared with a passion. We ran as fast as we could to where we had last seen him. Thank heavens he was still there, but the crowds had thinned.

"Rama, we desperately need you now. Stop everything. Lives are at stake," I exclaimed urgently. He shooed the stragglers away.

"Two of my companions have just overheard a secret conversation between the Governor and his commanders. He is so worried about the coming of the Great Messiah that he has ordered all newborn children to be murdered tonight after everyone has gone to bed. He gave orders to his soldiers to go door to door searching for and killing all babies. We have to spread the word and somehow get them and their mothers out of Al Barq before the soldiers come! Can you help us?"

He had me repeat it, pulling his beard when he heard that the Governor's own son was to be killed as well. Then, he cursed solidly for an entire minute before he regained his holy composure. "Where are you staying? Can you fight or offer some defense for all these women?" I told him we could, all six of us. "Okay. I'll trust you. You see, Jehosa has already revealed to me years ago that this might happen. He even said, 'Seek help from strangers to your land.' I'm prepared, though the poor families are not. Here, take this token to the innkeeper where you are staying, show him this — it'll convince him that you are one of us and that you are following my orders. Beneath the basement storage room of the inn, we have dug a tunnel that connects to the sewers. We have marked a passage with red dots that will take you through the maze to a point just outside the northern edge of the city. I'll send a messenger at once to the nearest village. They'll send wagons as fast as possible to that location. Your task will be to escort all that come through the tunnels to the outside and see that they are protected until the wagons arrive. I don't know how long that wait will be, I'm sorry. I'll begin spreading the word. I do hope that many young mothers will heed my warnings, but then Jehosa has said that many will not. Please, I implore you for all these mothers, do not fail me!"

"Sir, you have our complete assistance; they will not be harmed unless all of us are slain," Roy swore to Hama. "But may I offer a suggestion?"

"Thank you, strangers from the Greenway. That is all I can ask. Yes, a suggestion, young lad?"

"What if there was some kind of serious delay that would keep the soldiers occupied for some time this evening? That would give you more time for them to get to the inn. It's going to look very suspicious with lots of mothers carrying their babies into the inn and not coming out. Surely, someone will get wise to what's going on there," Roy commented.

"Ah yes, that is the only flaw in my plan. What could possibly delay them?" he asked suddenly very curious, again stroking his beard.

"Suppose there was a big fire in the infidel's section of town, perhaps the wealthiest section? Isn't a large scale fire the worst possible thing that can happen to a city?" Roy hinted.

"No, a plague is worse, but yes, a fire, a big one that threatened rich homes — now that would certainly require an all-hands effort. I see where you are heading with this. While everyone's attention is riveted on the fire, the women can get to the inn without too much fear of being observed. I like this, besides the infidels are harried as well. Yes, I think that would be an ideal distraction. How are we to set such a large fire? We cannot get very close to those houses."

"No, but we can see that the fire is set, and we can do it from a distance, if only we knew what buildings to set ablaze and when. We don't really want to kill innocent people," Roy explained. Suddenly I wished Thomas, our Lord of Fire, were here. I knew that he would love to be the one to set the blaze.

With a disbelieving look and with raising eyebrows, Rama said, "You can do this thing — start a big fire — from a distance?"

"We need only to be able to somehow see the target buildings; that's all. Might take us five minutes to get the fires going rather well," Roy said almost apologetically, figuring that a good druwid might get a roaring fire going in much less time. He knew Thomas could, but he wasn't here.

"I'll send a messenger to the inn early tonight. He'll identify himself with another token. He can direct you. If you can do this thing, many innocent babies will likely survive this night of unspeakable horrors. May Jehosa be with you and guide you. Now I must make hast. Once again, many, many thanks." With that, he bowed and hastened on down the street. We likewise headed back to the inn as rapidly as we could without drawing undo attention to ourselves.

When we arrived, we found the other four waiting anxiously for us; the girls had been crying; their eyes were red and robes wet. Raphael and Simon looked as grim as I have ever seen them. I knew they felt utterly powerless to stop this murderous madness. I ushered them into our room, shut the door, and quickly outlined all that we had discussed with the Prophet Hama. That changed everything. Four went from utter hopelessness to a vengeful enthusiasm.

"What are we waiting for?" Roy suggested. "Let's contact the innkeeper at once and get things ready!"

"Better that we talk about this in private," I cautioned. "Simon, take the token and bring the innkeeper here to our room." He smiled and took off at once.

"Too bad Thomas isn't here," Sarah Jane commented. "He'd love to be the one to set the fires." We all chuckled in agreement. "So who's the next best fire starter?" After some discussion, Sarah Jane and I were nominated. However, Roy would not hear of us going alone without him as our Protector. We three had the task to create the diversion that would allow those women with their newborn babies to have a chance of getting to the inn undetected. I hoped and prayed this would work.

Shortly, Simon returned with a very worried innkeeper, Rashid, who was about six feet tall but weighted perhaps two hundred fifty pounds, both heavy set and a heavy eater. His black hair looked slightly disheveled and his white apron bespoke of his doubling as cook. "This you got from my friend Rama?" he asked knowing that we had to have.

"Yes, unless we take very fast action right now, tonight all the newborn babies are to be slain on the orders of the Governor," I replied cutting to the quick. "Let me explain more fully and also what Rama has told us." A couple of minutes later, Rashid's face turned deathly pale. I spied a nervous twitch in his hands as I was explaining the situation. First, he continually wiped them on his apron, but by the time I got to the end, he had twisted the cloth into a tight knot and actually ripped it; his normally dark complexion had turned a ghastly grey. Evidently, this was something Rama had foretold, but he wished would not have occurred.

"Oh, dear me! Oh, dear me! I — I — I didn't really believe Rama, really I didn't. I just sort of went along with him. Oh dear. And now it is actually occurring. Oh my. This is really terrible, the heathens, the infidels — curse them all. May they rot in the ground with slimy worms eating their remains," he cursed, unable to find the right curse to match the horror of the situation. He took a deep breath, muttered a prayer to Jehosa, and finally regained his composure; the color gradually returned to his face, and he untwisted his hands and remains of his apron.

"Okay then," he said, "the first thing is to show you the concealed entrance in the storeroom. Next, you need to get all of the lanterns out, primed, and set into place. One of you will have to walk the path through the sewer tunnels placing them at the proper locations. We've rigged hanging hooks where each belongs so that people using the tunnels can safely see their way, but not to attract the attention of people out on the streets above. Yes, the lanterns must be placed and lighted; this will take about an hour to accomplish, yes. Then there are the blankets; Rama asked for a hundred blankets to be stored here for just such an emergency. Those need to be dusted off and made ready, perhaps taken to the exit location might be wise, yes I do believe that would be best. This will be a very long night indeed. Okay, so which one of you wants to help with the lanterns and the blankets?"

He led us down into his cellar storeroom, which was filled with dried foods, ale, and a little wine. Behind one wall of ale casks, a concealed door opened into a tiny room filled with blankets, all wrapped in canvas coverings to protect them. A thick layer of dust lay on them all. Obviously, they had lain here a very long time. Next, he led us to the wall of wine racks filled with perhaps fifty bottles. He showed us a hidden latch on the right side, which when released, allowed the entire wall to rotate, revealing a black opening with a damp, stinky odor, which slowly reached our nostrils as we stared into the inky dark. "Oh yes, the lanterns," he said to himself. Behind another concealed door was a smaller room stacked with several hundred lanterns. He fired up one lantern and showed us where to hang it just inside the door.

Once hung just inside the black opening, we spied steps leading downward. "You must take the lanterns and hang them from hooks like this one. Every place that there is a junction where a choice in direction is to be made, look for the sign of Jehosa three feet from the start of that passage," he explained.

"Wait, what is the sign of Jehosa?" I asked realizing we didn't know this key piece of information.

"It is a five-pointed star embedded in a circle," he hastily explained. "Here, like this." He drew one on the dirt floor and then scuffed it out with his boot once we had seen it. "I'd better get back to the kitchen or I'll be missed. Come get me if you need anything. If Rama is right, soon you may have some helping hands."

Once he had left, Roy commented, "Spooky. Our Lightning Circle symbol is a six-pointed star within a circle. Spooky."

Since this appeared to be a lengthy task, I setup a relay team approach. While we three women began dusting out the canvas sacks with the blankets, we also handed the lanterns down the steps to the men who in relay fashion passed them on to Roy, who took point, finding the path, the hooks, and hanging the lanterns. Soon, we were also needed in the relay line, passing the lanterns on to the men as they got further and further away from the inn. An hour later, we six lugged the blankets down the dimly light tunnel complex to a secluded valley one hill beyond the city.

The steps led down some twenty feet into the sewer system. Our path twisted and turned for perhaps a mile before the sewer lines ran out, and a side tunnel led directly on for another mile or so to a concealed opening in the side of the hill. Here we deposited the blankets in neat piles ready for use later this night. By the time we had finished, several other men had joined us to help. Two remained in the hidden valley; both were armed with swords, though we knew they probably would stand little chance if they had to face a Centurion warrior.

When we got back into the inn's storeroom, a young lad perhaps only fourteen was waiting for us. "I am Caliph. Rama told me to take you to where you can see the infidel's storage warehouses." He was nearly completely hidden by his robe and head turban. "It is getting dark; we should go now." His voice sounded scared but resolute.

"Thanks Caliph," I said calmly. "I'm called Bethany. You're leading me, Sarah Jane, and Roy. Okay, the rest of you do what you can. We'll see you all later on." The others bade us good luck and to be cautious. We followed Caliph as he snuck out of the back door of the inn, which opened near the stable. The sun was long gone; twilight faded as we slunk down the side streets, staying in the shadows as much as possible — four clandestine figures in the night. We hiked about a quarter mile before we entered the Centurion section of town. Here, Caliph slowed our pace trying to avoid and hide from any infidel that might be out in the street. Fortunately for us, the streets were nearly deserted. I figured they were getting their briefing for the night's massacre.

Finally, we reached the side of a two-story warehouse, which appeared dark and deserted. Caliph whispered, "Empty; climb up to roof; follow me." He led us around to the rear where a date tree grew quite close beside the building. We watched as he crawled between the tree and the building, and proceeded to chimney upwards.

"Clever," I whispered.

"If he can do it, so can we," Sarah Jane laughed quietly. It was harder than it looked! In the end, we all made it up to the top and the roof, but it took us more than twice as long as it did our guide. Further, we arrived quite out of breath from the exertion.

Once we recovered, Caliph pointed out the granary buildings and the warehouse now used as the armory. I made doubly sure that we knew precisely which buildings he indicated. I wanted no mistake on targets, for neither Sarah Jane nor myself wanted to accidentally burn down homes in which innocent people lived, even if they were infidel families. Once we were both satisfied of our targets, which by the way were about three-quarters of a mile distant though clearly silhouetted, we began our chants. Roy and Caliph watched. Soon walls of red, burning flames appeared above the targeted roofs and slowly descended onto the dry roofs. In this climate, the roofs were tinder dry and flared into flames almost as soon as our flames touched them. However, we needed to make this a big fire, so we made sure that all four roofs were in flames before we cancelled our druwid flames.

Caliph, shocked beyond all belief, kept muttering prayers to Jehosa. I firmly believe that he now thought of us as goddesses! We watched for a few minutes to see if this plan would work. It did. In a few minutes, Centurions came pouring out of nearby buildings, screaming "Fire! Fire!" Soon it would be an all-hands effort to put out the roaring rooftop blazes.

Quietly, we descended to the street. I found going down nearly as hard as going up, because of the effort needed to avoid falling down. Then even more cautiously, we crept back into the Arad sector of Al Barq. No Centurion saw us, of that I was certain.

We weren't prepared for the sight at the inn, when we finally returned. Dozens of women carrying small babies flocked to the inn. All were terrified, crying, and attempting to keep their babies quiet. We suddenly realized how frightening and awful this whole situation was for these people. On only a moment's notice, their whole lives were uprooted. They were forced to leave the rest of their families behind, along with all of their possessions, bringing only their precious babies. Theirs was an act of utter desperation, hoping to save the life of their newborn children. My heart went out to all these brave women whose courage was something to behold.

Once inside the inn, I found a dozen men helping, explaining to each new arrival what they were to do and where they were going. From each woman, they made sure that she and her husband had coordinated which distant town or village to which she would be heading. I learned that over the next two weeks, three-quarters of the remaining locals would at night, secretly and without fanfare, depart the city, eventually rejoining their wives and babies. Further, sometime later, we learned that after a month had passed, not a single Arad person remained in the town that had once been their largest city.

Now, I found controlled chaos was the order of this early evening. Of necessity, we grouped several women together and then one of us would lead them down the tunnel passage safely to the waiting area outside of town. I lost count of the number of trips that I personally made, back and forth. The worst came a little after midnight. Suddenly the still, quiet night was pierced with women's voices screaming in violent protests. I had visions of the bronze skinned, armed infidels breaking into a sleeping home, ripping a baby from its mother's arms, and killing it. All night long, we heard these random screams piercing the night. Even down in the sewers, we heard them, which tended to steel the resolve of the women we were leading to safety.

By the time the screams began, those who tried to get to the inn at the last minute found the going difficult and hazardous. Many women, I suspected, just didn't believe this could happen or weren't reached by the Prophet Rama in time. Perhaps, he was still going door-to-door, barely one step ahead of the infidels. As I returned from the tunnel to get the next group, Roy, Simon, and the innkeeper, Rashid, took me aside. Simon spoke for them, "We have a new serious problem developing. The Centurions are getting close to the inn. They are about two blocks away now. Eventually, they're going to see the frantic, panicking women rushing into this inn, and you know what that means." Rashid looked petrified, unable to speak. You could smell his fear; his eyes darted everywhere, as if infidels were already inside his inn.

"You have an idea, I really hope?" I commented, knowing I had none at all.

"We're going to have to stay here by the door and fully utilize my special training to make any that come here go away. I'll have to influence greatly many minds before the night is done. I need Roy to back me up in case one gets by me. Do we have your permission to so mess with their minds and kill any whom I cannot affect?" Simon asked, though he knew I knew there was no other real choice. I had never before asked him to completely mess with another's mind on such a scale as this. Yet, considering the circumstances, I gave my complete approval, knowing it would be up to the four of us to provide all the escorting through the lengthy tunnels.

Roy gave me a brief report on what was going on whenever I arrived back at the inn to escort the next small group of frightened, desperate women. Periodically, three Centurions came pounding on the door demanding to see the women who they'd just seen entering. Simon would say aloud and enforce into their minds, "I'm sorry; we are closed. There are no women in here. Several did pass by here on their way up the street. Hurry, you might catch them." And, as if hypnotized, they would repeat, "Closed. No women here. Up the street. Hurry men. Catch them." Unfortunately, about one in ten couldn't be so dominated and altered by Simon, and these pushed their way past him to get inside. Roy, concealed just inside, quickly dispatched them using backstabbing techniques, though Simon also had to kill as well. Their bodies were carried down and thrown into the sewers and left to rot and feed the rats.

The hideous wailing of women did not stop until dawn. Only then did this night of terror end. I was completely exhausted, having walked many, many miles back and forth through the tunnels. My robes stank horribly. When we six had led the last to safety, without a word, we collapsed on the ground beside those we had rescued. Six other men stood guard while we slept a bit.

Later we found out the tally. We had rescued three hundred women and their babies. However, the infidels had murdered over four hundred, some of those were their own children — Governor's orders. That morning, the Med Sea was littered with their small, ghastly white bodies floating out on the tide past the six docked ships. Thus, the night of Mass Murder finally came to a quiet end. Until this day, every time I hear a woman wailing, images of this night vividly come back into my mind. I cannot get rid of them; neither can my friends.

About ten that morning, Rama and another six men appeared from the tunnel bringing a bit of food and water with them, rousing us.

After relaying the news to us, he commented, "There is no way any of us can express fully how much we thank you for what you have done for us. It goes beyond all possible words. Know that Jehosa knows what you have done, and his divine light shall shine upon you forever. On the lighter side, my only problem is that now young Caliph swears that you are goddesses while Rashid believes your men are great wizards. I'm utterly unable to convince them otherwise," he smiled sheepishly. "I've heard fragments of some of the things you have done, and I too am deeply impressed. Indeed, Jehosa has chosen wisely our protectors."

Simon interjected sleepily, "Yes, well, all may end poorly yet, if the transportation does not come soon. There's no way we can properly feed this many people."

"Have faith, my son. Jehosa will deliver," Rama proclaimed with a total certainty. Indeed, near dark, the first of many wagons began arriving from nameless tracks across the mostly deserted countryside. None dared to travel the normal routes. They came to this hidden valley in secret and left just as secretly. Each wagon carried a half dozen women away to a new village and a new start in life. These were the lucky ones. We spent two days watching over this exodus before we made one last trip through the tunnels to the inn. We spent another day sleeping, eating, bathing, and washing our smelly clothing. That was a terribly somber day. Everywhere we went in the Arad sector, the mood of the people had changed drastically. Gone was the cheerfulness of life. In its place was a great sadness, a grief that knows no words. We, too, shared in that mutual sadness. It was the darkest day we'd ever experienced, but worse was to come much later on.

Chapter 19 Through the Southlands and into Megalos

The cooler days of early September were welcomed by us all, now two weeks into our journey further south. The grief hanging over the city of Al Barq was so great that we left the very next day, just riding southward along the paved road built by these baby slayers. Did you know that one can feel the collective emotion of a large group of people? Try it sometime. Our mood was just as dismal. However, after a somber week on the trail, we gradually pulled out of the sadness.

Simon now rode at the front with Roy at his side; Sandy and I came next, for I had given Simon carte blanche to do anything he wanted to do to these butcher's minds. We had no real plan except to get to Megalos. Once there, we were certain we'd think of something. Grieving as we were, whenever we encountered any Centurions along the road, Simon didn't hesitate to alter their minds to let us pass unchallenged in any way. It was probably foolish of us, but you have to remember the mood we were all in at this time. A man may make great works of physical wonder, such as paved roads and running water bathhouses, and yet still be suppressive and viciously mean to his fellow men. I guess what I'm trying to tell you is not to judge men solely on their wondrous, long lasting creations, as later historians actually did.

Of the Southlands, we had little information for it was largely unknown to the Greenway. In a way, we rather enjoyed the month that it took us to cover some seven hundred miles, mostly due south. The Southlands is a vast brown and green savannah, miles of sparse grasslands interspersed with nearly barren hills with only an occasional strange tree here and there. True, water holes were abundant, especially along the paved road, but the land supported the animal kingdom rather than men, though some men lived here. Sarah Jane declared that was an understatement. Everywhere we rode, we passed enormous herds of wild beasts, oxen, deer, antelope, zebras, giraffes, giant elephants, and creatures that looked like wild boars. Yes, there were lion prides and hyenas galore — even large dog packs. Here in the Southlands was where Nature placed the vast majority of her animals!

There were men here too, black skinned men whose language we did not speak nor understand for it was nothing like we had ever heard before. There are enough similarities between our own language and that of the Sea Princes, Juda Arad and even the Centurions for us to quickly pick them up. The language these men spoke was foreign to us. Yet, the few we met were friendly enough as well as patient enough to work out hand signs and drawings in the dirt.

We learned that many of the people native to the Southlands were tribal oriented, living in small villages scattered throughout this vast land. (We estimated that you could fit four Greenways into the Southland and still have land left over. Our estimate was considerably off, however. Later years would show just how much larger it actually was.) Others were nomads who wander the land, never staying long in any one location. Though their standard of living was dismal from our viewpoint, they were not ignorant. On the contrary, we found them to be highly intelligent and spiritual, but prone to superstitions. Yet, these people also hated and feared the Centurions. All this we learned during our third week of travel.

Just as the second week since we had left Al Barq behind came to an end, we spied a half dozen buzzards circling overhead, some distance from the brick road. Naturally, we had to go see what was happening. About a mile west of the road, we found a tall, thin black man, probably in his early twenties, unconscious on the ground, leaning against one of these strange trees. Even more naturally, with six healers present, we just had to see what was wrong with him and try to save him. So we tied our horses to the tree and began to observe him to find out what had happened. I was the first to spot it, for I had done just this very same thing with my dad, though it seemed so long ago to me now. "Viper bite in his leg," I declared. "See the two tiny pin-pricks?"

"A bad one, he's about dead," pronounced Sarah Jane with a sigh.

"Can we do anything to save him or is it already too late?" asked Raphael.

"Well, we can try to suck out what poison is in this streak up his leg and plaster it with alum to slowly suck out more. I don't know whether he will survive. Yet, we have to at least try," she declared and we set to work. Roy, Sandy, Simon, and I set up our camp here by the tree and got water boiling. Meantime, Sarah Jane, with Raphael assisting, worked her magic on the young man. When she finished, she declared, "That's about all I can do now. If he survives the night, there is hope."

All that night, we took turns sitting beside him, wiping his feverishly hot body with a cool, wet rag. At times, he spoke in a delirium; his words we couldn't understand. Forty-eight hours after we found him, he finally awoke weak from his near death ordeal. He recoiled from us the instant his eyes found us sitting on the ground beside him. In his condition, he was able to only move about four inches further away. He paused, like a frightened animal, staring wide-eyed at us. We must have seemed very strange to him, for we were dressed in hides of deer, that is, we were wearing our comfortable leather clothes once more, having tucked the robes and turban cloths away in sacks. We all sported light tans compared to his nearly naked jet-black body. He wore only a loincloth and crude sandals. The viper had struck just above his left ankle.

At the moment, we didn't know what he was thinking. Later we surmised that at first he thought we were Centurions, but a closer look changed his mind. We weren't bronzed skinned, nor did we wear their dress nor did we have their plates of metal on our chests. We were dressed in the skins of deer with which he was familiar. His conclusion was that we were different, though he understood not a word we were saying to him, attempting to say we were friends, we rescued him, how was he feeling, and was he hungry. Simon reacted the best of all of us. He took one of the water pouches, held it up, and let some water flow into his mouth, that is, he took a drink. He then offered it to him. Hesitatingly, the man reached for it, emulated Simon's exaggerated motions, and took a long drink.

Next, Simon retrieved a piece of the roasted rabbit that we had still simmering by the fire, took a small bite of it, then offered it to him, still chewing his mouthful. The man put down the water and took the rabbit, tasted it, and hastily devoured it. He was indeed hungry! Simon offered him all that Sarah Jane thought wise at this point in time. Next, she pointed to his leg and the various salves and herbs she had on it. He looked and drew up his nose at its smell. She gently examined his leg and then made gestures that showed how she had sucked out the poison with her mouth, spit it out, and healed him up. He grinned as he caught on to what she was describing. Evidently, they did similar treatments for viper bites. Thus, it was that we began to communicate with he whose language was so completely foreign to us, as ours was to him.

He could not travel for several more days until he regained his strength and recovered more fully. We all spent the time learning more about each other. Through gestures, signs, and drawings in the dirt, he was an excellent drawer we discovered, quite talented, we learned that he was called Runatilli, a "land walker." That is, he was a nomad.

His fear and hatred of the Centurions we discovered the next day when a patrol marched over to our campsite. Simon, without the hesitation, forced them to leave; all had images of highly diseased, black natives lying around awaiting death to take them. The warriors wanted no part of this and left at once. When they were gone, Simon explained by signs and drawings what he had done to their minds. When Runatilla grasped what Simon had done, he laughed for the first time and shook his hands wildly.

A half day later, after showing him some gold coins and some gems, we learned that this land abounded in gold, silver, emeralds, opals, and diamonds. For as long as anyone could remember, the Centurions had been capturing Southlanders and forcing them to work in their various mines. Fortunately for the Southlanders, these mines were mostly here in the far eastern regions of the Southland. The natives thus simply moved further westward to avoid these slave-takers.

Another half a day was spent trying to figure out what Runatilla was doing out here in the middle of nowhere, as we referred to this vast empty land. We learned in his culture, each man at least once in his physical life must make a Mali, which we determined to be a kind of solo walk through the land seeking a Oneness with Nature, finding his place in the universe or perhaps reaffirming it, we weren't totally certain on this detail. Thus, we realized that he thought of himself as a spiritual being just as we druwids did and that he only inhabited this body a short while. This viewpoint, I found exceedingly interesting. Exploring a hunch, I drew a picture of myself, rather crudely, since

I'm not talented in drawing, but my long hair made it easier for Runatilla to grasp that I was drawing my body. Next, with signs and drawing a circle a ways behind my head, I tried to communicate that I wasn't really inside my body's head. Finally, he gestured and smiled, drawing himself beside my picture, placing himself even further behind his body's head. We looked at each other, grinned, and nodded "Yes."

I formulated a theory. This was a land of vast, open spaces. Could vast, nearly empty spaces help one move outside of his head? Could this be one of the benefits of their Mali? Or perhaps what they were seeking, becoming free from the body's influence? As usual, I had raised interesting questions with no hope of finding any answers to them.

When Sarah Jane felt that he had recovered enough that we could leave him, which was fully three days later, we indicated, again by signs and drawings in the dirt, that we were going to leave, heading south once more. He kept shaking his head "No," and saying "Yeowie, Yeowie," along with some other words we did not understand. As usual, Simon took the time to have him draw what he was trying to communicate to us. Again, it took us several hours of intense attempts to grasp what he was trying to tell us.

We had saved his life. Hence, he had a Yeowie, which was an ethical contract to follow us about until an opportunity came for him to return the favor. Until his Yeowie was satisfied, he had to tag along with us. Suddenly, we had a new problem. We couldn't bring him along and yet, our sense of ethics wouldn't let us force him to betray his sense of ethics. Sarah Jane whispered that she didn't think he was well enough to walk along beside us, and he wouldn't climb onto a horse to ride either. We spent the rest of the day explaining where we were headed.

After much drawing and signing, on both our part and his, we learned that where the closest portion of the island of Megalos came to the Southlands, the Centurions had built a huge city called Sud. From his gestures, Sud had no equal in all of the Southlands. To our minds, this made sense. If an island nation were off conquering the known world, of necessity, they would require a large port city on the mainland, preferably one that was very close to the island.

Simon tried to get his Yeowie satisfied by having Runatilla guide us to Sud. Unfortunately, this failed utterly. By drawings, he told us that this paved road ran straight to Sud where it ended. I complimented Simon on a nice try, though. Next, Simon drew pictures showing him that we intended to go over onto the island for a while. Runatilla shook his head and indicated that he could not follow us there. Instead, he drew more pictures showing us that he would wait for us just outside Sud, waiting for our return. Finally, we could abide by this arrangement. In fact, we fully realized that we were putting off until much later how he was going to satisfy his Yeowie.

The next day, we continued our southerly journey with Runatilla, carrying his long, slender spear, walking along side of us. Either he didn't know how to ride a horse, or it was a taboo, or forbidden among his people; we could not be sure which. We learned much later that riding a horse would be interfering with his Mali.

Out of deference for our new friend, we didn't ride directly on the road but, following Runatilla's guidance, we paralleled it perhaps a mile to the west. The next two weeks were fun and easy going. We avoided all possible confrontations with the Centurions, not wanting to risk Runatilla's well-being or to scare him. We spent the vast majority of the time learning some of the basics of his language. When we actually halted on a low rise two miles from the sprawling city of Sud, we could communicate the basics with him.

He said, "Sud. Runatilla wait here. You go. You come. We go." That pretty well summed up what we had in mind. Next, we had to try to explain that we could be gone for days, weeks, maybe even a month. Would he wait that long? Yes. What about food? He made a wise sweeping gesture encompassing all the land about him, "Food everywhere. No starve. Me wait."

After some discussion, we rode further west to a point about four miles from the city, where we thought that our friend would be relatively safe from discovery. We agreed to find him by this lone tree. He said he would come here each sunset to see if we had yet returned. So shaking his hand, we said farewell for a while. He was all smiles, saying "Not worry. Me safe." Then we rode back to the road and headed into the city.

These last few miles into the city offered several encounters with both ingoing and outgoing parties of Centurions. Thrice, we overtook a group marching in unison toward the city. We moved off the road and passed them by; we were unchallenged. Twice, we moved off the road to let a party coming from the city to pass through us. Evidently, as long as we gave way to them, we weren't bothered or even questioned, though we did receive several long looks, but I detected those were not hostile looks, rather lustful. Apparently, they liked the way we three women looked, and I was very glad for the company of our men.

Sud was a vast, sprawling type of city, not the well-designed, well-thought out sort of town, but one which was added to as the need arose. The streets closest to the docks and coast were laid out perfectly square — a nice crisscross pattern. This section was only about one tenth of the city. The streets of neighboring sections ran at cock-eyed angles to these, fanning out toward the north. Even later additions on the northern side had streets askew to those in the middle. Yes, as the need for more space, more buildings was required, why they just added a section anyway that was convenient at the time. Some towns are laid out around the surrounding hills, while others are laid out according to a symmetrical design, not Sud. However, navigating the city was not a real chore since the land gradually sloped down to Tarra's South Ocean and the Shallow Firth in specific.

However, you must appreciate the geography here. Just off shore from Sud is the island of Megalos, from which the Centurions come. It is their home island, some four hundred miles long but only fifty or so at its widest. Here at the Shallow Firth, the water is but three feet deep at low tide, five at high tide.

Only two miles separate Sud from the western tip of Megalos. Yet, the water remains a barrier. As we rode into Sud, we saw numerous ferryboats making the brief passage by poling their way across. Some carried soldiers, but most carried wagons, boxes, and other supplies and goods. A great many large pottery vessels contained liquids and other food items, keeping them dry in the sealed containers. Some carried what looked like iron ore bound for Megalos. One even carried two war chariots toward Sud. Evidently, there was a significant industry in operation on the island kingdom. Trade was brisk.

As we approached the main entrance from this long northern road, three guards stepped out in front of us, challenging us. We halted. Quite bored, the corporal said in a monotone, "Pass tokens please?"

"I'm sorry," Simon tried the straightforward approach. "We didn't realize we needed a pass to enter the city. How do we get one?"

"Ah," he looked slightly less bored now. "Well, normally in that case, we'd escort you to the Governor's office where you may beseech Governor Horatius for one. If he grants you a pass, then we can let you into the city. Barbarians such as yourselves are allowed to stay only at one of three inns. Again, we'll escort you to one."

"Great, let's go see Governor Horatius," Simon stated agreeably.

"Sorry, his office is closed. You'll have to come back on Monday," he said with a distinct sneer in his voice. His two companions chuckled to themselves as if this was somehow funny.

"But this is only Saturday afternoon. What about tomorrow?" Simon inquired failing to see what was so funny.

"Ah, closed on Sundays. It is the holy day of Sol. We are a deeply religious, civilized people. No one works the day we worship Sol. So you'll just have to come back on Monday," he said with a grin.

"But where are we to stay? Where are we to eat until then?" Simon attempted to illicit some sympathy in order to get some idea of what was expected of us in the meantime.

"Well, you should have thought of that before you came here. Why, you can camp out on the savanna out there somewhere," he declared, pointing out into the hillside way beyond the city. Now they all laughed at our expense, but I still failed to see the humor.

Changing the subject, Simon then asked, "Do we need a pass to take the ferry across the Shallow Firth?"

"Heavens yes!" he declared obviously getting more interested in us. "For barbarians to take the ferry to the home land, you must have a pass from Emperor Hiro first."

"And how do we get such a pass? If Emperor Hiro lives over there and we need a pass from him to take the ferry, how do we get it? It seems a paradox."

Now they all roared. Finally, the corporal said, "Naturally, you *can't*. Not unless the Emperor sends for you, which he never does. You can't take the ferry without his pass. Now off with you; camp out there somewhere and don't come back until Monday." All three continued chuckling, as they returned to their post, a small wooden structure that protected them from the elements and had just enough room for them to sit down.

We had little choice at the moment. They were watching our every move. We turned around and rode back the way we had come, veering to the left behind the first hill that would obscure us completely from the city. We halted. "Now what?" asked Simon. "I played it straight, but look where that got us. We can try a different entrance point and I can enforce my will on the guards — make them satisfied that we have a pass and all that — force them to take us to an inn."

"It boils down to whether or not we wish to continue our guise of grain traders. We've come this far and must cross over to Megalos and see for ourselves what they are really like. It's going to be hard to do that if we constantly have to sneak around. Let's play it straight for the next few days and see what we can learn. If it gets us nowhere, then I don't see why we cannot cross this shallow water ourselves. We won't melt. I don't care if I get wet," I replied thinking aloud my reasoning thus far. "Besides, they didn't say we weren't *allowed* onto Megalos, just that we needed the Emperor's permission to cross on one of the ferries." We all grinned at this last observation. True, they didn't say that explicitly, though it might well have been implied. Thus, we camped out just out of sight of the city for two days.

Finally, on Monday morning, dressed in our best city clothes and not our usual comfortable leathers, we rode up to the same guard post. "Ah, you are actually back," the corporal said with a hint of surprise in his voice. "I guess you want us to escort you to see the Governor to get that token pass." We nodded. "Okay, Rex, watch things till we get back. You dismount and follow us." We did as he instructed, leading our horses single file behind the two guards. The streets were already quite busy; wagons of goods or basic ores were coming and going. In the distance, we heard the sounds of hammers upon anvils. Sea birds cawed in the clear blue sky, arcing their way over the docks looking for fish remains cast away from the fish preservers, who occupied several large buildings close to the water's edge. Additionally, many people passed by wearing long sheet-like robes tied over one shoulder. I wondered what they were called and if this was the local dress custom and why? It looked like they might fall off at any moment, revealing what modesty dictates should not be so displayed, at least in my opinion.

Finally, we halted before a large, well-built, white limestone building, single storied but with an open courtyard here at its front. We tied the horses at the hitching rail, which I thought was very conveniently located. Again, single file, we followed the Corporal through the ornate ironwork front gate. We entered a cozy waiting room with very plush purple chairs. "Wait until you are called," the corporal said rather coldly. He went to make the arrangements. We sampled the chairs, remarking on their fine workmanship and construction. Some ten minutes later, the corporal reappeared along with another man, completely bored, who said, "Governor Horatius will see you now. This way please." We followed.

Inside the large drawing room whose walls were covered with elegant tapestries depicting strange, lewd forest scenes with various men and women engaged in romantic activities — I won't get more specific for I found them rather offensive — the Governor sat behind an enormous mahogany desk. Two chairs sat directly in front of him and numerous others sat back against a wall. The desk was dwarfed in this huge room, perhaps an allegory for the presumed importance of the robust figure sitting before us. Governor Horatius was very over-weight, with well-trimmed, bushy black hair and eyes to match. He was clean-shaven, but he rather over did the scent, which came on strong to my nostrils. Simon and I took the two seats while the others sat at the back of the room.

He pompously cleared his throat, "I'm informed that you wish a pass to enter Sud and stay at an inn. Barbarians. Every day it seems that we get more and more of you barbarians coming here. Ah well, I guess that goes with the results of our successful campaign to bring civilization to the world. State your names or what you are called, your place of origin, and your purpose in coming to Sud." He was looking straight at Simon, so I mentally gave Simon the go-ahead to speak for us. He kept it simple and direct, giving our first names, Greenway, and that we desired to work out grain trade agreements. Evidently, this suited the Governor who did not question us any further. "Very well then, these tokens are good for one week only. Keep them on your person at all times for you may be asked to show them at any time to any guards. Security, you understand. One cannot be too careful with all these barbarians around. However, you young kids pose no threat, and we are always looking for more grain." He handed Simon six grey tokens in the shape of a coin. "That's the image of our illustrious Emperor on the front. Remember, one week only. Next Monday, different colored tokens are issued. If you need to stay longer, you must return here. So be speedy in your deal making."

That was the end of the meeting. He signaled to the corporal who was standing by the entrance door. He beckoned us to follow him out. Simon at least said politely, "Thank you."

Once outside, the corporal said dryly, "Three inns: Red Dragon, Green Dragon, Blue Dragon. Which will it be?" Of course, we had no idea what kind of inns these were, and Simon had to query him further. The Blue Dragon was closest to the docks and the fishery; the air around there had a very fishy odor. The Green Dragon was closest to the edge of the city, while the Red Dragon, the most expensive, lay near the heart of the business district. Since we needed to arraign theoretical grain for metal farming tools, we decided on the Red Dragon.

Forty-five minutes later, the corporal left us at the entrance to the inn. I think he was glad to get back to his duties instead of shepherding barbarians around the town. Simon decided to see about the arrangements and I accompanied him. As usual, we obtained three adjoining rooms and stabling for our horses. It was expensive here, a gold coin a day per person and another one for the horses. I traded in a small gem to pay for a week's lodging. Once we all had shown our token passes, we were given the keys, a map of the inn, and a map of the central business district, the latter proving most useful.

After stabling the horses, we found our rooms. Luxury was an understatement. Plush is a far better description of this inn and our rooms. Each room was large, about thirty feet square. The floor was carpeted with stone underneath. Rich tapestries hung on the walls except the back wall. Here, great sliding doors opened onto the giant courtyard entirely enclosed by the inn's rooms. Trellises with hanging foliage marked the entrance to this formal, well-tended garden. Many flowers were in bloom still and gave a heady, comfortable fragrance to this space. Various stone tables and chairs were carefully located to give one a sense of privacy.

One door across from us had a large sign denoting restrooms; another denoted the public bath, and the third, the diner. Naturally, we had to check out all three of these and this magnificent courtyard. We found the bathhouse interesting, in that it had hot and cold tubs, so that one could soak in the hot and then cool off quickly in the other. The first order of business was a bath. Okay, so we rather overdid it and finished in time for lunch in the dining room.

Raphael found the design and the style of architecture fascinating, and by the time that our week was up, he had made numerous sketches of the place. I think he had ideas of making something similar back home. That afternoon, we divided into three teams, each taking a small sack of grain, and began visiting the various trading companies. I won't bore you with the mundane trade deals we tried to make. We made more than we could possibly honor. The only real requisite was pottery urns; the grain had to be shipped in these giant sealed urns to preserve the grain from the sea travel. Shipping costs came out of our profits, interestingly enough.

When our week's stay was finished, we had our trade deals, but we had no real information on the Centurions and their plans for future conquests, the Greenway, in particular. Our last night here in the inn of luxury was spent in the public bath, planning our next move. None of us wanted to play games trying to get the emperor to give us a pass to take the ferry. We decided just to cross ourselves on our horses. The only real problem was the timing; it had to be at low tide. So part of our time during this week was spent observing the sea. Luck was with us. Simon estimated that low tide would occur around nine the night of the day that we checked out of the inn.

After our week was up, we checked out of the inn by midmorning and rode slowly out of the town past the guards who had accosted us that first day. Cheerily, we bid them goodbye. They, of course, were not cheerful in their replies, very glad to see more barbarians leave their city. We rode north along the paved road until noon. With no one in sight, we circled around, headed due west, and then south. Our plan was to circle wide around Sud and to cross the Shallow Firth several miles south of Sud, completely out of sight of the city and any watchers. Yes, this was going to be a dangerous move on our part, but then we had to see Megalos proper. After all, what could they do but run us off the island.

By nine that night, we were in position with only a bit of crescent moonlight to guide us. We stood quiet beside the waters, which slowly lapped onshore in front of us. The dark mass of Megalos lay only two miles from us, quite hilly, rocky, and ominous. Satisfied that we were completely unobserved, we began the crossing single file, Roy taking the lead. At first, the horses didn't want to venture into the waters. Soon they found that it wasn't deep, only three feet barely up to their bellies. We were lucky in that the bottom was not heavy mud, but rather sandy and solid for the horses. Still, we went very, very slowly.

Finally, the horses climbed onto the deserted shores of Megalos. We had arrived! Here the beach was narrow and rocky cliffs barred further progress for some time, until Roy found a path angling up through the hills. Having little other alternatives, we took it, though it seemed manmade. We climbed ever upwards, passing by black rocky formations only dimly illuminated taking on fantasy-like shapes. The only noise was that of our horse's hooves clanking upon the rocky path. Unfortunately for us, this path led to a large villa that was inhabited.

As we finally crested the hill and came out onto level ground, we found ourselves staring at a large complex of buildings, strange ones at that. The nearest one to us was illuminated by many lanterns. A man dressed in these strange bed sheets tied over one shoulder was actually standing in front of us painting — an easel held his canvas at a person's height. "Greetings strangers in the night," the man spoke as we crested the hill and became visible. However, he scarcely took his eyes of his work in progress, adding more brush strokes as we rode closer.

The man was standing in the middle of a building, if that is what it is called. I say building for I have never seen such before. Great marble pillars some fifteen feet tall rose up on all sides, six per side, holding an enormous arched stone roof overhead. There were no side walls what so ever. As I glanced around at the many other buildings, most looked rather similar to this one, only a few had actual walls. The man was in the middle of the "room" painting away. We rode up and dismounted. I could see that his painting was of the sunset over Sud and actually was quite good, but then I am not a painter.

"Niccolo Helios, artist extraordinary, inventor, writer, philosopher, thinker, and inventor of writing, at your service. Who do I have the pleasure of meeting on such a fine evening as this?" The man was in his thirties, with long black hair and the usual piercing black eyes. He had no moustache, but paint splatters dotted his face, particularly around his mouth. "And what do you think of my latest masterpiece: Sunset? Do you think I have captured the essence of the sunset?"

I handed my reins to Roy and ventured into this strange building to have a closer look at his painting. "Well, yes, in fact it does look very realistic.

It's almost as if you captured a picture of a real sunset here. Well, all except this flare over here," I pointed out a small streak that would not really be in a sunset unless the clouds were really weirdly shaped that evening.

"Ah observant eye. You are right. I was still working on that section when you arrived," he replied and turned to observe me. We were wearing our working leather clothing as usual. His eyes traveled from my feet slowly up to my head, pausing for the longest time at my eyes. We made strong eye contact. "Barbarians, I presume from your outlandish, highly impractical clothing. Yet with an observant eye, you can't be stupid as the Emperor would have us all believe."

"Indeed not," I replied. "I believe the word barbarian is being completely misused around here. We're from the Greenway, a land far up north. Perhaps, you have heard of it? Anyway, I'm called Bethany and these are my companions," I announced and introduced the others who had tied up the horses and walked slowly into this room staring, or rather gaping, at its construction.

Niccolo was highly intelligent and also observant. "Ah, I see you're the leader, Bethany. Interesting, are all the women of the Greenway the leaders of an expedition? I suspect this must be an expedition. You are far from home."

"No, men and women are equals in our land. We pick the best qualified person for the job. I happen to meet the requirements for our leader position. How did you know that I was the leader?" I asked slightly curious; the only indication I'd given of my position is that I ventured into the building first and answered his original questions.

"The first person to make contact and answer my queries almost always is the leader of the group, fairly obvious. That is a most intelligent way to choose. I only wish Megalos would listen to such logic. Alas, I'm afraid power begets corruption."

Simon interjected, "Nay, that is a cop-out. Power only tempts an individual, just as a pretty woman or man may do so, or the weight of gold, or the sparkle of gemstones. It is only temptation; it is the person who makes the decision for good or ill."

Niccolo paused, looked Simon in the eyes for a moment before he replied, "My compliments. You've caught me in my own trap. Yes, you're correct. I spoke hastily. On the other hand, I'm quite impressed with your knowledge and wisdom, Simon. Perhaps, you aren't barbarians after all. Yes, it's true that the Emperor has declared all peoples not from Megalos to be barbarians — a royal decree. I argued unsuccessfully that this was a falsehood; few would listen; it isn't wise to seem to go against the Emperor. Too many who have end up quite dead. Enough of my problems. It's rare indeed, when I come across people with intelligence and wisdom. Come. Let me show you around my villa."

"This building is my art studio," he gestured to the large building or roof rather that we were under.

Raphael spoke up, "Sir, I'm a designer by training. This is the strangest building I've ever seen. Its architecture is splendid, but why are there no side walls? I've been wondering that since we got here."

"To stay cool," came the quick reply. "Megalos is blessed or cursed, depending upon your point of view. It's hot all year round. We really don't have seasons such as I've heard tell about in the northern lands. Man adapts. We can't control the weather, so we make our living quarters as comfortable as possible. Always, there is a light sea breeze blowing, either in or out. With no walls, we stay cool, or relatively so."

"Then that is why you wear these tied sheets?" I asked

He laughed, "Tied sheets? Why I guess if you have never seen a toga, then they do look a bit like that. No, they are very cool," Niccolo answered. "During the daytime, here on Megalos you'll certainly be sweltering in that heavy leather clothing you're wearing. Come. I have many togas. I'll give you each one. Tomorrow, you'll see or rather feel for yourselves."

"Sir, who designed these buildings?" Raphael asked, unable to shake off his fascination with them.

"Oh, I designed this studio to meet my painting needs. It sits here on the highest point of the villa, and it always has good lighting. Come. Let me show you my gallery of my summer's paintings." He led us to another building, much smaller, and it had actual walls, though it still used the same style pillars to support a similar arched roof.

While he was lighting several lanterns, Raphael asked, "Are all these built of limestone?"

"Polished white limestone, marble actually. We have more than we can ever use here on Megalos. It's the bedrock of the island. When all the marble has been used, Megalos will be under the sea. That's a joke, by the way. We build all our main buildings, even the many temples to Sol, out of marble. Once a building is built, it stays built; that is, there is virtually no maintenance. Our works shall last for eternity it is said, but I say, how long is eternity? That's another joke by the way. Here, now you can see my gallery." The next twenty minutes we spent gaping and marveling at some thirty of the finest paintings we'd ever seen. Some were portraits but most were landscapes. All had a realism about them that made them seem like they were a copy of the actual world. Like any artist, he thoroughly enjoyed our comments, especially since they were extremely complimentary.

"Whatever do you do with so many fabulous paintings?" asked Sarah Jane. "Do you sell any?"

"Some I do indeed paint on a commission basis. Take this one here of the High Priest of Sol; he has paid me two hundred gold pieces to do his likeness. I'll give it to him when I get back to Galantas for the fall Senate session. I'm actually one of the hundred Senators — those who make the laws, see that they are enforced, and meet out justice; though nowadays, the Senate has become merely a puppet for the Emperor, I'm sad to say. I'm supposed to head back to Galantas in two days. These others — these are my pride and joys — these are the ones I make for no other reason than the joy of creation. I prefer to paint what I want to paint. Often, I'm able to sell many to those who have an eye for my work."

"I can understand that, I think," she replied. "Take this small one here, sunrise over a small island. Is it for sale? I'd like to buy it if it doesn't cost too much. It is small enough I can carry it in my sack."

"Strange indeed that you would choose that one out of all these here. You see, one morning as I lay in that half-sleep before waking, I had a dream that a beautiful woman would one day come to me, one who loved Nature, and she asked me to paint this scene. When I awoke, I painted it just as in my dream. Here you turn up asking for it. Strange indeed. By chance are you lovers of Nature?" Niccolo asked, his voice full of curiosity.

"Yes, we all are for that matter," Sarah Jane answered. "This is indeed more than a little bit weird."

Niccolo stared first at her and then the rest of us. "I should have guessed that you were, if only from your clothes and bearing. Sarah Jane, one this small would sell for around fifty gold pieces. However, it is yours for nothing, if you'll let me paint your portrait in the morning. Your face has a fascinating beauty and charm about it. Please let me paint your portrait."

"Oh how delightful! Certainly. But I've never posed for a portrait. What do I have to do?" she asked excitedly. Sarah Jane was certainly pretty, far more so than Sandy or me, and she was just a bit vane about it. She loved getting looks of admiration and longing from men. I didn't, well except for Roy, that is. Perhaps, I'm just overly self-conscious about my looks.

He handed her the painting, saying, "You only need to hold still for an hour or so. Excellent, let's get started after breakfast! What a dream come true. Strange indeed. There is more. Come on; let me show you a couple of my marble sculptures."

We turned out the lanterns and walked to the next building. Again, this one had no walls. In its center stood a huge marble table and ten chairs. Off to the seaward side, two life-sized statues stood dark against the sky. He lighted only two lanterns and set them on the table such that their light illuminated the statues in a special way. "Behold Nikka and Tikka, the twin founders of the Centurion Empire some five hundred years ago. Well, at least they are how I see these regal figures." While we marveled at the incredible workmanship and artistry, he explained legends say that these Hodhekansis twins united all the warring tribes on Megalos, unified them into one civilized nation, founded the Senate to govern them, and built the capital city of Galantas from which to rule. One twin pointed to the sky while the other pointed to the ground; he didn't comment upon any significance that had.

After he turned out the lanterns, he gazed at the heavens above. I asked, "Do you also observe the stars? We all have studied the heavens extensively."

"You have?" he inquired, rather amazed. "What shape is Tarra? What is the relationship between Tarra and Sol?"

"Round, of course; everyone knows that. Tarra goes around Sol; that's why there is the motion of the stars at night," I replied wondering if he did not know this.

"Eureka!" he cried, grabbed hold of my hands, and danced us around in little circles. He was very excited. Finally, just as I thought he might be mad, he said, "No, they don't. You do not know how refreshing it is to meet others who can see what the universe actually does! Most men consider Tarra to be flat; sail too far away and you fall off Tarra. Never mind what they say when I reply, 'okay, fall into what?' Even our silly priests believe that Sol moves around Tarra! I have spent many hours in my youth trying to convince them otherwise, but that contradicts their faith, so no matter how hard, how convincing I was, they wouldn't change their ideas. Here, strangers from the far north, you know the truth. How utterly delightfully refreshing! I had thought that the mariners from the Sea Princes, the greatest navigators on Tarra, would know the truth. When I questioned one last year, to my amazement, he too felt Tarra was the center of the universe and flat. Ah well. Come. Let me show you one of my inventions. You most certainly will find this one to your liking. It's over there in that building with only a half a roof."

We followed him as he ran over to a contraption in the center of this even stranger building. He took a sheet covering off, revealing a contraption made of bronze. It was a very long tube supported on a clever metal base that allowed it to be pointed all about the heavens. Up close, I noticed the gleam of light reflecting off glass. It had a large piece of glass in the end pointed skyward. The tube gradually narrowed to a tiny end, which he held in his hand. Another tiny glass was affixed here. He pointed it to the thin sliver of the moon low in the western sky. "Here, look through here," he said.

I won't describe the remarks we made as we gazed upon the crater-filled moon. It was as if we were flying just above its surface; we were that close to it. "It's my far-seeing eye," he proudly proclaimed. Raphael and Niccolo spent the next ten minutes discussing its construction, while the rest of us gazed in utter, complete fascination. Interestingly enough, when I moved it slightly to gaze at a star, the star remained a tiny point of light. His invention greatly surpassed the one that Rosita had given me months ago, which we used to observe the Centurion attack.

"The moon must be relatively close to Tarra, while the stars are infinitely farther away," I commented on my observations.

"How so?" Niccolo asked.

"Well, if you take a gold coin and view it right up here by your nose, it looks huge. Move it to an arm's length away, and it looks relatively much smaller. Now move it a mile away and it is a point at best. The moon looks big, even bigger and more close up, in your special eye, but the stars remain tiny points. Conclusion, stars are much farther away. Now I wonder how we could figure out just how far away they actually are?"

"Bethany, you have just posed the very question I have asked myself for the last year! Amazing. I have devised a theory, but as yet I haven't been able to put it into actual practice. Let me explain, see if you can find any error in my reasoning." Hastily, he drew a large circle in the dirt just outside the building, his hand-held lantern bobbing back and forth. "Here in the center is Sol. The circle represents Tarra in its orbit about Sol. Now here these two stones can be two stars, one close to us one much farther away. Stand here on this side of Tarra's orbit and look at where the closer stone is in relationship to the further stone. Okay, now move over here on the other side and look at the closer stone. See it moves a tiny bit in relationship to the distant star. From mathematics if we can measure this angle that it appears to shift, we can then calculate its distance in terms of the distance Tarra is from Sol."

"Yes, I see. It should work," I exclaimed grasping his reasoning. "Have you seen this tiny angle? How can it be measured?"

"Well, I put tiny copper wires into a grid in this end and have marked several stars and their relative locations. I've viewed them for the last six months and have not been able to see any difference. Rather discouraging."

"Ah, but if you picked two stars, which were equally distant, then you would expect to see no difference. Try some other ones," I suggested hopefully. "But which ones?"

"Ah, that is the key question. Well, I'll continue to observe. Maybe one day I shall see that tiny difference and can then set about calculating the relative distance. The stars must be very distant from Sol." We talked for a while longer before he realized that we and he were getting tired; it was now quite late.

He then bade us fetch our horses, put them in his stable, and join him in his main quarters for a late night snack of bread and cheese. His main dwelling had no walls, but thin gauze sheets separated the various rooms. Soon we found ourselves relaxing on soft comfortable beds with the intoxicating sea breeze gently flowing over us. I snuggled up to Roy and fell into a relaxing, deep sleep. These centurions certainly presented us with immense contrasts. I actually liked this Niccolo Helios — just the opposite for their Governor, the Baby Murderer. What kind of civilization can give rise to such opposites, I wondered as I fell asleep this first night on the island of Megalos, home of the Centurions, our enemy and yet. . .

"Wake up, please," a feminine voice intruded into my subconscious. She repeated herself several times before I awoke and rustled Roy awake. Dawn had come; daylight filtered through the gauze thin veils separating the rooms. Just outside our room, I saw a black skinned, young woman, probably from the Southlands, I thought.

"Yes, we're awake now. Thanks. Who are you?" I asked rising and stretching.

"Kaytlyn, missy," came the brief reply. "Master has left you these togas. He is awaiting you at the breakfast table."

"Thanks," I replied. "Say, are you from the Southlands?"

"So I'm told. I was born here to serve the master," came her equally brief reply.

Roy whispered, "A slave." We exchanged glances; this was another unexpected aspect of Megalos society that we should've been prepared for but had forgotten all the earlier clues we'd heard. We both whispered a brief curse under our breaths and tried to figure out how to get into these sheets called togas. In the end, I refused to have nothing on at all under it; Roy, likewise. By the time that we pushed our way through the gauze sheeting and headed across the green lawn to the open air-dining house, the others similarly attired in their new togas joined us. Sarah Jane also whispered "slaves." We exchanged knowing glances as well.

We found our host sitting by the table looking out over the land toward the ocean and the southern tip of the Southlands. "Beautiful day for a portrait," he exclaimed. "I trust you slept well? Ah, I see you have mastered the art of donning togas. Today you'll see just how cool you stay during the heat of the day. It's always hot in Megalos. Come, share a breakfast." He snapped his fingers and two other young dark skinned women rushed to his side bearing trays of food and drink.

We sat down and helped ourselves. By way of conversation, I asked, "So how many slaves do you have? Are they all women?"

Perhaps, he detected a bit of disgust or distaste in my voice. He replied, "Oh I have seven here at my country villa. One male looks after the grounds, and the other six handle all the domestic chores, from doing the marketing, to cooking the meals, to washing the laundry. Very convenient. This way, I can spend my time painting or inventing. Don't get me wrong, I treat my slaves very well. In fact, these are all at least second generation slaves, very expensive."

"What do you mean second generation?" I asked, though I already suspected I knew what the answer would be.

"They were born here. You see, first generation slaves are very hard to control; they are rebellious and attempt to flee at any opportunity. Those are cheap because of all the trouble and training they require. A second generation slave knows nothing but of life here. If you treat them well, they are quite satisfied with their lives."

"Well, we believe everyone ought to be free to live their lives as they wish so long as it does not harm others," I replied to clear the air so Niccolo wouldn't have any misconceptions about us.

"Well, there are some that mistreat their slaves, I'll give you that much," he affably spoke. "Mine love their lives here serving me. Just ask anyone of them." I thought about doing so but decided against it. It was plain that Kaytlyn was content with her life as a slave. If I tried to punch in all of the things that she was not likely free to do, such as marry, have her own family, and seek her own goals in life, why, I would only upset her and perhaps jeopardize her position with her master. There was no point in creating upset here, so I just bit my lip and kept quiet.

Fortunately, Sarah Jane spoke up, "So when do I get my portrait done?"

He smiled, "As soon as we have finished eating, while the early morning light is good. It makes your face look very mellow, very virginal. I shall try to capture that today." He signed, "But then tomorrow, it's back to Galantas and the Senate. I must be there day after tomorrow for the opening fall session, though I'm not sure there's any point in the Senate's meeting. Politics, hate it. Say, you are welcome to come with me as my guests if you like to see the Senate in operation."

"Sure, that would be an honor," I replied. "We can see how a civilized country governs itself."

He laughed, "Civilized? Ah well, so we think." He paused reflecting on the past. "Yes, twenty years ago, I'd have been proud for you to witness a Senate meeting. However, ever since the fool Hiro took over as the Emperor of Sol, everything's gone downhill rapidly. I swear he has a pig's brain in his head. Don't repeat these words; they are enough to get you executed."

We laughed and promised to say nothing. "Tell us more about this Emperor Hiro. Why can he dictate over the Senate?" I asked, seeking a better understanding of just how Megalos was governed.

"In theory, the Senate makes the laws, and the Emperor, who is reputedly Sol's ambassador on Tarra and thus above all laws save those of Sol, carries them out. But Hiro's a fool and power hungry. If any Senator goes against his personal wishes, Hiro has him eliminated. The only Senators who can stand up to him are those with great wealth or great artistry, such as me. He can't touch me; the repercussions would topple him from power over night, so I content myself with being a thorn in his side. That's about all I can actually do."

"So how does one become Emperor? It seems like an extremely important position," I queried.

"The twelve church Elders meet and elect the Emperor who is supposed to be exceedingly holy, the servant of Sol on Tarra. However, just between thee and me, the position can be bought. The church is always looking for ways to gain more power and control over Megalos. Why they would elect a fool such as Hiro is beyond me. He is the opposite of holy. We Senators all thought that Julius Theocopolis would be elected, not Hiro. There is rumor that Hiro holds some dark secret over the church and that is how he got elected, rather bought off the church so to speak. Whatever hold he has over the church, it's working. He gets away with murder, literally even. But come. Let's get on with Sarah Jane's portrait while the light is perfect." We headed back to the building where we first met him last night.

He positioned her where the sun could illuminate the side of her face, told her to hold still, and went to work on a small canvass. "Why don't the rest of you take a long walk around my villa here? Get Kaytlyn to show you around."

We accepted his invitation to explore and satisfy our curiosity. Kaytlyn enjoyed showing us all around, identifying the various buildings and such. She seemed proud of the fact that she lived and worked here; we would learn why later on. His villa covered the entire top of this particular hill, perhaps three square miles of grassy lands. The buildings were all similar in design and shape, save only a few that had actual solid walls. What got our complete interest, especially Raphael's, was the complex irrigation system. A stone aqueduct snaked across the land from a distant hill. When it reached his villa, the aqueduct ended by dividing into six smaller bronze pipes. Some ended up watering the land, which was why the grass grew so abundantly here. Some provided water for the laundry basin, for cooking and drinking, and for the elegant bathhouse. At each junction, there was a metal valve that one could open or close as needed to regulate the flow. Raphael, clearly intrigued with this system, drew numerous drawings outlining the setup.

A gong sounded; Kaytlyn explained that was the signal that lunch was waiting. We hurried to the dining building, just as a beaming Sarah Jane and Niccolo arrived. "Gosh, you are going to have to see my portrait!" she exclaimed. "He is really good."

"Nay, I had a good model to guide my hands," he replied modestly. "Come, let's eat." We dined on roast lamb and yams as the main course. When I asked where the servants ate, he replied, "Here with me when I'm alone or in the servant's building when I'm entertaining guests. Enough of the servants. After we eat, I'll show you my most prized invention. I call it writing." Naturally, we insisted on a full explanation while we were eating.

"I've invented twenty-five symbols that I call letters. With these, one can put words down on parchment. The combination of one or more letters makes a word. A series of words make a sentence. This writing is going to be revolutionary. With it, anyone can keep accurate records of everything and anything. And you can write down stories for the ages. A hundred years from now, people will still be reading my stories!" Niccolo was very excited and animated as he explained.

"You mean that you can somehow put down on parchment what someone says?" asked an incredulous Sandy; communication was her specialty, and I could see that she took a keen interest in this invention.

"Absolutely. All you need to do is be able to read what has been written. Here, I'll give you a demonstration. You say something and I'll write it down. Then, I'll get Kaytlyn to come here and read it back to you to prove it. I've taught her to read and write. Actually, she manages my villa when I'm away at the Senate meeting."

Sandy thought for a moment. It was hard trying to think of something to say knowing that Niccolo was going to write down every word you uttered. "Bethany loves to ride a horse really fast so the wind blows her long hair behind her. How's that?" Niccolo scratched furiously on a stray parchment. Once he'd finished, he read it back silently to himself. Satisfied, he signaled for Kaytlyn.

"Yes, master?" she said when she appeared. She was swallowing a mouthful; I gathered she was eating too and had not anticipated her master's summons so soon.

"Here, please read what I have written to our guests."

She cleared her throat and spoke clearly, "Bethany loves to ride a horse really fast so the wind blows her long hair behind her. How's that? This is what the parchment says."

Sandy's mouth open and shut several times, though no words came out. Finally, she managed to utter, "That's absolutely what I said! I have to learn more about this writing and reading invention. The potential of this invention is mind-boggling! Have you made it broadly available to others?"

"Well, yes and no. Some of my friends have taken a fancy to it. It does take some learning to be able to do it with speed and efficiency. If we ever get the right emperor, a royal edict will force it into widespread usage in Megalos. I have really just been waiting for the right circumstances." We chatted more about this invention until lunch was done. "Come. I'll show you my story scrolls. I've written down over a hundred of our ancient stories and legends."

In one of the few buildings that had actual solid side walls, along one side was a huge wooden set of "pigeon holes," more like a contraption to store hundreds of bottles of wine on their sides. Tightly rolled scrolls protruded from most of these. He grabbed one at random and read us the story of Helena, the Warrior Princess, who once saved her village from raiders. As he read, the uses of being able to write down something to be read back later began to flood through our minds, Sandy's in particular. He showed us one scroll that held the set of letters and another that contained a giant list of words.

"Why don't you look over these now? I have to go to Megalos in the morning. I'd be honored if you would come with me as my guests. However, I have much packing to do and orders to set down for the servants. They run this whole place when I'm gone. If they have any questions or problems, why, Kaytlyn just writes it down on a scroll and sends it to me in Galantas. I send her back an answer. Works perfectly. So entertain yourselves with this library of scrolls for a while. Also, don't forget to take a peek at Sarah Jane's portrait. It's still drying. I'll join you at dinner time, I think." We thanked him and watched him hasten off to find his servants.

"Wow, think of all the possibilities this can offer!" exclaimed Sandy. "We could write down all our legends so our children's children could read them."

"Think of the commercial uses," put in Simon. "Merchants could use it to keep accurate records. One could send a parchment with one's order to a merchant who could then fill it — all without having to go there personally and oversee it, and not have to repeat it or try to remember all the details. Man, this would be incredibly useful. I wonder how it's done?"

"Come on, gang. We have the time and the key scrolls. Let's make copies and see if we can figure it all out and adapt it to our language," Sandy insisted. I found it rather boring work, but we six spent all that afternoon making up our own scrolls of words and such. We kept his set of basic letters for they also seemed to fit our language well. I doubted that they would work without some alterations for the Southland natives, though, for their language was very different indeed. In principle, I thought something could be devised so even that language could be written down. Mid-afternoon, we all realized that the "words" were spelled just as they sounded when spoken. After that break-through, we tackled the problem in earnest and made great headway. By dinner, we had spelled out more than five hundred basic words of our own language, more than enough to get started on this project. As we walked to the dinning building, I realized that even if we somehow lost these precious scrolls, knowing the basics, we could re-invent it all. That was comforting.

Since Niccolo wanted to leave at dawn, we went to bed right after diner, packing our few things first to make fewer hassles in the morning. It took me a long time to actually fall asleep. New uses of writing kept appearing in my mind. However, one thing I knew that we should under no circumstances write down was our complex druwid training lessons. If those should fall into the wrong hands, real trouble could easily follow from their misuse. I resolved to see to it that druwid lessons were never written down. Later, Alabaster contacted us, primarily because Sandy had contacted him to tell him about the writing invention. He agreed with me that druwid principles and lessons should never be written. Only then was I able to fall asleep.

Chapter 20 Megalos: The Senate and Emperor Hiro

At seven the next morning, we six with our packhorse rode down the grassy hilltop behind Niccolo. His horse was laden with numerous sacks and packs; he intended to be gone at least six weeks. Once we left the edge of his estate, the lush grass gave way to a dry, rocky hillside where only tough grasses grew along with twisted trees.

"Irrigation," Niccolo explained. "The choice parcels of land are the hilltops, but they are barren unless watered. We invented a complex irrigation system of aqueducts, which bring water from the reservoirs located in the tall, central peaks of Megalos down to all the other hilltops. The system is hundreds of years old now, built by our ancestors. You see, all the major cities and towns are crowded along the coastline and up the low lying valleys, all of which have a source of natural fresh water. Believe me those cities are very over-crowded. The wealthy and those who can afford it make their residences upon hilltops, like mine. The aqueducts make that possible and spread the water uniformly about the entire island."

Raphael asked many technical questions about this system, which our host gaily answered. Niccolo seemed an endless reservoir of knowledge. "We'll pass by one of the largest reservoirs that feeds all the city of Galantas by evening. Then, you can see better how it works," he explained as we rode along heading down hill.

Finally, we came to a well-worn brick road. "Ah, this is called the Inner Circle Byway. It encircles the whole of central Megalos in a giant loop. If we rode down to the coast, there you would find the Beltline Roadway, which also loops around the entire island, visiting every major town and city along the coast. There is a heavy amount of traffic on it, which I want to avoid. Besides, I hate riding through endless, over-crowded towns — all that hustle and bustle and jostling about — turns a fun ride into a nightmare. Besides, it would take us four days to get to Galantas instead of two."

As we rode along the rocky hillsides were not entirely vacant. Here and there, shepherds tended flocks of sheep. We also passed several cattle farms, which Niccolo explained provided fresh milk and meat in abundance. A number of mines dotted the landscape. Some were played out and abandoned, but others were being worked for their ore, principally iron and coal. Occasionally between hills, we could see far down to the actual coast and cities. We knew they were large because of the dense smoke rising from all the foundries making metal, forging it into weapons, armor, and more mundane, useful items. Simon was definitely impressed with the level of economy and industry here in Megalos. Again, I had to remind myself that these people were also the baby-killers and brutal conquerors of other countries, perhaps the greatest suppressors on Tarra.

Just as the sun was setting ruddy red in the west, we rounded a bend and spied the largest of the reservoirs. Cradled at the cirque between two of the largest peaks on Megalos was a vast lake more than a mile across. A huge dam blocked its flow, forcing the water to flow down a network of aqueducts, the largest heading down toward Galantas itself, the capital of Megalos and the seat of power of the Centurions. Raphael had us pause for several minutes while he studied the enormous construction. I took this opportunity to ask a question I had wanted to know for a long time. "Niccolo, why are your people called Centurions? Or are only your soldiers so called?"

He smiled, "Because our civilization is centuries old. Nothing more grandiose than that, I'm afraid. Personally, I think that is rather silly."

Raphael asked, "Aren't you a bit worried about what would happen if the dam gave way? Suppose the lake got too full or there was an earthquake that damaged it."

"It is ruggedly built. It has stood undamaged for several hundred years. Yes, if it gave way, the wall of water would wreak some devastation as it thunders down the valley to the ocean. More importantly, it would leave Galantas without much water and that would be a serious problem, though several other smaller aqueducts also bring some freshwater there." Raphael nodded. I could see his mind racing down other paths, but I did not say anything at the moment.

By late afternoon the next day, we rounded yet another bend in the paved road and Niccolo proudly exclaimed, "Behold, Galantas, the greatest city of Tarra!" We all halted utterly spellbound at the vast sight before us. Nothing could have prepared us for the sights we now saw. Galantas went beyond our wildest imaginings! Stretching for miles covering several hills lay the marble city with enormous public buildings, all formed with massive columns and giant arched roofs, most with open sides: the White City.

"There, that is called the Royal Coliseum; we hold sports festivals, combat demonstrations, even plays there." It was a vast bowl shaped building whose sides rose well over a hundred feet at its rim. "It can seat a thousand people at one time," Niccolo explained. "There is the Royal Palace of the Emperor, and there is the Temple of Sol, the largest temple in all of Tarra! Our destination is over there, the Senate Building. See that gigantic rectangular building? We Senators sit on either side, and the current speaker who wishes to address us stands on a raised platform between the two sides. Acoustically, it is simply amazing. You can talk in a normal voice and be heard everywhere in the Senate! I still haven't worked out how that is possible." We stared in wonder at the white marble city, thousands of columns reaching toward the sky, holding equally marvelous arched marble roofs. It was certainly a wonder of the world.

"Come my friends; we must hurry. It'll be dark before we reach my dwelling near the Senate. Lex will have supper waiting, though he'll certainly be surprised that I bring six with me." We rode on, barely taking our eyes off the sights, only enough to make sure our horses stayed on the road.

Soon we were heading down the wide city streets and could see these buildings up close, although only in the twilight. Still, their white, polished forms gleamed. Even at this late hour, the streets carried a good deal of traffic, mostly workers heading home. I noticed that in our togas and sandals, we didn't look at all out of place, save that our skin was not bronzed by the constant sunlight. Finally, we pulled up at his stables, dismounted, and unpacked our many sacks and packs. Niccolo told us to leave the care of our horses to his stable staff; he promised that they would be well looked after; we trusted him on this point.

His residence here in Galantas was a square shaped single story building with marble side walls. The center was an open courtyard with formal garden. As we approached the main entrance, two Centurions stood guard and jumped to attention as Niccolo approached. "Guards, these are my honored guests. Allow them total access to my home here at any time, night or day."

"Yes, Senator!" both barked in unison.

We entered and Niccolo hastily explained, "These are my personal guards whose job is to protect me from assassinations and the like. Had I not given them those orders, they would never let you inside without me along. Here, I live inside a box with solid marble walls. Protection, you see. No one can enter and stab me while I sleep or eat, or you folks for that matter. Inside this house, we are safe. Outside in the street, it can be another matter entirely, especially if you have made enemies. So try not to do so; that's a joke, by the way." We did not find it particularly amusing, though.

First, he led us to three rooms on the north side of the square. "My quarters are on the south side. Dining facilities are on the eastern side, and the kitchen and servant's quarters on the western side, which tends to be the hottest, though the marble walls do dampen some of the late afternoon sun's heat. Unpack, wash up, and head for the dining room. I'll find Lex and let him know we have guests to feed. See you in a few minutes." Lugging his many sacks and packs, he lumbered on down the hall, made the turn, and disappeared. We chose rooms, unpacked a few items, found washbasins, and cleaned up a bit. Since we were famished and it was now full dark, we headed on down the long hallway, which was illuminated by oil lanterns, to find the dining room.

When we finally found it, Niccolo was already there along with Lex. His servant was an elderly slave with greying hair cut short. He showed a fatherly attitude towards us, always being polite and considerate of our needs. We sat down before a highly polished, marble table, absolutely exquisitely made! While we ate, Niccolo introduced us to Lex and told him a bit about ourselves, primarily that we were visitors from a far northern land. Lex was the kind of person that it is impossible not to like instantly. We chatted with him for quite some time even after we had finished eating and our host had excused himself for bed. Finally, we said goodnight to Lex and headed for our rooms. He explained that presently he would make his final rounds for the night, dimming out most of the lights. Once again, we had a good night's sleep though we did stay up a little longer chatting about the city and its marvels.

Over breakfast the next sunny morning, Niccolo, wearing a grey toga, explained, "Today, we go to the opening of the Fall Senate. As you will soon see, we Senators all wear grey togas. The common folks and guests of our land, such as you, wear white. Those with priestly duties don royal purple togas. Those in the artisan and construction trades wear brown ones. City guards wear red togas. Only the Emperor Hiro wears the yellow toga, which is the symbol of his office. His couriers, though, wear pale yellow ones. Let us hope that you don't get to see that yellow one." My thought was that there was a significant caste system here in Megalos; one's toga denoted one's position. Well, they were at least cool. The heat here was rather oppressive.

Walking through the streets of Galantas was an interesting experience for us. Before we left Calgary, we had spent hours practicing survival on city streets, trying to avoid pick pockets and out right thefts of our possessions. Here, we certainly needed all that training! The streets, though wide, were packed with throngs of people. Mostly I saw white and brown togas passing by us. Had Niccolo not been with us, it would have been more of a pushing and shoving match to navigate through the packed streets! However, the mere presence of the grey toga leading we six like tag-along dogs, helped immensely because everyone gave way slightly to Niccolo. Evidently, Senators were either respected or honored by the common people. The only others who were not being jostled about were those guards wearing red togas. Everyone gave a wide berth to passing city guards.

After about a half mile, we entered an arched entrance into the Senate Building. Many others wearing grey were also filing in along with us. Many said hello to Niccolo and he, they. Several asked him about us, but he just said we were his guests from the north. Once inside, the central area was a raised stone platform on which the current speaker would stand. On two opposing sides, marble stairs and bleachers rose ten levels tall. The most important Senators sat on the bottom row close to the speaker's platform. Niccolo led us to the top row, the tenth, explaining this row was reserved for any public observers. He also reminded us that even from this distance, due to the acoustics, we should have no trouble hearing each speaker. "Watch and learn," he said and then went back down to the bottom row. We dutifully sat down on the stone row. When the meeting began, we estimated there were about a hundred Senators present, fifty on each side facing the speaker's platform. One man rose and stepped onto it raising his hands for silence. The background chatter died away.

"Greetings fellow Senators and guests. I, Kilkis Lonika, President of the Senate, do declare the Fall Session is now officially in session. I trust you all enjoyed your summer break." The crowd muttered a response — some good, some not so good. "As usual, we begin this session with an update on the Northern War delivered by Emperor Hiro's worthy assistant, Helicon Theococos." He stepped down and a man wearing a pale yellow robe quickly stepped on stage amid some light clapping. From the sounds of the clapping, I deduced that most were doing so solely out of custom or duty.

"I bring you greetings from Emperor Hiro. He has asked me to relay to you the good news of the Civilization War. This summer, our illustrious generals have made steady progress conquering the Land of the Seven Sea Princes. I can formally announce that Pieta has fallen along with Bonilla and Vito. As I speak, our forces are closing on Barcella. By the end of this campaign year, it and Velona should be ours — all the key cities of the Sea Princes!" At this point there was a good deal more enthusiastic clapping and a bit of cheering from some of the Senators.

"However, I have even better news. As you know, the amazon band of female warriors, who call themselves the Sisterhood, were, and still are, the only effective fighting force in that entire barbarian land. However, Governor Lexus Thebes of Pieta has worked out an absolutely brilliant plan with the Sisterhood. He is using these women to help bring law and order into Pieta. By all reports, he has had fantastic success, unlike Zargarb, which is still a hot bed of rebels and troublemakers. So successful has Governor Lexus been that Emperor Hiro has personally awarded him the Golden Sun of Service!" Quite a few clapped loudly. "Further, the Emperor has ordered all other Governors to follow in the able footsteps of Governor Lexus and make effective us of these amazon women warriors to bring law and order back to the cities."

"But what of our losses?" called out one Senator. We couldn't see who it was.

"Ah, yes, where did I put those strings?" he said, fumbling inside his toga. He spied Niccolo and said, "Yes, I know Niccolo, we ought to use your writing system. Ah here they are," he pulled out a series of strings similar to those that Alabaster used with his census count. "The losses are hardly worth mentioning. But here they are. Zargarb: 750, Solamina: 10, Pieta: 5, Bonilla: 7, and Vito: 4. You see, once we have the amazons on our side, the losses for bringing civilization to the Sea Princes is negligible!" Again, a good deal of cheering and clapping interrupted him.

Yet another Senator spoke up, "I've heard that there has been some nasty business with that religious land we took many years ago. What is the situation there? Why after all these years is that land still barbaric? Have we made no inroads there at all? Who's responsible for this debacle?"

"Ah yes, well, as you know the Arads are devoutly attached to their pagan religious movement. And, ah, well, it seems that there has been some signs, some rituals, that according to their pagan prophets mean some kind of savior has just been born who is supposed to have the power to drive us out — if you can believe that! Drive the mighty Centurion army out! Ha. But these religious zealots believe utterly in this superstition. An example had to be set."

"What example?" called out the Senator.

"Ah, well, since their savior has just been born, the Governor thought it prudent to have all newborns eliminated. This way, their savior is gone. Now we can get them back on the path towards being a civilized land."

"You mean to say that he ordered babies to be killed? All of them? Which cities?" spoke up a female Senator across from us on the other side.

"Well, yes. There's no way to know which baby is their designated savior, so we eliminated all of them in Al Barq, where we feel their savior was most likely to have been born. Now that this savior has been eliminated, the pagans will listen to our civilizing wisdom instead of their pagan prophets." I detected several beads of sweat trickling down the speaker's face. He knew he was on a very touchy ground.

"But already it has produced excellent results," he added quickly to stem the uproar of protests coming from many Senators, mainly the women. "I can report that nearly all the remaining Arads have left Al Barq. Their capital city is now completely our own city. That is excellent news indeed." (It was all I could do to stifle my laughter.)

"There was no backlash against our forces in Al Barq?" asked a dubious Senator.

"None whatsoever!" That seemed to appease most of the Senators, who were mostly worried about their Centurions being attacked over this action.

"And what about all the rebellions in the heart of Juda Arad? Did sending all those expensive War Chariots take care of the problem?" asked another Senator.

"Ah, well, not exactly. They haven't had sufficient time to make their full impact felt upon the zealots. I'm sure their presence will quell all rebellions," he added quickly.

"I heard that a substantial number of these expensive War Chariots have been destroyed. How do you account for that?" asked the same man.

"Well, Senator, some have been damaged in transit to their stations. We've had some minor setbacks in getting the chariots from here to their destinations. Nothing out of line. It is, after all, a very long trip. We're on top of it. Minor detail, nothing to worry about. After all, they're all just a bunch of primitive, religious zealots."

"In other matters, the Emperor Hiro has asked me to report that another five hundred pounds of gold has been deposited in our treasury from our Southland mines, along with four hundred-fifty gemstones. We are doing as well as we expected."

At this point, since the financial report was always last on the reports, the President rose and took the platform, "Thank you for your honest and frank report, Helicon." The man quickly left the stage and continued walking on out of the building, thankful that it had gone as well as it had. He knew there would be trouble over the baby killings and the loss of so many chariots. He breathed a sigh of relief that no one had bothered to ask just how many of the hundred chariots had been damaged. Fifty, that is, half of them had already been destroyed beyond repair! He knew that if those war chariots could only get to where they were most needed, why, the rebellions would evaporate; no one could stand up to a charging war chariot, of that Helicon was certain.

The woman Senator who had voiced the opposition to the baby killings walked onto the platform. "I wish to submit a proclamation to the effect that there will be no further baby killings. Already, we have followed the advice of our holy priests and ordered our conquering Centurions to rape all the city's women so there'll be plenty of new babies to replace the many men that we killed taking that city. Now we kill their newly born children? This seems to go completely opposite of what our priests have requested. Should we not call forth a representative of Sol to ascertain their opinions in this matter?"

The President interrupted her. Senator Lucrezia, your proclamation properly falls under new business. We haven't yet attended to the older business. You may introduce it at the proper time, but now that we know your intentions to so do, I'll save some time and issue the request to the High Priest of Sol later today. Perhaps by the time we get to new business, their representative can addressed us. It may be that no proclamation will actually be needed." She seemed satisfied and returned to her seat.

"Now then, who wishes to speak first on old business?" He emphasized the word "old."

One Senator stood up and said, "What about the flooding in Helos? Has that problem been addressed yet?"

Another Senator stood up and answered, "Yes, we have formed a committee to look into the annual flooding and make some recommendations. So far, the committee is still looking into the problem."

And so it went for the rest of the morning. Problem after problem raised, committee after committee created to look into it and report back. I wondered if anyone around here ever actually did anything about anything! Shortly before breaking for lunch, I spied Niccolo falling asleep, leaning on a neighboring Senator. I chuckled; these meetings were incredibly boring for the most part. Simon pointed out that this could be a weakness, everything went to a committee, and little spontaneous problem solving was done.

During the lunch break, Niccolo introduced us to a number of other Senators, many of whom asked us from what northern land we came. We decided to tell the truth, told them we were from the Greenway, and were here seeking to open up grain trading for metal farming equipment. They seemed genuinely appalled when we said that there were almost no metalworkers in all the Greenway. One asked how the grain would be delivered, and we replied via the ships of the Sea Princes. "Ah, that is one of the primary reasons we have taken over the Sea Princes — to see that their marvelous ships are put to good use," that Senator commented self-satisfied.

The afternoon session began nearly as boring as the morning had been, until a man in a purple toga hastily entered the building and walked toward the speaker's platform. "Ah, His Holiness Rexus Thadrain has volunteered to come and explain the church's position in the matter of the baby killings." Everyone hushed as the elderly man took center stage. He was about fifty years old and tufts of grey hair stuck out from his headpiece. He carried a holy staff of office, and I gathered he must be fairly high in the priestly order here in Galantas. Everyone listened intently to his words.

His deep bass voice resonated, "Good afternoon noble Senators. Your

426

esteemed President has asked the Priests of Sol to address you concerning the matter of the slaying of babies in the lands of Arad, specifically, Al Barq. I understand that there is some talk of passing a proclamation banning such. Let me begin by explaining our position, which, until now, has been followed very well. When an army conquers another, many lives are lost, usually the young and able men of that land. Any land, which has suddenly lost so many of its current able-bodied generation of men, would soon find its very survival in jeopardy. We can't civilize that which has died. Thus, the Church requested that our conquering men bed as many of that land's women as possible, thereby creating new life for the future. It is only right and just that we make some attempt to replace that which we have taken from them. Now the Emperor has assured me that this incident in Al Barq is an isolated one and will not happen again. Remember too, that the lands of Arad were conquered many, many years ago, and thus, these newborn babies were not desperately needed to replenish their numbers. I grieved when I heard the news from Al Barq — prayed for the souls of those who had not had a chance for life. Tears I shed for the innocent. I met with the Emperor shortly thereafter and discussed the possibility of ordering our Centurions to bed all the women in Al Barq to make amends for the killing of this whole generation. However, he has informed me that such is not possible, because most of the Arads who lived in Al Barq have left the city. Who knows where they went, perhaps out into the desert to die of thirst? In any event, recompense is not possible at this point. Besides, the Emperor has assured me that this will not happen again. So it is the Church of Sol's opinion that no proclamation needs to be made concerning the matter — unless you wish to make a proclamation that if so many are ever killed again, that the Centurions are ordered to bed as many local women as possible to make amends." With that, he stepped down, bowed to each side, and left without taking any questions.

Never have I heard rape so wonderfully justified, so eloquently presented. I couldn't believe what I had just heard. After killing all the young men and husbands, they felt it their duty to rape their defenseless women just to make more babies. Wonderfully insane logic! I was furious, but bit my tongue and said nothing — likewise, the rest of my Circle. I was very glad when the Senate adjourned for the evening.

Over dinner at Niccolo's home, he asked us how we enjoyed watching the Senate in action. "Well, doesn't anyone around here ever take any responsibility for getting something done?" I asked more than a tad annoyed.

He laughed, easing my tensions. "So you too have observed that. Darn committees. These days, that's all they do is make committees. I'm on a committee to address a problem of pastures in the south of Megalos. Heck, I know nothing about shepherding, and furthermore, I don't want to know more about such! Thirty years ago, it was a different story. Ever since Emperor Hiro ascended the throne, the Senate has gone totally downhill, in my humble opinion. I think the Senate has become a joke. Nevertheless, I'm obligated to fulfill my duties as a duly elected Senator for life." He sighed and took a long drink. He was interrupted in even this by Lex.

"Master, a representative has arrived from the Emperor. It seems he wishes to meet your new guests from the north. He has asked that they join him for supper." Suddenly Niccolo's face paled and he nearly choked on his ale.

"Stall him a few minutes," he quickly ordered Lex, who left at once to carry out his master's wishes. He looked at us and said, "This is indeed terrible news. What have I done to you? Oh dear me. Look, when you get there, try to avoid all food and drink he offers you. He is going to try to poison you into a stupor. Probably he will chain up your men and bed you women later tonight. No one can go against his orders. He has done this many times before calling it "getting acquainted with" our neighbors. I'm truly sorry I have brought this doom down upon you all; please, please forgive me. I was so enthralled by your spirit, your keen insight, and intellect that I tried to ignore history."

"Thanks for the warning, Niccolo," I replied a little shakily. "We don't hold you at all responsible. It is solely the doing of this Emperor fellow. Say, can you do one thing for us?"

"Sure, anything!" he replied, seeing a way that he could make up for having placed our lives in jeopardy.

"See that our horses are saddled and ready to go at a moment's notice. See that our sacks are tied onto the saddles as well. I have a feeling that we may need to make a hasty exit."

"Certainly. I'll see to it myself. If you need a hasty exit, take the same road that we came here on. If trouble comes, if you can somehow get into the Southlands, you might have a chance. I'm so deeply sorry to have brought this down upon you kids," he said apologetically again. He led us down the hallway to the entrance gate where Lex was waiting with a man who wore a pale yellow toga.

As soon as he saw us, he said covertly, "Ah, here you are. The Emperor Hiro requests you dine with him right now. Please follow me." I didn't like his attitude in the slightest. He didn't even look at Niccolo; it was as if the Senator was not present!

"Do we need to fetch our horses? Do we have far to go?" I asked politely knowing the answer already.

"Walk, not far. Follow me; the Emperor hates to be kept waiting." He turned and headed down the street at a rapid pace. We had no choice but to follow. Niccolo's guards looked grim as he darted past them. Certainly, an evening visit with the Emperor was not something one desired. Quite why, we were about to find out.

As we walked along, Sarah Jane mentally sent to me, *I'll keep an eye out for poisoned or drugged food and drink. I'll let you all know as I determine what is safe and what isn't.*

Great. I'll try to keep his interest, I replied to my companions.

It's a shame we don't have our weapons. I'm afraid we're going to need them before this night is over, Roy sent.

We have to use our brains and our minds. They don't know we can communicate this way. Let's use it to our advantage, Sandy added cautiously.

The palace was only about a half mile from Niccolo's home, and we made it in record time, I suspected from our incredibly fast walk. Besides, all the people in the streets gave this man in the pale yellow toga a very wide berth.

A polished marble wall ten feet tall surrounded the immense palace and grounds, which occupied at least a large city block. Four entrances were placed at the cardinal points, all heavily guarded with ten men each. As we followed our guide up the walkway, the guards quickly searched us for concealed weapons. I smiled, realizing how wise we had been for not trying to sneak some inside. Finding nothing, the guards nodded to our guide who said, "This way." We entered through the arched entrance way onto the palace grounds proper.

Now the palace was actually a complex of buildings. One tall structure with no walls, but had magnificent marble columns supporting its arched roof, was gaily illuminated with banners and flowing ribbons. We spied a number of people lying beside each other, feeding each other what appeared to be grapes, fondling each other, and even bedding! Shocked, I quickly looked away from this crude scene. Fortunately, the guide walked on past this open building towards the largest building, which had marble walls. Still it was a magnificent structure, and I marveled at its construction as we walked up the polished marble steps, our sandals clapping on the hard stone.

Inside were a series of connecting hallways, highly ornate; many tapestries hung upon the fifteen-foot tall walls. Great golden lantern clusters hung from the ceiling illuminating the halls in a yellowish glow. We walked down one hall to a set of double mahogany doors. The guide opened them and beckoned us to enter. We stepped into a huge room equally well lighted but full of people. An overpowering flowery flagrance assaulted our senses. Around the perimeter of this giant room, people were lying on their sides eating grapes and sipping wine and, yes, flirting with each other. I spied several couples actively bedding, but they halted as we entered. In fact, a total silence fell the moment we walked into the room.

No mistaking the Emperor. At the back center of the room was a grand marble throne and sitting on it was a thin man perhaps in his late thirties with a canary yellow toga draped loosely over his body. Several women were sitting around him feeding him grapes or offering him a sip of wine. He spoke at once, "Ah, here they are, our barbarian guests from the northern lands. Welcome to my palace. Come sit by me." He motioned for us to come on over. Quickly, the three young women rose and vacated their positions moving off to his right side. "Yes, sit here beside me. I'm Emperor Hiro, Sol's chosen one, ruler of all the civilized lands of Tarra. I'm the Emperor of Tarra. And you are?"

It was decision-making time. Should I speak for our group as was my right and duty, or should Simon, who was far better at this sort of thing and a man, do it? The choice was simple; this man obviously was a womanizer. I spoke, "I'm called Bethany, and these are my companions." I introduced them, beginning with the women. He looked each of us over with his beady eyes, staring long at our breasts and legs. He paid almost no attention to the guys when I introduced them; his eyes focused on us women.

Once the formalities were completed, several servants brought in platters of food, goblets, and a several pitchers of wine. "Why don't your men sit over there beside those lovely women? I'm sure they would love to hear stories of your land," the Emperor commanded, well suggested, but under the circumstances, it was an order. Seeing no alternative, Roy, Simon, and Raphael moved some thirty feet away from us to where a dozen women, who had been fondling each other when we entered the room, smiled, and beckoned them sit beside them. *His court is full of nothing but whores*, I thought to myself. *What have we gotten ourselves into?*

Sarah Jane muttered softly her druwid chants. The Emperor noticed her, and I quickly interceded, "Oh, she mutters nonsense whenever she gets excited. Pay her no mind. It's a shame that you did not invite us earlier. We had already dined when your ambassador called. I'm afraid we're all rather stuffed at the moment." I hoped this would buy us some time.

"I'm afraid I didn't learn of your presence in my city sooner. I'm always the gracious host for visitors. Here have a grape. There is always room for a grape," he offered me the plate. "Look everyone, I offer the barbarians grapes and wine from my own table!" Various cooing sounds echoed from his court as if this was somehow a noble, grand gesture.

Take the one closest to him, Sarah Jane sent to me. I did so, keeping my eyes on Hiro, who seemed a bit troubled that I chose that grape out of all those on the plate. "Have one yourself," I said, and offered him one of the tainted ones.

"Ah, I'm afraid I'm full of grapes. My lovely women have been stuffing them in my mouth all evening before you came." He passed the plate over to Sandy and then to Sarah Jane. He seemed very annoyed that they each took one that was not drugged. I could see that this was going to be a long night.

He asked me to tell him what our land was like, especially winters. He had only heard of this thing called snow. I killed time by a very long winded explanation of our weather. After the first minute, he showed no interest at all in what I was saying. He even rudely interrupted me by yelling for more wine even though the pitchers had not been touched as yet. Quickly, the three pitchers were replaced by another three, this time, all drugged according to Sarah Jane. It was obvious that his sole intention was to get us all drugged. He was not subtle about it at all.

While I was doing my best to fend off the Emperor, Sandy covertly kept an eye on how the fellows were doing. They were in dire trouble with a dozen women fondling them, rubbing their legs sensuously, trying to get them to take a sip of wine or rubbing a grape against their lips and then to the men's. One even picked up Raphael's hand, placed it on her exposed breast, and began rubbing it! Sandy turned away at that point. Things weren't going at all well.

Next, Hiro asked for his musicians, and several men carrying stringed instruments entered and began playing. Now this was interesting and would have been enjoyable had Hiro not continued to get us to drink and eat. Again, he called for more wine though the pitchers remained untouched. While the musicians were playing, he again called out for the musicians to begin to play as if either he couldn't hear the music or, as I began to suspect, he was merely insane or psychotic. I wondered how the High Priests could've ever elected this buffoon.

Just then, Simon sent to us all via Sandy, *I have a plan. Raphael will drink and get drugged. Then, Roy and I'll use our powers to make them think we have been drugged as well. Perhaps, you three can do something similar.*

Great, just be careful, I sent back. To Sandy and Sarah Jane, I sent, *Look, I'll drink his wine. I'm terrible at doing what Simon does with minds. You two, see if you can fake it.*

You wouldn't believe the relief that spread across Hiro's entire face when I finally drunk deeply from his offered wine cup! I muttered something about it not tasting so good. I felt an immediate warming, tingling sensation in my stomach. Soon my arms became weak, and with the relaxing music, I slowly laid down beside the throne, much as many of the women were doing across the room from me. I wondered if they too were drugged. Then darkness seeped over me as I heard Hiro once again call for more wine and music.

I came to in a field of blackness, mostly because I felt my body being jostled about. I was entirely outside my head looking down. It was Hiro himself who was carrying my limp body into what must have been his open-air bedroom, because I thought I saw stars where there should be walls. He laid my unconscious body down on his bed and left me there. He walked over to a table and lit several candles. Now I could perceive the room vaguely instead of that blackness. Next, he washed himself off at a water basin. He was still wearing his yellow toga.

Satisfied with his preparations, he came over to his bed and gazed wickedly at me. He muttered, "Now I'll have my way with you, barbarian. I wonder how good this will be? She is so young and actually could be quite pretty if she had a mind to be more conscious of her looks. Ah well, but then she is just a barbarian. Now off with her toga, I want to see the rest of her young body!" He snickered and let out an evil laugh.

Now, his intentions became utterly plain to me. No more guessing. I had to act, but my body was totally zonked out from the drug in the wine. *Wait a minute! I'm not my body! I'm the druwid, not the body. I should still be able to do everything.* I made the body speak, though it was totally lying there in a stupor. I made the body rather brusquely utter, "Do not do this thing. If you try, I will kill you."

He jumped back in utter shock, staring at my unconscious body. His expression was one of complete and utter disbelief. Cautiously, he touched my near lifeless body, poked it, lifted its eyelids, and generally satisfied himself that it was completely drugged. He shook his head and began removing his toga. Once again, I caused the body to utter, "This is your last warning. Do not do this thing. If you try, I will kill you."

Again, he jumped back three feet, holding tightly onto his toga staring wide-eyed at my still unconscious form. After a few minutes of standing motionless and staring at me, he finally again poked the body and lifted its eyelids. Finally, he said, "I must be dreaming. She is totally out of it, unconscious. This bitch is trying to scare me somehow. I'll have my way with her. I'll show her! She can't harm me, only spook me somehow." He tore off his toga and, naked, walked confidently up to his bed.

I expanded my awareness upwards into the nighttime sky, coalescing the black energies of Nature. I felt him carefully taking my toga off. Surprise, I wasn't naked beneath it, as were his courtesans. I had on my underclothing that I normally wear beneath my leathers. This slowed him down as he tried to figure out how to get them off my body. I concentrated on the black energies, formed them. Oh, this was so easy for me to do. Finally, just as he was pulling my nickers down my legs, I connected a line between him and my black energy mass. I watched as the tiny blue energy line raced from his body upwards to the cloud knowing what would happen in the next split second.

Once the tiny line reached the black mass, a huge amount of energy came lashing downward from the sky — a giant lightning bolt flashed through the open side wall and straight to his head. Unfortunately, he was touching my legs slightly, and I, too, got a bit of the electrical jolt, and my body bounced six inches into the air, completely disorienting me. The thunder that followed knocked out all the candles leaving me in total darkness once more. Stunned, I forgot to stop what I was doing and kept the tiny blue lines going upwards from his body to my comforting black energy mass in the cloud, unseen, but high overhead. Bolt after bolt came blasting down from the sky, a gigantic display never before seen in Galantas. I sensed bits of marble falling on my body, but groggy from experiencing the backlash from my own lightning bolt, I continued pulling them down from the sky. Imaginary images of Isabel standing alone against the might of the Centurion army and calling down lightning bolts to destroy them came into my mind along with other imagined images of our own renegade druwid, Erline Herbiscus, smashing raiding Galts into oblivion. I knew what they felt, how they felt, and it was so wonderful, so powerful, so comforting.

Stop it. Stop it, Bethany. It is done. Stop Bethany. It's Sandy. It is finished. We have to get out of here now. Stop it, Beth, please, I beg you.

Her words, crude and brash, came unwelcomed into my mind. *How dare anyone stop me! I am power incarnate. I am a goddess!*

Please stop it now. Roy needs you. Roy loves you.

I am here Beth. I do love you. Please, we must get away. Here, I will join with you, the gentle, yet urgent voice of Roy spoke directly into my mind. I felt the presence of Roy; kind and gentle, he seemed to envelop me and surrounded me with his love. Suddenly, I realized that he, too, was out of his body and was attempting to hug me, two eternal beings, two spirits attempting to occupy the very same space. Love does that — being or joining one with another. I let my comforting black energy mass float off and latched onto Roy. The lightning bolts ceased instantly. I hugged Roy back.

Am I dead? I asked him.

No, your body is drugged and in a stupor. Sarah Jane says that it'll wear off in time, but time we don't have. We must get away now. I'll carry your body, Roy sent. Since we were still locked together, I felt the sensations from his body as he lifted up my limp form and, together with Sandy, walked out of the debris-filled room that had once been the Emperor's bedchamber. I began seeing through Roy's eyes. Just outside the room, the others had gathered. Simon was carrying Raphael with Sarah Jane's assistance. The looks on their faces told me just how frightened they actually were. All around us, people were screaming, running terrified in all directions. Palace guards pushed past us and into Hiro's bedroom. Simon muttered a chant, and we headed down the hall as fast as we could go, which was not very fast considering two of us were being carried by the remaining four. I heard Roy call out, "Sandy, start grabbing any weapons you come across. There, grab that sword." I saw her bend down and pick up a sword that had been dropped in panic.

I heard, "The Emperor has been killed!" coming from somewhere behind us. Over and over, the words came, "He's been killed. Struck by lightning. Where are the barbarians? They have escaped. Capture them. This way." I heard heavy footsteps thundering on the marble stone somewhere behind us. Any moment I expected to feel the clamping weight of a Centurion's hand upon Roy's shoulder.

Instead, when the footsteps drew painfully close, Simon muttered, "They went that way. We're evacuating the wounded women. Go get them." Again, I marveled at how well this master illusionist could so easily sway men's minds. Then I suddenly realized that doing so for him was as easy as bringing down lightning was for me. In that instant, I felt very close to Simon and he, me, as he picked up my thoughts. He sent, *Yes, true. Hold on; we'll be out of the palace shortly,* he placed into my mind. In that instant, I realized that he, like me, had to fight off the temptation to force any and all to do his will. He could be a god if he so chose, just as I or Erline could be.

Unfortunately, a quick departure was not the case. As we drew closer to the gate that we had entered earlier this evening, we found it had been securely locked, and ten Centurions stood guard, allowing no one to pass. We ducked off to the right some distance from the gate, hiding in the shadows beside the ten-foot tall marble wall. The men were breathing heavily from the strenuous exertion of carrying both Raphael and me. "Now what?" whispered Sandy. "We have got to get out of here!"

Roy panted, "I can't fight ten of them at once. We need a plan. Simon, can we climb over the wall?"

Simon panted back, "No way, not without ropes and not with these two."

"Then we are trapped like dogs in a pen," cried Sarah Jane, tears forming and trickling down her chin. "We've come all this way only to have it end here. Let's at least put up a good fight."

As their Wid, I'm supposed to create the plans. It was up to me to get us out of here. *Roy, look at the guards and the gate, please. I need to see them.* He moved a little so I could see what he saw through his eyes, our beingnesses, that is, we, the immortal spirits, were still intertwined. I loved this new sensation of an almost total joining of ourselves. Once more, I found the black energy masses far overhead. They were greatly diminished from just a little while ago, probably because I had taken so much from them. There was still enough. It just took a little longer to amass it together. I strung the familiar blue energy line from the gates up into the sky to the dark cloud of energy. Boom. A giant bolt of lightning returned down that path, smashing into the elegantly carved, mahogany gates, smashing them into splinters, wounding several guards. *Simon, tell them to flee or the next bolt hits them.*

Stunned, Simon yelled, "Get away from that gate! More lightning is coming. Run for your lives!" It worked. The frightened, shocked guards needed no second suggestion to flee. They ran as fast as they could away from the gate. I felt Roy's strong arms pick up my still unconscious body and felt the straining of his leg muscles as he carried me toward the now open gate. One of the guards had been killed by flying door splinters. I saw the spiritual being drifting upwards from his lifeless body. Suddenly I remembered Alabaster's request to try to find out what happened to these beings when their bodies die. I kept an eye on the Centurion as he floated up above the palace. When he was several hundred feet up, I saw that he saw something white open up like a tunnel. In a flash, he took off down that imaginary tunnel. Physically, I saw that he headed not for the Appian Way, but for somewhere far out in the uninhabited Red Desert. *How weird*, I thought. *Something strange is going on here. I wonder what it is?*

Roy missed a step, and I got jolted back into my body as it accidentally banged into the side of a building, giving me a sharp pain in my shoulder. "Sorry," I heard him mutter aloud. "We're never going to get them back to Niccolo's this way. I'm tiring rapidly."

Simon replied, "Even with Sarah Jane's help, I don't think I can carry Raphael much further. Let's stop and catch our breaths." Again, we halted. "You all stay here in the shadows. I'm going to go find something to help us. If I'm not back in say five minutes, you all go on as best you can." Sandy protested but gave him a farewell kiss. Bravely, she held up a Centurion sword, along with Roy, intent on protecting us as best she could. Sarah Jane knelt beside us two unconscious ones, seeing if there was anything she could do to help bring us around. Unfortunately, there wasn't a thing she could do. All her supplies, her herbs, were back in our rooms at Niccolo's home or rather attached to our saddled horses, if Niccolo had lived up to his promise to see that they were saddled.

I will say one thing, when a being is not connected to a body so solidly, time seems to run differently. A short span can seem an eternity, and an eternity can seem to be only a brief flicker. After what seemed to me to be an eternity, Simon reappeared pushing a stolen vender's pushcart. "Put them on this quickly. The Centurions are starting to search for us in the streets." Again, I felt Roy's muscles strain, as he lifted my body and placed it gently in the cart. Both men then pushed it along at a rapid pace with the two women, now holding the swords, leading the way.

Thank goodness, druwids have a near perfect sense of direction. Spying men rushing down some streets, we had no choice but to take unfamiliar side streets. To me, it seemed as if we were traversing a maze whose walls kept changing, and the desired route out constantly varying. Finally, I got so confused, so spinney, that I had to let go of Roy and moved up into the sky to get a large scale overview. Now I could see where we were going and relayed some directions to the others. I found I could see the Centurions way down on the streets and give orders that would allow us to bypass them.

Finally, we arrived at the back of Niccolo's home. Lex was standing by the opened door, looking back toward the palace. He had our horses ready, tied neatly to the hitching rails. "Ah, here you are. Oh my, are they hurt? Your horses are ready to go as you instructed. Niccolo is watching for you at the front door."

"No, they are okay, just drugged," Sarah Jane replied. "Thank you for having the horses ready! The Emperor is dead; the lightning bolts killed him. Did you see the lightning flashes?"

"Oh my. Oh yes! Never have I seen such a display of Nature. So Nature got him in the end. Serves him right. While you are getting ready, let me go get Master Niccolo. I'm sure he wants to say farewell."

My attention now went onto the problem at hand dutifully raised by Sandy. "How on earth are we going to get them on their horses? They aren't in any condition to ride, much less sit in a saddle. Do we tie them on somehow?"

"We don't have much of a choice," Roy commented. He heaved my body like a sack of potatoes up and over the saddle. He tied my hands and legs around the middle of my horse so I wouldn't fall off, but I sure would have a sore stomach the next day. It took both the men to get Raphael up onto his horse. By that time, Niccolo came running up to us, followed by Lex some distance behind him. Both were breathless from running through the long hallways.

"Are you all safe? Oh, are they wounded?" he asked. Sarah Jane explained that we were drugged and still unconscious. "What happened up at the palace? Did you see that incredible display of Nature's unbridled fury? Never have I seen such a lightning display, and there wasn't a storm cloud in the sky!"

Simon replied, "Ah, yes. I'm afraid Emperor Hiro took most of those lightning bolts to his head. There is very little left of him now. He tried to bed Bethany here just before Nature struck him down. We had to kill a few

Centurions to escape. I'm afraid that a hue and cry for us has gone out."

"Well, at least you didn't get hit. That's what matters to me. You know, I almost think this must have been what Nature did during that Great Battle at Zargarb, where we lost so many soldiers to the Sisterhood. Nature can be frightening when she unleashes such a fiery storm as this one was."

Simon agreed and added, "Niccolo, use this situation to your advantage. You have the opportunity to choose a new Emperor. Choose wisely this time. In fact, you may say that your god, Sol, so disapproved of the lecherous ways of Hiro that Sol struck him down in a blaze of lightning. That would be highly believable under the present circumstances."

"An excellent idea indeed. I shall, though it'll give more power to the Church of Sol. That may just be a good thing."

We were ready to depart, and the four shook hands with Niccolo. "When the Centurions get here," Simon added, "tell them the truth that we returned from our evening with the Emperor and left for home, riding down this street here. That way, you are telling the truth. So long and good luck." He was the last to mount and then off we went. Simon led Raphael's horse; Roy, mine; Sandy, the pack horse. Sarah Jane attempted to navigate our way out of the city without running into the Centurions, who were scampering down the main streets looking for us. Once again, I saved the day by floating high above the buildings. Looking down, I could see where the soldiers were and directed us around them. Several times, we came dangerously close to running into a swarm of Centurions. It was well past midnight when we finally climbed up the hill overlooking Galantas.

As we rode slowly past the last guard post, Simon called out to the guards, "Too much wine." The guards completely bought that explanation; there was even a grain of truth in that statement. Slowly, we rode on into the night. I knew that eventually the guards at this last outpost would report our passing and that the hue and cry would soon follow. I envisioned hundreds of cavalry charging after us. Unfortunately, we could only go at a slow pace until Raphael and I regained consciousness.

My body still felt dead to the world. Things still looked dark to me, yet by morning they would look even glummer.

It was late at night. I'm normally asleep at this late hour. The excitement and necessity of operating while exterior to my drugged, unconscious body gave way to the monotony of a slow ride along a paved road late at night. I soon fell asleep.

"Wake up, sleepyhead," Sarah Jane's voice seeped into my dreamy mind. I was imagining Roy and I were dancing, swirling around a dance floor somewhere within a billowing white cloud. I didn't want it to end.

"Huh?" Then, my nose picked up an awful scent, and I awoke with a cough. Sarah Jane, satisfied that she had me now fully awake with her herbal remedy, sat down beside me.

"How do you feel?" she asked.

The hot, bright midmorning sun threatened to blast my eyes into a white oblivion. "Not so good. I feel weird, like my head is swimming in a black spider web. My chest feels as if I've run into a tree branch. My eyes ache from this bright light. I feel nauseous and my head is spinning around in little circles. Besides, I was having a pleasant dream of dancing on a cloud," I retorted, annoyed with being awakened and feeling this out of sorts.

"I think that is normal. You were given quite a knockout drug last night," Sarah Jane optimistically diagnosed. Suddenly last night flashed rapidly through my mind. I sat up straight and looked worriedly around. We were all here, sitting beside the road in the small shade provided by a rising hillside. Raphael looked as bad off as I presumed I looked. She went on, "Plus, the wine didn't help. I expect you're a bit dehydrated as well. So here, drink this and then see if you can eat a bit. We're stopping for breakfast." I drank some water, but my head only swirled even more, probably a side effect of the wine.

"Where are we?" I asked, if only to get myself out of the center of conversation.

"Dunno, somewhere along the same road we came on with Niccolo," Simon answered. "We haven't yet made that big reservoir, which is the half-way point as I recall."

"Active pursuit?" I asked, fiddling with the offered food, though not eating much.

"Debatable. Yes and no. Roy believes he spotted a bunch of riders behind us some distance. He spied them on one of these wide curves where you can see the road many miles behind us. They disappeared quickly as we rode on and lost that viewpoint. We estimate that they are several hours behind us, though that may not be as much of a head start as it sounds. We've been forced to go at a walk, while I expect our pursuers are galloping and trotting."

"We stopped now only so we could get you both revived and to eat, but also because of something Roy spotted. We are not sure what to make of it," Simon continued. I noticed that instead of looking at me while he was talking, he stared far off the way we had come, while Roy stared ahead.

"Hey, there they go again!" exclaimed Roy. "Look there and then back there." Light flashes — patterned flashes. "It's got some rhythm to it, some patterns I can't decipher. I don't think it is a natural phenomenon."

"Looks as if someone is sending light signals," I replied. "Cripes, that means they are signaling Centurions ahead of us!" Suddenly, the full impact struck me. It is one thing to try to outrun those that are pursuing us and quite another to run headlong into those ahead of us awaiting our arrival!

"Well, we have learned a bit more about their long distance communication methods and means," declared Simon, attempting to put a bit of optimism into the stark reality of being pursued. "This is the other reason we stopped — to try to figure the significance of this light signaling and how to respond. Any ideas?"

"Well, certainly, if those ahead of us now know about the death of their

Emperor and our escape, why, they ought to be planning how to interdict and capture us as we get closer," I surmised. "We must get off Megalos; otherwise, we're trapped, doomed. Where could we go and hide for any length of time on an island, even one this large. Eventually, we'll be discovered or turned in, perhaps for a reward. The only way off the island that we know about lies at the Shallow Firth. So we must get there, no question about that. I sure wish we could somehow delay those coming after us because then we would only have to deal with those ahead. I think we ought to get going soon."

Hastily, we packed up and continued at a bone-jarring trot — I hate trotting — down the road. "So gang, mind filling me and Raphael in on what happened last night," I asked.

"Well, once you passed out, Sandy and I pretended to fall asleep. We watched as Hiro carried you off by himself. I think it was rather silly after that. The others congregated around us five. Crazy would be more like it; some women came over with some men and began undressing us and well, you know what they probably attempted to do after that. Similarly, it wasn't just that bunch of women that went after the three guys either. Hiro sure has a weird court! Simon suggested we let them struggle to get off our togas and figure out how to undo our undies. When they nearly had Simon's pants off, he jumped up and said 'Boo!' I swear those people had to be somewhat drugged themselves, for they reacted badly or should I say slowly as if something unexpected like this had never happened. Then came the wrestling match. Everyone tried to pin us down and force their intentions upon us. Sandy and I gave a few of them black eyes, but we really needed the fellows to get us free. Simon and Roy got into a free-for all brawl with the men in the room who came over to tackle them. I'm afraid that several had their arms and legs broken in the scuffle. Then, a couple produced swords. That's when things turned down right nasty. Roy killed two with their own swords while Simon spooked the others, making them run out of the room. Only when the lightning bolts came flying were they able to get free and drag Raphael over to us. While Sandy and I tried to drag Raphael along, Simon and Roy went looking for you. We don't know how you managed to call down the lightning, but it sure helped us find you. His palace sure has a lot of rooms."

"Finally, we got close by following where the bolts seemed to strike. We panicked because they were coming at the rate of one a minute! We thought perhaps you had lost control; I guess we were right. Sandy tried to make contact with you first and then Roy helped. From what Roy said, his help was really needed. You were completely berserk when we found you, but your body was unconscious. How can you call lightning when you are unconscious? That is what we have been debating all along."

"I got jostled awake only to find myself outside the body," I tried to explain. "I was watching him undress and trying to undress me. I knew what he had in mind, and I wasn't about to let him do it. Right there gang, I realized something. We are spirits, beings, not bodies. If we can call lightning, then it is we, the beings, that are doing it. I reasoned that I should still be able to do my thing without the body. After all, what has the body to do with calling lightning? We have to discipline ourselves to ignore the body and reach out to Nature's energy masses anyway. I found it far easier to do it without the interference of the body. However, I'll admit that my first strike accidentally also hit my legs. The sudden electrical surge in my unconscious body confused me greatly, and I'm afraid that I lost control for a while. Then, all went black because one bolt knocked out the candlelights. I couldn't see, so I kept it up fearing the worst, until you all came."

"So you are saying that we, too, should be able to perform our druwid actions while the body is unconscious?" asked a very curious Sarah Jane.

"I couldn't," broke in Raphael, "because I was unconscious. Doesn't unconscious mean not conscious? I don't understand. I was out like a light until this morning."

"I know what you mean," I answered. "When I'm asleep, I'm unconscious too. Somehow, I was jostled awake and found myself out of my body. Perhaps, it was a side effect of that drug. I've never been drugged before."

We discussed this for a while before I remembered what I had seen about the dying Centurion. "Say, one other peculiar thing. Remember when we watched where the Sea Princes spirits went when their bodies were killed in that battle? They went somewhere up into the Appian Way. Well, I watched one of the Centurions just after his body was killed. He didn't go there at all. True, he seemed to be following some kind of white light thing, but he went straight as an arrow to somewhere into the Red Desert, definitely not to the Appian Way. Most peculiar, don't you think? I wonder what is going on?"

Simon broke in, "I don't think now is the time to discuss religion. Ahead lays that reservoir. We might find a welcoming party there waiting for us. What should we do? I don't think it wise for us to use lightning bolts this time. That would undermine Niccolo's proposed 'Act of Sol' explanation, and it would definitely begin to tie us and the Greenway to the battle at Zargarb. I think it too risky to use our ultimate spells. So what do we do? Fight it out with swords? They're going to hear us coming a long way off — what with these hoof beats on the stone roadway. I've just discovered why I don't like these roads!"

Roy added antagonistically, "Yes, probably we can expect an ambush ahead."

"Well, if I could just get out of my head and float way up high and look down, I could see and guide us," I said rather pessimistically. "Only, I don't know how to let go like I did last night. Guess you could try to drug me again," I said jokingly. *Seriously, if I could somehow manage to let go of my body enough and move way up high, why the possibilities are unlimited, but I can't.* "Okay, we need a plan, gang. Let's pause a minute from this darn trotting so I can think."

We halted, much to my relief. We were rounding the eastern rim of the pair of hills, which cradled the reservoir between them. The road snaked around this hill to the base of the reservoir and then around the western hill. The hillside rose steeply to the top perhaps a thousand feet above us. Below, I spied a rock quarry from which they originally mined the stone, which was used in its construction. It gave me an idea. "See that abandoned stone quarry below us down there?" I pointed out. "How about cutting across country, making for the quarry? Once there, we ought to be able to find a track out of there. After all, they had to move all those heavy stones up and out." Since no one had any better ideas, Roy led the way trying to find a safe path.

The hillside below us was either talus slopes or highly rocky — either could be deadly to our horses' legs. We dismounted and began to lead them, occasionally slipping and sliding ourselves. I was beginning to feel I'd made a wrong decision to cut across the hillside when Roy finally found us a trail of sorts. It was narrow allowing only single-file passage, but it was safe and seemed to lead us where we wanted to go, the quarry. Unfortunately, it led us not to the quarry but to the lowest portion or base of the actual reservoir!

"Hey, this is really great!" exclaimed Raphael. "I wanted to inspect it up close like this, but I dared not ask Niccolo since he was in a hurry. While you figure out what we do next, I want to examine it." He walked up to the very base and looked up the sheer marble wall that dammed up the waters. Far above him, the aqueducts provided passage for a controlled amount of water, most destined for Galantas. Five hundred feet above us, the road wandered up to the control building and then on westward toward Niccolo's villa. While we were waiting, a stone fell from on high, narrowly missing our packhorse.

Looking up, we spied a Centurion far above us; he was scanning the roadway that we would have been on had we not taken this detour. Silently, I prayed that he didn't look down. I had visions of boulders falling on our heads, and there would be very little we could do to avoid them. We waited breathlessly. Finally, he moved back from the edge, and we could no longer see him. "You are right, Roy. They are indeed waiting for us," I whispered.

"You stay here; I'm going to look for a path to the western side," he whispered back. I took his reins and watched him move silently along the stone wall. Soon he disappeared around the edge of the hill.

"Say, you know there is a flaw in their dam here," Raphael announced. "One good earthquake and this dam is going to burst. I wonder what the chance of an earthquake occurring about now really is?" he said half in jest, half seriously. He showed us the flaw; a tiny crack had appeared in one of the base stones. He explained that here at the base, the stones held back an enormous weight of water. Of course, the odds of an earthquake right about now were nil, but I liked his intention.

Never underestimate Raphael, especially when he is in a critical situation involving some construction or design. We were waiting patiently for Roy to return when he said, "Hum, I think that will do just fine. Bethany, you are going to get your much needed diversion!" Sarah Jane looked quite proud, her face beaming. *If there was ever any doubt that she was in love with him, this would certainly dispel it,* I thought to myself, and immediately wondered if I had the same reactions when Roy did something great! "How much rope have we got?"

As quietly as possible, we went through our supplies. Between us, we managed to find three fifty-foot sections. One he used to tie all seven horses together. Next, he fastened two together and coiled it over his back. "Now comes the hard part. I have to scale that cliff up to that large boulder there." While we watched and kept a sharp eye out for Centurions, Raphael began to climb up the cliff side. He went very slowly, feeling out each handhold and foothold. Roy returned while he was still climbing, and we explained what he was doing, sort of, because we really didn't know what Raphael actually had in mind.

"I found the quarry path that leads off and up to the main road some distance west of here," Roy whispered. I smiled my approval. It took Raphael about a half hour to make the climb and secure his rope around the boulder. He let the other end fall down toward us and then repelled back down. In less than a minute, he stood beside us quite out of breath from the climb. Next, he tied the rope to the end horse.

Raphael explained, "Okay, here's the plan. We get the horses to take up the slack and then with a big pull, why, we should be able to loosen the boulder, which, due to the nature of this valley here, should come down and smash into the ground just about where we are standing."

"And that's going to do what?" I asked, "Besides alerting them to our presence?"

"Not sure, but I think the flaw will get magnified. Come on; time's a'wasting," Raphael declared. We moved out, staying as close to the rock face as possible until all the ropes connecting the horses grew taught. On Raphael's signal, we urged our horses forward. They pulled and strained. Suddenly without warning, the boulder broke free and began its accelerating descent, while the horses, free from its pull, lunged forward, nearly knocking us off our feet. Quickly, we kept them going as fast as we could safely scamper to make sure we were out of the way of the falling boulder and small debris that came along with it. A thunderous crash echoed through the entire area, magnified by the bowl shape of this end of the valley between the two hills. We turned around. There was the boulder bouncing high off the ground where we had been standing earlier.

From high above, over a dozen Centurions looked down from the top of the reservoir to see what had happened. We kept moving and were soon around the side of the hill where we couldn't be seen from above. We halted and collected the rope and untied the horses, while Roy kept a sharp lookout to see if we had been spotted. For once, luck was on our side. The soldiers were looking at the fallen boulder, which still rocked and swayed a bit, and they didn't see us. We mounted up.

"Looks like it didn't do anything, Raphael," I consoled, "but it was a worth the try. Guess we needed a bigger boulder. After all, that is pretty solid marble down there." I figured he might be heartbroken if his plan had failed.

Even Sarah Jane looked a bit glum; she had high hopes for his success.

I wasn't prepared for his answer, "Women! Always in a hurry. Gotta see an immediate effect don't you? Well, you just need to have patience. Let's ride. I think that we really need to get out of this valley in a hurry. Lead on, Roy!" We followed Roy's lead, but due to the tricky footing, the horses merely walked at a fast clip. Finally, I spied Roy's trail. It ran from down below at the quarry, I presumed, up to the main road on this western side. Once we climbed out onto the trail, we could now make far better time and chose to trot along. The ground was not paved, which was far better on the horses than the stone roadway of the Centurions.

Some twenty minutes later, we finally joined up with the paved road. We had no more than set foot on it when we heard a sickening cracking sound from behind us. Looking back, we could see nothing. More stone cracking sounds reached our ears; we looked at a smiling Raphael, who said, "Told you to have faith. That is the sounds of the bottom stones cracking along that flaw line. Shortly, I suspect the reservoir's contents will come rushing down the valley we just left. Now whether or not it also takes out this roadway where it goes by the dam, I don't know. However, I suspect it's all going to go. If so, that should really slow them down."

We cheered Raphael, who grinned and nodded his pleasure. Simon pointed out, "It'll do more than that, my friend. If this whole reservoir goes, there goes the primary water source for all Galantas. Now that is what will really set them back. In fact, it may divert resources from their attacks on neighboring lands for several years even!" Little did we know that would actually be precisely the case, combined with several other actions, one of which was the new political situation in Galantas in which the Church of Sol took on a more dominate role. Meanwhile, we watched and still saw nothing. Then a roaring, crashing sound deafened our speech. A great wall of water and stone came smashing, thrashing, crashing down the valley, carving out a deep new gorge. I spied bits of the red roadway stone among the debris sailing like mad down the valley. The Centurions to the east of us had no quick way to follow us. We had eliminated half of their threat. Once the big wave had passed, Roy led us on down the road. We still had another day of riding before we would reach Niccolo's villa and the crossing point back into the Southland. Certainly, we could expect the Centurions to be looking for us, particularly if they thought we had anything to do with the reservoir destruction.

We had only been on the road an hour before Roy spied a large number of those light signals going back and forth. We didn't doubt that the destruction of the reservoir was the hot topic being relayed ahead of us. He cautioned, "You know, there may likely be a great deal of people coming our way, if only to inspect and repair the damage. Traveling on this road is not going to be very safe much longer. Ideas?"

"I agree," Simon added, "can we leave it and bushwhack our way? We know where we want to go, so can we just find a different route?"

"Nope, just look at the rugged, rocky terrain around this road," Roy pointed out. "If we bushwhack, it'll take us days to get there. Further, we risk laming a horse or two, which we can't afford to do. Besides, we may well run into other villas and small villages down there. The best we can do is to ride like the wind on this road and pray we don't get ambushed."

"Okay, then let's do it. Gallop as much as possible. If we get waylaid, just keep on riding as fast as we can go," I ordered. "We don't stop for anything." The others took me literally; off we went at a gallop, horse's hooves clapping loudly on the stone roadway. Others could hear us coming from a long way off now, but there was little other choice left to us. Ordinarily, I love galloping, but today, every large boulder, every outcropping, around every turn, I expected to see soldiers suddenly appearing and attacking us.

Two hours into our ride, it happened. We rounded a bend and met a hail of quarrels. "Attack!" yelled Roy, but he needn't have; it was obvious. "Keep on riding," he yelled, urging his horse into a full canter. Swiftly we passed by the dozen men, who had positioned themselves in a perfect ambush position on the hillside above us. In less than a minute it was over and the damage was done.

"I'm hit!" screamed Sandy. Sure enough, she had a quarrel sticking in her left shoulder. Fortunately, it had missed her head.

"Me too," called out Raphael, "in the back, but I can still ride."

"Oh no, my horse is hit; he's faltering!" I exclaimed, as I spied the black shaft protruding from my horse's left front flank. "We have to slow down!"

Roy did slow us down. "Can you all hang on if we go slower? We have to put some distance between them and us before we stop. Otherwise, they'll overtake us, and we'll have to battle it out on foot." Painfully, we rode on for a couple miles before my horse finally refused to go any further. In fact, he nearly fell. So we halted. Sarah Jane helped Sandy dismount while Simon assisted Raphael down. I gently dismounted and looked at the wound my horse had received.

"Okay, damage report," I called out. "My horse isn't going any further. I can get the quarrel out, but I think we'll have to leave him behind. How are Sandy and Raphael?"

"Neither is life threatening," Sarah Jane reported. We breathed a sigh of relief. "She passed out from the pain, when I extracted the quarrel. Raphael's in a good deal of pain but he can ride."

"Okay, then here's what we do," Roy took charge. "Bethany, you ride double on Sandy's horse, hold on to her, and keep her upright in the saddle. Sarah Jane, you ride beside Raphael and keep an eye on him. Simon, you bring up the rear with the packhorse. Let's keep one horse relatively fresh just in case. This may not be the only ambush. Mount up." We did so. The guys gently lifted the unconscious Sandy into the saddle, and I awkwardly climbed up behind her, took the reins in one arm, and put my other around her to keep her upright.

"I think I can manage this if we don't go too fast," I suggested. Raphael looked a little pale and sat very stiff in his saddle, trying not to move his back, which hurt intensely. Off we went once more, albeit far more slowly. "Our speed got us out of that one, but not anymore," I commented, realizing just how lucky we had been because we were galloping past the crossbow men. At this slow pace, many quarrels could be fired at us, we were now easy targets.

We hadn't gone more than a mile when Roy called out, "I hear galloping horses ahead, let's get off the road. Find cover, over there, behind those boulders." We followed his lead, I had a great deal of difficulty trying to steer Sandy's horse because, with her in front of me, I couldn't see very well. Roy came back and led us to shelter. No sooner had we all gotten behind the boulder than a dozen cavalrymen came galloping down the road. They passed us by without spying us. "One benefit of the stone road is we don't leave tracks," he commented. I hadn't thought of that aspect before, interesting.

Five more times we made a hasty exit from the road, hiding from approaching riders. Each time, twelve cavalrymen passed by, so I guessed that twelve was their basic unit organization. Finally, just as the sun was sinking in the west, we spied the side path that led up to Niccolo's villa. Roy took it without hesitation, but asked me, "Bethany, should we make our presence at the villa known? That might get Niccolo or his servant-slaves into trouble, though." Again, I had to make the decision. Certainly, our two wounded definitely needed a long rest and some further attention to their wounds. We needed to spy on Sud and see what was waiting down there at the crossing point. However, if it became known that Niccolo or his staff helped us, they could face severe repercussions.

"No, we don't want to alert his servants. When we get to his green land, let's halt and wait for full dark. Then late at night, let's circle the estate and make for the path from which we originally came," I declared. Soon, we passed under the archway trellis onto the green land of Niccolo's villa. Roy veered to the left, and we halted at dusk, hiding from the villa by staying well below the hilltop. We dismounted, made a makeshift camp, fixed some dinner, and looked after our two wounded members. This was probably the fastest that we ever managed to do all of these actions, for it was starting to get dark, and we couldn't risk lighting either a fire or a lantern, so we had to be efficient and fast.

Sandy came to and Sarah Jane pronounced, "This is all I can do for them until I have better light. I can't see anything anymore." Sandy mumbled her thanks and managed to eat a bit but drank considerable water. Raphael, sat stiffly, but ate and drank his fill. Then, we relaxed and dozed, waiting until midnight before we attempted to move from this location.

I was dreaming of dancing with Roy, when Roy nudged me alert, "It's time we moved out, Bethany." I brushed the sleep from my eyes and helped get our gear stored. Then, following Roy's lead, we walked, leading our horses. We circled entirely around Niccolo's villa and in an hour reached the very path that we'd ridden up days ago when we first met him while he was painting. "Lots of lights down there," he commented. "I can't tell anything for sure from this distance. I guess we have to go down to the water's edge and have a look see." Down the path we went, still on foot, leading the horses, for it was quite dark now. The moon had set, which was to our advantage actually, because the Centurions waiting for us on the other side would have a hard time seeing us.

Sarah Jane supported Raphael, while Simon assisted Sandy. Me, I was left leading several horses, while Roy went ahead of us making sure it was safe. I know he felt the burden of now having to really protect us, so I tried to be as useful as I could leading several horses. It was tougher going downhill than it was coming up. Besides, our walking wounded had a great deal of difficulty with each falling step. Finally, I felt the soft give of sand beneath my feet, and the ground leveled out. We had reached the beach.

"Now what do we do?" I asked the obvious. True, here the Shallow Firth was only a few miles across, but all along the opposite shore, bonfires periodically illuminated the shoreline. These Centurions were not dumb; evidently, they had figured out that we must have just crossed on our own without taking the ferryboat. Now they lined the shore for several miles on either side of the city.

"We can't do anything without more information, Bethany. We need to find a place to hide until daylight so we can see precisely what we are dealing with," Roy explained. "Back up; let's get everyone out of sight now." Stumbling, we reversed our steps until some trees blocked our view of the shoreline. "Wait here until I return. I'll find us a place to crash for the night."

Roy was off, moving silently, like a black shadow in the night. For a moment, I admired his stealth, his cunning, but then the moaning of Sandy brought me back to reality. While Simon attempted to comfort her and keep her quiet so as not to reveal our presence, I took charge of all six horses.

How long Roy was gone was impossible for me to say; it was dark on a dark night, and time is measured by the changing of things. Nothing changed but our breathing and that of the horses. After what I deemed an eternity, Roy reappeared nearly surprising us all, and would have except that he alerted us mentally as he drew near. "This way. I've found a perfect spot," he whispered. Thankfully, he took half of the horses with him.

We crept back up the trail we had just come down and took a side branch. Soon, the sound of trickling water caught my ear. Instantly, I realized just how thirsty I was; the horses, likewise for they walked with renewed interest. Roy led us to a concealed grotto just big enough for all of us. Through its middle, a small rivulet of water cascaded down from somewhere far above, perhaps a leak in the aqueduct system, who knows. We tied the horses, gave them a long drink, and fed them. Meanwhile, Sarah Jane and Simon made the two wounded as comfortable as possible, and both fortunately fell asleep almost at once. Roy suggested that Sarah Jane and Simon also get some sleep with their partners, which neither protested.

Roy and I sat beside each other; I rested my head on his shoulder, and he put his arm around me, comforting me. "Don't fret, my love; tomorrow, I'll find us a way across."

"I'm not, Roy. You were good tonight. I didn't hear you going or coming. Say do you realize you called me 'my love?'" I jested playfully. "I like the sound of that, you know."

He kissed me gently on my forehead. "I meant it, Bethany. I'm hopelessly in love with you. I hope you don't mind," he said rather sheepishly.

"Don't worry, Roy; for some time now I've known I'm in love with you too," I replied, knowing that the ice between us on this subject had just melted.

"Really, you do?" he asked almost in disbelief.

"Yes, silly, can't you tell? Honestly, I can't get you out of my mind. Whenever I'm dozing, I keep dreaming of us off somewhere doing things together, you know, like dancing and such. Isn't it ironic that we six divided up to have pretend marriages to avoid suspicions while traveling and we six all end up in love with our pretend partner?"

"Yes, but I was in love with you even before I met you. My mentor, Herbert, he told me lots about you that he heard from Ellen. So I felt I almost knew you before we met at the solstice party that first time," Roy confessed.

"What? You already knew about me?"

"Well, yes. But you had better get some sleep; you are still recovering from that awful drugging. You sleep and I'll keep guard."

"Can I just sleep like this, leaning on you?"

"No, but you can lay your head on my lap. You really do need to get some sleep." I did and felt his loving arms around me. I felt protected and loved all at the same time. I believe I was also asleep nearly at once.

I awoke with a rock poking my back. Stiff and sore from lying on the rocky ground, I grumbled and got up. Roy was already up and about checking on the horses. One by one, the others awoke. While I rustled up some breakfast, again cold, for we couldn't risk any fire to give away our location, the others took a good long examination of our two wounded. Sandy's had grown infected, and she no longer had the use of her left arm. Sarah Jane had to perform emergency work on the nasty wound. Raphael fared better; his was a clean puncture wound, but in a painful spot in the left middle of his back between two ribs. With every motion he made came twinges of pain. Sandy, on the other hand, kept drifting in and out of consciousness. Without a fire and hot water, Sarah Jane had her work cut out for her. Long after the rest of us had finished eating, she finally joined us. "I think I got all the infection out. She's running a fever now, not good."

While she ate, I examined our grotto. We were behind a rocky spur that completely hid us from the coastline. The trickle of falling water flowed down the middle of our camp and on out to sea. "That's how I found it," Roy commented when he spied my eyes tracing out its path.

"Clever and in the dark no less!" I praised him. "Okay, you all stay here. Roy and I are going to go for a look-see at what we face. Somehow we have to get across." Hand in hand, Roy and I walked down and out of our secret place. As we got closer to the beach, we knelt down and crawled along on our bellies, eventually getting to a point where we could see clearly the entire shoreline. There was the sprawling city of Sud. What really surprised us were the sheer numbers of soldiers lining the distant shore. For over a mile in both directions from Sud, the Centurions patrolled, looking across the narrow waters at the coastline where we were hiding. "Looks like you were right about the light signals. They know we are coming here and are more than ready. Now what are we going to do?"

"I rather thought that was your department," Roy teased me playfully. "Don't worry," he added quickly, "we'll think of something. We always do." He gave my hand a loving squeeze.

We watched the soldiers for quite some time, ascertaining their patrol movements and such. Occasionally, we spied a ferry going across. If only we could just ride across on one of those boats, but to do so would mean our certain capture or worse. We estimated a hundred soldiers were watching and waiting for us. "What about crossing further down?" I asked.

"Look at the color of the water, Bethany; you can answer your own question."

I did and I did. Not too much further south from where we originally crossed the waters looked substantially bluer, much darker. Conclusion, the water's depth grew rapidly from about where we were at on southward. We would have to swim across, which was impossible for our wounded. "Could we try crossing further north?" I asked hopefully, though I already knew his reply.

"Not likely. They built Sud right at the narrowest, shallowest portion. Undoubtedly, they are patrolling all along the bank where it is shallow enough to cross. No, we need another plan, a natural disaster perhaps."

"Well, they fell for a fire once," I suggested. "Perhaps they will do so a second time."

"You mean start part of the city on fire?" he asked, remembering our adventures in Al Barq.

"Yes, if the fire is big enough, they are likely to call an 'all hands' to help put it out. During the confusion, we cross. I'm afraid that's the best I can come up with right now. Maybe Simon will have a better idea." Satisfied that we had seen enough, we crept back to the others.

After explaining our situation, Simon said, "Well, if it were only a few, I'd say let's use our illusions and control their minds. However, I can't control so many at once. Now the fire sounds like a reasonable way to go, but there is only one fatal flaw, Bethany."

My heart sank; there went my sole idea. He explained after a pause, "The distance: the city is well beyond our range. We could never bring down fire on it from this far away." In that instant, my face became as glum as my mind. "No, we need something else. I think you are on the right track. We need some kind of cover or diversion to hide our crossing. Let me think on it a while."

I checked on how Sandy and Raphael were faring; at least that gave me something to occupy my mind. Meanwhile, Roy climbed up to a better vantage point to stand watch over us. I found Sarah Jane just finishing laying both down to sleep. From my face, she knew we had no plan as yet, so she said,

"Why don't we get some needed sleep? Wake me if anything comes up; I'm really beat." I smiled and joined her, lying on a blanket on the ground, not that I was particularly tired, but I needed to think of a way for getting us safely across this narrow stretch of water.

Think, Bethany, think. Use what is at hand, that's the rule. Okay we're here at a beach by the ocean. We were not raised by the sea, on the contrary, deep inland. None of us had ever seen the sea before we journeyed to Calgary. I spied Simon rejoining us. After giving Sandy a kiss on her sleeping forehead, he laid down beside me. I whispered my thoughts thus far to him, adding, "The sea must be the key, don't you think?"

"Hum, yes, Bethany, I think you're on to something. I've heard that fog is a real problem for the ships when they want to dock or leave port. If we could have a thick fog roll in tonight, that might do it. If we crossed quietly enough, perhaps only a few Centurions directly in front of us would have to be handled someway. Controlling the weather is quite a challenge, though."

"I think it is our best hope. Can we do it?" I asked hopefully for we had an idea at last. We discussed it briefly and settled on this as our only real hope. Next, we got the four of us into agreement on what needed to be done, namely we needed a mass of cold, moist air to settle over this hot land. Being druwids, we then joined forces and began to search for and pull toward us what was needed. Controlling the weather is not something that happens fast, like calling down a lightning bolt. Rather, after a half day of work, we had begun to make Nature work for us. During this time, Roy back tracked the way we had come and began systematically hiding the plain trail that we had left in the sands just in case Centurion patrols should come looking for us on this side.

The afternoon came and went, likewise dinner. However, by sunset, we saw the fruits of our work. A dense patch of fog was now rolling in from the south. The long rest did wonders for Sandy, who now was able to ride, at least one handedly. Raphael did not feel quite so stiff and sore in his back. These were good signs. After we ate, we packed up and made ready. By nightfall, the fog was thick and damp. We left our hidden grotto and made for the beach once more. Only barely could we see the bonfires on the opposite shore, just faintly perceptible at best.

"Okay, it's now or never," Roy proclaimed. "Remember, stay in single file, stay close, and try not to make any noise. We'll go very slowly unless trouble occurs." None of us really needed to be cautioned about staying close. We could only see a few feet ahead. Roy took the lead, sword drawn. Simon followed him, also with his weapon at the ready. Raphael came next followed by Sarah Jane, then Sandy. I brought up the rear.

Spooky. Scary. These are very appropriate adjectives to describe how I felt riding out into the Shallow Firth in the middle of the night in dense fog only barely able to see the rear of Sandy's horse, knowing that at any moment the Centurions might detect us and charge into battle. Every slosh of the horses seemed to be crying out to the enemy, "Here they come!" Yet, we were going so very slowly that after a while, the sloshing seemed to blend in with the normal rushing sound of the waters onto the shore. I realized that in part this was why Roy insisted on such a slow pace. I smiled reflecting on the fact that he was one step ahead of me in his reasoning.

It was agonizingly slow. The spot we picked to cross the Shallow Firth was three miles wide, and I estimated that we were going at best only a mile an hour, very slowly indeed. I fretted that this was going to be three hours of agonizing worry and fright. After a short while, I fell into the rhythm of the action, and my fears subsided. Actually, the hardest thing to do was to maintain concentration on the horse in front of me. More than once, a slight panic flooded over me when I could no longer see Sandy's mare! It seemed to float into view and then fade, but that was the effect of the fog.

Finally, I could vaguely see a bonfire ahead and the barest outline of three men standing around it. Roy veered us just south or left of them hoping to bypass them if possible. Sneak in between their patrols seemed a sound move. Roy made land. I could tell by the sucking sounds of hooves in the sand. I saw the forms move toward him. Then I heard a voice from behind them in the darkness issuing orders for them to go to their right; it was Simon's. Somehow, he had "thrown" his voice at a distance; I didn't know that he could do such a thing. The guards seemed confused. They saw horses coming ashore to their right but were issued orders to go left. They hesitated, confused, issuing challenging orders, saying they saw something this way. Now Simon was ashore.

Then, mass pandemonium broke loose. *Speed it up now*, Roy sent to us all. As I monitored Sandy's horse, I heard shouting from both our left and right. Some was Simon's confusing orders; some were their leaders' orders. I heard the clank of steel upon steel. Both men had taken up a flanking position fending off the Centurions, while the rest of us made the shore. Once my horse got its feet firmly onto the shore, Roy sent, *Ride hard straight ahead now! Don't stop for anything*. I kicked my horse into a canter, dodging this way and that to avoid Centurion soldiers that suddenly appeared out of the fog. I had no idea where I was riding, just following more or less Sandy and the others. I heard Roy and Simon closing in behind me. Twangs. I began hearing the telltale strings of crossbows firing. Something whizzed past my head, but I gave it no heed, concentrating on avoiding running into a soldier. Something hit my back, a sharp pain; something warm seeped down the right side of my back. I found my movements somewhat restricted, but I kept on galloping. Gallop to safety was my only thought, that and trying not to lose track of the three others ahead of me.

Now we were going up, I could tell by my position in the saddle. We had climbed out of the beach area onto the hilly ground surrounding Sud. The fog thinned. Sounds of pursuit, sounds of orders and confusion — all fell away. Only the thundering hoof beats of our horses echoed in my ears. I felt hot. My heart was pounding. I could see the others ahead of me riding around a hill heading away from the city. We were going to make it! If only my right arm would keep working. I noticed its strength kept lessening and lessening, but I didn't know why. I spied Roy riding passing me, resuming his position in the lead. I heard Simon bringing up the rear behind me. We were going to make it.

Simon seemed to be slowing down. Did I dare call out to him and risk giving away our position? No, I thought better and made mental contact instead. *I can't keep up. Hurt,* was all I could get from him, that and a sense of pain he was feeling. I relayed it to Roy who slowed our pace. When we were several miles from Sud, Roy called a halt. Only then did my back really begin to ache. I reached around and felt a wooden shaft sticking out of my back. I had a sickening feeling in that instant. I had been hit too. Feebly, I spoke, "I'm hit too." I dared not move and took the reins awkwardly in my left hand for the right was now too weakened to be of much use.

Sarah Jane circled around to Simon and me, but attended him first. He had two quarrels in his back along with two nasty sword cuts in his leg and arm. As Roy looked at my back, I saw that he too was bleeding from his arm and leg. "Don't fret," Sarah Jane muttered, "I got a quarrel sticking out of my back too. One of you is going to have to pull it out before I can be of much use to you. Roy told me to hang on to my saddle. I did and felt him grasping the shaft. He gave a mighty pull. Oh the pain! I had barely felt it hitting me, but my whole body screamed as it was pulled out. So this is what it was like to be wounded, I thought. I didn't like it at all. Next, he did the same to Sarah Jane, who said merely "Thanks," through gritted teeth. "Bethany, check on Roy's wounds; I'll get Simon."

Ignoring the warm, flowing blood trickling down my back, I leaned over to examine how bad Roy was injured. It was hard to see here in the dark, but it was clear enough to me that he would need sewing up and soon. Yet, it was midnight and dark, and we couldn't afford to stop and light a fire. I relayed the information to Sarah Jane. Roy commented, "We can't stop here. We must keep on riding." I knew that he was right.

"Simon too," came Sarah Jane's brief reply. "Okay, just get some clean bandages out and tie up the wounds tightly to stem the bleeding. We'll let our quarrel wounds just bleed, Bethany. Besides, with puncture wounds, a good bleeding is to our benefit. We'll have to sew the guys up when we make camp."

Raphael came to my aid. My right arm was just not working worth a darn, and I was grateful for his help in bandaging up Roy. He then helped Sarah Jane as well. Within five minutes, we had stemmed the blood flow. As we prepared to ride on into the night, Roy asked weakly, "Where do we ride too?"

Without any hesitation, I said, "Head to the tree where we may meet our friend, Runatilli. Can you find it in the dark?"

Raphael replied, "I'll take point. I think I can find it. If not, we'll certainly be far from Sud by morning. We ride in pairs; look out for each other. Sandy, you ride up front with me. Stay close. Let me know if the pace is too fast for you." Off we went, Roy fell in beside me, and Sarah Jane and Simon brought up the rear. Mentally, I was glad that we had plenty of healing supplies with us. Alabaster's gift would be highly needed when it was light. As we rode on, I began to tire rapidly. Roy muttered something about the adrenalin rush being gone, but I figured it also had to do with being wounded and losing blood. I noticed that Roy began bobbing in the saddle, a sure sign that he was fatiguing rapidly. Painfully, I pivoted to look at how Simon was holding up. He too showed signs of passing out. Sarah Jane nodded to me that she had already observed the signs. I became even more frightened a short while later. I coughed and tasted blood; this was not a good sign. I told Sarah Jane this, and her reply made me even sicker; she too was coughing blood.

I was almost panicking — at that stage where fear and worry gain the upper hand and shock sets in. Roy was starting to lose consciousness. Frantically, using all the strength I could muster with my right arm, I grabbed one of the reins from him and began leading his horse so he could concentrate on just holding onto the saddle. Sarah Jane had already done this for Simon. I was weakening fast; I knew we'd have to halt soon. I think Raphael or Sandy picked this up for at last, he halted. The last thing I remember is sliding or falling out of the saddle, hitting the ground hard.

Chapter 21 Flight Across the Southlands

I awoke with the hot sun on my face; it felt soothing, though annoying. "Oh gods!" I exclaimed as I attempted to sit up only to feel an intense, sharp pain shoot through my back, right arm and chest. I laid back down.

"Good to see you are awake," Sarah Jane commented, she was lying next to me. "Raphael and Sandy have been put to the test. We've gotten everyone sewn up, herbal ointments applied — done about as good as we can expect on such short notice. Imagine not even being able to boil hot water! This field doctoring is the pits. We can't do a good job this way. I sure hope none of us pick up nasty infections as a result."

"Well, it couldn't be helped, Sarah Jane, really. I'm just thankful we weren't injured worse. We could have been killed or worse, captured," I replied somewhat propitiatively.

"Haven't you got it backwards, Bethany? Isn't killed worse?"

"Nah, being their slave prisoner is worse in my mind. You realize that Emperor Hiro was insane and a sexual pervert? All he wanted to do was to bed me like a horse. No thanks. Say, where are we?"

"To be perfectly honest, I think we are lost. We are actually right here," she jested with me, adding, "only we don't know where here actually is compared to where we want to be. Raphael is out scouting trying to get his bearings. Sandy is lying on the hillside acting as look out unless she has fallen asleep. None of us got too much sleep last night, especially those two. She helped Raphael with everything, though only using her left arm. I do hope the feeling comes back in her right arm soon. What a sorry lot we are! The entire party is walking wounded!"

"Well, we have one thing going for us then," I commented.

"What's that?" she asked playfully, trying to keep her attention off her back as well.

"If we don't know where we are, it's just as likely the Centurions don't either." We laughed. We both knew that, if they had an ounce of tracking skills, our trail wouldn't be hard to follow. Say, how come the horses are still saddled?"

"In case we need them. None of us is in any condition to saddle them or unsaddle them, for that matter. If trouble comes, we only need to collect a few things and get going — though I hope he comes back soon with some idea where we should go. I've been lying here wondering how I would manage to get you all on the horses if the Centurions should come. I'm glad you are awake. Can you see if you can manage any movements? It hurts if I try to do much. I figure the guys are going to be in even worse shape. They took several nasty sword cuts." Once more, I tried to set up. This time I was prepared for the flash of pain and managed it. Next, I got to my feet, which was actually a whole lot easier to do. I found myself moving around as Raphael had done, keeping my back stiff as a board.

"Want something to eat or drink?" I asked, adding, "Now that I'm up."

"A bit of jerky and some water, if you can manage." I set about the task. What normally would take me seconds to do now took ages, as I carefully measured my motions to minimize the stabbing pain in my back and weak arm. "Say, what are we going to do if the Centurions do find us like this? I don't see any alternative but to bring down fire or lightning on them. We can't fight close quarters; we can barely ride."

"Yes, for good or ill, we don't have too much choice at the moment. Perhaps they won't find us for a while," I replied trying to be as optimistic as I could. I realized that when one is in pain, there is a great tendency to slip lower in emotional tone, even down to utter apathy and hopelessness. I brought some food and a canteen and carefully sat down beside Sarah Jane. Now I could see why she was sitting up; it was the least painful position from which we could get into any other physical position. From the sun, I guessed it must be midmorning.

A little while later, I spied Raphael riding up to Sandy's position and together they came down the hill toward us. I waved, but the look on his face gave away his message long before he actually arrived. After he dismounted slowly because of his back and tied his horse to ours, he said ruefully, "I'm sorry, Bethany. I've let us all down. I have no idea where we are or where we're to meet Runatilli. None of this terrain looks at all familiar. I ventured out a mile or so. I found nothing I recognize. What should we do?"

"Send for Thomas," I jested. "Of all of us, he would be able to find the place where we are supposed to meet that native. Seriously, it's not your fault, Raphael. It was dark and foggy, and we rode helter-skelter last night."

"Well, I'm afraid it's worse than that, Bethany. I spied a Centurion patrol a ways back. I believe they are tracking us. We're going to have to mount up and get going somewhere and soon."

"See, your mission was not a complete failure. We now have advance warning so we can get going," I pointed out the bright side. Also, I knew that I was the second best woodsman present; I was going to have to lead. "Come on; let's get the others up, and see how well we can ride."

With great difficulty, we managed to get Roy and Simon astride their horses. Again, we helped them by leading their horses so they could concentrate solely on staying in the saddle. Fifteen minutes later, we began moving out once more. "We'll head northwest. I figure they'll figure that we want to head north and stay close to their roadway, so we won't. Perhaps that will help us elude them," I suggested as we rode slowly away from this semi-concealed valley. No one objected or had a better idea.

For several reasons, I decided to follow the gullies, such as they were here. First, we rode nearly level avoiding going up or down, which made it far easier for the wounded men to stay on their horses. Second, we would be harder to spot. I grew paranoid about cresting a hill only to be spied by the enemy several hills behind us. The day grew hot; we began sweating a lot, as did the horses. Our passage was very slow, barely a walk. With every step, we got farther away from Sud. That felt encouraging at least.

By late afternoon, the land suddenly changed and changed so drastically, that I came to a complete stop. The rolling hills that lay near the coast suddenly gave way to a vast nearly flat savannah. Tufts of grasses grew here and there along with scattered strange looking trees whose spindly trunks twisted skyward dividing into equally twisting branches. Strange birds cawed in the distance. Far off I spied a herd of large animals, probably a variety of deer or antelope. Once we would set foot in this land, we could be seen for miles! This was not good at all. I gazed as far as I could in all forward directions but could spy no watering holes or creeks. We had to have water; our water gourds and bags were half-empty already.

A feeling of hopelessness seeped unbidden into my mind, one that I could not force out no matter how hard I tried. I think the feeling was mutual; no one said a word; we just stared off at the vast panorama before us. "Okay gang," I said drearily, "let's take a lunch break. Maybe we can figure something out." Careful to avoid stabbing pains, we dismounted and then helped Roy and Simon get down without opening up or pulling out the threads. We ate a somber meal, all staring out across the savannah as if we might see some hopeful thing that we had overlooked.

Suddenly, Sandy exclaimed, "Someone is coming over there behind us!" We looked and struggled to our feet. A sole dark skinned man with a spear in one hand was running our way. As he drew closer, we all exclaimed in unison, "Runatilli!" He came trotting into our midst, his face illuminated by a huge smile of welcome!

Even though he had been running, he was not out of breath, "Good see you. Been waiting. Missed the tree spot, you did. Me find you anyway. Bad trouble comes behind." He spied our bandages.

"Runatilli, we're lost and very, very, very glad to see you!" I exclaimed, giving him a hug. "We got wounded leaving Megalos. None is life threatening yet, but we need to find a safe place where we can have a fire and better tend the wounds. What do you mean trouble comes behind?"

"Me knows you coming. Sees fog round Sud last night. Never see fog there. Sign you coming. Me follow tracks. Me see Black Tracker follow tracks too. Plenty bad man, Black Tracker. Me runs. You no go out that way. Runatilli knows safe place. You follow Runatilli."

"Gladly! Lead on!" I heartily exclaimed, totally relieved. Help had arrived! He took up a position behind us, telling me which way to head. Instead of heading out onto the savannah, we veered north paralleling the edge of the hills. Occasionally, I glanced back at Runatilli to see what he was doing. He had found a dead branch and was slowly erasing our hoof prints! Bright man I thought to myself. We rode along for about five miles before he came running up front saying that now he had to lead. We turned eastward into the hills for a short distance to a steep hillside and headed up its valley. I could see that it was going to become a dead end fairly soon. Halfway up,

Runatilli veered to the left and disappeared only to reappear shortly. He'd found us a cave!

Its entrance was askew to the valley so one could only see it if you knew where it was at or came upon it by chance. Its opening was just big enough for a horse barely to squeeze in, and I noticed a large amount of dung on the ground just inside the entrance, which grew in quantity the further we went inside. He halted, "You have light?" he asked. I fumbled through my sacks for a lantern and got it going so we could see. We were in a bat cave! Hanging from the ceiling were thousands of bats, thousands! The floor beneath them was several inches thick with their dung. It was cool and quiet. Quickly, more lanterns were lit, and Runatilli led us deeper into the cave. Once past the bats, the cave opened up into a large cavern whose ceiling was more than twenty feet overhead. At its northern end, an underground spring bubbled to the surface, and a tiny stream carried the water across the floor and into some underground passageway.

"Runatilli, this is perfect! Very well done indeed!" I cheered. He smiled back.

"Me go hide rest of tracks; bring back wood for fire." He was off, leaving us to make camp. Poor Raphael, he was the only one capable of really unsaddling the horses, though we girls made a sorry attempt to work together with our good arms, but found it so awkward that we settled for unloading the sacks and packs, setting up a camp, and laying down some blankets for Roy and Simon, who quickly went back to sleep. Rest was just what they both needed at the moment. By the time we had some semblance of a camp setup, Runatilli reappeared with an armload of branches. After unloading them, he went in search of more. By the time he returned for the last time, he had brought us ten loads, and we had a crackling fire going and hot water boiling for the first time in days!

The first thing that I did was make a large pot of tea. Oh how I missed the simple comfort of hot tea! Next, we set about cleansing all wounds, starting with Roy and Simon. An hour later, Sarah Jane was finally comfortable about all the healing, though the threat of infection was still quite high. Finally, I sat down beside Sarah Jane, had another cup of tea, and chewed on some jerky. Naturally, in this position, my aching back pains greatly subsided. I could think clearly once more and remembered Runatilli's warning. "Say, Runatilli, who or what is this Black Tracker you spoke of earlier?

He was chewing on one of our jerky sticks. "Bad man from Megalos. Whenever captured people escape, he is sent to get them back. Black Tracker is greatly feared among my people. He tracks like one of us. He always finds those that try to get away. Plenty bad man after you. Me knows. But Black Tracker never finds Runatilli. Runatilli better. You safe now. Rest now. Me watch." With that gentle assurance, sleep came over me. One by one, we laid down and fell rapidly asleep. We slept soundly for the first time in days; we felt safe. As I drifted into sleep, I realized that all one needed to do to get a good sleep was to "feel safe." I resolved to try this approach the next time things were not safe — convince the body and mind that it was safe and sleep well.

If you have ever slept in a cavern underground, then you know what I mean when I say one's sense of time can go completely awry — body rhythms confused. I wonder how the bats deal with this. I awoke and got up only because of a tremendous urge of "nature's needs." My back didn't hurt as much as I struggled in the dark to add to the bat dung piles. Lighting a lantern, I spied my companions sleeping peacefully on their blankets. Hungry, I ate a little and then wandered towards the entrance and the pale stream of light filtering down here deep inside the cavern. The bats, I noticed, were gone. It was night and the moon was making the light. That could only mean it was early evening, as the moon when I last saw it was nearly a quarter. I found Runatilli half standing-half sitting by the entrance, staring out at the vast moonlit savannah that we had nearly entered. "Evening," I said softly.

"You sleep long. Feel better?" he replied just as softly maintaining our common sense of the beauty of the evening and vista before us.

"Yes, is it the next day's night?"

He smiled, "Yes, you sleep long."

"I guess we needed it. All of us were lucky to escape alive."

"You did something important to get Black Tracker after you."

"Well, yes, I killed their Emperor Hiro, and the others killed a number of the guards." I wondered just how much I ought to tell him.

"Ah, that good, very good. Black Tracker wants you bad. He not get you if Runatilli with you."

"Thanks, you saved us from a really bad situation."

"Where you go now?"

"Home, we need to head for home, but we can't go back the way we came. They will be guarding their paved roadway which we followed down here."

"Black Tracker sure to check road. Road not safe."

Inspiration struck. I found a stick and drew a rough map of Tarra. "Here we are down here; this is the Southlands. Here is the Med Sea. Here is the Appian Way. Here is our homeland, the Greenway. Can we go this way to get there?" I drew a like diagonal up and across the whole of the Southlands to a point just below Velona in the Sea Princes.

"We can go to here," he drew another line marking the southern boundary of the Red Desert. "No cross sands. Moon people there. No cross."

"Moon people? Why not cross the desert? No water?"

"Moon people only seen at night. No water. Any who go into sands get rotting sickness. Black and red spots over feet and arms. All die soon. No cross."

Suddenly I was all ears! "But the Moon people live there, and they don't get sick. So they can cross the desert," I protested hoping to get more information.

"Moon people live there. They strange people. No cross."

"Well, either we try the desert or we go through Juda Arad, and I think

Black Tracker will be waiting for us there if he doesn't find us before then. The only route northward is through the Arad. I kind of hoped we could cut across the Southlands, then the desert, and maybe get a boat ride from there to the Greenway," I explained my thinking.

"You all get rotting sickness. You die if you cross sands," he insisted strongly.

"Hum, I'd like to meet one of these Moon people. Have you ever seen any?" Besides, how can one get sick walking over the sands of a desert? It made no sense to me.

"Long ago, I walk to desert. Me watch. Me see robed Moon people at night. No understand them. They no understand me. Moon people strange people."

"Well, then, let's cut across the Southlands until we get to the desert and then see if we can find any of these Moon people. I'm very curious about them. We've never heard of them. We thought no one lived in the Red Desert. Say, are the sands red?"

"Yes, red. Black Tracker no cross sands," he said, which sounded hopeful to me.

"How do we cross the Southlands without the Black Tracker following us?" I asked.

"On foot, easy; on horses, not so easy. Me think."

I left him to ponder this while I went to check on the others and get a fire going to cook some warm, hot food. Besides, I really, really wanted a cup of hot tea. Okay I also really wanted a bath and to wash my grungy long hair, but this I knew would have to wait. When the fire crackled, the others, one by one, awoke, rubbed the sleep from their faces, answered "Nature's call," and then wanted to eat. Sarah Jane insisted on a close examination of everyone's wounds as well as having me check on her back. To her credit and Raphael's, all wounds were healing. Luckily, no signs pointed to infections as had happened to Sandy. We were again very lucky people.

While we sipped our tea after eating and inspecting, I discussed what I had learned about the Red Desert and the Moon people. None of the others had ever heard of these either. All had thought the desert was uninhabited. None had heard of the rotting sickness. Then, none from the Greenway had ever ventured there, at least that we knew. Sandy decided to contact Alabaster and report in what had occurred thus far; she said she would ask him about the desert.

Meantime, Runatilli joined us with another stack of firewood. "We go tonight," he explained. "You follow Runatilli. You walk horses, not ride. No travel in day; sleep day. Take lots water. Me worried Black Tracker find us. Black Tracker already came by here looking. He not find us."

That was more than a scary thought; the enemy was definitely on our trail! "Roy and Simon might not be able to walk long distances," I protested. "They each got a good leg cut from the Centurion swords. The rest of us probably can walk." He agreed to this, what else could he do? One look at the two guys told all; both had a heavily bandaged leg. Dutifully, though, we filled every container we could find with the cold clear spring water here in the cavern.

"Any chance Black Tracker will come back here and find us?" I asked.

"No. He came during night. He go out on savannah. Me thinks he wait for us at water hole. So we no go there. Need lots water." Now his plan began to make some sense to me. If I was the tracker looking for us, having followed the trail this far before I lost it, I'd gamble that the party was heading out across the savannah. The first available watering hole would be a good place to attempt to pick up the trail once more. Certainly, the roadway would be heavily watched, so he only had to circle around until he finally picked up our trail once more.

"Runatilli go now. Buy two oxen."

"What?" I asked. Whatever does he want with two oxen?

"Hide horse tracks." Now it became clear. I should have picked that up at once.

"Here, let me give you some coins to buy the oxen." I gave him two gold coins, but he only took one, smiling his thanks.

"Be back tomorrow night. You be ready go," were his parting words. We promised him we would be ready. After he left, Roy and Simon decided to go back to sleep to help their bodies heal more quickly. Sandy and Raphael joined them. I wanted another cup of tea, so I didn't. Sarah Jane, also now fully awake, didn't want to sleep just yet. She took the opportunity to sort through her sacks rearranging things and looking for anything else that might hold water.

"Say, look at this, Bethany! Look what Niccolo stuck in here," she said very interested. She held up a small parchment book, one that Niccolo had written. I examined its cover with her. Together we sounded out its title: A Treatise on the Origins of Megalos by Niccolo Helios. "What is a treatise?" she asked. I answered that I thought it meant a learned study of something. We leafed through it and saw that there were just under two hundred pages of carefully written script. She was very surprised with the gift and also quite proud to be the owner of a book, the first book ever in all the Greenway, if only we could get it safely home.

Finally, as the fire died down, we doused all the lanterns save one and joined the others. I still couldn't sleep knowing that it was only early evening. Besides, I had already slept through one night and day, so I laid back watching the others, especially Roy. He looked regal, powerful, and handsome as he lay like a baby sleeping peacefully. After some time, I finally couldn't resist the urge to go lay beside him and snuggle with him. Instinctively, his arm draped around me as I snuggled close to him. He knew it was me. I too slept the sleep of babes.

The intense flutter of thousands of bats returning to their roost awoke me. Since they lived in the outer portion of the cavern, I wasn't too concerned. By the time night came, we all were well rested and definitely on the mend physically. As agreed, we had packed and were fully awake, ready to go when Runatilli finally returned just after full dark. He had two oxen with him. The plan was simple. We would walk single file following his orders, while he brought up the rear with the two oxen, whose heavy, sliding feet would help obscure our passage. As we began under a first quarter moon, we could easily see the landscape, which looked amazingly beautiful and serene at night.

Whenever we came across a trail made by some herd animals, he had us follow them for some distance to obscure our passage further. Fairly soon, I detected the unmistakable signs of a trail or track that led in the same general direction we were heading. He explained it led to the watering hole. I looked even closer and even in the dim light saw the signs of a number of riders. So Runatilli was right, someone was out ahead of us, undoubtedly the Black Tracker. Who else would be out here riding horses? For a time, I wondered if we shouldn't go find this tracker and eliminate him for the betterment of the natives of the Southlands. However, I didn't know how many others he had with him and decided against such fantasy.

Unfamiliar night sounds can be scary, especially if you have never heard them before. This first night a cacophony of sounds greeted our ears as we walked along. First came the deep bellowing of some great cats off in the distance. More worrisome were the dog-like barking of the hyenas, which Runatilli cautioned us, could attack us if we showed some weakness. Night birds of many types added their calls to the evening sounds. I still believe that this was how Nature had intended the world to be, sans humans. Once we made a detour around a pride of lions who had made a kill and were feasting upon the remains of what I thought might be an antelope.

Yet as the evening wore on, the temperature grew steadily cooler and quite hospitable, unlike the searing sun of daytime. With the moon to guide us, I rather enjoyed the walk. My senses opened up to the lands about us. However, once the moon went down, it was quite a different story; walking only by starlight was quite challenging. Yet our guide knew where he was taking us. Villages were given a berth of several miles to avoid putting its occupants into danger on our account, should the Black Tracker visit them in search of word of our passing. More importantly, this first night, the next watering hole, where one might expect to camp, was bypassed by four miles, circling way north of it. We apparently made good speed, for Runatilli called a halt before sunrise, camping on the north side of a small outcropping of reddish rocks beside a small stand of trees. He cautioned us not to go onto the rocks because many vipers lived there usually sunning themselves this time of year on the rocks, which also held the heat of the day far into the night. He also warned us about scorpions, if we laid upon the ground for any length of time. He himself simply sat on the lowest branch of a tree and went to sleep completely safe from curious vipers and deadly scorpions.

Hence, we attempted to follow suit. None of us had ever tried to sleep in a tree on a branch before. Needless to say, we didn't sleep at all well this first time. This was especially true because of the occasional passing animals — of which we got great views!

The next evening, we were lucky to come upon a herd of twelve elephants slowly moving in the same direction we were going. Runatilli had us follow in their footsteps until, after several miles, they moved due west. Obviously, this helped hide our passage across the dry ground. Because we had sufficient water, we also bypassed the second watering hole. However, this second night, we slept in an abandoned gold mine, long unused and could sleep comfortably once more.

The next night, we ran into a band of hunters returning home with their day's kill, an antelope hanging upside down between two poles being carried by four men. The party of a dozen chatted with Runatilli, but they talked so fast that we could not follow them. Our mastery of his language was not yet that good. Later Runatilli reported that indeed the Black Tracker had visited their village the day before asking about us. Since they had not seen us and so reported to the feared Centurion, it was not likely that he would return to that same village. Nevertheless, we grew more apprehensive about being tracked and found.

Our fears didn't materialize, and after a week, we were about a hundred fifty miles from Sud, still heading mostly northwestwards. At this point, we doubted the Black Tracker would venture this deep into the Southlands. From here, the obvious choice would be to head due northeast and enter Juda Arad, about where we had left it as we entered the Southlands heading south along the paved roadway. However, we continued our general heading for another few days.

This part of the journey was fun because Runatilli changed patterns, and we traveled by day and made far better speed. Further, we could enjoy the magnificent sights of the many herds of animals we found. Yes, had it not been for the constant threat of the Black Tracker, this would have been a thoroughly enjoyable vacation type of journey! Finally, after nearly a month and some six hundred miles, we arrived at a deep gorge with a shallow, wide stream running from the east to dump its load into the ocean far to the west. It was called the Divo Rivo, meaning the "dividing river."

On our side, the vast savannah of the Southland stretched for hundreds of miles. Just across this river lay rolling dunes of red sand, reputedly waiting to give any trespasser a certain death by rotting sickness. Here, Runatilli would go no further, and he repeatedly warned and begged us not to go any further. We made camp here at the top of the gorge where we had an ideal view of the Red Desert for many miles. We spent several hours staring at it and saw absolutely no life signs, not even a bird! It was indeed a desert of death that lay before us.

We are druwids. We seek knowledge. Just why this particular desert could kill, could produce a rotting sickness, begged for our understanding. We spent hours speculating about how a mere desert could be responsible. In the end, none of us had the slightest notion how this could be true. Because the threat seemed so real, via Runatilli, we decided on a course of action: gain more knowledge without actually setting foot in the desert. Being healers, one and all, we asked Runatilli if there were people around here on his side that had accidentally gotten this rotting disease. If so, would he take us to them so that we might see for ourselves and see if we could heal them. This seemed to be a safe line of inquiry.

He said that there was a small fishing village somewhere around here. The village was cradled on this side of the river on a wide plateau that sometimes flooded. Perhaps someone there might have it. However, he did not know whether the village of Titi was up river or down river from our location. He left us to camp and relax while he went in search of the village. We took the time to catch up on small chores like mending holes and tears in our leathers and undies, as well as stitching much needed new leather soles onto our well-worn boots.

During this time, Sarah Jane showed everyone else her new book. "Everyone have a look. Niccolo has given me my first book! He must have stuck it in when he gathered our stuff while we were off to see the emperor." We all gathered around and stared at the thick parchment pages held together by a stiff leather binding.

"Well, what's it called? What's it about?" asked Raphael, who strained to look over her shoulder to see for himself. She had already shown it to me.

Carefully sounding out each word as we were taught, she read aloud, "A Treatise on the History and Origins of Megalos by Niccolo Helios as Told to Him by the Historians. Bethany says that a treatise is a kind of learned discussion. It might give us some insight into their country and customs. Perhaps there might be something in it that we could use to defeat their army." Carefully, she thumbed through the pages to the end; it contained some two hundred pages. "Say, will you look at this! Here is an account of Governor Lexus Thebes of Pieta entitled 'How Governor Lexus Thebes of Pieta Changed a Conquered City into a Civilized City in One Week.' This I got to read!" She let Raphael do her mending while she read aloud this section.

Here I set down the words of the Governor himself as told to me by Historian Demosthenes who was personally told the details by the Governor. Governor Lexus Thebes took control of Pieta on June 10, 559 AH. (Note to the reader: here I have substituted the current year as we now identify them instead of the now ancient system in use at that time. Again, AH is After Hodhekansis, the twins and founders of Megalos.) Based upon the ruinous situations my predecessors have had with their conquered cities, I decided to take a more decisive role. Thus, it was that I recruited the Sisterhood to be on our side, for they are the only effective fighters in the whole of the Sea Princes. They, and they alone, besides our undefeated Centurions, can command authority over the citizens. By seeking out and actively forming an alliance with these amazon women, promoting them into positions of leadership, the entire city of Pieta has been transformed back into a civilized, thriving city in less than a month. Even the Prince and the Church obey their every order. Emperor Hiro, upon learning of this monumental achievement, awarded me, Lexus Thebes, the Golden

Sun, our highest political medal of meritorious service to Megalos.

"What?" cried Raphael. "That's not what happened at all! It's all distorted; he did nothing but agree with Simon, or rather Simone. They have it completely backwards," he protested. Sarah and I looked at each other, and we both instantly realized another aspect of the written word. One can write anything one wants, and, because it can be read by others, it can be accepted as the truth, when in fact what is written is completely erroneous.

"Look on the bright side," I broke in, "there is no mention of Simone or our involvement. Thus, the role we druwids played remains a secret." The others nodded, but still they chatted about how wrong it all was.

"Look, this means that whatever we read in this book may not accurately reflect what actually took place. We need to keep that in mind if we find anything we can use against them," cautioned Simon. Again, everyone agreed. However, I must admit that this dampened my enthusiasm for this newfound media of communication. Their "history" was almost fiction.

Still, Sarah Jane spent hours reading sections of their history. "Say everyone, listen to this.

Megalos was first settled by two brothers, Nikka and Tikka, who came out of a land called Arwan, which by many accounts was located somewhere in the uninhabitable lands that we now call the Red Desert. Approximately five centuries ago, the brothers arrived here and founded Galantas, aligning the wild tribes that inhabited the island, converting them into followers of Sol. They chose this location because the surrounding landscape reminded them of their former home in Arwan.

"Now gang, doesn't this sound like there used to be cities and towns where there is now desert? The Red Desert must have been a habitable land at one time. I wonder what happened to change it into a desert of certain death? Did all those people perish? How? Why?"

Raphael chuckled and teased her, "For each page you read, you end up with more questions than answers. By the time you get done with the whole book, why, you'll know less than before you began." She playfully poked him in the ribs.

"Do you suppose that these Moon people that Runatilli talks about are actually descendant of the Arwans?" asked Sandy, which was my thought exactly.

"Supposition: some calamity befell ancient Arwan, a calamity that created a desert of death," I replied thoughtfully. "However, as we well know, people are a hardy lot. It is next to impossible to kill everyone off. Some always seem to survive somehow. So I really wouldn't be at all surprised to find out that these Moon people may actually be descendants of Arwan."

"True," Simon cautioned, "but they might also be nomads that have, for whatever reason, moved into this land at a much later date. Such is equally plausible."

"Yes," I teased him, "but that isn't nearly as interesting as my idea." We all laughed. Without much more information, all was the merest of speculation on our part.

"Well this book thing would be a whole lot easier to use if it had some kind of referring pages," commented Sarah Jane, "where I could look up Red Desert and find a listing of all the page numbers where it was mentioned. I'll let you know if I find out anything more about it." We returned to our mending activities while she read further.

Several hours later, Sarah Jane caught our interest once more. "Listen to this, gang.

The famous prospector, Helke the Lucky, first discovered the diamond mines in the Southlands, which, of course, led to our current vast interests in that land. However, it was Helke who also placed the first of the taboo markers on the tracks leading into the Red Desert, for he himself ventured onto those sands only to die a horrible death from the rotting disease shortly thereafter.

Isn't that interesting?" We naturally agreed. Even the Centurions knew that this desert killed. No wonder they chose instead to conquer Juda Arad. It was the only other land passage to the northern half of Western Tarra.

Slowly two days passed before Runatilli returned. He was unable to locate anyone who had the rotting disease; those who contracted it seldom ever lived more than a few weeks. However, he did find a Moon people village on the edge of the river, and a local Southland village had been known to do some trading with them. His suggestion was for us to go to that village and actually meet these Moon people. He was doing his best to find ways to convince us not to set one foot in the Red Desert.

Thus, it was that a day later we stood high on the Southland river bluff overlooking the Red Desert to the north and an actual village of twenty adobe homes cradled tightly onto the northern shore of the river. This village was actually not in the desert proper, but lay several hundred feet below the sands in a totally sheltered cove. A narrow path descended from where we stood down to the southern shore opposite the tiny hamlet. From our position looking down, we saw six small reed boats carrying fishermen out onto the broad, but shallow, river. Runatilli, however, would go no further. It was clear he greatly feared being even this close to the Red Desert. Hence, he stayed at our position high atop the river bluff while the rest of us descended to the river's edge.

Simon called out to the fishermen, but they barely glanced at us and otherwise took no notice of us, apparently intent only on fishing. Their manner of dress was indeed strange, the strangest yet that we had encountered. They were covered with some kind of cloth wrapping, rather like a robe or cloak, made of crude homespun that fit them tightly, outlining their body's form. Their hands were entirely wrapped in cloth rather like the gloves that we wore in the winter. Similarly, their heads were also wrapped with the same type of cloth, leaving only small holes for the eyes, nose, and mouth. In short, no skin was exposed whatsoever!

As we watched the hamlet from several hundred feet across the river, we noticed there was very little room in the village for our horses. Hence,

Simon tested the river's depth and announced that we could probably safely wade across. He suggested we not ride across. Since the fishermen did not respond to our calls, leaving the horses on the bank, one by one, we waded across the river single file. This got the attention of several women, who came out of the adobe huts and stood waiting our arrival.

Simon spoke first, "Hello. We are travelers from the far north." It was exceedingly difficult to see any kind of response, let alone their reactions because they were similarly covered head to foot with the crude cloth wrappings. Their black eyes stared back at us. "I don't think that they understand me," he added to us. Quickly, he tried in all the languages that we knew, but none brought the slightest sign of comprehension.

At last, one woman with unusually large, though completely covered, breasts spoke what appeared to be several sentences. None of us understood a word that she said, though Sandy did suggest that it did sound an awful lot like the Centurion's language. After ten fruitless minutes of trying to understand one another, Sandy had a last ditch idea. She reached into the woman's mind, trying to pick up her concepts. "Eureka. Boy this is weird, but I can talk to her this way," she told us.

"It's like she is reciting something. Roughly, it goes like this:

Wash thy feet before entering. Expose no flesh out of doors. Touch no one save thy mate and then only after both have bathed. Be cautious of strangers for they may bring sickness. Eat no offering that grows upon the surface save that that lives under waters. Stay ever alert for the winds of Atlas for they bring the sands of death. Accept in trade nothing that comes from the land's surface. Thus sayeth the Holy Defense Code of Amin, messenger of Sol.

"What do we make of all this?" she asked, adding, "Her language is some kind of distant cousin of the Centurions."

"Hum, sounds an awful lot like some kind of religious ritual. Perhaps we ought to demonstrate that we understand and can follow their code. Let me go get our turbans, we can wrap them around our heads mostly. Maybe our winter gloves might work too." He sloshed back across the river, rummaged through our sacks, and came back with his arms full. Hastily, we wrapped our heads as well as we could and donned our winter gloves. In our leathers, we now appeared reasonably similar to these Moon people.

By now, seven women were watching us along with ten children, that is, we assumed the smaller ones were children; we had no way to really verify that though. They stayed some distance behind the women and appeared to be quite shy. Well, at least their body motions so suggested it. Sandy placed into the woman's mind whom she had been observing, *Our feet are washed in the river. No flesh out of doors. We touch no one. We are visitors. Is it permitted to ask you questions about the Red Desert?*

Instantly a change came over her. Although we could only see her eyes, they now appeared to open wide, and she ceased her chanting and said a number of fast exclamations and sentences, which Sandy could not read because they came rushing through the woman's mind like a surprised whirlwind. Since she and the other women seemed to be conferring with each other and one yelled aloud to the fishermen, we assumed that contact had been made. We waited for their official reaction. Soon one of the men began paddling towards the shore; we presumed that he might be their leader or head priest or keeper, so we dutifully awaited his arrival.

As he paddled, Sandy made the gentlest touch upon his mind, only to find that he, too, was reciting the same liturgy that the woman had been, going over and over it in his mind. We watched as he reached the shore, carefully got out of the thin reed boat, pulled it onto the shore, went back into the water to wash his covered feet off, and then walked to stand in front of the seven women, facing us. Again, he uttered a series of rapid sentences, which we did not understand, catching only a possible word here and there. Sandy used her mental contact once more with him with the same startling effect.

Actually, if someone began to place understandable thoughts into your mind, you would be just as surprised and shocked as he was. Only we, who had been thoroughly trained in telepathy, wouldn't be. Sometimes I have the tendency to take too many things for granted. Sandy placed in his mind, *Our feet are washed in the river. No flesh out of doors. We touch no one. We are visitors. Is it permitted to ask you questions about the Red Desert?*

He formed the idea, *Traders?*

Sandy shrugged, *I'm not certain we have anything that you might need or want.* Thus, Sandy entered into a long, silent dialog, explaining who we were and where we were going. She sketched a crude map in the sandy beach, which they recognized after she redrew the map upside down so that they saw it right side up. These were not hostile people. I saw nary a weapon or anything that could so be used. Even his fish hooks were made from carved bones. No metal was visible anywhere. I must admit the half hour that Sandy took to explain things to him was incredibly boring to the rest of us, who stood waiting patiently a couple feet from the river's edge. Actually, for the first time in our long journey, I fully appreciated Sandy's unique talents. Without her skills, we would have gotten nowhere with these Moon people.

Thirty minutes later, Sandy triumphantly proclaimed, "Okay everyone, I've made a breakthrough. He wants to see our grain samples, and he says that our horses are in dire danger where we have left them — the rotting sickness. So, will someone go get all our remaining grain samples, our healing packs, and then lead the horses back up the bluff? Maybe Runatilli will watch over them. He wants us to join him in his house, believe it or not. This is a breakthrough."

The men waded across the river once more while the rest of us watched as did the villagers. Simon and Raphael returned carrying several sacks, while Roy led the horses back up the river bluff. Because of the Moon people's unusual customs, we all waited until Roy rejoined us. Then, with Sandy in mental contact with the village leader and his wife, we entered his adobe home.

Sandy relayed to us all mentally, *Okay, first, inside this door, we wash our feet off. Follow my orders exactly. Here we go.* Strange was this home, for it had no windows at all nor any fire place. In fact, other than the door, there was no contact with the outside world. The door opened into a lantern-lit small area whose floor was filled with water. Dutifully, we sloshed about in the water following the pattern of set by our hosts. Immediately beyond this entrance pool was another door which we then entered. Their home was even stranger on the inside. Only one room held a small table and two chairs with a bed along one wall. Another wall held pottery-encased food items. A large section along another wall was devoted to numerous growing fungi. Our hosts sat on the chairs and motioned for us to sit on the floor in front of them. We did so.

After an uncomfortable pause while Sandy mentally communicated with the man, she finally said, "Our host is Luminous, and his wife is Bethala, and this is the village of Legos, one of three Moon people villages that are out in the open. They keep chanting all those sayings repeatedly in their minds, so I'm having a hard time with this communication. But I believe that their religion is called Amin or Hamin, and they keep reciting something called Holy Defense Code of Amin. So where should we begin?"

I suggested she relay who we were, where we came from pointing out just how far away from the Red Desert it was, that our people were farmers, that we grew much grain, and that it was safe to eat it. Wherever we go, people always want more of our grains. Sandy took a deep breath, relaxed, and began the difficult task of communicating these ideas. The only thing in her favor was that their language was akin to that of the Centurions (much like Middle English is to Modern English on your planet, as I understand it). It took her quite a few minutes to get all this fully relayed so that they both understood. Wrapped in their cotton coverings with only their eyes and mouth visible, we lacked most of the normal body language signs, which made it doubly hard for Sandy. Finally, the man nodded, satisfied with her ideas. Slowly, he began to unwrap his head while his wife did the same. Sandy indicated we should follow suit.

Now we could see our hosts. Their skin was a pale bronze color, much like that of a Centurion, who had not been out of doors for a very long time. The bone structure of their faces also matched. Hence, it appeared obvious to us that these people were perhaps distantly related to those who inhabited Megalos. Luminous and his wife Bethala both looked like they were in their early thirties, no longer youthful, but not yet age lined. Both stared at each of us in turn. They had nearly identical, very short hair not more than an inch long, probably because of always having to cover their heads. He did have a small moustache though. Once they had un-wrapped their hands, they wanted to examine the grain.

The next ten minutes were spent watching them greedily sifting, smelling, and tasting each sack of grain, commenting excitedly between themselves about each sack. Finally, he made a great encompassing gesture with his arms, then brought them together, and opened up his hands toward us with a quizzical look on his face. Sandy went to work once more and finally said, "He would like to trade for all the grain. At first, I thought he needed it to eat, but then I found out that he wants to use it as seed to grow more. His people are desperately short on grains. I'm not sure where their fields are located."

Ceremoniously, I tied up each sack and handed them one by one to Luminous, whose face began to smile more and more broadly, until I thought his face would crack! One did not need to be a telepath to know that, from his viewpoint, I was giving him a gift far more precious than equal sacks of gold coins or even gems! I returned his smiles. Quickly, his wife began to prepare an offering of thanks. She handed us each a clay cup, filled it with a greyish liquid, and set a plate of dried mushrooms before us. Both our hosts ate a piece and took a sip, indicating it was safe to eat. Sandy repeated their parable, "Eat not untested food or drink; only eat that which another has already eaten and deemed safe."

"Wow, this is some kind of fungus wine," declared Simon. "It's potent!"

I have never eaten dried fungus but tried it. It was much like eating a cracker except for the dry, powdery taste. From our hosts' expressions, they wanted to know if we liked it, so we all smiled, nodded, and said it was good. Well, I thought the wine certainly was.

I then asked Sandy to see if she could find out more about these people, their life style, anything. We knew nothing of their existence. However, I also told her to desist at once if our hosts felt we were somehow prying. While Sandy attempted to work all this out sending mental ideas interlaced with a few words in the Centurion language that seemed close enough, we enjoyed the fungus wine. A half hour later, Sandy took a big drink and relayed what she had found out.

"They are called the Moon people by outsiders because they are seen only at night, except here in these three villages by the river. It is death to be outside in the desert in the daytime or so their scriptures tell them. Their entire population lives in vast underground chambers, growing fungus for food, clothing, and wine. Apparently these chambers are well lighted. The desert sands contain some kind of poison. Nothing alive lives in the desert for long before it dies of the rotting sickness. Even just touching the sands can cause this disease. They have lived underground for probably centuries. Their survival depends upon strict following of this Holy Defense Code of Amin. From the moment that a baby learns to speak, it is taught to recite this holy code. All throughout the awake hours, everyone recites the code over and over, for one tiny slip, one minuscule breaking of the code, means a certain painful death by the rotting disease. Apparently, in their distant past, the God Angibus destroyed the land, turning it into this poisonous desert. Sol's High Priest, this Amin or Hamin, I'm still not sure which, was given this code by the benevolent Sol so his people might survive. Only those who follow the code without the slightest deviation are allowed to live. When someone comes down with the rotting disease, all know that he or she has broken the code in some way. So their death is accompanied by everyone knowing that they have transgressed from the code, and are also humiliated in the eyes of the other Moon people, rather grim, if you ask me."

Sandy continued, "What is most peculiar is that they can safely travel across the desert at night. Something about 'Walk where there is no red glow' whatever that means. Still, surface travel even at night is apparently fraught with peril. If a dust storm comes, you must get underground before the slightest dust arrives or you die from the rotting disease. That's why everyone washes their feet before entering — to wash off any infected sand or dust. Kind of like a preventative measure, I think. I believe there is something real behind every one of these parables they recite. Golly, what a dangerous place to live. Oh yes, these three fishing villages provide the only outside source of food. It is deemed safe to eat because the fish live under water." Sandy finished with another long drink of wine and a satisfied look on her face.

After complimenting her for such great work, I asked her to find out more about this rotting disease. Sandy explained that in our land, we were known as healers and that perhaps we might be able to help. Both hosts chatted cautiously among themselves before Sandy got her answer. "Ah, it seems a young boy in this village has come down with it. He is only five years old. He crawled up the riverbank and touched the sands of the desert to feel what sand felt like. Now his hands are rotting. They said that, if his parents agreed, we could take a look at him. He warned us not to touch his body with our exposed flesh or we too would contract the rotting disease. He said to use only our gloves or hand wrappings." Sarah Jane and I conferred and decided that she, Sandy, and I should go. If all six of us went, we might be too many for the parents to face.

Carefully, we followed Luminous' example and covered our heads and hands once more with only our eyes and mouths open. Then we followed him back outside to a nearby home. We waited outside with our healing sacks, while he talked with the parents. Soon he beckoned us to follow him inside. In one corner separated by a wall of cloths from the food and growing fungus lay the disease-stricken boy. Both parents' eyes were wet; we assumed from crying. Sarah Jane went to work, while Sandy tried to communicate with the boy's parents.

Sarah Jane methodically examined the boy, "He has nausea, has clearly got diarrhea, and has vomited recently. He is running a high fever. His arms are covered in red sores that are bleeding just under the skin. Ah, he is losing his black hair too; look at all of it here in his head wrap. What kind of a disease is this anyway?" Clearly, she was completely baffled. Indeed, none of us had ever seen anything remotely like this.

"Well, he needs fluids," I suggested, "since he is losing it all over the place."

"That's obvious," she replied didactically. "It's like all these bleeding sores are trying to eject something from the body, like a poison. He is in dire need of most all nutrients as well. We also need something to help force the poison out." As usual, she was thinking aloud, and I followed her reasoning.

"I'd feed him liver soup," I suggested. "Only where would we get liver here?"

The air, incidentally, was filled with the aroma of fermenting wine. The boy's father was brewing a large batch. I think this was what inspired her. It took fifteen minutes for her via Sandy to convince the parents to let her utilize what she could find in their food stores and brewing. I watched fascinated as her sheer healing genius shone. First, she carefully extracted a large amount of the yeast byproduct from the brewing vat. Next, she discovered strawberries, yes, strawberries. We didn't ask where they got them; rather she just used them, adding them into the mix. She ground up many mushrooms and added it to the growing mix. Soon she had made two gallons of an awful looking and foul smelling liquid, far worse than liver soup. Next, she worked with the boy to get a quart of it down him.

Then, we all waited. Sarah Jane explained the boy might stand some slight chance if the concoction would stay down. Miraculously, it did. Two hours later, she put another quart into him. She, via Sandy, instructed his parents to get another quart into him every two hours until morning. Then we all returned to Luminous' home. Sarah Jane had no idea if this would actually cure the boy, but her concoction contained all the nutrients she thought his body craved at this time. Time would tell.

Sandy explained to Bethala that we were trying to heal the boy, and she looked most disbelieving. That was to be expected. Since the evening was approaching, we decided to head back to Runatilli and make camp for the night. Via Sandy, we told them we'd be back in the morning to check on the patient. Luminous gestured again at the six sacks of grain, and Sandy determined that he was still wondering what we wanted in trade for them. I had her relay to him, "Nothing. Accept our gift. We no longer have any real need for the grain and he does." Once he fully understood, he smiled, nodded, and said what sounded like "Many Thanks" akin to how it was said in Megalos.

We joined Runatilli, made a hasty camp, and fixed dinner. The single topic on all our minds was the boy and would Sarah Jane's invention actually help. Equally discussed was just what kind of a disease was this rotting disease anyway. None had any solid ideas. Sarah Jane explained her reasoning though, "He has lost lots of nutrients and fluids. His body is fighting something and expelling it; so let's help it do so by providing a massive amount of easy to absorb nutrients." It seemed simple enough. Her concoction certainly provided that.

The next morning, we three women went back across the river to check on our patient. Miraculously, he showed marked improvement! The raw, bleeding sores on his arms had scabbed over; the slow bleeding had ceased. His other symptoms were much lessened, and he seemed somewhat stronger. Hence, Sarah Jane's orders remained the same, a quart every two hours throughout the day. Since they would quickly run out of the concoction, she spent an hour showing them how to make more. It was awkward because she had to have every order relayed telepathically by Sandy and then respond to their questions in a similar manner. Slow going.

The rest of the day, the men decided to help the villagers catch and dry fish. Actually, I think this was just an excuse to get out on the water, relax, and go fishing. We all needed a break, a way to unwind. I spent some time practicing my music high on the river bluff overlooking the river. Runatilli even taught me one of his songs, which glorified those who walkabout.

That evening after the sun went down, Luminous signaled to Sandy, and she found out that a small group of nearby Moon people were due to arrive this evening. He wanted to know if we wanted to view the desert and see for ourselves what their teachings told them about it. So when it was full dark — the moon wouldn't rise until very late this night — we six, along with our host, wrapped from head to foot in cloth with only eyes and mouths exposed, slowly made our way up the river bank to the edge of the Red Desert. Sandy kept reporting that Luminous kept chanting repeatedly, "Expose no flesh out of doors. Walk where there is no red glow. Stay ever alert for the winds of Atlas for they bring down the sands of death." She added, "I guess we ought to do the same."

When we reached the actual desert sands, we halted. As we gazed out upon the rolling sands and low dunes, Luminous pointed and Sandy translated. "Walk where there is no red glow. If you look where he is pointing, you can barely see a hint of a reddish glow. Now he is pointing to a safe path with no red glow. Boy, it sure is very faint. You could never see it in the daytime or even when there is a moon. Oh I get it, that's why they travel only at night. Duh." We all understood now.

However, what was this red glow that killed all living things? That was the real question. I hate questions with no answers, but I'm afraid the answer was not going to be known to me for many centuries. Sandy indicated to Luminous that we all saw the red glow and understood his parables. Still, he didn't let us venture out onto the sands, rather we waited, watched, and observed. Sandy added a bit later, "Don't forget to be alert for winds that might blow the poisoned sands onto us." Overall, it seemed a very unforgiving, hostile environment in which to live or travel. Yet, even in these nearly impossible surroundings, people lived, survived, and multiplied.

About an hour later, we spied three shadowy shapes walking slowly our way, though not in a straight line. Obviously, they were avoiding the patches with sand that glowed slightly red. Interestingly, more than once, they had to backtrack because they reached a section of sand entirely covered with the reddish glow. Simon pointed out that since the winds often move the sand around, there were likely no permanent trails in the desert; one would have to pick out a safe path each time he went from place to place. How very different this was from the Greenway. I began to appreciate our homeland even more.

Luminous waved to the three travelers and they waved back. Soon, they closed the distance and we all returned to Luminous' home. We carefully washed off any traces of sand on our feet before we entered the actual room.

Once we all un-wrapped our faces and hands, communications difficulties arose at once, with Sandy doing her best to translate. The three appeared to be in their twenties, but stared wide-eyed at we six strangers. Luminous did his best to introduce the three, but Sandy was only able to grasp one name, Tiki, the leader of the three. Next came a long round of trying to explain who we were and where we came from and all that. What helped the most was that we have given Luminous and hence the larger group six sacks of seed grains — that plus the startling fact that we were making some progress in healing a boy who had the rotting sickness.

Once the three grasped this last fact, Sandy, Sarah Jane, and Luminous had to take them to see the boy. By now, he had recovered sufficiently to speak once more, but all he really said, besides the fact that he felt bad, was that the concoction tasted bad. Sarah Jane was pleased that so far it had been successful at least in arresting the boy's eminent death. It was far too soon to speak of "cured" but the parents had some small hope where there was none before. Even the three newcomers were impressed with the results — so much so, that they chatted between themselves so fast that Sandy couldn't grasp any of it.

Once the excitement died down, the three carefully loaded the precious grain sacks into another set of sacks and then into a third sack. We found out that they were going to take it to the nearest growing room, where the seed could be planted. They had intended to come to pick up the dried fish, leaving several large sacks of dried fungus for Luminous and the villagers to eat. The arrival of grain was vastly more important for the survival of the Moon people. They packed it carefully first and then began to take what they could of the dried fish.

While they were thus engaged, Simon carefully drew a large map of Western Tarra, indicating where we thought we might be and where we desired to be, on the shores of the Med Sea just south of Velona. Once the three were done packing, he asked via Sandy, if it was possible to somehow travel across the desert from here to there. Again, Sandy's skills were pushed well beyond her limits. Fully ten minutes went by in total confusion until at last she understood and told us, "No, there is no way to cross that many miles of open desert but there was a way to get there by going mostly under the desert." It was 'over' and 'under' that had gotten her so confused.

"Ah ha!" exclaimed Simon. "Sandy, ask him if they or others could lead us from here to there. In trade, once we get to the sea, we can have a boat load of seed grains waiting for us as the payment for our safe passage from here to there." Suddenly, we all realized his plan: trade grain for passage. When Sandy finally got the question fully understood by the Moon people, their eyes lit up like the moon; their faces became animated, like a kid entering a store and seeing the candy jar. I chided myself for not having realized this sooner: for these people a boatload of seed was more valuable than a boatload of gold or gems.

Next, came a discussion on time. How long would it take? How would the grain get delivered and so on. Since Sandy more than had her hands or should I say more appropriately her mind, fully occupied, I reached out to contact Alabaster. I explained our situation, that we needed to be picked up by boat on the shores of the Red Desert directly south of Velona, and that we needed to use a boat load of seed grains as payment. We were in luck, though the snows had already come, the port was not yet iced shut. There was still time to get a load out. I asked for our old friend Captain Bartoloma and his Lucky Lady.

Though Tiki was very eager to do this trade, he didn't have the authority to grant us such a passage through the heart of their realm. He promised to ask their High Priest just as soon as he got back to his chambers, and would return personally with the reply. From his enthusiastic reactions to the deal, we all felt confident the answer would be affirmative. Besides, we couldn't leave just yet. Sarah Jane had a patient to handle. She wouldn't leave until the boy was either dead or well on the road to recovery, and either way, time was needed to tell.

Chapter 22 Crossing the Red Desert of Death

A week passed until we heard word that our request to be guided across the Red Desert had been granted. Payment would be a boatload of seed grain. The boy continued to show signs of recovery. Each day, he seemed stronger; the sickness, a little less. It looked hopeful and Sarah Jane agreed that she could finally leave. Alabaster reported that the Lucky Lady was available, and Captain Bartolomo was more than eager to assist. I believe the news that an entire civilization lived in the uninhabitable Red Desert came as a total surprise to both men. Captain Bartolomo's intense curiosity wouldn't let him rest until he had seen personally these Moon people. Besides, Velona was currently under siege, ahead of schedule. Evidently, the Centurions met far less resistance than they had earlier.

We had rather lost track of the date, but fortunately, Alabaster came to our rescue. It was actually the second week in December when we began our crossing. Once the deal was finalized, we gave Runatilli our six horses and all the tack. We would be traveling underground mostly, and the horses couldn't follow. I explained to him that if he took the tack to Juda Arad, he could get a good exchange for them. I never found out what happened to our horses. Some days I would imagine the black-skinned tribesman galloping carefree across the savannah; others, well, I won't say the other things I imagined. Interestingly, Runatilli presented me with a special farewell gift, a set of bolas. He explained their use and said that he could bring down an antelope with them or even one of our horses. He demonstrated it use on a small tree. Roy, who was watching, noticed its use immediately. He saw possibilities using them against the Centurions, promising to explore the possibility when we got home.

Tiki, via Sandy, explained that he would be leading us to his chamber. Once there, his High Priest would make the final decision; the High Priest, we learned, made all the important decisions for Tiki's group. Unless the priest found something very wrong with us, we would be on our way. The journey across the sands would begin tonight after full dark, once the crescent moon set. We knew why we had to wait now and spent the remaining hours preparing our gear. Carefully, we packed everything double, sacks within sacks. In the event of a mishap, the poisonous sands would have a hard time reaching our food, healing supplies, spare clothes, and such. I was glad we no longer had to transport all that grain. My guess is that our packs weighed thirty pounds, while the men's were closer to forty or more. We would have to carry them all the way across the desert, which Simon estimated would be some three hundred miles as the crow flew, though we all expected our route to be far longer.

Sarah Jane made very sure that all of us could make up her concoction that seemed to help with the rotting sickness. We hoped and prayed that we wouldn't get it and vowed to be vigilant. Yet, we had no statistics by which to measure just how dangerous it would be to try to cross the desert. However, all of us felt that this was a better option than heading back into Centurion controlled territory. There, we were now hunted people. Certainly, the Black Tracker would be alert for signs of our appearance anywhere in the region. No, however dangerous this new venture may be, we all thought it preferable to creating more trouble with the Centurions.

Tiki had also brought six of their wrapping suits. He pointed out that sand could easily get in by coming up our loose-fitting pant legs or through our sleeves or even around our necks. Following his demonstration, we began wrapping his coverings over our clothes. The wrappings were about a foot in width and long. Leaving a little overlap as it spiraled upwards from our feet, we quickly became completely encased. When we finished and looked at each other, we appeared no different that Tiki! We were now official looking Moon people!

At last. we were off, following Tiki in single file. After we climbed up the riverbank and reached the edge of the sands, he paused for a long time. Sandy whispered that he was checking on the winds and examining the sands for the faint reddish hue. Even though he had only just come here from the desert and was retracing his path, still he acted as if he had never walked this way, reciting repeatedly in his mind the Holy Defense Code of Amin. This wasn't some idle game we were playing. One careless misstep in the Red Desert could mean a horrible death. Tiki also had the added responsibility of us six; our lives depended in large measure upon his skill and knowledge.

At last, Tiki began walking slowly out onto the sands, and we followed his footsteps, single file. Interestingly, Roy brought along a walking stick and brought up the rear. Once we had gone some distance, he poked in the sand, dug a little hole, and even examined some nearby sand that had the reddish glow. "The red is actually a very, very fine dust that is either laying on the surface or has been covered up. Where we walk, just under the surface is more of the reddish glowing dust. It is as if some god has dusted the entire desert with some kind of poisonous powder. How can this be? What in Nature could have caused all this?" While we were all fascinated with his observations, none had an explanation or even a remote idea. An act of some god remained a plausible reason.

We hike on in silence, yet totally alert, eyes watching the ground beneath our feet and just ahead of us. Thankfully, Tiki was going slowly. In fact, this was actually his top speed crossing open desert. Sandy discovered this while monitoring his mind. Yes, she still was doing such, for in a life and death matter, we didn't want to leave it to hand gestures alone — too much room for mis-communication. If a bird would have been flying overhead watching us, he might have thought we were doing a drunkard's walk, for we zigged this way and then zagged that way, never going in a straight line for very long. Always, we walked upon sand that did not glow slightly red in the starlight. Five hours we spent and covered five miles at most, but actual distance in a straight line was more like two or three!

Up ahead, we saw a dark, tall mass; presumably we were at the base of a big dune. Here Tiki pointed to it and said cheerily several words, which Sandy translated. "Here is entrance to my chamber." She wasn't sure if it was the entrance or an entrance. We headed toward the dark dune. When we got closer, I spied the unmistakable columns so common in Megalos, holding or defining rather, a doorway ten feet tall and six wide. We walked under the arched stone roof and found a metal door facing us. In the near total darkness here under the roof, we couldn't see if there were any designs carved or etched in the metal. Tiki grabbed hold of one of the two enormous rings and pulled. The door swung open effortlessly to our amazement. A dim light illuminated the entryway just beyond.

Immediately inside the door was a pool of water about six inches deep into which one had to step if he were to enter. Tiki motioned for us to step inside, and one by one, we did, standing in the water. Once we were all inside, he pulled the door closed. Now he showed us how to properly wash off our wrappings — both feet and hands. Next, dripping wet, we stepped out onto a stone floor and unwrapped ourselves. Tiki indicated that we were to leave the wrappings in a pile, so we added ours to his. Evidently, the next person who needed to go outside would merely reuse these. I wondered if someone would come along and perhaps wash them beforehand.

Now we walked down a long tunnel that was about six feet tall and six wide. The sides were stone, perfectly cut and polished so that light shone off its surface. Every ten feet a light fixture hung from the ceiling. These were no ordinary light fixtures that we had ever seen or heard of! They appeared to be made of some kind of transparent glass with the source of light encased within the glass. Raphael noted that a small metal pipe ran along the ceiling connecting to each of these light fixtures. He speculated that these pipes may have something to do with the light, though he had no idea what that might be. I sensed that we were in for more unusual, strange things.

Every so often, a metal side door appeared, but Tiki kept on walking straight down this corridor. Sandy thought it prudent not to ask about these doors, figuring someone would explain if we needed to know. She did ask, "Is it much further?" She translated his reply, "About a mile ahead." While we walked down this incredibly long tunnel, awe began to creep into all our minds and thoughts! I had rather expected to be in an underground cave or something, but nothing like this! Since sounds echoed loudly, we kept our chattering to whispers.

Finally, Tiki halted before an especially large set of double doors, elaborately carved with two doves sitting upon two vines with many leaves. While we recognized the doves, the nature of the vines eluded us. Perhaps if Thomas had been with us, he might have recognized the vines; after all, he was our Loremaster. Tiki said that the High Priest dwelled inside. We straightened up our clothes as best we could, took a deep breath, and followed Tiki inside, after he pushed open the doors. We weren't prepared for what we saw when we entered!

A pale blue light fully illuminated this chamber, which was approximately thirty foot square with the door we entered squarely in the middle of one side. The sides rose upwards to seven feet but the ceiling was really a dome, rising from the sides to a lofty twenty feet above the floor. Ringing the joint between the walls and the bottom of the domed ceiling were long glass tubes that provided the pale blue glow, which illuminated the room. The ceiling was painted black with stars covering it; it was as if we were looking at the nighttime sky. All the stars glowed with different brightnesses. I recognized many familiar star patterns at once! It was as if I were somehow looking at the night sky outside. Every foot of the walls were covered with painted frescoes or paintings, realistic looking scenes of life. Magnificent would be a gross understatement. The room smelled of lilacs in springtime. I heard water bubbling from somewhere within the room. Great pots of living plants were positioned around the central area of the room. I spied lilacs in full bloom in two pots.

While we just stood and stared in complete and utter disbelief, a soft woman's voice caught our attention. "Over here, please." Her speech was very slow and confident, enunciating each syllable carefully. So similar was it to Centurion, that we could actually understand her. Our eyes turned toward her. On the opposite wall from the entrance door stood a raised dais surrounded by growing flowers and a little fountain or spring. She was dressed in a light, loose-fitting, blue robe. She stood and motioned for us to come to her.

She was perhaps thirty years old, stood nearly six feet tall, with very long black hair and the brownest eyes I have ever seen, contrasting sharply with her completely pale-bronze skin. She was exceedingly pretty — the guys later corrected me, saying she was absolutely gorgeous. Gaping in awe, we approached her. She, again speaking slowly and exceedingly clearly with perfect diction, said softly, "I am Galentia, High Priest of the Edhessa Chamber. Welcome. You can understand my words?"

As Wid, it is my duty to respond for the Circle. I spoke up using my best Centurion speech attempting to speak as slowly and clearly as she, "Yes, we can, if we speak slowly and clearly. Thank you. We have had to use mental telepathy to grasp the other's ideas. We are able to understand you. Thanks for speaking so clearly. I am Bethany, the leader of my Circle." Oops, her beauty and sincerity and, well I don't know what all, caused me to slip and use "Circle" when I ought to have said group. I recovered quickly and introduced the others by first names only. "We come from a land far north of here, beyond the Med Sea, beyond the Appian Way, a land called the Greenway." I had no idea if she knew anything about lands beyond the Red Desert, but I explained anyway in case she did.

"So your Circle is led by a woman. Is this not unusual?" she asked politely.

"Unlike so many other lands, in the Greenway, men and women are equal partners in all things," I replied truthfully. "We believe in using the person most qualified for any given job." I had no idea if this had any relevance here with the Moon people. I desired to be quite honest with her.

"Your men here follow your orders?" she asked probing just a bit. I detected that she really was after information about us just as we were about her.

"Certainly, for I am their leader. If I wasn't qualified to be their leader, they would not," I answered. This she seemed to accept.

"Why is your land called the Greenway?" she asked politely. I suspected she had never heard of our land.

"Because there during most of the year everything is green and growing. We have vast fields of grasses and forests. Our people are mainly farmers, and we grow far more grain than we can use. Our people love and respect Nature, for the most part. My Circle certainly does."

"Do all your people possess this mental ability to talk into our minds? It seems most god-like," she asked next. Obviously, Galentia was very well informed of our activities, but this was a particularly tough one to answer truthfully.

"We are druwids, lovers and protectors of Nature and the common people who inhabit the Greenway. They call us the Guardians and the healers, for we are skilled in the healing arts. Only few of us have the skills to read other's minds and we do so only out of dire need." I realized that our having probed their minds might have been a transgression from her point of view, so I added hastily, "Forgive us if we have offended your people by so doing. We don't speak their language, and we had to find a way to communicate with them — especially when we found that boy who had the rotting sickness. We had to try to help him." I hoped putting it this way would make our use of telepathy appear beneficial to her.

"Reading minds is a gift from the gods. You have used it wisely. The young boy is no longer at death's door, I am told. Is this true? Have you cured him?" she asked, but I sensed a much deeper significance behind her words.

"It was all Sarah Jane's doing. She is our best healer and has already saved many lives. When we left, he appeared to be on the road to recovery, though we don't know if he really will fully recover. At least he is now doing remarkably well, considering. We have never heard of this disease nor have any idea how to cure it. Sarah Jane's concoction certainly has helped him. She has trained all of the riverside villagers in how to make it. Hopefully it may help in the future as well."

"And you freely share this information? You want nothing in return?" she distinctly probed.

"Certainly not! We are healers. We all assumed that we would be instructing others of your people on how to make this concoction as we crossed your land." This seemed like a likely spot to interject what we really wanted. "We are desperately trying to return home and greatly desire to be aided in crossing the Red Desert. On the shore of the Med Sea, one of the boats of the Sea Princes will pick us up and leave the boatload of seed grain from our land in return."

"Ah, the seed grain. Yes, I'm told that you will give us one of the little fishing boats loaded with seed grain in return for your passage across the Red Desert. Is that correct?" Again, she was probing, I could sense some deeper thoughts behind her question, but refused to use telepathy on her to find out more. Then I realized our error. A boat to them meant one of their one-man fishing vessels, but to us a boat meant the Lucky Lady.

"Oops. We have a communication error here. I apologize. We meant one of the Sea Princes boatloads. Let's see, that would likely be a stack of grain that would fill about a quarter of this room. I hope that is sufficient payment. If it isn't enough, we can arrange for more," I hastily replied, assuming the worst.

Tiki, who had been standing silently by the entrance door all this time, nearly choked and coughed. Galentia's eyes opened incredibly wide and her mouth was open but silent. After a moment, she found her voice and said, "Surely you are jesting with me, teasing me?"

"No, I'm sorry, but back in the Greenway, the winter snows have come, and the fall harvest is done. The excess grain for this year has already been sold and shipped. On such short notice, we could only manage to get enough to fill a quarter of this room. If you desire more than that, please accept our promise to deliver it in about nine months, after next year's fall harvest," I explained humbly, hoping that this would appease any errors on our part.

Again, Tiki nearly choked to death and Galentia stared at me in utter disbelief. At last, she exclaimed, "No! No, that is more — much more than enough payment! A little fishing boat quantity would have been sufficient payment! Do you realize that you have just offered to pay us more than the ransom of several kings? The most precious thing in all the Red Desert is seed grain! You only need to give us say this much." She indicated about a three-foot cube of grain.

"Oops. Mis-communication," I laughed. "Well, I'm afraid the grain is likely already on its way here. If we give you enough to fill a quarter of this room, can you make use of it? It won't go to waste? If it will, I suppose we can take what you don't want back with us."

"Use it? Dear child! Certainly, we desperately could use it. We could use ten times that much. It means life to our people! You only need to pay us this much," again she indicated about a cubic yard of grain.

"Well, if you can use all that we have coming, why, then it is yours. Consider it a gift from the Guardians. We feel very honored that we can really help your people with a simple gift of grain," I replied without any feeling of superiority. If these people needed grain, that we could easily give to help them out. "If you need more, perhaps we can work out some kind of yearly exchange of grain for something," I added as an afterthought.

"You are truly generous beyond all words, beyond all imaginations, beyond all that we hoped for. Yes, we could use more seed stock, but I'm afraid that we likely have nothing to offer in exchange for this most precious grain.

Tomorrow is another day." Her face had the impression of having decided something, "It is late; we should be asleep by now. Tiki will show you to some rooms for the night. In the morning, Bethany, please use our bath. You have lovely long hair that is in dire need of a washing. Besides, I'm sure you will like the lilac scent that we put in the waters," she smiled knowingly at me.

My hands went instinctively for my hair; I smiled back. "Yes, it is long overdue. Thanks."

"We shall talk much more tomorrow, after you have had a chance to bathe and eat. Until then, I'll leave you with this. You are the very first outsiders that have ever passed into any of the many Chambers of our land — the very first, but more about that tomorrow. Sleep well, Bethany, druwid of Greenway."

We bowed and Tiki, grinning broadly, led us on down the hall to another side door. He asked, "Do you need three rooms or one? I know not your customs." Again, Sandy had to translate, for his speech was nowhere near as clear as Galentia's. For tonight, we opted for one. We were all dead tired and more than ready to sleep. We piled into the room, which fortunately had three simple oil lanterns. The bedding consisted of giant piles of pillows and such. Once I hit the pillows, I was out like a light. Well, not quite that fast, I felt Roy's arms around me and mine around his; then I was asleep.

The next morning, well I assumed it was morning because my biological clock said so; we awoke and found that some breakfast had been placed into our room while we slept. After eating, a young woman knocked on our door. When we opened it, she motioned for us to follow her. Two doors down from our room was the bathing room. Clean towels and washcloths had been carefully laid out for us, lined up neatly along one wall. In the center of the ten foot square room was a recessed bath made from stone. Several ledges stepped down to the center, which was six feet deep. One could sit on the top step with only the lower part of your body in the water. The next step down had most under water except one's head. The room felt warm and humid; the aroma of fresh lilacs permeated the space. In case we didn't have clean clothes to put on when we were done, six sets of robes were also laid out for us near the towels.

None of us hesitated a second! One minute later, we were all gaily splashing water on each other enjoying our first real bath in a very long time. Naturally, the guys soon grew bored, stepped out, dried off, and returned to our room. We women soaked for the longest time and then helped wash each other's hair. Mine being the longest gave us all the most trouble, but then I didn't care. I'm just a bit vain about my long tresses; I love them, but not the four hours it usually takes to fully dry it. At last, we too got out, dried off, put on the robes, and joined the guys.

Shortly after we joined the men, Galentia appeared outside our door. "Enjoy the bath?" she said using her perfect diction and speaking sufficiently slowly for us to grasp her language. I noticed that she wore a robe similar to the ones that we were given, only hers was the palest blue enhancing her long black hair and brown eyes. We all heartily said that we did and thanked her.

She then said, "Would you like a brief tour of the Edhessa Chamber? I'm sure that you have many questions. I know that I would." Eagerly, we joined her by the door; we needed no second invitation. She then began a long description of the chamber as we walked along the major hallway.

"Edhessa Chamber is home to five hundred of us. The outside world calls us the Moon people, but we call ourselves the children of Amin, for it was he alone who saved our ancestors after the angry, fiery outburst of Angibus, who scorched the land turning it into a desert of death. Our legends say that most of our original people perished either in the fiery blast or from the rotting sickness that followed shortly thereafter. But father Amin invented the Code, and all those who chose to follow his code survived. To this day, we, the faithful, still follow his Code, for failure to do so results in the rotting disease and death."

"Long ago, Amin brought his faithful here to these underground chambers to survive. Today, we, his children, still live, holding strong his Codes in our hearts. As you probably have observed, here in the chamber we have everything we need to live. Everything is recycled to give life to the future. When one of us passes away and goes to join Amin, his earthly body is placed into the compost room, where it decays and returns to the earth from which it is made. The only exceptions are those who die from the rotting disease; those we bury outside the chamber according to the parables of the Code. Ah, here is the Growing Room." She paused and opened a side door.

Inside was a huge, well-lighted room, quite humid. Rows upon rows of growing boxes sprouted massive fungus growths as well as ordinary garden vegetables. We were shocked to see an entire garden of this magnitude thriving completely underground! "How is this possible?" we asked nearly in unison.

She smiled, "Only by the blessings of Amin. Though you may think this is large in scope, I assure you that it is only a fraction of what it used to be. Even in my short years, I have seen the quantity decreasing. That is why the new seed is so vital to us. The elders say that our output is less than half of what it was when they were children."

"I had no idea," I exclaimed. "Look, Galentia, if what we bring isn't enough to totally reverse this, please let us know somehow. We will bring double that amount next fall." I knew that I expressed our common feelings. Simple grain could help save an entire civilization. Somehow, I knew that these were people well worth saving, unlike their distant relatives, the people of Megalos.

Again, she looked wide-eyed at me, almost in disbelief. "Your generosity is overwhelming. You ask nothing in return?"

Simon sent me a warning signal, but I already knew. "Well, we know that for your own mental well-being, you should exchange something. Getting something for nothing, especially when it is so valuable, leads to degradation. If we can find something we could accept, we should, but if we cannot, I would rather accept the responsibility of having contributed slightly to your feelings of degradation than to see you suffer or succumb. Either way, you get all the grain you need. If we can also find something you can exchange, we will accept it."

"Wisdom in one so young! There are many who reach the end of their life without realizing that, druwid Bethany. I humbly bow to you," and she did. I felt awkward having her, their High Priestess, bowing to me. She sensed my reservations and added, "It is not permitted by the Codes for us to physically touch. I sense that you would be more comfortable with a hug or hand shake, but I'm forbidden by the Holy Codes." She seemed sincerely ill at ease, as if she were wrestling with the effects of breaking her sworn code.

"I accept your bow. I honor your Codes, Galentia. Do not break your vows on our account, I beg you," I replied earnestly. She smiled in appreciation.

"Say, how do these lights work?" Raphael asked, his curiosity had gotten the better of him. Besides, he felt slightly awkward watching the intense interactions of Galentia and me.

"These are the Eternal Lights of Amin," she replied. "I don't know how they work. There is a switch on the wall over there that we can pull down to turn them off at night. They have worked ceaselessly for as long as the children of Amin have lived in this chamber. No one knows how they work. Only Amin does. We do not ask."

Raphael was dumbfounded, as we all were. Here was an unlimited light source, strong enough to simulate the sun, consuming nothing that we could see, lasting for generations without needing any assistance. Truly, this was a gift from the gods or more powerful beings!

"We have ten such gardens in this chamber," she continued with our tour. For a few minutes, we were speechless! "These next two rooms hold the kitchens. We eat in shifts so we don't overload them. Ah, here is one of my favorite rooms, the children's playroom." We peeked inside to see two dozen youngsters, none over the age of six, playing quietly. Some had dolls that looked like the grownups walking in the desert; some were playing with building blocks. All smiled and waved at Galentia who smiled back.

At last, we found ourselves back in her room where we met her last night. "Come here; I want to show you our history. It's painted on the walls for all time." We had noticed the frescoes last night, but didn't realize their significance. "It begins here," she said with a distinct note of sadness in her voice. "Here Angibus is casting down fires from the sky creating the Red Desert." We saw a green land with stone buildings much as those in Megalos. People were running in all directions from the flames as the buildings crumbled. It was not a pretty fresco. In the top portion, a disembodied hand seemed to be causing the flames and destruction. Angibus, no doubt.

"Here is Lord Amin leading the faithful into the Chambers." We saw a white robed man leading a scant number of people into an opening just like the one that we had entered last night. Behind them, the scenes of destruction seemed to be smaller in relief, giving a sense of hope to those fleeing underground. She continued with the many other frescoes depicting life as it may have once been and as it was now or rather in the past when these were painted.

"May I as a question?" Simon spoke up during a lull, when Galentia seemed preoccupied with her own thoughts. She blinked and returned to the present and nodded her ascent. "Why have your people not abandoned the Red Desert and moved out into the world to find a new home? Why are you still living generation after generation here underground? I don't understand this. If I were here, I certainly would evacuate and find a new home elsewhere."

This seemed to cause her some mental anguish, and her answer was long in coming. "In the beginning, we believed the destruction so massive that one could not survive outside long enough to leave. That is what we believed at least. As for now, that is simple. We, none of us, have the knowledge or skills with which to survive elsewhere. Yes, we all could leave the safety of the Chamber, but once outside then what? We have occasionally monitored our black-skinned neighbors across the river, building dwellings, cooking, and even hunting once. None of us knows the first thing about these things. Surely, we would all starve long before we learned. Yet, I must speak truthfully. When the grains began to fail, I encouraged the bravest in this Chamber to observe the black ones as they gathered their fish from the river. A very few accepted the challenge to move out there, dwell on the surface, and devote their lives to fishing so that we may supplement our dwindling food supply. Only recently have they been successful. For a few moons now, we have been able to send fish to other Chambers further into the desert to help them. We have made a small first step."

"Congratulations on your wisdom and success," Simon acknowledged sincerely. He had that look in his eye that meant he already had a bright idea. Though I was dying to know what it was, now was not the time to inquire. I stifled my curiosity for the moment. She blushed, genuinely appreciative of his kind words.

"And here," she continued, "is the reason I'm showing you these frescoes. Legends speak of the coming of the Outsider — one who comes unlooked for during a time of great need. She comes bearing a gift of life, asking nothing in return. Here you see the prediction; she is the white robed lady with her hands opened wide. Here, she is healing the sick." Shocked beyond words, I stared at the frescoes and the white woman. She had long brown hair nearly down to her thighs; as my eyes traveled down her form, I spied a hint of leather boots beneath her robes! Sandy gasped and pointed to five similarly clad figures in the background, but they were too indistinct to make them out clearly. Tingles of electricity shot through my body; I felt a rush of emotions too mingled to make any clear sense of them, just letting them flow: fear, awe, pride. It was frightening for the white lady closely resembled me! While my friends commented, I could not find my voice. Even if I had, I didn't know what to say!

"It sure does look like a likeness of Bethany," Simon suggested, but cautioned, "Yet it could be any woman. Lots of you like to have long hair. We can't clearly see her face."

"Well, I say it sure is a remarkable likeness and a good fit," Sarah Jane exclaimed, undaunted by Simon's hesitancy. "Look, we're here in a time of great need bringing the grain they need in a quantity that they actually need and are just giving it to them. I have helped at least that boy recover somewhat from the rotting sickness, so we are attempting to bring healing, though we don't yet know if my invention will actually cure him or not."

"But how could someone know and predict our coming?" protested Roy. "We didn't even know ourselves that we would be coming here until we got here. Heck, we didn't know these people even existed a few weeks ago. I say it's merely a coincidence. Look, if an outsider ever came, it's fifty-fifty that it would be a female. Besides, aren't you women more of the healing, nurturing types than men? It would make sense to depict their savior as female."

"Yes, but Amir, who saved them, was male," countered Sandy. Roy didn't respond.

I did instead, "S-s-spooky! U-u-uncanny!" I finally managed to utter and leaned on Roy; my legs felt so weak!

Undaunted, Simon countered, "But if you accept that this is a representation of us, then how could someone know about this event so long ago? A prophet? Besides, if so, what about our free-will? Do we or do we not have control over our own destiny, our future? I'd hate to think that some all-powerful being up there somewhere is pulling our strings, making us do his will! I refuse to be someone's puppet!"

"Say, Galentia," Sandy inquired having moved further down the wall, looking at subsequent frescoes, "what is all this? It looks like your people are going out into the world once more."

In the softest voice, Galentia spoke, "It is said that after the coming of the White Lady, others of her kind will come to teach us how to live and then lead us out into the world once more."

Simon turned a ghastly white and nearly choked. I've never seen him this pale; his eyes bulged in mighty protest. "They stole my idea!" he managed to mutter at last. We all stared at him. I suddenly realized this was his bright idea that he had formed only minutes ago. "I — I was going to see if we couldn't send back some others to teach them the skills they need to live a normal life. They stole my idea!" So much for free will, I began to conclude.

"But maybe it is just a normal idea that any kind hearted person would naturally get," Sandy offered. "Look, anyone kind enough to give them the grain that they needed to live would certainly want to do something to help them overcome their virtual imprisonment underground. It would only be the honest, natural thing to do, don't you think so?"

Slowly the color returned to Simon's face. "Yes, thanks, Sandy, yes, it would be a logical, natural conclusion. I guess maybe they didn't steal my idea. Anyone would likely have such, but it was my idea all right. I'd decided to ask

Alabaster to send a Circle back here with the next load of grain to teach them. I just hadn't worked out where they could go to live. I'd thought of the Greenway, naturally, but with the war with the Centurions so close, I had my doubts about our land. Coincidence again." He seemed greatly relieved that he found a logical explanation for this.

Galentia spoke once more, "You see, I reached my decision after meeting you last night. While you were sleeping, I sent runners out to the other Chambers telling them of your coming. True, it will be weeks before all the Chambers know the news, but know they will! I also realize you need to be on your way across our desert; you have needs of your own." What she was going to say next was postponed, for a young woman knocked and entered hastily. Tears were streaming down her cheeks. We knew something had happened.

"He has passed away, Galentia. It is time. You must come at once. The rites are needed," the grieving woman said. She was young, perhaps only a few years older than us.

Galentia replied, "Certainly, Jolina. We all knew that Hector's time of separation was close at hand. His body was old and frail." Turning to us, she added, "This is Hector's daughter. Her father has just passed away. I must see to the Separation Ceremony. You have similar ceremonies when one of your kind's body dies?"

"Absolutely!" I replied. "May we watch?" I added. She beckoned us to follow her.

As we walked swiftly down the main hall, I recalled she had said that they even recycled their dead. Besides, I was curious about their ceremony. Was it similar to ours?

We entered a small room filled with nearly twenty people of all ages. A safe assumption would be that these were his relatives, children and perhaps grandchildren too. Grief was the overwhelming emotion that filled the room. We sensed it and felt it as well. Quietly, we pressed back against the wall and watched Galentia. On the bed lay the old man; he had a peaceful look upon his face, as if he welcomed death when it came.

From her neck, she unfastened her pendant and swung it over the head of Hector. "Hector Kronos you were known in life and it was a long and purposeful life. Never did you deviate from the Holy Codes of Amin. By the powers invested in me, I now release you from this shell of a body that you may seek life anew with Amin. From the dust of Tarra your body came. Now that is it no longer alive, we dutifully return it to Tarra so that it may renew the dust of Tarra that more life may yet be created." As she waved her pendant over his head, I spied Hector moving out of his head, grateful for his holy release.

Sandy, I see him leaving. I want to watch and follow him a bit. Look after my body please, I sent her. Indeed, he appeared to my senses as a light grey, misty form somewhat larger than his body's head. He floated up above the room to the ceiling and looked back down. He saw his body lying properly prepared and saw his relatives dutifully grieving. Most importantly, he saw Galentia bending over his body with her glowing pendant. "All is as it should be" was his thought. Slowly he floated up out through the ceiling, moving through the solid stone as if it were mere vapors. Ah, to an immortal being, all this earth is but a vapor. I relaxed, concentrated, and slowly followed him upwards. Alabaster wanted data on what happened to all these spiritual beings when their bodies died. Here I had an opportunity to see, and I resolved to follow him as best I could. I'd never done anything quite like this before and was improvising as I went, though I must say, it was nearly effortless to do so. I still felt a tiny, thin connection to my body way back down there, so I knew that I could return to it if anything dangerous happened.

Up he went until he reached the desert's surface and then up still more until he could look down and see the vast emptiness of the Red Desert. I'd guess he was maybe some fifty feet above the sands. For a minute, he paused, looking simultaneously in all directions. So I did as well, but I must say, looking with a three hundred-sixty degree vision was uncanny and unnerving. I was so used to looking solely out of my body's eyes. I realized he was actually orienting himself. Satisfied, he now headed, much to my surprise, not northeast toward the Appian Way, but rather mostly to a little north of east! This did not fit the earlier pattern, so I followed from a safe distance.

Relatively speaking, he didn't go far. Up ahead, I spied what had to be his destination. Rising above the desert sands were three enormous pyramids, perfect pyramids forming an equilateral triangle. Straight into the middle of the formation he moved. I stayed far off at a distance and watched; I felt Sandy's mind joining with mine and knew that she and perhaps the others were also witnessing what I saw.

Now please realize that for me, there is a huge difference between viewing the physical universe through my body's eyes and viewing it as a spiritual being without the presence of a body. This latter I have only done on a relatively few occasions and my "vision" is not to be trusted. Well, that is not quite right. Rather say that my perceptions and judgments of distances and sizes leave much to be desired. I offer here no estimate of the height of these pyramids or my distance from them as I watched, other than to say they appeared tall to me.

I watched as Hector floated into the center of the triangle. Immediately, some kind of energy beams activated flooding him with a strange glow. I saw his mental pictures of his life flashing by his mind in vivid color. However, the energy beams seemed to be randomly scrambling them, distorting them, altering them. When that agonizing process finally ended, the energy flows changed colors and a message began to be implanted into his mind. So loud was that message that I could hear it clearly even at the distance I was from the process. "Follow the Holy Codes of Amin." The message was repeated over and over. Meanwhile, I spied some motion on the sides of the pyramids!

As my attention shifted to the stone, to my horror, I saw crawling up the sides of each pyramid what appeared to be three enormous praying mantises!

Each was a third the size of the pyramids and each was intently watching the process. Now I love to watch a praying mantis crawling on a leaf or twig, but these were gigantic, like monsters. To my utter horror, they seemed to be controlling this entire operation. One made a motion and the vocal message changed. "Return to the Chambers. Find a new baby body. Follow the Holy Codes of Amin. Go now."

Suddenly the energy beams disappeared. The mantises slunk back down the sides to ground level. Hector, completely confused, spinning in circles, disoriented, latched onto a mental picture of a Chamber. To my complete surprise, he fairly dove toward it, like a lightning bolt he moved! Swoosh and he flew by me without even perceiving my presence. However, the eyes of the mantises spied me as they followed Hector. Now I was the total focus of their attention!

It's funny how in a single instant of time one can realize that he has seen something that he should not have seen. Fear bordering on terror seized me for an instant as I had this very realization. In my mind, I heard one of the mantis's commands, "This way please." His intention was clear. I was yet another Moon person whose body had passed away and had come as did Hector. I was supposed to float between the pyramids. No way! Like Hector before me, I dove as fast as I possibly could back towards my body, hoping and praying that my unexpected response would take them off guard, that I might escape them. Admittedly, I had no idea what they could do to me as a spiritual being, but I certainly was not going to stick around and find out!

I nearly made it before I felt one of them reach out and latch onto me with some kind of energy beam, attempting to pull me back into the middle of the pyramids! The harder I resisted it, the harder it pulled on me, threatening somehow to tear my beingness apart. Panic struck me once more, and I lashed out the only way I could. Wham! I sent a lightning bolt back down at the mantises. In hindsight, I see now that this was the only way I could have escaped their entrapment net. Being blasted by a bolt of energy was the absolute last thing that they expected to get. Startled, they lost control of their sucking beam, and I flew into my own body with such violence that I knocked it solidly into the wall and passed out.

Roy and Simon, who had been following all that happened via Sandy's mental link with me, grabbed my body and supported it. The ceremony was over, and they led me back to our room, leaving Sandy to mutter some excuse. I vaguely heard her say, "Too much excitement. She needs to rest a bit to absorb all this." By the time that they got me into our room, I had recovered. A bit of fungus wine helped as well.

"Did you all see that?" I muttered. From the frightened faces looking down at me as I lay on the pillows, I didn't need to see their affirmative head nods. "We have to get out of here fast. They may come after us!" However, we didn't get to talk more as Galentia appeared.

"Ah, I see that you are doing better. I hope the ceremony did not frighten you," she apologized.

486

"No, it is just so similar to our own passing ceremony that my breath was taken away," I answered with a half-truth. Certainly, I couldn't tell her the complete truth; she'd probably think I was crazy, mad, or hallucinating, but this was no hallucination that I witnessed!

"Okay. I do wish you could stay with me for a long time. There is so much I would like to ask and to know. You have urgent business of your own, and I know that you need to be on your way. I won't hold you up any longer. If you ever have some free time, I would dearly love for you to come and visit a while. Our Chamber is always open to you." I took this as a very high honor. She added, "Since you desire nothing but safe passage across the Red Desert, I have decided to give you something in return. One moment, please." She quickly left the room and returned before we had time to speculate.

"I want you to have this." She handed me a small box. "Go ahead; open it up," she eagerly urged. I did. Inside was a golden lantern. "See that switch on the bottom. Press it." I did and immediately, the lantern glowed brilliantly. "Press it again and the light goes off. This is one of our eternal lights. No matter how long you leave it on, it still shines brightly. It never runs down. It needs no, what do you call it, oh yes, fuel. It needs no fuel or any care, save to wipe any dust off it. We call these Eternal Lanterns of Amin."

"Galentia, I'm speechless. This is a priceless gift! Thank you ever so much! This we will prize highly!" She glowed, for her present, her gift, was found to be just as valuable as she considered it.

"It is the very least I can give, but now you must go. The moon has set. Tiki has volunteered to guide you to the next Chamber. Because the further from here that you travel, the more scarce the food supply becomes, I have taken the liberty of packing a lot of extra rations for you so that you'll not be imposing too much on the other Chambers. Word has been sent so they will be expecting you. As you know, you travel by night and sleep by day. Good luck to you, and thank you for the grain of life and the healing potion. We have already begun making a supply of it for emergencies." With that we bowed, said our farewells, and thank you's, for still she followed the Holy Code of Amin; touching another, as in a hand shake or hug that I longed to give her, was totally taboo.

I carefully placed the box in my sack. As we left the room, others were waiting in the hall with a food sack for each of us. The food sack was double sacked so that if the poisonous sands somehow got into the outer sack, the inner sack would still protect its contents. Soon we stood at the entrance chamber and began the laborious task of wrapping our bodies in protective cloth until only our eyes and mouths were exposed. Without a word, Tiki opened the door and we stepped out into the dark night and onto the poisonous sands of the Red Desert.

While we could have discussed the frightening occurrence by using mental telepathy so that Tiki wouldn't hear, we didn't dare to do so. All of our attention had to be focused on our passage across the desert. One misstep could spell disaster, possibly even death from the reddish-hued dust. In fact, I found I had to dismiss completely all thoughts of this encounter from my mind in order to concentrate upon the path. Besides, we each were now carrying two heavy sacks instead of the single one. With the soft sands yielding beneath our feet, we had to keep focused on each step. Besides, after a good fright, there is nothing like a long walk in the dark like this where you can't afford even to reflect on the frightening experience. It helps to put it out of your mind.

Periodically, Tiki would pause to sense for even the slightest hint of wind. Only the faintest whiff of moving air could be detected. I wondered what we would do it a sudden sand storm came up while we were out here. I presumed that we would all be exposed to the rotting sickness for sure. That was not an encouraging thought.

We walked all night long, with only a few minutes rest allowed. By sunrise we had to be within the next Chamber or we couldn't see the red glow of the poison and would likely walk right through it contaminating ourselves. In the end, we just barely made the next Chamber as the first hints of dawn appeared in the star-filled skies above us. Once we entered the Entrance Room, Tiki shut the door, and while we all washed off our feet, Tiki sighed heavily in relief. "Didn't think we would make it. That was too close," he said with Sandy translating. After cleaning our feet, we all unwrapped and left the wrappings in the room. Tiki then opened the door leading into the long hallway of this Chamber. Just inside was a man dressed in similar priestly robes.

"Welcome to Kronos Chamber, Holy Ones. We're honored to have you spend the night with us. Let me show you to your room. I'll arrange for food and refreshments to be brought directly to your room. I am called Priaeus, the High Priest of this Chamber." Again, Sandy translated; she was getting better and better at this. Besides, we, too, were now beginning to pick up several words on our own.

"Thank you for your generosity, Priaeus," I replied tiredly, "but we know that food is scarce and have brought ours with us. We would appreciate something to drink, though. And yes, we are tired; that was a very long walk." Without further words, he led us down the hall a ways to a side room. Our room was nearly identical to the room we had occupied in the previous Chamber. In fact, we soon discovered that all of the Chambers were nearly identical in all ways! Someone had built a large number of identical underground facilities. Raphael pointed out that we druwids did the same thing with all our emergency survival cabins throughout the Greenway. Still, a small wood cabin was one thing and all these vast underground chambers quite another.

We ate, drank, and fell asleep. I was dead tired. So were the others. I began by carrying a thirty pound pack, but tonight, the two must have weighted at least sixty! I had no idea how heavy the men's were. With each passing day, one sack would lighten — the food sack. As I fell asleep, I wondered if the food we had brought would last us until we reached the Med Sea. My biological clock was springing its mainspring. I was going to bed at dawn instead of getting up at dawn.

I got up in the late afternoon, as did the others. We drank, ate, and then went in search of the Priest. His room was precisely where Galentia's room was in her Chamber. There, we instructed six in how to make Sarah Jane's concoction. The hope that each person displayed more than compensated for all the communication difficulties we had with their language. Soon, it was time to go. Once more we followed our guide into the Entrance Room, wrapped ourselves carefully, and stepped out into the dark night. We had no time to discuss the scary incident and would not again this night. I guessed we would likely be walking all night long.

This was indeed the case. Only this time, we couldn't even take a rest break! Full dark was almost an hour less each night because of the moon. Again, just at dawn, we stumbled into the next Chamber and met that Chamber's Priest. Always many of the inhabitants peeked and gawked at us, me in particular, for I was their legend come true. I found it more than a little embarrassing to be such a center of attention and awe. Sarah Jane, on the other hand, reveled in all the attention that she received with her concoction for the rotting disease. For two more nights, this same pattern repeated itself. On the third night, because the moon was growing closer to full, we got a break. The sky was very cloudy and our guide left earlier than normal, arriving while it was still dark in the wee hours of the very early morning. Admittedly, our guide was utterly paranoid that a storm was coming and we'd be caught out in the open. With just a little bit of convincing by we druwids, no storm came while we walked. Though we tried to estimate the distance that we had traveled, because of the winding, twisted path followed to avoid the red death, we really had no notion, save that we were generally heading in the right direction, northwest.

At the seventh Chamber, we had to halt for several days during the time of the full moon for there would be no darkness sufficient for us to observe the red hue of death. At last ,we had some time to ourselves and to reflect on what we had all witnessed. Actually, I brought up the subject. "Okay, I take it that you all saw what I saw when I followed Hector a couple nights ago." Suddenly, everyone was totally serious; I had reminded them of the horrid scene they'd witnessed. From the looks on their pale faces, I knew they had and didn't wait for them to reply. "That wasn't at all what I expected to find. It was surreal. I really don't know what to make of what I saw. Do any of you have any ideas?" I threw it open to discussion, hoping that one of my friends might shed some light on what we had witnessed. Admittedly, I didn't really expect anyone would, though.

Silence greeted my ears. Finally, Simon ventured, "Well, let's begin with what we all actually observed. Then, draw conclusions. I know it was a pretty darn shocking scene to witness. I guess I'll begin, but feel free to jump in and correct me if I get something wrong here." We nodded that we would. "First, Hector was or rather is a spiritual being as we are. We all saw him as he traveled around without his body. The Moon people's last rites are similar to ours; there's no question about that. They recognize that they are beings as we do, inhabiting an earthly body. There is no question that at some level of awareness, Hector knew precisely where he had to go when he was released by Galentia's ceremony. He went straight for those pyramids without even the slightest hesitation, like one who was implicitly following orders. When he was hit by that first energy flow, which seemed to emanate from the three pyramids, he didn't resist it or try to leave. Rather he just stayed there. From my observation, it appeared to me that all those beams did was completely scramble all his life's memories into a complete, incoherent mess. If my memories were so scrambled, I'd find it very hard or next to impossible to remember anything from that time period. Anyway, next he was zapped by a different kind of energy, one which really seemed to confuse him utterly, and over the top of that, he was given an order to return to a Chamber and get a new body, presumably a baby body, and above all, follow their Holy Codes of Amin. Once that action was completed, he shot off like an arrow to carry out those orders. I've never seen anyone move as fast as he did at the end, though admittedly, I haven't seen too many free spirits in action, just a few. Still, it seemed to me that he went terrifically fast."

"Finally, I swear that I saw three enormous insect creatures that looked like praying mantises. They seemed to be the ones in control of the operation — their movements, actions, thoughts — all seemed to me to be performing this sequence of actions on Hector. I say insects, but these were no normal insects! Heck, they had to be at least a third the height of the pyramids, though we've no idea how tall the pyramids actually are. Now if they were, say, six inches tall, why, then the mantises would be the right size. Somehow, I get the feeling that the pyramids weren't six inches tall, but I guess there's no way to tell."

"I saw some pyramids in one of the frescoes on Galentia's walls," Sandy added. "They were in the background of one scene. If that artwork was at all reflective of their world, the pyramids ought to be hundreds of feet tall. Who ever heard of an insect that is fifty feet or more in length? I don't know of any animal on Tarra that is that big. It can't be real."

"Real or not, there were three spiritual beings in those bodies and they tried to force me into that same mess that Hector endured. I believe that they thought I was another being whose body had just passed away," I replied. "Rarely have I ever been that frightened. I was really terrified of getting my mind blasted like Hector had!"

"We all were, Bethany," Sandy consoled me. "Remember, we were watching, felt, and heard his orders just as you did. I was terribly afraid you'd get sucked into that energy and then we'd lose you!"

"I couldn't fight it. The more I tried to pull away from it, the stronger the sucking was! I panicked utterly. The only thing I could think of was to blast at them with lightning."

The others chuckled. Roy commented, "Well, after all, we are the Lightning Circle." We all laughed. "I don't think that you did any actual damage to them, Bethany, but it certainly gave them a totally unexpected action. I know you couldn't see what happened, but they were so taken by surprise that they lost control over their sucking force or beam or energy or whatever it was. That gave you the instant you needed to get the heck out of there. You have my permission to blast away anytime you feel the need to," he laughed. We all laughed, but he did speak truthfully.

"Okay, conclusion time," Simon attempted to get us back on course. "Those creatures are controlling life or the destiny or future of beings here in the Red Desert. They are forcing them to their will. And you, or we rather, saw something that we were obviously not supposed to see. I fear that they might try to find out who you are and come after you to prevent your telling others about what you witnessed, though no one would really believe you. It is so wild, so far-fetched that people will think you are hallucinating or just plain crazy. Nevertheless, I'm worried that they might try to catch us."

"Well, perhaps they are just watching over these people and have their best interests at heart," proposed Sarah Jane. "I mean this desert is deadly; we've seen and heard enough to prove that. So these people's survival actually depends upon following slavishly these codes. Maybe they are just trying to help the Moon people."

"It seems plausible," Raphael agreed, "except if we were going to do that, why would we purposely completely scramble all their memories of the life they had just finished living? It would seem to me that retaining those memories would be most beneficial in the next lifetime. You know, they would have certainty on the real need for the Holy Codes and all that."

"So what you are saying is that they don't have the best interests of the Moon people in mind?" Sarah Jane countered. "I see what you are saying, but then that means that they are really some kind of dictators controlling these people for some other purpose. That's evil."

"That's what I'm saying," Raphael replied seriously. "That probably means that they're after our butts!"

"If that is the case," Simon added with a dramatic pause, "then they must know of the Moon people's legends of the lady of mercy coming to their rescue — an outsider. Galentia did say we're the first outsiders ever to be allowed inside a Chamber, let alone seven of their Chambers so far. Undoubtedly, these creatures or things already know that. I think the real question is this: will they be able to find out where we're headed and so intercept us? If they can't find out where we are going, they might not be able to locate us, maybe. After all, a fifty-foot insect walking into a Chamber, assuming that one would even fit inside these corridors, would certainly cause quite a stir. Maybe they won't be able to find out where we are heading and be forced to guess which one we are going to go to next. Maybe we will be safe. Maybe."

Sarah Jane giggled, "That's way too many maybe's for me. It seems to me that the longer we stay in one place, the more likely they are to catch up with us. After all, all they have to do is question the folks at the last Chamber in which we spent the day to know where their guide was taking us that night. I should think that we are sitting ducks."

Roy, who had been quietly thinking, spoke up, "I agree with Sarah Jane. I think that it is a safe assumption that these beasts shortly, if not already, know our next destination Chamber. I agree with Simon, I don't think that they can afford to visit a Chamber directly. Look, even if they can cast an illusion over themselves as we can, they will not fit in here, not unless they can also somehow change their physical size. From a Protector's point of view, I believe we're quite safe while we are within a Chamber. No, if they want to intercept us for whatever reason, they most likely will do it at night, while we're outside walking in the poisonous desert hopelessly at the mercy of our guide. I've been leery of this very thing since we began. While we're out there, if anything happened to our guide, we're really doomed, to say the very least. If I wanted to get rid of this group of six outsiders while raising no questions whatsoever, I'd wait until they were about halfway to the next Chamber and then eliminate the guide. Let the poisonous desert claim six more victims. Neat and simple."

At last, I added my opinions to the pot. "I think we must trust Roy in this matter; he is our Protector. One of us should always stay very close to our guide to prevent anything happening to him. I think Roy ought to do that; he's the best at this kind of thing. What if we get attacked by these beasts? My lightning bolt took it by surprise but according to you all, it really didn't do any actual damage. What are insects the most afraid of anyway? Fire and ice. They freeze in the winter and get burned up in flames. If we get attacked, let's use these two weapons on them and see if that does anything to them."

Scowling, Sandy broke in, "Aren't we overlooking one small detail?" We looked blankly back at her. "Look, if these creatures are intelligent and are able to do these kinds of mind things on ordinary spiritual beings, then isn't it highly likely that they have weapons which we've never even dreamed of? Who knows, perhaps they can shoot lightning bolts back at us! Remember how Alabaster could not be harmed by our bolts? Well, we must do our best to emulate Alabaster, if they attack us with weapons we've never seen before."

This was a very sobering idea — that these creatures might possess weapons unheard of and whose damage infliction we could only speculate. No one said a word for a couple of minutes. At last, I offered Alabaster's own words to me, "Let the energy flow around you; do not resist it. Let it pass through you. I know it's terribly hard to do that. I sure didn't when those creatures nearly pulled me back. I forgot, but we all must at least remember to try not to resist."

Trying to bring a bit of life back, Roy commented in jest, "Well, I never met a bug that I couldn't squash. Let me get close enough and I'll physically get the bug." We smiled and his mission was accomplished. "Seriously gang, if the bugs appear trying to get us, they really have no choice but to kill our guide, even if they fail to get us. If they don't, think of the wild stories the guide will tell when he gets back to his Chamber! No, if they appear, they'll have to destroy the guide."

"Say, I have an idea," I put in when he finished, "why don't we have a look at this Chamber's frescoes and look them over very carefully to see if we can find any trace or illusion to these bugs or mantises? Let's see if they have entered into the lore of the Moon people. We can do this without asking them about the bugs directly. Besides, if they are ignorant of the bugs, they'll think we're mad. If they know about the bugs, then they might venerate them or hate them. Let's just see if we can find any trace of them in the frescoes." This everyone thought was a good idea, so we were off to find the Priest and admire this Chamber's ornate frescoes of history.

We spent several hours closely examining the huge frescoes but found not even the slightest hint of the bugs. Raphael whispered another idea for us to consider, "Hey, maybe it was these mantises who originally built these Chambers? Maybe all this we see here is some outside invader's technology. After all, a perpetual light is otherwise not possible, yet it exists here. Could these bugs actually be some form of advanced race not normally seen on Tarra?"

"Not very advanced if they use bugs for bodies," Roy commented.

"Well, if you ask me," Sandy added fearfully, "I'm terrified of them. They are so huge; they could rip us apart like we could a frog."

"That's only natural, Sandy," Roy consoled. "It's one thing to go off like we have and face the world of the Centurions, We can make good assumptions on how they fight and behave, but the total unknown of these creatures is quite another thing entirely. We have nothing at all on which to make any assumptions about them, save they probably aren't very friendly towards us. I'm a bit scared too." We all drifted off into our own thoughts.

Four days passed before the moon was rising late enough for us to have enough total darkness to cover the distance to the next Chamber. Our guide this night was Demosthenes, a young man in his twenties. With Sandy acting as our mental interpreter, we once again wrapped ourselves up, began our cautious journey across the red sands with only starlight to guide us, and the ever-present reddish hue of the poisonous sands. As planned, Roy took up his position as close behind Demosthenes as possible. I followed next with Sandy behind me. Simon brought up the rear and constantly looked back over his shoulder to make sure we weren't being followed. Nothing happened, so as the hours went by, we fell into the boredom monotony of staring at the ground to place our feet where the one before us had stepped, ever cautious of avoiding the dull glowing sands.

Without warning, Roy suddenly halted, freezing in his tracks. "Demosthenes is walking on the red glowing sands! Stop him, Sandy!" We too froze. Just ahead, our guide was slowly moving forward, directly marching onto the forbidden sands!

Sandy let out a shriek as she made contact with his mind. "Something has taken over control of his mind! I can't get through to him. Help me!" At once, I joined with her and felt the tug of Sarah Jane and Raphael also melding into the mental link. I felt that same strange, foreign mind, not the normal minds of Moon people!

Awkwardly, Roy whipped his sword out and stared frantically in all directions, but saw no signs of any other presence besides ourselves. Sandy, however, with the added boost of us managed to contact Demosthenes' mind, separating it from the invader. That action allowed her to make a guess of the location of what we could only assume was one of the bugs. "It's over there," she pointed towards a sand dune to the west of us about five hundred feet. Between us and it lay a field of glowing sands, impassible. Roy's sword was useless, but Roy was not. While Sandy and the rest of us attempted to force the intruder out of the mind of Demosthenes, Roy began chanting a fire spell.

As expected, a searing wall of flames appeared just over the far side of the dune. He let it fall down towards the unseen ground. Normally, we would never just drop fire onto unseen ground for fear of burning something, such as a tree or worse, a home, but sand does not burn and he let it fall. Meanwhile, Sandy had no luck forcing the intruder from Demosthenes' mind. This invader had a powerful connection. As Roy's flames reached the ground out of our sight, a sizzling sound came from that direction followed by a hideous shriek. In that instant, Sandy forced the distracted mind out of Demosthenes. The poor fellow began shaking and could not help but notice he was standing in a pile of red glowing sand. Sandy's mind flooded with his instantaneous recognition of his blunder, his violation of the Code, and his recognition of his imminent death from the rotting disease. It nearly overwhelmed her. We who were helping her also got some backlash as well.

It took all of Sarah Jane's power to force her thought into his confused, frantic mind. "We have a cure for this. Just wash your feet well when we arrive." He, of course, didn't believe her, that there was any such cure, and slowly fell further on down towards apathy. At least, he slowly stepped back out of the poisoned sands to where we stood.

Roy's flames were short lived for there was nothing to catch on fire. No further sounds could we hear, so I decided the best thing to do was to get Demosthenes back on the right path towards the next Chamber. With Sandy's help, he again began picking his careful way, bypassing the danger areas. Soon, we left this ambush zone behind us. Simon couldn't detect anyone or thing following us. Roy's conclusion was that the fire stopped it, though he didn't go so far as to declare that he had actually killed or even wounded whatever had been hiding behind the dune.

The rest of that night's journey was no longer boring. All of us kept a sharp watch on our footsteps and our minds alert for any further attempts at possession, especially our guide's mind. No further attacks came. As the moon rose dimming out the faint red glow of the poisonous sands, we arrived at the entrance to the next Chamber. I speak for all of us when I say we were never gladder to see an entrance before now!

Once inside, we washed off our feet very carefully, and Sarah Jane insisted that Demosthenes wash his three times. She took no chances. Once we had unwrapped, she had Sandy tell him that she wanted to examine his feet immediately. To everyone's surprise, she found a few tiny reddish splotches, which only confirmed to Demosthenes that he had the dreaded disease and was going to die soon of a horrible death. He moaned about having failed the Code. Sarah Jane just got to work and instructed the priest, who greeted us, to help her prepare another batch of her concoction.

An hour later, having shown a dozen of this Chamber's people how to mix her potion, Sarah Jane had Demosthenes drink a quart of it. As predictable, she sat up with him all night observing and insisting he down as much of the liquid as he could. Meanwhile, we entered our new quarters and cleaned up a bit before eating. Simon commented, "You know, that invader or bug or whatever sure knew what he was doing. By making Demosthenes lead us out into the poisonous sands, we all should have contracted this rotting disease and perished. It is obvious that they want us dead, and it is also obvious that they don't want to make themselves visible to either us or the Moon people. Conclusion: the Moon people don't know anything about these manipulators of their spirits. This is getting stranger by the minute. I just don't know what to make of it all." Neither did the rest of us. What were the goals and purposes of these creatures? We had no clue. Naturally, we all slept rather poorly.

The next morning, or rather late afternoon, we gathered around Sarah Jane and her patient. Carefully, she pointed out the barely perceptible red patches on his feet. In fact, many, many Moon people stopped by to inspect his feet. The red spots were actually much reduced in size from the previous evening. This was what so intrigued the Moon people. Ordinarily, by now, the patches should have been the size of small buttons. She and the Moon people found this highly encouraging! At her request, we delayed our departure another day so that she could continue to monitor his recovery. While these people kept speaking of her miracle cure, Sarah Jane kept Sandy busy explaining that she didn't know if her potion would actually cure the rotting disease, but it certainly helped the patient.

Meanwhile, the rest of us held a conference after eating our breakfast. The topic I presented was the ethics of our continuing to have a Moon person guide us across the desert, knowing that these creatures might attempt taking over control of the next guide forcing him to lead us out into the poisonous sands to die. In the end, we knew we couldn't find our own way across the desert; we were at the mercy of these Moon people and their generosity. Only the chance that Sarah Jane's potion would cure any rotting disease permitted us to continue using their guides. I summarized it this way, "If it weren't for Sarah Jane's concoction, I would order a retreat back into the Southlands, though still honoring our deal for the seed grain." Still, none of us liked being in the position of knowingly placing one of these Moon people in grave jeopardy on our account. The bugs were after us, not them. We really had only two choices: continue or retreat. We chose the former only because of Sarah Jane's potion.

Simon then counseled us all, "Okay then. These creatures don't want to become visible either to us or to the Moon people. Think about or dream up all the ways they might do their dirty work. We need to speculate so as to get some further ideas on how to prevent another accident to our guides." This was what we thought about the rest of the day, dreaming up ways and means these creatures could kill us from a distance. As you might expect, without any hard data on these creatures, we didn't come up with very many ideas. In fact, none. After all, from our point of view, taking over the mind of our guide was unexpected. What else could these creatures do that we did not know about? That scared me even more — the fear of the unknown.

Roy took me aside; something was bothering him. "Bethany, sometimes the best defense is a good offense. Ordinarily, I would advise that instead of waiting around for their next attack we attack them. I've been trying to think of a way to counterattack these bug creatures. However, I keep running into this darn confining Red Desert. There is just no way we can safely move about here. We are at the mercy of these Moon people and very dependent upon them. This makes me really, quite uncomfortable — I prefer to be the master of my own destiny, so to speak. What if these bug creatures should somehow convince the next Chamber of people that we are up to no good? The guide might intentionally be given the order to strand us out there. Or perhaps they might offer us food laced with some of that red glowing sand dust. Or, or, or. I guess what I am really asking is: are we strong enough to mentally attack these bug creatures, you know like you have done in the past when our need was great?"

"Roy, I just barely escaped being pulled into their mind-washing thing, whatever it is called. My lightning bolts really did not harm them, only surprised them, but perhaps your fires did some damage — there was that sizzling noise. We have no way of knowing whether it did actually harm it. If we tried something like what you are thinking, what if fire fails to harm them? Surely, ice is unlikely to hurt them, except maybe slow them down. Roy, if we expose ourselves and are actually unable to harm them, we're likely doomed. I know how badly you want to attack them — you are our Protector, after all. Roy, I just do not see how this can be done at the moment. By the way, you did very well out there last night. You spotted the takeover of our guide almost as it happened and got the bug distracted so we could get it out of his mind. My compliments, Mister Protector." He grinned and seemed satisfied, especially with my sincere compliments.

Raphael now wanted a private word with me. Roy backed away and Raphael spoke what was gnawing on his mind. "Bethany, remember what Alabaster asked us to do, the special thing we are to do?" I nodded; he was obviously referring to finding out what is happening with these spiritual beings after their bodies die. Where do they go? Why are more beings apparently arriving on Tarra every year? "Well, I've been giving this a lot of thought since that night when you followed the Moon person to the bug creatures." I muttered a soft "uh huh," and he continued. "I think these bug creatures are attempting to control and manipulate all the beings here in the south, south of the Med Sea that is. To what end, remains a mystery, granted. However, Bethany, if there are these creatures down here, totally invisible, completely unknown to all the inhabitants of Southern Tarra, wouldn't it make sense if yet another bunch of these outsiders were doing the very same thing up north somewhere in the Appian Way area?"

Unfortunately, I didn't follow his great leap in logic from one set of creatures to the second. "I don't see," I started to say but he interrupted me.

"I'm afraid a bit of Simon is rubbing off on me. Remember what he always says? If two people are arguing, fighting, the root cause is to be found elsewhere; there must be some other person known to each of the combatants that is fomenting, causing the trouble, a third person."

"Yes, he is always telling us that, but what has that got to do with this mess?" I asked. I bit my lip. Just as soon as I uttered my protest, I grasped his point. Yet, Raphael graciously spelled it out for me.

"Look, the Centurions are attempting to conquer all the northern lands, having pretty much gotten all these southern lands under their dominion. It's like us versus them. Two sides locked in a bitter struggle for supremacy. According to Simon, that is a sure sign that someone, or perhaps something in this case, is actually behind it causing all of us to fight. Niccolo didn't seem too keen to wage war, neither do we. Yet our countries are heading for all-out war. Enter the third person idea. What if these bug creatures are egging, forcing the Centurions to war against all northern peoples? Let's not speculate on how they are doing it to Niccolo's people, just assume that they are, somehow. Then, either these very same bug creatures are doing the same thing to the Sea Princes, the Arads, and us or, and this is a big 'or,' there is another group, separate from the bug creatures, who are inciting the northern lands to war!"

"I see where you are going with this," I replied thinking hard. He was several steps ahead of me, and I was his Wid. Not good. "Suppose for a moment that there was a different group controlling or impacting the northern lands. If so, suddenly much makes sense. If both of these controllers hated each other, they could be using us as pawns to fight their battles. Or perhaps it is just an amusing game to them — to see whose pawns are the stronger. I think we've hit upon the real underlying reasons for this insane conquest of the Centurions, Raphael. Given this, so much would suddenly make total sense! Raphael, you may have just given us a bargaining chip with these bug creatures. Suppose we told them: 'leave us alone or we will broadly tell the political leaders of these southern lands about you and what you are forcing them to do.' That might be enough to keep them at bay long enough for us to get out of this land of death. We'd better tell the others."

I called a formal meeting of our Circle and even had Sandy make a connection to Thomas so he could be informed. Raphael and I outlined our speculations. Simon merely sat back and smiled the whole time, as if he was the proud teacher listening to his students successfully tackle a tough problem. After some discussion, everyone reached the same conclusion that I had — we could go on the offensive against these creatures by using threat of exposure.

Interestingly, we found out Thomas and Thallia were on the Lucky Lady bringing the grain down from Calgary and would be meeting us when we finally reached the shore of the Med Sea below Velona. However, I had Sandy stress to Thomas just how deadly the sands were and made sure Thomas wouldn't let anyone ashore. That solved one nagging problem I had, what if one of the crew should come ashore and thus contract the rotting sickness?

All that remained was to figure out how to get into communication with these bug creatures, including what language to use. Sandy decided that for us, "Use concepts, not words." Easy for her to say; hard for me to carry out. Further, Sandy insisted that she be the one to make the contact, after all, this was a communication situation, and that was her specialty. We all argued over this but in the end, her logic was irrefutable.

Thus, after we all slept and ate, we formed into a circle on the floor, joining minds. Roy and I took up positions of Circle Protectors. It was his duty and I was by far the most experienced in performing our tasks sans body or outside of my body. The task for Simon, Raphael, and Sarah Jane was simple: in the event of any trouble, they were to use any means necessary to pull Sandy out of the enemy's clutches and back into her body as well as Roy and me, should we be attacked. We all relaxed and expanded our minds, our awareness — out and up into the daytime sky. It was daytime, late afternoon. I had forgotten all about the time of day.

Roy couldn't actually move out of his body, so he took up a position surrounding Sandy and myself. Sandy, to my amazement, didn't need to leave her body. Rather, she just expanded her awareness further and further out. I matched her but stayed slightly back. For an hour, nothing happened. I was just beginning to suspect that this wouldn't work, when Sandy felt a solid tug on her mind: contact. She had done it; she had reached one of these foreign minds. I watched fascinated as she sent concepts and ideas without using words. Now I could really see why she was our Communicator. I always had to use words. She just had the knack for this, but I also suspected it had a lot to do with all of her specialized training.

Now Sandy received a return set of ideas to which she had to respond. She sent the idea that up to this point in time, none of us had mentioned these creatures to anyone here in the entire southern Tarra where we were located. I also realized that would have been a logical question I would ask if I were in his shoes, assuming the bugs wore shoes. However, the next volley of ideas, Sandy refused to answer, sending back the idea that they didn't need to know who or what we were. Instead, she reiterated the idea that if they leave us alone so we can cross the desert, we'll leave this land promptly and say nothing of them to anyone here.

A long pause followed. I concluded they were discussing the proposition or perhaps whomever she had reached didn't have the authority to make such a bargain. We waited, but Roy and I remained fully alert for treachery. I was worried they might use that same sucking energy beam on Sandy that they had used on me, which I narrowly escaped. We waited. Finally, Sandy received a single concept back: "Agreed." The contact with the bug creature abruptly terminated, though Sandy had not broken it. The bug creatures demonstrated that they had total control over this mind communication mechanism. Quickly, we retreated our extended awareness back into our bodies and the underground room. In unison, we sighed in relief; it worked!

Simon cautioned, "Don't put too much faith in this. They might not live up to their agreement." Bummer. I was so hopeful that our troubles were at an end, at least from these creatures. He was right; we shouldn't let our guard down for one minute. It would be simple enough for the bug creatures to misguide our next guide, leading us into the poisonous sands. It was soon time to find out.

We checked on the recovery of Demosthenes; he was still doing very well indeed. This Chamber's guide wanted to leave as soon as it was full dark, so we packed up our few things and made our way to the entrance room. This time, we very carefully wrapped ourselves with the coarse cloth, for we more than realized just how important this protection actually was. It probably had saved the life of Demosthenes, along with Sarah Jane's concoction. Soon, we said our last farewells here and began the slow nighttime journey to the next Chamber.

The stars seemed exceedingly brilliant this night for some reason. Yet we walked and studied the sands beneath our feet with greater care than we had ever done so before. None of us wanted a repeat of the last night stroll on the desert sands. The trip was completely uneventful, and we entered the next Chamber having made good time. All of us took this as positive sign that the bug creatures would honor the agreement.

They did. Three weeks later, we finally arrived at the last Chamber which overlooked the Med Sea! All of us cheered loudly when we crested the last dune and spied the sea below. Of course, we had heard it and smelled it long before we actually saw it. The next night, our guide found a path that led safely down to the shore. There, Roy conjured a huge ball of fire high in the sky, letting it slowly descend into the sea before us. Far off to our left, Thomas replied in kind. For the next hour, we were treated to echoing flames falling from the sky as the Lucky Lady tacked towards our position. Finally, around midnight, we could clearly see the ship as it hove to just offshore and watched as a couple rowboats slowly made their way towards us. Never have any of us been so glad to see rowboats! We would soon be free of this horrible desert land.

Our guide had brought along six other men with him. We loaded all seven up with heavy sacks of seed grain. Their excitement, their reverence with which they lovingly carried the bags, was a wonder to behold. Sandy made sure that they all understood that there was more than ten times this amount to take ashore. For these people, that volume was simply beyond their comprehension. They took four nights to get all the grain unloaded and transported back to their Chamber, though each night, they brought more and more men and women to help. Yes, to them, we seemed as gods.

Our reunion with Captain Bartoloma, Thomas, and Thallia was a happy one. As we climbed aboard that first night, he cheerily called out, "Welcome aboard the Free Lucky Lady!" He emphasized the word 'free.' He went on to explain, "Yes, as of two months ago, I now own the ship outright! I have made enough profit to buy her outright. Now, we're on our own. Believe me, the profits are more than double!" Several of his nearby crew cheered affirmation of their newfound ability to make money. Naturally, he had to explain all the details over tea.

Then, he wanted to know all about these new Moon people. That the desert was inhabited was totally new to him. We gave only a few details stressing just how dangerous the desert sands actually were. He soon forgot about these new people for he could see no trading opportunities at the moment.

While we all longed to share our adventures with Thomas and Thallia as well as hear all about their journey with Isabel and the others, we knew that we couldn't speak freely while here on the boat. Some things are best not overheard by these Sea Prince men, even though we count them as our friends. We settled for hugs and handshakes all around and such news as could be safely spoken.

Chapter 23 Revenge

It was October 1, 559 AH and both cloudy and chilly. A light rain fell on the city of Velona, typical for this time of year. Pacing his throne room, Prince Jamil Alvelardo paid no attention to the weather. No, he had far more important matters on his mind. His long black hair bobbed as he paced about his elegant chambers, his bejeweled crown kept his hair from getting in his face. His advanced scouts reported yesterday that the Centurions were not waiting until spring to assault his city. "Curses on all the other weakling Princes! Not even one of them slowed the invaders down!" he said to his close confident, Hamil, an effeminate man perhaps twenty-five who dressed in richly colored, expensive clothing, compliments of Jamil.

"I know, I know, they are such weaklings, compared to you, Jamil," Hamil replied soothingly. "I'm sure you'll do much better. You're *so* strong!" he added smiling at his liege. He hated to see Jamil in such an angry mood. Hamil hated anger and did everything he could to avoid it, usually by covert means. He bit his lip as he suddenly realized that if his Prince went to war against this huge army, he would surely be killed and there would go Hamil's life. He owed everything to the generosity of Jamil. In return, he gave his Prince his undying loyalty, preferably not the dying part, though.

"So you think I should attack these invaders Hamil?" Jamil asked, wondering if Hamil was implying he was strong enough to conquer them.

Hamil got down on his knees and pleaded, "Oh no, Sire! Please, no. You would certainly be killed or worse. No. I meant you could easily defeat any one of these vile southern men in single combat, but you cannot defeat thousands all by yourself! Besides, we have all seen or heard how effective normal guards are against the Centurions — worthless, totally worthless. It is such a horrible shame that your guards are such impotent fighters — not like yourself. Now it is too late to do anything about that."

Smiling because he had made Hamil plead, Jamil responded, "Yes, you speak truthfully. I could take any one of them. My fighters are so pathetic. Only the Abominations, those accursed Sisters, have any chance of defeating Centurions. Look, they proved it in Zargarb. If only now we had an army of them," he looked longingly into space.

"Yes, Sire, but remember those Abominations sued for peace and have been given the authority to help run the cities. Curses on those idiot Governors!" Hamil consoled.

Standing completely erect to his full height, Prince Jamil declared, "One thing you can count on, Hamil, under no circumstances will I let those Abominations ever get control over Velona. Never. Ever! Women are only good for bearing children and that's all. Leeches, every damn one of them."

"So you have often told me, Sire. I agree. If we can't fight these Centurions, surely you're not going to just give up and surrender?" Hamil finally asked the slanted question he had intended to ask since he entered the throne room this afternoon.

"No, you're right; we can't fight them openly. Over my dead body will I surrender! Never has any Alvelardo ever surrendered, and I don't aim to be the first. My family didn't get control of Velona by being weaklings!" He lowered his voice, "Hamil, there are many other ways to defeat an opponent than open combat, many."

Hamil was just about to ask about what the Prince had in mind when another guard knocked on the door. At once, Hamil walked over to the door, swaying his hips as he walked and with a grand gesture, opened them. "Sorry to disturb you, Prince Jamil. Antonio Po is here to see you. Says it is very urgent and can't wait. Shall I send him in?"

Ah, my nemesis approaches! thought Jamil. "Yes, by all means send him in at once. It will not do to keep the High Priest of Tur waiting, unseemly. Show him in now." Turning to Hamil, he said, "How do I look? Presentable?" Quickly, Hamil adjusted the Prince's robes so that he looked the part of Ruler of Velona and then stepped aside to his usual position at his Prince's side. *It must be something very important to bring Antonio here to see me. He hates my guts.* Coincidentally, these were the same thoughts that Hamil had.

Shortly, the youthful High Priest strode tall into the throne room, purple robes swaying with his swift, sure footsteps. Antonio had a single purpose in this visit, and he fully intended to get it fulfilled. His power depended upon it; he couldn't fail. He'd already seen that all the other High Priests' grand ideas for power grabs fail utterly. He thought that stockpiling supplies and then coming to the rescue of those in need after the city fell had been a perfect plan. Six times now, he'd seen that tactic fail. "So glad that you can see me, Prince Jamil," he began courteously. He had to keep his temper or all would fail.

"Let me begin by asking if the rumors are true — that the Centurions aren't waiting out the winter before they attack Velona?" He already knew the answer. Actually, that was what had driven him to seek this audience. He had to act and act swiftly.

"Since you and I share power over Velona," Prince Jamil replied courteously, he could afford to be magnanimous at the moment, "I'll answer you honestly. Yes, the latest word from my scouts suggests — no affirms — that we're going to be attacked soon, probably within three months. Why do you ask?"

"Our people are very, very worried, Prince Jamil. They have heard about the fall of the other cities and the loss of so many thousands of lives. Naturally, all men of age are, how shall I put this, worried and scared that soon they're going to be ordered to fight to the death to defend Velona. Now don't take this the wrong way, I'm sure that all are completely loyal to you, Sire. Yet the statistics from the other six cities are in no way remotely encouraging — so many young men dead and for nothing. Each city fell rapidly. From my pulpit, I can see that the morale among the men in Velona is now very low indeed. I don't think I need to elaborate what that would mean to you should you call upon them to defend Velona." *There I've said it politely. How will he respond?*

Jamil knew he was on thin ground here so he replied honestly, hoping to give no edge to his bitter enemy. "Yes, I'm not blind. It is obvious that, should I call upon every able-bodied man to arm up and go off to fight for Velona, the result would be even less favorable than it has been with the other six cities. Rest assured, Antonio, I have no plans for openly fighting against these Centurions with force of arms at the moment."

Perfect! Here goes everything. Antonio Po nodded and said, "Ah, both excellent and wise, Prince Jamil. My compliments. If you aren't going to fight these invaders directly as the other Princes have done, surely you aren't just going to surrender and give up, correct?"

Jamil chuckled. *He's shrewd, this young priest.* "No, I have no intention of surrendering and giving up, if that is what you are worried about."

Antonio feigned a show of relief, but he long suspected that Jamil would never do any such thing, for that would imply an immediate power shift over to the Church of Tur, something Po could not ever fathoming Jamil doing — yielding the city power to the Church. Now Po was ready to spring his plan. "Thank you, Jamil. No, I'm glad that you're not. On this point, you and I think alike. I don't believe open combat against the invaders would be remotely wise nor would a total capitulation to their rule. On this, you and I completely agree. Do you realize that this is perhaps the first time we are united in our views?"

That brought a smile to Jamil's face. "True, Antonio. Very true."

"Then, I offer you a gift, Jamil. Until this confrontation is over, may we join our forces together to meet this common foe? You do realize that if we don't do something different and vastly more effective than the other Princes have done, then the Abominations are going to end up in charge here in Velona just as they are now in the other sectors? I don't know about you, but I can't tolerate this ever happening here! Over my dead body will those Abominations ever gain control here in Velona!" He said this with passion and a vengeance, knowing that it would strike a nerve with the Prince. He was not mistaken.

"Funny that you should mention those Abominations, I was just saying nearly the very same thing to Hamil here just before you came! We are in complete agreement on this point as well, Antonio. So what are you suggesting we do?"

Got him! Antonio concealed his excitement over his complete victory over Jamil and said, "Let us put the combined forces of the Church and the Royal Throne together. I'm sure that we can work together to find another way, don't you agree? Together, we are stronger than if we worked alone. I feel confident that together we can find a way to put an end to these invaders once and for all time."

"You are right, Antonio. Hamil, fetch us my best wine. I see that Antonio and I have much to discuss! Come, let us go into my dining room were we may sit as equals and share our ideas." Antonio smiled; this encounter had gone even better than he had hoped. He had calculated the Prince was desperate for effective ideas, and he assumed that he was correct.

For the next hour, the two men sat sipping wine and tossing out various ideas, none of which were practical. Finally, when Antonio thought that the Prince had run completely out of ideas, he suggested, "Sire, do you still have that plague ship in quarantine off that remote island?"

"Eureka, Antonio! You have just given me an idea on how to kill thousands of Centurions! Yes, it is still there. Wise of me to keep the ship intact. I know your father condemned me for doing it, but I said there might come a day. Sure enough, this is the day. What about this, Antonio? Suppose that when the thousands of invaders finally march into the city, that plague ship is docked here. Within a few weeks, surely vast numbers of the Centurions will be dead from the plague! When they are so terribly weak, we can then attack and drive them into the sea for Tur to eat."

"Brilliant! What about the hundred thousand folks who live here, not to mention us as well? What is to prevent us from getting the plague as well? Should we not evacuate the city?"

"Yes, yes of course. We can't leave our men who could fight here to die along with the enemy. Nor can we leave their families here to die as well. They'd end up deserting and trying to rescue their loved ones. Then the plague would spread everywhere. No, Antonio, we must evacuate the entire city, leaving it all for the Centurions alone."

"Ah, the people will praise you for sparing their lives and the lives of all their young men! But where can we put a hundred thousand people? How can we house them and feed them until new trading is fully operational?"

"I can order that all outlying towns and villages are to double in size, spreading Velona's people uniformly across our sector. I'm sure we can create an effective, organized migration, if only we can, as you point out, feed them until trade is re-established properly."

"Ah, the Church of Tur can assist here. We have the means to feed them for say a month at the moment. If certain things occur, we can even supply them for far longer. It will take great planning to get the supplies to the people at the right time and place. Coordination."

"Brilliant! Think of what we can achieve here, Antonio. In a few months, we shall slay thousands of Centurions unlike all the other Princes combined. We shall mete out our revenge, make them wish they had never heard of the Sea Princes! When they are at their weakest, we shall sweep down upon them with the wrath of Tur behind us. We shall drive them from our lands and then from the other cities. Then, all the other sectors will know our might. We shall unite all the Sea Princes under our rule! Then we can deal with these Abominations at our leisure. We'll have those women come crawling at our feet begging for mercy, and we'll show none!"

Both men laughed loudly. Neither could have pulled this off without the other's aid. For the first time ever in the Lands of the Sea Princes did the

Church of Tur and the Prince work together instead of opposing each other. Together, they would defeat the Centurion invaders.

Later Antonio Po walked home with light steps, convinced that in a few short months, surely by spring, he, Antonio Po, would be the supreme religious leader of all the Sea Princes. The invaders from the south and the Sisterhood Abominations, who he thought had played some role in his father's execution, would be eliminated. He was also convinced that he could now completely control Prince Jamil.

After the High Priest had left, Prince Jamil said "Hamil, see how perfectly I played that fool of a priest? I got him to reveal just how much food and supplies he has been secreting away, though I already had a good idea of it anyway. I got him to bring up the plague ship without my having to suggest it. If anything goes wrong, I can always say that it was Antonio who first suggested we use the plague."

Hamil's mouth opened wide, and he stared in awe and wonder at his Prince. "This — this was your plan all along?"

"Yes, but I just needed the right opportunity to come along. I figured it might. However, had Antonio not come today, I had other ways of procuring his complete support. So, Hamil, have you learned anything today?"

Both men snickered. Hamil added, "Won't it take considerable time to move Velona's people? Surely, some will protest and refuse to leave. What about the Sisterhood? Won't they give us trouble once they learn what we are doing?"

"Months, yes. The people will be told that a great sickness shall befall Velona. We can count on our High Priest to spread that word. People will believe the Church. I have plans for the Sisterhood. They must be kept busy, thinking that they are helping. Then, when the time is ripe, the Sisterhood will be history." He made a sweeping cutting motion across his neck. Both men laughed loud and long and then they retired to the royal bedroom.

Chapter 24 The Appian Way

Since we ended up parked here offshore for four days and nights transferring the grain to the Moon people, we asked Captain Bartoloma about how the war against the Centurions was going. The news, though not unexpected, was bad. All the cities had now fallen; Velona alone stood against the invaders. "But the Prince has a plan. It is being executed even as we sit here. Perhaps, we might even catch a glimpse of it in action when we head back." He couldn't have hoped for a more attentive audience. We insisted he tell us all about it.

In essence, the Prince, who had the benefit of watching the six other cities and their attempts at defense fail, had come up with a clever, diabolical plan. From our past encounters with the Prince, we knew that he would be hard pressed to put up an actual fight; he was not that kind of a man. Instead, over time, he slowly moved every citizen out of Velona and into the numerous northern towns and villages, giving each family their choice of location. In the last few months, all the outlying towns had more than tripled their populations, some greatly in excess of that. The Prince simply rerouted all of the normal overland commerce lines. Further, he had numerous small ports constructed all along his coastline, where only one or two ships could dock for a brief time, unloading and loading cargo. He intended to play a gigantic shell game with the Centurions, who would never know where any given ship would actually dock. Even so, the ship would only be docked for a couple days at most before all its cargo disappeared into the interior of the land.

This mass evacuation of the entire city had taken well over three months to accomplish even with the assistance of the Sisterhood, who had already made a bargain with the Prince, providing security for overland shipments. Now the Centurion army was approaching the edge of the abandoned city. Within a week, the Prince fully expected Velona to be completely occupied by the Centurion army. Their new Governor would have no one to govern. What the Prince didn't know was that fully three-quarters of the entire Centurion army was now encircling Velona! He had no idea of the total impact of his diabolical scheme. No one did.

"For the longest time," Captain Bartoloma continued, "I couldn't see why he would abandon the city. True, the High Priest claimed that they were abandoning the city because of sickness. People seemed to accept their word, though many protested. With the Prince and the Church both abandoning Velona, none cared to risk staying behind. Also, I figure eventually, the invaders will figure out his port shell game or simply fan out and enter every city in our land. I realized that the Prince would still have all of his vast wealth with him. The Church, too, for that matter. Now our Prince has become the wealthiest of all the Seven Sea Princes. I always say, follow the money trail."

This seemed to fit our ideas of how this Prince would think and operate. I hesitated; surely the Prince would seek retribution somehow. Never in a direct confrontation, for he had not the stomach for that. Bartoloma continued, "As we were leaving the docks at Velona for the last time on our way here, I heard the final orders being given." Here he lowered his voice to a whisper. "He's called for the Death Ship! As soon as I heard that, suddenly it all made sense to me!"

"What is the Death Ship?" I asked unable to contain my curiosity for even a moment.

"A year ago, Captain Diggory, a known cheat and scoundrel, took on an illegal cargo. Tur heard of his action and brought down his wrath upon that ship. Well, that's assuming you believe in Tur. While at sea, everyone on board got the plague and died a horrible death. When the ship was long overdue, the Prince sent out searchers to find her. The crew that found her told many tales of the horrid facial expressions on the dead men's faces. It was enough to scare the heck out of me, anyway. Besides, all those that originally found her also came down with the plague. The Prince ordered the ship to be quarantined on a deserted island not too far from that chain of islands you saw there at the Narrows. I know that the Church called for its destruction by fire, but now I see that the Prince was indeed farsighted. Anyway, as we left port, the Prince ordered the Swallow to tow the ship into dock in Velona and leave it parked there; it's the sole ship in port now. He's planning to give the Plague of Tur to the invaders!"

We all sat horrified and speechless for a moment. "I think now that his plan is that once all of the invaders have died from the plague, we will retake our city back intact," he added, confident of the success of a brilliant plan.

Sarah Jane was the first to find her voice, "Plague is a difficult thing to control. Do your people have the means to cure someone who has contracted the plague?"

"Er, no. If one gets it, one dies," he explained. "Pretty simple, actually, but I see your point. If the enemy all die of the plague, what is to prevent our people from encountering the same fate when we go to reclaim the city?"

Simon interjected, "Trial and error. I'll wager he plans to send in a few men and see if they die. If so, he waits another month and sends in another bunch. Eventually, when a bunch doesn't perish from the plague, he'll send in more. Diabolical plan. The only flaw is once the plague gets started, what's to keep it from spreading to all the outlying towns and villages?"

"That's one reason I'm staying at sea around here. Being a free Captain, I can now pick and choose my cargo and destinations. The Lucky Lady will not go within fifty miles of Velona until it is proven more than safe!" he declared.

Thomas added, "That presents a travel problem for us, Bethany. By the time we can get back to Velona or anywhere around there, the plague will have probably already started. It is January and the ice prevents any attempt at sailing back to Calgary until next April at the earliest. I assume you don't want to hole up somewhere until spring. However, Thallia and I have had a lot of time to try to figure out something that we can try. We think that the smartest thing to do to get home is to land at one of the middle cities, head north to the

Appian Way, and see if we can find a way across the mountains. It isn't going to be safe for us to try to cross the outlying lands around Velona. The Prince surely will have all paths carefully and closely monitored. You know we aren't welcome there." He alluded to the visit there last year, where he'd accidentally killed their High Priest causing us to make a rapid exit overland.

Still shaking her head in disgust, Sarah Jane commented, "Unleashing the plague. God, I hope he hasn't signed the death warrants for all your people. The plague doesn't care whom it strikes, friend or foe. I fear much ill will come from this, Captain Bartoloma, much ill indeed. Do all the other people in the outlying villages know that he is unleashing the plague?"

He shrugged, "Don't know. Eventually, they'll find out, though. You think that the plague will spread — spread everywhere?"

"That's what the plagues usually do. That's why it is called the plague, silly," she confirmed. The Captain no longer looked upon this plan as so ingenious. I immediately picked up his thoughts — he was fairly screaming them. "What's going to happen to my girlfriend back on shore? Can I get her out to my ship in time?"

Cleverly, I asked, "Do you have anyone on shore who you would like evacuated before it is too late?" He brightened up.

"You must be reading my mind," he joked. "Yes, I have a girlfriend. I don't know if she would agree to leave her family behind. Nor do I know if she would agree to spend her days on board the Lucky Lady. I've not actually proposed to her yet, mind you, but we're good friends. Still," his voice died away as he began thinking hard about his choices.

Later that night after the last of the Moon people left with their grain sacks and we all went below to our makeshift cabins in the hold, I asked Thomas about his plans to cross the Appian Way. "It is or was my understanding that no known way exists to cross these mountains. Surely, the winter snow and ice would make such passage even harder if not impossible."

To my surprise, Thallia winked at me, shook her head, and gurgled what had to be a "No."

Thomas whispered softly, "What I just said was for public consumption. No, there is no known way to cross the Appian Way, especially in winter. What we're going to do is head north to the Appian Way and then take the same route that we followed when I got Isabel safely home. We will ride across the lands to the Narrows before heading north. We have made good friends with Count Bassilica d'Grange there, you know the father of that young boy you met on our way to Velona when we had to spend a couple days repairing the damage from the passage through the Narrows. The Count has built a huge stone fortress, the likes of which no one has ever seen. That's one fortress that will not easily fall to the Centurions, especially since we are now backing him up. Already, we have shipped a large supply of grain and dried meats. They can withstand a very lengthy siege if it comes to that. You will see. I don't trust anyone in the Sea Princes any farther than I can see them. What I said up on deck is what we all need to continue to say in public. It will even seem that is what we are in fact doing just before we disappear off their maps, so to speak. Actually, it was Thallia's idea. She came up with it. I think she is even more paranoid than I am."

"Way to go, Thallia," Roy cheered. We congratulated her and she smiled confident of her abilities.

Thomas then added, "Besides, Thallia and I are going to get married just as soon as we get safely back to Calgary." Wow. We all knew that they were in love — but marriage. Thus ensued another, even larger, round of praise, congratulations, and well-wishing. *Marriage*, I thought, *marriage. A normal life. I had forgotten all about such things for over a year now. Gosh, that sure sounds wonderful*! I spied Roy looking intently at me; I smiled and looked at him just as intently. Okay, I could have read his mind, his thoughts, but I didn't.

Those four days of unloading passed slowly. Yes, we were up most of the night unloading grain — a tedious process of un-crating the shipping boxes, stowing the sacks into the two small row boats, rowing ashore, handing them to the Moon people, rowing back to the Lucky Lady, and then waiting for quite some time until they returned for another load. Boring, true. It was terribly difficult to stay awake. Our body's built-in day-night rhythms quickly readjusted from the many weeks of reverse operations, while we had crossed the Red Desert, traveling at night, sleeping by day. I was amazed to see just how fast my body firmly readjusted itself to the world. Finally, the last of the four tons of seed grain had been unloaded, and we could be on our way back to the land of the Seven Sea Princes.

During this time, because of the close quarters shipboard, we couldn't talk freely. Conversations were light and confined to the simple pleasures of life. Once we returned having deposited the last sack and said farewell to these people, Captain Bartoloma quickly set sail tacking north by east and then north by west, taking advantage of the current winds. Late that night, I fell asleep in Roy's arms feeling the familiar heaving and pitching of the ship beneath me. I found it comforting and relaxing, but more importantly, we were heading towards home.

The next day, I discovered Thomas still didn't have his sea legs. He was ill once more, though not as bad, for he had brought a number of herbs along with him this time, which helped him mostly overcome this bout of seasickness. Thallia constantly looked after him. Even though this was her first trip on the high seas, she took to the travel like a natural. Perhaps it was in the blood of all these Sea Prince people, an inherited thing.

Two days later, we hove to just south of Velona. "Come have a look," Captain Bartoloma called to us, and we all scampered on deck. "There lies Velona, deserted. If you look carefully, those tiny things are the approaching Centurions, just east of the city. Look over there to the west near the coastline." I saw two ships, one similar to the Lucky Lady with her sails white against the clear blue skyline. Behind her bare-masted came another ship. "It's being towed. That's the Il'Bonita, the Plague Ship, that's being towed. I wouldn't give a dull copper for the crew that's doing the towing, though. I'll wager they all come down with the plague. There isn't enough money in all the Prince's coffers that would entice me or my crew to haul that vessel into Velona!" Several crew members nearby catcalled their complete agreement with his statement.

All I could say was, "So that's the Plague Ship."

"Aye, and no closer do we come. Hard tack to starboard!" came his orders, and the ship now turned due east. He added for my benefit, "Now the winds are at our back; we will make good time heading for Pieta, but I worry that the winds may carry the plague to us. Is that possible or do I worry too much?"

Sarah Jane answered for me, "Superstition. Plague is not carried on the winds. I'm certain of that. You need to have some kind of direct contact. We're safe enough out here, but please don't get us any closer!"

We leaned on the guardrail, each lost in our own thoughts. I stared at the only barely visible shapes that must be the Centurion army advancing in their slow, methodical way, building a straight brick roadway into Velona. *Do they know what lies ahead for them?* I wondered. Roy broke in on my musing, "Say, that looks like an awfully large number of them. I can't really tell for sure from so great a distance, but it sure looks like a large army. Does it to you?" I looked again.

"By golly, Roy, you are right. For us to see much of anything this far away, they must be both large in numbers and close together. I'll bet they have brought every available soldier to this last battle, perhaps in an attempt to finish conquering the Sea Princes in short order. This bodes ill for the Greenway, because I'll bet anything that we are next in their conquering plans!"

"As evil as this sounds, Bethany, this may be a terrific break that the Greenway is about to get. If the plague takes hold in Velona, the Centurion army will surely be greatly reduced in numbers. If we are lucky, they'll not be strong enough to wage war on us for quite some time! I find myself rooting for the plague. Does that make me evil?"

"No, Roy, just practical. As much as I respect life, we haven't found any means to force them to stop their expansionist plans on the Greenway. I guess we take what aid we can as we can. Perhaps, the plague will do what we could not. I just hope that the innocent people of the land don't get it. Once a plague gets rolling, it is terribly hard to stop it. We've been taught that the plague has been known to wipe out every single person in an entire village, leaving it a ghost town."

"When we get back, do you suppose that we should adopt some new rules like allow no one into the Greenway who comes from the south to avoid any chance of accidental spread of the plague into our lands?" Roy asked.

"Eureka, Roy!" I exclaimed. He looked at me with a startled look, a non-comprehending stare. So I said formally, "Allow no one in who comes from the south. Wash your feet before entering. Do not walk on the red glow. Get it?"

He still didn't, so I elaborated. "The Moon people and their Code. That code is nothing more than some rules to be slavishly followed to avoid disaster. Someone long ago, probably in response to that great calamity that befell them — someone set down a set of guidelines to be followed to minimize future problems. Over time, it has become a Code of Conduct and even a religion!"

Now he understood. I could see recognition in his eyes. "Ah, now that you point it out, why yes, it does sound like a set of rules to be followed to minimize bad things happening. Bethany, you are a genius!" He gave me a loving hug. I reciprocated willingly.

"Hey, look at all the ships!" Raphael exclaimed breaking in on us. We looked up and saw a dozen ships sailing along similar routes as ours, some coming our way, some behind and ahead of us.

Almost in unison, Roy and I had the same thought, "This will never do!" We chuckled at our mutual words, and I volunteered to speak to the Captain who was manning the tiller.

"Captain, can we perhaps sail back out into the middle of the Med Sea? We want to enter Pieta without everyone knowing that we're arriving. With all these ships, everyone will know our every move, especially the Centurions. We might meet with a surprise attack when we finally dock."

"Aye, lass, I was thinking the very same thing." He quickly gave orders to change course, heading back out into the middle of the sea. We watched as the ships slowly fell away from us until an hour later, no ships could be seen anywhere on the horizon.

"Without being able to see the land," I inquired in a sudden panic, "will you know where to sail? We don't want to end up in Zargarb."

"That's why I'm the Captain. I've a good sense of speed and direction. I won't need to see land until we get close to Pieta, but there is a tiny two-ship port town about ten miles west of Pieta, where we sometimes lay up for repairs. If I left you off there, hardly anyone would know about it. Might not be any Centurions there. How's that sound?"

"Captain, that sounds just perfect!" I replied greatly relieved, especially without having to explain why we so desperately wanted to avoid all contact with the Centurions.

"It'll take about a week, give or take a few days, to make Pieta," he announced. "So relax and enjoy yourselves." After I relayed the news, that is exactly what we all did. The first order of business was a dip into the Med Sea, clothes and all. For us, this was a way, way overdue bath. The mid-January waters were still slightly warm, especially if you swam around to stay warm. So grimy was I, that I hardly noticed the cold.

We spent more time washing our clothes, mending them, and reorganizing our packs, which, by now, had become quite light. We certainly would need to get supplies, along with some horses once we made landfall. Miraculously, we still had a good deal of money left and all the gems that Alabaster had given us for emergencies. We felt confident we could acquire what we would need for this last leg of our journey. All this busy work occupied but one day. The remaining seven seemed to drag on endlessly! We were a Circle of Action, temporarily at sea with nothing to do, and, because of our need for secrecy, couldn't talk freely. To fight the utter boredom, we attempted to learn as much about sailing these ships as the good captain would teach.

Finally, the boat tacked hard to port, and I knew we must be close to our goal. I and everyone else, for that matter, were more than ready to set foot on land once more, to be free to move around on our own determinism without fear of poisoning. Time seemed to move slower and slower as the few hours passed, while the Lucky Lady tacked into the small port town. Indeed, I counted only fifty homes cradled close to the sea along with the sole dock, which ran out some fifty feet from the shore in such a way that one ship could be docked on either side. Our earlier months in this Land of the Sea Princes had been the warm summer time. Now, a light dusting of snow covered the land and the leaves were gone. Save for the sea, the sights reminded me of my home back in the Greenway. Okay, by now, I was really getting homesick; I think that we all were.

Slowly the Lucky Lady slid alongside the dock, and two dockhands tossed large ropes onto her deck. Her crew fastened them securely and then seven more ropes, as slowly the ship was snugged up tight to the dock. Once a gangplank was extended, we said our farewells and thank you's to the crew and Captain Bartoloma, and the eight of us headed down the walkway into the town.

The first order of business was to arrange a room for the night. Next came warmer clothing and then horses and supplies. However, in such a small town, all of our needs could not be met. The innkeeper, Randolfo, a burly man with a bushy beard and fairly long hair reminded me of a black bear. He was an astute observer. In his slow drawl, he said, "We don't often get many visitors arriving seaward, if you take my meaning. Of course, in Pieta proper, you could get all you need, but I reckon that you'll not be wanting to head just that way or why would you land here, eh?" He winked knowingly at us. "I know where you can get a few warm coats and one horse, not enough mind you, but with a few blankets, you'll mange. It's not really all that cold outside. If you take the north road out of here tomorrow, it connects to several small towns like ours here. You ought to be able to pick up more horses and coats along the way."

Two days later and forty miles inland, we had accumulated nine horses, winter gear for all, and enough grain and dried food to last us for several weeks. We saw no Centurions, but we thought we spied at least two Sisters guarding a small convoy of wagons heading south toward Pieta. Purposely, we made no contact with them. Thus, now fully equipped, we rode northward in earnest.

Though none of us really knew the way, Thomas led, picking out likely gullies to travel. It was a no-brainer. We needed to just go far enough north until we could climb out of these twisting hills and gullies onto the vast foothills of the Appian Way, the Paese di Dio, some thirty miles deep and impossible to miss. It took us a week to reach it, having headed up a dead end gully and forced to backtrack twice. During this time, we related all that had happened to us since Thomas and Thallia had left us to take Isabel home to the Greenway. True, Sandy had remained in telepathic contact with Thomas, but could only relay the most basic events. Now, we had all the time we could want to discuss everything in detail. Thomas had many questions, because many things raised his curiosity to a peak, particularly our journey across the Southland savannahs and the many strange animals there.

When the two were completely brought up to date, it was their turn to tell us about their adventures. For the most part, it was uneventful. Quickly they had reached the Paese di Dio proper. Then, it was a straight ride nearly due west, day after day, along the pass of the gods. After a few days, everyone relaxed, as the spectacular beauty and serenity of this unique land seeped into their very being. Even Isabel cheered up as she got more and more used to being active once more. However, as they neared each perpendicular to the major cities, a few Sisters would head down into the hills and gullies in search of supplies. Invariably, they returned not only with more food and fodder, but also with more Sisters, who desired to accept our offer of a new land and a new life. "By the time that we reached the end of the Paese di Dio," Thomas exclaimed, "we had fifty-five Sisters with us beyond our original party. Can you believe that?"

Then came the hardest part of the journey, crossing the extremely rocky and rugged western edge of the land where the Appian Way range lowered into the sea, separating the Greenway from the Sea Princes. "For most of the time, we had to lead the horses on foot; it was that rough! Finally, we ran into some of the Count's men, who were on watch duty. Once they had communicated our presence to the Count, he came out to meet us. Actually, he's a rather nice fellow, if you ask me. He led us by some devious routes to his fortress — some easy-to-ride paths that are all but hidden to normal eyes. I aim to retrace that path and so enter the Greenway. Besides, Raphael, you have just got see his stone fortress. It is huge and perched high atop a craggy, stony hilltop. Its walls are ten feet thick — solid stone, I believe. We've given him enough food and supplies now so he could hold off an army of Centurions for at least six months with no outside aid! If we come to his aid if he is besieged, he can possibly hold them off entirely. There really is not any other way through to the Greenway save through his valley. The fortress overlooks the valley, so any attempt to bypass it would be disastrous on the Centurion foot-soldiers."

By late November, Thomas finally had led his large party into the snow-filled streets of Calgary. "Alabaster gave them all a very warm welcome, allowing all the women to winter in his complex. He's promised that come spring, when the land becomes warm and green once more, we druwids will accompany those that want to move deeper into the more rural settings and help them get settled. You know, he cried when he saw Isabel and they hugged for a long time." Thallia nodded emphatically that this was true.

He explained that he had to stay and act as interpreter for the women for a time, as both sides rapidly picked up the basics of each other's language. "When your message for grain and a rescue came through, I was more than ready to head back to help."

Thallia added in her coarse speech, "Me too." We all picked up her intention, more so than her words.

"Well, I'm glad both of you came," I declared. "Now we ought to have a simple, nice ride home. What can possibly go wrong up here where no one comes?" I remembered what the Sister Florencia had said, "After spending a month up here, you become totally serene and completely at peace with yourself." I was looking forward to this.

I'll never forget riding up out of that last gully and onto the Paese di Dio. An unblemished sea of white snow lay before us. The snow-capped range rose high to the north, contrasting sharply with the deep blue sky. Unspeaking, we paused for some time to take in this incredible view. It was almost a sacrilege to ride out onto this plain, marking up the six-inch cover of snow with our passage. There are places of incredible beauty and places where Nature is most holy. This was one of those.

This first day, we headed due north until we were within a few miles of the Appian Way mountains proper. Then, we turned westward, expecting to ride nearly due west for hundreds of miles. For twenty days or about three hundred-fifty miles, we rode in the still silence of the Paese di Dio, seeing no other travelers. Six inches of unspoiled snow covered the gently rolling land. Our horse tracks seemed like a wound in the land, trailing far off into the distance behind us. Slowly, complete serenity seeped into and filled our hearts and minds. I was at peace with Nature and the universe.

On the twentieth day, we were somewhere between Barcella and Velona, when we spied something grey up and to our right in a mountain pass. It's hard to say who saw it first, as we eight were thinking and moving as one unit, such was the mood this land generated within us. There was no doubt that a figure was looking down at us, watching our every move. However, the same moment that we spied the form, it darted quickly behind some rocks out of view.

Now, had the figure merely waved, we would have waved back and continued on our way, wondering at most what shepherd chose to live way up here and perhaps even admiring him or her for their choice. It didn't wave; it chose to hide instead. That sounded the alarm for us; we had seen too much treachery to let this go unnoticed. Roy's comment pretty well summed it up for us, "That's not very friendly — more like a spy. Who could be spying on us way up here?" Of course, we just had to know the answer to that question.

For the first time in nearly three weeks, we abruptly altered our direction, now heading toward the Appian Way proper, which lay just a couple miles from us. In fact, we made for the location among the boulder-strewn pass where we had seen the form watching us. As we neared the pass, the sides of the mountain rose steeply on either side forming a quickly narrowing pass.

Roy and Thomas slowly maneuvered to the front — one to protect, one to scout. Both halted and dismounted close to the boulder behind which we guessed that the person had hidden. Their feet sank into about a foot of snow. For a moment neither said a word; the rest of us cautiously moved up behind their horses and dismounted as well. "What's up?" I asked, my words, though not loud, seemed very shrill and piercing in this land of nearly complete silence.

Roy whispered, "Come have a look." A bit of mystery or surprise was in his tone. I trudged to his side, taking deep steps in the snow.

"What *is* this?" I managed to say as I looked at the footprints our watcher had left in the snow. The others crowded around me for a look; several gasped. There clearly in the virgin snow were footprints left by the watcher, only these prints were unusual. Perhaps 'unusual' is not quite the right word, mysterious, weird, strange — all might be a better description. Clearly, our observer had two feet, left and right — one could tell from the curvatures. Yet the shape and size were foreign. Each footprint was twice the size of ours, as if made by some giant, assuming that the body was proportional to the feet. Size was not all that was wrong with these prints. The heel was very, very slender, perhaps a fifth of the width of the front, whereas with our feet, the heel is about half as wide as the toe area. That is to say, the toe area was enormous compared to the heel area. Besides this, the person was not wearing boots or any protective cover, for we could distinctly see the toes — all three of them — all equally sized and spaced across the front of the foot.

"Conclusions, Thomas?" I inquired, completely baffled at what I was seeing. I hoped our Loremaster could shed some light on these prints.

"Ah, ah, well, actually, I have no idea what this is," he finally managed to utter. "What kind of a creature is this? No animal I have ever seen or heard tell of leaves prints like this!"

"Maybe it's wearing some strange boots," offered Sandy in an attempt to make some sense of what we were seeing. "There has to be a logical explanation," her voice trailed off into silence.

"Looks like he moved behind this boulder and then climbed up those rocks over there," Roy finally said. "Let me move ahead a bit and see if I can pick up the trail in the snow. If he went further up the pass, I should be able to find these prints up there a ways. You keep a sharp look out. Watch my back." We agreed, but he knew without asking that was precisely what we'd have done without his even asking. We were a team. I held his horse's reins as Roy took effort-fill steps on up this narrow pass through the deep snow. Not only was the path heading steeply upwards, but also the foot of snow cover made each step precarious to take. He slipped and slid several times as he moved out ahead of us.

Shortly, Roy announced, "Yes! More tracks. He went this way."

Simultaneously, Sandy cried out, "Up there! There he is!" Indeed, we all caught a fleeting glimpse of the greyish form again darting behind some tall outcropping further on up this very pass some two hundred feet farther up from Roy's position. Slipping, sliding, and leading the horses, we managed to follow Roy, who continued his exploration of the pass ahead. Over the course of the next effort-filled hour, we continued to catch brief fleeting glimpses of our watcher, who always managed to stay several hundred feet ahead of us.

The very strenuous exertion of climbing a steeply rising path half buried in snow caused all to gasp and pant for breath in this thin air. It was arduous going, but if he could do it, so could we, at least that was my determined opinion. After that hour, we just had to take a break to catch our breath and cool down. I was sweating; my underclothes, soaked. Sarah Jane cautioned us, "Hey, I'm really working up a sweat here. This isn't good. It is deadly to be wet and outside in the cold of winter. When we stop, we're going to have to change into dryer clothing or risk hypothermia."

"Well, let's not stop," came Roy's reaction. "I've got to catch up with this guy and see what the heck is going on! But I need to catch my breath too. This is one heck of a steep climb, and the snow is making it really, really difficult. This guy seems to be very agile and always ahead of us, like he isn't plowing through the snow somehow." Roy was more than a little baffled — an hour, and we still had not appreciably closed the distance between us and him.

"Wow, look at the view behind us!" I announced, having looked back at the way we had come to better hear Sarah Jane. Easily, we had climbed over a thousand feet. Far off in the distance, we could see the marks of our passing in the snow, and where we had veered off our westerly course heading northward into this pass. The scene was remarkably beautiful, but unfortunately, I was starting to be chilled from the damp clothes.

The reality of our folly began to sink in — the horses had barely been able to climb the pass, even with our leading and pulling them. The ever deepening snow made their footsteps even more treacherous than ours; horses don't recover as easily from a slip as do people. With every step, we risked breaking a horse's leg or worse. I realized that going back down would be even more dangerous than going up! Compounding matters, the sun would be setting in about an hour; the shadows already were quite long. Here in this narrow pass, darkness had already begun descending, and we were wet. To make matters even worse, Thomas pointed out the dark cloudbank for to the south that was slowly moving our way; tonight more snow was likely. We had to find shelter out here where there was none!

Reflecting back, at the time, I didn't think too much about the fact that, as I realized all this, the others did likewise. Up here on the Paese di Dio, over the last twenty-some days, we had all become attuned to each other's thoughts. In fact, this was quite remarkable.

Thallia looked slightly afraid and gurgled as best she could, "Shelter!" Though garbled, we understood her and agreed. I don't think any of our faces reflected any sense of confidence back towards her, which only added to her worries.

In situations like this, a Loremaster shines. Immediately, Thomas took charge, "Gang, I must find us some shelter fast. You hang on to our horses,

516

and Roy and I'll see what we can find. You are right. We shouldn't try to go back down this late in the day. Don't worry so, Thallia. I'll find us somewhere warm to camp for the night. Trust me." She managed a faint smile in spite of her fears. To my amazement, both he and Roy headed on up the pass, following the watcher we had been following. I sensed Thomas's reasoning. The watcher too would have to find shelter and soon. Thus, it made sense that the watcher had some place to camp fairly nearby. There was not much light left by which to travel.

"Stomp your feet," Sarah Jane said quietly, as my teeth started involuntarily chattering from the cold. Immediately, we all followed her lead. We had to stay warm!

Meanwhile, Roy and Thomas climbed up and soon disappeared around a bend, leaving us wondering how they were doing. It was more than a bit nerve-wracking to have them completely out of my sight like this, but we knew we had mental contact when we needed it. I felt sorry for the "headers" who did not have this sense; in situations like this, they must really get spooked.

A few minutes later, Roy's head reappeared, and he yelled for us to climb on up to where they were. At least, it gave us something to do; we were on the move once more, expending lots of effort to get ourselves and the horses up this slippery, steep pass. I felt my circulation flowing again and began to warm up. Ten minutes later, we came tramping and stamping around the bend. We saw the two men scampering far ahead of us searching among the boulders. Spying our arrival, Roy scampered down to explain.

"This bend is fortuitous because it offers shelter from the wind, as it goes roughly east-west and blocks all winds from the south. What has us baffled is that our watcher's footprints came right up the middle here and on up to that boulder where Thomas is at and then they just disappear completely. We've searched several hundred feet in all directions. Nothing. Unless this person sprouted wings, something is going on. Thomas thinks there must be some shelter around here, and he is looking for it. Come on up to the rock." We continued our trudging, but it was nearly full dark in this valley, which was cut off from the world by tall, craggy peaks rising on all sides save on up eastward.

"Eureka!" exclaimed Thomas jubilantly. "Come look at this." Leaving the horses, we all felt our way on upwards to where he was standing. When we were all present, he said, "Look at this boulder and look at the mountainside behind it. What do you see?" I was about to say, "Thomas, this is not the time for a lesson," when I saw something. Around the edge of the boulder where it contacted the mountain side, the snow had melted. Something warm had to be behind this boulder! "Come on, every one; help me push this boulder out of the way. Let's see what is behind it." The boulder was about ten feet tall and must have weight a ton, but we put our backs to it and pushed. Surprisingly, it rolled to one side easily, as if it had been somehow designed to move in just such a fashion. A deep black hole appeared behind it; relatively warm air rushed out onto our faces.

A druwid is never without light. In unison, we seven conjured our "blue lights," moving them into the opening. We looked into a deep chamber, a cavern tall enough for even our horses to enter. "Hello?" I called out, remembering that most likely our watcher had somehow ducked into this very chamber. We listened to my echo and guessed that this was one big underground cavern indeed. "Well done, Thomas! Let's get inside. It looks deserted to me," I suggested. Roy went first to protect us all from what might be inside. Soon he gave the all clear sign, and one by one, we entered, leading the horses.

Once everyone was inside the chamber, the guys rolled the boulder back into place, while pointing out to us that it had actual hand holds cut into the rock here on the inside. Then, I remembered the gift that the High Priestess had given me, the Eternal Light. I dug through my sacks and produced it. One switch pressed and a brilliant light illuminated all in a hundred feet in whatever direction I pointed it. Slowly, I panned it all around us. The cavern must be enormous for I saw no signs of back walls. However, Thomas had me point the light toward the ground in front of us. We all saw the unmistakable outline left by wet feet! Our watcher certainly had entered here. The path headed straight into the chamber in a straight line. So naturally, we followed them for a bit.

"Wait a minute," I called out. "We ought to set up camp and systematically explore. We don't know how big this cavern actually is or if it's occupied. We don't want to get surprised or worse." Quickly, some twenty feet from the entrance, we setup camp. Within a few minutes, we had the horses unsaddled, watered, and fed. We had brought some charcoal to use sparingly to cook at least one hot meal a day. We girls set to work on cooking dinner. Once the charcoal was going well and dinner started, we took turns changing our wet underclothes. An hour later, we ate voraciously and then relaxed over steaming tea. Completely refreshed, now we felt like exploring our safe-haven. We got out eight oil lanterns; I left my oil lantern by the charcoal embers to mark our campsite, taking my special Eternal Light with me. No way was I going to leave this treasure unguarded!

Roy decided we should break up into pairs, and he sent us out in the four directions to explore. Naturally, I went with Roy who headed off in the general direction that the watcher had gone long before we entered. By now, all traces of his passage had gone, dried up. We walked slowly, me beaming my light in an arc before us. Some two hundred feet from the entrance, we finally found the opposite wall! This place was big. Interestingly, we spied another tunnel, perhaps five feet wide but seven feet tall leading deeper into the mountain. Presently, other bobbing lanterns joined us as the others, who were skirting the circumference, arrived at our position. The report was that the chamber was an oval with only this single tunnel leading out. Out to where was another question. Roy and Thomas both sniffed the air in this side tunnel and pronounced it stale but breathable. The only sounds were those we made and those of our horses.

"Well, I guess we ought to leave the further exploration for tomorrow," Roy concluded. "I'm tired and sleepy. I would hazard that we are safe enough to sleep here. What do you all think?" We chatted a bit, but we had to sleep sometime, and no one could discern any real danger here. The place was totally deserted as far as we could tell. None of us had seen any signs of habitation on the floor or markings on the walls as they traced out its outline, so we headed back to the camping area. Still, prudence dictated that two stand guard over those sleeping at all times. Roy and I took the first watch. We sat back, leaning on our saddles as pillows, covered up with blankets. I leaned onto his strong chest. Soon the only sounds we heard were those of the other six sleeping soundly.

"Speculations, Mister Protector?" I asked whimsically. Actually, I wanted his astute summary of our present situation. I already had formulated my opinion, but it's always wise to get other's input.

Roy knew what I wanted, "Honey, one thing is for sure. Someone does live up here in the Appian Way — someone who is intimately familiar with the mountains. This is a natural cavern, but that stone blocking the entrance was likely made to keep it hidden. What I find most curious is that our watcher fellow is nowhere to be seen, even now. Obviously, that solitary tunnel must lead somewhere, and personally, I'm dying to know where and what. I have this insatiable curiosity, my love, just gotta know. Something is going on and I want to know what."

"Hum, that's pretty much my thoughts too, dear. Tomorrow we shall see what we shall see. I guess we ought to be quiet so they can sleep." After a minute, I added shyly, "I love lying on you like this."

"I know; I like it too," he replied and gently rubbed my back. I barely noticed when he got up to wake Raphael and Sarah Jane for their turn. The next thing I knew, Thallia was waking me; she had breakfast waiting.

"I guess I'm the sleepyhead here," I suggested as I wiped the sleep from my eyes and stretched, noticing all the others were up and about in the dark cavern. Thomas and Roy were off examining the chamber. The others were readying the horses and cleaning up the breakfast dishes and waiting on me, of course, so I ate hastily and thanked them for letting me sleep in a while.

While I was eating, Simon approached me, "I've done a bit of calculating here. Assuming that we're going to see where that tunnel leads, I've measured how much oil we have for our lamps. I don't want to depend upon that Eternal Light lantern. If it fails, we're doomed to groping around in the dark. We have eight lanterns and oil bags. My guess is that if we burn one lantern for say a total of twelve hours a day, then we can make these lanterns last for about fifteen days, give or take. Incidentally, we only have enough food for two weeks anyway."

"Thanks, that sounds good to me," I replied encouragingly.

"Not really. We're going to be very short on drinking water. We've been relying on melting snow too heavily, I'm afraid. If we don't find some drinkable underground water, we'll have major problems," he said seriously.

"Well, in that case, we ought to collect and melt as much snow as possible before we leave here. Fill up every conceivable container," I suggested.

An hour later, we were packed, ready to explore the tunnel, and more than ready to find out who the watcher was. Thomas and Roy went first, with Thomas holding the Eternal Light so that in case of trouble, Roy was free to attack or defend. The natural tunnel, though roughly five feet wide, varied in size, forcing us to follow along single file. We women came next, leaving Raphael to lead the string of eight horses. We had tied them together so one person could lead them. Simon, carrying an oil lamp, played rear guard, just in case.

For hours, we tramped down the tunnel, which in places widened slightly and narrowed in others. It twisted to the right and later to the left, but always sloped slightly downward. We found no signs of any side chambers. The air continued to feel warmish and damp. Occasionally a bit of mold or lichen adorned the otherwise rocky surfaces. However, we did find numerous signs of spiders, which made their nests often in the corners where the walls met the rocky ceiling.

It must have been around noon, though in the near total darkness, who could say, when we heard the telltale ker-plunk of water dropping ahead of us. Rounding the next bend, the tunnel wall on the right opened wide to reveal a large hollowed out area. Against the far wall, water trickled down the surface and dropped into a well-worn bowl carved into the floor. "Nature provides" was our point of view. The water, though high in mineral content, was cold and refreshing. We allowed the horses to drink their fill, after which, the little pool was nearly empty.

"Say, come take a look at this," Thomas called out, motioning us to come over to where he stood against a far wall. We did. He had found a dried oak leaf.

"So what? It's just a leaf," badgered Sarah Jane.

"Ah, but what kind of a leaf?" Thomas persisted, evidently turning his find into an educational lesson for us all.

"Kind of looks like a gnarly oak leaf," I ventured a guess, in part to take the pressure off Sarah Jane.

"Precisely," Thomas replied. "And where do these trees grow?"

We thought a bit. Sandy answered this time, "I think we were told they grow only in the southern Langdoc region near the Appian Way."

"Precisely," Thomas repeated himself and waited for us to reach the same conclusion that he had. He waited in vain. "So, so. . ." he prompted.

"So what? It's just a leaf!" Sarah Jane exclaimed huffily, a bit put out by all this significance on an ordinary leaf.

"So do these trees grow on the Paese di Dio? No — no trees at all. So it could only come from the Langdoc region of southern Greenway. So, so. . ." he persisted.

"So what?" declared Sarah Jane, who now was completely exasperated with Thomas.

"How did this leaf get to this spot right here? That is actually very, very significant. You always carry a leaf or two in your pockets, Sarah Jane, just to drop off in some remote tunnel, right?" he teased.

She was about to say haughtily, "Of course not!" but thought better of it. Then, she realized what he was implying. "Probably some animal carried it in here, stuck in his fur or something. That means this tunnel likely has some other entrance on our side of the Appian Way!" Thomas smiled at her, satisfied that she had learned her observation lesson for today.

"I wonder how this tunnel was made," I pondered. "It certainly doesn't look man-made."

"Although I have never been to the Langdoc region, I've heard that it is a basically a land of nearly barren limestone hills with many water-worn caverns," Thomas replied. "About the only trees that grow there are these gnarly oaks. It certainly isn't good farming land or timberland either. I believe it's uninhabited for the most part. Right here, the rock walls seem to be of harder stone, granite perhaps. So maybe we are walking down an old volcanic vent. I'll bet it somehow connects with the Langdoc caverns, but then, that remains to be seen."

On we went following the tunnel. For a time, it ran nearly level, though full of twists and turns. Again, we encountered another wider section where water had seeped down forming a pool. Here we decided to make camp for the might, guessing that it was nighttime — based solely on how hungry we all felt. Thus far, we had found no other side passages and no sign of where the watcher had gone.

This enlarged section was also the home of several field mice that had a nest in one corner. They really did not appreciate our lighting up the 'room,' rather choosing to hide in their nest. Thomas had to examine their nest to see what it was made of. Elated, he pointed out various bits of twigs and other plants, including a hardy grass. This was further evidence that this tunnel somehow connected with the Greenway, the Langdoc in particular.

Over supper, we tried to estimate how far we had come this first day. Our best guess was perhaps some twenty miles. Some speculated that our watcher was heading for the Greenway, but since we had never heard of grey colored, giant people in our lands, this was unlikely. For some unknown reason, as I lay down to sleep, I began to imagine that right about now the plague that the Prince of Velona had unleashed upon the Centurions might well be running rampant down south of us. Probably scores were dying daily now. It was a fiendish action the Prince had taken, in my opinion.

I think my dwelling or fantasizing about the plague this evening was what made me acute to the sensing or detecting of spiritual beings moving past us, far above the Appian Way range. If not that, then I have no explanation for why I clearly spotted a number of beings, who had recently lost their bodies, moving past our position some thousands of feet above us. Maybe it was an effect of the mind-clearing Paese di Dio. Whatever the stimulus, I did spot a number of beings. "Roy, look up there. Can you sense them too? Dozens of beings." I gave him plenty of time to attune his senses; Roy was not too good at long distance sensing of spiritual beings.

After what seemed an eternity, but probably was only minutes, he whispered, as though they could somehow sense us way down here under the mountain, "Yes! Yes, I do. What are they doing?"

"Roy, wake the others. I'm going to try to watch them from a distance. This is something Alabaster specifically asked Raphael and me to find out: what happens to our people when their bodies die." He immediately began waking the others, while I closed my eyes and focused my full attention far above me. It was snowing outside. Interesting, but then I spied another being arriving from what had to be a southerly direction. I followed him from a good distance. As I said before, my perceptions when not using my body's eyes are often questionable; distances are not quite right, and colors seem weird to me. Spatial arrangements are distorted. Nevertheless, I did my best. The person seemed to be heading for a particular peak, and as I realized this, I felt the gentle tug of Sandy joining with my mind. I knew then that everything I was "seeing" she was relaying to the others, including Thallia. The person that I was following zeroed in on a particular, distinctive, triangular shaped peak — one of the taller ones, and then floated downward rapidly. Very slowly, I edged closer to peek.

Down below, there was some kind of flagpole rising from the ground. A whitish energy emanated from it, and I watched in horror as the being first moved toward it and then got sucked into the pole. Even from this distance, I could feel the pull on me coming from the pole. However, I had Sandy pulling back hard on me so I wouldn't be sucked in as well. I decided this was close enough. I looked around the greater area. To my complete surprise, I spied three grey forms manipulating some kind of machinery — our watcher, perhaps. Their bodies were just plain weird. They had grey skin, strange shaped feet, and yes, with three toes that were widely separated. All stood fairly tall, but all had skinny, spindly arms and legs — so thin that I wondered how they could even find the strength to stand upright. They apparently had no such problems. Their heads looked strange; the hairless top was quite large, but it narrowed considerably to almost tiny at their chins, somewhat like a top, though not quite that narrow. Their eyes caught my attention the most! Huge blue eyes, far bigger than our eyes, stared expressionless outward. No eyelids, no eyebrows; their lips, tiny. They were not humans like the rest of us on Tarra!

Now one began speaking into a tube; it was directed at the poor person stuck on that pole. I saw that the person's mind, which before held many images of their recent life, was nothing but a glowing ball of white, blinding energy. All their mental pictures were gone. The voice said, or perhaps it was really just telepathic thoughts, "Go now and get a new infant body. You will remember nothing of this. When that body dies, you will report here for further instructions." This was repeated at least a dozen times, over and over.

At last, a grey form pulled a lever downward, and the energy from the pole suddenly ceased, releasing the poor person. I watched as the person fumbled around, trying to perceive where it was at. However, all it could see was the images of infants in its mind. Suddenly, like a bolt of lightning, it took off heading north into the heart of the Greenway. I had no doubt that it was on its way to pick up a newborn infant's body. I looked up and saw that there was now a line of others waiting for their turn; I counted ten of them. In disgust, I watched as the next one slowly approached the pole, following these long ago implanted orders, watched the grey person pull the level up, and felt the energy flow sucking him into the pole and me nearly along with it.

I'd seen enough, so I slowly edged my way back, making very sure not to attract the attention of these grey people. Because there were so many waiting in line, this time I had no difficulty backing out of the area. Soon I reentered my body and put my full attention on the cavern walls around me. I said nothing for some time.

I heard Raphael speak, "Alabaster has secretly asked Bethany and me to look into what was going on with our people after their bodies died. I suspect now that he may have had some idea that our people were being somehow manipulated during the time between when they left their dead body and when they entered a new one. People, we're most definitely being manipulated! This is disgusting and has to stop!"

Sandy protested, "The mantis creatures are doing it down south, and these grey things are doing it up here. What is really going on here anyway? What are they trying to do with us — our people and why?"

"Well, these grey things look like they can hardly stand up," Roy commented. "If we can bring a small fighting force to bear on them, I think we can eliminate them."

"Yes, but we only have Bethany's distorted views of where they are located. We could search for years in these mountains before we found them," observed Simon. "But it would appear we should be able to take them out by force of arms. I'm not so sure of those enormous mantis creatures, though. They might be far stronger than us. They are certainly huge in size and probably strength as well."

"Maybe these tunnels will lead us to their location," Thomas said hopefully.

"Well at least this time your presence went unnoticed, Bethany. We don't have to fear a counterattack just yet, so that is a good sign," Sandy observed.

Finally, I spoke, "Gang, we have to get this information to Alabaster and let him decide what is to be done. I suspect, like Raphael, that he knows more about all this than he has said to us thus far. So let's first concentrate on getting home. Sandy, later on, see if you can contact Alabaster and let him know what we have found. Now more than ever, we need to explore this tunnel and see where it goes. This could be very important indeed. I'm now really, really tired. Wake me if you need me." I laid down and was asleep almost at once. Thankfully, I had no dreams. For a moment, I feared that I might have nightmares about all this, but I slept soundly.

The next day things began to become more complex. Midmorning, or what we assumed was that time, our tunnel divided. Actually, at the junction, it continued on straight but two similar sized side tunnels sort of "Y'ed" into it ahead of us, offering three different paths that we could follow. For once, no one suggested that we split up and search all three. No way did I want to become separated from the rest of my Circle! Things had become a lot scarier; danger lurked near, I felt.

In the end, we decided to continue on straight. Mid-afternoon, we encountered another similar junction and once more decided to continue on straight. By evening and an estimated twenty miles further along, we camped at a major junction of five tunnels. Here four others joined the one we were following, coming in at various angles. Once more, water had found its way downward and over the long years carved out a drinking pool. This time, the water had a strong aftertaste of minerals, but it was palatable.

During the third day of travel, although we encountered more side passages, we kept the mantra of "go straight" as our guiding principle. Of course, none of us had the slightest idea if this was the correct or even an optimum choice. With so many side passages, if we had gone right here, left there, why, we would be completely confused by now and could never have retraced our steps, if it led to a dead end.

The fifth day, the walls of the tunnel we were following changed to soft limestone. This we took as a very positive sign for it meant, we thought, that we were getting closer to the Langdoc region of the Greenway and home. Now a new problem arose. The tunnel system changed subtly into more interconnecting chambers, leading in all directions. There seemed to be no pattern where the next chamber would open up at, sometimes on the left, sometimes on the right, sometimes ahead of us and at all angles in between. We found ourselves in a maze of limestone caverns! So the sixth day, we held a long conference to try to make the best choice to follow. Still, however, I found myself relying heavily on the wisdom of Thomas, who so far had not erred in leading us. When we asked him how he could choose which cavern to follow next, he said, "By smell. I take the one that smells the freshest." We laughed, but it made perfect sense!

By the seventh day, the air felt just a bit chillier than it had and fresher. Heartened that we must be getting close to an exit, we marched onward with a renewed determinism to get free of this underground maze and actually set foot in the Greenway for the first time in over a year, even if it was in the most uninhabited region.

As we were walking along, Sandy came close to me and whispered, "Bethany, can I have a word with you sort of in private?" Well, I'm not one to have secrets within my Circle; it isn't wise. She seemed awfully worried, so I consented but reserved the right to let the others know if I felt they should know.

"It's Alabaster. I still haven't been able to contact him. I've been trying a couple times a day, since we discovered those grey people. Now, I'm getting awfully worried. This is the first time that I haven't been able eventually to reach him. I think something is very wrong. I don't want to alarm the others, in case it is just me failing to do my job."

"I know; let's work together on it," I answered trying to be as hopeful sounding as possible. "Two heads are better than one or two minds in this case," I teased, but she didn't smile. However, she looked grateful for my assistance. As we walked along, together we attempted to reach Alabaster telepathically.

After some ten minutes, I looked at Sandy, "Golly, you're right. Something isn't right here. I'd better let the others know." The relief she felt was plainly obvious on her face; she was now sure it wasn't her mistake.

After I told the others of the problem, Simon offered a reasonable explanation, "Maybe he's just sleeping. He seems to do a lot of that. Maybe he's just sleeping more these days; after all, it is the dead of winter." That seemed a logical explanation, and we were content with it and continued our march. Still, Sandy periodically attempted to make contact to no avail.

Near the end of the eight day, we came to another junction of three chambers, or more precisely a merging of three chambers. From one, there came a strong rush of cold, fresh air. This one Thomas chose to enter and follow. To our amazement, we suddenly found ourselves standing just outside the underground, on a ledge overlooking a vast snow covered section of the Langdoc! We had made it. More importantly, we had just found a way to cross the Appian Way. Now we regretted that we had failed to mark our passage through the chambers and tunnels or even make a map showing the choices. While we thought that we might be able to retrace our route if we entered from the Paese di Dio, going back the way we had come we probably couldn't. Ah well. We were the first people to have crossed the Appian Way. That was something.

However, I swore everyone to complete secrecy on our achievement. I had this gut feeling that keeping these interconnecting chambers a secret known only to us might have some vitally important significance in the future. I was only off by a few hundred years in my hunch.

For a few minutes, we stood here high above the rolling, rocky, nearly barren snow covered hills enjoying the spectacular view and the realization that we were in our own land, albeit not the inhabited portion, but that was just a slight technicality. Though we didn't know precisely where we were, to get to Calgary, all we had to do was head west until we reached the ocean and then follow the shoreline. Cutting diagonally across the countryside was more risky; we could overshoot and wind up far south or north of the city.

Just as we were mounting up, Sandy got a telepathic contact, loud and strong. *Able Communicator here.* His emotional tone was that of heavy grief. *I've finally been able to reach you. I have some really bad news. Alabaster Benjamin Crowley has passed away.* There was a long pause; she sensed he was crying, barely able to maintain his concentration to keep up the mental connection. *He died last night. He went to sleep and never woke up.* Now it was Sandy who nearly lost her concentration; grief welled up inside her. She relayed it to us, giant tears streaming down her face. *Where are you? It is of the utmost importance that you get back to Calgary just as soon as you possibly can.*

For a moment, Sandy lost her concentration, saying aloud what she intended to transmit, "We're close. We're somewhere in the Langdoc region heading toward Calgary." She caught her error and sent it mentally to Able.

Langdoc? But how? Never mind. Get back here to Calgary just as fast as you possibly can. Please hurry! That is all. He broke the connection, primarily because his grief overwhelmed him.

Tears rolled down all our cheeks; we stared in complete disbelief at each other. Alabaster, dead! He was the founder of the druwids — the Guardians, the Protectors! He was our leader. Whatever would happen to us now, just when we needed a wise leader to battle the Centurion invasion, which was likely to come as early as this spring? Why couldn't he have held on just a few more days so we could give him our full report and get his wisdom on what we should do next? Could we have gotten back any faster? Did we dally around on our return and cause this mess? Many thoughts passed through my head in a whirlwind of recriminations. Roy, good old Roy, he sensed my utter confusion and said, "Bethany, there's nothing we could have done to get back any sooner. In fact, following the tunnel probably cut several weeks off our return time. We did our best. That is all that was ever expected of us. Come on; let's ride like the wind."

"Well, not that fast. The ground is snow covered, and we don't want to have a horse break a leg this close to home!" protested Thomas. "I'll gamble a bit and head diagonally. Let's ride. Roy, you come up front with me. Two abreast. We can make several miles before dark. Keep your eyes open for any kind of place where we might spend the night." We were off — not the galloping, long hair flowing behind my head style, which I dearly love, but more of a slow, carefully picking your way through the rocky ground half-hidden by the blanket of snow.

Whenever a large hill appeared, Thomas would climb to the top and stare off in the distance to get his bearings. Then, he would lead us east by north. By full dark, we had to halt and fix dinner. Still we hadn't found any place to camp, save out here in the wide open spaces. By the time that we had finished eating, the moon rose and was just past full. It provided reasonable light, so Thomas risked a moonlight ride. We continued until nearly midnight, when we found a small cave at the base of a rocky slope. Here we huddled and spent a chilly night. At the crack of dawn, we were up and riding in less than a half hour.

On the sixth day since we left the underground chambers, we spied the unmistakable signs of Calgary in the far distance — smoke clouds rising into the cold blue sky from countless chimneys. Late that afternoon, we rode into

Alabaster's druwid complex of buildings from which we had left over a year ago. We arrived on the last day of February, saddened beyond belief.

Chapter 25 Decisions

Protector Finch, eyes red from recent crying, soberly met us at the gate, allowing us inside. "Welcome back, Lightning Circle. I wish it could be under better circumstances. Martha's inside waiting for you. Go easy on her; she's taking this really hard — honestly, we all are, for that matter. I just can't believe that he is really gone. I keep expecting him to wander down at mealtimes." Tears trickled down his cheeks once more; he said no more, leading our eight horses toward the stables, while sacks in hand, we walked up to the front door.

Able Communicator, waiting there for us, opened the door and motioned for us to come in saying, "Dining room, please." His voice was filled with a deep sadness, and he no longer held his head high. I had a great lump in my throat and really couldn't speak if I had to. Silently, we walked into the large room with the beautiful, huge oaken table. Martha, wrapped tightly in a woolen shawl, sat silently there, a cup of tea barely touched in front of her. Martha Lindwood, the Loremaster, looked old, very old, as if she had aged twenty years, since we left last year. From her face, we knew she had been crying quite a lot. She looked positively morose.

Thallia went to fix us all some tea; she instinctively recognized that we seven needed a few minutes alone with Martha. She looked up as we sat down, "If only you had been two weeks earlier," and she began crying again. I got up and went over to her and held her in my arms.

"I know, I know," was all that I could say without completely breaking down myself.

After a time, she said, "I keep seeing that night in my mind, over and over, wondering if I could have done something to save him? Did I miss a sign that he was in trouble? It's all my fault that he's dead."

"Nonsense, Martha, you did all that was humanly possible, I'm sure," declared Sarah Jane. "Able said that he died in his sleep."

Perhaps this was what Martha was looking for, a sign that she wasn't responsible for his death, but then perhaps not. Either way, she straightened up and said, "Yes, I tucked him in a bit earlier that night. He seemed just a bit more tired than usual. When he didn't come down for breakfast, I went to check on him. I was the one that found him," and she cried a bit more over the memories of that fateful morning. We let her take her time to regain her composure.

Sniffing, she explained, "We gave him the Parting Ceremony, though he was not around. We have no idea where he has gone for that matter. Not even Able has been able to make contact with him. We think this is very strange indeed. Then, maybe this is his will. His ashes have been cast upon the seashore as per his request. All that is left now is his memory, I'm afraid."

"Oh no it's not," protested Roy, "his entire network of druwids survives him. His legacy to mankind lives on in all of us." She brightened up recognizing the truth of his pronunciation. Something in what he said triggered something in her, for she sat upright and attempted to look as formal as possible. Protector Finch, Able, Pete, Wilma, and Jane, the other remaining members of his Circle had silently entered the room and were standing behind us.

She looked at them, as did we. "Here goes," she said, I believe mostly for her Circle's sake. "Long before Alabaster passed away, he left us, me, with certain instructions and orders to be carried out in the event that he should die. My Circle will bear witness that I speak his precise words to you. These were his last orders:

Martha, in the event that my aged body should pass away, a new Circle must be put in command of the entire druwid network that I have built up over these many years. The Greenway is in perilous times. All that I have worked for these many years is in total jeopardy. Sooner or later, we likely must face an invasion from the southern lands. Should the Lightning Circle return from their assignment, it is my last command that they and they alone shall assume the leadership of the druwid network of all Greenway. If they return, put them in charge at once and have those that remain of my Circle give them their complete support in all that they do. If there is even the slightest chance that the invasion that I foresee can be somehow avoided or lessened, it is they, the children that may find a way. If the Lightning Circle does not return, as they might not, because I sent them into the mouth of the lion, then I leave the choice of leadership of the network in your hands, Martha. Seek guidance from the other Circle members. Finally, should Bethany or Raphael return, ask them to continue my secret counting; they will understand what I mean. Swear to me that you will do this.

"I so swore, and with the witness of my Circle, I have now fulfilled his last orders," Martha looked relieved, as if an enormous pressure lifted from her mind.

"I so swear that she has repeated his words correctly," stated Judger Jane, indicating formally that Martha had completely fulfilled her pledge to Alabaster.

My mouth wagged, but nothing came out. "But," Roy tried to protest though no other words followed.

"But we do not," Simon tried to find the words to elaborate on Roy's protest. This was the only time that I ever heard Simon at a complete loss for words.

Judger Jane formally pronounced, "This complex is now entirely yours to use as you see fit. If you wish, we will find other quarters in the morning. You may count on our full support. Alabaster wouldn't want it any other way. Here is the master set of keys that Alabaster kept," she handed them to me, adding, "In the morning, we'll present you with our keys as we move out."

Finally, I found my voice, though squeaky, "You'll do no such thing! You all stay just where you are now for the time being. Our old rooms will do just fine for now." I watched their reactions, and I knew I spoke wisely, for a great relief was plainly visible on all their faces. This, after all, had been their home base for so many years. I had no intention of kicking them out into the snow. I continued, "I can't imagine why Alabaster chose us to lead over all the many other Circles. In the short time that I knew him, I saw that he always had a strong reason behind his every action. While we know very little about running the druwid network, you all do, and we are counting — no, make that, depending upon you for help. It is going to have to be a team effort if we are to save our land. However, we have been, as he said, in the lion's mouth and have learned a great deal about our enemy. We have made new friends and allies in distant lands. Actually, I ended up killing their Emperor — an event, which may create a positive change in their outlook, perhaps not; time will tell. The cowardly actions of the last Sea Prince may have greatly weakened their army, giving us more time to prepare than Alabaster had anticipated. So I am just beginning to sense what he may have meant by 'the Lightning Circle might find a way to save the Greenway.' On the other hand, I had hoped to just return, give him a full report, and let him make the decisions on what to do next, but this is not to be."

"On our journey, we have met many people in many lands. Maybe this was what he wanted us to discover. I can honestly say that all men and women everywhere are basically good and want to do what is right and just, though some pick what we would consider bad ways to achieve it, such as the Sea Prince unleashing the plague upon the Centurions in Velona. Men and women everywhere just want to be free to live their own lives, flourish, prosper, and raise their families. This I have seen with my own eyes. I have also seen just how much more aware and able we, the druwids, are than the normal people of Tarra. Thus, be it known that I, Elizabeth Stanton, do here by dedicate my existence to helping the people of Tarra achieve the freedom they deserve. As ordered and by my own choice, I begin here in the Greenway." I had just made my eternal commitment, my goal and purpose in existence.

Simon picked up the formal declaration immediately even as Judger Jane did. He said formally, "I so bear witness to Bethany's decision. Be it also known that I also so dedicate my life to these ends." One by one, the rest of my Circle followed his lead, not from a sense of duty or loyalty, but from deeply held convictions that, for us, there could be no higher purpose.

When the last of my Circle had finished, Judger Jane spoke up, "I'm slowly beginning to see that perhaps Alabaster was right in his choice. I must tell you that from the moment I heard his orders to put you in charge, I wasn't for it at all. I tried several times to convince him otherwise, just for the record. Of course, he only smiled his usual disarming, all-knowing smile. Now I see that you aren't children any longer and that you have even a stronger intention that I have about all this. Rest assured that I'll give you all the support that I'm capable of generating."

"Thanks, I can't ask for more," I replied tactfully. Secretly, I was glad to hear that someone had tried to convince Alabaster not to choose us. That he remained adamant gave me just a bit more confidence. "One small detail, one of the first actions we must take is to find your Circle a replacement Wid. Think on the matter, and let's discuss it in the morning." Just then, as if on cue, Thallia entered carrying a large tray with steaming tea, rolls, and cheese — Thomas's doing I suspected.

The smell of food reminded us just how hungry we were. Over the snack, Martha said that many of the Sisters were staying here in the complex, including Isabel, and that they all would want to see us. However, I said, "Tomorrow. Tonight, I only want a long, long, long, hot soaking bath and to wash my hair properly. I've not had a descent bath in over a year."

"And a good night's sleep in a bed with real sheets," Roy added good-naturedly.

"I'll second both of those!" declared Sarah Jane.

"I'll third it!" Sandy added quickly.

Martha winked, "For once, I'm way ahead of you! Yes, I have already had the master bath prepared. It is steaming and can hold six of you at one time. Two can use the smaller bath. Soak all you want. When you are done, I'll even help comb out that lovely, long hair of yours." So it was, I took a two hour bath. I will admit it; I truly enjoyed it, one of life's small pleasures. Roy washed and rubbed my back, but even he couldn't stay in for more than an hour before he grew too bored. We four girls stayed until the water turned cool.

Later, we joined the guys in our old commons room off which the four bedrooms connected. The instant we entered, they became very quiet; obviously, they had been discussing something behind our backs. Roy managed to say, "How was the bath? All refreshed?"

I didn't fall for it; neither did the others. "Okay, out with it. What have you been discussing?" No answer. They looked rather sheepishly at the floor, the chairs, anything but me. I looked at them one by one, knowing that I was going to have to use Wid technology on them to find out. "Okay, I'll hazard a guess. You are upset because we have been moved into the top leadership position and not just given a town to protect, something like that, right?" From the instant flushing of faces, I knew that I wasn't too far from the mark. "Well, I myself was hoping to get assigned to maybe Karka so I could be near my family."

"Why us?" Roy offered. "Why us? We don't know anything about heading the whole organization. Martha and the others do; why not them? Besides, we'll just be stuck here in Calgary and never get to go anywhere; leaders are like that. I won't get to protect anything really anymore. I'll be a fish out of the pond."

"I'm not trained to run the country either," Simon added. "Look, I'm good at adjudicating smaller matters between people. Here, I'm only going to get broad matters of state, mega-boring. What will I get to conjure anymore? Nothing. I love being out in the world."

"Worse for me. I crave roaming the land, the forest, the meadows, the valleys," Thomas added his protest. "Here, I'll be stuck. Okay, maybe we can go for a walk or ride nearby, but they are not going to let us go any real distance away."

"I'm the only one that this assignment doesn't particularly bother," Raphael finished up, "because I can build my great buildings anywhere. Calgary will do just fine, perhaps better than some because there is a wealth of man power and supplies here. I'm okay with this deal, but they aren't."

"Thanks for telling me," I said sincerely, giving me time to think. "You boys have forgotten one very import detail in this matter." I paused for emphasis, making sure I had their attention. "We run the show; we give the orders. Why can't we give ourselves assignments that allow us to travel, Thomas, or do some spying, Simon. As for protection, we all know that the invasion is highly likely to come, and then you'll have more to protect than you can protect, Roy. I, for one, don't want to spend the rest of my life cooped up here in Calgary. No, fellows, we'll make as many opportunities for travel as we can. Besides, you're all being selfish, thinking of your own well-being. We have all the Greenway to worry about now and that is a whole lot bigger than any of us. Now we had better get some sleep. Tomorrow's likely to be a challenging day for us all." Without waiting for their comments, I headed to bed, letting them think about my words.

The next morning after breakfast, we made the rounds, visiting with all the guests. First stop was Isabel. We found her in the study instructing her devoted Angelina and Alicia in the art of observing what is really present. First, it was loving hugs all around between all of us. "My you do look so much better!" I complimented her. Her skin tone was back to normal, and her hug had some strength behind it. Perhaps more importantly, her eyes shone brightly; she was alive!

"Still not one hundred percent, but nearly so. I owe you and Sarah Jane so much, Bethany. I'm giving back to these two. They never seem to get enough learning. Perhaps a pair of Wids in the making," she jested, proud of the developing skills of the two Sisters. Both young women looked vibrant and radiant! Evidently, life in the Greenway completely agreed with them; both seemed immensely happy. Just as I had predicted, Alicia Bortolo and Angelina Torquora were treated with immense respect for their lengthy sacrifices to save Isabel. Obviously, they wanted to hear about our adventures, and we promised to tell them all about them later in the evening when we could get all those that wanted to hear them together in one place.

Then, we visited Leonia Torelli, Cherie Leggio, and Louisa Bertronelli. All three had decided to make a new life here in the Greenway, having heard Isabel talk about it all during their trip across the Paese di Dio. I was gratified to find that Leonia had totally recovered emotionally from the loss of her hand. In fact, Leonia just had to tell me, "You are so right about the Greenway men! It's a paradise here. And," she blushed and faltered a bit, "I've met this really nice merchant, and he's already taken me to several dances. He's not the slightest bit concerned about my having only one hand. He's such a good dancer, and he's so romantic!" She was bubbling, and I found her enthusiasm contagious!

Cherie added with a laugh, "You didn't tell us that there are hundreds of really nice men to choose from here! Louisa, Leonia, and I agree: the Greenway is utter paradise! We even don't mind all this snow. We've already been taken on several sleigh rides!" We laughed along with these women. I realized just how much I missed the normal things in life.

Finally, Thallia took us to the room that Severnia Tolli, the Sister who had saved her life so long ago. She too was happier than we had ever seen her. Severnia explained that Thallia had "saved" her life by bringing her here. She already had her eyes on a young man; and he, her. For these women, the Greenway offered a new chance at life. All told, we found just over a hundred Sisters had come to the Greenway, and about half of them were good fighters. The others had useful skills. Really, we benefitted as much as they.

The first part of the afternoon's conference was spent in giving a very detailed report of our journey, findings, and conclusions to Alabaster's Circle, part of which they had already heard from Thomas. However, the incidents with the mantises and the grey creatures were highly problematical. Should I relate our observations that these things were attempting to control our people? Who would believe such nonsense? After all, it was fantastic, bordering on delusionary. I chose to omit the descriptions and glossed over the particulars, saying that both needed firsthand, direct observations — that I, we, had seen them without the use of our eyes. I didn't know how much, if anything, that Alabaster had told them about any suspicions he had, either of their existence or their secret operations. Besides, we had larger problems to worry about, such as keeping our people alive and avoiding a terrible war and suffering. I had no evidence that either of these strange creatures were attempting to control or direct human lives, only what happened after their bodies died. I kept it within the Lightning Circle for the time being. Dinnertime came just as I finished our official report. Together, we ate, putting aside official business.

However, as soon as we ate, we resumed our conference. Judger Jane asked, "So do you have any immediate plans — things that should be done? Can we help?"

"Simon, correct me if I mis-speak," I replied. "First, we must know just how bad this plague in Velona really is. How many of their soldiers are dead? How soon can they be replaced? That sort of thing. This requires someone visiting that sector of the Sea Princes, relaying firsthand information. Second, we need to do everything we can to help Count Basilica d'Grange build up his fortress, because, if they attempt to invade overland, of necessity, they must get past him before they can get to us. So everything we can do to make his stronghold invincible must be done. Third, we need to find out who their new Emperor is and what their intentions now are — specifically, will they continue their aggression and wars. Fourth, if they choose to invade the Greenway by sea, how can we defend ourselves? We must find a way. Fifth, we must attempt to let those back in Megalos know that we are a civilized people. To that end,

I'm going to adopt their system of writing that we learned from Niccolo Helios. From now on, all trade leaving here shall be accompanied by a written cargo manifest so when they receive it, they can see that we can write as they do. Who knows, but that might sway them from attacking us. Hence, we need to get many people to learn to read and write — at least those who conduct our export business. Sixth, in the event that they do invade us, we need to devise some plan for the defense of the people we safeguard. Finally, seventh, if we are invaded and conquered, we need to make provisional plans for those druwids who may survive." There was an eight, but I told only my Circle: find out what is going on with these grey creatures and find a way to stop them.

"You have presented a reasonable statement of the situation," Simon witnessed for me.

Poor Martha, all these drastic actions obviously needed to be done, but all were beyond her skill. She sighed and said, "None of these involves the normal day-to-day operations of the Greenway."

"Right, Martha. Just as soon as we get you a new Wid, that will be your Circle's task, manage the normal affairs here in the Greenway. After all, your Circle is extremely adept at doing just this, right?"

She smiled as she realized what I had just done, "Yes, dear child, you are indeed a Wid. Our Circle has done that for so many years now that I've lost count. We're comfortable doing this. I'm afraid none of us are the best choice to deal with your needed actions. Speaking for the rest of my Circle, we'd be most honored to continue to serve in this capacity. Thank you, Wid Bethany!"

"Just Bethany, please. No need for formalities among us," I responded. "After all, I still look on you, Martha, as my surrogate mother." Everyone chuckled or smiled for there was a hint of truth in that. She had been sort of our Circle's mother during our stay here last year.

Raphael broke in, "Say, can I ask one very important question that we really need to know?" Since no one objected, he continued, "Just how many Circles do we have in total now?"

"I can answer that one," Planner Pete replied. "While you were gone, we held a ceremony inducting the Circle that completed the forth tier. Until you returned, our Circle was at the top of the hierarchy. Beneath us is the second tier of seven. The third tier beneath them contains seven for each or forty-nine. Now the forth tier is complete, seven beneath each of those, making three hundred forty-three Circles operating at the lowest levels protecting towns and villages. With your return and with both our Circles remaining at the top, the total of complete Circles numbers four hundred and one. However, I do point out that many members are advancing in age. Before we can begin work on the fifth tier, we must see to the needed replacements. I fear we may only be able to provide enough for the replacements. I know that Alabaster's dream was to have seven tiers. He often said that if our strength ever achieved a full seven tiers, we would be unconquerable. However, I just don't see how we shall ever be able to even build the fifth tier."

"Wow, so many?" I replied in surprise. I had not realized just how strong we potentially could be. "Now to the matter of your Wid. I have just the person in mind to fill it. Great wisdom is needed here, along with a solid reality of what we are facing. It's my decision that Isabel should become your Wid. For in fact, it was due to her actions that so many positive changes occurred in the Lands of the Seven Sea Princes. While she might not know much about running the day-to-day things here, she has the knowledge and experience of what we may ultimately have to face, the invaders. Isabel will add depth to your Circle's bastion of wisdom, if you'll have her with her physical disabilities. What say you?" I had long wondered what Alabaster would do with Isabel. Surely, she would have to be integrated with another Circle, but with no hands, she could not very well be sent out to a rural village to be their protector. Besides, if the attack came, she would want to be on the front line, and that's where I would want her as well. Calgary would seem to be the first place the Centurions would attack. I wish I could have talked with Alabaster about this and gotten his opinion.

Protector Finch spoke first with a chuckle, "She's fine with me. That's one druwid who doesn't need protecting! I'd be honored to have her. I guess we can just have her two assistants — those Sisters never leave her side — wait just outside the door, when we need a private conference."

Martha looked relieved. "For some time now I've been all worried that we'd get a new recruit who's but sixteen. I could be her grandmother, so I'm pleased too. I'm sure we can work with Isabel just fine. We all knew her before she took on that assignment to the Sea Princes years ago. I'm certainly going to be far more comfortable with her, than a youngster, no offence, Bethany." I smiled at her frankness.

Judger Jane had the final word, "She is a true survivor. That's just what we need in our Circle, survivors. Will she agree to do it? Her training isn't that of a Wid."

"Ah, that's the next thing I have to find out. I'm almost certain that she will. I expect to hear her only objection is would you want a helpless cripple in your Circle. Besides, if the fight comes to Calgary, I certainly want that woman here on the front line. The impact she can have on the enemy is staggering. She knows them, their battlefield tactics, and will be positively invaluable here at the top of the organization."

Next, Judger Jane presented an overview of the organization, what their current activities were under Alabaster, the state of our treasury, and so on. She presented me with Alabaster's master set of keys, all twenty of them. She had tied colored strings on many indicating what doors they unlocked. Three keys remained a complete mystery. "We've left his room just as it was when he passed away. We assumed you'd want to move into it, seeing as how you are now the master Wid."

"Well, for the time being, I'll stay with my Circle, where we are now. I'll use his room as an office and you all can too. I have a tremendous amount to learn and discover. I know Alabaster had many secrets that he didn't reveal to us. Perhaps I'll learn about them from what is in his room. Besides, I love a challenge: what do these three unlock?" Everyone laughed, though I already knew that one unlocked the secret underground chamber, which held centuries of birth-death records of the entire Greenway. Two were a complete mystery to these six druwids.

Leaving the mystery, I asked, "Is there an appropriate room for Isabel or is where she is now satisfactory?"

"I'll make up one of the guest rooms for her and her two assistants. That way, she can be close to the rest of us," Martha replied, the housekeeper in her rising to the occasion. When the meeting adjourned, I went in search of Isabel.

I found her getting ready for bed. Her two assistants were brushing her hair. It had grown longer since I had said goodbye to her back in the Sea Princes. Her complexion had returned to normal, and her strength had revived as well as her spirits. "Ah, two visits in the same day," she teased me as I entered. "I'm honored. What can I do for you tonight?"

I leaned over her, took a hold of both her stumps as if they were hands, and looked her squarely in her eyes. I felt her slight jerk or attempt to withdraw her stumps, and then she accepted my gesture as I intended it, and forgot about her disfigurement. "Isabel, you have just been promoted. You're now the Wid of Martha's Circle, taking Alabaster's place. I have spoken to all of them, and they are excited and most happy to have you as their Wid. What say you?"

She blinked in complete disbelief. Her lips moved repeating the word 'Wid' but no sound appeared. She stared at me looking for some sign that I was teasing her, playing with her, that I wasn't serious. She saw at once that I was completely serious about it. Only then did tears form in her eyes and trickle down her face. "I — I don't know what to say, Bethany. You really want me — as helpless as I am — to be their Wid? How can I possibly take the place of Alabaster? Me?"

"Yes, you. You're perfect for the job. You're not expected to *replace* Alabaster. No one can. Actually, the Lightning Circle as a *group* will try to fill his shoes. No, they need a Wid to help run the day-to-day operations of the Greenway, but they also need a Wid who is very familiar with the enemy that we're likely going to have to face in the near future. They desperately need your guidance in such matters. Beside, Isabel, I need you here with me in Calgary. If the Centurions attack us, Calgary is likely to be their first target. I want your lightning bolts right here. You know — payback time. We'll have a contest between us to see who can cause the most damage," I jested.

She laughed at my tease, breaking her tension as I hoped it would. "She tried to pull her stumps out of my grip as she said, "Even with these useless appendages? They really can have me as I now am?"

"Yes, you and I both know that the only real problem with your appendages is your own consideration of their worth or lack thereof. There are plenty of hands around here to help you when you need it," I gestured to her two apprentices who nodded eagerly.

"Yes, you speak wisely. I must admit to you that I'm doing better in my considerations of their lack of worth. I don't feel nearly so embarrassed in public with them anymore. Let people stare all they want to — I'm not so bothered about that anymore. Still, I flinched when you took my arms just a minute ago. It does feel good to have you holding them. Thanks. You know that you have saved both my life and my dignity? How can I ever repay you?"

"By accepting this new assignment and doing your best," I replied. "Honestly, Isabel, I really, really need you as their Wid. They've no idea what we're likely to face. We both do. Please, say yes, please."

"Bethany, I'll share something I realized on the long ride across the Paese di Dio. We all live to *help* others. When we're completely convinced that we can no longer help anyone, we're dead. That is, when we feel that we can no longer pay back the help that we're receiving, we're doomed. I was at just that point when you found me. You've shown me that I can give back help to others, though I now require so much help myself, but I can give back valuable help. That alone is what has brought me back from the brink of death. So yes, I'll be their Wid. It will be wonderful to be back among an operational Circle as a contributing member after so long an absence. Thank you." She pulled me closer and gave me a strong hug.

As I left her, I said, "Okay. Tomorrow, Martha will fix up a new room so you and your two assistants can be with them." I left her with a great big smile on her face and her two assistants pelting her with questions about what this was all about; she would have some explaining to do.

We set about taking over the leadership of the entire druwid network. There was much to do and to learn, especially for me. I sent Raphael and Sarah Jane off to inspect the fortress down south both to learn what additional aid we could provide them as well as for Raphael to see their design so he might construct similar fortresses here in the Greenway. They also were to attempt to find out the effects of the plague. Sandy and Simon were set the task of devising a written language for the Greenway and then teaching the reading and writing of it to all those engaged in foreign trade. In order that the script be readable, the encoding had to be similar to that in use in Megalos or the Centurions would find it unreadable. Yet, it had to relay our spoken language. Sarah Jane also assisted in its development as she was the most proficient in the reading of Megalos writings. Of course, I gave stern warnings that at no time should anything related to druwid knowledge ever be written down. I sent Roy, Thomas, and Thallia on a mission to travel up and down our coastline so they could become familiar with the land, spot likely invasion beaches, and where we might best defend. In addition, I took on the task of going carefully through everything in Alabaster's room, looking for knowledge and useful items as well as what the other keys unlocked.

The days passed swiftly, and the snow cover began melting. Daffodils pushed through their new green shoots and soon brilliant yellows dotted the entire entrance way of our building. The Vernal Equinox Ceremony was now only two days away. However, the details I left to Martha's Circle. True, the Lightning Circle would be formally presented to the other seven second tier

Circles and other visiting representatives from more distant Circles. Since her Circle had always conducted the ceremony, I had no intention of changing tradition. My plans for a co-Circle team approach were working out splendidly.

However, this lovely morning, the guys were acting just a bit secretive. True, Raphael and Sarah Jane had only returned a few days before. Still, they were keeping something not only from me but also from Sarah Jane and Sandy. I suspected Thallia knew what was going on, but I didn't dare mind-link and force it out of her.

We had finished breakfast and were relaxing with our tea, when Roy, Raphael, and Simon excused themselves and said, "You ladies stay here a while. Thallia, you make sure they do." He had a mischievous look in his eyes, and Thallia grinned, so I knew that she was also in on their scheme, whatever it was. About ten minutes later, the three men came back into our commons room, each carrying a bouquet of daffodils. Roy knelt before me; Raphael, before Sarah Jane; Simon, before Sandy. Standing back, Thomas and Thallia put their arms around each other. In unison, the guys stated, "You are the love of my life. Your eyes are my moons; your radiance, my sun. Your breath gives me life; your glance swells me with hope. If you feel the same, will you marry me and *soon*?" Well-rehearsed, they simultaneously presented us with the bouquets.

The unexpected suddenness took us by surprise and filled me with a ground swell of happiness and joy. Tears flooded my eyes, and my heart pounded as I said, "Yes, oh yes. Soon!" I got up, put my arms around Roy, hugged him tightly, and then we embraced lovingly. From the corner of my eye, I saw the others similarly engaged. So were Thomas and Thallia. So this was their big secret! They could have many more like this, I thought.

Thomas spoke next, "We wanted to get married on the Vernal Equinox, symbolic of the return of Spring and a renewing of life, but then there are our families to consider. I figured you'd want your parents to be present too. That means we would have to travel to Karka, at least assuming that we can get away for that long."

"Thomas that is a wonderful idea, married on the return of Spring! How utterly romantic!" I exclaimed. "Let's do it! Who knows when or even if we can get a couple months off to travel to Karka. Let's do it now. If we can go to Karka, why, we can hold a Greenway ceremony for our families' benefit — rather like getting married twice. What do you all think?"

Naturally, everyone was in complete agreement with my suggestion. Gaily I dashed off to find Martha to tell her the news. This equinox celebration was going to be an important, significant one for us! When I got back, the girls were discussing what we should wear. With the big day only two days away, time precluded too much planning. Besides, this would be an official druwid night's celebration, and we'd need to wear our official leather garments. We opted for a new set of leathers, including Thallia, for it wouldn't do for her to be dressed completely different from us. We just left off the identifying druwid markings on her set.

While we spent much of the next two days preparing for our big day, or rather night, the ice sheet broke in Calgary's bay, and the following day, the Lucky Lady sailed into dock — the first ship to land this year. Captain Bartoloma brought in a load of dried fish, meats, and some metal farming equipment in exchange for grain. However, he had vital news for us concerning the plague. He relayed that, as of two weeks ago, fully one half of the entire Centurion army had died! Much of the wooden structures of Velona had been burned in an attempt to stamp out the plague, but to little avail. The other Governors, hearing of the plague, had issued a formal quarantine; no one was allowed out of the city. Needed supplies were brought by wagon to the edge of town and left. Later, those trapped in Velona would come out, haul them into the city, and disburse the vital supplies. The situation in Velona was grim indeed. Thus far, no one outside of Velona, namely all those that had fled the city prior to the arrival of the Centurion army, had gotten the disease. I kept my fingers crossed. Plague can be very unpredictable. However, his news convinced us that no invasion would occur in all likelihood this year. Even if the plague ended now, with their strength so reduced, to continue attacking other lands, they would have to bring up re-enforcement troops. That would take time. By then, winter would descend and any invasion would have to wait. This news was very encouraging to us all. It gave us lots more time to prepare.

Sarah Jane and Raphael reported that the stone fortress of the Count was exceedingly well built and strategically positioned. If the Centurions intended to invade the Greenway overland, they first would have to take this fortress, which now was well armed and well manned. Thanks to our efforts, it was also well supplied. Raphael had a long conversation with Count Basilica and reported that this man considered himself separate from the authority of the Prince of Velona and wouldn't be following the Prince's orders or allowing the Prince's guards into his fortress. Because of his location so distant from Velona, the Prince cared little for his independent status.

However, while they were there, Lucretia Botini, the training leader of the Velona sector of the Sisterhood arrived along with five hundred Sisters! Until recently, the Sisterhood had been escorting the many convoys of people moving out of Velona into the outlying towns and villages. The Prince had paid them well to ensure that the mass migration went without any bandit attacks. However, only a couple weeks ago she learned the real reason that the city was evacuated, that the Prince had set the plague upon the conquering Centurions. For her and the Sisterhood, this was the last straw. After sending word of this and her plans by secret courier to the other sectors, she had brought all the Sisters in the Velona sector to Count Basilica's fortress. One night, the sisters in each town and village just disappeared, never to be seen again.

Lucretia seemed very glad to see Raphael and Sarah Jane present and asked them to attend her official conference with the Count. She began, "The reason Velona has been abandoned is that our illustrious Prince has brought the plague into the city in hopes of killing the Centurion army."

Count Basilica, an imposing man in his mid-thirties with black hair and moustache, replied, "Ah, now events begin to make sense. The plague! The fool! Does he think he is immune? Tur help us all!"

Lucretia continued, "So, I gathered all the Sisterhood in our sector together and gave them two choices: either migrate at once to another sector or come up here with me. Most have chosen to follow me here, Count Basilica. We have but two choices. Some wish to seek asylum here with you, Count. Some want to forsake our lands entirely and travel to the Greenway. I must ask you, Count, would you accept so many Sisters here in your fortress and treat them with respect? Personally, I haven't made up my mind whether to go to the Greenway or to wait it out here in your fortress. A lot depends upon you. What say you? Do you look upon us as Abominations?"

The Count pulled on his moustache thinking quickly. "Here in my fortress, space is at a premium, and we're all living in close proximity to each other. We're not like the Prince. I believe you'll find that we respect our women far more than the city men do. As you know, I don't believe that you have ever recruited a Sister from here because of some mistreatment. Is it true that the Sisterhood of Zargarb stood and fought the invaders, inflicting many casualties upon them? We've heard all sorts of rumors."

"You heard truthfully. Some hundred Sisterhood fighters gave their lives to defend Zargarb when everything else had failed. They took five times their numbers with them to the grave. If we stay here, we owe you no less loyalty," Lucretia answered him honestly.

"Sister Lucretia, I would be a fool if I didn't accept your request for asylum here. I suspect that I'll need every able-bodied fighter in the not so distant future. The only real problem is that we don't have enough housing within the fortress to provide five hundred more with a place to live. We probably could arrange for perhaps half that number. If the rest could find sanctuary in Calgary, some hundred miles to the north, then when the battle comes, they could ride to our defense, if they desired to help. Those that stayed here would have to follow my orders, though. I can't have two different sets of orders flying around. Would they need to be housed separate from all others? I know that in Velona your Sisters are used to staying in separate housing from the other citizens."

"You realize that these women have been traumatized by men or even brutally attacked or maimed? Many are terrified of men and want to stay as far from them as possible, but I see your point. What about this idea? Let those that can handle living in closer quarters with your people stay here and those that would find that too difficult to do go on to Calgary. I know when the fight comes, most will want to return here to help defend. After all, the Lands of Sea Princes is our rightful home too. Would that work?"

"Splendid! Welcome Sisters to Fortress d'Grange!" the Count enthusiastically gestured. So began a unification of forces. Two hundred-fifty Sisters followed Lucretia on up to the Greenway, led by Raphael and Sarah Jane on their return trip. Another two hundred-forty took up residence within the stone walls of Fortress d'Grange.

Naturally, we welcomed all the Sisters, and Isabel had her hands full trying to find housing for so many, okay, not literally. She and Martha had a hectic, though enjoyable challenge. While perhaps only half of these Sisters were actually fighters, we still counted our blessings that so many were now concentrated here where we would most need their special skills. After all, they were the only fighters who had slain any real numbers of the invaders.

Raphael's report on the Count's fortress was highly encouraging. All we needed to do was provide them with grain and dried meats and they could hold out indefinitely. Further, Raphael thought he could build a stone fortification for us here in Calgary. It wouldn't protect the whole city, but, properly placed, it could command a prominent position, one that could not be ignored. Of course, the only drawback was the years that would be needed to build such a fortification. We didn't expect to have years to prepare.

In contrast to all this encouraging news, Roy's and Thomas's report on our coastline was the opposite. If the Centurions chose to invade by sea, there were more than a dozen places where ships could be easily beached and troops disembarked. I had no hope of defending all them. Thus, we knew that somehow we must discover where they intended to attack us first.

To my surprise, the merchants of Calgary really took to the new skill of writing and reading. Among the people of the Greenway, it took off like a wildfire; by the end of the year, hundreds and hundreds of people were demanding to be taught how to write and read. The logging of facts and accounting had just been revolutionized! Those in business immediately saw in it a tremendous potential and wanted to know how to do it. Any misgivings I had about perhaps only we druwids would take to writing and reading were forever dispelled.

All this added together cast the future in a bright light for me. We could afford to get married and begin our families. The world was not about to end tomorrow. Later, when the weather warmed and the land greened, we could journey to Karka, be reunited with our respective families, and hold a civil marriage ceremony for their benefit. Yes, this Spring had brought renewed life to us all.

Curiously, in these past weeks I still hadn't found what those two additional keys unlocked. Though I had examined everything in Alabaster's room carefully, I found nothing there that I didn't already know. The night before our wedding ceremony, Roy and I found ourselves in Alabaster's room, sitting on his bed speculating on what these two keys might unlock.

Roy was of the opinion that they opened something very secret and valuable. "Have you and Raphael measured out everything in this complex? Are there any other discrepancies like that side stairs to the hidden cellar rooms? How about this room? Checked everywhere for any secret compartments?"

"Alas, we have, Roy; three times to be exact. I've thumped all over this room. I swear that there are no hidden places in here. Actually, Alabaster's room is just that, a sleeping room with clothes and personal stuff. There's nothing of any importance in here at all. Yet, I can't see him wandering far — he always got so tired so easily. If he had something valuable, surely it has to be near here; but where is a complete mystery."

We laid down on Alabaster's bed. I rested my head on Roy's shoulder, moving my long hair idly to my left side. Together, our minds joined, and we thought about the mystery of the two keys. Perhaps that action helped make the connection, who can say.

Bethany. Bethany, Alabaster here. Oh, I see Roy's here too. That's okay. Alabaster had suddenly, without warning, made telepathic contact with us! I nearly shrieked — I was that startled. After all, I thought that he was dead and long gone, starting over with an infant body somewhere. Roy merely choked and coughed. We both sat straight up, staring about the room, which was dimly illuminated by an oil lantern on the desk. We didn't see him.

You are alive! I sent back without thinking. Oops, I thought: *Bethany, that was really stupid! Of course, he exists.*

Roy sent to me, *Calm down. He understands.*

Where are you? Are you okay? I started on a better approach.

For your safety's sake, I won't say where I am now. I'll say this, I'm where you were the first to go. Roy picked up on this and suggested that he was in the caverns that we found when we crossed the Appian Way. *Bright lad,* Alabaster placed in Roy's mind. *Let's see, ah yes. As you know or may not know, my body was taking more and more of my attention and energies just to keep it alive. Bodies are supposed to grow old and die, you know. I just didn't let mine die, but at last, it was taking so much of my attention to keep it running, so I just finally let it go. I have so much to do, you know. I've paid a visit to those creatures you encountered in the Appian Way and am about to go pay a visit on those mantises you discovered in the Red Desert. But can I have a complete report on your return please? All the details of our special project in particular, please.*

So I related our experiences in the Red Desert as well as what we had seen in the Appian Way. He asked for clarification on a number of details. When I finished, he sent, *You aren't imagining it. For quite some time, I suspected that there was an outside influence at work. Several years ago, I too saw them at work, having followed a fellow whose body had just died. That you too saw them confirms what I had suspected. My latest round of observations shows that they are still doing it with the many that are dying in Velona. Now how goes everything in Calgary? Has Martha given you my final message? Any problems?*

I quickly outlined what all I had done, including using Isabel as their replacement Wid. It took me several minutes to fully brief him. *Ah, things have gone even better than I had hoped. Very well done, Wid Bethany, well done indeed. Yes, Isabel was an excellent choice. Now I suspect you have some questions for me?*

We both chuckled, his was an understatement. *First, we have two keys here that no one seems to know what they unlock.*

Ah, they unlock my personal gift to you, Wid Bethany, and my heritage to the druwids. I regret not having spoken of these to you before. However, I expected still to be around when you returned. In the secret counting room along the north wall behind the desk there lies a secret door, which opens into a long underground corridor. It leads to the stables — you know, in case we need to make a fast getaway. Along the hall, there are two side rooms and the keys open them. The first room you find on your left — the entire contents of that room are for you to use as you see fit. The second room a little further along on your right contains all the druwid artifacts I've accumulated over these couple of centuries. Roy, you should take the legendary Sword of Agnar, as it should be used, not hidden away.

I took a deep breath knowing that this might be the last time I ever had the chance to speak to Alabaster. *Second, what should we do? I mean the Centurions are still likely to invade us, though we have slowed them down greatly. I have the Count defending the land entrance down south, but there are a dozen places at least where they could invade by sea, and if they come through the Northern Steppes, Galt lands, we've nothing to stop them there.*

My dear child, I can't advise you on what you should do. The druwids are now in your hands. I can say this, though: so far, you have done splendidly, just what I would have done. You'll do what you think best at the time. Try to know all the facts first before reaching a decision. That is what I always practice, and it serves me well. As you know, it takes two sides to have a fight. In a war, neither side really wins, and the pain and suffering of the common man who pays the price of war is great. If only conflicts could be settled by taking the two opposing generals into a room and let them fight each other, think of all the suffering that would be avoided. Surely if the druwids go to war, it will be the end of them. If the Centurions discover that we have the power to bring down lightning, you'll be hunted down like animals and destroyed, one by one. Our numbers still are not large enough. On the other hand, as you and Simon or Simone so cleverly showed, we druwids can work miracles in the background of history. Your great challenge is to find a way to survive.

But I have to get going. I think these grey creatures are on to my location. This will be the last time I contact you. It's for your safety. I don't want them to know about you just yet, or your life would be in dire jeopardy. Don't try to contact me either, because if I responded, it would likely give my location away to these strange creatures. Just know I'm trying to do something about their interference in our lives. Goodbye Bethany and Roy. Thank you both for taking over for me. I love you both. As suddenly as he had appeared in our minds, he was gone, leaving a great loss, a great sadness upon me once again. It was as if I watched him pass away twice! Tears flowed and I really needed to hug Roy close to me for some time. Roy was my rock, my foundation.

We lay there still as a mouse for over an hour. The oil lamp went out, run dry. In my mind, I replayed all that he had said, over and over. Finally, my grief left me. Roy broke the silence first, "Bethany, do you realize what a tremendous gift Alabaster has given you? When we lose a loved one, we never get to chat with them after they're gone. He came back to you and chatted, answering your lingering questions. Pretty amazing fellow!"

"Well, I guess I haven't made a fool of myself trying to run things in his place," I replied. "Golly, it's late. Maybe we should go see what is in those two rooms. If we go now, few would notice our absence."

Together, after casting our blue lights, we refilled the lantern and relit it. Next, we got the keys and my Eternal Light gift from the Moon people, and headed down into the secret counting room. It took Roy only minutes to carefully move the desk and open the secret door into the escape tunnel that led to the stables. Using my Eternal Light, we walked down the narrow passage. Six feet high and four wide, it was a narrow tunnel indeed. However, it hadn't been used in many years. Cobwebs often blocked our passage, and the dust was a half-inch thick on the stone floor. Soon we stood before the first door on the left. I inserted one of the two keys; it was fifty-fifty. This one didn't work, so I tried the other, and the lock clicked open. We pushed the door open and shone the light inside. We weren't prepared for what we saw.

Alabaster had given me a treasury room! I guess it is safe to say that a man of Alabaster's power doesn't live for two and a half centuries without accumulating some wealth. Here were boxes of gold, silver, and gems by the hundreds. If we were to transport all these valuables, they would fill two wagons! I was speechless. Roy commented, "Well, looks as if we can fund just about anything that Raphael can dream of building!" My sentiments exactly.

Locking the door, we headed on down the tunnel to the first door on the right. Opening it, we shone the light inside and then entered. Artifacts, bits of history, lay nicely arrayed upon several tables. Various swords, daggers, crowns, amulets, statues, and other items covered every inch of tabletop space. One large two-handed sword immediately caught Roy's eyes. It held a huge red ruby in its pummel and had some gold fillet around it. Carefully, he drew the legendary Sword of Agnar from its leather scabbard.

Holding the sword with great reverence, Roy recited the story we had long ago been taught surrounding this sword. Nearly three centuries ago, in a hamlet where Calgary now stood, King Agnar, the first and only King of all the Greenway forged this mighty sword. Some say that Agnar came from Volksholm and was a descendant from that hardy race who lived in the lands of ice and snow of the far north. He stood over six feet, had huge muscles, and so could wield this mighty sword. With it, he drove out all the northern invaders and established himself as King of Greenway. Thus, Calgary was founded. After he died in a hunting accident, his several sons fought among themselves and divided the Greenway into parcels, none of which lasted more than a few years. It was at this time that Alabaster founded the druwids, and the Guardians took over protecting the inhabitants of the Greenway.

"How did Alabaster get this sword?" I mused. "Could Alabaster have actually known King Agnar?" Roy smiled and suggested anything was possible when it came to Alabaster. I filed that question away to be asked if ever he should contact me again. Nothing about Alabaster would ever surprise me again!

We retraced our steps and carefully put the desk back into place, hiding the secret entrance to the tunnel. When we finally entered our commons room, all the others were asleep. We kissed goodnight and went into our separate rooms. As I laid down on my bed, I realized in just a few more hours we would be wedded. Once again, so much had happened or was about to happen that I couldn't get to sleep. My mind was racing down numerous paths that night.

The next morning, the girls roused me out of bed early. "Come on; we've got to take a hot bath and get ready. Martha wants to leave before noon. Come on sleepy head," Sarah Jane teased me. The excitement of this day drove all other thoughts from my mind. We bathed, dressed, and ate breakfast. By the time we were ready to go, the guys had already saddled our horses. Yes, we four appreciated their consideration. As we mounted up, I discovered we were indeed a large party. Not only were there seven from the Circle of All Greenway and our Circle of seven more, but also a large number of the Sisters joined us. Most wanted to witness Thallia's wedding as well as ours. Over fifty men, women, and children rode out of the compound this late morning.

The standing stones nearest Calgary were about five miles out of town off to the southeast in a secluded valley far from any farmsteads. Once we all arrived, Martha handed out decorations and soon gay colored banners flapped in the light wind denoting the very special occasion. Others from more distant Circles began arriving too. Food and drink were laid out; the party began. Several folks played various instruments, and quickly dancing became the thing to do for those of us who were young or young at heart.

After the early supper came our ceremonies, all done in proper druwid fashion. Martha and Isabel presided over the wedding proper, for this is one of the duties of a Wid. Each of the four couples had a golden chalice filled with a red wine, symbolic of the blood of our lives, which were now being joined into one. Isabel spoke the vows, while each couple drank from their chalice, sealing their pact before all Nature. First, she explained to our guests, "Tonight, you are witnessing a druwid ceremony to wed these couples. Ours is a simple ceremony, in Harmony with Nature. Later, they will renew their vows in a proper civil ceremony in Karka, where their families are located. If you also witness that one, you'll likely see a wedding that is more like what you are accustomed to seeing in your own lands of the Sea Princes."

"We are gathered together this evening to bear witness to the joining of these four couples in Nature's sacred covenant of marriage. In order for Nature to create a future, a man and woman must join together. Neither alone can produce a child, but through the gift bestowed by Nature, the two, acting as one, produces the future, our children. And so has Life proceeded since the dawn of time. Each of these couples has sworn to join together forming a union of one from this night forward. Each has sworn to honor and respect the other, to abide by the decisions they mutually create, and to treat each other as equals in all matters. Tonight, we also celebrate the coming of Spring, once again renewing all life on Tarra. Symbolically, they begin a new life together in total harmony with Nature itself."

She continued with the ceremony, but I drifted off into the significance of this day — Nature's return of Life and ours just beginning, so utterly romantic! I did manage to come out of my reverie in time to hear her say, "By the powers invested in me, I pronounce these four couples wedded. I now ask you to seal your vows with a Holy Kiss." Roy and I eagerly embraced, and everyone began cheering and clapping. Once we finished, she continued, "And now the hour has come for our two Circles to celebrate and honor this Holy Day. The sun is setting. Please take your places beside the stones. The rest of you are welcome to observe. Please note the spot where the last rays of the sun strike — this mark here on this stone. It marks the coming of equal days and nights once more. The sun will not strike this spot again as it sets until the Autumnal Equinox." Quickly, we took our positions behind the seven outer stones. Many of the Sisters crowded close to Isabel so they could see the sun's rays on the mark in the stone. Once it had occurred, they asked her many questions about it. She enjoyed sharing bits of astronomical lore with them.

One footnote to the reader, in the Greenway, when a couple marry, it is customary for the couple to decide upon their new last names. Sometimes, the men take the women's last name; others, the women take the men's. It is also possible to take them both in whatever order they desire or even choose a totally new last name that neither has. For example, Roy and I could be known as Roy and Bethany Randell, Roy and Bethany Stanton, Roy and Bethany Randell Stanton, Roy and Bethany Stanton Randell, Roy Randell and Bethany Stanton, or Roy and Bethany WhatSoEver. In the Greenway at this time, a couple chose what had the most meaning for them. We chose to be called Roy and Bethany Randell Stanton because Roy insisted that the Wid was more important than the Protector was. The others were now known as Raphael and Sarah Jane Penton, Simon and Sandy Glaston Donegal, and Thomas and Thallia Wilkins.

As soon as the official ceremony had finished, the music began once more, and everyone came to congratulate us and we them. Then, it was party time once more until the hour grew late. Another footnote: in the Greenway at this time, no one gives the bride and groom presents, for that is the sole province of their parents, who usually give household items with which to start their new home. When we would hold our civil ceremony back in Karka for our parents and families, our folks would give us suitable presents, bearing in mind that, unlike normal couples just starting out, we did not actually need anything at the moment, especially with the wedding present Alabaster had given me last night.

It was the idle thought of my parents giving Roy and myself some presents that reminded me of Alabaster's visit and gifts last night. On the long ride home, I told the others that I had a secret surprise for them when we got back to our commons room. Roy beamed and grinned broadly, so the other six knew that he was somehow involved in the secret.

A couple hours later and around one in the morning, we eight finally plopped down on the soft chairs in our commons room. "This had better be really good," Sarah Jane teased, "I'm all ready to bed Raphael here. It is our wedding night, you know." Everyone chuckled, for we all were thinking the same thing.

"Okay gang, I'll give you the short version," I teased back. Quickly, I told of the telepathic meeting Roy and I had last night with Alabaster. I related how we had found the secret tunnel and the two secret rooms. I ended with a very brief description of their contents. I was done in less than two minutes. "There, satisfied?" I teased back, knowing that none of these six was. We then spent nearly a half hour discussing everything in full detail. I promised that we would discuss this more fully in the morning. Finally, we four couples got to spend our first night together as man and wife.

The next morning, we women had that radiant look about our faces, while the men had that totally contented, satisfied appearance. Arm in arm, we four couples headed down for breakfast, knowing that we would take tea back in our commons room, and after that, we'd discuss the heavy impact of Alabaster's words and gifts.

Sipping tea while facing my Circle, I began by saying, "First, though Alabaster specifically left his accumulated fortune to me, I intend see that you all always have everything you need. Specifically, Raphael, anytime you need construction money, just let me know. We can finance just about anything! However, this also presents a new problem and a large one. If Calgary falls to the Centurions, we can't leave a fortune like this down there. They are surely likely to search this compound very thoroughly — what with it being the seat of the Guardians. Also, all the historical items can't be left here either, nor can Alabaster's records of our population."

"Well, why don't we transcribe Alabaster's counting into writing on some scrolls?" suggested Sarah Jane, ever the practical one. "A few scrolls are easier to transport and store than a mountain of sticks and strings." We agreed this was the wisest course to take, though it took the seven of us close to four months to accomplish the task converting Alabaster's census records onto scrolls.

"It seems to me that the treasury and the historical items must go wherever we go if Calgary falls," Raphael suggested. "Where will we go and when? Do we have time to build some kind of fortress?"

"Ah, herein lies the problem," I replied. "It may be that we'll never be attacked. It may be that the entire Greenway may be conquered just like the Sea Princes, Juda Arad, and the Southlands. They might come later this year or five years from now or never. If they come, should we, the Protectors, do the fighting? We can't stand alone. Our numbers are too small, even if we could somehow get all the druwids to come here to Calgary. Do we try to organize an army of Greenway men and women? Will they even want to fight this battle? Their chances of success are even worse than the Sea Princes, for our people are basically farmers not fighters. Remember Alabaster's last bit of advice to us: 'On the other hand, as you and Simon or Simone so cleverly showed, we druwids can work miracles in the background of history. Your great challenge is to find a way to survive.' Our whole organization is based on having one of us in each village to help the people there, especially with healing and driving off the Galts and Axemen."

"If we, the druwids, openly go to war with these Centurions, they'll have no choice but to hunt us down, one by one, and kill us, for they can't tolerate anyone who possesses the kind of power that we do. Our existence would be a constant threat to them; they would have no other real choice but to wipe us out."

"Are you saying that we just give up the Greenway without even a fight?" protested Roy. Simon echoed his sentiments.

"I'm saying that if we go into open battle like Isabel did, then if we didn't totally defeat the Centurions, they would, in time, wipe out every living druwid in the Greenway. What other choice would they have?" I replied.

Simon straightened up and pretended to put on his Arbitrator Hat. "Okay, in a situation such as this, there are only five actions one can take. First, one can attack the enemy. Second, one can try to avoid or bypass the enemy somehow. Third, one can ignore the enemy and carry on with what one is doing. Fourth, one can succumb and totally surrender. Fifth, one can run away from the enemy. In the case of the Greenway, the country can't ignore the invaders should they come nor can the country flee. This leaves only three choices: succumb, attack, or somehow avoid the enemy. The situation is compounded by our side having two different participants: the local militia and the druwids, as well as the fact that the Greenway, as a country, has no controlling ruler, such as the Princes. Let's face it, gang, we're supposed to be protecting and aiding our people here, not acting as divine rulers making the decision whether to go to war or not on their behalf. That ought to be their decision, not ours."

I added, "Precisely, Simon. In addition, it must be clear that if they choose to go to war, then they must understand that we can only participate indirectly, behind the scenes, and not openly on the battlefield. I sure don't want to be responsible for bringing down the destruction of the entire druwid network that Alabaster created. No way. So our part must be subtle and seem like Nature intervening."

"Agreed," Simon acknowledged. "May I suggest that we get in contact with all of the Communicators of all the Circles? Have them explain the situation to those under their care and get their wishes in this matter."

Thomas broke in, "What would be the choices that we give to the people?"

"Do they want to mobilize their own men and women, go to war, and fight the Centurions or do they want us to try to work out some way to avoid a war, letting them 'occupy' as much of the Greenway as they demand? The Centurions can't ask for gold each year; there is none in the Greenway and precious little silver, for that matter. More than likely, the yearly payment would be in grain or dried meats."

Sandy added, "A side benefit might be that the Centurions would build paved roads between the larger towns."

"All in favor?" I took a vote. It passed unanimously. Sandy and I went to explain what we wanted done to the All Greenway Circle. They also thought this was a wise move. We let Communicator Able implement the action, because this had always been his major function as Communicator for the topmost Circle. Sandy and I rejoined the others.

Next, Roy and I led the others, including Thallia, to the secret tunnel and showed them the contents of the two secret rooms. All were dumbfounded at the immense wealth in our possession. An hour later back in our commons room, we held a discussion on what to do with the treasury and the heirlooms. On one point, we were all in complete agreement: if the Centurions came, it had to be moved, because this complex would probably be thoroughly searched. Sandy also pointed out that if the Centurions occupied Calgary, then we wouldn't be safe living here either. On the other hand, the All Greenway Circle would be safe, with the possible exception of Isabel. We all agreed that we would have to move somewhere else, but where?

Talk about a hot topic of discussion! We spent the rest of the day tossing out idea after idea. Some thought we needed to be fairly close to Calgary, the heart of our land. Some thought we needed a fortification to defend ourselves as well as any other druwid who felt threatened by the Centurions. Others thought we needed to be deep in the forest, so we could easily sneak out and in without being seen. Others preferred to be in the middle of the Greenway where the population was small and the Centurions less likely to ever go in force. Others felt we needed to be near the coast so we could make use of the Sea Prince boats if the need arose. Guess who finally coalesced all the ideas into one bright plan? Thomas, our Loremaster.

"Gang, I have an idea that might work. As you know, I've traveled around here quite a lot more than the rest of you. Just south and east of here lies Mont Blanc at the very edge of the Langdoc region. While the mountain is fairly barren, a dense oak forest grows at its very feet. There are numerous limestone caverns in that region as well. Suppose we build a stone fortress on Mont Blanc, rather like the one that Count d'Grange has done. We would have ample forests, water, farmland, and still be within twenty-five miles of Calgary and the coast. If we really were harried, we could ride out across the Langdoc to the caves and retrace our path to the Sea Princes to escape. Those caves are only a little over a hundred miles from Mont Blanc. Besides, I'll wager some of the Sisters would also like to join us in a place safe from the Centurions. In fact, we could found a small town there within the fortress walls. Oh, Thallia, there ought to be beautiful, virgin meadows there as well. No one lives anywhere near there. The Langdoc region isn't good for much of anything. We would be remote, but not far away. What do you think?"

"Hurray!" we chorused, as we instantly fell in love with his plan. It answered all of our needs, if only there was time enough to construct it before the Centurions came.

"I've a theory about that," Simon broke in on our cheering. "If I were the invaders, before I sent in an invasion fleet, I would send in either a spy or an ambassador, whose task would be to scout out the land. You know, find the best places for an invasion, find their weak points, find where the booty may likely be, and find out what value the land holds for us. Perhaps they have already done just that. We could ask around and see if any bronzed-skinned men have been here in Calgary in say the last year or so. Or they could be using Sea Prince sailors as spies. Either way, if we could meet this person, we could see what we might be able to arrange to avoid this war. The more I keep thinking about this whole mess, the more I can envision ways to bypass going to war with them, that is, assuming the people here don't want war and would accept being occupied by the Centurions as an alternative."

"I think you are precisely correct, Simon. We should investigate and see if they have already done just this. If not, we should maintain a sharp lookout for such a person and arrange a meeting with him. Consider it done. I'll see to the necessary details," I concurred. The number of bright ideas coming from a Circle once more convinced me of the wisdom of Alabaster's druwid Circles, with each member being specialized in some key area. I wondered how he originally thought of this aspect in the first place — another question to ask him if he ever made contact again got filed in my mind.

In two days' time, by March 24, 560 AH, I had people on the go once more. Half of my Circle, including Thallia, went off to scout out Mont Blanc for a suitable location for our new fortress home. Simon and Sandy began searching Calgary for any clues that a Centurion spy had already been here. Roy and I began work on crating up the historical items and monetary funds for transport. We wanted to be able to make a fast getaway should the need arise.

Chapter 26 The Plague and the Centurions

It was mid-December 559 AH, General Thrace Theocopolous pulled on his neatly trimmed, black goatee. Light snow covered the ground as his loyal soldiers worked double shifts to follow his orders to build the roadway to Velona before the end of the year. Leader of the entire First Phalanx of Megalos, General Thrace faced a mid-morning meeting with his two key subordinates: Major Hercules Thesis, Commander of the First Phalanx, Forward Assault Group, and Major Bracious Kronos, Commander of the Second Phalanx, Forward Assault Group. The Governor-to-shortly-be of Velona, Helix Nickolopous would also attend; the General had been informed, probably to pin down just how soon he would be allowed to move into the city and into descent quarters. General Thrace loved camping out of doors with his men under less than homey conditions, but he found that the Governors were softies, nearly unable to cope with army life on the road.

This has turned out to be a piece of cake, General Thrace thought to himself. He'd assumed command more than a year ago, when the entire strike force was still in Juda Arad awaiting deployment. The entire success of this whole campaign to conquer the Lands of the Sea Princes had been due to his leadership and advance planning. Though admittedly, he had suffered a totally unexpected setback just as he was conquering the first city-state, Zargarb. Who could have foretold that the amazon women would join the fight and prove to be the only adversary worth mentioning for as long as the General could remember? In fact, as he mused upon this detail, he couldn't recall any other group of fighters in the entire history of Megalos who had offered any real challenge. That stormy day, he'd lost five hundred excellent soldiers, the only significant losses in the entire campaign. No, it had to have been the combination of the freak thunderstorm that caused all their problems. After all, the intense lightning destroyed nearly half of his entire chariot fleet! He was thankful the other half had been held in reserve and saw no action during that battle. Foresight of Sol, he claimed, but really, he felt that he didn't need them that day.

However, ever since Governor Lexus had struck a fine bargain with these amazons, they hadn't intervened at all during his conquest of the other five cities, and he didn't expect them to hinder him here at Velona. However, the two years he had spent out here in the wilderness had taken their toll. General Thrace longed to return back to Megalos and his family. He hadn't seen his wife and two children for over three years. He wondered how big little Alexia had become; she ought to be four years old now. In fact, this was the primary reason General Thrace had pushed up his timetable of conquest. Velona would fall within days, and then he could return home for a much-needed respite. So could all his Forward Assault Group, and he knew just how badly they wanted to return home, even if only for a few months. The Rear

Guard Group had the responsibility of holding onto the conquered territory. Thrace was very glad that he hadn't taken that commission! Those men wouldn't likely see home for at least six years or more!

Another thing weighed heavily on his mind. Only a month ago news had reached him by overland courier that Emperor Hiro had been killed in some kind of freakish lightning storm that had also heavily damaged the royal palace. He'd never liked that man, so his loss wasn't what worried him. No, who would be the replacement and what would his new orders be? Those worried him. With Hiro, General Thrace had always gotten precisely what he'd asked for, in both men and equipment. Would the new Emperor be so generous? There was also the very troubling news that same freak storm had somehow loosened boulders at the major dam that fed the aqueducts that provided most of the water to Galantia where his family lived. Did they have water to drink and bathe? He'd sent several posts back to his wife, but as yet had not heard from her. This he found most disturbing; she had never been so tardy in replying to his letters. No, General Thrace intended to put an end to this campaign within a few weeks and head home, preferably commandeering one of the Sea Prince boats to take him to Juda Arad.

It was time for the meeting, and General Thrace made last minute adjustments to his wardrobe. Satisfied he looked the perfect General, he gave the order to admit his fellow officers and the Governor. The three men entered, Governor Helix Nickolopous moved quickly and quietly to the rear; he feared this commanding General. Major Hercules Thesis, Commander of the First Phalanx, Forward Assault Group, spoke first, "The road is nearly done. My forces are positioned around the eastern half of Velona. No resistance to date."

Major Bracious Kronos, Commander of the Second Phalanx, Forward Assault Group, added, "My forces have circled around to the western side and have the city cut off from the rest of the sector. We await the assault orders, General."

"Nothing suspicious going on? Still no puny Prince cavalry attacks?"

"No, General, no signs of activity from Velona. Sir, may I speak frankly?" Major Hercules inquired. The general nodded his assent.

"Well, it's mighty strange here. By now, we should have fought many of the city guard forces. At least we did so with the other six cities. Do you suppose that they are holding all their forces back to fight door-to-door in an attempt to make us pay dearly for taking the city? Are we seeing a new tactic in play?"

Major Bracious added, "Tis very strange. We haven't even seen but a few isolated smoke tendrils. Could no one in the city be using cooking fires anymore? And why would they not? Is there any point in not using fires to cook and warm bath waters?"

"Well, this Prince has the advantage of having watched the tactics used by his six other Princes — to no avail, I might add. I would expect him to try some other tactics to defend his city. I know I would, but then we're so much smarter than these barbarians are. Still, my plan stays. We'll assault the city just as soon as the road is a quarter mile from the outskirts. By the end of December, Velona will be ours, and we can all be on ships headed for home and a well-deserved break." This brought smiles to both major's faces. They too longed for home. For them, this had been a most boring campaign, ever since the initial battle for Zargarb. Besides, every Centurion hated the cold and snow, even if the snow here in the Sea Princes was never more than a light dusting. These soldiers came from Megalos, where the weather was hot all year round, and their skins bronzed in response to all that sunlight.

At last, Governor Helix spoke up, "So I'm led to believe I'll be able to take charge of Velona within a couple weeks?"

The general only nodded, thinking to himself, "Half-wit — hasn't heard a word I've said — politicians!"

Undeterred, Governor Helix continued, "Well as you know, it's vital that I get in touch with these amazon women who call themselves the Sisterhood. Please, as soon as anyone of you comes across one of them, please send her to me. I'm obligated to seek a pact with them similar to what Governor Lexus has done. Emperor's orders, you know." He seemed satisfied he'd made this point quite clear. These military men often cared little about running and governing a land, only in conquering it. No, it took men of superior knowledge and skill, men like Governor Helix, to change the heathen city into a civilized bastion.

By the time that their supply road was finished, General Thrace started to become worried. No, not worried so much as annoyed. Why hadn't these stupid Velona guards failed to come out upon the battlefield and attack them? Their complete absence — not even a scouting party — began to weigh on his mind. Unusual, yes. His mind raced through all the tactics and strategies with which he had been trained. Nothing matched, except the possibility of hand-to-hand, house-by-house defense. Surely, this must be what the Prince intended. However, General Thrace wouldn't let such actions delay him. So he ordered the assault, only this time, both phalanxes would converge into the city at the same time from all sides, save the ocean. From a hilltop, he could make out the masts of at least one ship still in port, which he took as a good sign. Still troubling were the distinct lack of normal signs of city life. Had all the people been ordered to stay indoors? It appeared so. He raised his right arm and brought it down swiftly, signaling the simultaneous attack of over five thousand Centurions. He watched as his strong men marched in unison into the city from all sides. He waited for the telltale sounds of combat. None came.

Within a few minutes, he spied a dispatch rider galloping out from the city toward his position. News, he thought. "Sir, the city is empty!" the rider said. The news took a moment to sink in to his mind-set.

"Empty?" he queried in disbelief.

"Yes, sir. Not a soul anywhere. The people have all vanished! The majors are systematically going door-to-door, but so far they haven't encountered anyone, not even a dog. What is going on here anyway?"

"Take me to the majors at once," he barked, insisting on viewing the obviously safe battlefield personally. Yes, his aide had raised a key question. Where had they all gone? Suddenly, he saw his return trip to Megalos evaporating rapidly. This wasn't what he had in mind at all. A hundred thousand people just don't disappear into thin air. Perhaps they were gathered in one heavily fortified sector of the city. *Yes, that has to be it*, he decided on the brief ride into Velona. Governor Helix, on the other hand, stayed upon the hilltop, awaiting the outcome.

General Thrace met his two majors, joining for a conference, because neither knew what to do at this point. It wasn't in their training. Quickly, General Thrace ordered the cavalry to ride down the main streets all the way to the docks in an attempt to flush out the defenders. Meanwhile, the majors were ordered to continue their house-to-house search. Finally, riders came back to him to report that they met no resistance at all and that there was only one decrepit old ship in port. By nightfall, they had secured Velona, moving into the choicest buildings. Naturally, Governor Helix took one of the finest buildings in town. Over dinner, Governor Helix and General Thrace conferred; the governor wasn't at all pleased with the situation.

"This is a disaster, General; it's all your fault! There's no one here to govern. How am I expected to civilize when there are no people? What are you going to do about it?" He was extremely upset. Suddenly all his hopes of reaching another judicious settlement, as had Governor Lexus, just evaporated. Instead, if something wasn't done soon, he would become the laughing stock of Megalos — a governor of an empty city!

"Some new treachery is afoot here. A hundred thousand people don't just vanish. They have to be here somewhere. There aren't enough boats in all of the Sea Princes to move so many people elsewhere. They'll turn up. We'll find them. Meantime, I see no reason that my men shouldn't avail themselves of all the comforts of the city. It appears that nothing is sabotaged. Even their crude bathhouses are fully operational. However, there does seem to be a distinct lack of edible supplies to be found. I'm afraid for the near future, Governor, you'll still have to dine on our trail rations. We'll know more in the morning. Now if you will excuse me, I have much to do yet tonight. I have a whole population to locate." The General stomped out of the meeting fully annoyed, not with the Governor, rather with his own foolishness. He had become so overconfident of total success that he had failed even to send in advance lookouts, preferring to give them a well-deserved break from the constant action. Now he deeply regretted his decision.

Meeting with the two majors, he issued the only orders that he could, under the circumstances. "The Prince must have evacuated the whole city right under our noses. Thus, we have a hundred thousand people to find. My guess is that they are to be found in the outlying towns and villages. Normally, we leave those to the Rear Guard, but it'll be our hides if we leave this for them to handle. No, I'm afraid we must delay our trip home a little longer, men. Tomorrow, send out cavalry patrols. Fan out from the city in all directions. They must be around here somewhere. Actually, this plays well into our hands.

Divided up into many smaller pieces and so out of communication, we can even more easily defeat them. I'll draw up some search patterns for the morrow. You prepare your forces. We want to take them out just as soon as we encounter them." With that, the General returned to a fine home that his staff had decided was befitting a conquering general. He stayed up late drawing out the searching patterns that would rapidly find the opposing forces. The Prince would soon see the utter folly of this surprise move.

By the end of the next day, the first reports had come back to General Thrace. The news was not encouraging. That the Prince had moved the entire population from the city had been proved. A dozen smaller towns and villages close to Velona had been searched. Uniformly, they found many, many new and hastily built dwellings. Each was estimated to be at double or triple its usual size. However, no one offered any resistance to the Centurions; they found no armed forces. Uniformly, at each, they were informed that the Prince was not here. No one knew where he was at or how to get a hold of him. Neither did anyone know the whereabouts of the Church of Tur leaders. The amazon women had all disappeared. Thus, it went for the next three days.

Finally, General Thrace accepted the situation. "Governor, I give you the city and the outlying towns. Evidently, both the Prince and the Church have fled for distant parts unknown. All the towns and villages we've visited are leaderless and have offered not the slightest bit of resistance to our forces. Thus, I conclude that the city is secured. There is no threat of any counter-attack. I think you have your work cut out for you, since you're going to have to go to each village and establish your Rule by Law. I've sent for the Rear Guard, but my men will accompany you for the time being. In fact, I've placed Major Hercules Thesis at your complete disposal. He'll follow any orders that you give him. The rest of the men will bunk here in the city until the Rear Guard arrives, and we can arrange for transport back to Megalos."

The Governor bit his lip. This had not gone at all according to plan. Instead of an easy turnover of power, now he had to do everything repeatedly at each new town and village. "But what of the amazons? You haven't brought one to me yet. Surely, you have found them in these villages."

"No, and that is a bit strange. They are nowhere to be seen. As far as we can tell, those women are uniformly hated. We checked for them in every village we searched. I'm sure the men there would have given up any amazons that might have been hiding out there. You wouldn't believe the animosity the men here have toward them. Actually, they are called the Abominations. I guess you and the Rear Guards will have to locate them. Perhaps, they are in hiding somewhere. You might check and see if they have migrated to some of the other sectors. Maybe they are all helping in Pieta. Who knows?"

"Very well, General. I guess this isn't a fiasco after all. Plainly, the Prince is such a coward that he fled. Seeing him flee, the ordinary folks followed suit. Makes sense. I'll take charge now, General. It is time that I bring law and order to Velona, or rather to this area it seems." With that, the General took his leave and returned to his headquarters in a grand building overlooking the Church of Tur.

When he arrived, one of physicians attached to the First Phalanx was waiting for him. "May I have a word with you, General?" He nodded. "Some of the men have fallen ill, I'm afraid."

"Well, do something about it," he barked, irritated to be bothered by such trivial details. "You are the physician, aren't you?"

The man fidgeted, knowing that he had already raised the ire of the General, but he had to state the facts. "I mean a hundred men have gotten sick, sir."

"Well, maybe it is the water? Could they have poisoned the drinking water?"

"No, sir, some of the ill men swear that they have not drunk from the local wells. Others have. There is no pattern here. We'll work on healing them. I just thought that you should know." Quickly, the physician excused himself and returned to his quarters, the temporary shelter set up to house the ill.

The next day, General Thrace, having little else to do, decided to visit his sick soldiers and to cheer them up with the news that they would be going home fairly soon now. When he arrived, he was shocked to see that the building overflowing with ill men. Another hundred had turned up on the doorstep during the night. The ugly pussy splotches that covered their faces and arms both stank and looked horrible. Suddenly, the General realized what was happening. "The plague," he uttered.

"Yes sir," came the reply from the same physician, who had alerted him the night before. "That's my diagnosis. Have we displeased Sol in any way that he would unleash the plague upon us?"

"Nonsense. This is not Sol's doing. You forget. We are his Chosen Ones. It is just one of those unexplained events of Nature. You do have a cure for this, don't you?" Finally, the General realized the critical question that he needed to ask.

"Well, we are trying everything that we know," the physician sidestepped his question, but the General stared at him. "So far, nothing has worked. I'm sure it's just a matter of time until we have the cure. Don't worry."

"Worry? Well, not yet. You keep sending me daily reports on your progress," and he quickly left the infirmary just as fast as he could. Gone was his noble idea of comforting his men. In fact, he stayed inside his headquarters and never left that building again, alive, that is.

During the next few days, the reports grew steadily gloomier. Half of those that first took ill had died. Hundreds of new cases were reported each day. On the sixth day, no reports came, and the General ordered one of his aides to go find out why. The man returned very pale, the physicians had taken ill too. The General felt out of sorts, kept examining his face in his mirror, and looking at his arms. Yes, two days later, tale-tale blots appeared. He panicked and wandered through the city looking for any of the physicians. Only one remained untouched; quickly, he was ordered to treat the General and only the General. General Thrace died four days later.

Now as soon as the plague was diagnosed, Governor Helix knew what had to be done. This was his province. He ordered a citywide quarantine. Guards were posted to see to it that no one left the city. Any that entered could not leave. By dispatch, which was risky — sending a rider back to the advancing Rear Guards might expose them to the plague — Governor Helix notified the chain of command of the plight of the army within Velona. The Rear Guard proceeded to encircle Velona and enforce the quarantine. Governor Helix really felt like he was in command. He would triumph over the plague and go down in history as the Governor who successfully oversaw an entire city battling the plague. That he might also get the plague never crossed his mind.

Within a week, supplies ran dangerously low, so following his orders, the Rear Guards brought wagon loads up to the edge of the city and left them there. Those inside the city then went out, brought them into Velona proper, and saw to their distribution, all under the control of Governor Helix. In fact, the Governor chuckled privately to himself when he heard that General Thrace had died from the plague. He had never liked that man.

By the end of January, he faced a new problem. So many had died that now there was no place left to bury them properly. Consequently, he issued burning orders. The shanty town houses were filled with the corpses and set ablaze. Disposal now became neat and tidy, save for the rotting stench, if the winds blew inland instead of seaward.

By mid-March, the plague had run its course. No new cases had been reported for a week now, and those that had been ill had either died or recovered. Governor Helix composed his final report to the new Emperor. Of the ten thousand men of the invasion force, fewer than one thousand remained alive within Velona. Half of the city had been burned down, but that was just slums anyway. No one would morn their passing. It actually made space for new construction. The Rear Guard fared better. Of their one thousand men, only a hundred had perished, due mostly to the effectiveness of the Governor's Quarantine Plan. He wrote that had he been slower in reacting, why, the plague might have spread to all the other cities and maybe even all the way back to Megalos. He embellished his accomplishments nicely. Thus, he lifted the quarantine.

His next action was to renew his contacts with the nearby towns and villages. To his amazement, he found that the plague had spread to these as well. More than half of each town had already perished. So quickly, he reinstated the quarantine, this time to protect the Centurions from being infected by the local population.

During this time, the other Governors, hearing of the outbreak of plague in Velona, ordered their borders closed and sent many of their rear guards out to strictly enforce it. No one was allowed into any other sector for the next six months. Their fast reaction to Governor Helix's warning prevented the spread of the plague into the other sectors of the Sea Princes. Hence, Governor Helix was credited with brilliant thinking, fast action, and received an official commendation direct from the new Emperor himself.

On June 1, 560 AH, after all quarantines had been lifted, a caravan of men rode into Velona, purple robes swaying in the light breeze. Quickly, Governor Helix prepared himself to meet these emissaries of the Church of Tur and finally get some answers. When the six robed men finally arrived at his mansion, the Governor stood on his porch to greet them. "Greetings. I'm Governor Helix Nickolopous, at your service." He bowed confidently.

"Well met. I'm now the High Priest of Tur in Velona, Marcello Po, the son of Antonio Po. I'm afraid he fell to the plague. We're leaderless and wish to sue for peace. We bring you the treasury of the late Prince of Velona, who also fell to the plague." At the mention of treasury, the Governor's eyes lit up. This was almost too good to be true.

"Why thank you, please come inside and take some refreshments with me. We have much to discuss. You're all most welcome here." He led the six inside, noting that these men were barely of age, if that! So young to be in such powerful positions, he mused, but realized that they would be easy to twist into following his orders. His task of governing Velona just have became a thousand times easier, he thought.

He poured them all some of his best wine. After eating some bread and cheese, Marcello Po explained all that he knew. Yes, the Prince had ordered the evacuation of Velona long before the Centurions arrived. The plan that everyone was told was that once the Centurions were in the city, Tur would unleash a great sickness upon them. Then, when their numbers were greatly reduced, the Prince would marshal his guards and retake the city, wiping out every last Centurion. It was rumored that he had made a deal with the Sisterhood to assist him in this task.

However, by the time the plague began, no one could find any Sisters. They had somehow vanished in the night. No one knew where they went or were. None had been seen for six months now. The Prince and his wagon loads of treasure, heavily guarded of course, simply traveled from town to town, always ahead of the Centurion patrols. Unfortunately, the plague spread widely, and the Prince and most of his guards fell victim to it and died. "My father may have had some connections with the Prince. I suspect he and the Prince may have shared information, but alas, he too has succumbed to the plague. Whatever he knew died with him. I'm now the undisputed High Priest of Tur and thus by default the leader of all the people of the Velona sector. None of the Prince's family has arisen to challenge me. I took charge of the Prince's treasure wagons. I hope that by giving them to you, you'll look favorably upon all the citizens of this sector. All our people have been ravaged by the plague. We need assistance, food, and supplies. Some towns are in dire need, Governor. Can you help us?"

Governor Helix just couldn't believe his incredible good fortune. He was being handed rulership of Velona on a literal golden platter! There wasn't any resistance. To these people, he would appear the beneficent savior! "First, let me give you my condolences on the untimely death of your father. Second, you are wise for your young years. Yes, Your Eminence, you have come to the one person in this entire sector who can and will help your people at once. I'm sure that the treasury you have brought will pay all the yearly taxes for everyone for at least a couple of years, allowing your people to get back onto their feet, so to speak, and there should be more than enough to pay for getting food and supplies here at once. I will personally see to it that food shipments begin before the week is out! Will you please consider moving back into your rightful Church of Tur complex here in Velona? I'm sure that will help convince others it's now safe to return to this once great city. Together, you and I — we can rebuild her to be a thriving metropolis!"

These were the very words that the young Priest had hoped he would hear, perhaps even better. Now, he, High Priest Marcello Po, would be seen by all his people as having the wisdom to lead them back to survival, even perhaps thriving, if the Governor's words rang true. He, Marcello Po, had just done something that no one before in the entire history of the Land of the Sea Princes had done. He had merged the two offices into one — the Prince of the City and the High Priest of Po were now one and the same person! He had total control, excepting for this Governor, which he now knew could be bought with gold. He failed to mention that the Church of Tur's treasury was more than three times the portion that he had given the Governor. Much of the Prince's wealth had been spent on the mass migration of Velona's population last winter. Thus, he, Marcello Po, was now the most powerful Sea Prince in history. He humbly sipped more of the Governor's excellent wine.

Chapter 27 The Preparations

It was mid-July 560 AH, when the Lightning Circle met as a group. The spring and early summer had been one of intense activity, with many going down separate paths. Thomas had indeed found an ideal site for their new fortress-home near the top of Mont Blanc at the very edge of the Langdoc region. Already, Raphael had begun work on the site, hiring many craftsmen from Calgary to do the work. The fortress perimeter would encompass the entrance to an underground cavern complex wherein our treasures could safely be hidden. Further, there were some possibilities that the cavern complex might also provide a secret exit several miles to the southeast.

Simon and Sandy probably talked with every inhabitant of Calgary, well maybe not that many. They fully explored the idea that the Centurion's had already scouted out the Greenway in preparations for the expected invasion. To date, not a single shred of evidence to this effect could they find. Thus, we concluded with a reasonable sense of surety that they had not yet spied upon our city. Simon now continued to watch the docks for incoming people, as well as strangers who arrived overland, looking for a possible emissary from the Centurions.

Word got to us of the impact of the plague in Velona. So many dead! Lucretia was more than gratified to know that she had done the right thing by evacuating all the Sisters from that sector. She had probably saved most of their lives from the plague. We heard that both the Prince and Antonio Po has died of the plague as well, dashing the grand scheme for retaking Velona. His youngest son, Marcello Po, had bargained with the new Governor, and together they were restoring the entire sector. Lucretia pointed out to us that now one man held both seats of power: the Prince and the High Priest. We, of course, had no inkling of its significance.

The results of the Greenway-wide survey came back. Almost to the town, they voted not to go to war to fight off the Centurions. No one wanted war. Our job was to make that happen.

On the human side, all four of us, Thallia, Sandy, Sarah Jane, and me, were now with child. We and our mates were all thrilled. Come December, we expected to start our families! Thus, we decided that now was the time to travel back to Karka to visit with our respective families and to hold a civil marriage ceremony for their benefit. We expected to spend six weeks traveling there and back again and spend two weeks with our families. All told, we would be gone for two months. Certainly, we did not expect any Centurion actions for quite some time. Their entire attack force had nearly been wiped out; only their Rear Guards remained mostly untouched by the plague.

Some twenty Sisters accompanied us. Half wanted to see the country, and the other half wanted to move there, to a place of relative peace and quiet, where life was simple.

I won't bore you with the details of these two months, save to say that for us, these two months were blissful. During that time, we forgot our many duties and responsibilities. All we had to do was enjoy the ride, the countryside, and our families back in Karka. I will say this, our parents were extraordinarily proud that we were now the leaders of the Protectors. We gave our parents enough gold coins so they could survive without working for several years. Thus, we knew that they wouldn't suffer because we weren't present to help them directly . It was the least we could do.

Actually, we found that our families were now thriving in their new homes; all were doing very well. We met our old Guardian friends and found that Ellen had now been replaced with a young man, a new Loremaster, so their Circle was again complete. We promised our families that they could come and see our new fortress-home once it was finished. Of course, they all were a bit hesitant at the incredible distance to be traveled, but we promised that we would come and escort them both ways. I know mom and dad really appreciated that; they had seldom ventured far from their home. In fact, we had so much fun visiting with our families, that we actually extended our stay another week!

Oh yes, in case you were wondering about King Randolf. He continued to leave Karka and Blankford alone, preferring to expand his dominion to the south with far easier prey. All told, it was a most enjoyable trip indeed, and we arrived back in Calgary just in time for the Autumnal Equinox celebration.

Upon our return, two matters needed immediate handling, ignoring the obvious new construction. First, I had received a letter reply from Niccolo Helios! Second, Isabel reported that she had found ten volunteers who would go to the Moon people and help them learn how to survive above ground. Interestingly, most were retired druwids, including Kos Aran and his wife, Yanna, who had looked after us when we were in Karka! Coming from all over the Greenway, these volunteers were scheduled to arrive in Calgary and catch the last ship out before the winter freeze. They would take necessary supplies and another large batch of seed grain with them to ensure the continued survival of the Moon people. I, of course, had to see to the many details of this action and even arranged for our old friend Captain Bartoloma and the Lucky Lady to ferry them to the Red Desert. As the volunteers arrived, Sandy and I had to teach them the basics of the Moon people's language as well as educate them on what to expect.

The letter from Niccolo was most interesting. I had written him a simple letter, saying we arrived home safely, thanking him for the history book, and asking him how things were going in Megalos. I fully expected many prying eyes would read my letter to him long before he received it. It had only taken seven months for the round trip. His letter arrived in a box. Actually, the box was protection from the elements. It was sealed. Inside were two letters. The first was very short and said:

Dearest Bethany,

So glad to hear you arrived home safe. All is well here. I've attached a longer letter. However, I suspect others may read it. If the seal on the box looks tampered with, know that it has. However, the second letter is in code. The key is the name of the pretty woman whose portrait I painted during your brief visit.

Your Eternal Southern Friend,

Niccolo Helios

We examined the seal. Someone had indeed opened it and crudely tried to reseal it. Niccolo had been indeed prudent. Of course, the key to the encryption was Sarah Jane. I gave Sandy the task of unraveling the "gibberish" that the very long second letter contained. It took her over a week to do it all proper. She gaily pointed out at last how he had done it. "Look at this. See I write down the letters of his invention in order. Then, below them, I write out the letters that spell Sarah Jane. Now every place I need to use the first letter, 'A,' I substitute instead, the letter below it, the 'S.' The gibberish now makes sense. You know, this is a very useful invention: how to send messages to another that can only be read by the proper receiver. I think this is incredibly clever!" I thought so too. His real letter, as translated by Sandy, read:

Dear Bethany,

I cannot tell you how grateful I was to receive your kind letter letting me know that you all returned safely home. For months, I was so worried. I heard that you had evaded the guards at Sud and headed off into the wilderness of the Southlands. When I heard that they hired the best tracker in Megalos to hunt you all down, I feared for your lives. Again, I apologize for having gotten you into so much trouble here in Megalos.

Here in Galantas, the official word is that Emperor Hiro was slain by the freakish lightning storm that struck that night. That same storm also caused major damage at that main dam I showed you, the one which supplies all the water, or most all of it, to Galantas. Actually, the dam was in bad shape for many years, but no one would do anything about it, save form more committees to study the problem. It ruptured. Personally, I was thrilled to hear that it failed. Naturally, Galantas had to be evacuated in a hurry — almost no water. The entire Senate term was cancelled, and I got almost a year's vacation from politics!

I took your advice and spread the word that all this was Sol's retribution for lascivious conduct by our late Emperor. Needless to say, that went over very well with the priests of Sol, who took up the call and spread that far and wide across Megalos. They are still preaching it even today. We now have a new Emperor, Titus, is his name, who is but a puppet of the Church of Sol. I believe strongly that he only does what the Church tells him to do. This might be a good change. Already the lewd conduct has ceased, but I guess time will tell.

Did you hear about the disaster in Velona? In case you have not heard, here is what we have been told. Our glorious army, led by General Thrace, finally conquered the last of the Sea Prince cities, Velona. He did it without swinging a single sword! Apparently, that Sea Prince was so afraid of our forces, that he evacuated the entire city! Our army simply walked in and took it. Pretty amazing. Then disaster struck. There is no stopping Nature, I guess. The plague struck our conquering army!

Fortunately, Governor Helix was quick to respond and quarantined the whole city to prevent its spread. However, our conquering army was devastated by the plague. The actual numbers are a bit shaky; it depends upon whose version you believe. Some say that only a handful of soldiers remain. Others say that only half the army died from the plague. I don't know which to believe; however, the new Emperor is saying that only half died.

The plague also took its toll on the inhabitants in that land. Reports are saying that half of their entire population perished as well. Grim statistics. At this writing, the Governor reports that he has engaged the complete support of their High Priest in restoring the entire sector. He even got a commendation from the Emperor for all his good works.

Finally, I did some checking on that matter that most concerns you and your land. The Church is still backing bringing "civilization and Sol" to the barbarians of Tarra. However, due to the devastation of the plague and other matters here at home in Megalos, further actions have been put on hold. My best guess is two years, maybe three at the outside.

By the way, congratulations on introducing writing into your land. How did I find out you wonder? Commerce. It seems that all the commerce we get from the Greenway now has written cargo manifests, written in what appears to be our own language, or at least fairly close to it. I'll let you in on a little secret. Because of this, there are some among us that are beginning to believe that this Greenway place might not be so barbarian-like. That is a positive statement, by the way.

Write when you can, but use the code. I would not come visiting me for several years, though.

Your Friend,

Niccolo Helios

Raphael was the first to respond, "Two to three years. Terrific. I may have enough time actually to complete much of the first stage of our fortress. Wonderful news indeed."

Sandy pointed out how they once more rather twisted the facts and that those alterations were being believed, for the most part. Me personally, I was very pleased indeed that Niccolo had followed our suggestions and that he had also written me back. Not all the people of Megalos were our enemies. I took some comfort in that data, plus the two to three years. We had been successful in slowing them down. Still, the business with the plague bothered me. True, we were the primary beneficiaries, not the poor people down in the Velona sector — strange how the Prince had actually helped us and not his own people. He had taken a cowardly gamble and lost everything, his life and his throne. I relayed the hopeful news to Martha's Circle; even Isabel seemed greatly relieved, heaping praise on all that we had accomplished. I also pointed out that it was most likely the plague that had so greatly delayed the invasion of the Greenway.

However, Isabel now wanted a conference so all could be certain that we were leading the Greenway in the right direction. We fourteen sat once more around the large oak table in the dining room. I began by giving a summary of the status of our affairs, including the supposed time line from Niccolo. "We now know that our people want us to try to find a peaceful solution to the Centurion problem. For various reasons, we may have several years to bring that about. Already some back in Megalos are wondering if we really are barbarians because of our new skill, reading and writing." I received several kudos for having instigated that when I did; even in so short a time, writing had become *the* thing to learn in Calgary. I continued, "I guess the next question we should ask is, 'How should we follow this up?' I'm open to suggestions."

Isabel asked, "Could we perhaps send an ambassador to Megalos with the purpose of making some kind of peace before they come invading? Perhaps invite them to come and join us? Would that be wise? Or should we just wait until they send someone to scout us?"

"Or maybe send an official letter to their Emperor," suggested Sandy. "After all, we only escaped there by the narrowest of margins. I think it I awfully risky to send just one person."

Simon scratched his head and thoughtfully said, "You know, why don't we send an official letter requesting they send an ambassador to the Greenway? We can say honestly that we have seen the great benefits they have brought to the Sea Princes, and we were wondering if they might consider helping us out. You know, hit their ego, their pride. Besides, we all do agree that the roadway they likely will build would be of great benefit here at harvest time. Grain can be moved far more swiftly and easily to Calgary over paved roads instead of dirt tracks."

"Brilliant, Simon, you took my idea right from my mind," teased Judger Jane. She added, "Yes, this would be the best route to follow. Get them to come here now, long before they begin making attack plans. We can always try to negotiate the best deal that we can, you know, smallest yearly taxes. I'm not sure how their Sun God Cult will play out with our people, though. Considering the numerous "gods" they now worship, one more probably wouldn't make any difference to them. We do need to open up communication lines with them; there's no question about that. Failure to do so will only likely lead to their unilateral invasion, which we want to avoid. I agree, from your experiences, it is just way too dangerous to send a single ambassador from the Greenway. However, and this is a big however everyone, just what do we tell them about ourselves, the druwids, and our mission here?"

"Yes, this is perhaps the most critical aspect of allowing them into the Greenway," I replied. "We can't tell them the whole truth; they would certainly perceive that we pose the single largest threat to their rule here. If they know all about us, our days are doomed. However, I have given this some thought. We can safely describe ourselves as healers. Our purpose is to live out among our families and friends, and provide healing when someone gets hurt or sick. Because we are good at this, we are known as the people's Protectors or Guardians. While a half-truth, it's one of the primary things the average villager depends upon us to do. We can also safely say that for some time now we have been trying our best to fend off the raids from the Galts and the Axemen; we would appreciate any aid that they can provide, any security, so that we can go back to doing what we do best, healing the sick and injured. That would seem very plausible, I think, to outsiders. For sure, we make no mention of calling down fire, ice, and lightning. If they hear rumors of such, they'll not believe it. We must make very sure that all the druwids never put on such a display when there is any possibility of a Centurion watching."

I continued, "However, should any druwid get into trouble with the Centurions, they can come in secret to our new Mont Blanc fortress. It should be operational in a few years' time. We can hide them there. We have miles of underground caverns directly attached to the fortress-to-be. We can provide a safe haven for any that need it. The Langdoc region is mostly uninhabited, so there wouldn't be any real reasons for the Centurions to go there."

Thomas spoke up, "This is all well and good, but what if we did nothing and the Centurions never get around to invading the Greenway? Here we go inviting them to take over our land now, when maybe they never would have done so. Aren't we jumping to conclusions here? Maybe they'll find no reason to take over this land."

Judger Jane answered him, "You have a valid point. Until the recent events unfolded, we were confident that we might be their next target, but I stress the might be. Even Alabaster wasn't totally sure they would in fact attack us. With all these recent changes, especially at their head of government, in fact, we're even less certain that they really will come and invade our land. Yet, it's a certainty we'd be under their jurisdiction if we invite them to come and take over the Greenway. On the other hand, Thomas, if we wait until we're certain of their invasion, by then it may well be too late to attempt to settle it peacefully on our terms. We may be forced to accept far worse conditions of occupation, if they have a deployed army to back up their demands. Thomas, we are behind the backs of two horses — either way, we get dumped upon."

Simon jumped in, saying, "Another factor for doing it now is that, at this point in time, they're in the weakest position they have ever been in since launching their crusade to civilize Tarra. This strengthens our bargaining position significantly, though, as you said, what if they never would have come here? What a conundrum we face. Sometimes I wish we could see the future so we could make more rational decisions."

Sarah Jane added her opinion, "Well, why don't we see if we can open up a dialog with them and see if the Greenway could become friendly with Megalos. I mean, offer them lots of grain for a low price. Initially asking for payment in gold or gems, explaining that we don't have either, but then accepting, when they naturally refuse that, iron-forged farming equipment. Let them get the idea that we are so utterly devoid of anything but grain that they might not consider wasting their resources invading us. We can also ask them for assistance in building paved roadways. Or perhaps ask them for advice on how to defend ourselves from the Galts and Axemen, explaining that we're farmers and have little fighters or weapons. I guess what I'm suggesting is we try to befriend them first. If this fails, then see if we could somehow sue for some kind of acceptable peaceful occupation. I hate giving up our sovereignty if we don't have to succumb."

Laughing, Judger Jane replied, "You do have a point. Here we all sit like it was doomsday, but in fact we don't know that they wouldn't be amenable other possibilities. The new governor in Velona might be a good person with which to open up a dialog; after all, the situation is grim down there because of the plague. Perhaps we can establish a peaceful co-existence with these Centurions. If not, then we can try to arrange the best occupation settlement that we can. Above all, an actual combat confrontation should be avoided."

"She's right, Bethany," Isabel added. "We really should give diplomacy a try first, even though we suspect we're next on their conquest list. I think the timing is right for such an attempt with that new governor. One additional thing is in our favor: his ego. We know that the governors are vying with each other for power and control. I think this new governor might jump at the chance to bring the Greenway under his thumb without the use of the army, especially so, if we offer to pay for their services in building the roadway and for help against the Galts. Honestly, I don't relish an all-out battle with these Centurions again; I've seen too much death and pain in my life, but I'll do it again, if I have to, don't mistake me."

"Okay, then here is my ruling," I concluded. "First, let's try the straightforward approach and send someone to speak with this new governor of Velona. Second, if that fails, let's request a diplomat from Megalos to come here to arrange some form of peace, the best that we can negotiate. Meanwhile, let the construction of the new fortress go at top speed. Also, let's make sure that the Moon people are serviced properly as well. I also think it prudent that we begin to store up some grain, so that, if and when Megalos places demands upon us, our people are not placed in jeopardy. Isabel, can your Circle see to the creation of a grain reserve?"

"Yes, we can. I think that would be the prudent thing to do, under the circumstances. If we have some reserves, perhaps at hidden locations so they can't be robbed by the Centurions, then, when and if demands are made, we can respond, saving our people from near starvation." she replied.

"Okay, great. Now we have to decide who should go to Velona to contact the governor," I brought up the tough decision. "Though things have changed since we were there, still, I don't believe that any of the Lightning Circle should go, nor any women, considering the way that women are generally treated there. We don't know if that has changed appreciably in Velona yet. Further, how many should we send?"

"More than two would probably not be wise," Judger Jane replied. "For safety, probably two should go. But who? Considering the magnitude of this situation, it probably ought to be someone from our two Circles. After all, we're the leaders. However, we don't have very many choices, now do we?" she said looking at the seven in her Circle, four of which were women.

"I'm afraid I'm a bit too old and frail to make such a journey," Able Communicator answered forlornly. "But a Communicator would be an ideal second person, I admit."

Planner Pete and Protector Finch looked at each other. Finch spoke with a chuckle, "Well, it looks like we get to go. There aren't many other choices, are there?"

"I'll take on the diplomat hat, if Finch protects my rear," joked Pete. "Jane, you're going to have to train me a bit more on diplomacy tactics if I'm to be successful."

"I'll help too," Simon added, "I've had a good deal of experience dealing with governors, well with one anyway."

After a bit of last minute training, I sent these two volunteers off to Velona to bargain with the new governor. Roy arranged for their passage on the next boat to the Sea Princes, and I gave them each a pair of pouches — one with a hundred gold coins and one with five hundred in gems for an emergency. They sailed on the last day of September 560 AH.

Mid-October, the two returned with a potential treaty. Yes, a treaty. As expected, Governor Helix Nickolopous took the offering. Winter was coming, and the importing of so much food was draining the treasury he had gotten from the late Prince. Pete reported the deal would be finalized in the spring, once the ice had broken up and the appropriate representatives could come to Calgary and assess the situation. The base agreement was: in exchange for ten boat loads of food yearly, they would build a paved roadway across the Greenway, provide soldiers to thwart the occasional raiding bands, and provide a government for us. Any food delivered in excess of the tithe would be paid for by iron farming equipment. All food would be transported to Velona, and from there, the Governor would arrange for its disbursement. There was no mention of the Guardians or Protectors. Also, there was no mention of the number of soldiers who would come, but the Governor assured Pete that the Greenway would not be responsible for providing them food or shelter. However, if we did, we would be recompensed. Also, no mention was made of establishing their Church of Sol in the Greenway, but we figured they would be doing just that. If all this happened, the price wasn't too high at all, especially since we would greatly benefit from their paved road system.

Thus, the threat of invasion was thwarted; the druwid movement was still kept secret and operational, but the Greenway would be an occupied land.

When the two tried to return their unused funds to me, I said, "No, you two keep what's left. You've earned it. Thank you for a job well done." Both were very pleased and shared it with the others in their Circle and their immediate families. Of course, the All Greenway Circle now had to do a lot of advance planning in order to coordinate raising the necessary tithe so as not to place a hardship on any single town or village. That was a tall order.

As the first snow fell, both our Circles actually relaxed for the first time in several years. The threat was all but defused, and we could reasonably expect life to be mostly normal from now on, at least we hoped so. However, Simon pointed out, "You know, give them a couple years at their road building and I'll bet they'll then assault the Galts in the Northern Steppes from the south in Juda Arad and from eastern Greenway. I know if I were a general that would be a terrific idea — to hit them from two sides simultaneously." I did not doubt his wisdom.

During the middle of December 560 AH, our children were born. I had a little boy who we named Robert Roy. Sarah Jane had a boy, John Henry, after their fathers. Thallia had a girl who they named Lilly Elizabeth, honoring Nature and me. Sandy also had a girl who they named Misty Simone — Simon couldn't resist perpetuating his joke. All of us were quite proud and all were healthy. And in the early spring of 561 AH, we moved into the still under construction fortress on Mont Blanc, ensuring our safety when the Centurions arrived after the ice melted, freeing the port in April.

Chapter 28 Mont Blanc and the Deadly Miscalculation

It was early June 564 AH, the start of the fourth year of the Centurion occupation of the Greenway. Our Governor Hextor Piraeus, a bronzed-skinned, middle-aged man who always seemed to have a smile on his face no matter the circumstances, had taken up residence in one of the larger stone buildings located in the heart of Calgary and which overlooked the port and docks about a mile downhill. Thus far, all had gone well. Perhaps a thousand Centurion soldier-workers had come to build their paved roadway and bathhouses. In fact, their road now connected Brownsville in the middle to Calgary. It had quickly become very popular with our people, who found travel and transportation of grain and other supplies took about one-half the usual travel time. As I had suspected, only a very few side roads were built to connect to this main route, because the other villages and hamlets were far too small to justify the expensive paved roadways. Last spring they extended the road beyond Brownsville and were now actually finishing connecting to Karka. We suspected they intended to push their road all the way through the Greenway to the border of the Northern Steppes, where they could easily begin their conquest of the Galt held lands. Such made good sense, though the Governor had yet to acknowledge this was their true intention in extending the roadway to all these small, distant eastern villages.

Since no protests, no rebellious populations were encountered, only a handful of Centurions remained at any one location, mostly to provide security for the Governor, should he desire to travel, which he seldom ever did, preferring the warmth and comforts of the large city, Calgary.

The yearly cost of grain and other dried foods had not posed any significant problems on our people because of three factors. One, we druwids continually counseled our villagers on how to increase their productivity and hence crop yields. Two, more and more metal farming equipment had been imported. The improvement of a metal plow over wooden ones made believers out of the most die-hard conservatives. Three, we druwids, and the Lightning Circle in particular, had been quietly using some of our own funds to purchase and store extra production for protection against harder times.

Yet another factor that played into our hands: the actual construction of the brown brick roadway necessitated turning a fair number of our people into stonemasons and cutters. Most of the Greenway lands were rich black dirt; hardly any good stone for roadway construction was locally available. True, one could find enough boulders to make fences and such, but this wasn't the stone needed to be turned into paving stones of a roadway. However, the Langdoc region, nearly barren limestone foothills of the towering Appian Way, proved to be a prime source of the limestone that the Centurions prized in their road construction. Hence, our people were first taught how to quarry limestone. Because they were quick learners and expressed a great interest in learning how to build with stone, during the second year of occupation, the Centurion engineers began to teach methods of stone masonry to the most promising of our populace. In fact, here in the fourth year, nearly a quarter of the road construction crew were our own people — an action that Raphael greatly encouraged.

Thus far, to our knowledge, neither the Governor nor the Centurions knew the true nature of us druwids. As far as they were concerned, we were just the local village healers. Pete became our primary contact point with Governor Hextor, and he kept us up-to-date on all actions these Megalos people undertook. Yes, the Governors Hextor and Helix Nickolopous of Velona had become rather famous back in Galantas, because without firing a single arrow, they had extended their dominion over their next intended country. Indeed, Niccolo and I continued our correspondence, always in the secret code, and he told us that the Emperor had given both men his highest commendation.

Niccolo also told us that the Senate committees were now doubled in number. Ideas flew in all directions, but absolutely nothing actually was done. In fact, they still had not determined just how to repair the dam that we had destroyed in our escape from Megalos five years ago. Instead, water was being hauled overland into Galantas now. The remaining water flows from the alterative aqueducts had been rerouted to only supply the public bathhouses. Niccolo's opinion was that they had lost the technology of how their ancestors had built these marvelous water systems — hence, all the committees to study the situation!

On the political front, however, the Priests of Sol now dictated policy; their new handpicked Emperor was merely their puppet, a figurehead. According to Niccolo, the Priests' real drive seemed to be in the direction of the conversion of all heathen religious practices into a worship of Sol only. To that end, a spate of new church construction had begun, primarily in the Lands of the Sea Princes. True, Niccolo reported that there was much talk of the planned invasion of the Northern Steppes, so their expansionist policies were still very much alive. I felt very relieved that we had been able to spare our country the devastations of war.

Our new fortress home on Mont Blanc was now called simply Blanca. Raphael utilized the newly trained stonecutters and masons to speed along his grandiose construction plans. The outer wall was finished and stood twenty feet tall and over ten at its base. The mile long wall surrounded Blanca, which lay on the northwestern side of the peak, commanding a view of many miles in all directions. Within the walls, twenty two-story stone buildings housed our growing families and those who chose to move to our new town; many were Sisters seeking a new, quiet life. Thomas found that sheep could be easily raised on the stony hillsides nearby. Thus, sheep and woolen products became our trade goods by this year.

Incidentally, we had moved all our treasure and historical items from the Calgary complex's hidden vaults into our new secret chambers hidden within the limestone caverns behind our buildings and within the walled compound. Raphael had carefully designed the new hiding places to look like the cavern walls, so unless you knew just what you were looking for, you couldn't find our secret rooms. This detail would become exceedingly vital in a couple hundred years, but that is another story for later.

As I alluded, our families thrived. Robert Roy was now four years old and running everywhere. In fact, Robert, John Henry, Lilly Elizabeth, and Misty Simone were best friends and played with each other all day long. Ellen Sarah, my second born, was now three; Al Helmut was two. Raphael and Sarah Jane also kept pace with me and were the proud parents of Ellie Ann and Tom Paul. Likewise, Sandy and Simon had Henry Alabaster and Frank John, while Thallia and Thomas had May Lina and Thomas Ben, Junior. Yes, we women were kept very busy with all the two, three, and four year olds! It was a source of immense fun for us all, really.

Blanca now boasted fifty full time residents, ignoring the construction crews that were finishing another six homes. It seemed as soon as one construction project was completed, Raphael though of yet another building that just had to be built!

Oh yes, what of the Count and his fortress? Fortress d'Grange remained unconquered by the Centurions. They found no need to attempt to build an overland route from the Sea Princes to the Greenway; the land was just too steep and rugged and offered little return on their investment. To this date, Fortress d'Grange remains the only town in all the Sea Princes that isn't under their dominion. The Count alone is still a very independent man! And yes, we are still supplying him in secret.

However, on June 6, Sandy received a frantic telepathic message from Mary Ann Twindle of the Blankford Circle and came to get me at once. I was out playing with the children; it was my turn to look after the young. From the pale look on her face, I knew something was wrong, just as soon as I spied her walking hurriedly toward me. "Mary Ann has news. We need to talk right now." Leaving the children in the care of one of the Sisters who had moved to our new town, we ducked into my kitchen, where it was quiet and wouldn't be disturbed.

"Mary Ann sends word that big trouble is brewing. As you know, the Centurions are building the roadway, now just east of Karka. They are approaching the territories controlled by King Randolf and the renegade Erline. She reports King Randolf has annexed all the lands down to the Langdoc region and is now putting pressure northward on Erline's lands. Frank and Herbert have just returned from spying on King Randolf and reported to her that perhaps a thousand Galts are amassed just to the east of Redun and the King's forces. She surmises that King Randolf has secretly been bringing a large force of Galts into his territory. It follows, she says, that the

King has made some kind of alliance with our enemies! Meanwhile, Jason, sent to spy on Erline, reports that she knows of King Randolf's intentions on her domain because she has amassed an army of her own somewhat north and east of the Galts. It appears that those two are going to war soon. Worse, the Centurions are building their roadway right through the middle ground — where the battle is likely to be joined. Mary Ann reports that there are now about a thousand Centurions stationed just outside Karka and further eastward along the new roadway. Finally, she says that she suspects that either the two are going to war with each other with the Centurions caught in the middle or, more sinister, those two are in cahoots and together are planning to wipe out the entire Centurion army, attacking from two sides. However, she also said that there could be other possible scenarios. Whew, that was a lot to receive!" Sandy exclaimed.

"Well, looks like we need to get everyone together right now," I replied. "Good job, Sandy. Let's get the others." Within fifteen minutes, we sat around my living room table. "Gang, Mary Ann once underestimated King Randolf. We must not make that mistake ourselves. Sandy, tell them the news you just received from Mary Ann." Confidently and proudly, Sandy relayed the message she had received from Mary Ann, via her old mentor, Willow. The other five sat stone-faced through her brief explanation, so I couldn't get an initial reading on their reactions.

"Well, darn," exclaimed Simon in disgust, "just when things were going so positively. She's right. There could be many different strategies in play here, besides the obvious two she mentioned. Can we afford to do nothing? I mean, theoretically, the Centurions are supposed to be providing protection from the Galts now. Why not let them deal totally with this development? Just go explain to the Governor what we have heard and let him handle the situation as he sees fit."

"If Erline weren't involved, I'd be inclined to do just that, Simon," I answered thoughtfully, "but she is a renegade druwid still. If the Centurions go after her or put undue pressure on her, she is liable to blast away with lightning bolts or fires. That may well give us, the druwids, away to the Centurions. We can' have them knowing just what we are capable of doing."

"I'm inclined to agree with Bethany," Roy came to my defense, "there's no telling what Erline may be up to doing. We can't risk it. We can't go talk to King Randolf either. I mean just ride into his fort and ask him what his intentions are — we'd have more luck getting a pig to fly!"

"Maybe we could talk with Erline?" Sandy suggested. "After all, we haven't bothered her at all for all these years. Perhaps she will at least listen to us."

"Talk is all well and good, but what are we going to do about the situation if it turns out that King Randolf is in cahoots with the Galts? We can't take on thousands of Galts at one time," the ever-practical Thomas added, more than a little concerned.

"Yes, what?" put in Sarah Jane, who felt just as frustrated as Thomas, and altogether annoyed that this might place on hold the new buildings that Raphael was designing and building. One was for her — a dance hall.

"One thing is for sure," Simon answered them, "we can't just threaten that King with the wrath of the Centurions. He's never seen them in a combat situation, and he will not realize just how deadly these fighters actually are."

"Gang, there is no use speculating on what we should do," I interjected, "until we really know what is actually going on there. Until we know what the gen is, we can't take any countermeasures. It's just speculation upon speculation. No, I'm afraid we're going to have to go and inspect the situation for ourselves — find out what the true situation is. Then, we can perhaps formulate some decisive action against it. There's no use in all of us going. Besides, we might need some of you to interface to the Governor or to the All Greenway Circle. Then there are our children. So, I'll volunteer to go and see what I can find out. I'll take Roy with me, for a Protector would never let a Wid go into a potentially dangerous situation as this portends," I teased Roy, winking at him. He smiled back; I was precisely correct, but he would want to go with me anyway. The others seemed quite relieved with this; it meant they could stay home and continue with the many construction projects and the raising of our families. Also, I really didn't mind taking a fast trip back into the Karka area. Perhaps, I could visit briefly with my family there; and Roy, with his.

The next day, Roy and I said our farewells to our children. I gave them all strong hugs and kisses. I felt just a bit strange going off like this and leaving them behind. This was the first time both Roy and I would be away from them for so long a time. Though we intended to ride fast down the new paved roadway, which would cut the travel time to Karka to just under two weeks, still, we expected to be gone perhaps six weeks. I didn't know it then, but this was to be the last time that I would ever see my children.

Ten days later, we rode into Karka; we'd averaged a whopping forty miles a day! This new paved road really helped cut travel time. We spent the night and half of the next day visiting our parents and then hit the road to Blankford, arriving at Mary Ann's home at sunset as arranged. Her home, designed by her Planner, Jason Whiteoak, was a log cabin style, rather unusual in appearance. Great logs formed the walls with mud acting as filler between them. Though not large, it was very homey with the bedrooms just under the slanted roof above the main floor. We had a long chat with Mary Ann, but she really had no additional news for us. However, I could see she was very worried about this situation, bordering on a panic, because once before she had erred in her estimation of King Randolf, and it had nearly cost the lives of my family, Ellen, and me.

When Mary Ann heard that we intended to ride into Erline's land and establish contact with her, she insisted that we take along her Protector, Herbert Jackson. Many years ago, Herbert had actually traveled through that part of the Greenway before Alabaster ordered all contact with her to be broken. Thus, we had a guide, and I was very grateful for that detail. I had envisioned roaming around the unfamiliar countryside asking for her whereabouts; not a good plan at all.

Thus, the next morning, re-supplied, we three set out for the fortified town of Urkut, which lies about a hundred miles east of Karka and which is the home of the priest-warrior, Erline Herbiscus, our renegade druwid. We expected to make Urkut in three days, but on the morning of the second day out of Karka, we detected someone was spying on us, following our movements. Herbert suggested that we ignore the unseen watcher and continue on to Urkut, where we would probably find Erline already expecting us. Good plan. Didn't work, though.

On the morning of the third day, some twenty-five miles from Urkut, as we broke camp, without warning, two dozen armed men encircled our small camp. They had snuck up on us during the night. Though heavily armed, they did not threaten us, just made it impossible for us to leave in any direction without going through them. One tall, burly man dressed in bear furs and with one of the largest swords I've ever seen, slowly walked up to us. "Greetings, Guardians. Your clothes give you away. You are trespassing onto Erline Herbiscus' land. You aren't welcome here."

Time for diplomacy, I decided, not a fight. "We're on a goodwill mission to meet and talk with Erline," I said solemnly. "We haven't come for a fight nor do we desire one. We just want to speak with her. Can you direct us to her, please?"

"Aye, I could, but I won't — not without asking her first. You don't look threatening. Okay, I'll send a message to her. If she approves, I'll take you to her. Meantime, you stay right here. Probably take a couple days. My men will watch you. Mind you, they have orders to kill you if you should try anything. Now what should I tell her that would convince her to meet with you?"

He was being civil; this was very encouraging, dispelling my preconceived notions of giant bands of barbarians or wild men. "Tell her Wid Bethany of the Lightning Circle wishes to speak with her. I have some vital news regarding King Randolf and the Galts down south of here." That ought to prick her interest level, I thought to myself. I had no way of knowing if she had heard about the wild start that our Circle had when I had nearly gone insane and become a renegade like her. If she had, I should have her interest.

I watched the man, as he headed south, not east toward Urkut. I concluded she probably wasn't in Urkut, rather she was forward on her defense lines, probably opposite the King's line of men. Thus, without a guide, trying to find her would be hopeless. We would run the risk of encountering the Galts or the King's men. Actually, I thought this meeting was fortuitous indeed. Thus, we remade camp on a more permanent basis and relaxed. The guards moved off a good distance, but maintained their encirclement of our camp.

For two days, we just sat around our camp. I took the time to practice my flute that the musician had given me several years ago. Herbert had Roy tell him about our many adventures down in the Sea Princes and Megalos. Roy was very eager to tell tales to his old teacher. I thought they were two peas in a pod, only the one was much older than the other was. After all this time, I still couldn't get excited talking about fighting tactics, but the two Protectors never tired of it. The days passed slowly, but calmly. Note: the one thing that I didn't do was to imagine what Erline might say and what I might say to her. I never wasted my time doing such idle thinking.

Late that second night, the burly man returned. Stone-faced, he walked straight up to me before speaking in his deep bass voice, "Amazing. Lucky you are. Erline the Mighty has agreed to see you. Tomorrow, I'll lead you to her." Without saying another word, he turned and walked back to his men and their camp. I smiled, thinking only a fool wouldn't see us.

The next day, a storm was coming. We rose to a dark, cloudy sky and said little. Mounting up, we followed our guide and six others, as he headed nearly due south. The day only grew darker as we rode, but the heavy rains held off, as if in courtesy to our passing. By evening, after covering some twenty-five miles, nearly all due south, we rode upon a tall, heavily forested ridge that was several hundred feet above the surrounding lands. We spied numerous campfires dotting the entire ridge line, stretching for miles in both directions. Evidently, Erline was already preparing for war. Only against who remained the question. Our guide led us unerringly to one of the larger campfires.

As we dismounted, some men came forward to take our reins for us and see to the horses. I glanced around looking for this warrior-priestess. Suddenly a large pile of bear skins rose up, revealing a very large, well-muscled, woman, Erline. She looked the part of a wild-rogue warrior-priestess! For an instant, even I flinched at her domineering, huge form. Her arm muscles were every bit twice the size of mine and even bigger than Roy's! She stood over six feet and probably weighed at least two hundred fifty pounds, all solid muscle. She wore her hair long and wild looking, with braids and beads dangling in random patterns. Across the top of her head was a helm with two ox horns protruding to either side. She carried two swords, one at either side. I spied daggers in her boots and guessed that she had other concealed weapons as well. I wasn't surprised to hear her speak with a deep alto voice.

"I'm the Warrior-priestess, Erline Herbiscus. Never, til now, have I allowed druwids onto my lands. You are the first, but I have heard about this Lightning Circle, for little escapes my eyes and ears. I wish to meet you. Come. Sit by my fires tonight. Eat first, and then we talk. Mind you, this is a war camp. You'll not find the nice amenities of city life here. Latrine's back yonder." We dutifully sat on logs around the fire, as other men brought plates piled with food and drink. I was indeed quite hungry, and we did as she asked, ate our fill. All the while, she watched us closely. I could feel her stare, her confront. She, like us, had been trained to observe. She had to — otherwise she would not be able to call down lightning or fire. It felt like her eyes were somehow burning into my mind, my thoughts. Purposefully, I quieted all thoughts, save enjoying the meat and ale.

When we were finished and had wiped our hands, I began, "First, Alabaster has passed away. Did you know that?" I figured to break the ice by letting her know that her old nemesis was now dead. "Actually, the Lightning Circle is now the leader of the Guardians, and I'm their Wid." There, that ought to let her know the current situation.

"That is already known to me," she replied solemnly, "and why I agreed to see you. In case you're wondering, I voted to allow the Centurions access to the Greenway."

"Thanks. Wise decision. We traveled all the way to their main city in Megalos. There was never any doubt about their plans to conquer the Greenway, once they finished taking the Land of the Sea Princes. We managed to delay them a bit, and I think we managed an equitable arrangement, at least thus far. Have you heard about the benefits of the paved roadway?"

"Yes, if the Guardians decide that they can't stop the Centurions, then this foe must be powerful indeed. I've never known the Guardians to back down from a fight before. Even our trade goods are getting to market in the fall far faster than before. But as you say, time will tell all, revealing whether this has been a wise decision," she replied in a non-committal manner.

We were each feeling the other out; neither revealing critical information, but testing how much the other knew and where each stood. Thus, from her reply, I assumed she wasn't planning to wage war upon the Centurions. Hence, I said, "Recently, we have learned that your neighbor to the south, King Randolf, has very likely made some kind of bargain with the Galts. As we speak, some thousand Galts are encamped near his fortress in Redun. We fear that he intends to attack you and take over your lands. We came to warn you."

The solemn meeting was broken by her deep outburst of laughter. "You, you came to warn me? Yea gods! If I had to wait until you came to warn me about King Randolf's treachery, we'd be conquered already!" She and several of her nearby men roared with laughter. When they finally stopped laughing at our expense, she added, "This is called Hogback Ridge here, and this ridge line marks our southernmost border. I have arrayed my army all along the ridge to defend our lands and teach this upstart of a King the lesson that the Guardians ought to have taught him years ago!"

I guess my face told her she had hit the mark. She continued, "You have come here seeking to meddle in this war, trying to find a way to avoid valiant combat. Am I not right?"

"In part," I did not lie. Besides, she had much basic druwid training and probably could tell if I did. "None more than I desire to see this King put in his place. Remember, he almost killed my entire family when I was a child. Yes, you are right. I wish to try to find a peaceful way to avoid this war, but for entirely different reasons. We have had three years of friendly relations with the Centurions, nary a problem. But now with the road construction drawing close to here, if suddenly you two go to war, they can only view it as a civil war within their controlled lands. I know these beasts. They'll retaliate and stomp down hard on both sides, likely wiping you out and shipping all competent fighters off to become slaves in their southern salt mines. That is just what they did all throughout the Sea Princes. I know many others refer to you as a renegade, but I have always thought of you as an ally, defending the eastern sections of the Greenway from the Galts. I don't want you to suffer at the hands of these Centurions. Yes, they are formidable fighters. I don't doubt for one second that you could defeat any single Centurion in combat, perhaps many at the same time. However, they don't fight that way. They march in formations numbering in the thousands and slay any in their path. I've personally witnessed this. Yes, it is possible to deal with a small group of them by using stealth and secrecy, but against their attacking formations, nothing can stand for long."

I stared into her keen deep blue eyes, and she, mine. For a minute, neither spoke. Finally, she broke contact, using my title, said, "Okay, Wid Bethany, come sit with me, tell me about these Centurions, and their fighting style and tactics. I would learn, though I hope never to need the information." I relaxed; I had broken the ice; she would listen. I was hopeful I had half the problem resolved. I discussed all I had seen of these Centurions during our time in the Sea Princes, Juda Arad, the Southlands, and on Megalos. We talked until nearly midnight.

When I had finished answering her last question, she pronounced, "Wid Bethany of the Lightning Circle, you have convinced me. I will stay my hand against King Randolf until such time as he actually invades my land. Only then will I strike. Mark my words: he is soon to strike. We've been expecting his assault upon us to begin any day now."

"Thank you, Erline. Tomorrow, I'll see if I can speak to King Randolf. Do you think if we ride into his lands holding the universal white flag of parley, he'll honor it?" I asked.

"Only a damned fool wouldn't honor the white parley flag," she replied. I felt more confident and thus made my fatal mistake.

The next day was even darker than the previous one. Light rain began to fall, as we three prepared to ride down the ridge out into the forests below. Somewhere out there King Randolf must be with his men. Our plan was simple. Ride forth under the universal white parley flag and take our case to the King. King Randolf might not know that several thousand Centurions were nearby, busily at work on their road construction. Further, if trouble arose, I knew it would only be a matter of months before thousands upon thousands of Centurions would pour into the Greenway from the Sea Princes, march across the road to attack, and slaughter the King and all his men. Of that, I was quite certain. My task now was to convince King Randolf of this fact, but first, we had to reach him.

Both Roy and Herbert protested our riding into his territory, even under the parley flag. My second mistake came, because I didn't listen to the protests of the Protectors, whose job it is to see to my safety. "Look, I can see no other way. We must talk to King Randolf. If only we can get him to see how awful it will be for him — that he will eventually be utterly annihilated by the Centurions, then he surely will stop his actions." My reasoning was that of a sane, reasonable person. King Randolf was neither. I ought to have known that already. Okay, I did, but I just didn't want to pay attention to that detail, my final mistake.

Light rain began to fall on us as we headed down the steep side of the ridge. Herbert carried the white parley flag held high. Herbert was on my left, Roy on my right. We stayed as close to each other as possible. Once we had reached the land below, the dark forest was ominously quiet, like the calm before some mighty storm. No birds sung. Animals had long ago burrowed or taken refuge into their homes or fled the area. As we rode on, I felt like eyes were watching us, though I saw no one. Even so, periodically, I called out, "We come to parley with King Randolf. Lead us to the King, please." My voice sounded high and shrill, the only sound other than our horses.

After covering perhaps a mile and at the bottom of a small forested hill, I heard an unmistakable voice call out, "Fire! Kill them all!" It was that of King Randolf himself.

Herbert reacted by waving the parley flag. He whispered, "That's the King's voice!" Suddenly a volley of arrows flew at us. Most were hastily aimed or else their shooters were relatively unskilled or their shots rushed. However, several came right at me. I watched in slow motion as Roy grabbed one arrow out of midair just before it would have struck me in my chest. With his other hand, he snatched another destined for my head. Herbert, encumbered with the flag, still managed to snatch another arrow, which would have hit my heart. Both men took several arrows to non-critical areas as a result.

However, they did not have an available fourth hand to save me. Another arrow in the hail of arrows that flew at us came right at my forehead. Frozen as I was, only a few seconds had elapsed; I could only watch as it came at me. I felt its impact, a sharp pain resounded in my head. At the same instant, everything went entirely black. I could feel nothing anymore, see nothing, and hear nothing. I could not move. My young body was dead, though it remained sitting in the saddle. A bit later, I moved out of its head and my vision turned back on. I could see in all directions at the same instant and was rather confused for a moment. I saw Roy and Herbert grabbing my horse's reins, and they retreated as fast as they could. I saw a second hail of arrows fly at them, hitting horses and the backs of the men and my dead body, but none was life-threatening to either man or beast. I floated along with them, completely dazed and confused.

When they had gotten out of range, they halted to examine my body. Roy was crying so badly that Herbert had to do the examination, pronouncing me dead. Quickly, he had the presence of mind to pull the arrows out of himself, Roy, and the horses. He fairly yelled to Roy to tie my body onto the horse. Poor Roy, he had failed completely, and I was dead. Only then did the grief I felt flood over me, but I couldn't cry. I did the only thing I could. I reached out and made telepathic contact with Roy.

Roy, get out of here fast. I really blew this one. It's all my own stupid mistake. You both did all you could have to protect me from my folly. But Roy, you must survive. Get out of here and get back home. Promise me you'll look after our children! Promise me! Think of our kids!

Roy's mind was so flooded, so overwhelmed with grief that I could hardly get through to him. I know that I would be likewise, if the situation were reversed. He was my mate, my partner in all things, save death. I just had to reach him!

Allow me to help. It was Alabaster! He had seen it all and now had joined with my mind. I sensed his great strength, and his presence calmed my mind, setting aside my grief. Alabaster reestablished contact with both men, introduced himself, and consoled both men. Somehow, that man had enough presence to dissolve even deeply felt grief. I don't know what else to call it but presence. Roy came to his senses, so to speak, and I got my message through to him.

I swear! I swear! Roy returned in my mind, but tears rolled down his face heavier than the rain, which had now begun in earnest.

Now Alabaster placed into all our minds, *It is time for haste. Herbert, you and Roy get Bethany's body out of here. Have Mary Ann give her the proper passing ceremony. The problem of King Randolf will shortly be completely solved. Bethany, Erline, and I will end it here. So return home and grieve; but know that Wid Bethany achieved all that she desired. She prevented another war and Centurion intervention. I will look after her now. You have done well, both of you. Now ride; ride like the wind, and for heaven's sake, do not look back!*

I placed a parting kiss into Roy's mind, but I don't know if he recognized it as such. *Come Bethany, it is time for action. When I saw the treachery of King Randolf occur, I summoned Erline and her forces, but it's really the three of us that are going to do the dirty work. I have summoned an immense storm. We should have all the power we could possibly need to put a complete end to King Randolf and his Galts. Ah, Erline. So glad you could join us.* I sensed a three-way mind link in operation.

I tried to tell her not to do this. So he wouldn't even honor a parley flag! So sorry for you Bethany.

It was my mistake, I managed to mutter humbly. Now, I felt completely foolish, full of grief, but also anger.

My plan is simple, the soothing thoughts of Alabaster floated in my mind. *Using this incredibly strong summer storm as a cover, we shall bring lightning down on everyone, especially King Randolf. This man is completely insane and has caused so much pain and hardship that he must be slain. I can see no other way. So, shall we?*

Erline needed no further encouragement. I could see matchstick men or soldiers scurrying about. I found it utterly trivial to make the connection between them and the mustering energies in the sky. The sheer volume of lightning strikes that occurred during the next ten minutes, for I assumed that it was ten minutes — remember my time sense and size sense are distorted when I'm out of my body — was something to behold. Even the charging fighters of Erline halted and waited out the ferocious display. Never had they witnessed such an intensity of lightning. All were totally used to Erline's waves of lightning, for she used it often in every battle she had fought all these years, but this display was an entirely different thing. Some claimed that there had been over a thousand strikes in less than ten minutes time.

As I floated among the trees, I came upon King Randolf, cowering from the storm. Briefly, I touched his mind. *Just as soon as this wicked storm passes, why, I'll kill the rest of those that are trying to get away.* The man was insane, no question of that. I made the connection five times, and five times, I watched a bolt blast into his body.

That's enough on him; he's quite dead, Alabaster helped me regain control once again from my passion. *Say, look where he is going!*

I paused and spotted him as he left his electrocuted body. He rose up high into the air. For an instant, I saw in his mind that same yellow burst of energy. Then, like an arrow, he flew off toward the grey creatures, high in the Appian Way west of here. I noticed that hundreds of other beings whose bodies had just been slain doing precisely the same thing!

What they are going to get when they arrive at that mountaintop, I wouldn't wish on any being, Alabaster said with a note of sadness in his thought. I remembered what I had seen the grey creatures doing, totally scrambling all their memories and such. *I believe we're finished here. We can stop our attack now. Erline, will you clean up this mess?*

With great pleasure! Are we then at peace with each other after all these long years? she asked.

Yes. I have often said that who can foresee what role Erline may yet play, have I not, Bethany. I concurred. I detected what had to be a mental smile coming from Erline. *Yes, dear child, we are at peace, you and I, though for my part, I was never not at peace with you, though I know many others were. After today, I think you may find your standing greatly increased among the druwids, but Bethany and I have other business to attend to, so I bid you farewell, Erline.* I humbly and quietly added my thanks to his.

Oh, yes, can you make sure Roy and Herbert are doing okay? I added.

You have my sworn promise to see them safely to Blankford. Wid Bethany, you have my complete respect. It has been good to know you. May our paths cross once again.

With that, I felt Alabaster break the connection with Erline. *Follow me; let's get out of here.* I floated after him, up and over the hills, heading further south until I recognized the beginnings of the barren Langdoc region, the foothills of the Appian Way, and uninhabited, save by a very few shepherds.

Once there, we floated down onto a large boulder. *I think you'll be more comfortable if we perch on this rock. It's rather solid.*

I, I screwed up back there, didn't I, I began, wondering how I could have been so blind.

You accomplished your mission; you achieved your goal. There'll be no civil war to give the Centurions an excuse to wage war on our people in the Greenway, he countered. That was true. I had achieved what I had set out to do. I brightened up considerably. *It's only a body that you lost, and your time with Roy and family, those matter more, I expect. At least, it did with my wife and me when I lost her.* I realized he spoke the truth, and this was his way of comforting me.

Why *were here in the first place?* I asked.

I've been spying on our grey creatures. Still have no idea how to stop them or what their objectives might be. By the way, I did spot the mantis creatures doing much the same thing down in the Red Desert. Most strange. Needs more study. I'm aware of much that goes on in the Greenway, but I'm not omniscient, Bethany. I didn't know how your proposed parley with the late King Randolf would go. However, you're right; you cannot reason with an insane person. Tell me, Bethany, what plans do you have now?

Darn, I don't know. I always thought I'd live to a ripe old age as you did. I don't know what to do now. Should I head down there and try to get a new baby body? Perhaps, Sandy or Sarah Jane or Thallia will have another child soon. I could ask them. I'm sure they would if I asked. Alabaster didn't reply with his usual that's a good idea. Silence, instead.

Finally, he said, *I can't ask anything further of you Bethany. Already you have made the ultimate sacrifice for the druwids and the Greenway. If that is what you want to do, I know your Circle will love to have you back.*

Okay. So what do you actually have in mind, old man? I teased. I could tell that he had something else in mind for me to do. I still can observe.

Well, you know in your report of your journey, you spoke of the coming of the Great Messiah down in Juda Arad. His coming is supposed to herald the driving of the Centurions from Juda Arad. Is that correct?

More like they all expect that this Great Messiah, the Son of their God, is somehow going to drive the Centurions from their land. At least that is what the prophets all seem to believe and say. Why?

I find that most curious, don't you? I have my hands full up here in the Greenway, especially with these grey creatures. If you wouldn't mind, could you go to Juda Arad, pick up a body, somehow get connected with this Great Messiah, and see what is going on? Perhaps we can learn from him how to defeat the Centurions. I will contact you later on, and you can report all that you learn at that time. What say you? Up for a bit of mystery?

You know that we make our own futures. Sure. This Great Messiah thing has always been in the back of my mind, so to speak. Two of their three harbingers of his coming were directly due to druwid actions. Sure, I'll go. Only promise me that you'll look after Roy, the others, and even my family back in Karka, if you have the time. I know they're going to be terribly upset with me going and getting my body killed. They're going to be very sad and will miss me, especially my three children. I felt my own twinges of grief coming back, but stifled them for the moment.

I promise to look out for all of them. Bethany, thank you for doing this for all the people in the Greenway. Okay. Go now. I believe you know the way better than I do. Later, I'll contact you to find out what you have learned and help get you back to the Greenway. Then, I felt what must have been a mental kiss — that of a loving father to his daughter. I loved this man, well, this being, actually.

Slowly, I floated up and looked to the east and south. Higher and higher, I rose until I was above the Appian Way. The view was spectacular. Then, I began moving southeast. Soon far below me I spied Zargarb and got my bearings. I knew that their Great Messiah had been born in Jerilum in 559 AH. Prophet Emil Tamir had said as much when he rode off toward that town just after we had spotted the new star in the sky that night near Al Barq. Was the young child still in that town or had he been moved for safety's sake, especially after that night of the baby murders? I certainly would have moved him. So my first task, I decided, would be to find out where this Great Messiah was now located; he must be around five years old now.

I spied Jerilum below me. Suddenly I realized something. Already, I was feeling the excitement of this new adventure. Had I not gotten my body killed, more than likely, back in Blanca I was facing years of mostly boredom. All crises handled there. No adventure; no mystery; no excitement. But love, love was there, and I felt my grief once more. I still felt that I had really screwed up this time.

Chapter 29 Bethel, Juda Arad

It was early July 564 AH in Jerilum, as I hung out around the large square where I had once heard the Prophet Emil Tamir speak. I was resting atop the Church's entry way watching and waiting. Eventually, one of their prophets was sure to speak in public. After three days of waiting, he showed up, giving his rousing sermon once again. Only this time, I noticed there was an air of hopefulness in his voice that hadn't been there before. Further, the townspeople also listened more intently to his words and prayers.

When he finished, I floated down and hung out close to him, hoping to pick up the information I needed — where their Great Messiah was being raised. I suspected I could do a telepathic mind link and get it out of him. However, that might frighten him into having the Great Messiah moved to some other town. No, I would just have to be patient, but I found the task incredibly boring.

My patience was rewarded two nights later. Emil met in secret with another prophet to discuss how things were going with their savior, who I rightly assumed must be their Great Messiah. I learned that he was a young lad in the town of Bethel. Of course, I had absolutely no idea of where that town was located. I decided to follow this other man. Sure enough, he led me to Bethel!

Bethel was a small rural village of some five hundred people in total. Most depended upon their small herds of sheep. It didn't take me long to locate their Great Messiah. He was the only child among the many children running around in the streets that had an adult constantly watching over him, protecting him from unseen dangers. What dangers? I couldn't see any. This village was remote and in the far eastern portion of Juda Arad. No Centurions were here, and none was ever likely to come here for that matter.

Now all I had to do was find myself a new baby body to occupy. None of the women seemed with child right now. For a moment, I panicked, wondering if they would ever have more babies here in this village. Patience, I told myself. I bided my time, content with watching the young messiah run and play. To me, he was just an ordinary child, save one thing. He, like I had been, was not in his head. He was always at least five feet above and behind it. If nothing else, he was prime druwid material, I thought.

Again, some time passed. As I have said before, I am a poor judge of time when not in my body, or in this case, a body. Maybe it was a month. A young five year old girl was running and playing in the street and accidentally ran into the side of a wagon bringing supplies into Bethel. Instantly, she fell down and was unconscious. I moved closer, my natural instincts to heal rising to the forefront, though I had no idea how I could do anything without having a body with which to do it. She had taken a nasty bump on the head, but that was all. Oh no it wasn't! When she fell to the ground, she landed on a very surprised viper that had struck out in retaliation! I spied it slithering away, its back half-broken.

I watched as a crowd of people gathered around the unconscious girl. Much to my amazement, the being whose body it was decided that it was now dead, rose up out of the body, paused a moment, and then shot like an arrow off toward the Appian Way. Here was my good fortune: a body already made and ready to go, except that it was dying from a viper bite that the well-intentioned people didn't see. I watched helplessly as the adults did nothing!

I had to take action. I spied their Great Messiah trying to get a look between the legs of the adults. I placed the concept into his mind: *She has been bitten by a viper. Tell the grownups.*

Surprised, he looked all around for me, but, though not spotting me, then did as I asked, yelling, "Viper bite! Viper bite!" Sure enough, words spoken by their Great Messiah carried great weight among these people. Soon they had located the tell-tale bite mark on her right arm. However, they all stood, stared, said prayers, and still did nothing. Finally, one elderly gentleman arrived and was told what had happened. He moved the others out of the way and examined the girl. Now I noticed what had to be her parents. They were crying furiously in the background and being comforted by several other adults. I watched as the old man took out a knife, made the necessary cuts, and began to suck out the poison. I cringed a bit because he didn't even boil the knife first!

Sometime later, after he had sucked all he could out of the wound, he began to bandage the small wound without even putting any herbs on it to further leech any residual poison out! Clearly, these people were in desperate need of a true healer! I looked around and found what I would have put on it. Then, once more, I placed that idea into their Great Messiah's mind and had him speak it to the old man. Once again, I was doubly impressed with the results. Literally, anything that he spoke was carefully marked by the adults! Further, this time, he had spotted me, slightly above the unconscious body. Then, I felt the touch of his mind and a great, peaceful feeling came over me. Soon, I had the wound properly bandaged to my satisfaction. Only then did I make the solid connection with the body, latching onto its head. I felt the headache from the bump and the dizziness, nausea, and paralysis from the bite. I figured the body would survive. As an extra incentive, I gave this new body an order: *live!* I felt the body jerk in response to my command. Then, slowly my vision turned off, as I slipped more fully into this new body, which was now in a deep sleep.

I felt my body being carried lovingly some distance, placed into a warm bed, and covered up. I felt someone kiss my forehead. Ah, I was loved already. *Success. I have a new body about the same age as their Great Messiah. Now I'm all set to see what goes on. First part of my new mission accomplished! Now I think I'll go to sleep for a while. I seem to be so very tired.* I slept like a baby.

The End.

Other Books by Vic Broquard

Without Warning (fantasy)

The Trident Series: (fantasy)
> Volume 1 The Trident and the Book
> Volume 2 The Trident and the Scepter
> Volume 3 The Trident and the Resurrection

The Adventures of Elizabeth Stanton Series: (science fiction)
> Volume 1 The Evolution of the Path
> Volume 2 The Great Messiah
> Volume 3 Of Kings and Queens and Troubadours
> Volume 4 Chaos in the Aftermath
> Volume 5 Power Plays
> Volume 6 Age of Exploration
> Volume 7 Abducted
> Volume 8 The Emperor and Empress
> Volume 9 A Job Worth Doing
> Volume 10 Degradation
> Volume 11 The Second Crusade
> Volume 12 When Worlds Collide
> Volume 13 Dark Ages

The Lindsey Barron Series: (fantasy)
> Volume 1 The Rod of the Apocalypse
> Volume 2 The Board of Governors
> Volume 3 The Crown of Moses
> Volume 4 Dominus for President
> Volume 5 The National Health Care Program
> Volume 6 States Justice
> Volume 7 Cross and Double-cross

Zoran Chronicles Series: (fantasy)
> Volume 1 A Dragon in Our Town
> Volume 2 Dragons, Power, Courts, and War

Planet of the Orange-red Sun Series: (science fiction)
> Volume 1 When Kingdoms Fall
> Volume 2 Dark Ages
> Volume 3 Age of the Towers
> Volume 4 Difficillis Exitus
> Volume 5 Age of the Lords

The Return of the Wizards: Twelve Companions – The Making of Wizards (fantasy)